SQUISHED

SQUISHED

Megan Wagner Lloyd
and Michelle Mee Nutter

An Imprint of
SCHOLASTIC

Library of Congress Control Number: 2022930701

ISBN 978-1-338-56894-3 (hardcover)
ISBN 978-1-338-56893-6 (paperback)

10 9 8 7 6 5 4 3 2 1   23 24 25 26 27

Printed in China   62
First edition, March 2023

Inking assistance by Veda Kasireddy
Color flatting by Maddi Coyne

Edited by Cassandra Pelham Fulton
Book design by Steve Ponzo
Creative Director: Phil Falco
Publisher: David Saylor

For my family
M. W. L.

For Ethan
M. M. N.

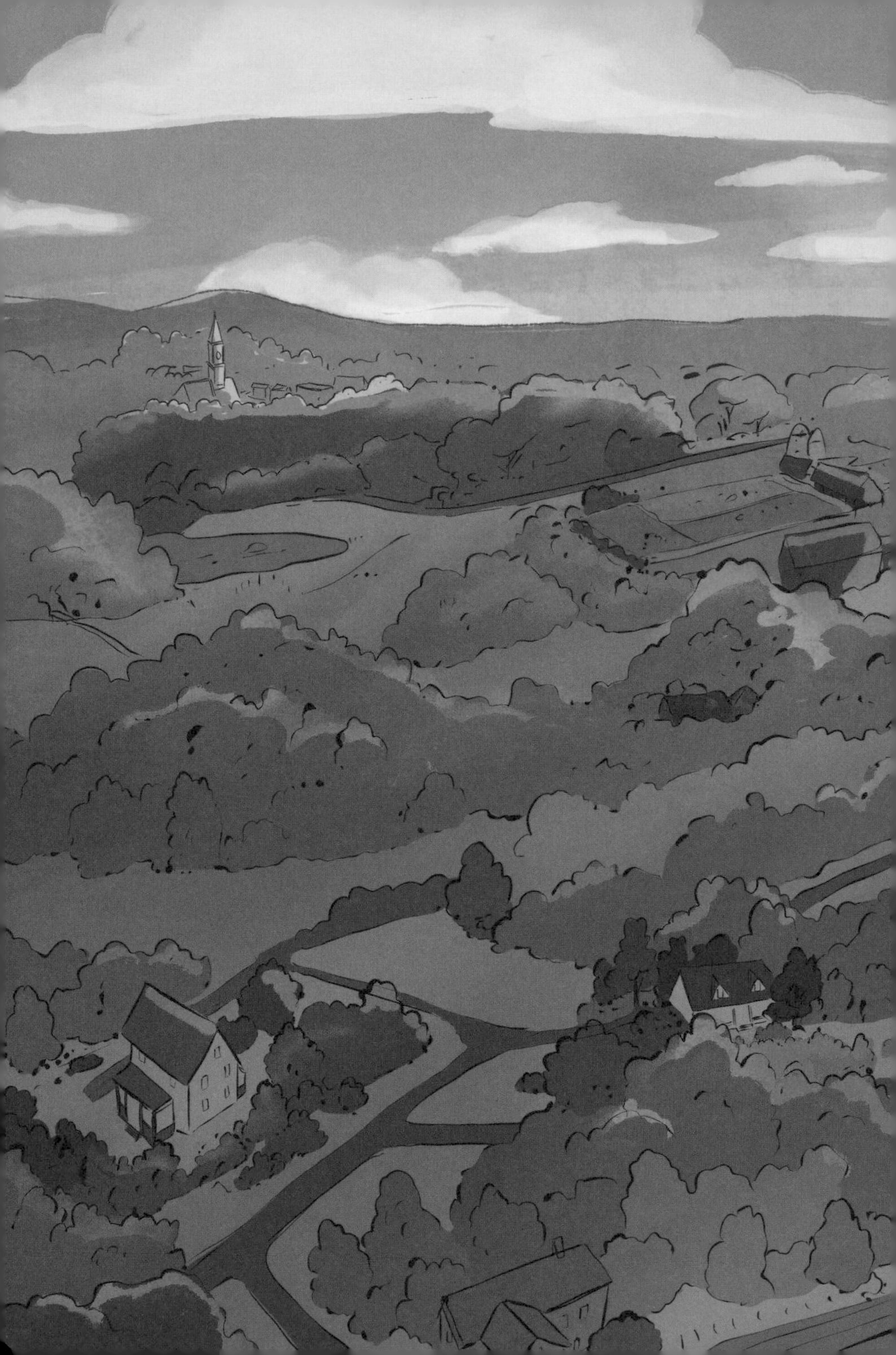

Chapter One

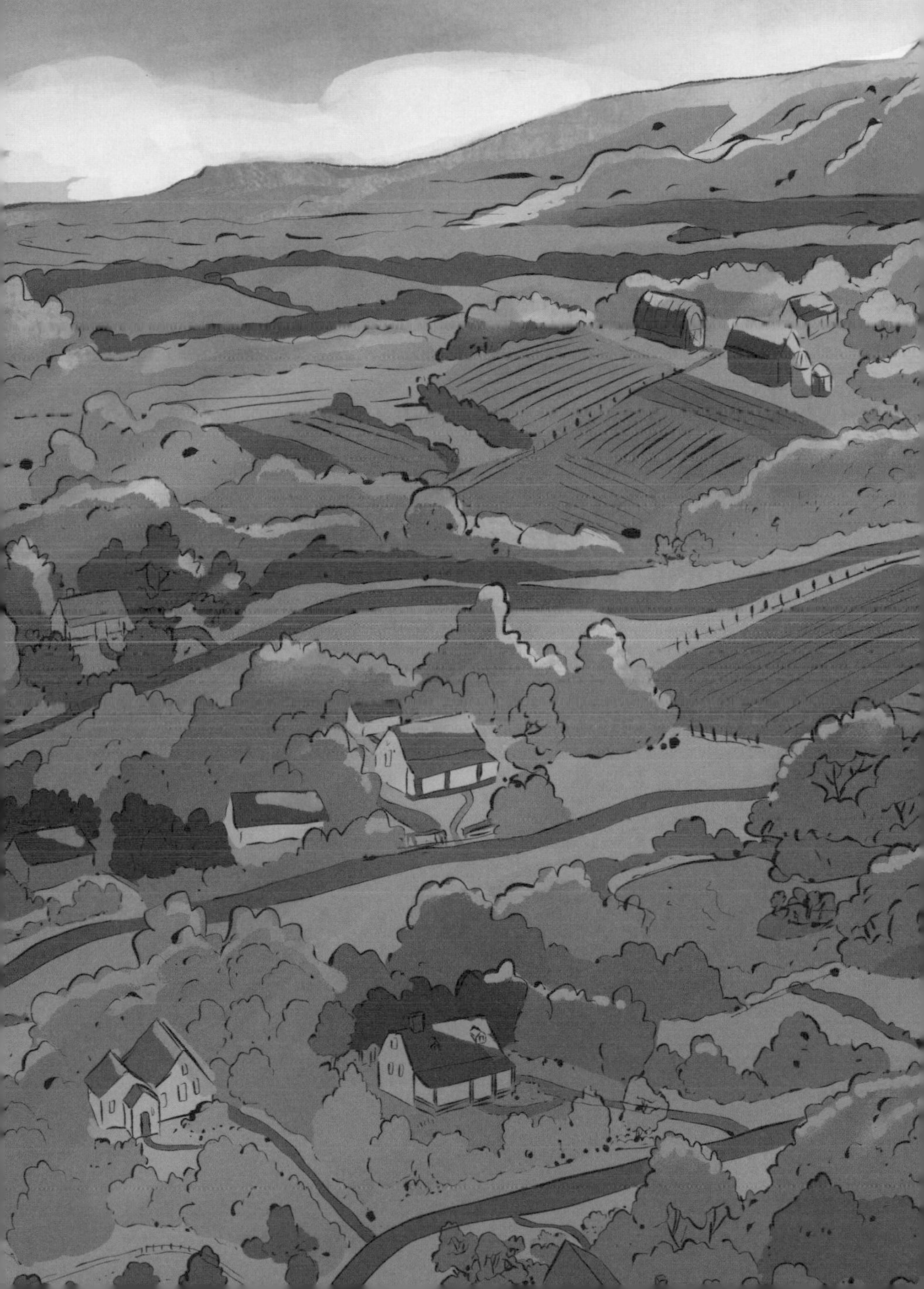

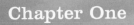

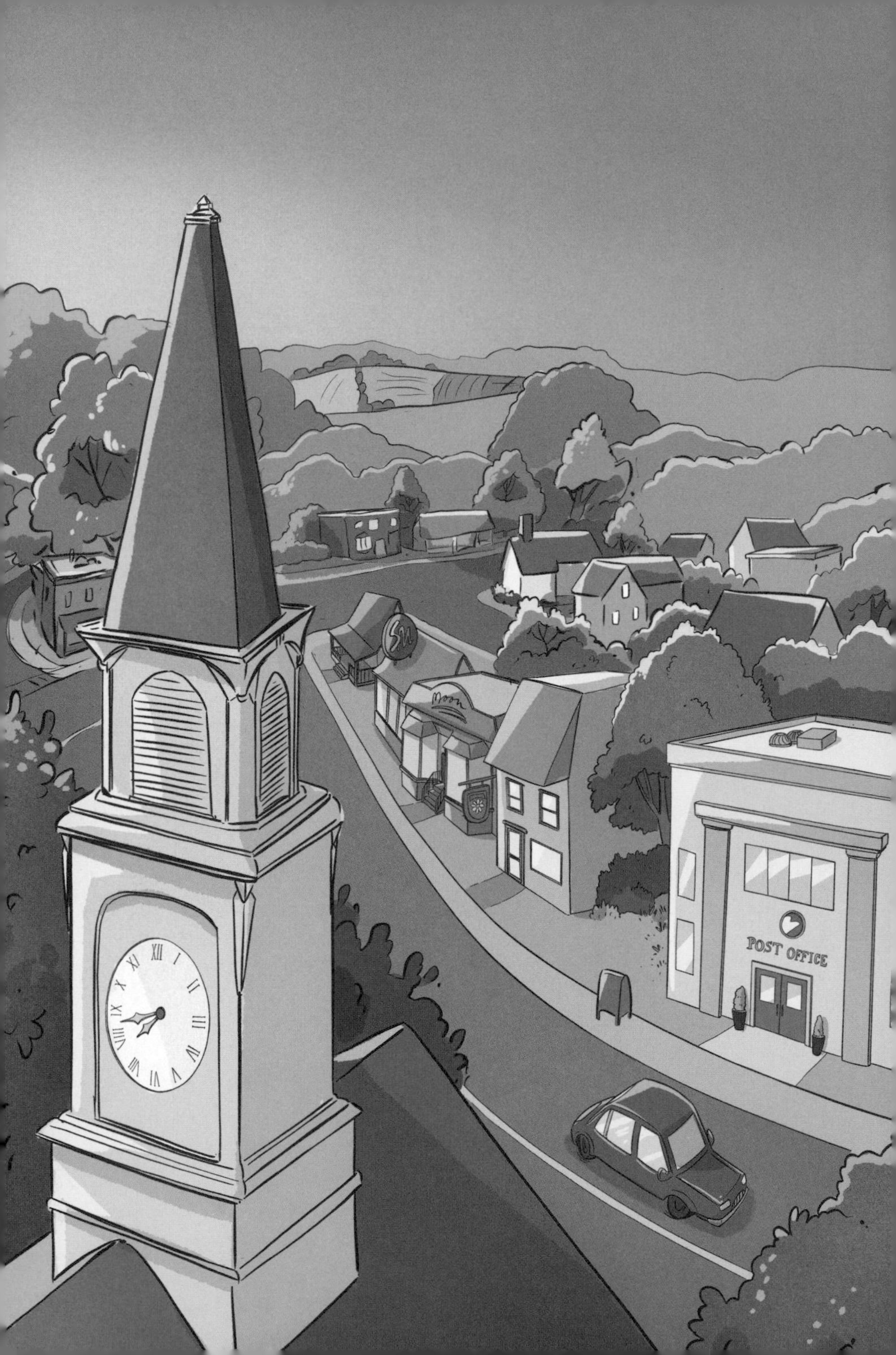
Su
Moon
POST OFFICE

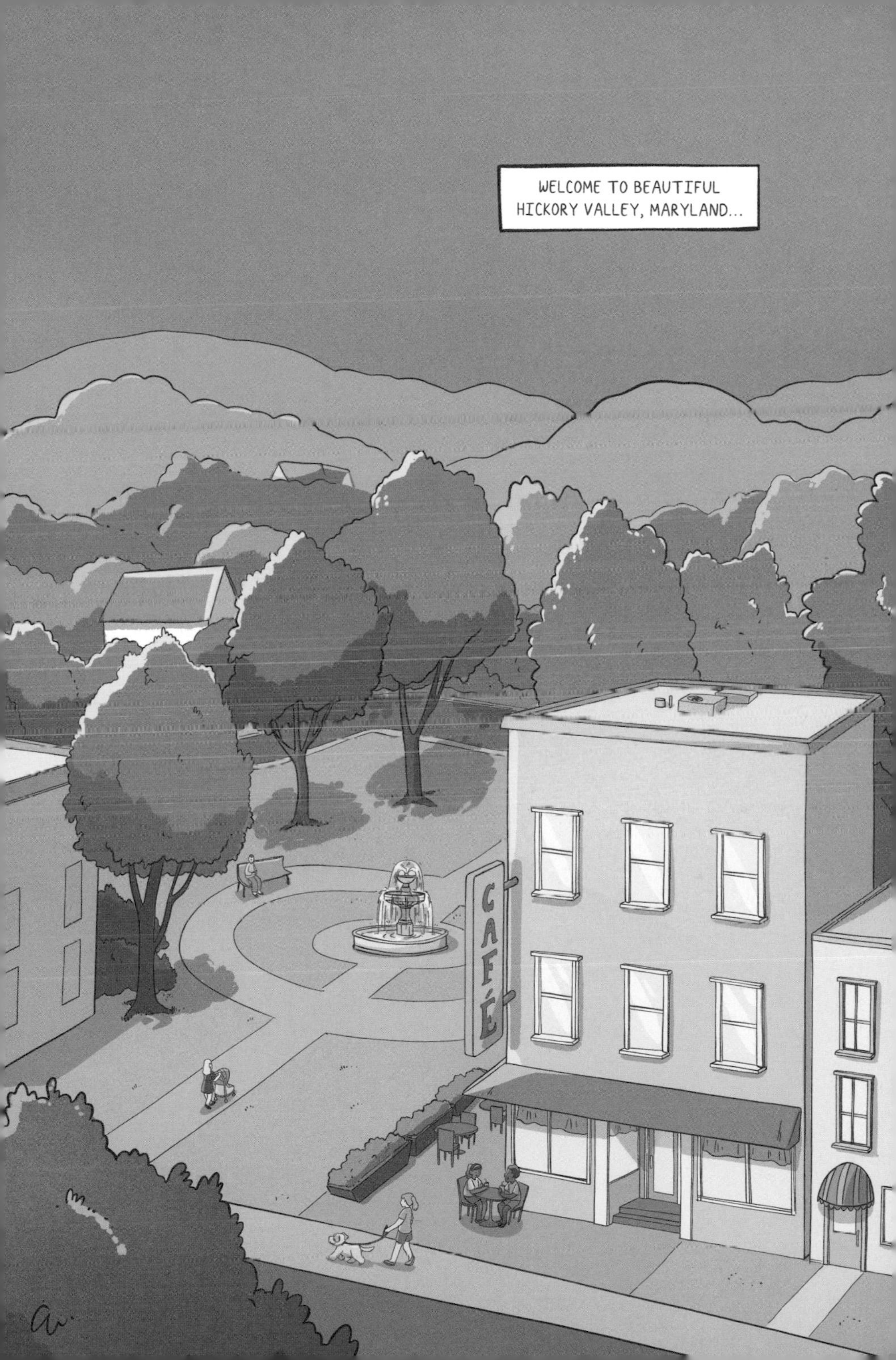
WELCOME TO BEAUTIFUL HICKORY VALLEY, MARYLAND...
CAFÉ

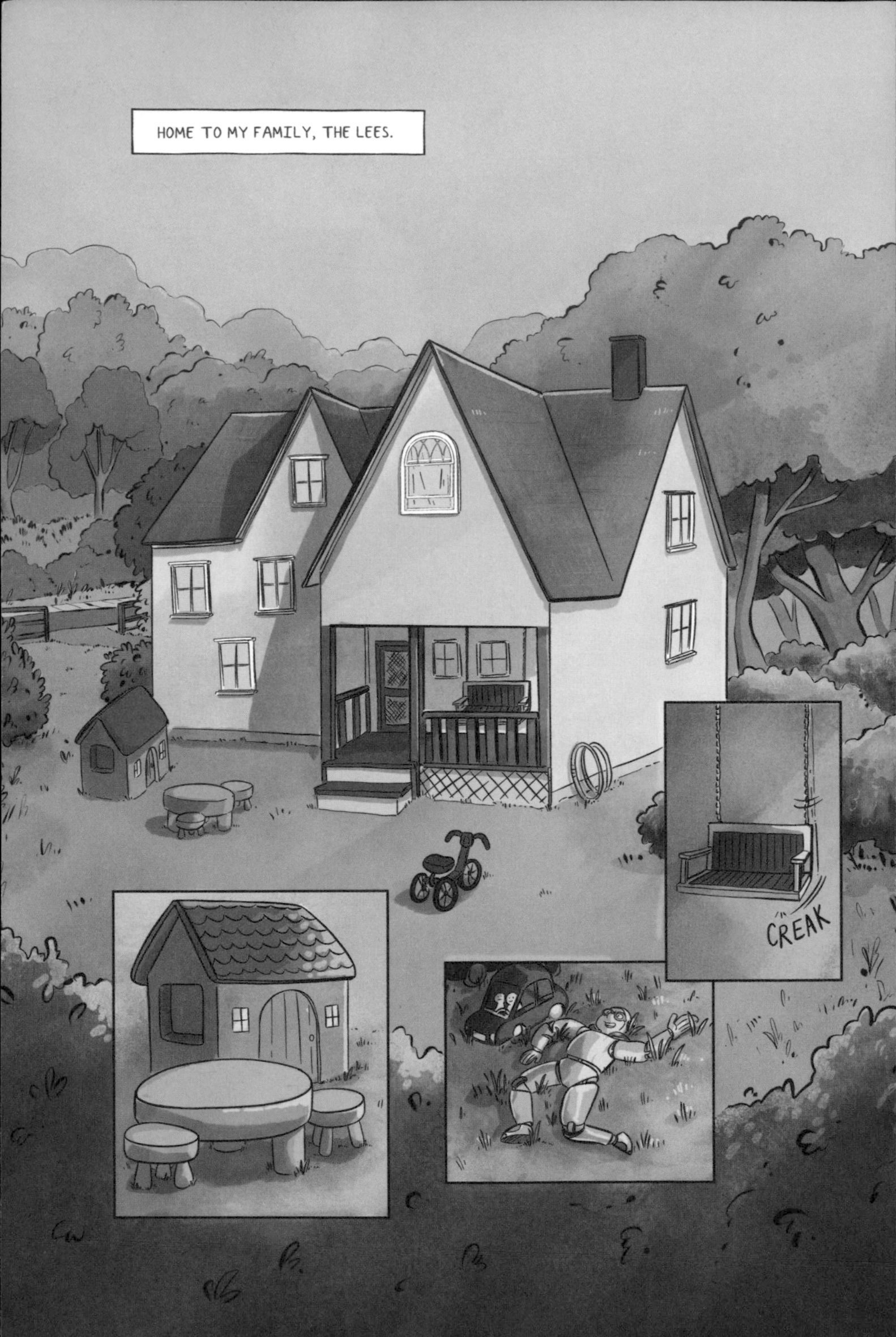
HOME TO MY FAMILY, THE LEES.
CREAK

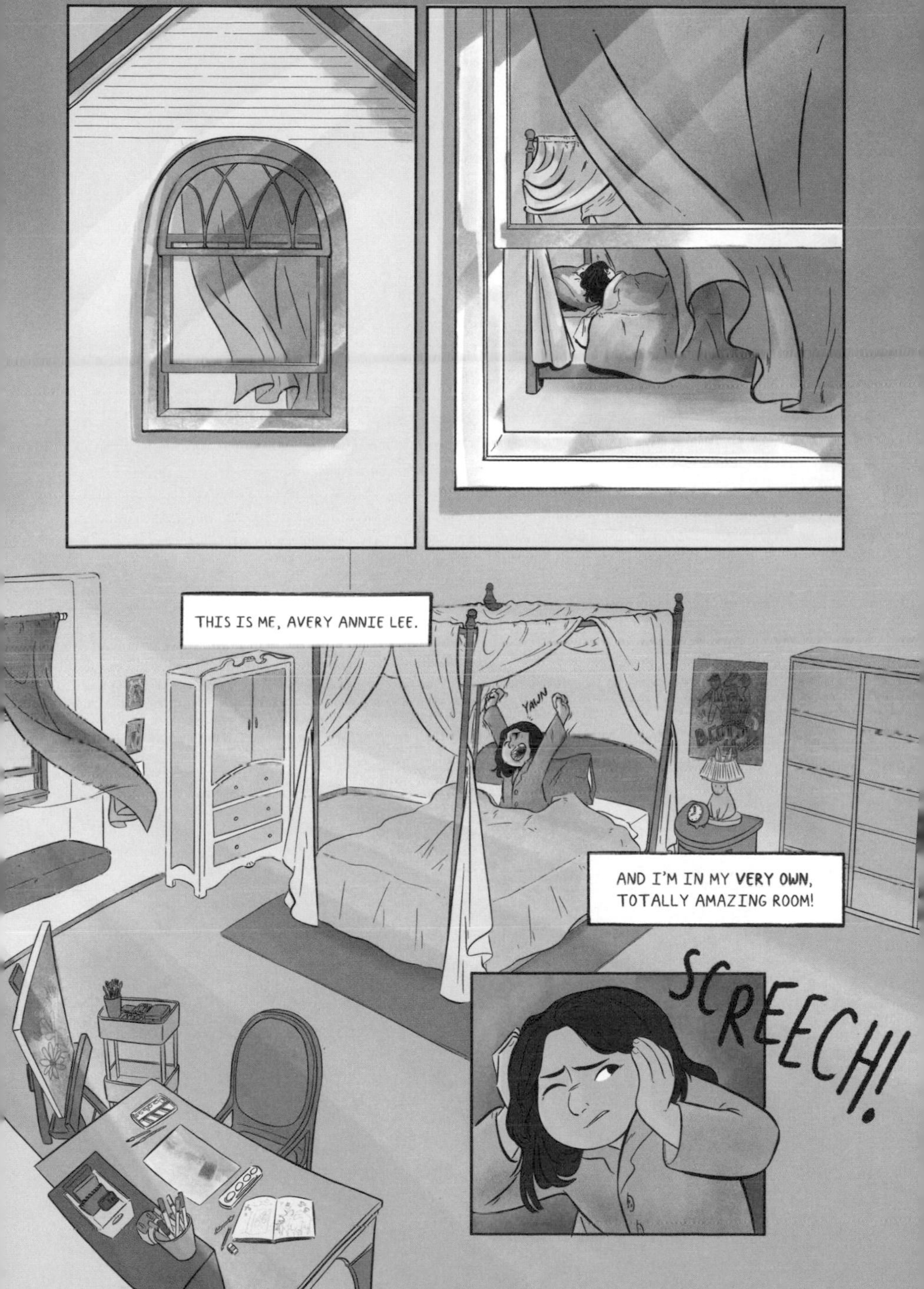
THIS IS ME, AVERY ANNIE LEE.
YAWN
AND I'M IN MY **VERY OWN**, TOTALLY AMAZING ROOM!
SCREECH!

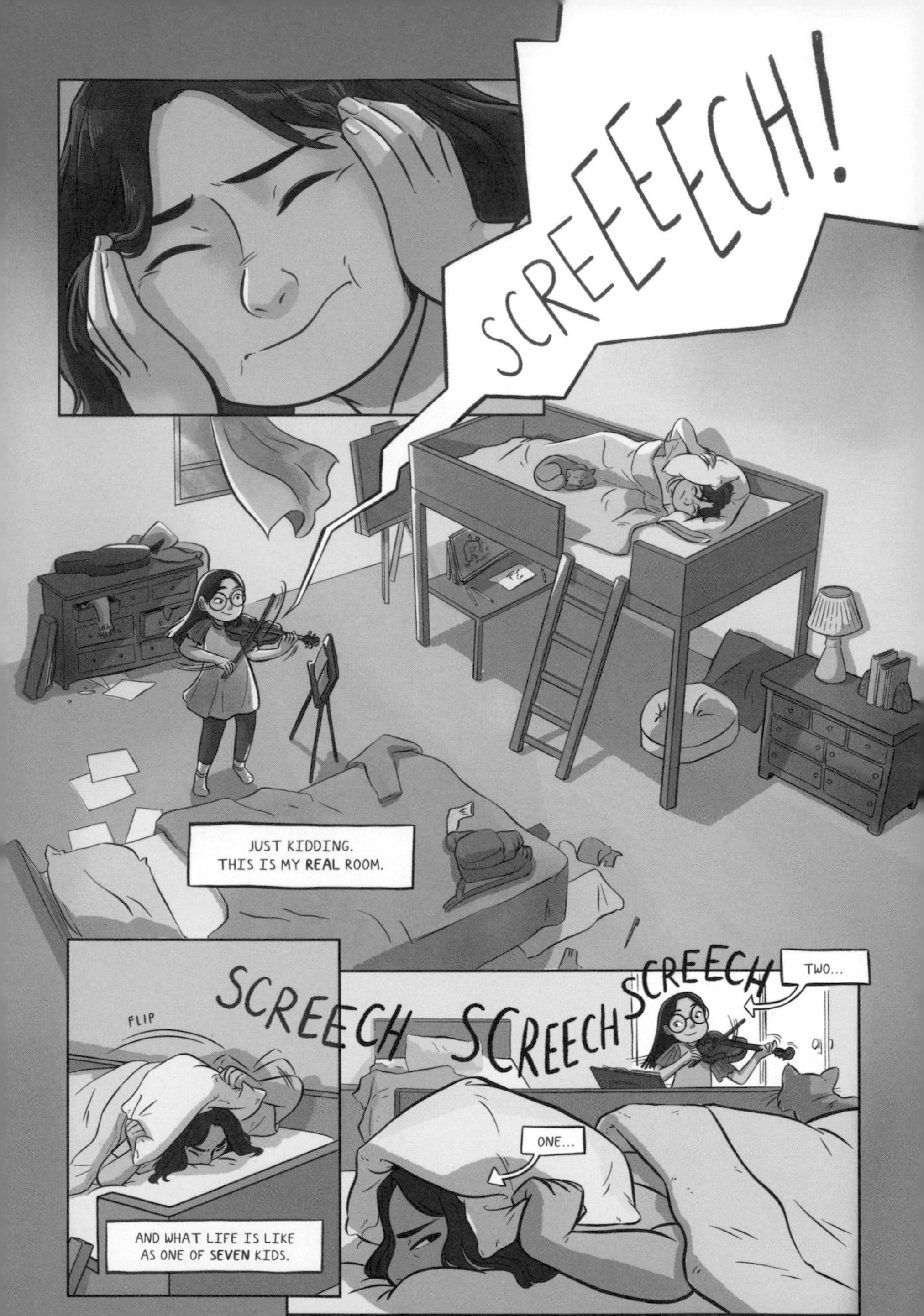
SCREEEECH!
JUST KIDDING.
THIS IS MY **REAL** ROOM.
FLIP
SCREECH
SCREECH
SCREECH
TWO...
ONE...
AND WHAT LIFE IS LIKE
AS ONE OF **SEVEN** KIDS.

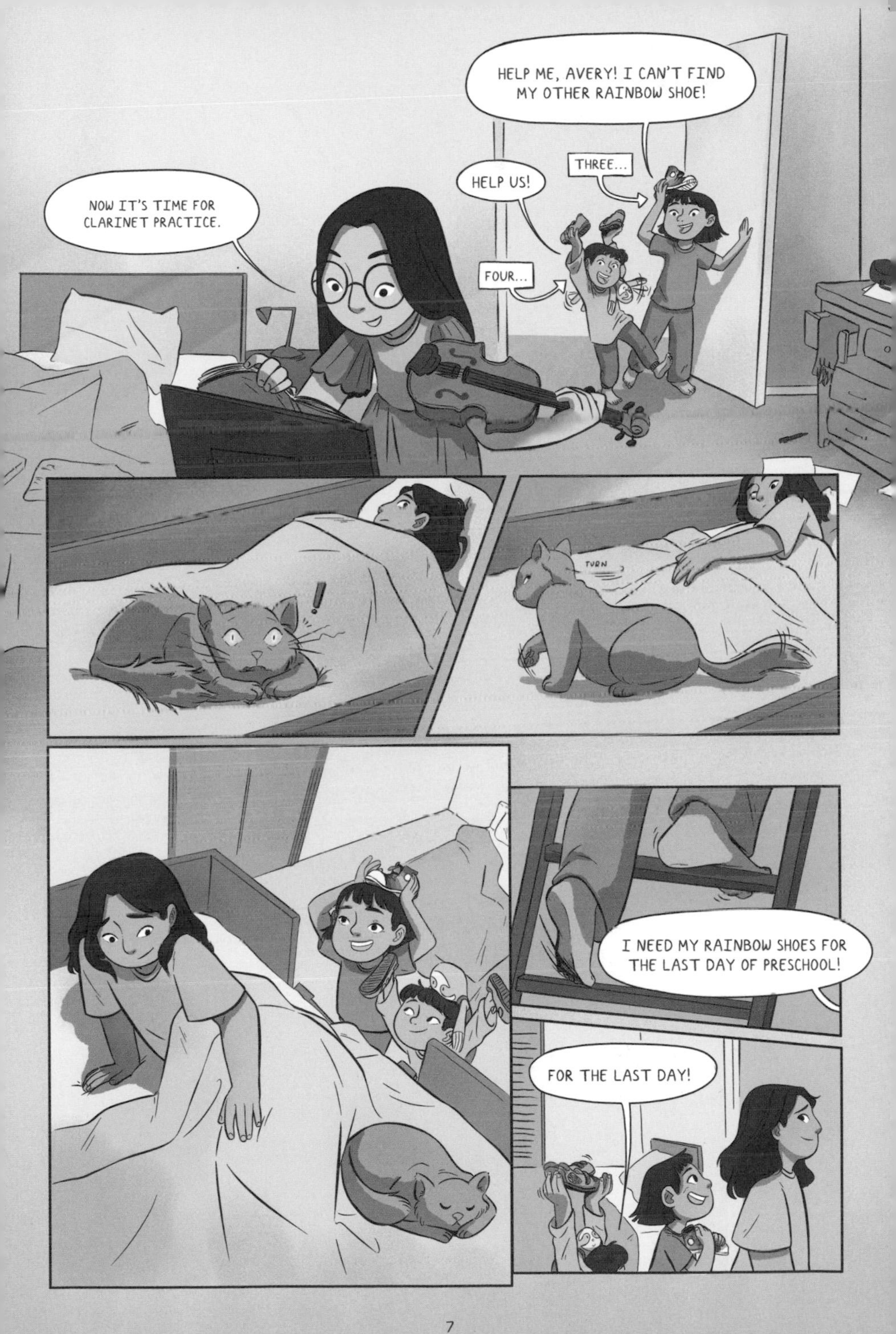
NOW IT'S TIME FOR CLARINET PRACTICE.
HELP ME, AVERY! I CAN'T FIND MY OTHER RAINBOW SHOE!
HELP US!
THREE...
FOUR...
TURN
I NEED MY RAINBOW SHOES FOR THE LAST DAY OF PRESCHOOL!
FOR THE LAST DAY!

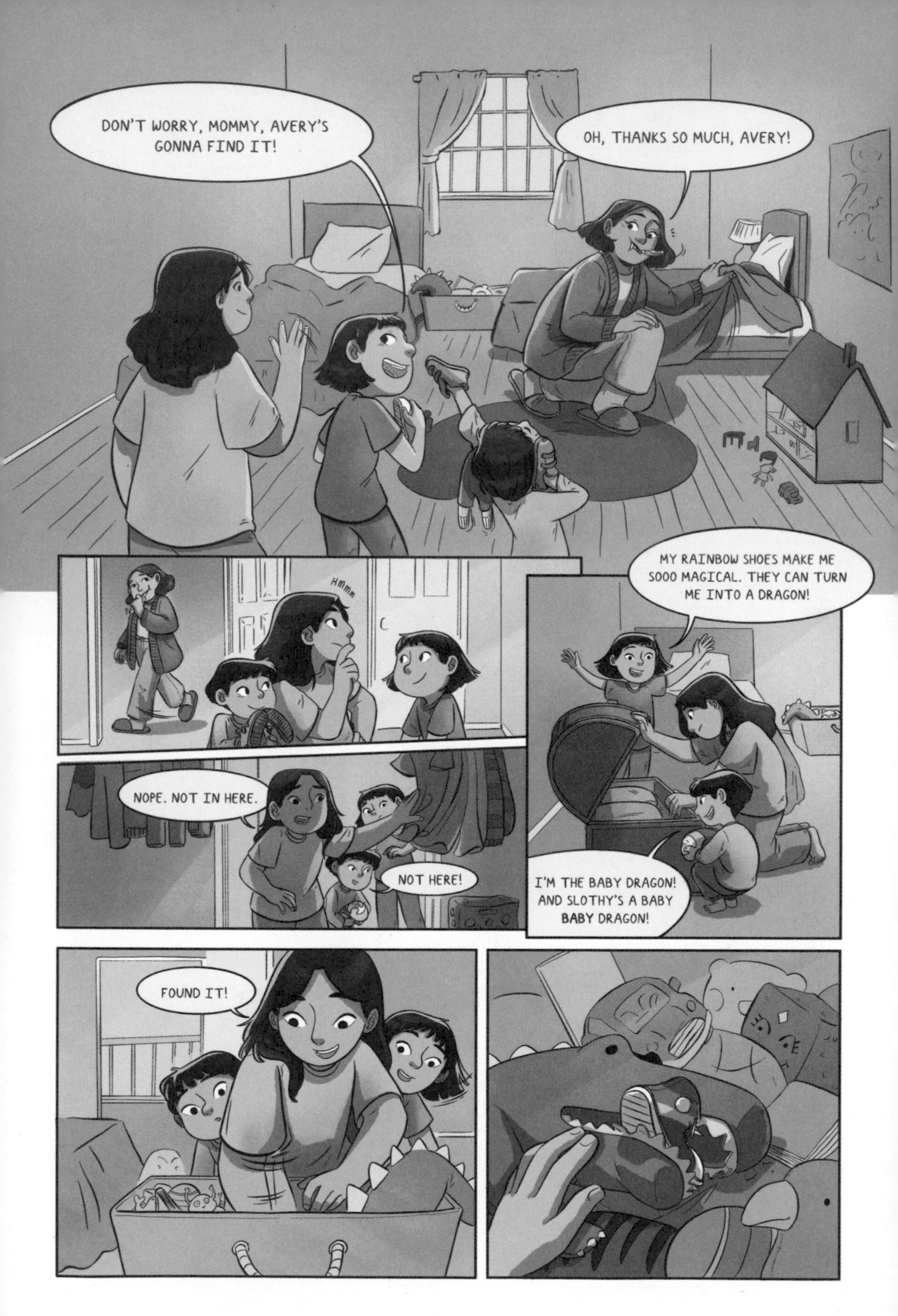
DON'T WORRY, MOMMY, AVERY'S GONNA FIND IT!
OH, THANKS SO MUCH, AVERY!
HMmm
MY RAINBOW SHOES MAKE ME SOOO MAGICAL. THEY CAN TURN ME INTO A DRAGON!
NOPE. NOT IN HERE.
NOT HERE!
I'M THE BABY DRAGON! AND SLOTHY'S A BABY **BABY** DRAGON!
FOUND IT!

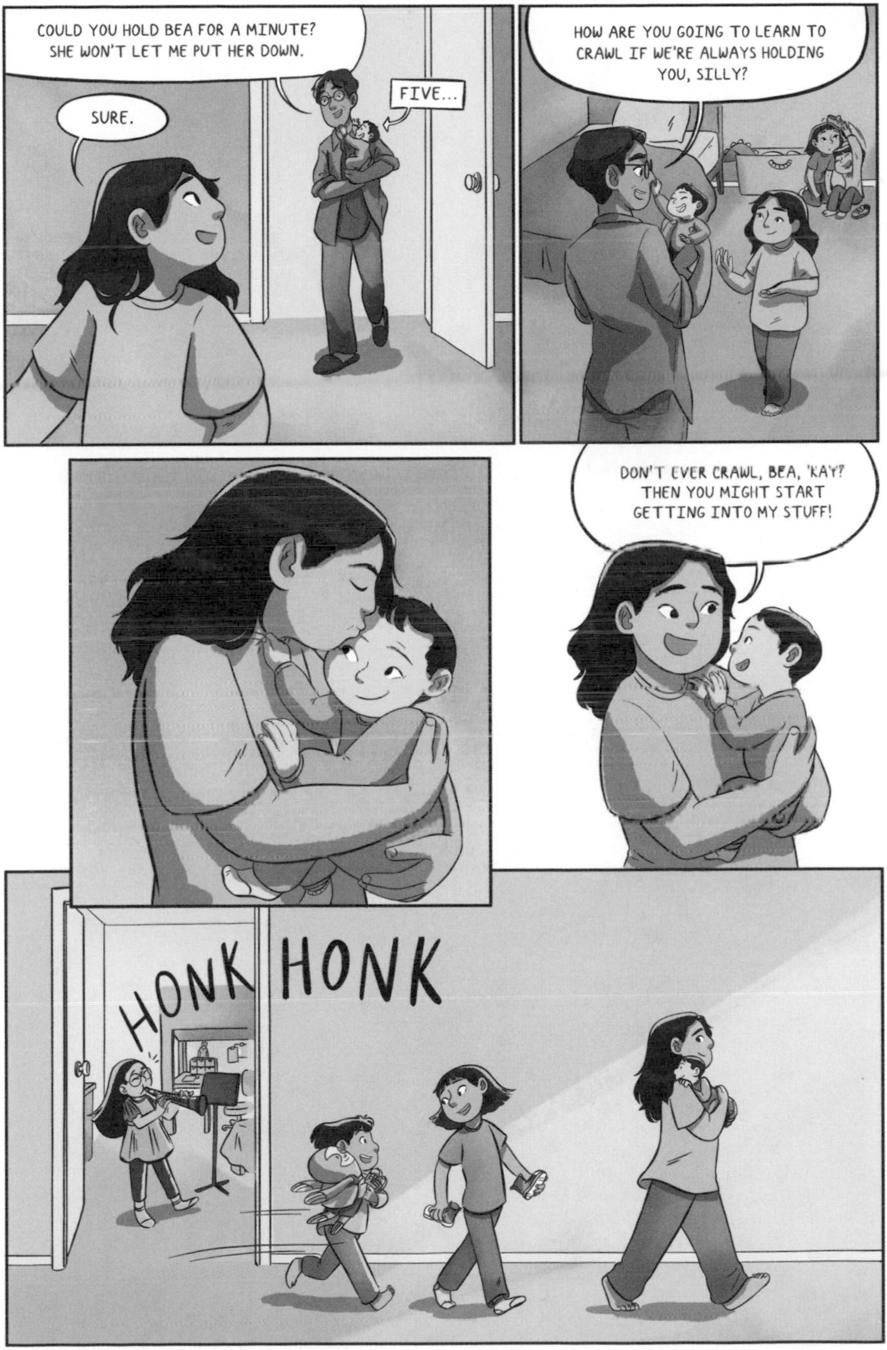
COULD YOU HOLD BEA FOR A MINUTE? SHE WON'T LET ME PUT HER DOWN.
SURE.
FIVE...
HOW ARE YOU GOING TO LEARN TO CRAWL IF WE'RE ALWAYS HOLDING YOU, SILLY?
DON'T EVER CRAWL, BEA, 'KAY? THEN YOU MIGHT START GETTING INTO MY STUFF!
HONK HONK

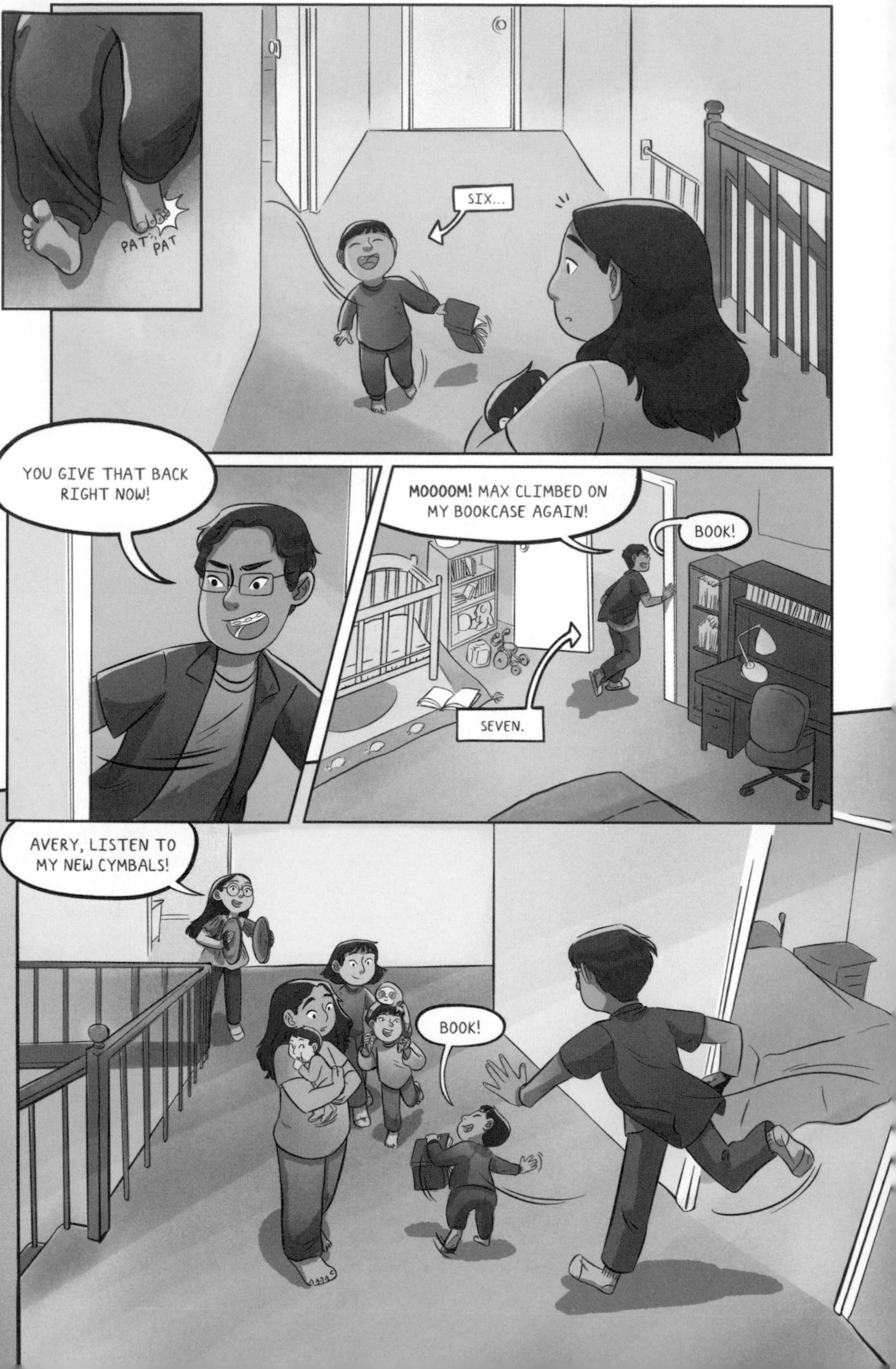
PAT PAT
SIX...
YOU GIVE THAT BACK RIGHT NOW!
MOOOOM! MAX CLIMBED ON MY BOOKCASE AGAIN!
BOOK!
SEVEN.
AVERY, LISTEN TO MY NEW CYMBALS!
BOOK!

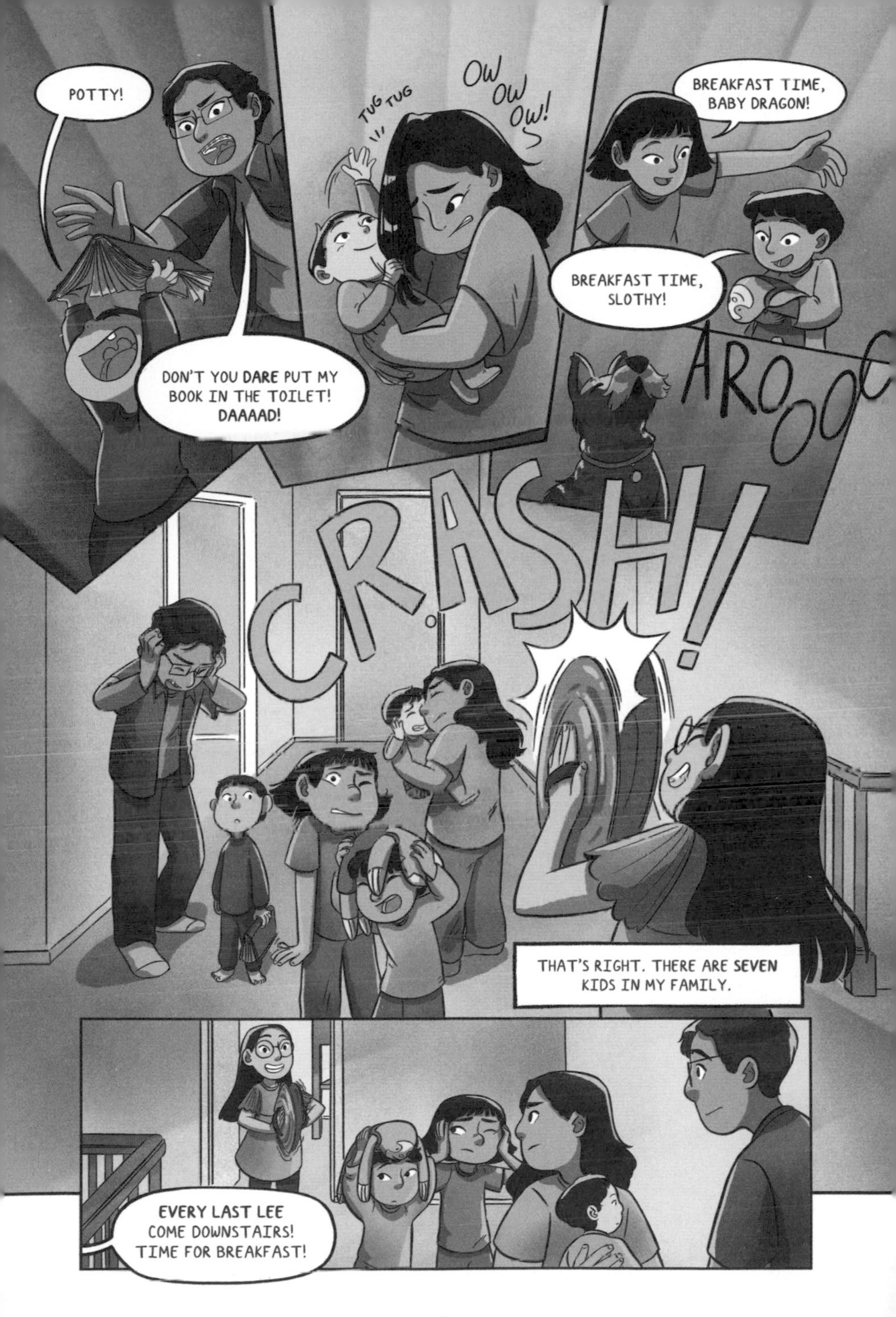
POTTY!
DON'T YOU DARE PUT MY BOOK IN THE TOILET! DAAAAD!
TUG TUG
OW OW OW!
BREAKFAST TIME, BABY DRAGON!
BREAKFAST TIME, SLOTHY!
AROOOO
CRASH!
THAT'S RIGHT. THERE ARE SEVEN KIDS IN MY FAMILY.
EVERY LAST LEE COME DOWNSTAIRS! TIME FOR BREAKFAST!

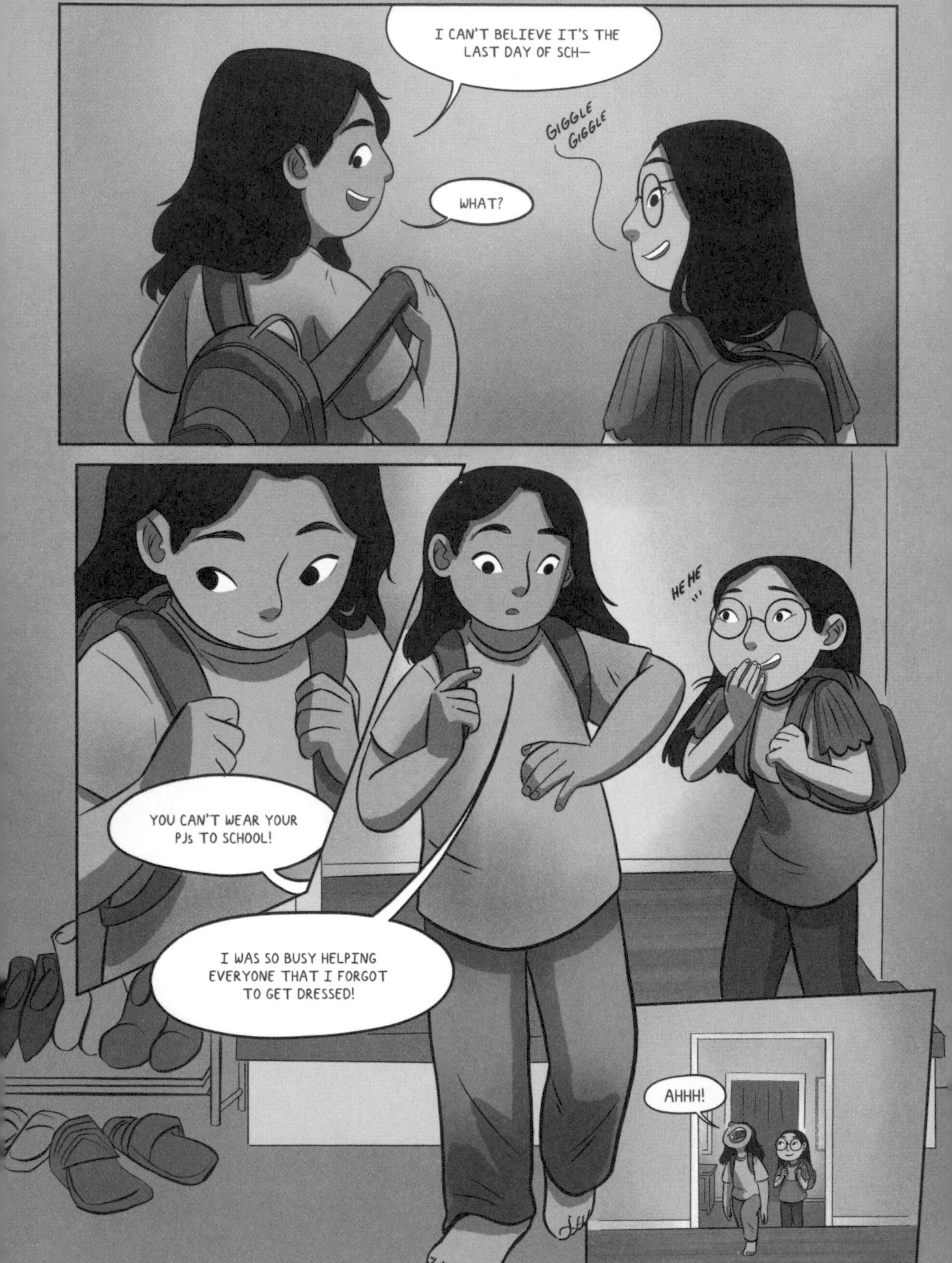
I CAN'T BELIEVE IT'S THE LAST DAY OF SCH—
GIGGLE GIGGLE
WHAT?
HE HE
YOU CAN'T WEAR YOUR PJs TO SCHOOL!
I WAS SO BUSY HELPING EVERYONE THAT I FORGOT TO GET DRESSED!
AHHH!

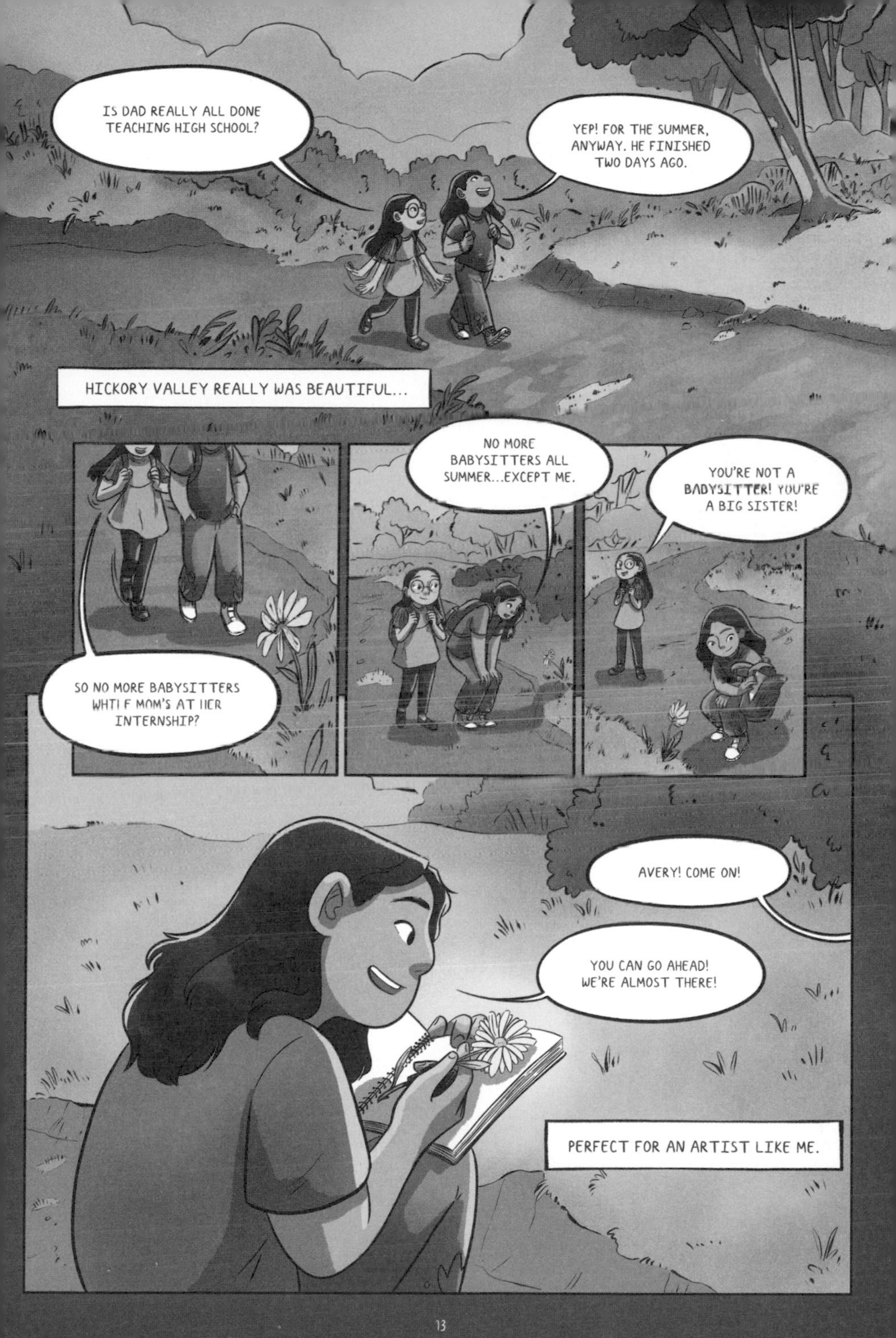

IS DAD REALLY ALL DONE TEACHING HIGH SCHOOL?
YEP! FOR THE SUMMER, ANYWAY. HE FINISHED TWO DAYS AGO.
HICKORY VALLEY REALLY WAS BEAUTIFUL...
SO NO MORE BABYSITTERS WHILE MOM'S AT HER INTERNSHIP?
NO MORE BABYSITTERS ALL SUMMER...EXCEPT ME.
YOU'RE NOT A BABYSITTER! YOU'RE A BIG SISTER!
AVERY! COME ON!
YOU CAN GO AHEAD! WE'RE ALMOST THERE!
PERFECT FOR AN ARTIST LIKE ME.

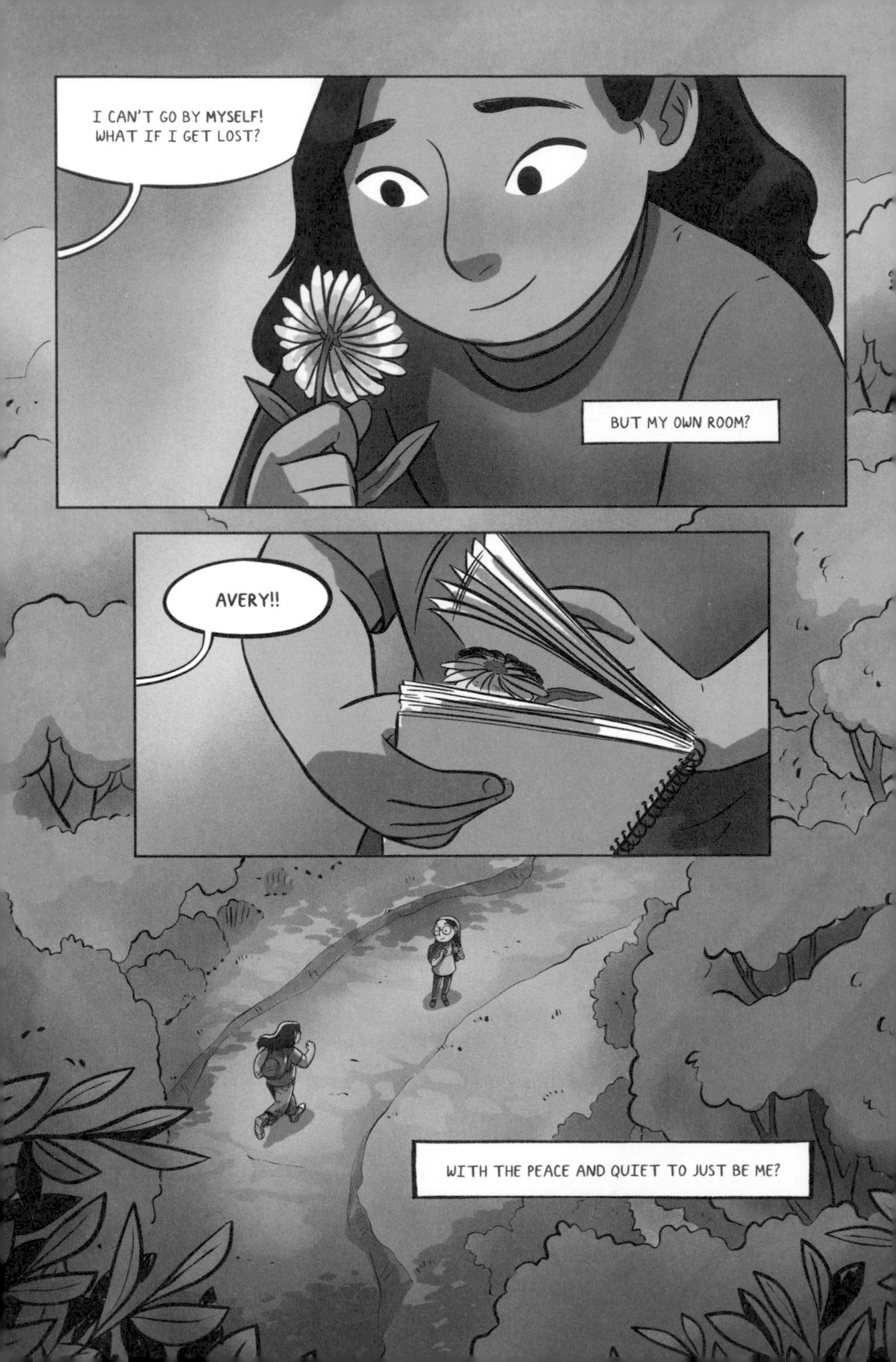
I CAN'T GO BY MYSELF! WHAT IF I GET LOST?
BUT MY OWN ROOM?
AVERY!!
WITH THE PEACE AND QUIET TO JUST BE ME?

THAT WAS MY DREAM.

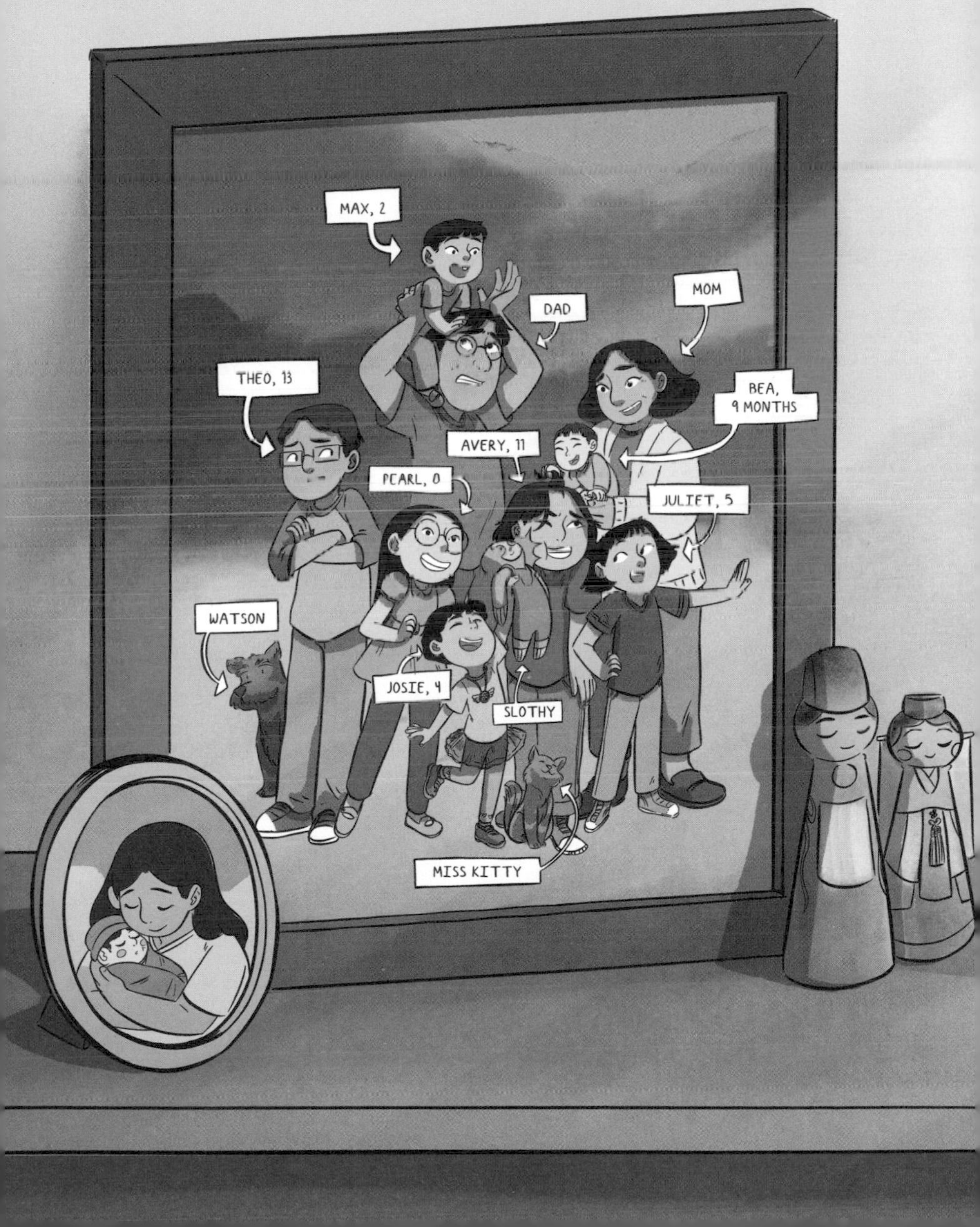
MAX, 2
DAD
MOM
THEO, 13
BEA,
9 MONTHS
AVERY, 11
PEARL, 8
JULIET, 5
WATSON
JOSIE, 4
SLOTHY
MISS KITTY

Chapter Two

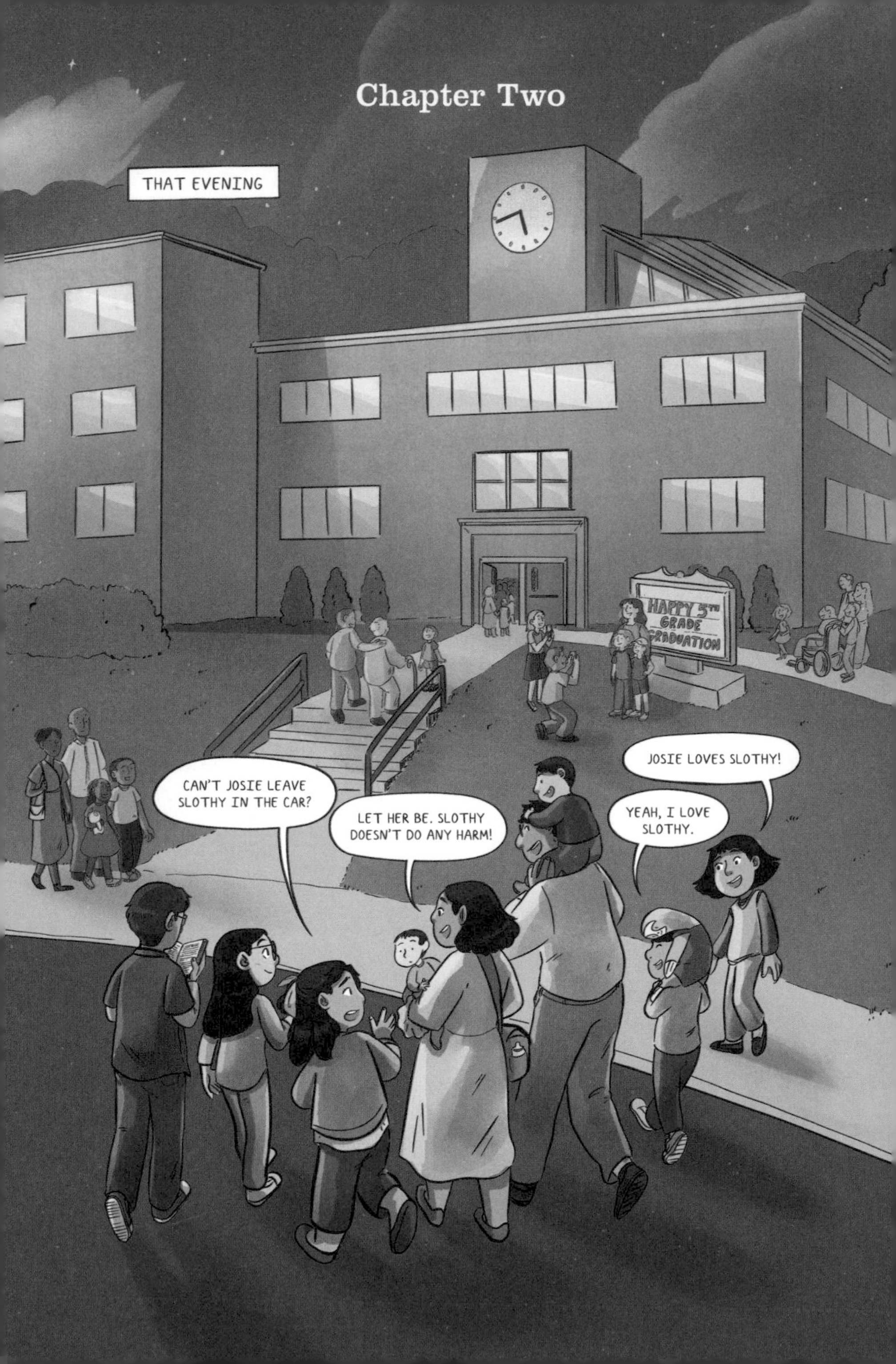
THAT EVENING
HAPPY 5TH GRADE GRADUATION
CAN'T JOSIE LEAVE SLOTHY IN THE CAR?
LET HER BE. SLOTHY DOESN'T DO ANY HARM!
JOSIE LOVES SLOTHY!
YEAH, I LOVE SLOTHY.

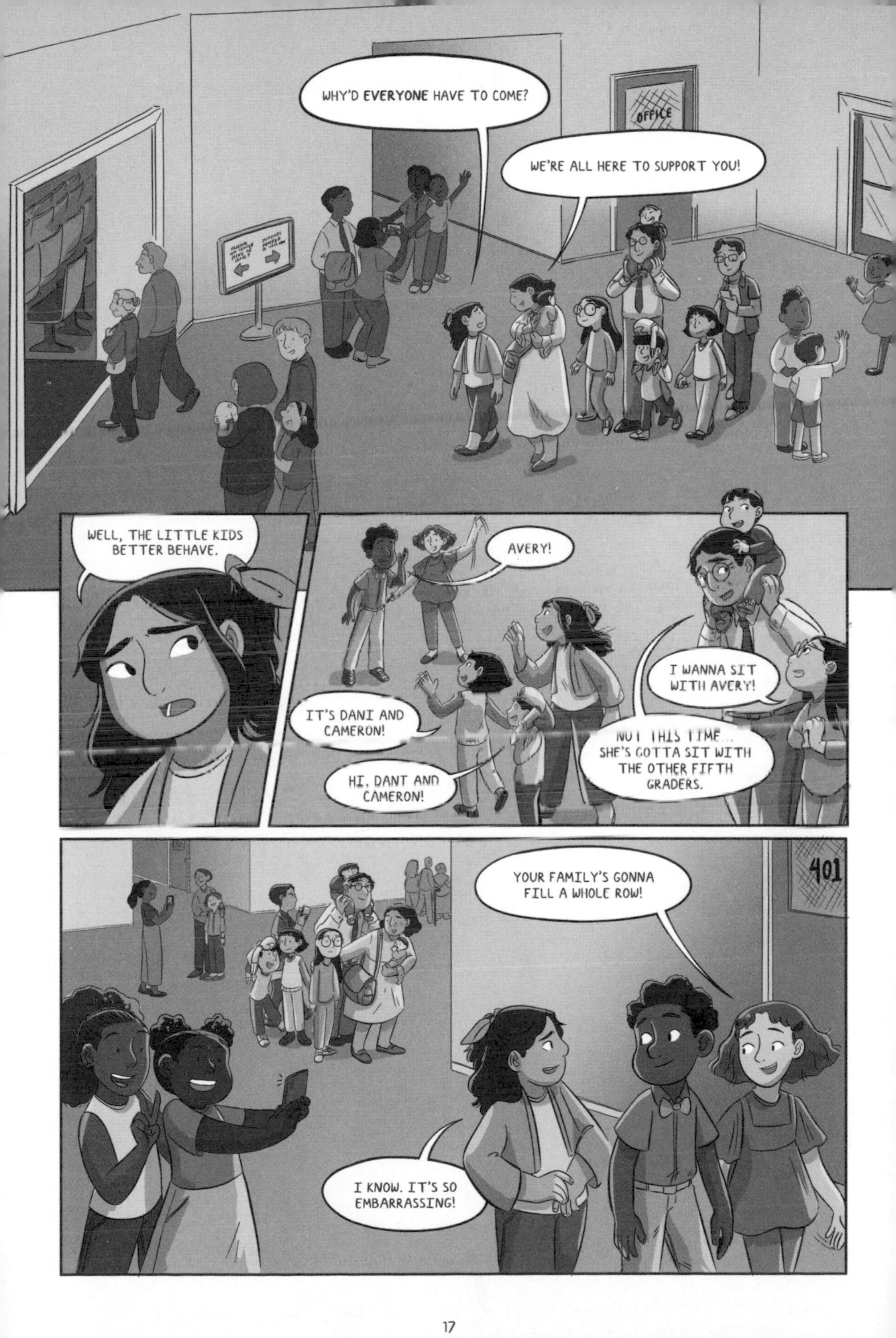
WHY'D EVERYONE HAVE TO COME?
WE'RE ALL HERE TO SUPPORT YOU!
WELL, THE LITTLE KIDS BETTER BEHAVE.
AVERY!
IT'S DANI AND CAMERON!
HI, DANI AND CAMERON!
I WANNA SIT WITH AVERY!
NOT THIS TIME... SHE'S GOTTA SIT WITH THE OTHER FIFTH GRADERS.
OFFICE
401
YOUR FAMILY'S GONNA FILL A WHOLE ROW!
I KNOW. IT'S SO EMBARRASSING!

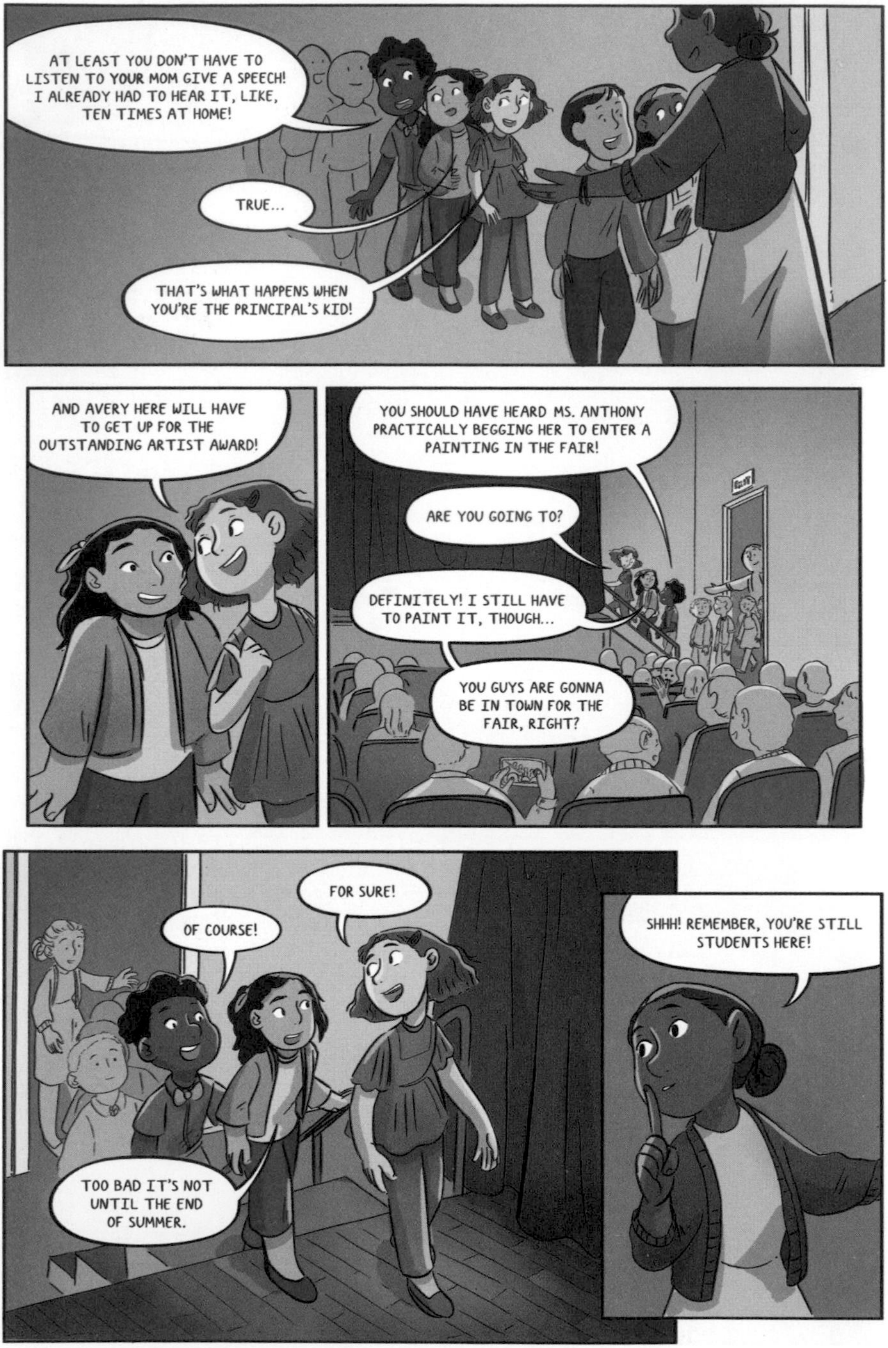
AT LEAST YOU DON'T HAVE TO LISTEN TO YOUR MOM GIVE A SPEECH! I ALREADY HAD TO HEAR IT, LIKE, TEN TIMES AT HOME!
TRUE...
THAT'S WHAT HAPPENS WHEN YOU'RE THE PRINCIPAL'S KID!
AND AVERY HERE WILL HAVE TO GET UP FOR THE OUTSTANDING ARTIST AWARD!
YOU SHOULD HAVE HEARD MS. ANTHONY PRACTICALLY BEGGING HER TO ENTER A PAINTING IN THE FAIR!
ARE YOU GOING TO?
DEFINITELY! I STILL HAVE TO PAINT IT, THOUGH...
YOU GUYS ARE GONNA BE IN TOWN FOR THE FAIR, RIGHT?
OF COURSE!
FOR SURE!
TOO BAD IT'S NOT UNTIL THE END OF SUMMER.
SHHH! REMEMBER, YOU'RE STILL STUDENTS HERE!

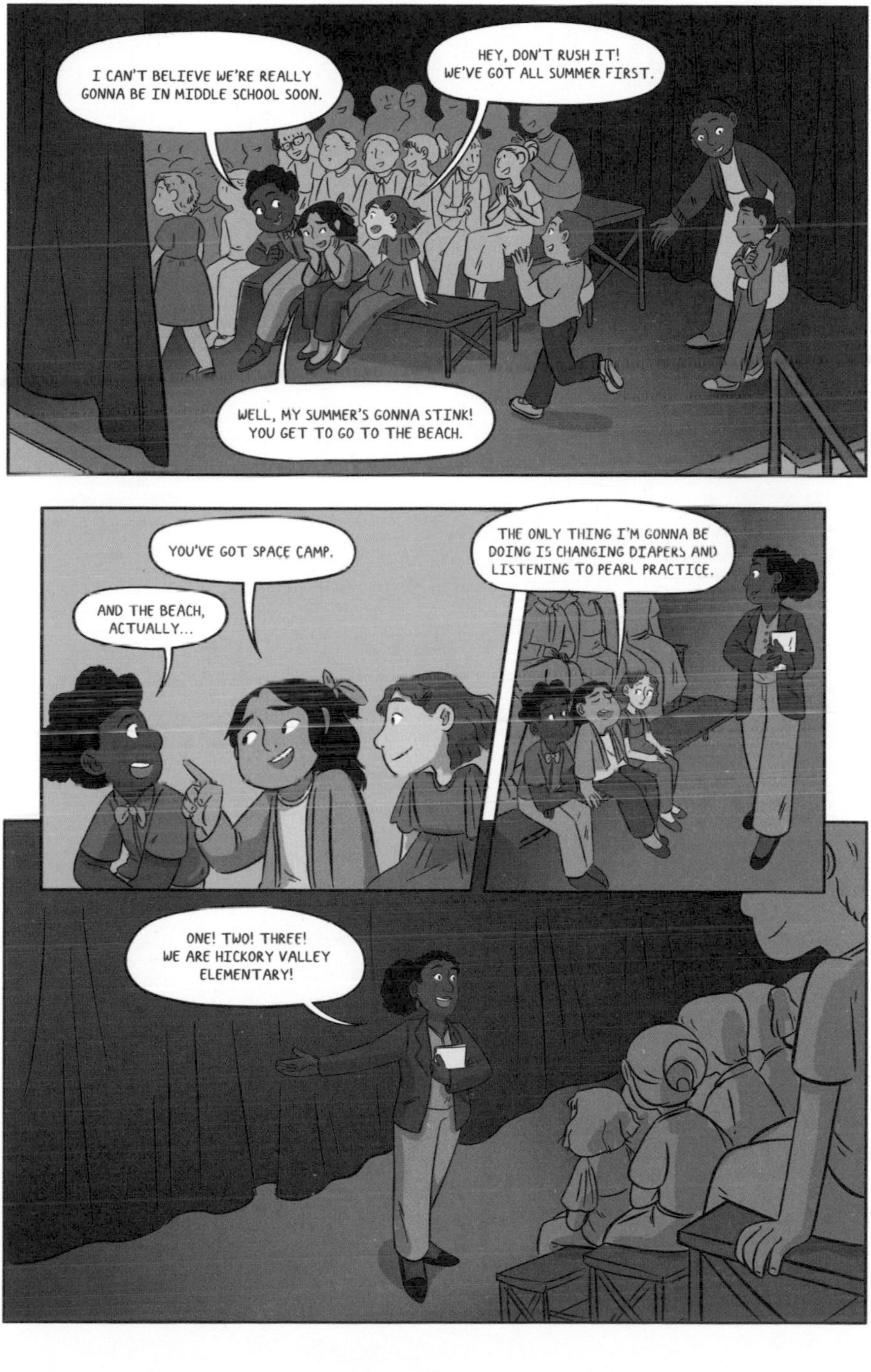

I CAN'T BELIEVE WE'RE REALLY GONNA BE IN MIDDLE SCHOOL SOON.
HEY, DON'T RUSH IT! WE'VE GOT ALL SUMMER FIRST.
WELL, MY SUMMER'S GONNA STINK! YOU GET TO GO TO THE BEACH.
YOU'VE GOT SPACE CAMP.
AND THE BEACH, ACTUALLY...
THE ONLY THING I'M GONNA BE DOING IS CHANGING DIAPERS AND LISTENING TO PEARL PRACTICE.
ONE! TWO! THREE! WE ARE HICKORY VALLEY ELEMENTARY!

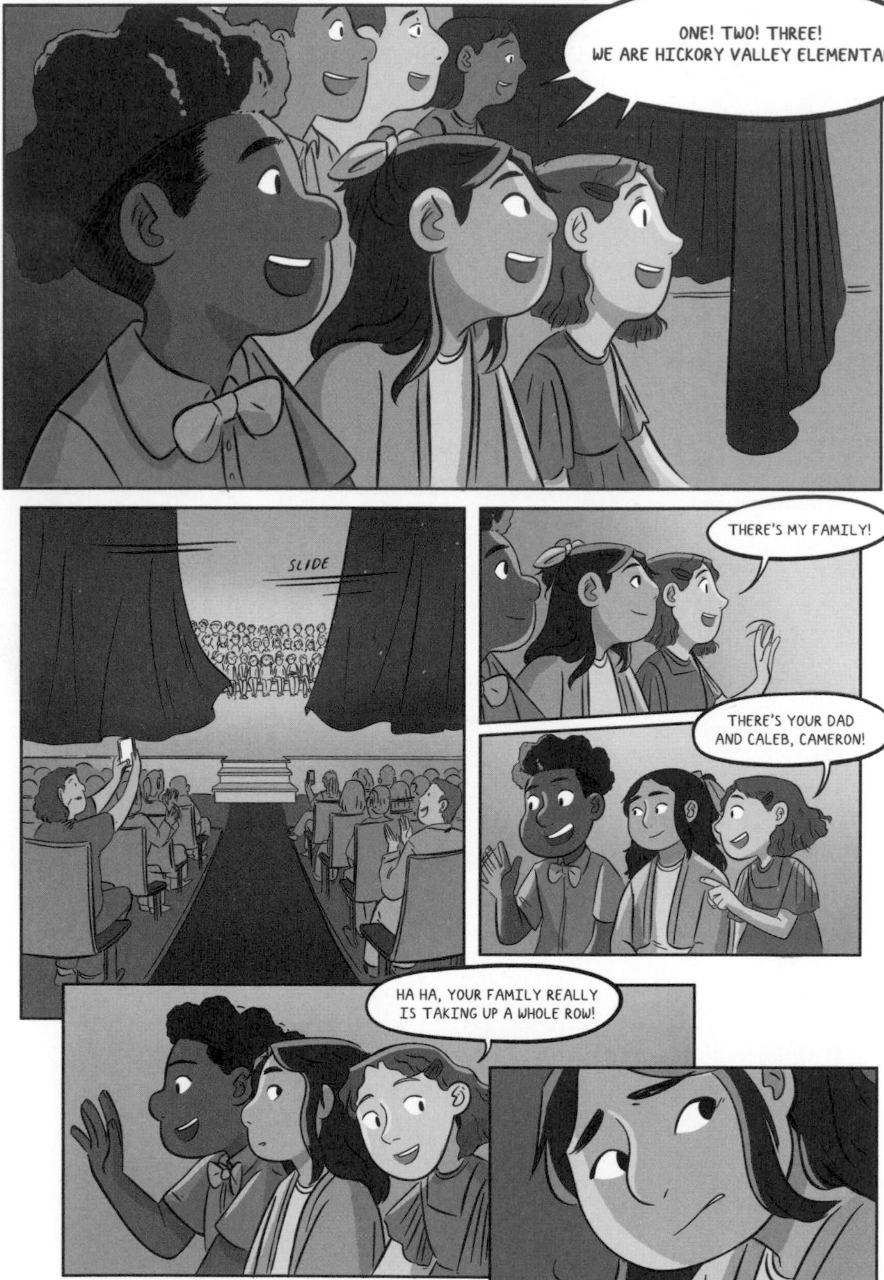
ONE! TWO! THREE!
WE ARE HICKORY VALLEY ELEMENTARY!
SLIDE
THERE'S MY FAMILY!
THERE'S YOUR DAD AND CALEB, CAMERON!
HA HA, YOUR FAMILY REALLY IS TAKING UP A WHOLE ROW!

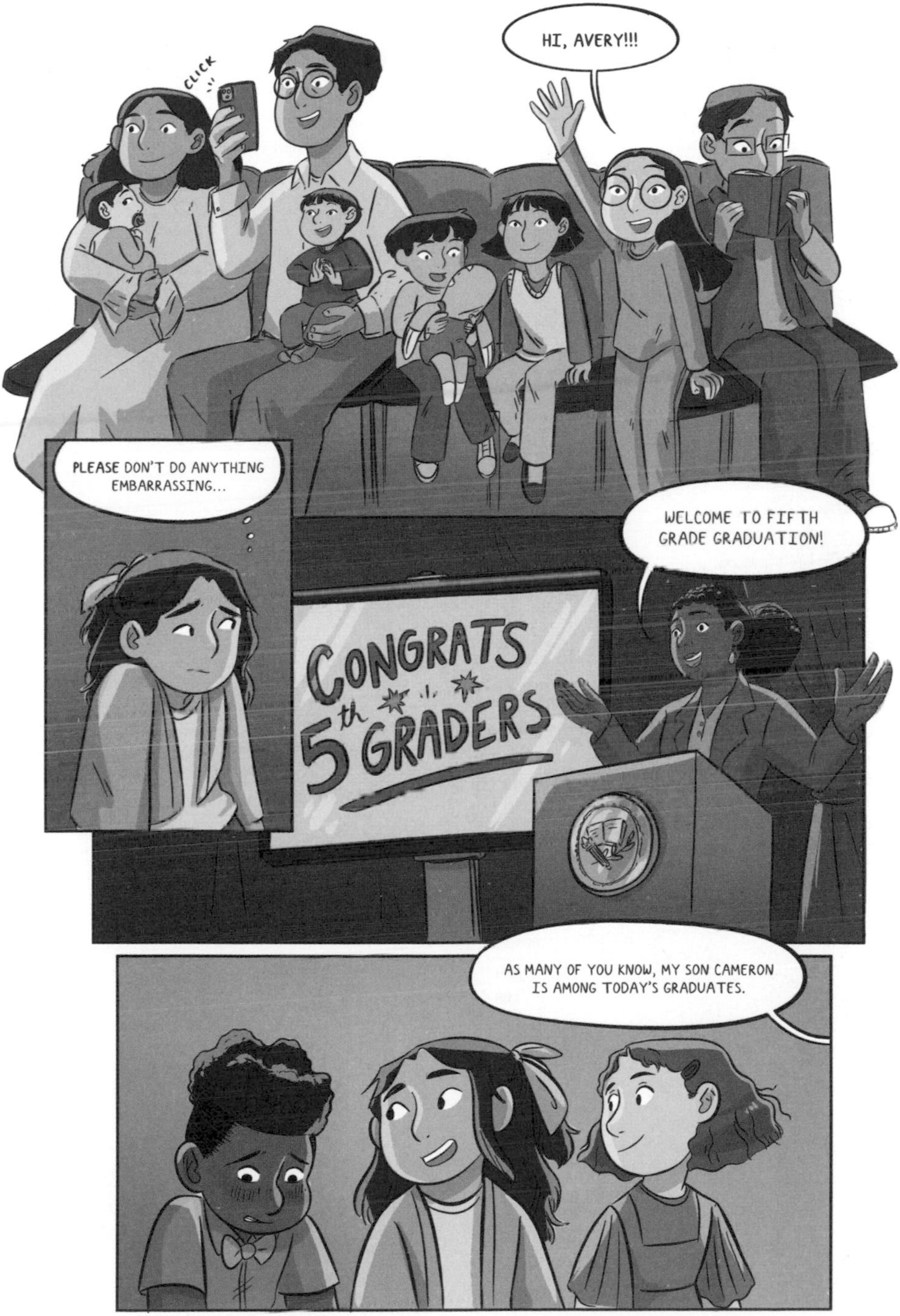
CLICK
HI, AVERY!!!
PLEASE DON'T DO ANYTHING EMBARRASSING...
WELCOME TO FIFTH GRADE GRADUATION!
CONGRATS 5th GRADERS
AS MANY OF YOU KNOW, MY SON CAMERON IS AMONG TODAY'S GRADUATES.

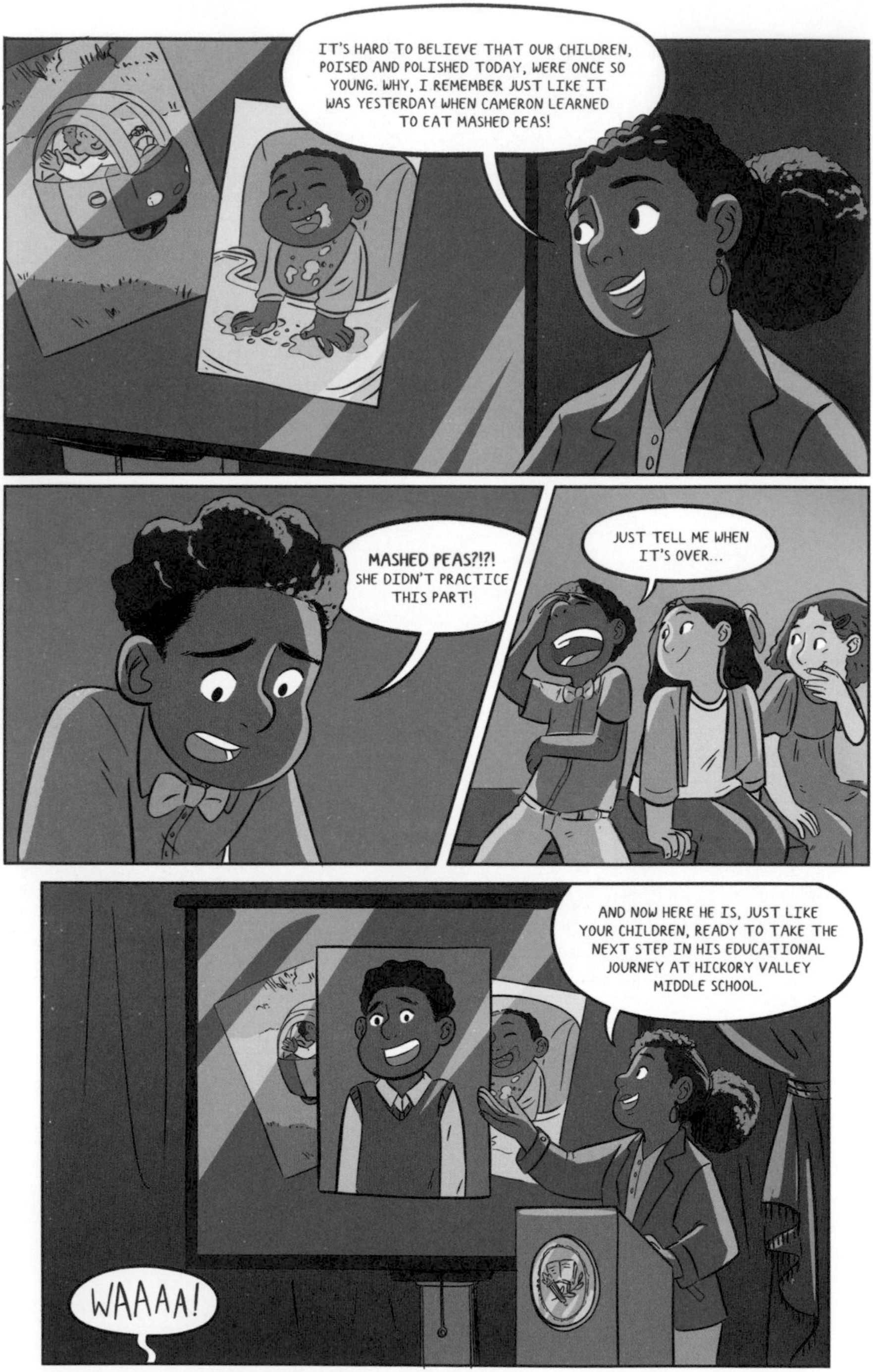
IT'S HARD TO BELIEVE THAT OUR CHILDREN, POISED AND POLISHED TODAY, WERE ONCE SO YOUNG. WHY, I REMEMBER JUST LIKE IT WAS YESTERDAY WHEN CAMERON LEARNED TO EAT MASHED PEAS!
MASHED PEAS?!?! SHE DIDN'T PRACTICE THIS PART!
JUST TELL ME WHEN IT'S OVER...
AND NOW HERE HE IS, JUST LIKE YOUR CHILDREN, READY TO TAKE THE NEXT STEP IN HIS EDUCATIONAL JOURNEY AT HICKORY VALLEY MIDDLE SCHOOL.
WAAAA!

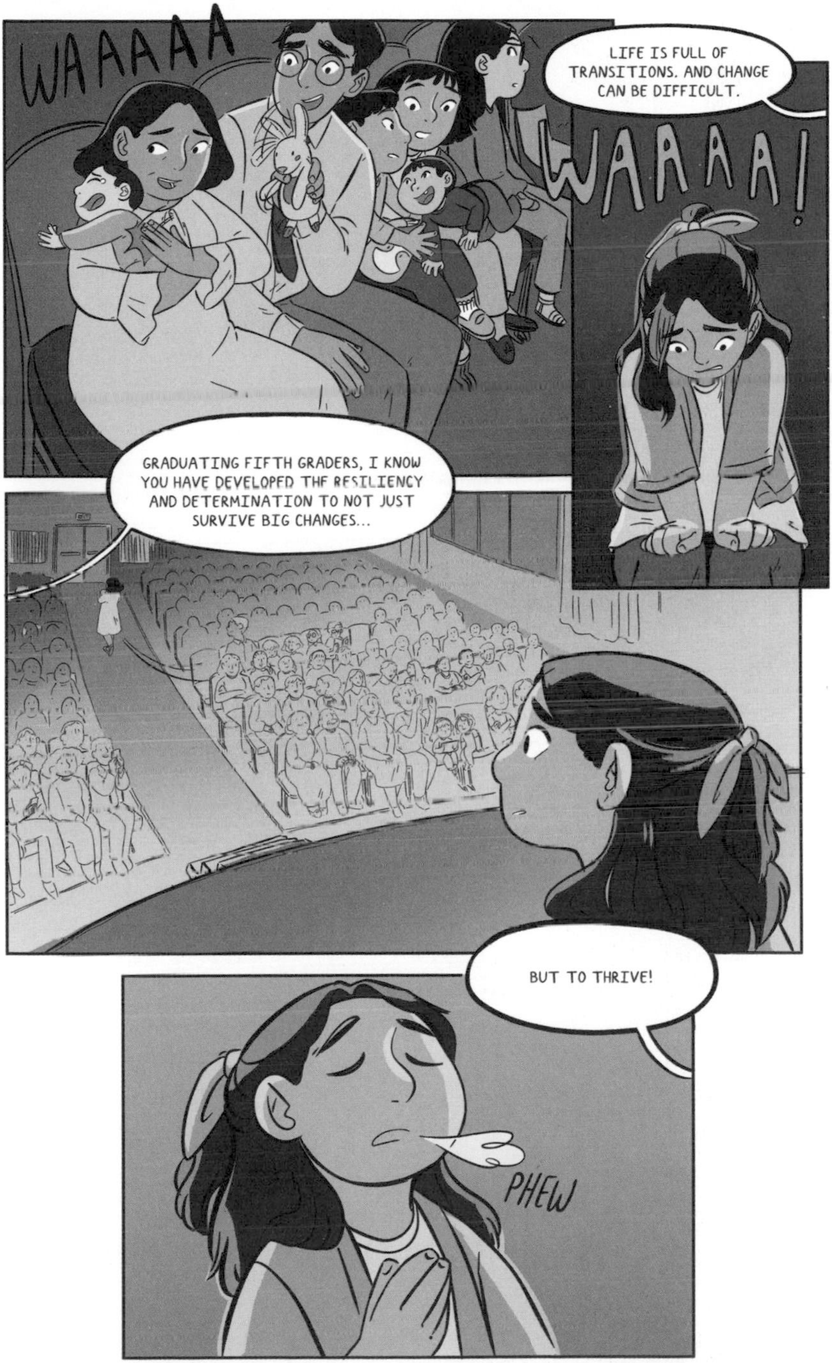
WAAAAA
LIFE IS FULL OF TRANSITIONS. AND CHANGE CAN BE DIFFICULT.
WAAAAA!
GRADUATING FIFTH GRADERS, I KNOW YOU HAVE DEVELOPED THE RESILIENCY AND DETERMINATION TO NOT JUST SURVIVE BIG CHANGES...
BUT TO THRIVE!
PHEW

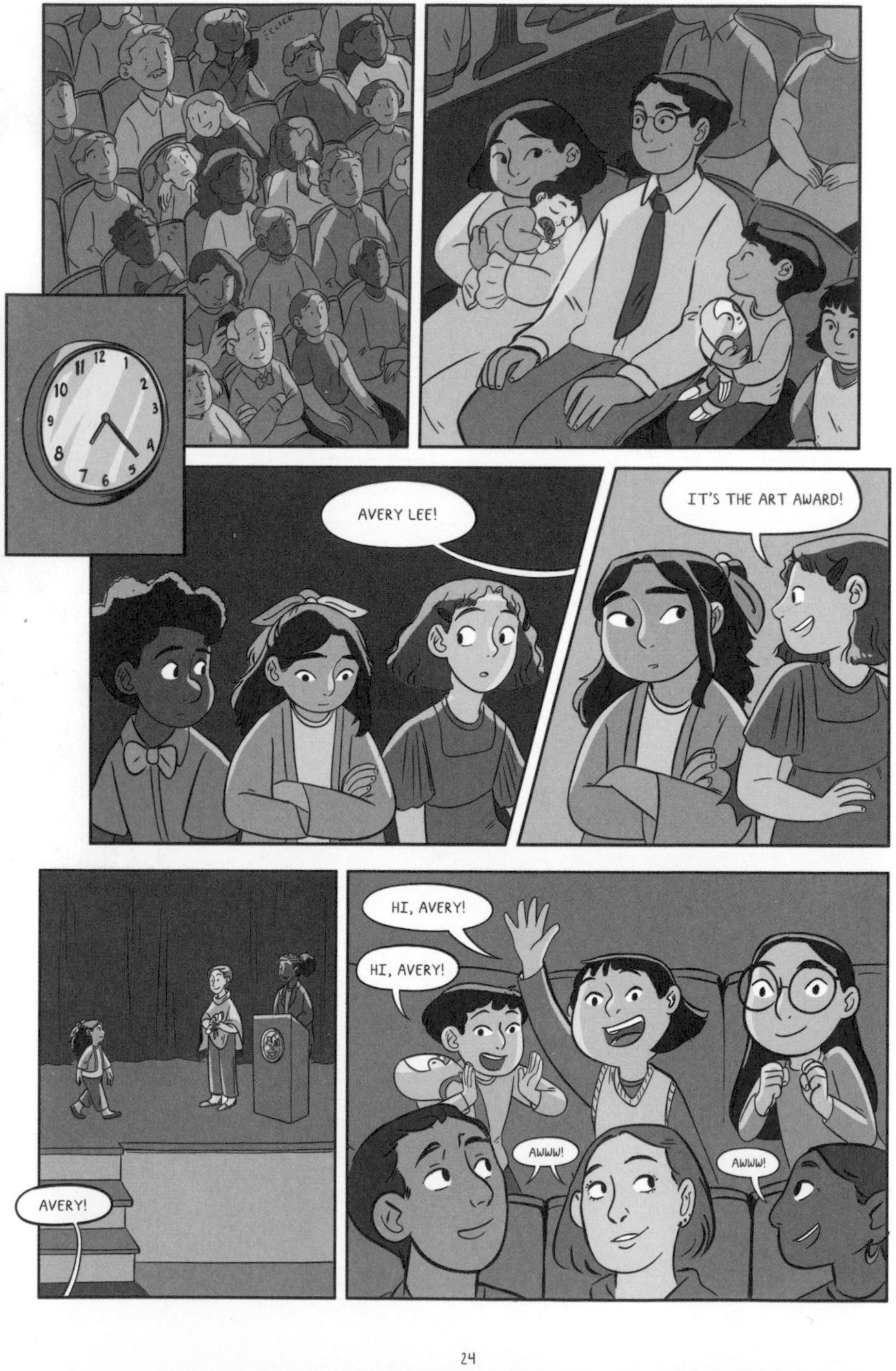
AVERY LEE!
IT'S THE ART AWARD!
AVERY!
HI, AVERY!
HI, AVERY!
AWWW!
AWWW!

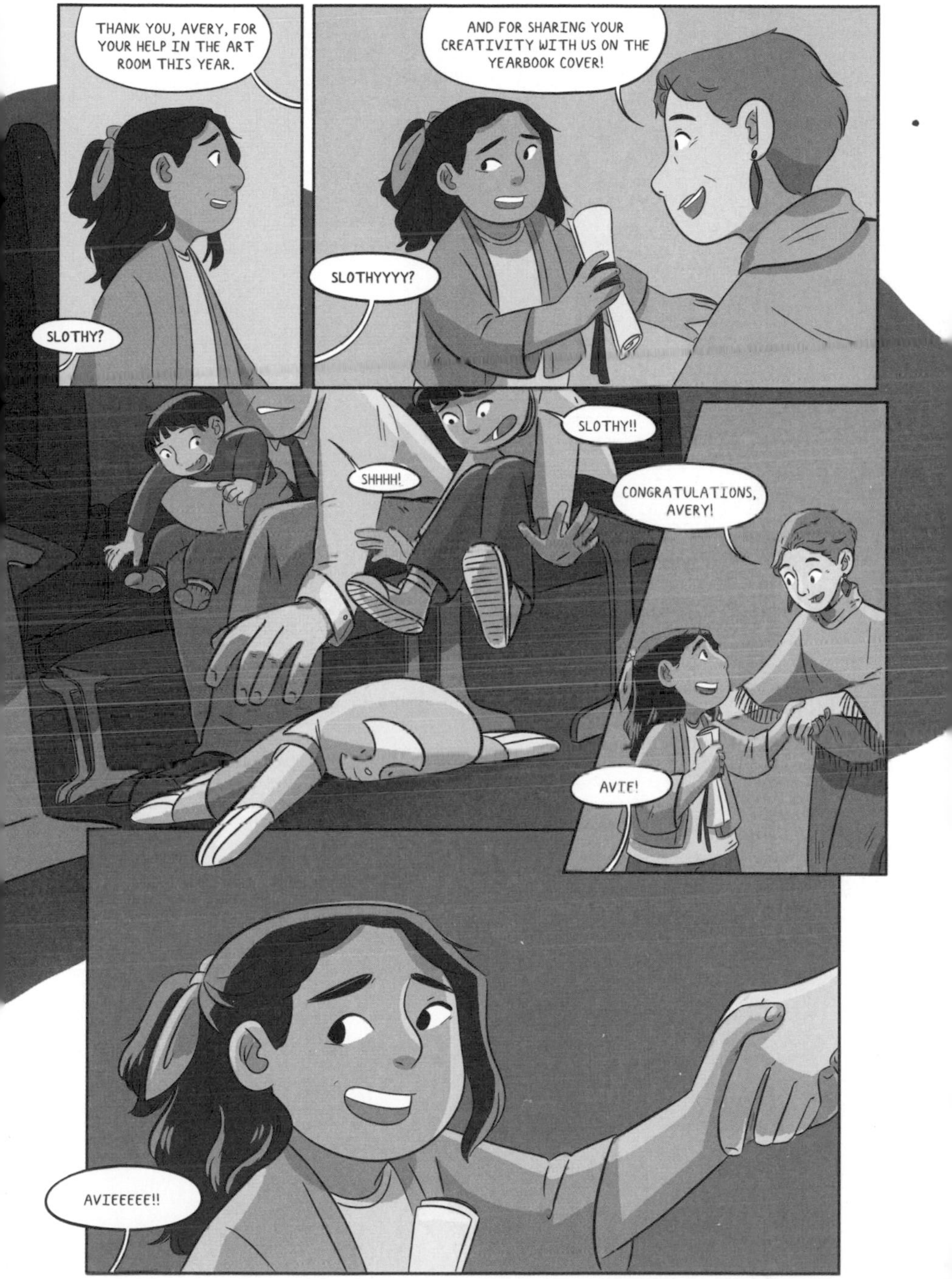
THANK YOU, AVERY, FOR YOUR HELP IN THE ART ROOM THIS YEAR.
SLOTHY?
AND FOR SHARING YOUR CREATIVITY WITH US ON THE YEARBOOK COVER!
SLOTHYYYY?
SHHHH!
SLOTHY!!
CONGRATULATIONS, AVERY!
AVIE!
AVIEEEEE!!

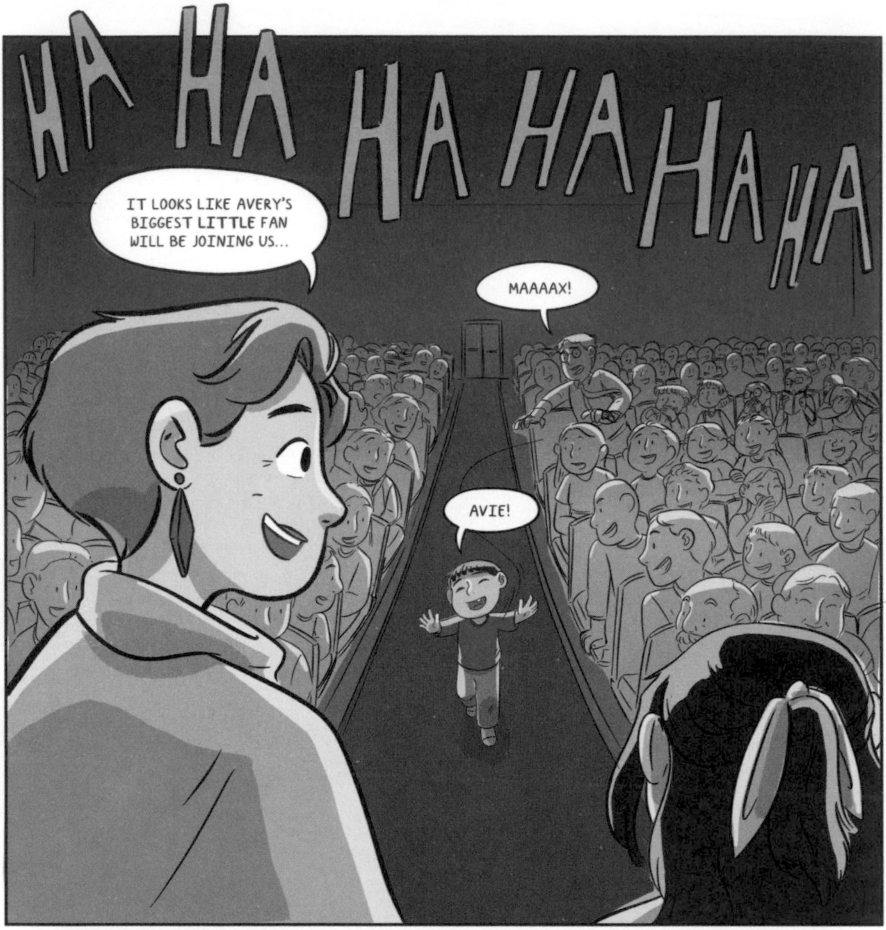
HA HA HA HA HAHAHA
IT LOOKS LIKE AVERY'S BIGGEST LITTLE FAN WILL BE JOINING US...
MAAAAX!
AVIE!

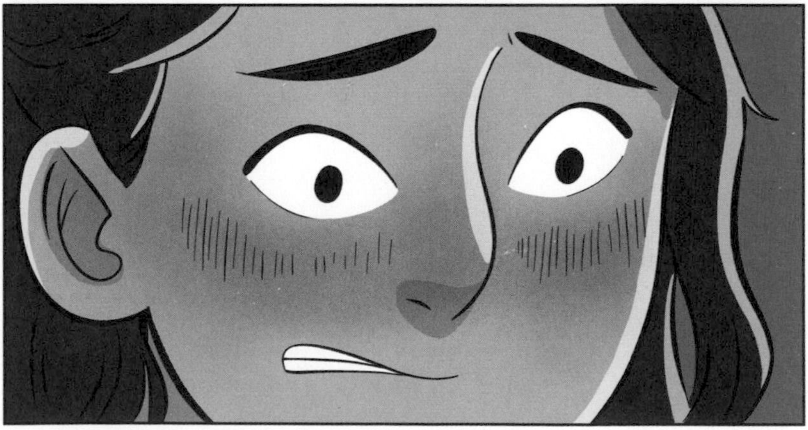

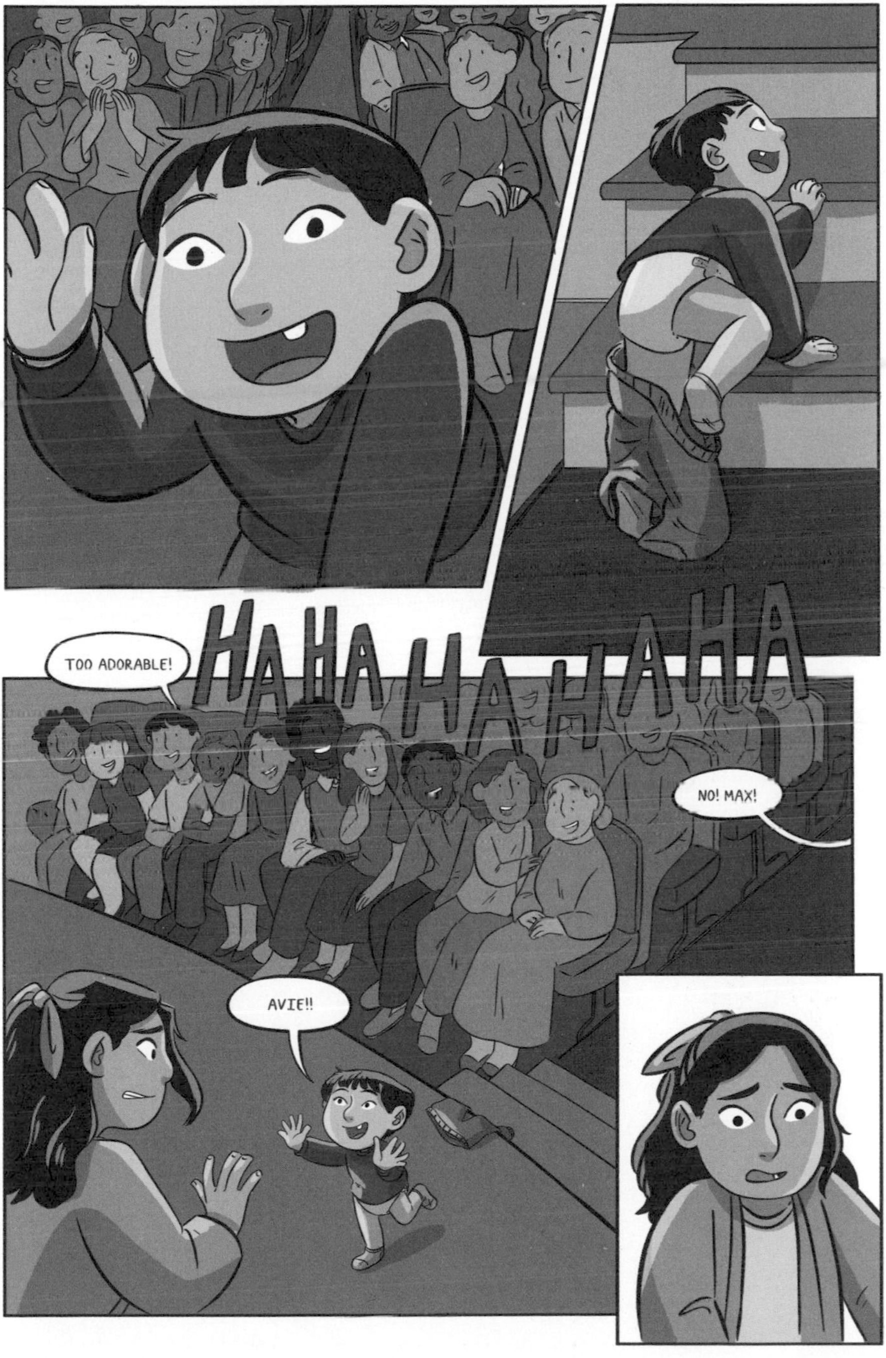
HAHAHAHAHAHA
TOO ADORABLE!
NO! MAX!
AVIE!!

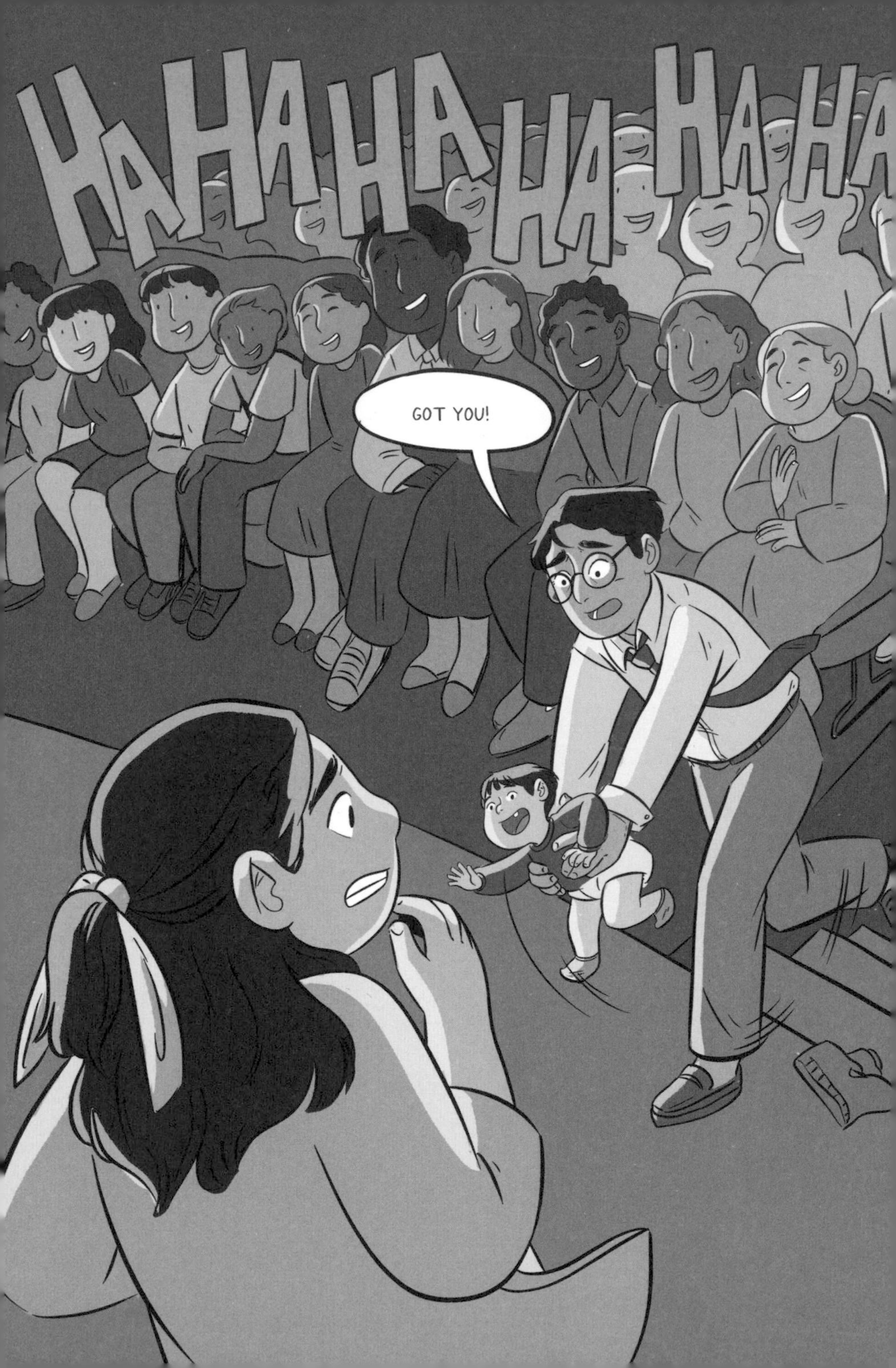
HAHAHAHAHAHAHA
GOT YOU!

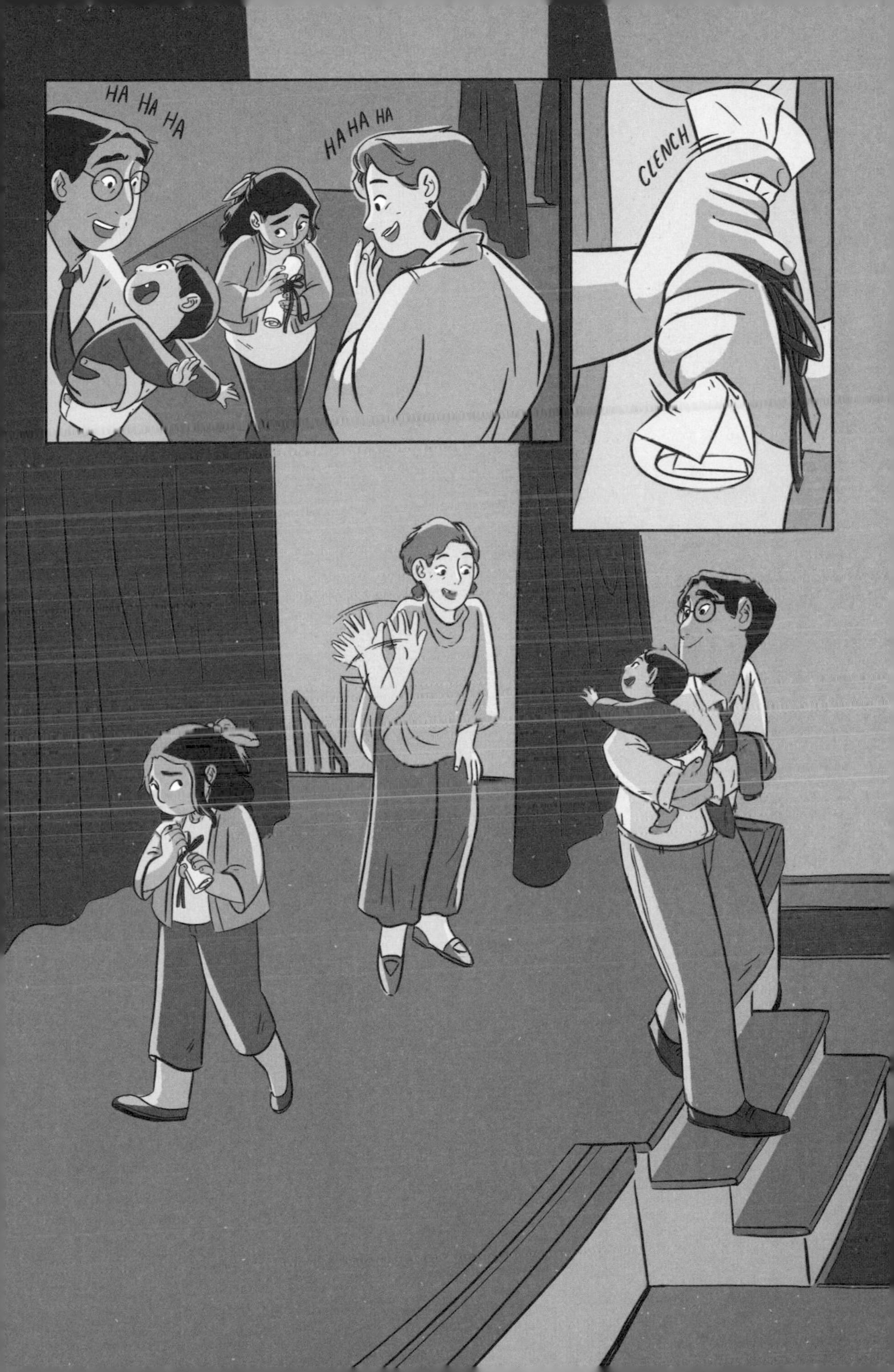
HA HA HA
HA HA HA
CLENCH

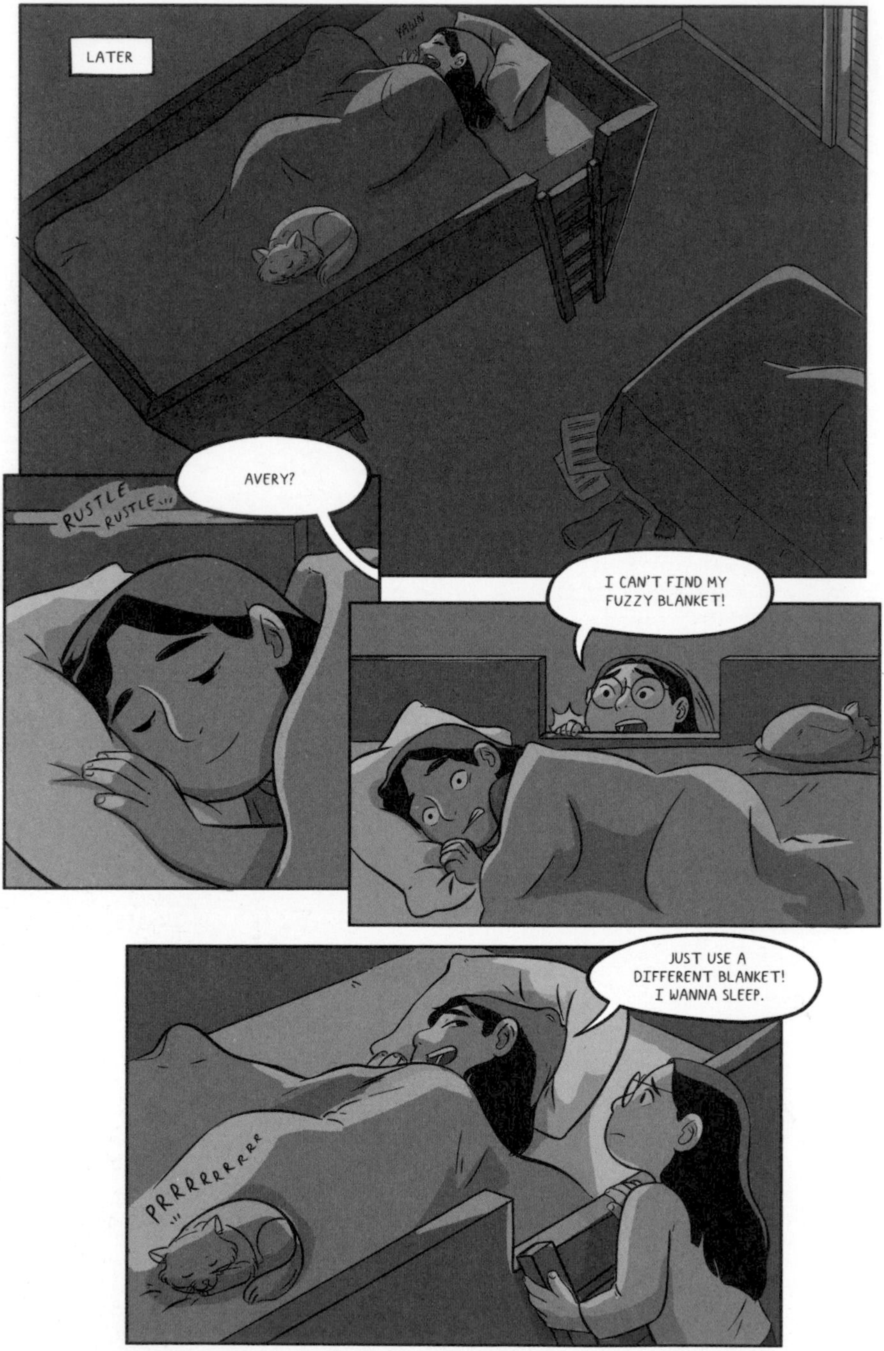
LATER
YAWN
RUSTLE RUSTLE...
AVERY?
I CAN'T FIND MY FUZZY BLANKET!
JUST USE A DIFFERENT BLANKET! I WANNA SLEEP.
PRRRRRRRRR...

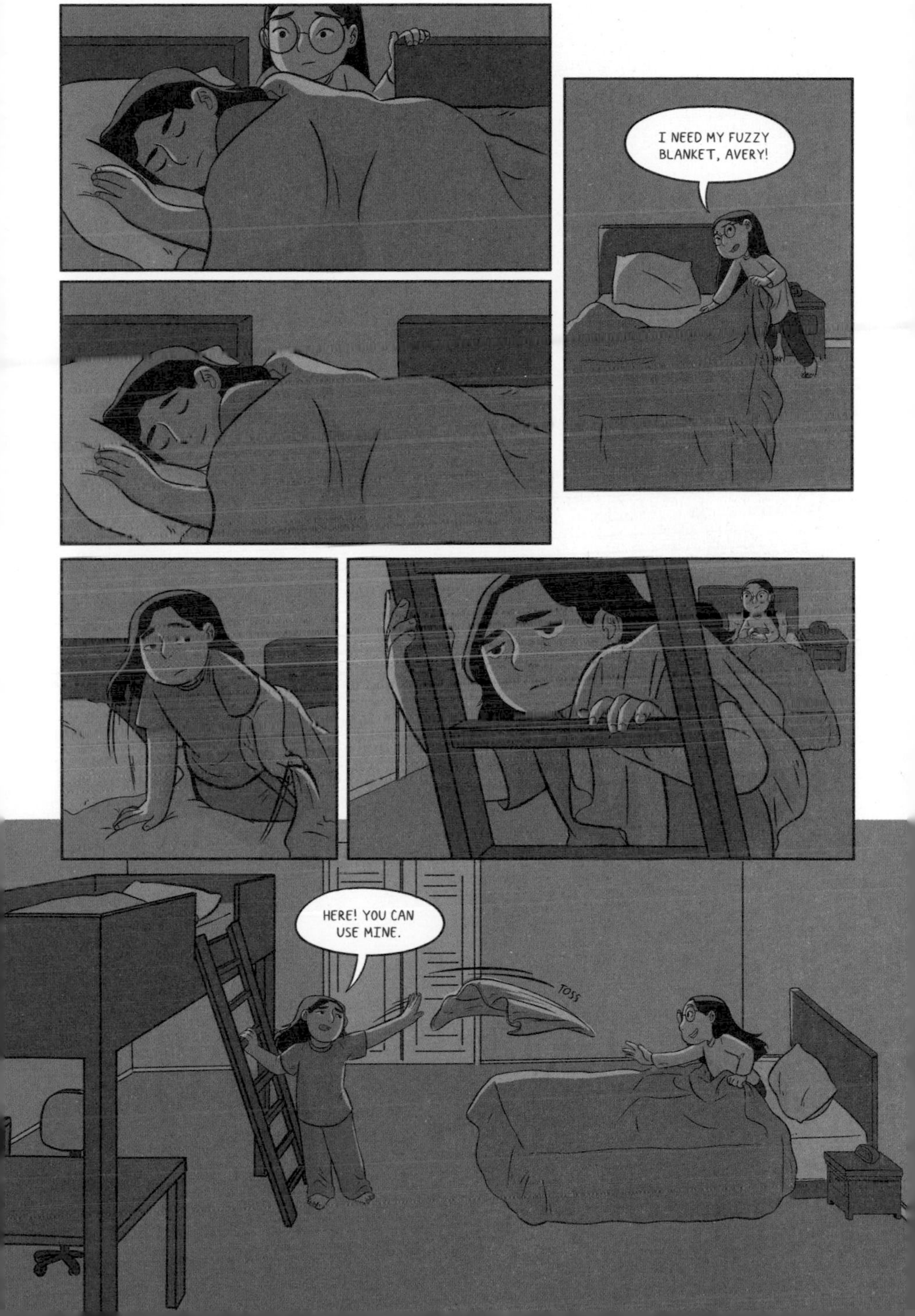
I NEED MY FUZZY BLANKET, AVERY!
HERE! YOU CAN USE MINE.
TOSS

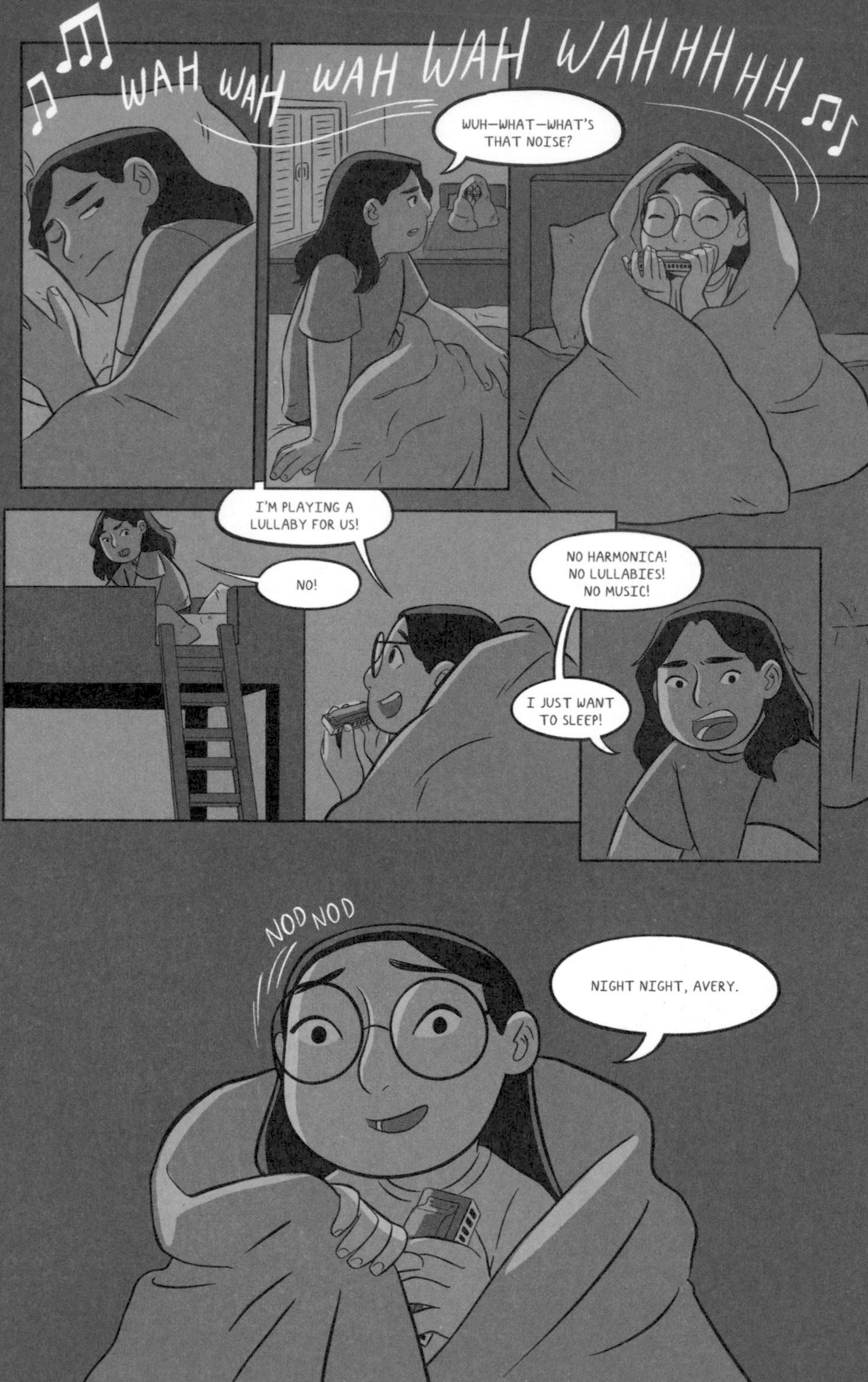
WAH WAH WAH WAH WAHHHHHH
WUH—WHAT—WHAT'S THAT NOISE?
I'M PLAYING A LULLABY FOR US!
NO!
NO HARMONICA! NO LULLABIES! NO MUSIC!
I JUST WANT TO SLEEP!
NOD NOD
NIGHT NIGHT, AVERY.

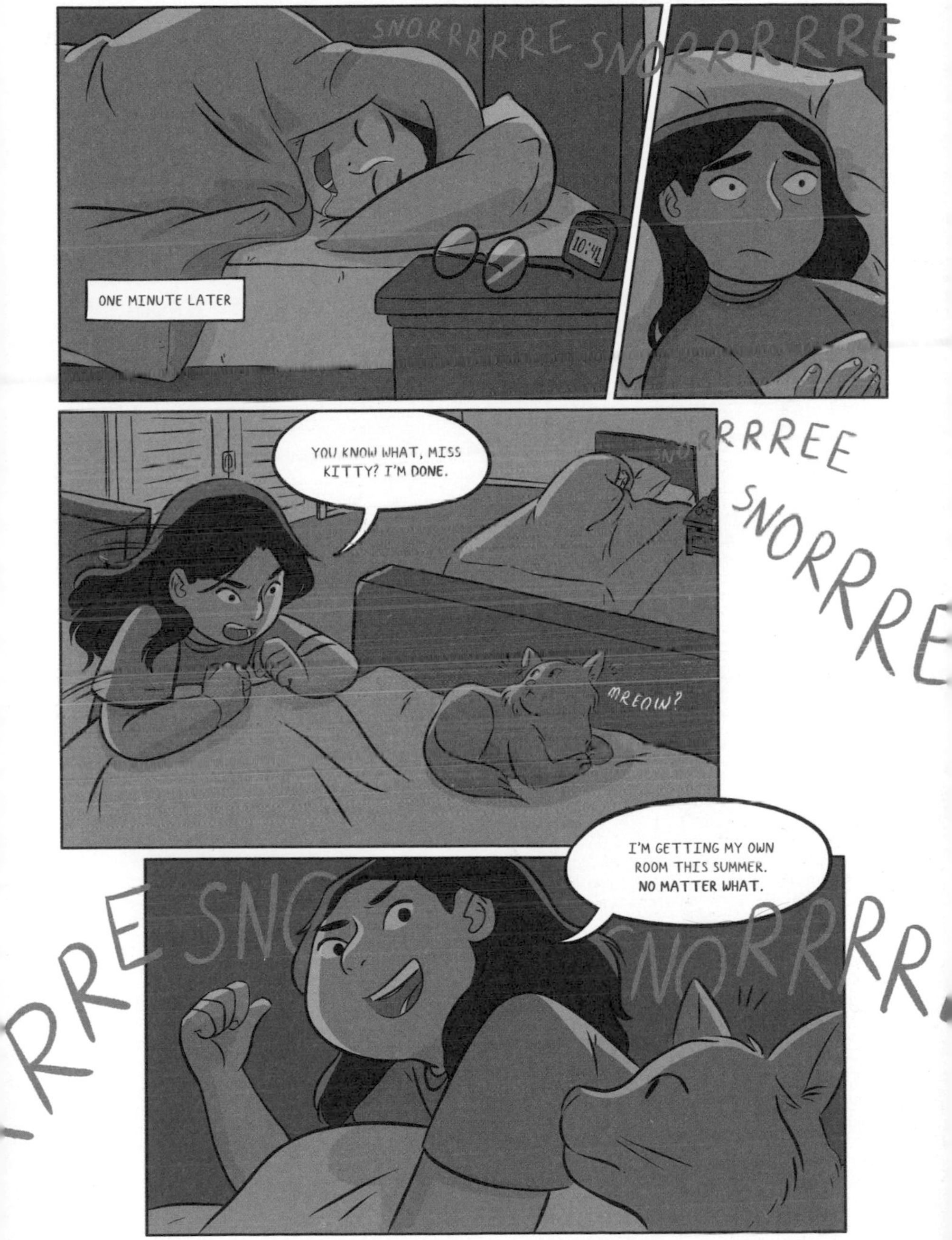
SNORRRRRE
SNORRRRRE
ONE MINUTE LATER
SNORRRREE
YOU KNOW WHAT, MISS KITTY? I'M DONE.
SNORRRRE
MREOW?
RRE SNO
I'M GETTING MY OWN ROOM THIS SUMMER. NO MATTER WHAT.
SNORRRR

Chapter Three

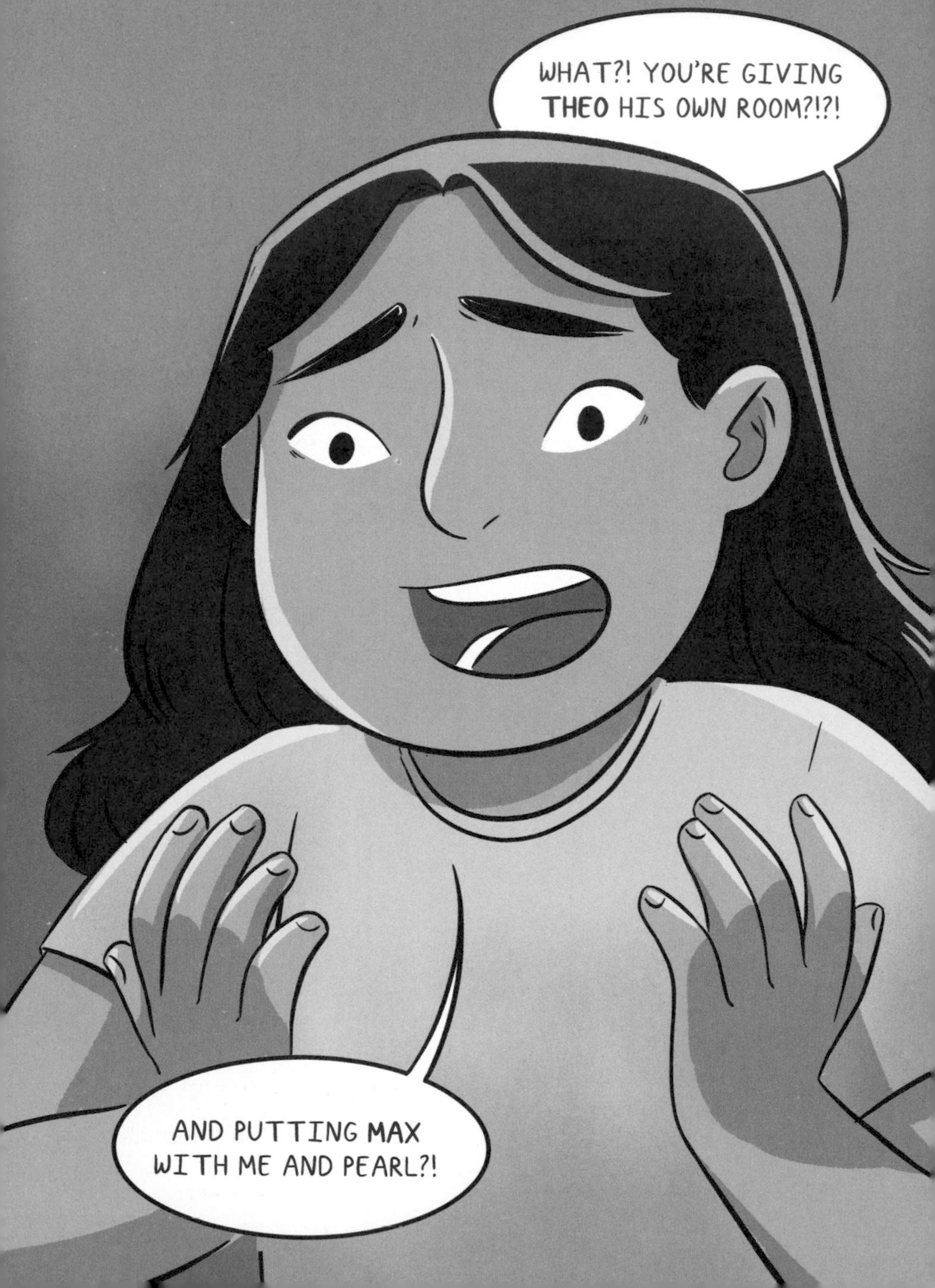
WHAT?! YOU'RE GIVING THEO HIS OWN ROOM?!?!
AND PUTTING MAX WITH ME AND PEARL?!

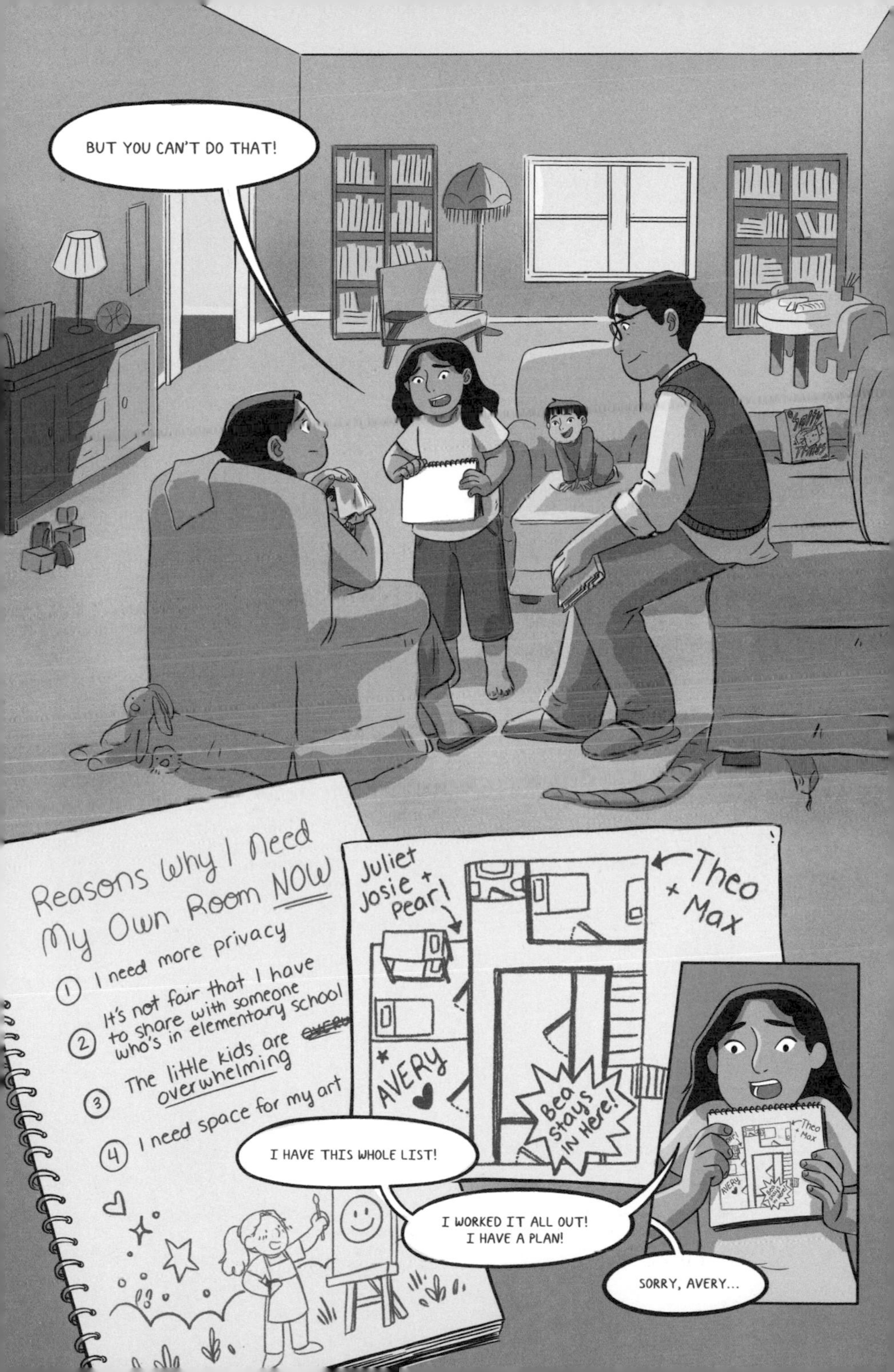
BUT YOU CAN'T DO THAT!
Reasons Why I Need My Own Room NOW
① I need more privacy
② It's not fair that I have to share with someone who's in elementary school
③ The little kids are overwhelming
④ I need space for my art
Juliet Josie + Pearl
Theo + Max
AVERY
Bea stays in Here!
I HAVE THIS WHOLE LIST!
I WORKED IT ALL OUT! I HAVE A PLAN!
SORRY, AVERY...

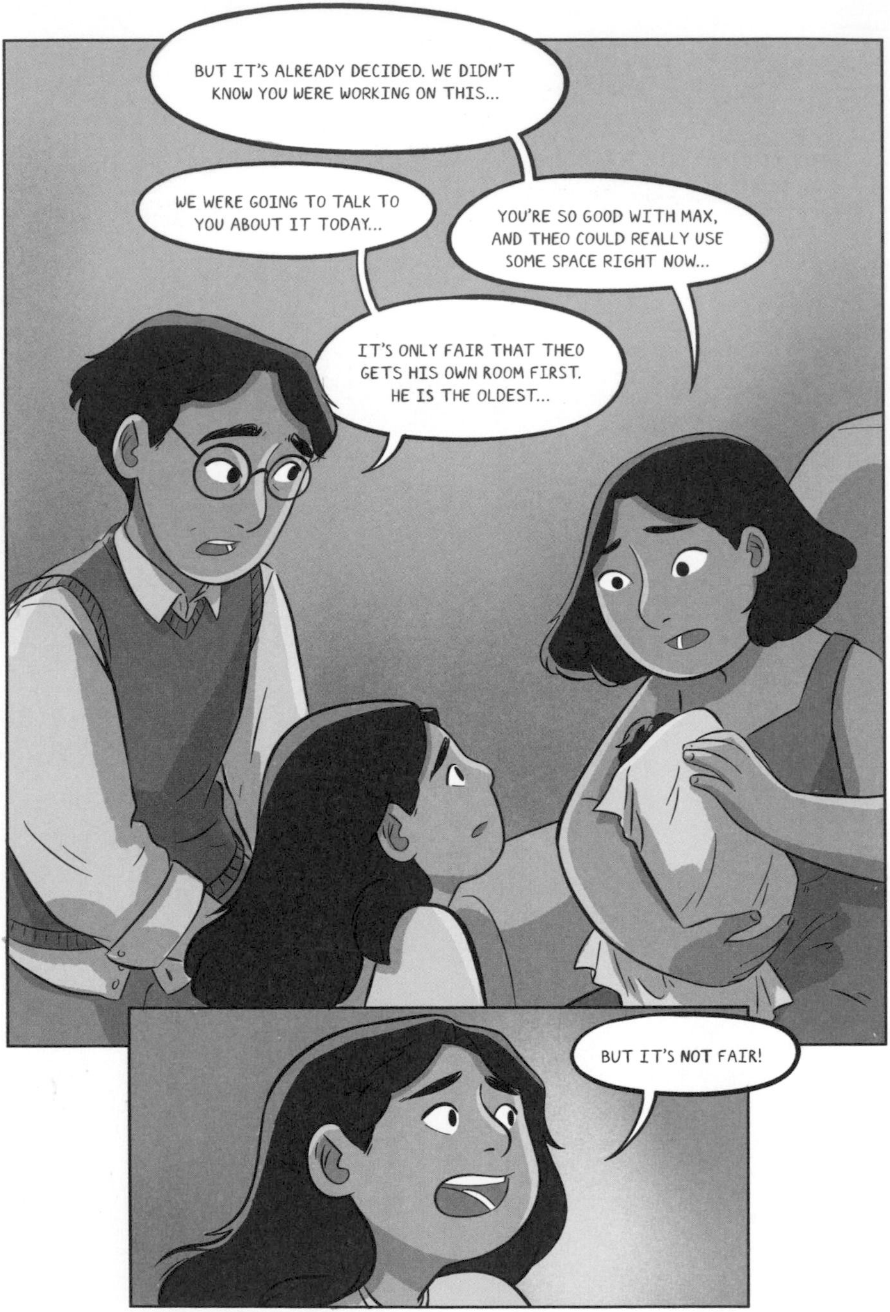
BUT IT'S ALREADY DECIDED. WE DIDN'T KNOW YOU WERE WORKING ON THIS...
WE WERE GOING TO TALK TO YOU ABOUT IT TODAY...
YOU'RE SO GOOD WITH MAX, AND THEO COULD REALLY USE SOME SPACE RIGHT NOW...
IT'S ONLY FAIR THAT THEO GETS HIS OWN ROOM FIRST. HE IS THE OLDEST...
BUT IT'S **NOT** FAIR!

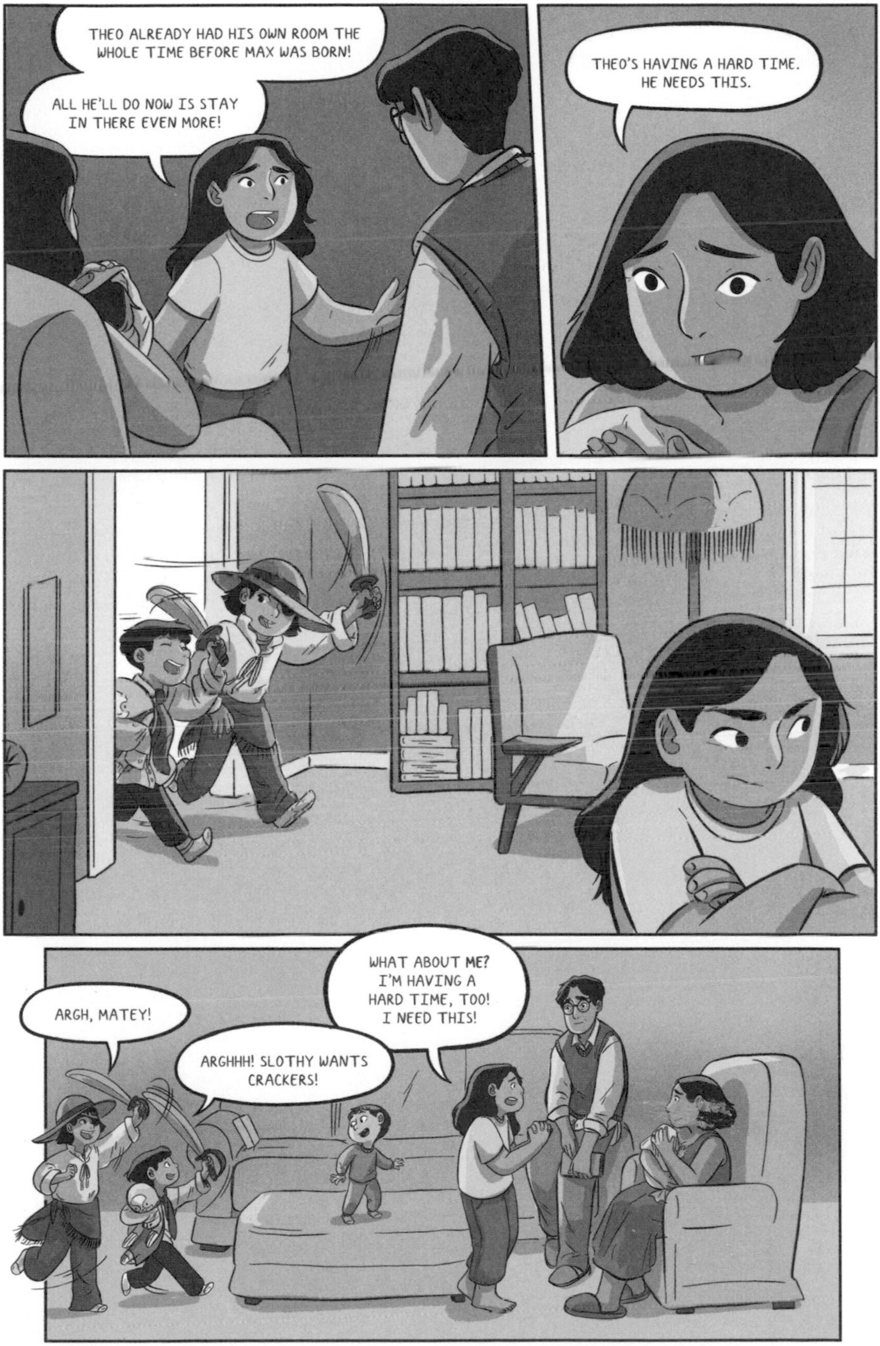
THEO ALREADY HAD HIS OWN ROOM THE WHOLE TIME BEFORE MAX WAS BORN!
ALL HE'LL DO NOW IS STAY IN THERE EVEN MORE!
THEO'S HAVING A HARD TIME. HE NEEDS THIS.
ARGH, MATEY!
ARGHHH! SLOTHY WANTS CRACKERS!
WHAT ABOUT ME? I'M HAVING A HARD TIME, TOO! I NEED THIS!

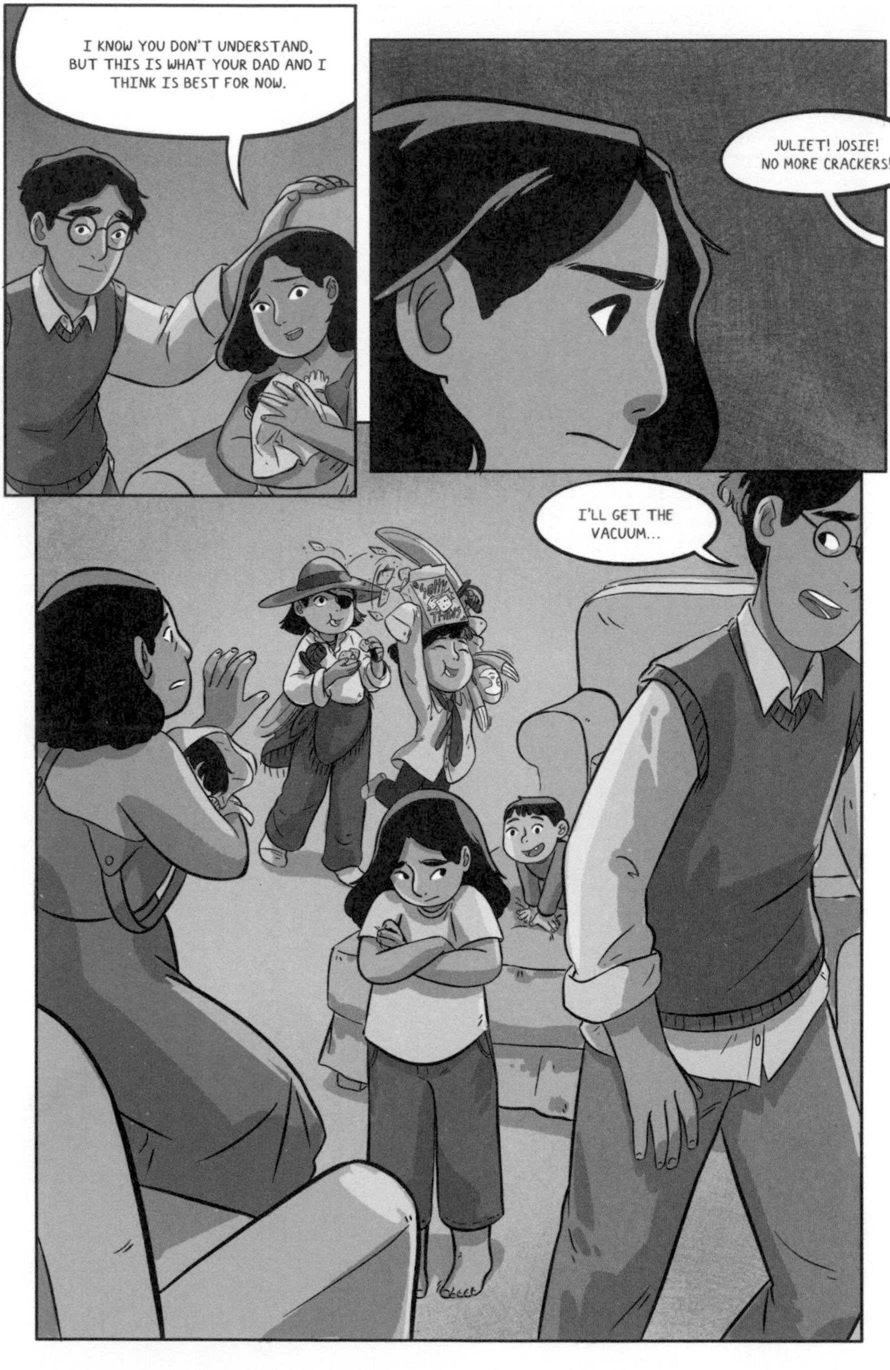
I KNOW YOU DON'T UNDERSTAND,
BUT THIS IS WHAT YOUR DAD AND I
THINK IS BEST FOR NOW.
JULIET! JOSIE!
NO MORE CRACKERS!
I'LL GET THE
VACUUM...

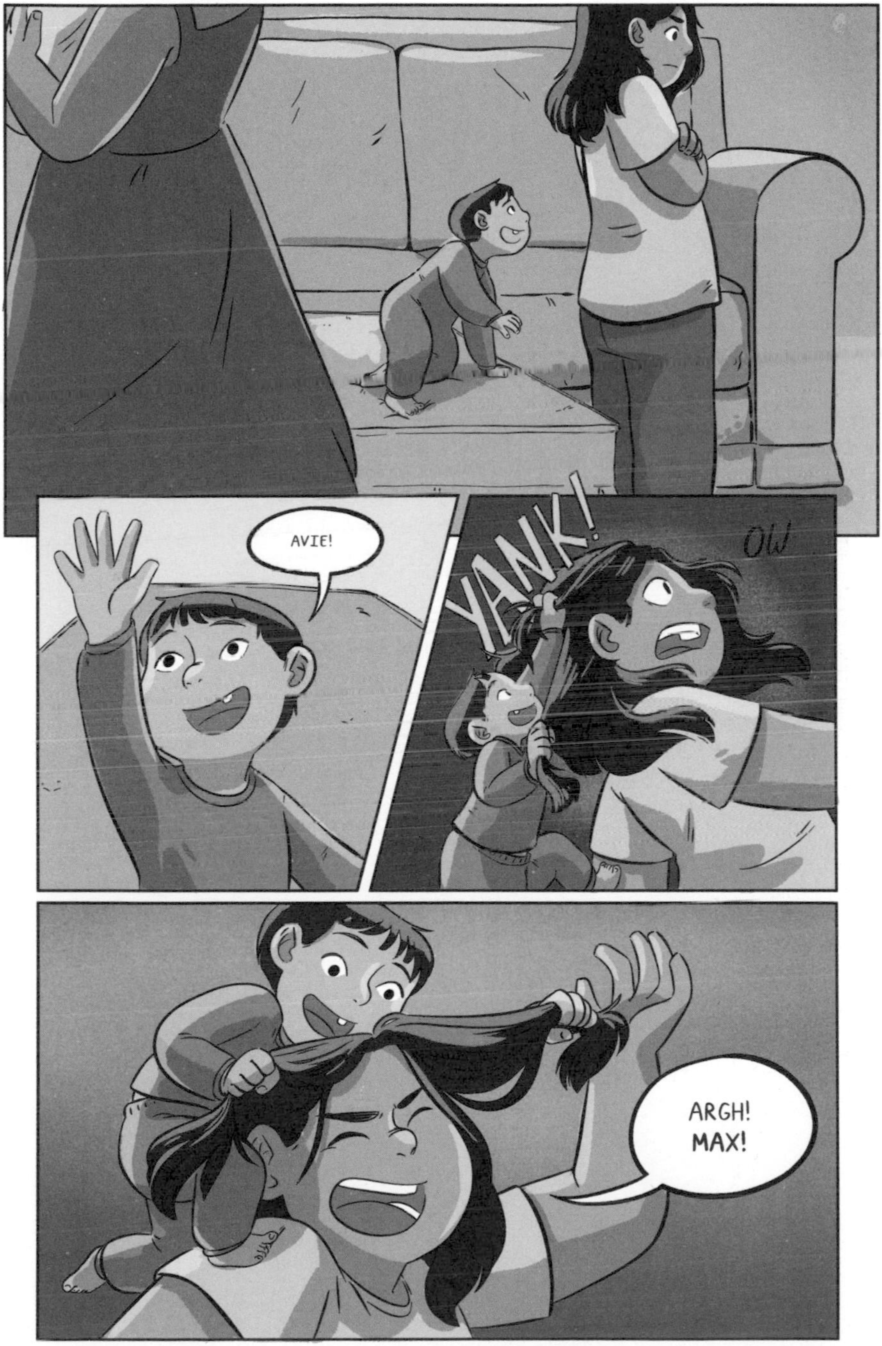
AVIE!
YANK!
OW
ARGH!
MAX!

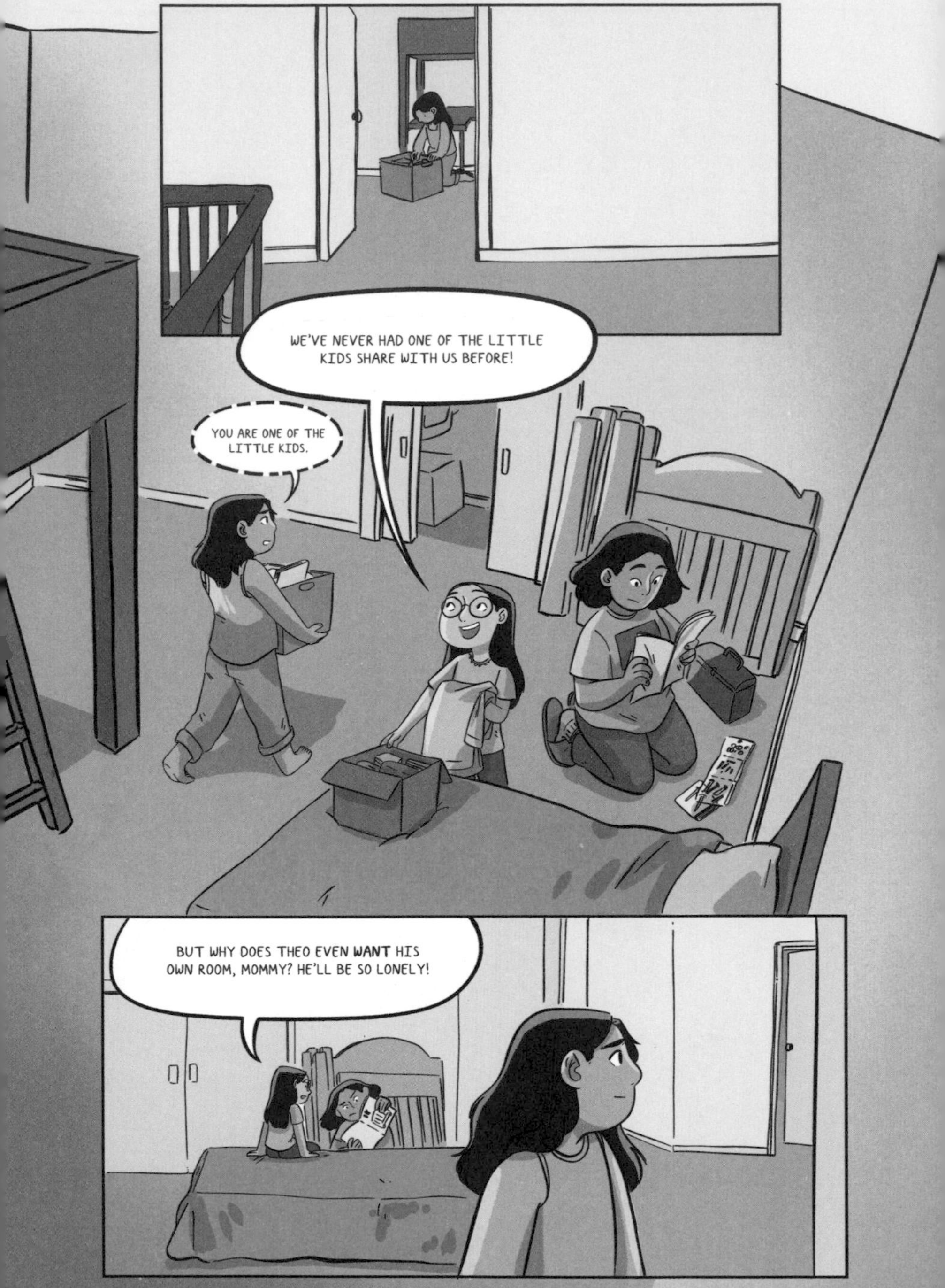
WE'VE NEVER HAD ONE OF THE LITTLE KIDS SHARE WITH US BEFORE!
YOU ARE ONE OF THE LITTLE KIDS.
BUT WHY DOES THEO EVEN **WANT** HIS OWN ROOM, MOMMY? HE'LL BE SO LONELY!

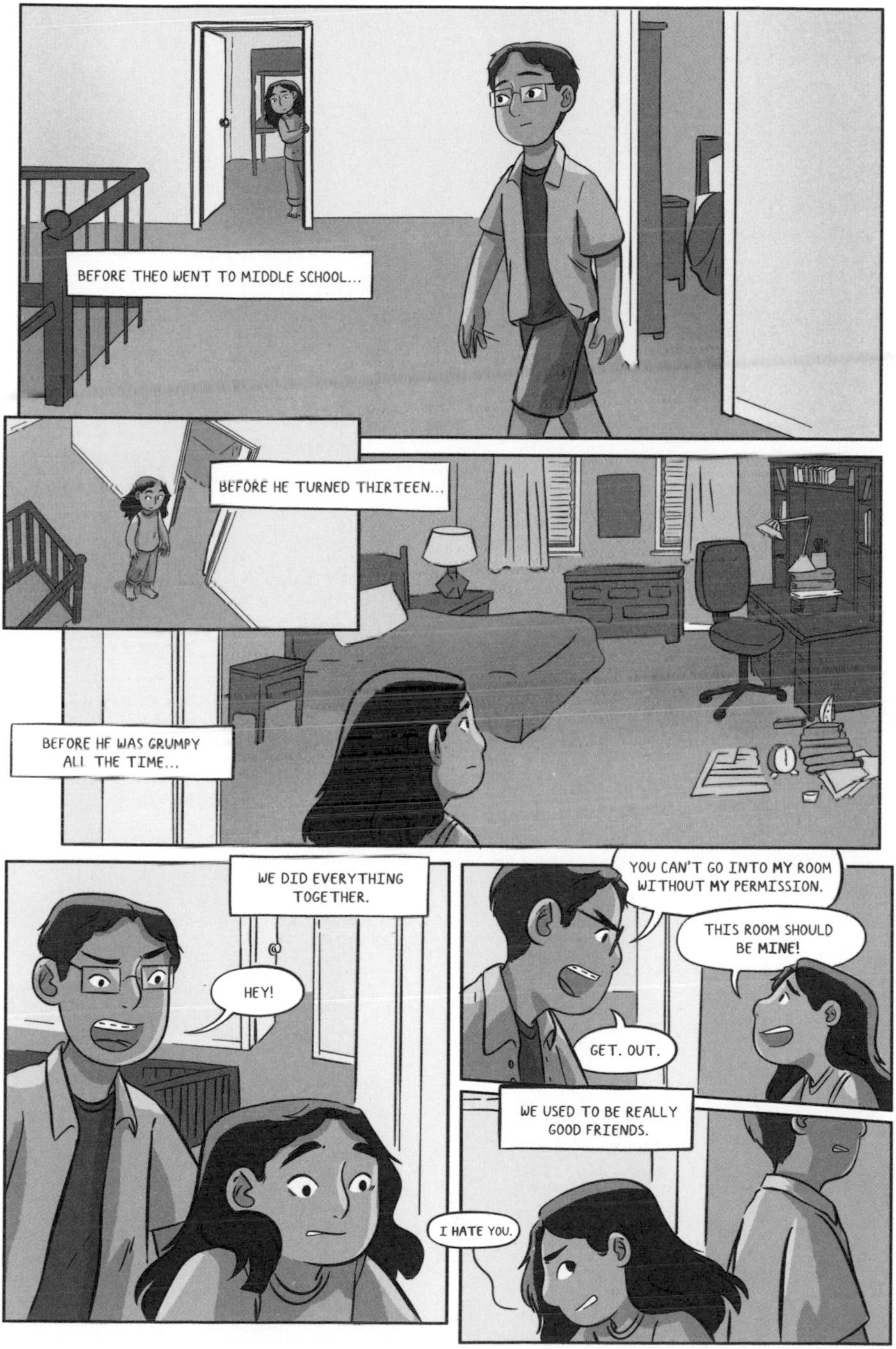
BEFORE THEO WENT TO MIDDLE SCHOOL...
BEFORE HE TURNED THIRTEEN...
BEFORE HE WAS GRUMPY ALL THE TIME...
WE DID EVERYTHING TOGETHER.
HEY!
YOU CAN'T GO INTO MY ROOM WITHOUT MY PERMISSION.
THIS ROOM SHOULD BE MINE!
GET. OUT.
WE USED TO BE REALLY GOOD FRIENDS.
I HATE YOU.

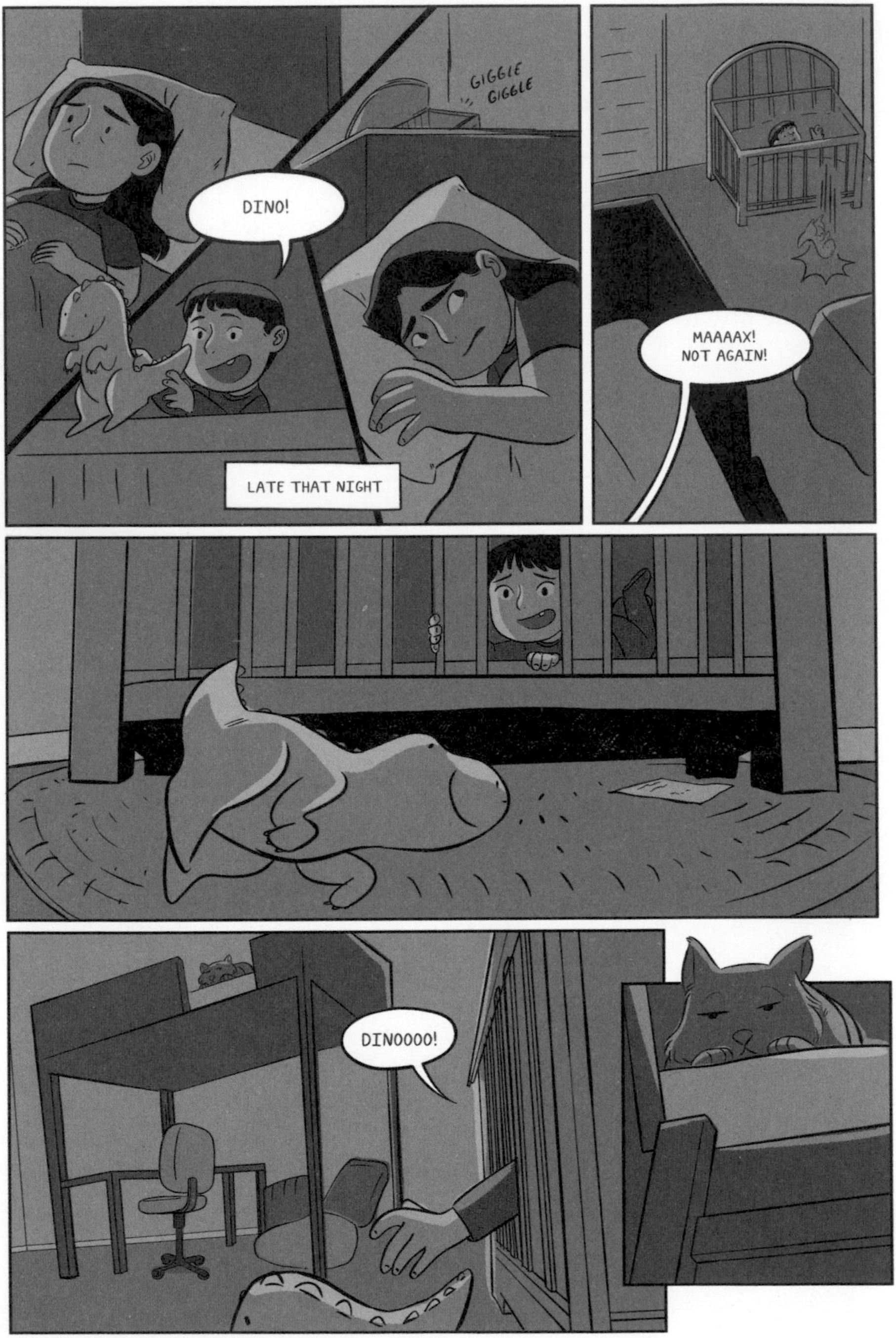
GIGGLE GIGGLE
DINO!
LATE THAT NIGHT
MAAAAX! NOT AGAIN!
DINOOOO!

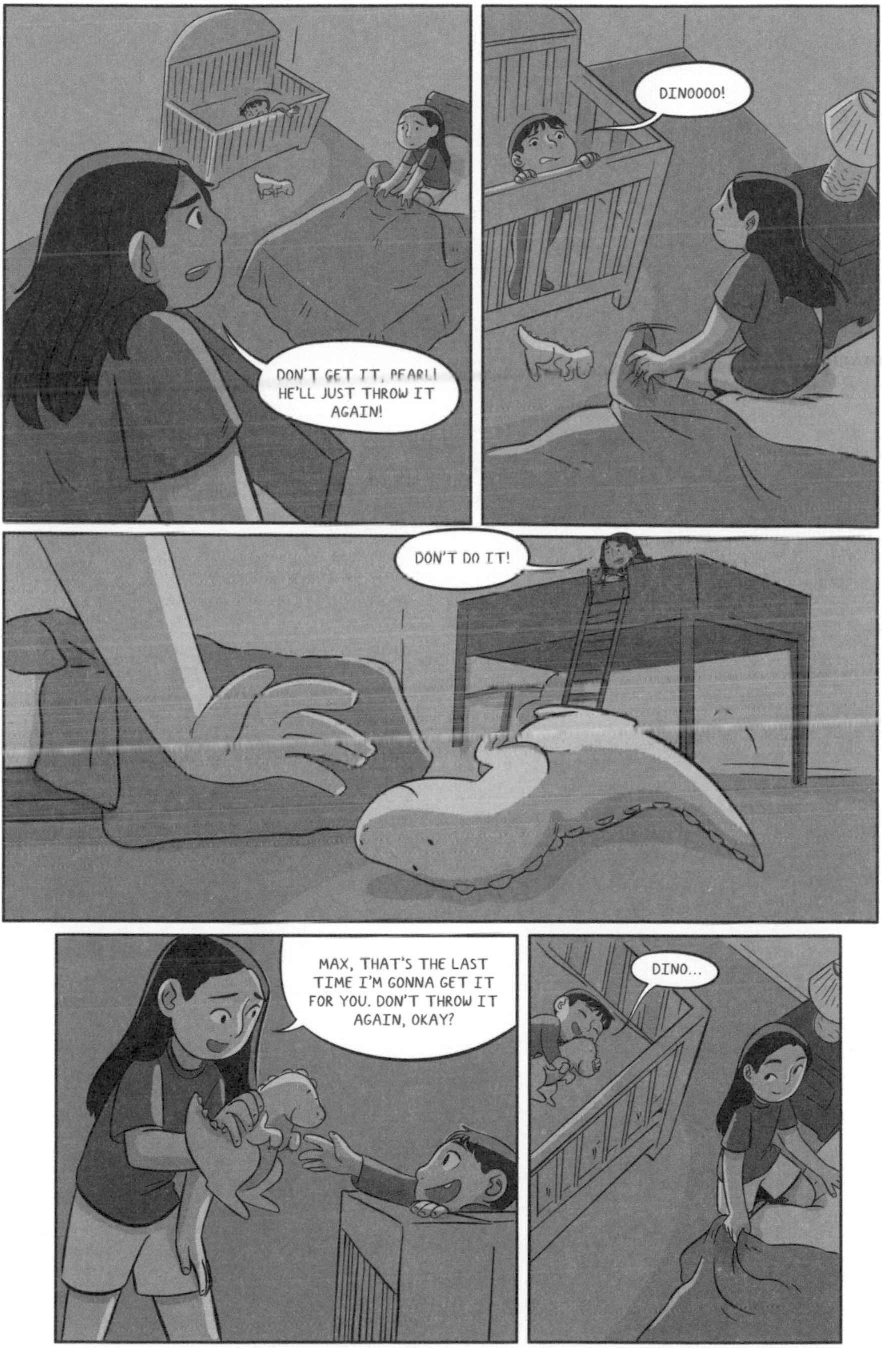
DON'T GET IT, PEARL! HE'LL JUST THROW IT AGAIN!
DINOOOO!
DON'T DO IT!
MAX, THAT'S THE LAST TIME I'M GONNA GET IT FOR YOU. DON'T THROW IT AGAIN, OKAY?
DINO...

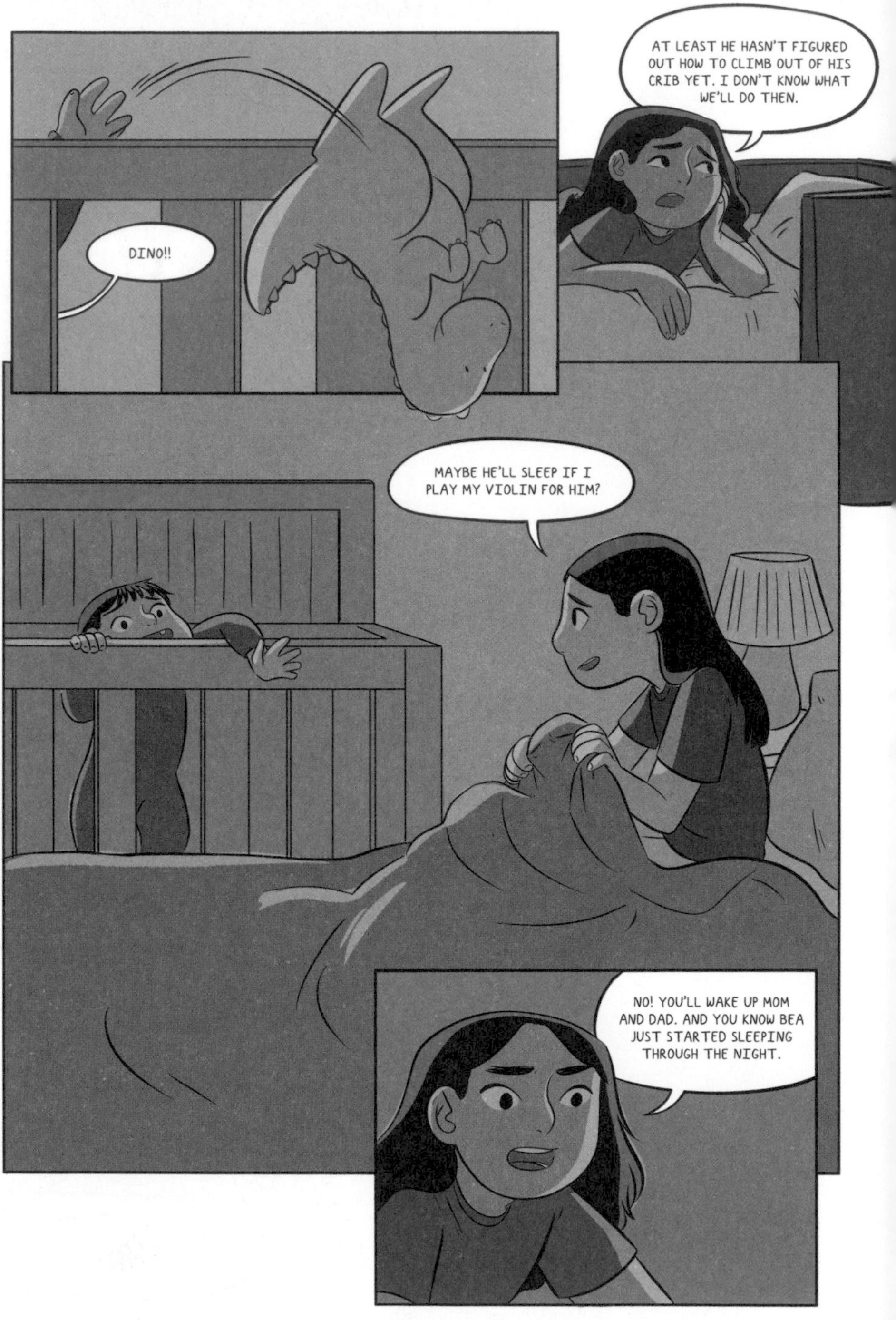
DINO!!
AT LEAST HE HASN'T FIGURED OUT HOW TO CLIMB OUT OF HIS CRIB YET. I DON'T KNOW WHAT WE'LL DO THEN.
MAYBE HE'LL SLEEP IF I PLAY MY VIOLIN FOR HIM?
NO! YOU'LL WAKE UP MOM AND DAD. AND YOU KNOW BEA JUST STARTED SLEEPING THROUGH THE NIGHT.

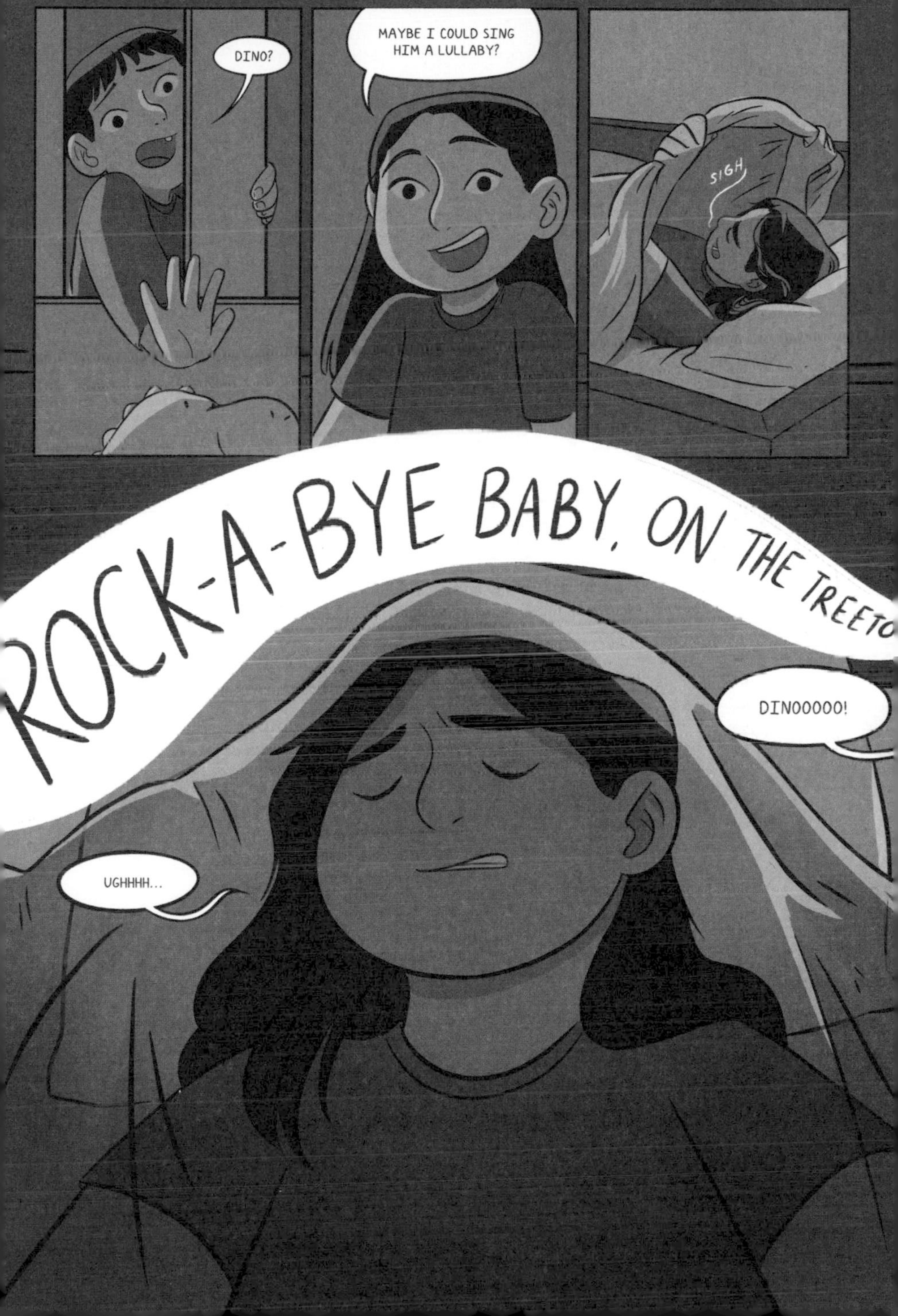
DINO?
MAYBE I COULD SING HIM A LULLABY?
SIGH
ROCK-A-BYE BABY, ON THE TREETO
DINOOOOO!
UGHHHH...

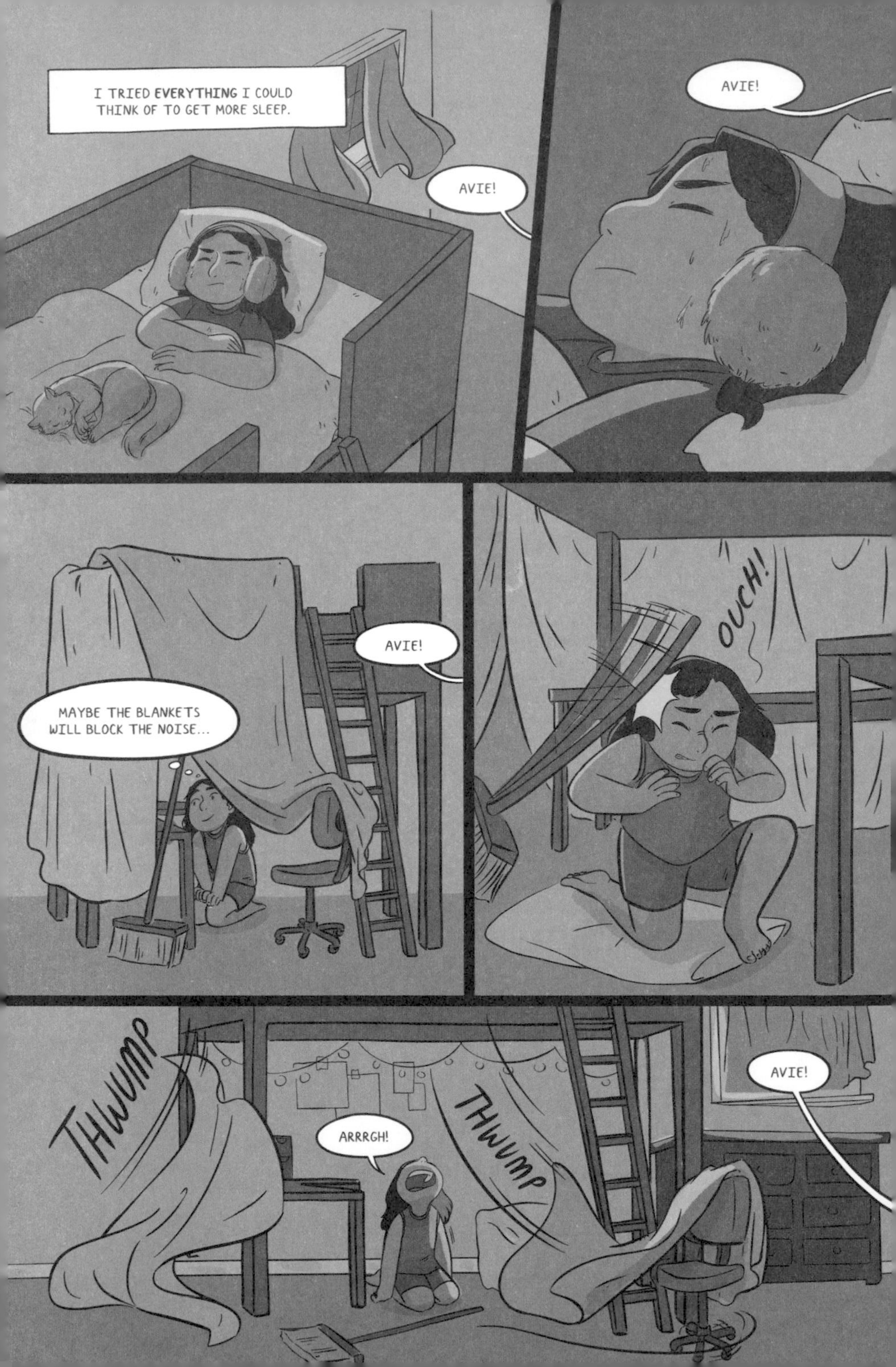
I TRIED EVERYTHING I COULD THINK OF TO GET MORE SLEEP.
AVIE!
AVIE!
AVIE!
MAYBE THE BLANKETS WILL BLOCK THE NOISE...
OUCH!
THWUMP
ARRRGH!
THWUMP
AVIE!

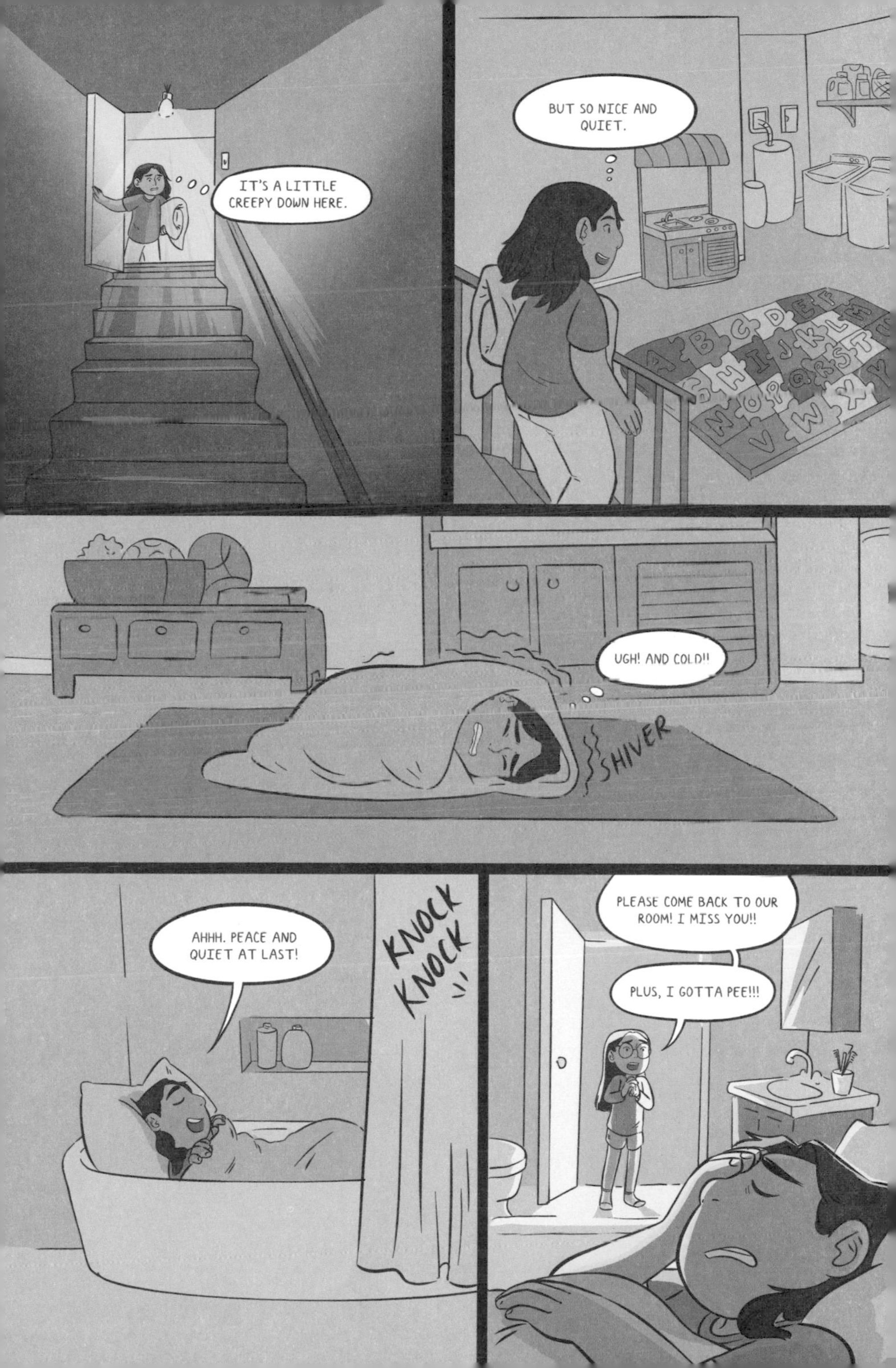
IT'S A LITTLE CREEPY DOWN HERE.
BUT SO NICE AND QUIET.
UGH! AND COLD!!
SHIVER
AHHH. PEACE AND QUIET AT LAST!
KNOCK KNOCK
PLEASE COME BACK TO OUR ROOM! I MISS YOU!!
PLUS, I GOTTA PEE!!!

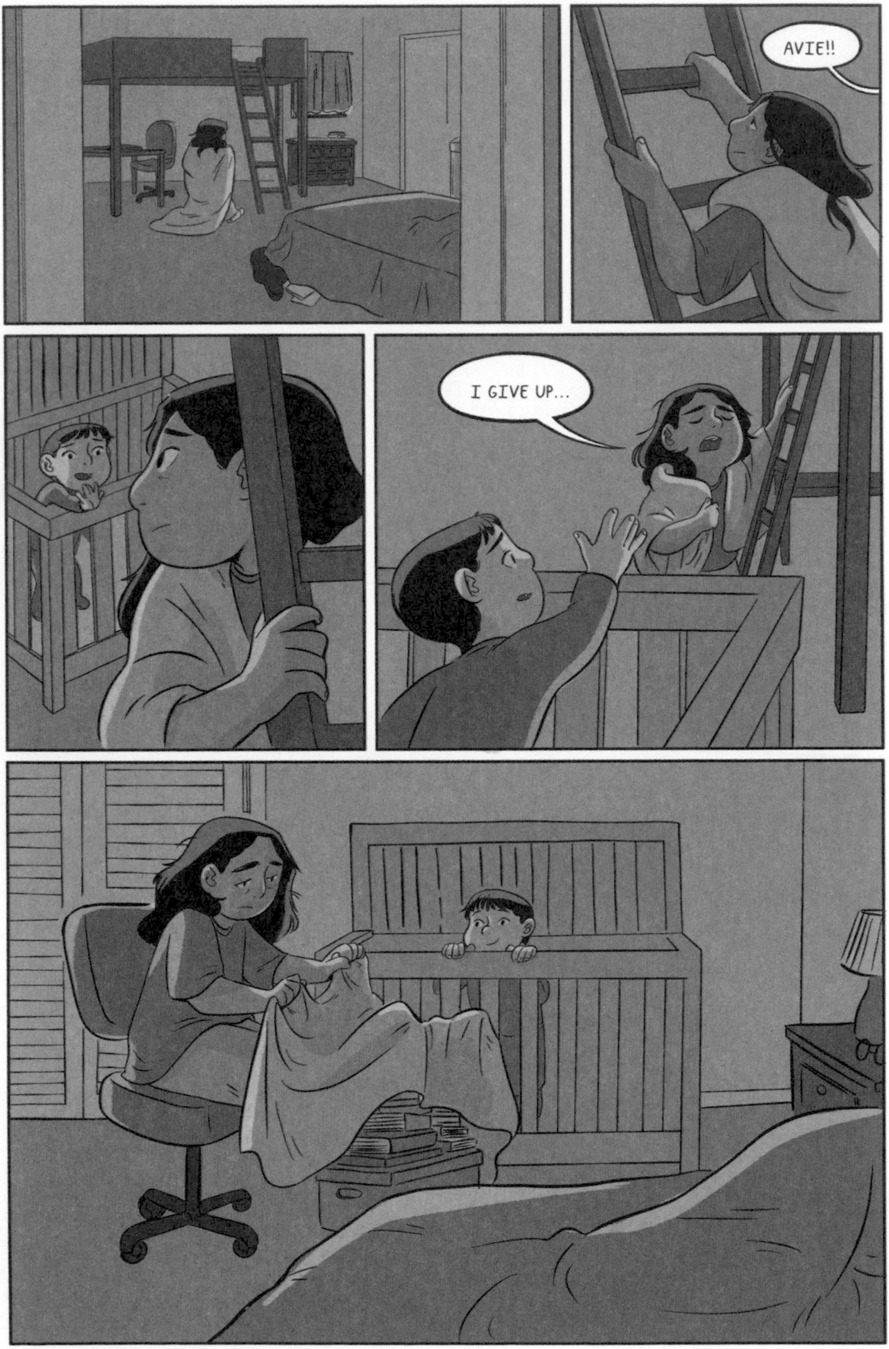
AVIE!!
I GIVE UP...

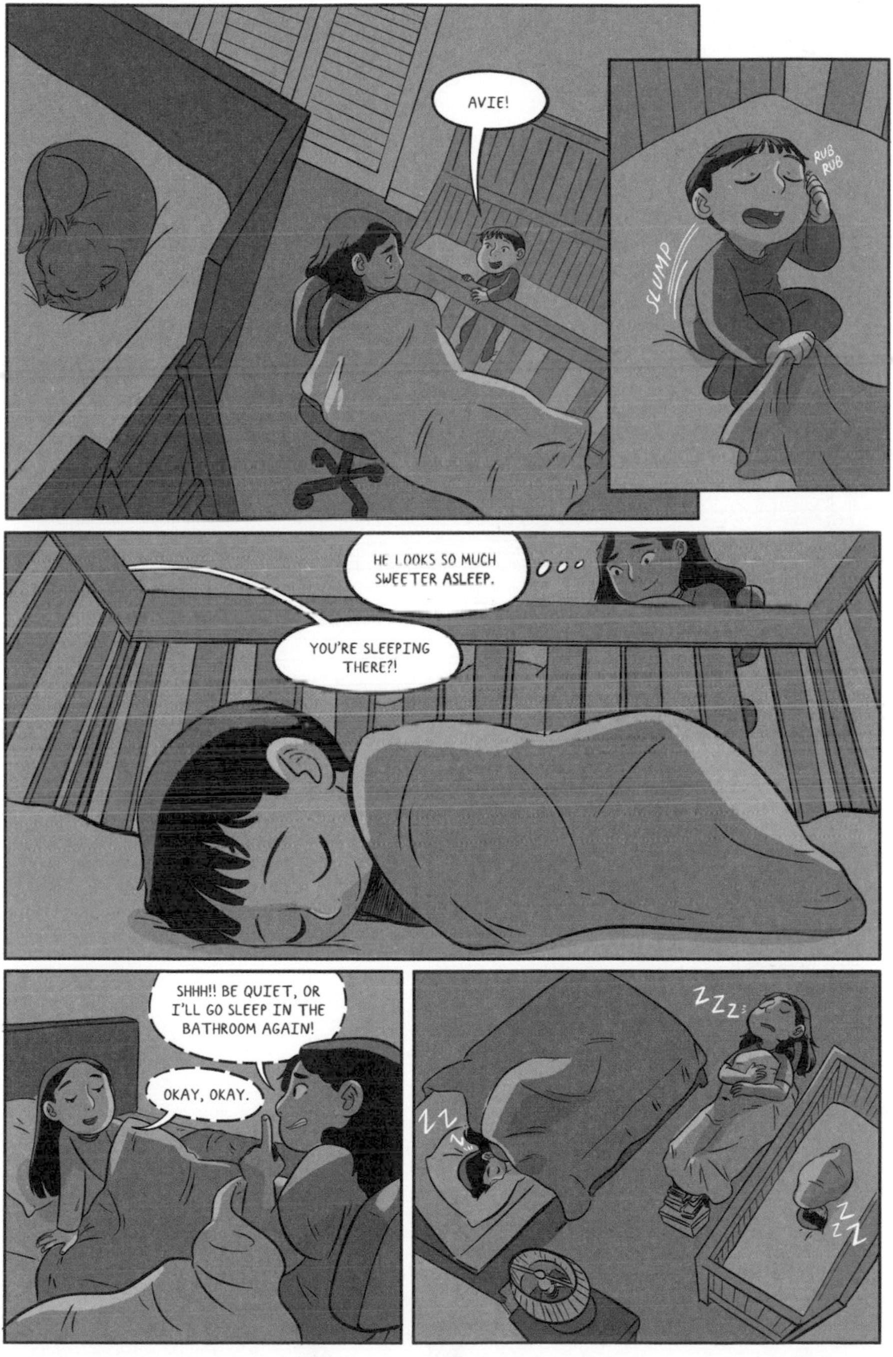
AVIE!
RUB RUB
SLUMP
HE LOOKS SO MUCH SWEETER ASLEEP.
YOU'RE SLEEPING THERE?!
SHHH!! BE QUIET, OR I'LL GO SLEEP IN THE BATHROOM AGAIN!
OKAY, OKAY.
ZZZ
ZZ
ZZ

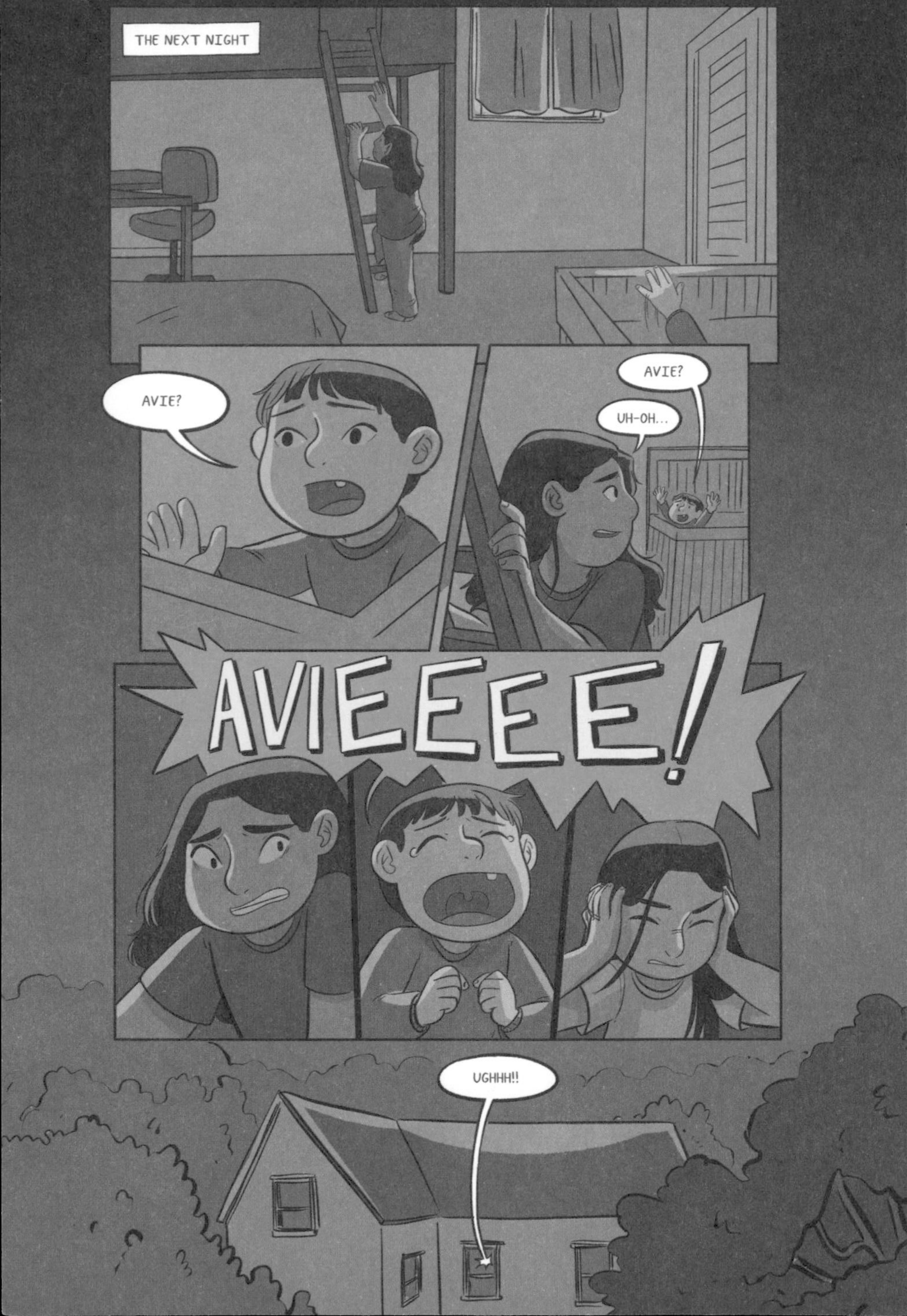
THE NEXT NIGHT
AVIE?
AVIE?
UH-OH...
AVIEEEE!
UGHHH!!

Chapter Four

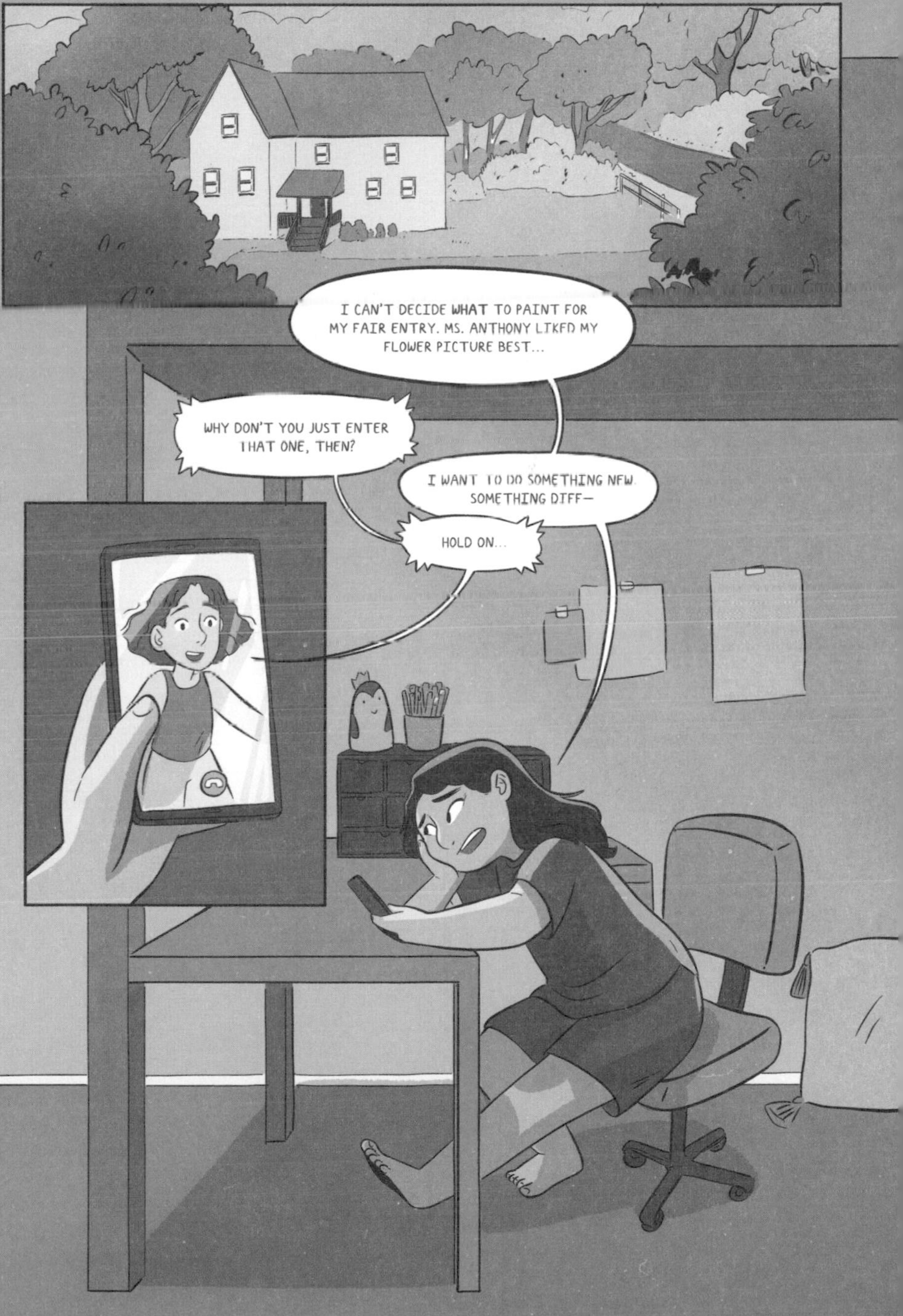
I CAN'T DECIDE WHAT TO PAINT FOR MY FAIR ENTRY. MS. ANTHONY LIKED MY FLOWER PICTURE BEST...
WHY DON'T YOU JUST ENTER THAT ONE, THEN?
I WANT TO DO SOMETHING NEW. SOMETHING DIFF—
HOLD ON...

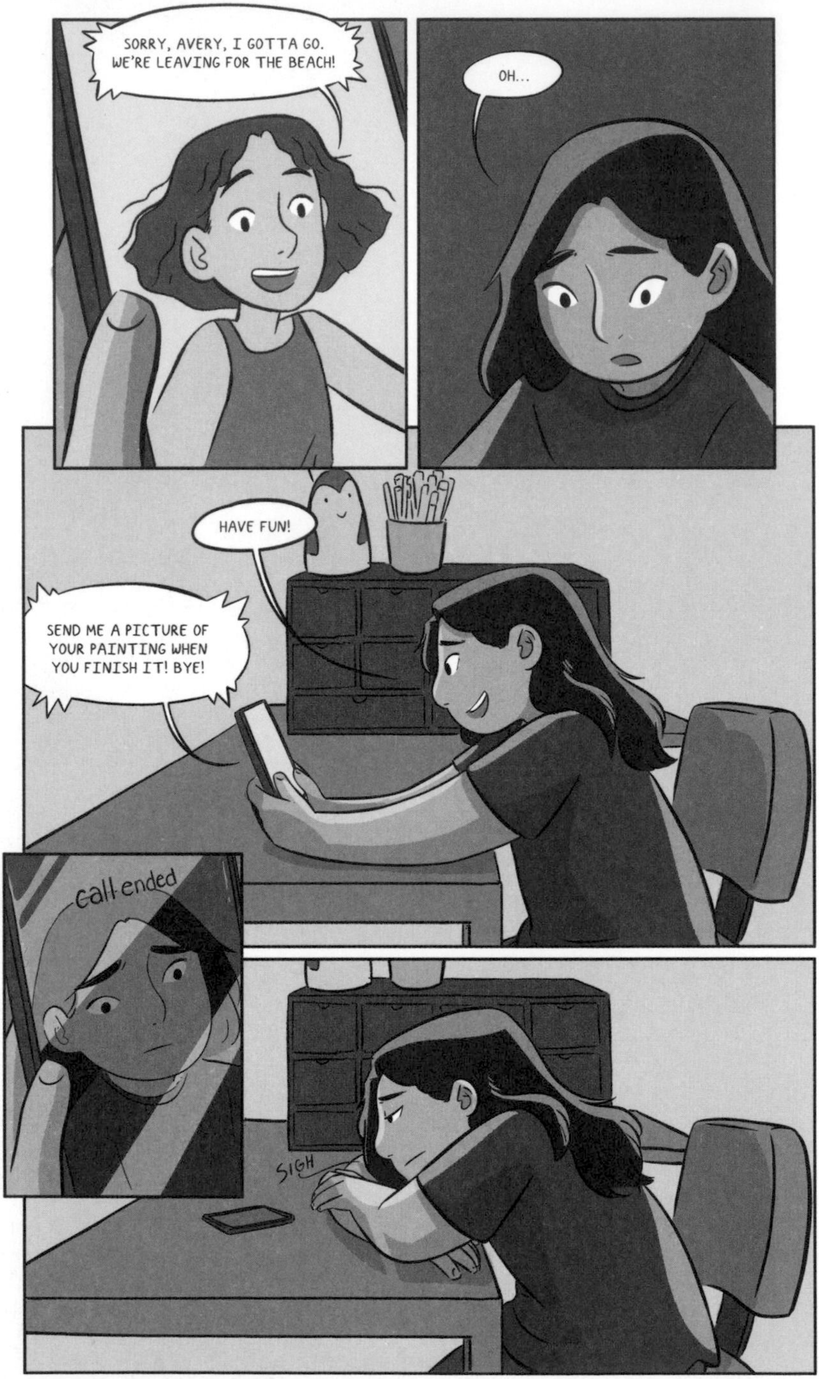
SORRY, AVERY, I GOTTA GO. WE'RE LEAVING FOR THE BEACH!
OH...
HAVE FUN!
SEND ME A PICTURE OF YOUR PAINTING WHEN YOU FINISH IT! BYE!
Call ended
SIGH

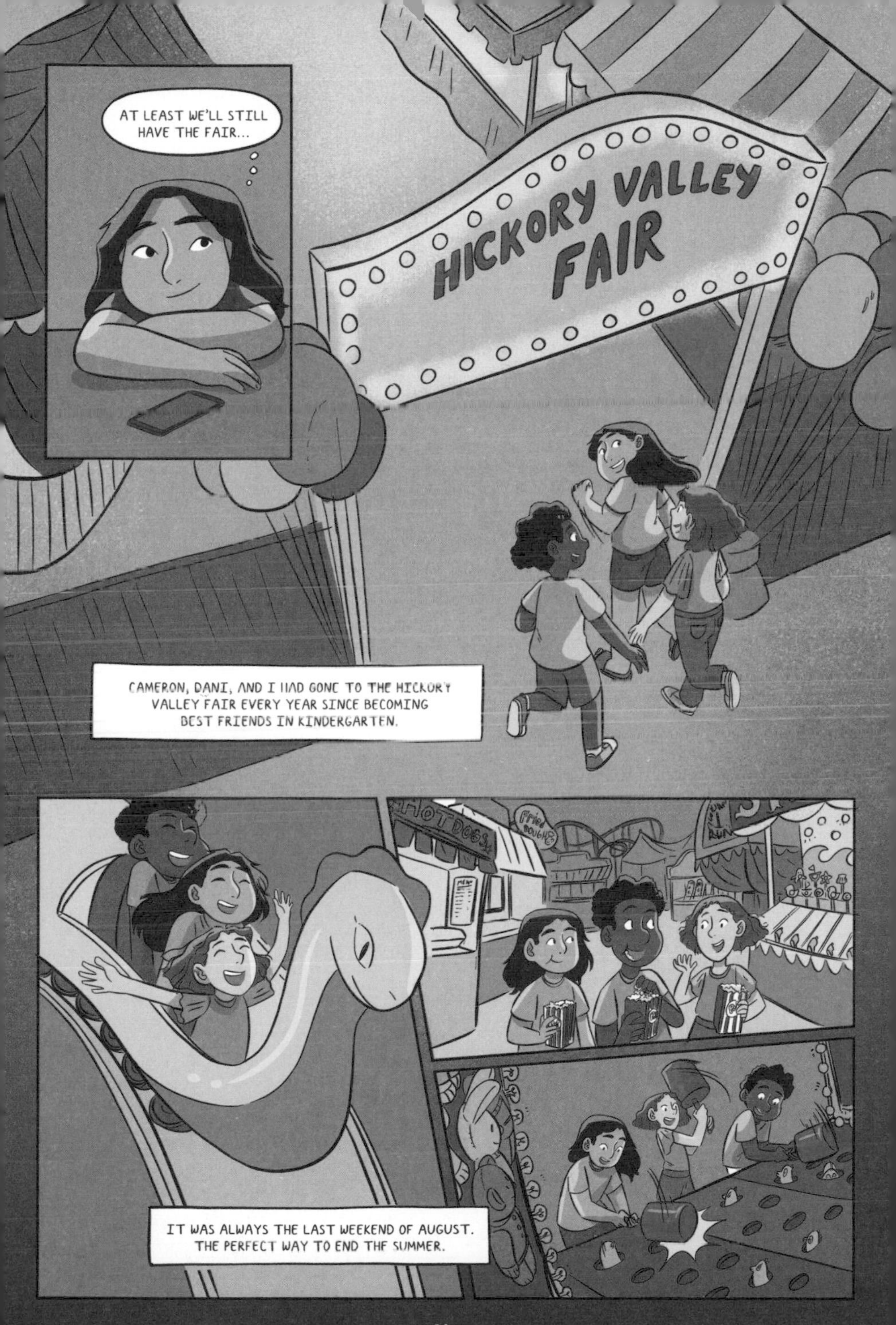
AT LEAST WE'LL STILL HAVE THE FAIR...
HICKORY VALLEY FAIR
CAMERON, DANI, AND I HAD GONE TO THE HICKORY VALLEY FAIR EVERY YEAR SINCE BECOMING BEST FRIENDS IN KINDERGARTEN.
HOT DOGS
Fried DOUGH
IT WAS ALWAYS THE LAST WEEKEND OF AUGUST. THE PERFECT WAY TO END THE SUMMER.

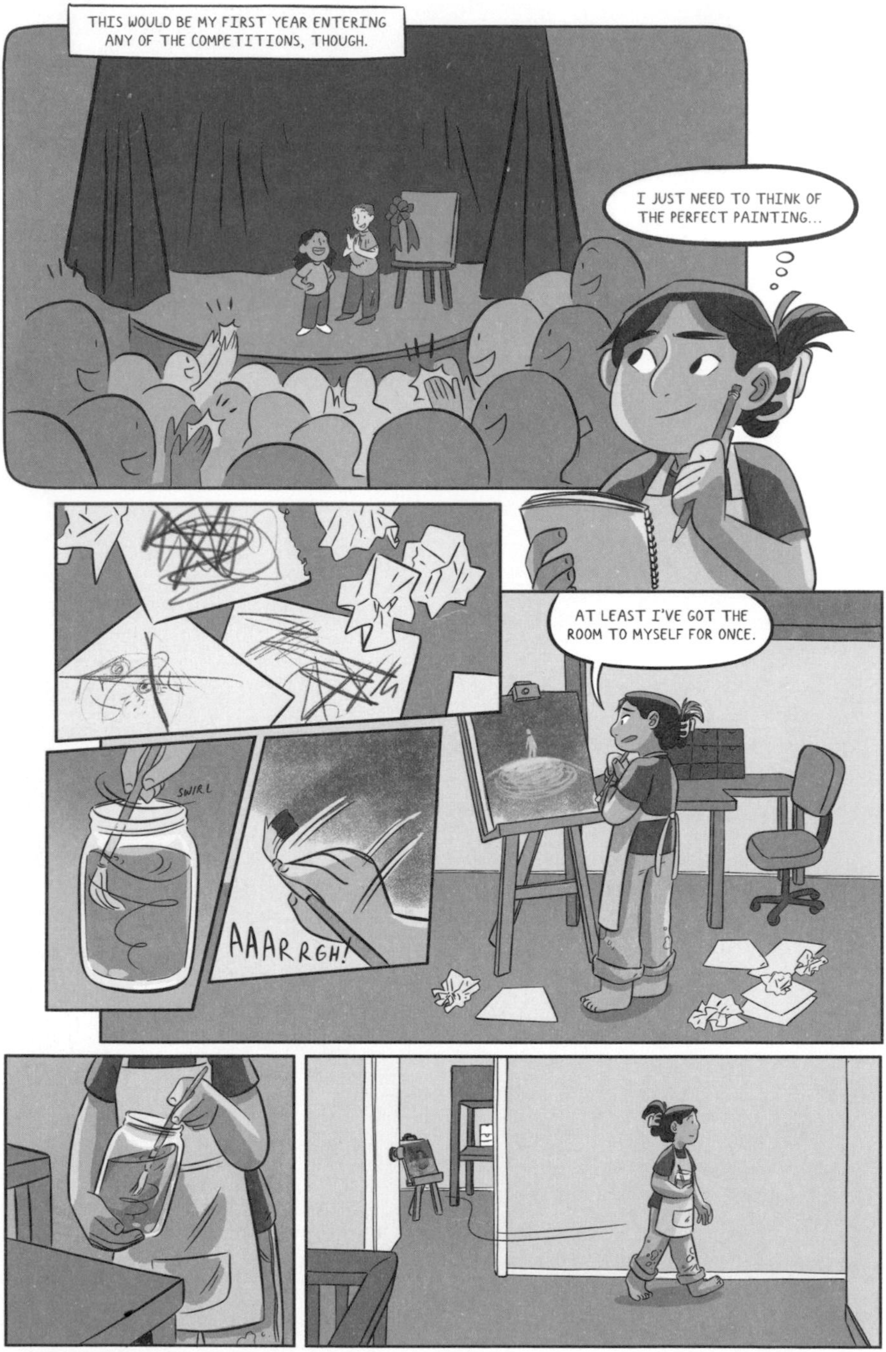
THIS WOULD BE MY FIRST YEAR ENTERING ANY OF THE COMPETITIONS, THOUGH.
I JUST NEED TO THINK OF THE PERFECT PAINTING...
AT LEAST I'VE GOT THE ROOM TO MYSELF FOR ONCE.
SWIRL
AAARRGH!

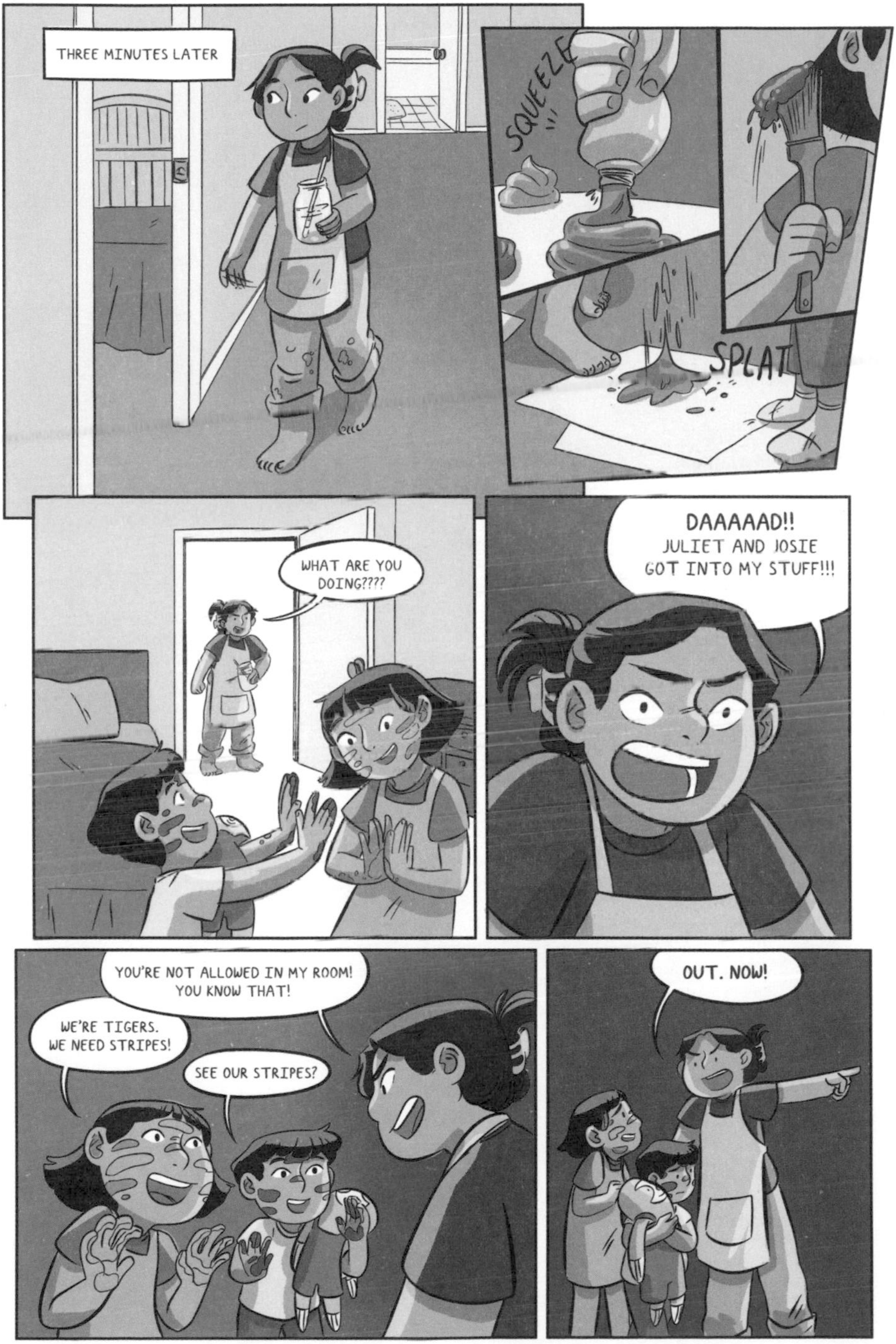
THREE MINUTES LATER
SQUEEZE
SPLAT
WHAT ARE YOU DOING????
DAAAAAD!! JULIET AND JOSIE GOT INTO MY STUFF!!!
YOU'RE NOT ALLOWED IN MY ROOM! YOU KNOW THAT!
WE'RE TIGERS. WE NEED STRIPES!
SEE OUR STRIPES?
OUT. NOW!

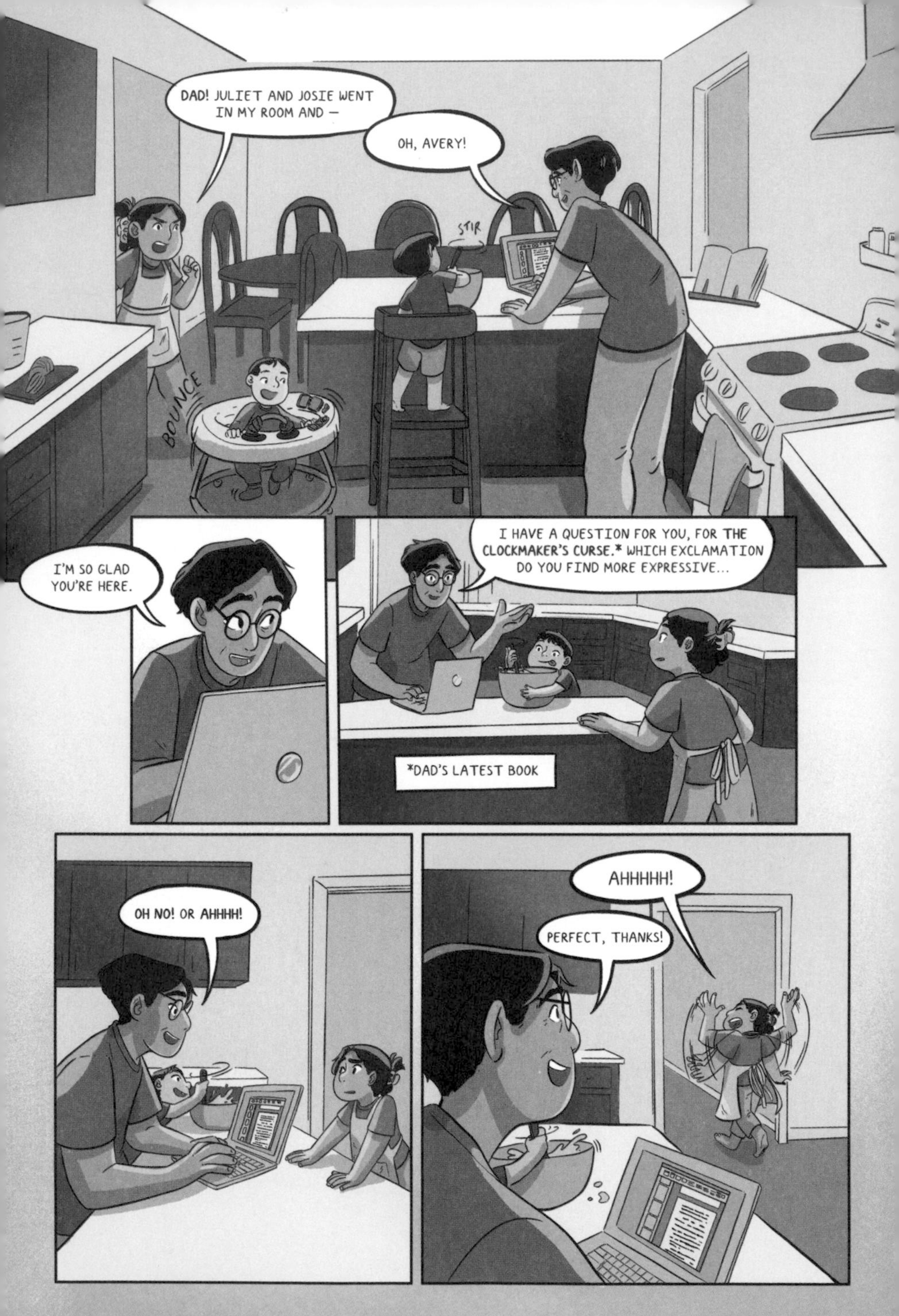
DAD! JULIET AND JOSIE WENT IN MY ROOM AND —
OH, AVERY!
STIR
BOUNCE
I'M SO GLAD YOU'RE HERE.
I HAVE A QUESTION FOR YOU, FOR THE CLOCKMAKER'S CURSE.* WHICH EXCLAMATION DO YOU FIND MORE EXPRESSIVE...
*DAD'S LATEST BOOK
OH NO! OR AHHHH!
AHHHHH!
PERFECT, THANKS!

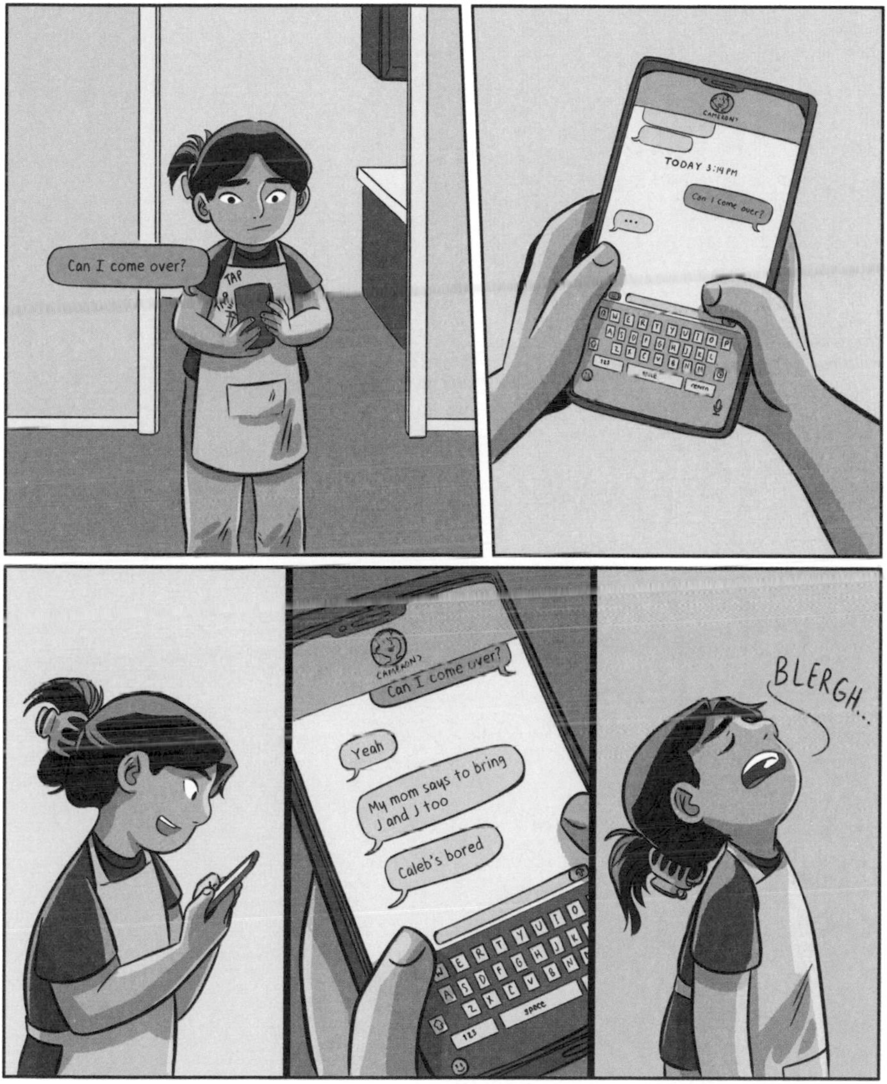
Can I come over?
TAP
TAP
TODAY 3:14 PM
Can I come over?
...
Can I come over?
Yeah
My mom says to bring J and J too
Caleb's bored
BLERGH...

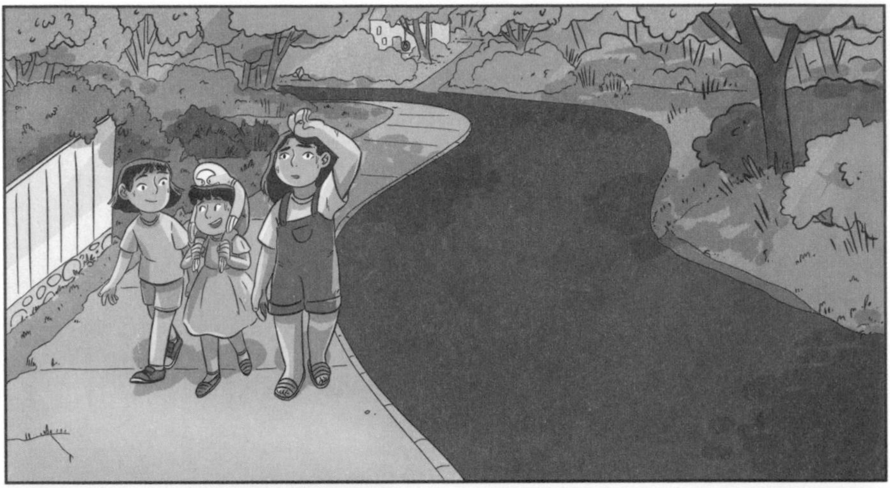

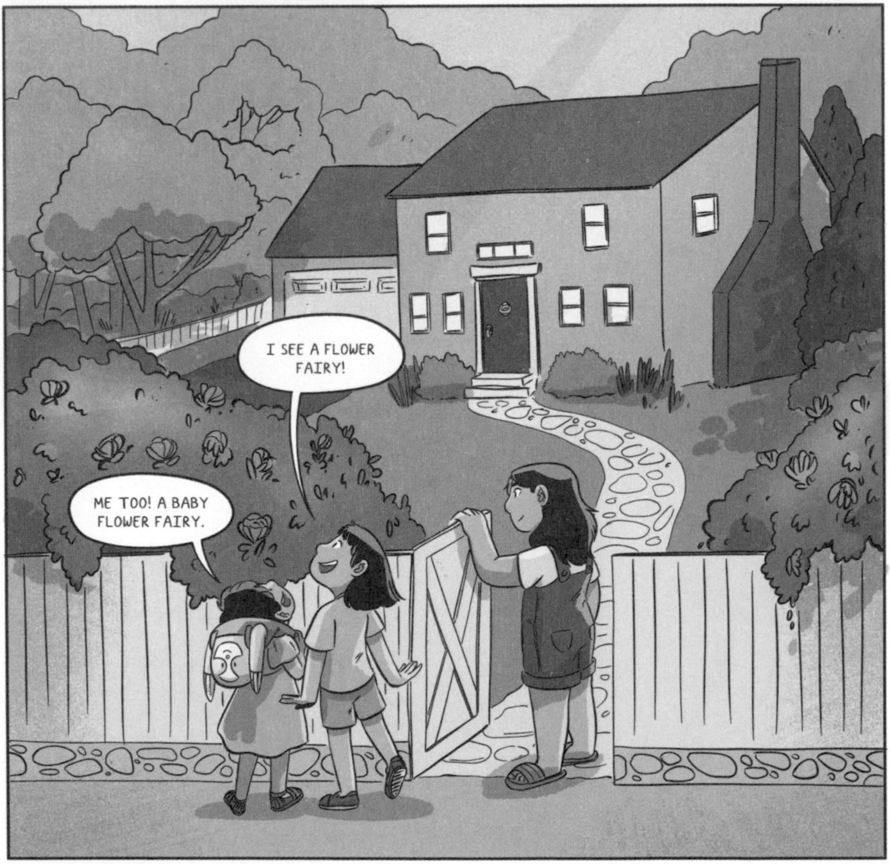

I SEE A FLOWER FAIRY!
ME TOO! A BABY FLOWER FAIRY.

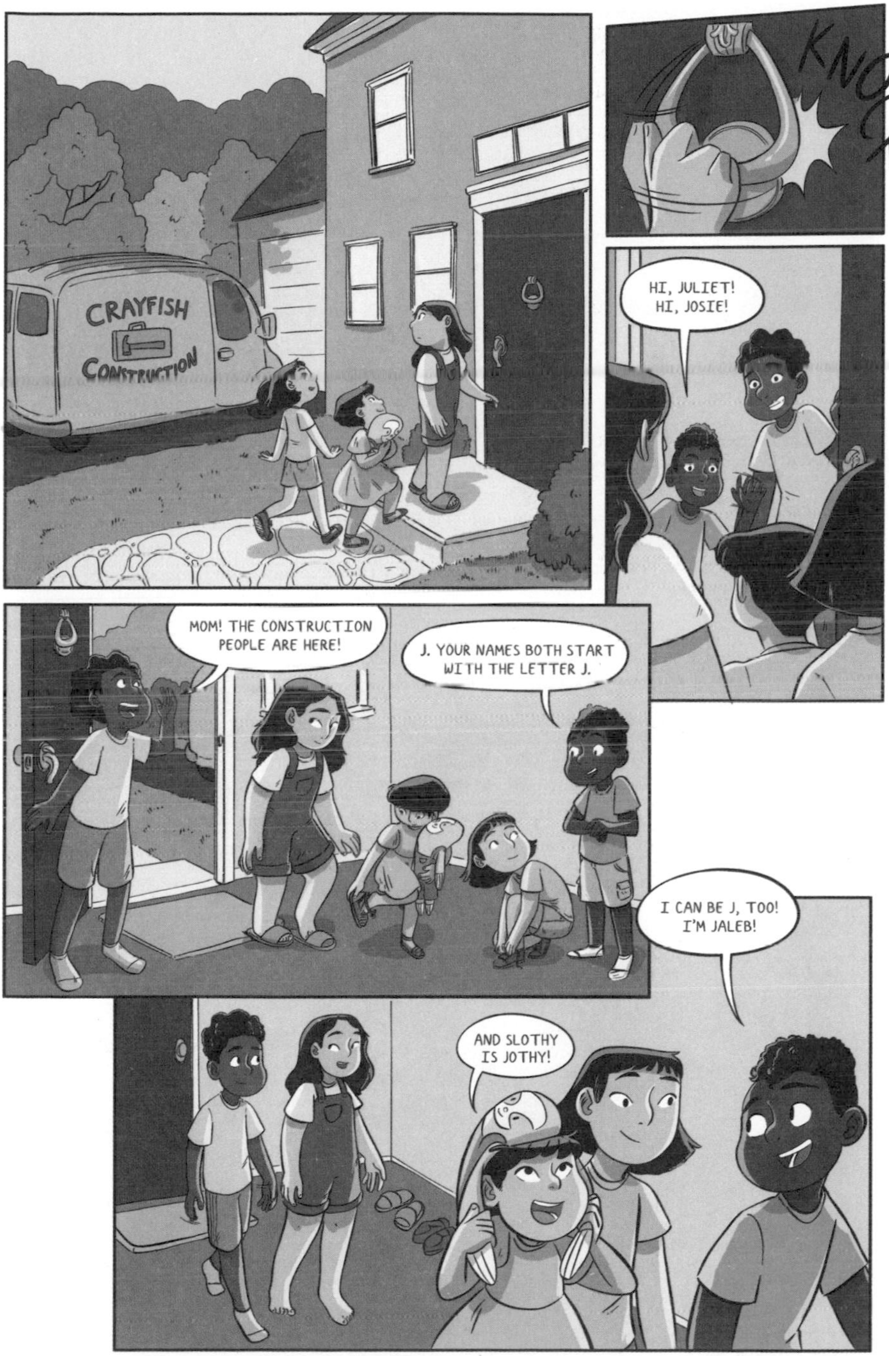
CRAYFISH CONSTRUCTION
KNOCK
HI, JULIET! HI, JOSIE!
MOM! THE CONSTRUCTION PEOPLE ARE HERE!
J. YOUR NAMES BOTH START WITH THE LETTER J.
I CAN BE J, TOO! I'M JALEB!
AND SLOTHY IS JOTHY!

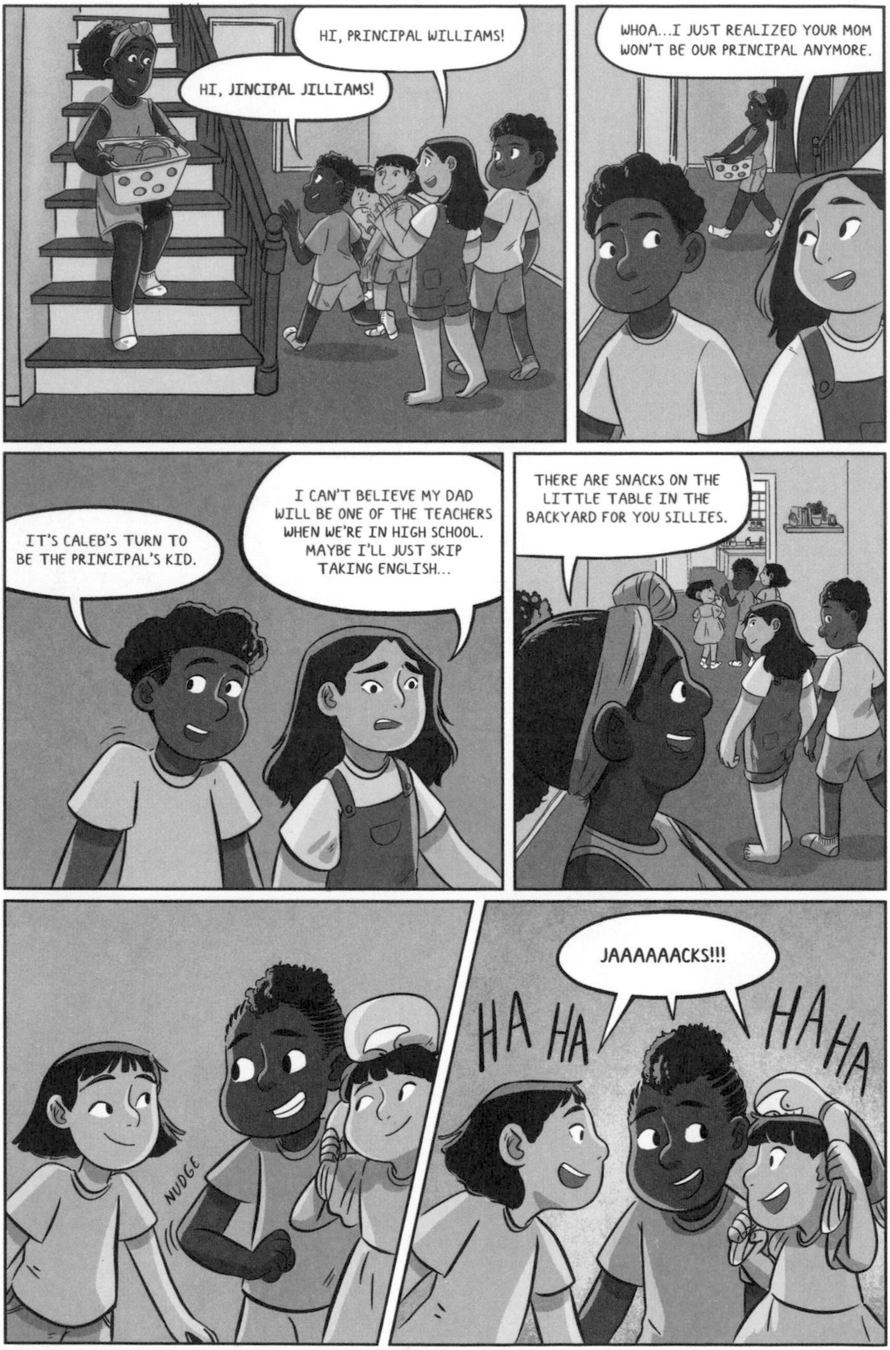
HI, PRINCIPAL WILLIAMS!
HI, JINCIPAL JILLIAMS!
WHOA...I JUST REALIZED YOUR MOM WON'T BE OUR PRINCIPAL ANYMORE.
IT'S CALEB'S TURN TO BE THE PRINCIPAL'S KID.
I CAN'T BELIEVE MY DAD WILL BE ONE OF THE TEACHERS WHEN WE'RE IN HIGH SCHOOL. MAYBE I'LL JUST SKIP TAKING ENGLISH...
THERE ARE SNACKS ON THE LITTLE TABLE IN THE BACKYARD FOR YOU SILLIES.
NUDGE
HA HA
JAAAAAACKS!!!
HA HA

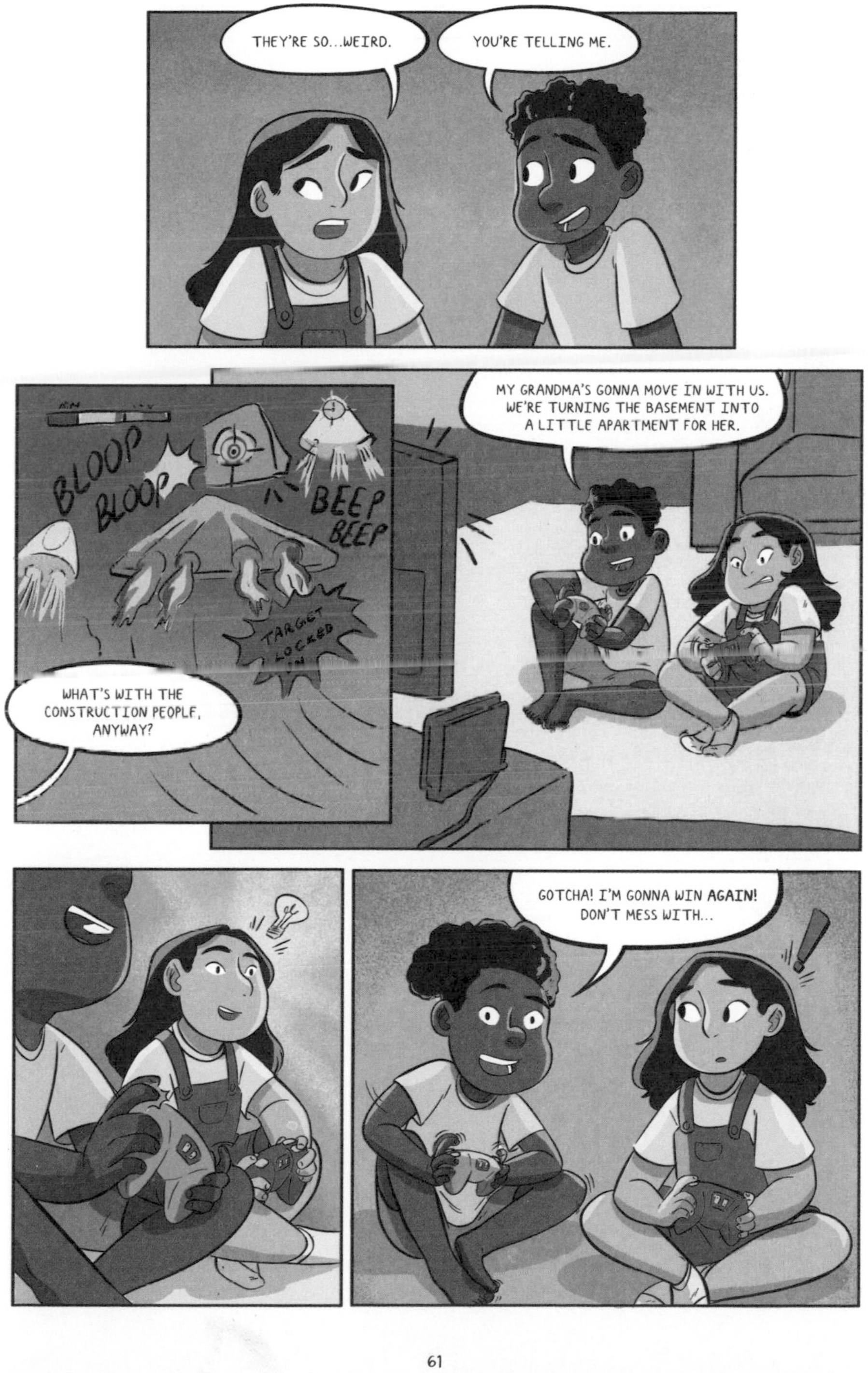
THEY'RE SO...WEIRD.
YOU'RE TELLING ME.
BLOOP BLOOP
BEEP BEEP
TARGET LOCKED IN
WHAT'S WITH THE CONSTRUCTION PEOPLE, ANYWAY?
MY GRANDMA'S GONNA MOVE IN WITH US. WE'RE TURNING THE BASEMENT INTO A LITTLE APARTMENT FOR HER.
GOTCHA! I'M GONNA WIN **AGAIN**! DON'T MESS WITH...

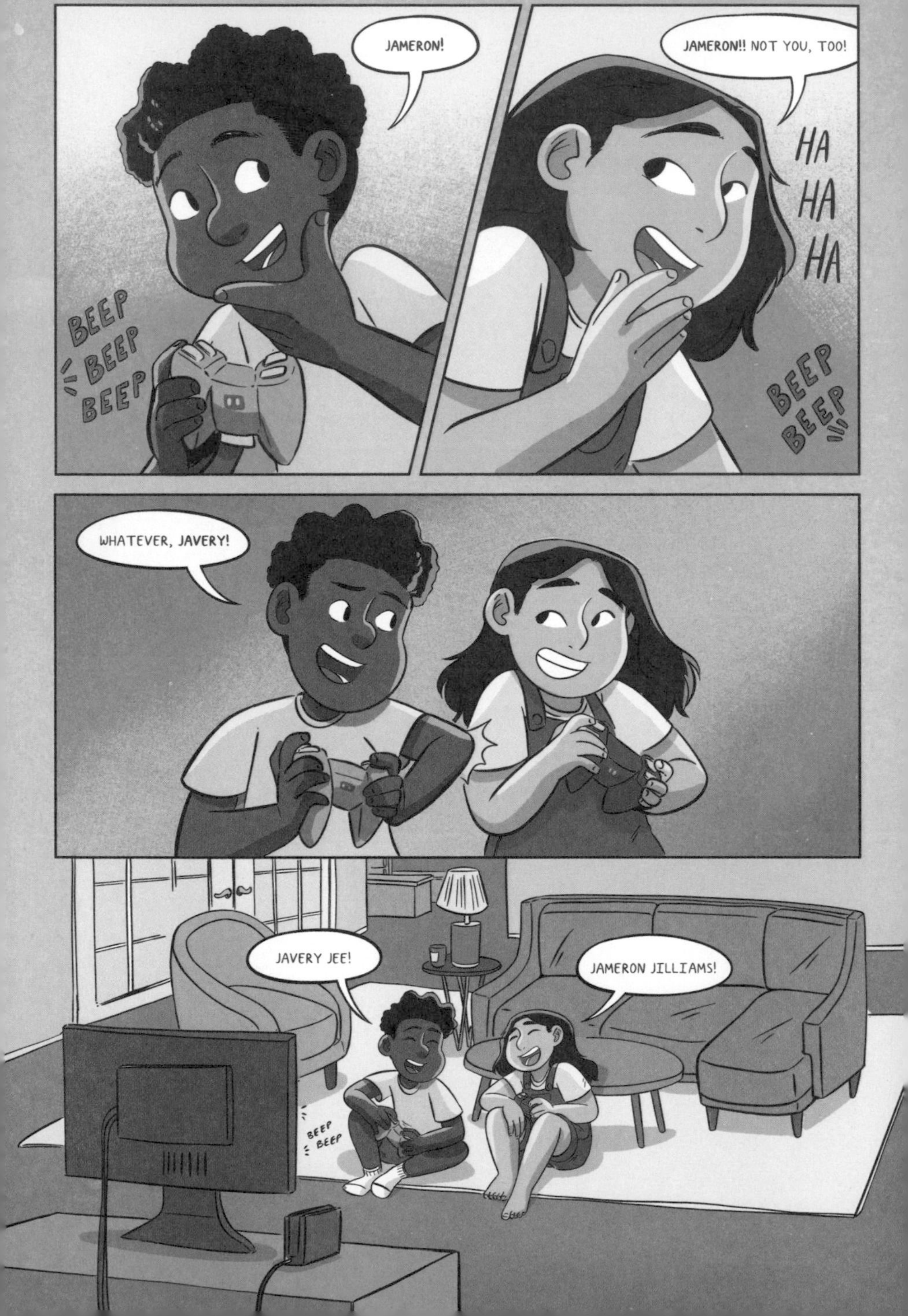
JAMERON!
BEEP
BEEP
BEEP
JAMERON!! NOT YOU, TOO!
HA
HA
HA
BEEP
BEEP
WHATEVER, JAVERY!
JAVERY JEE!
JAMERON JILLIAMS!
BEEP
BEEP

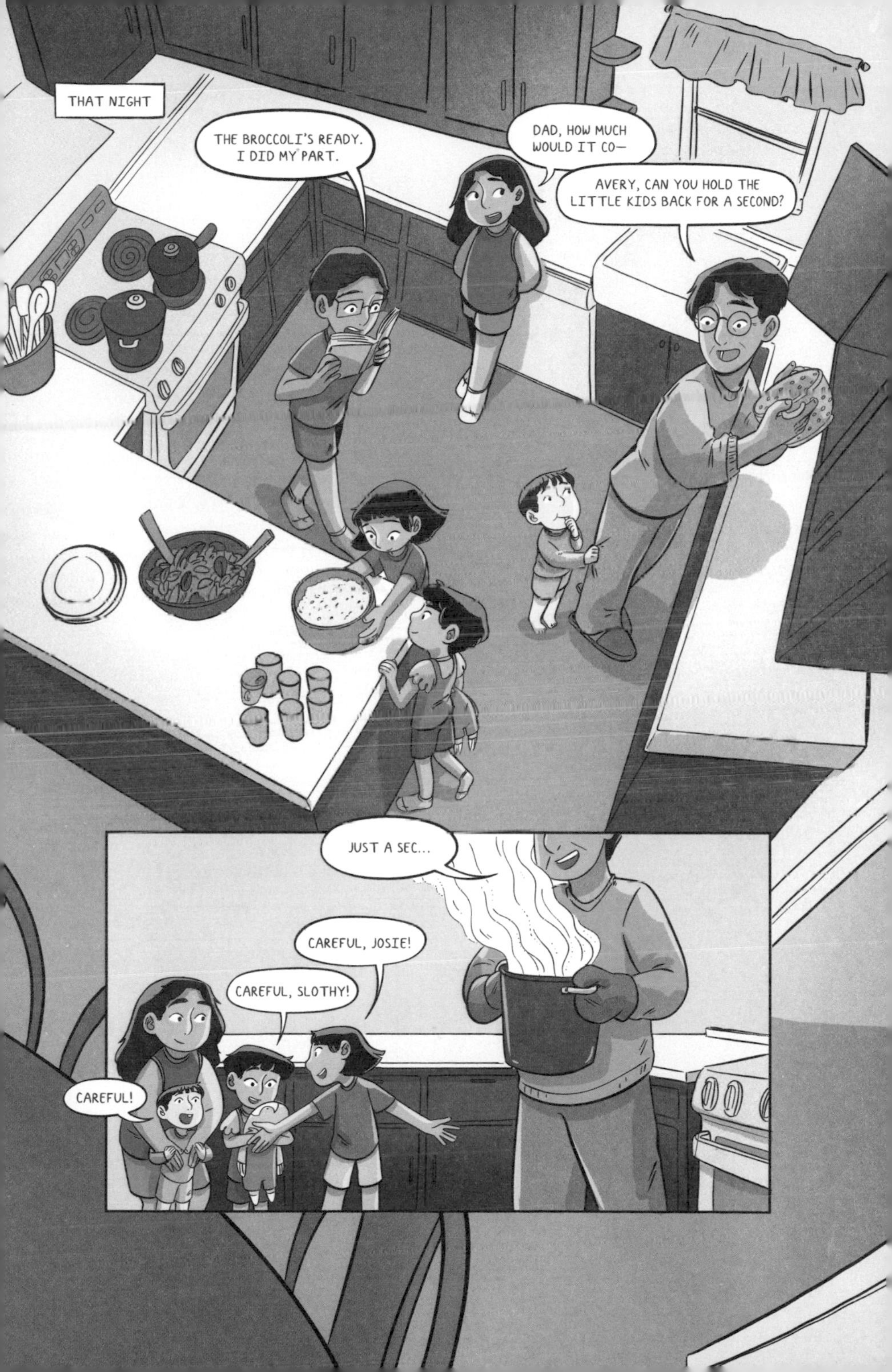
THAT NIGHT
THE BROCCOLI'S READY. I DID MY PART.
DAD, HOW MUCH WOULD IT CO—
AVERY, CAN YOU HOLD THE LITTLE KIDS BACK FOR A SECOND?
JUST A SEC...
CAREFUL, JOSIE!
CAREFUL, SLOTHY!
CAREFUL!

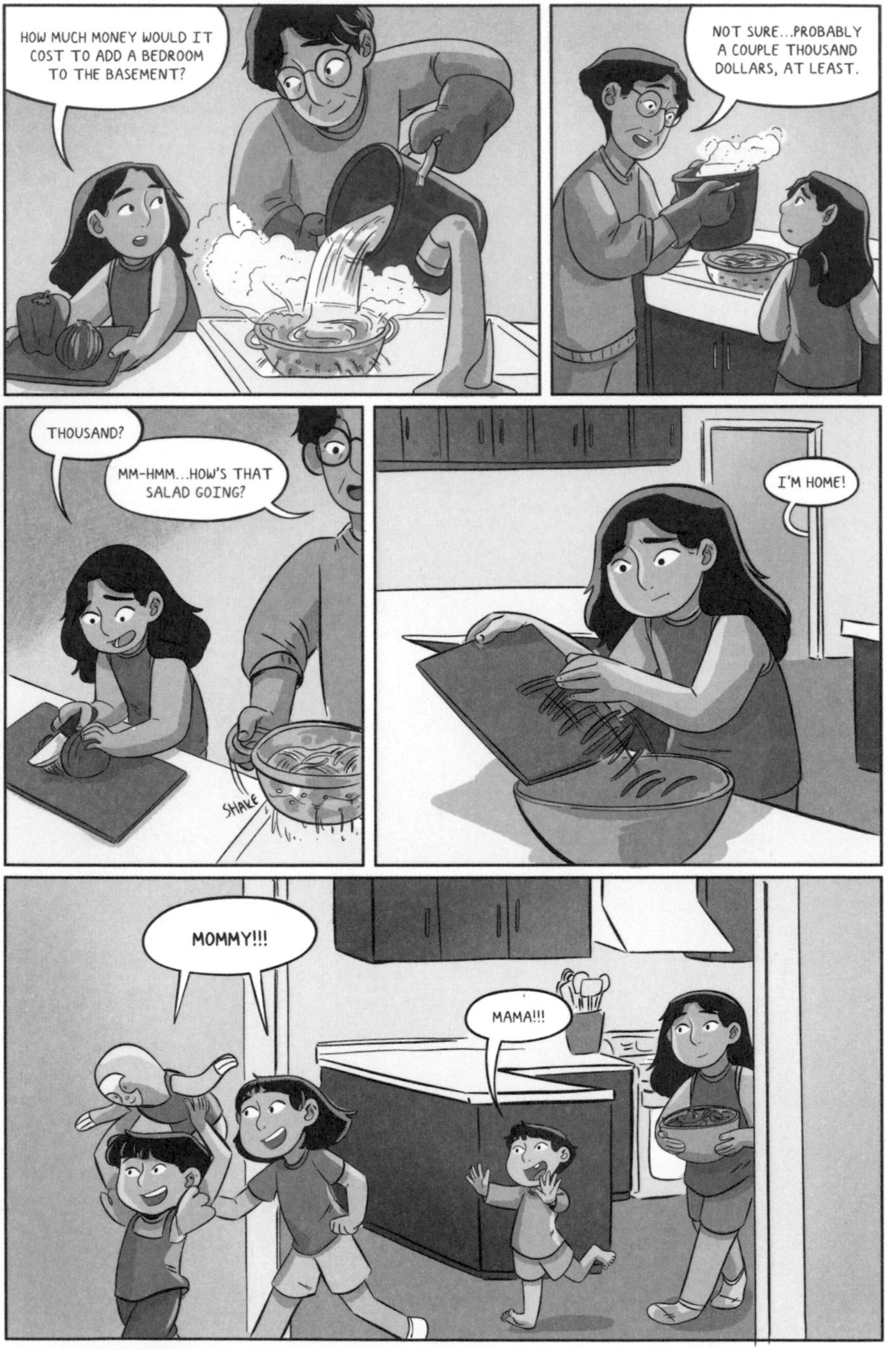
HOW MUCH MONEY WOULD IT COST TO ADD A BEDROOM TO THE BASEMENT?
NOT SURE...PROBABLY A COUPLE THOUSAND DOLLARS, AT LEAST.
THOUSAND?
MM-HMM...HOW'S THAT SALAD GOING?
SHAKE
I'M HOME!
MOMMY!!!
MAMA!!!

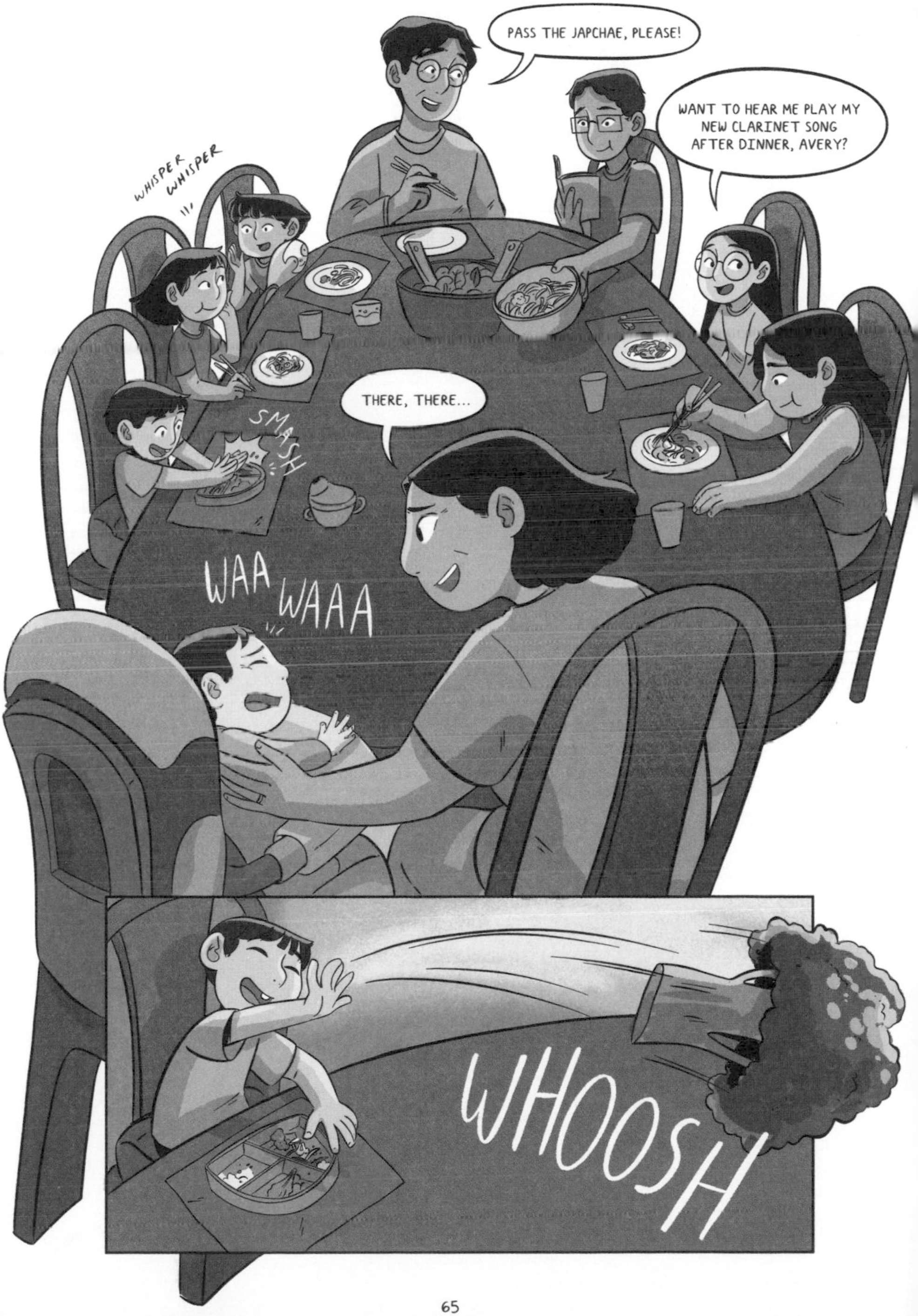
PASS THE JAPCHAE, PLEASE!
WANT TO HEAR ME PLAY MY NEW CLARINET SONG AFTER DINNER, AVERY?
WHISPER WHISPER
THERE, THERE...
SMASH
WAA WAAA
WHOOSH

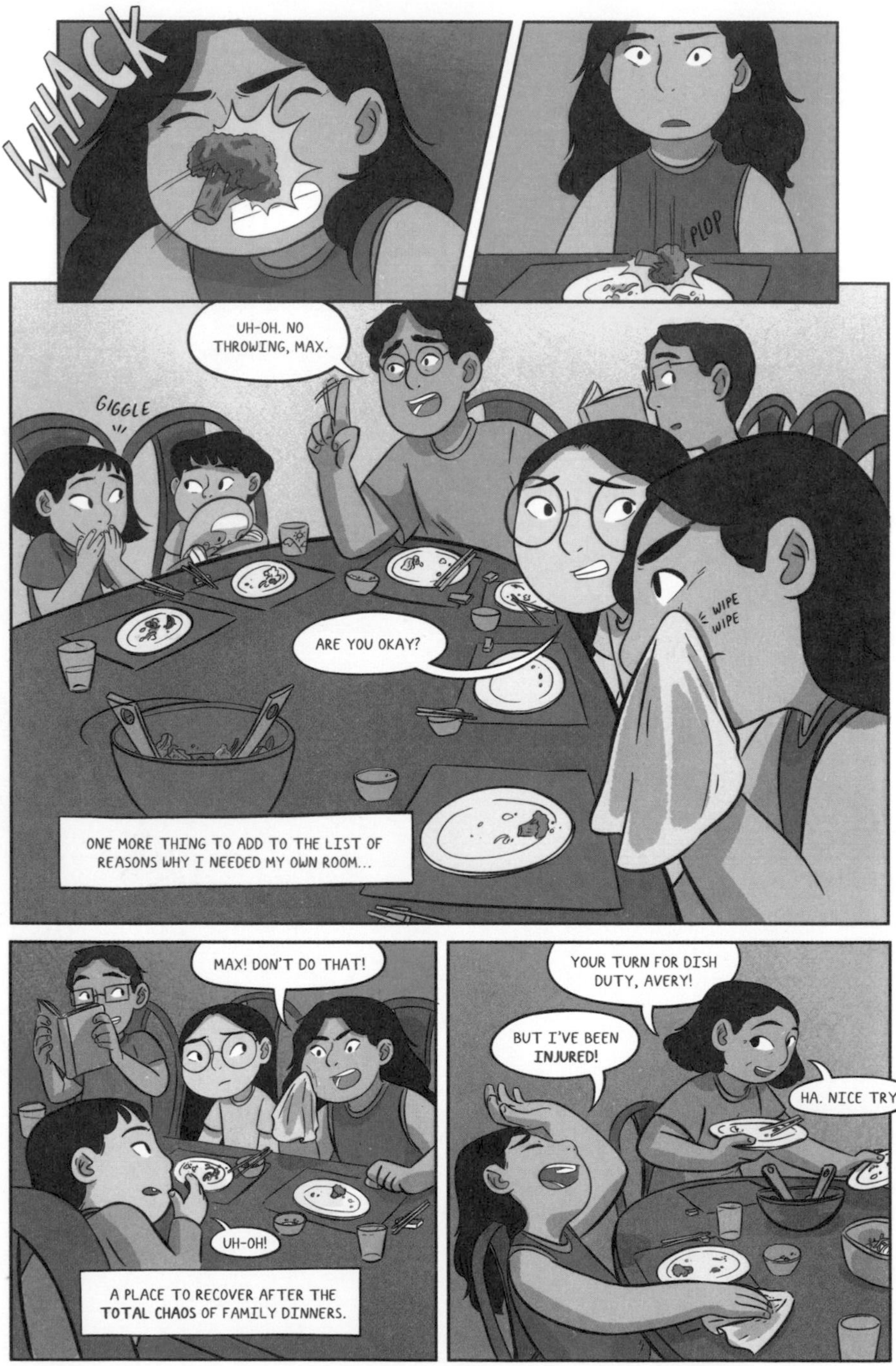
WHACK
PLOP
UH-OH. NO THROWING, MAX.
GIGGLE
ARE YOU OKAY?
WIPE WIPE
ONE MORE THING TO ADD TO THE LIST OF REASONS WHY I NEEDED MY OWN ROOM...
MAX! DON'T DO THAT!
UH-OH!
A PLACE TO RECOVER AFTER THE TOTAL CHAOS OF FAMILY DINNERS.
YOUR TURN FOR DISH DUTY, AVERY!
BUT I'VE BEEN INJURED!
HA. NICE TRY.

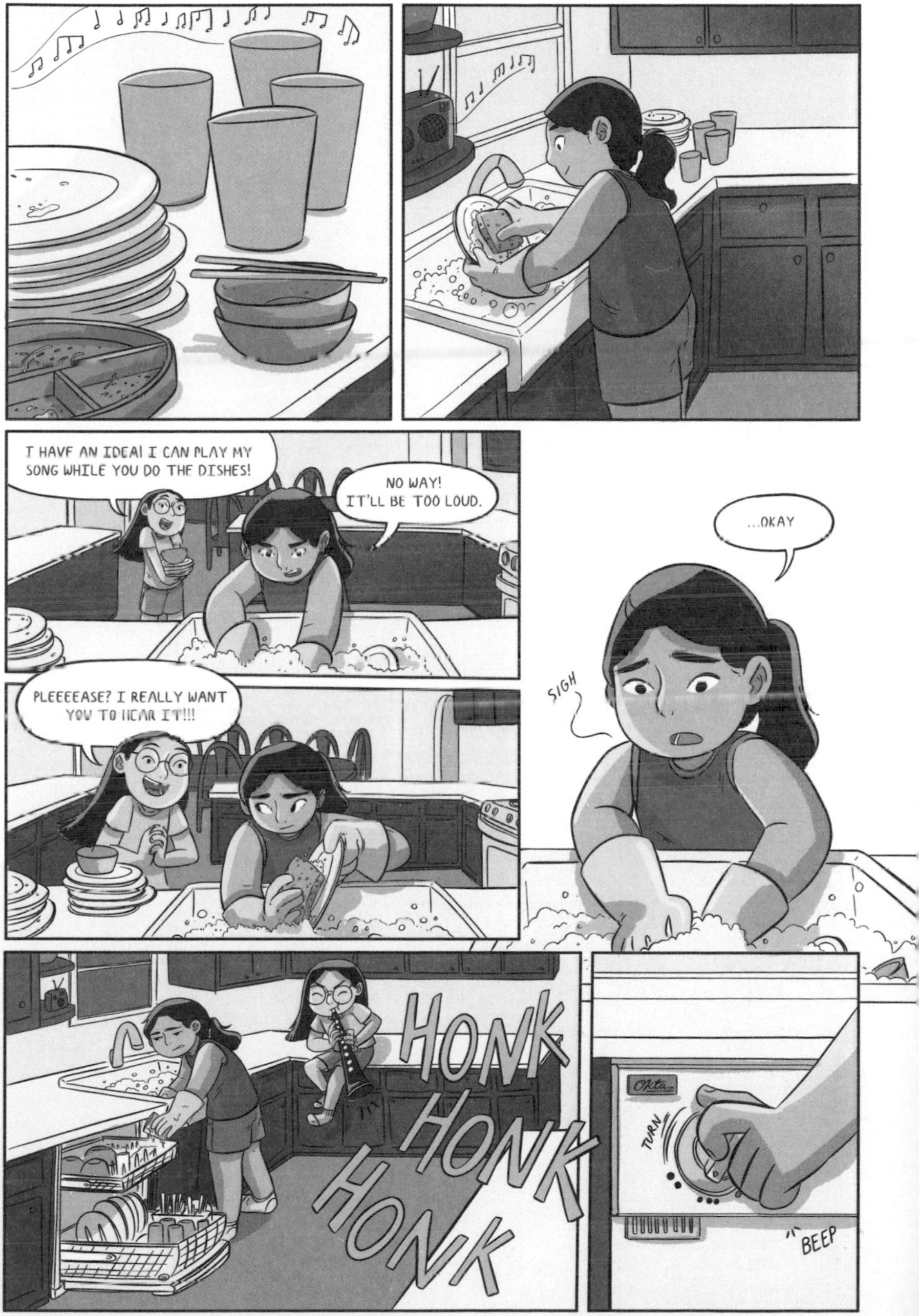
I HAVE AN IDEA! I CAN PLAY MY SONG WHILE YOU DO THE DISHES!
NO WAY! IT'LL BE TOO LOUD.
PLEEEEASE? I REALLY WANT YOU TO HEAR IT!!!
SIGH
...OKAY
HONK
HONK
HONK
TURN
BEEP

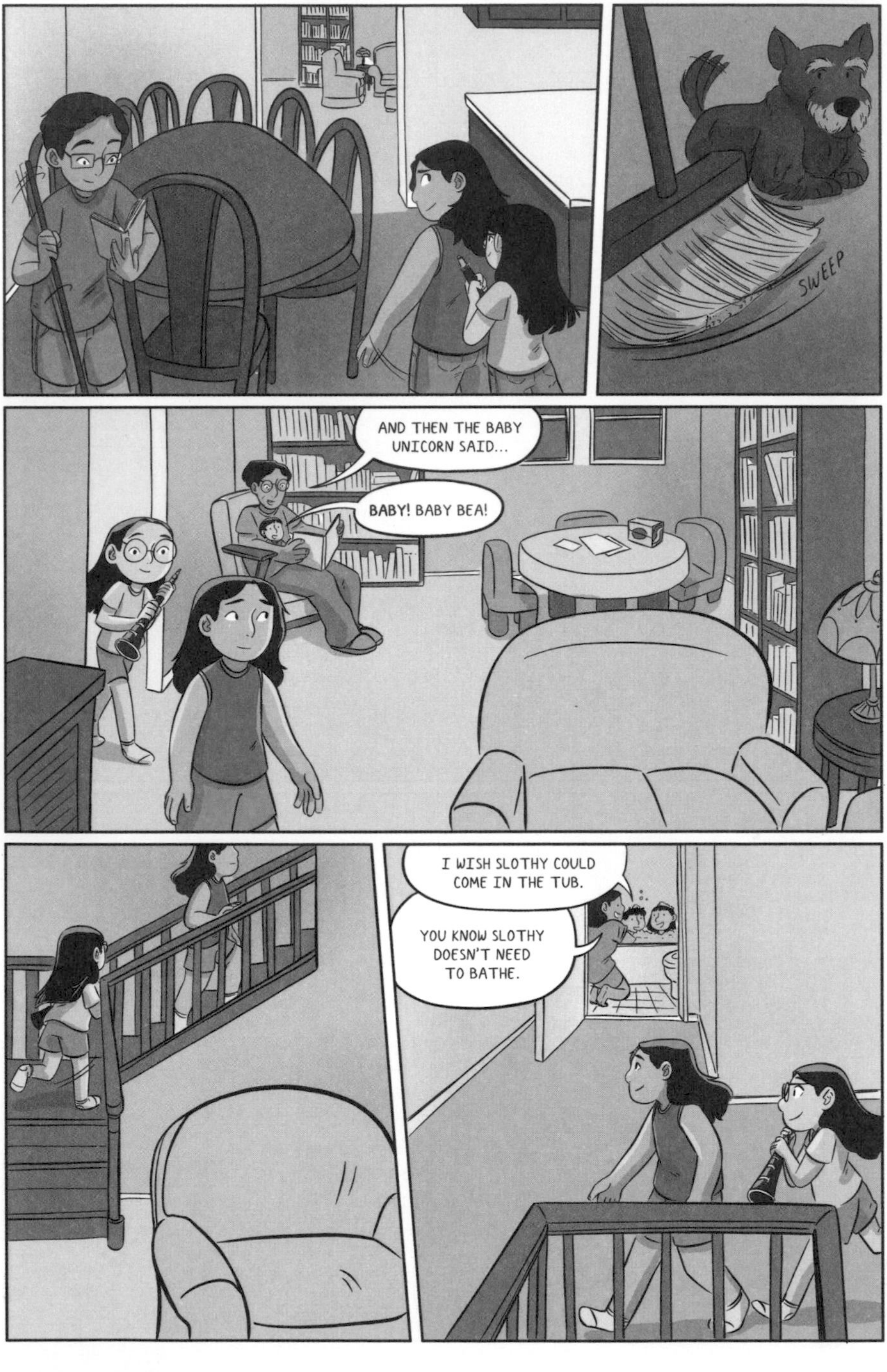
SWEEP
AND THEN THE BABY UNICORN SAID...
BABY! BABY BEA!
I WISH SLOTHY COULD COME IN THE TUB.
YOU KNOW SLOTHY DOESN'T NEED TO BATHE.

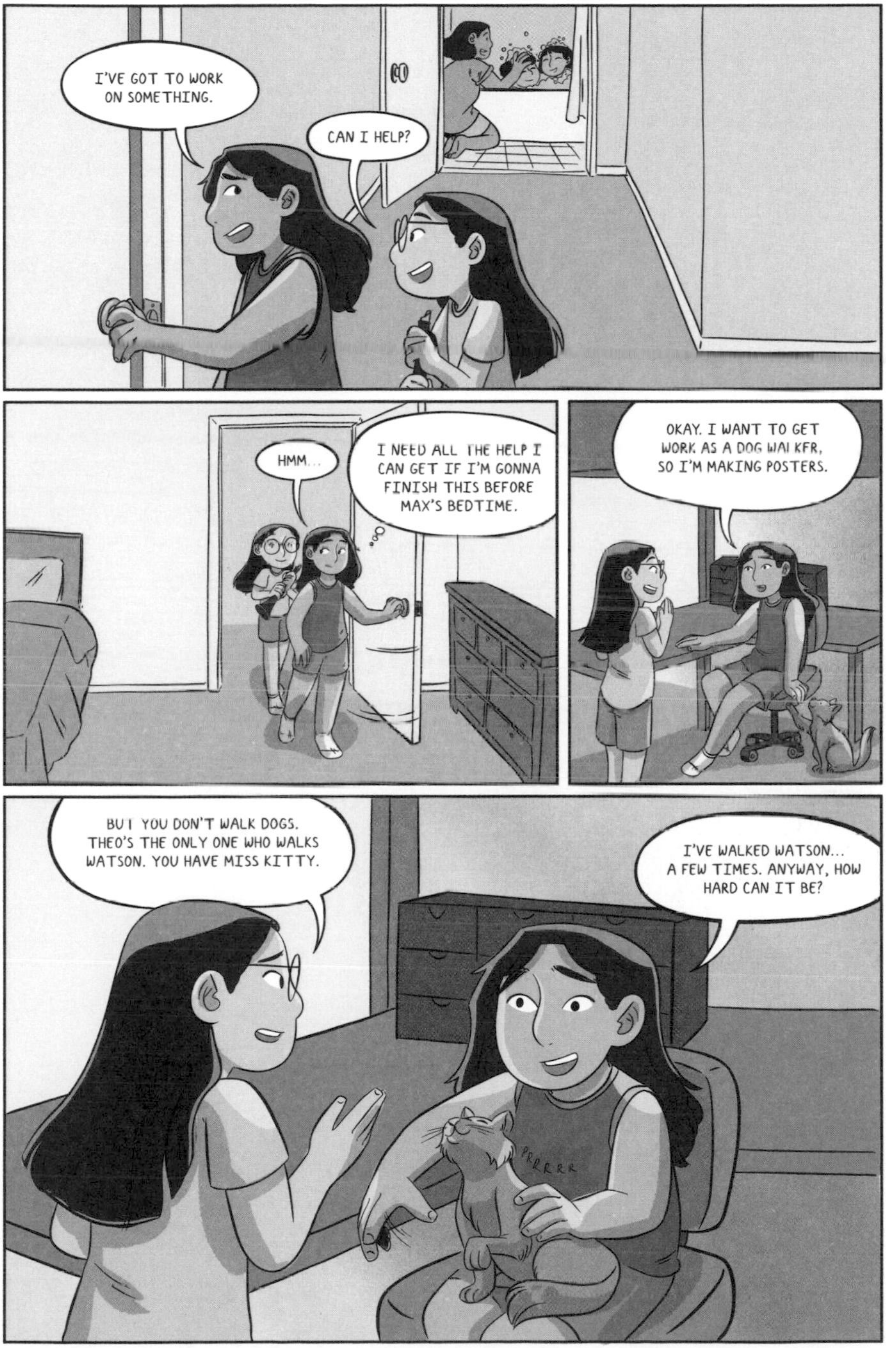
I'VE GOT TO WORK ON SOMETHING.
CAN I HELP?
HMM...
I NEED ALL THE HELP I CAN GET IF I'M GONNA FINISH THIS BEFORE MAX'S BEDTIME.
OKAY. I WANT TO GET WORK AS A DOG WALKER, SO I'M MAKING POSTERS.
BUT YOU DON'T WALK DOGS. THEO'S THE ONLY ONE WHO WALKS WATSON. YOU HAVE MISS KITTY.
I'VE WALKED WATSON... A FEW TIMES. ANYWAY, HOW HARD CAN IT BE?
PRRRRR

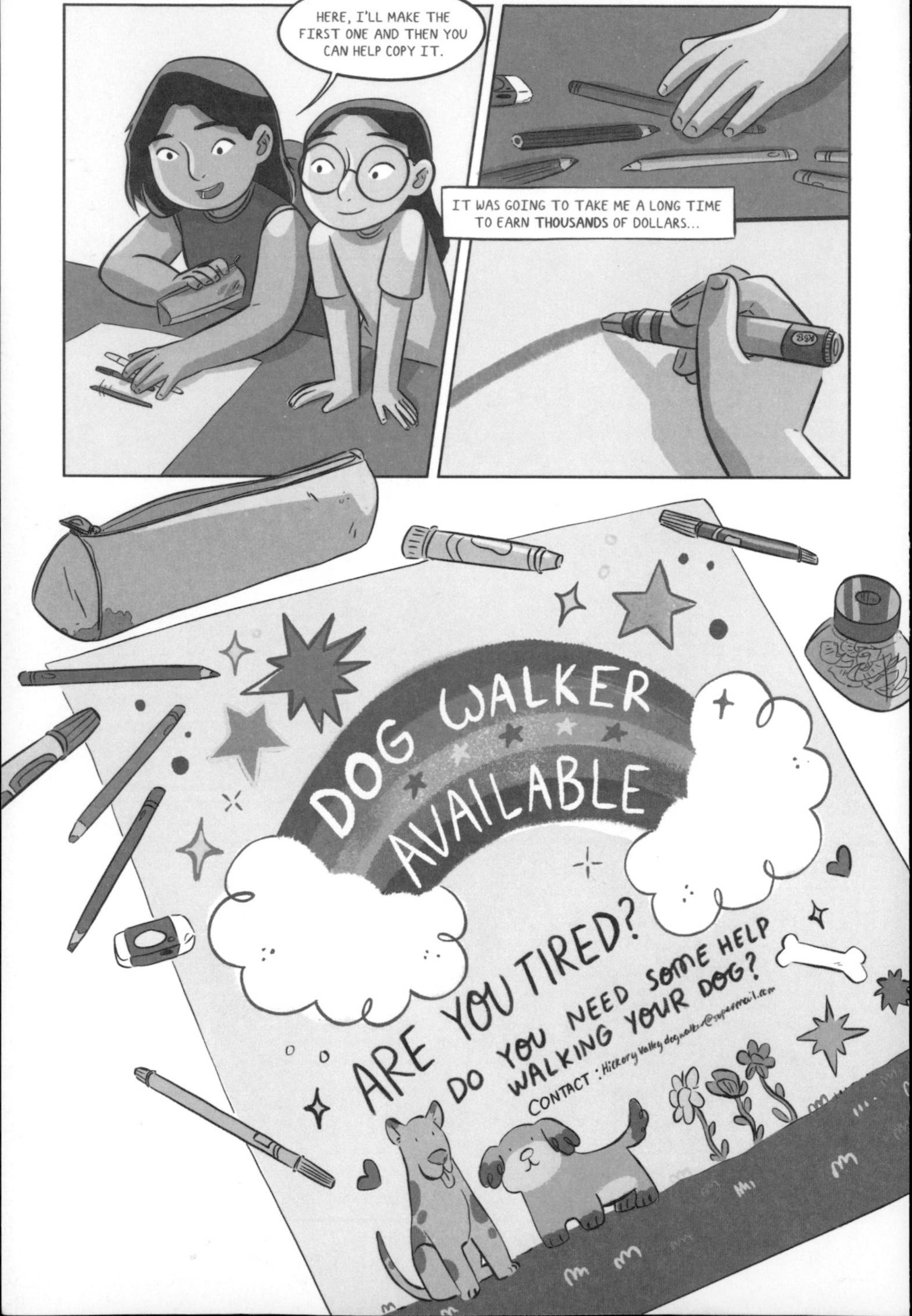

HERE, I'LL MAKE THE FIRST ONE AND THEN YOU CAN HELP COPY IT.
IT WAS GOING TO TAKE ME A LONG TIME TO EARN **THOUSANDS** OF DOLLARS...
DOG WALKER AVAILABLE
ARE YOU TIRED?
DO YOU NEED SOME HELP WALKING YOUR DOG?
CONTACT : HickoryValleydogwalker@supermail.com

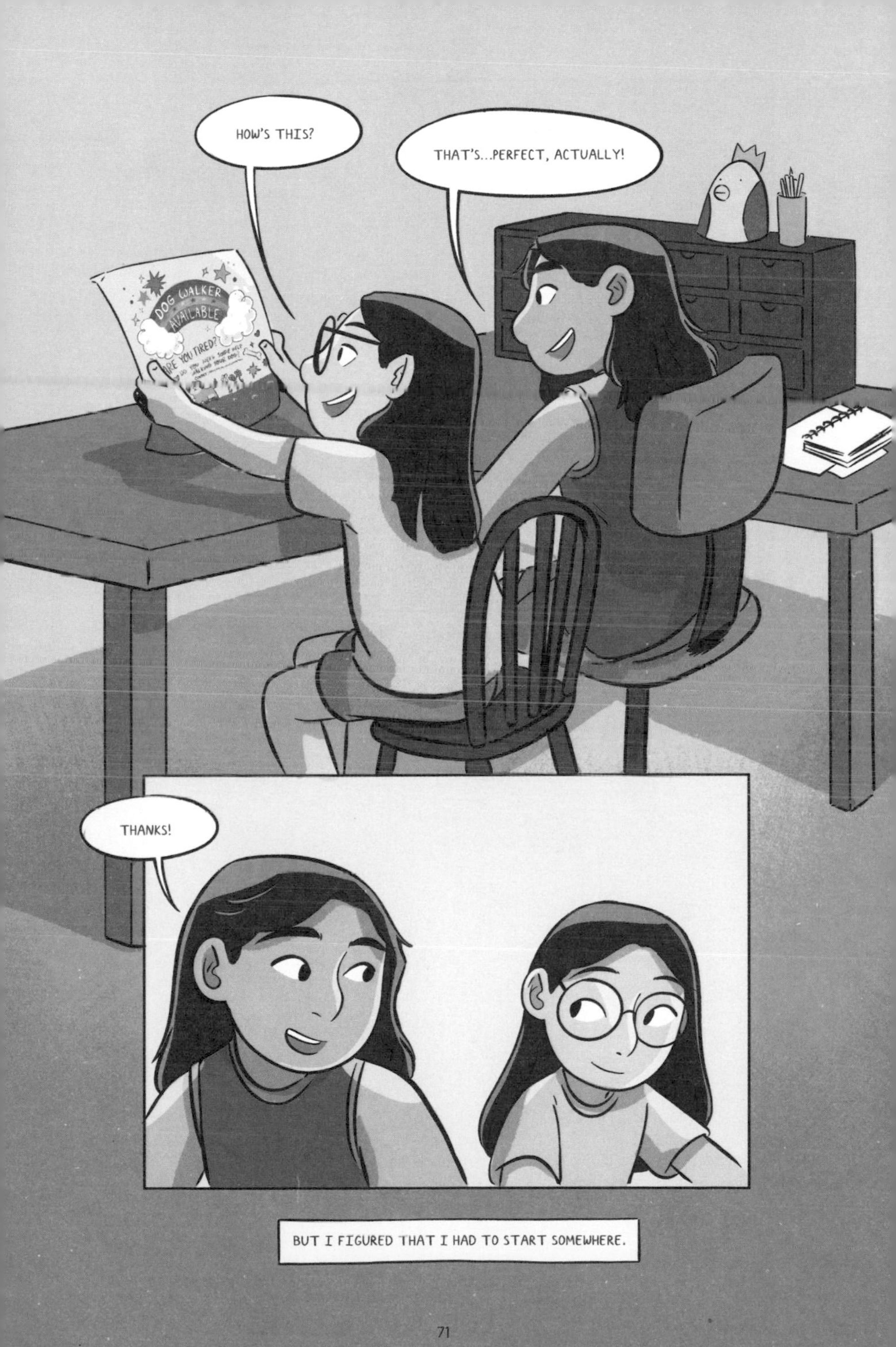
HOW'S THIS?
THAT'S...PERFECT, ACTUALLY!
DOG WALKER
AVAILABLE
THANKS!
BUT I FIGURED THAT I HAD TO START SOMEWHERE.

Chapter Five

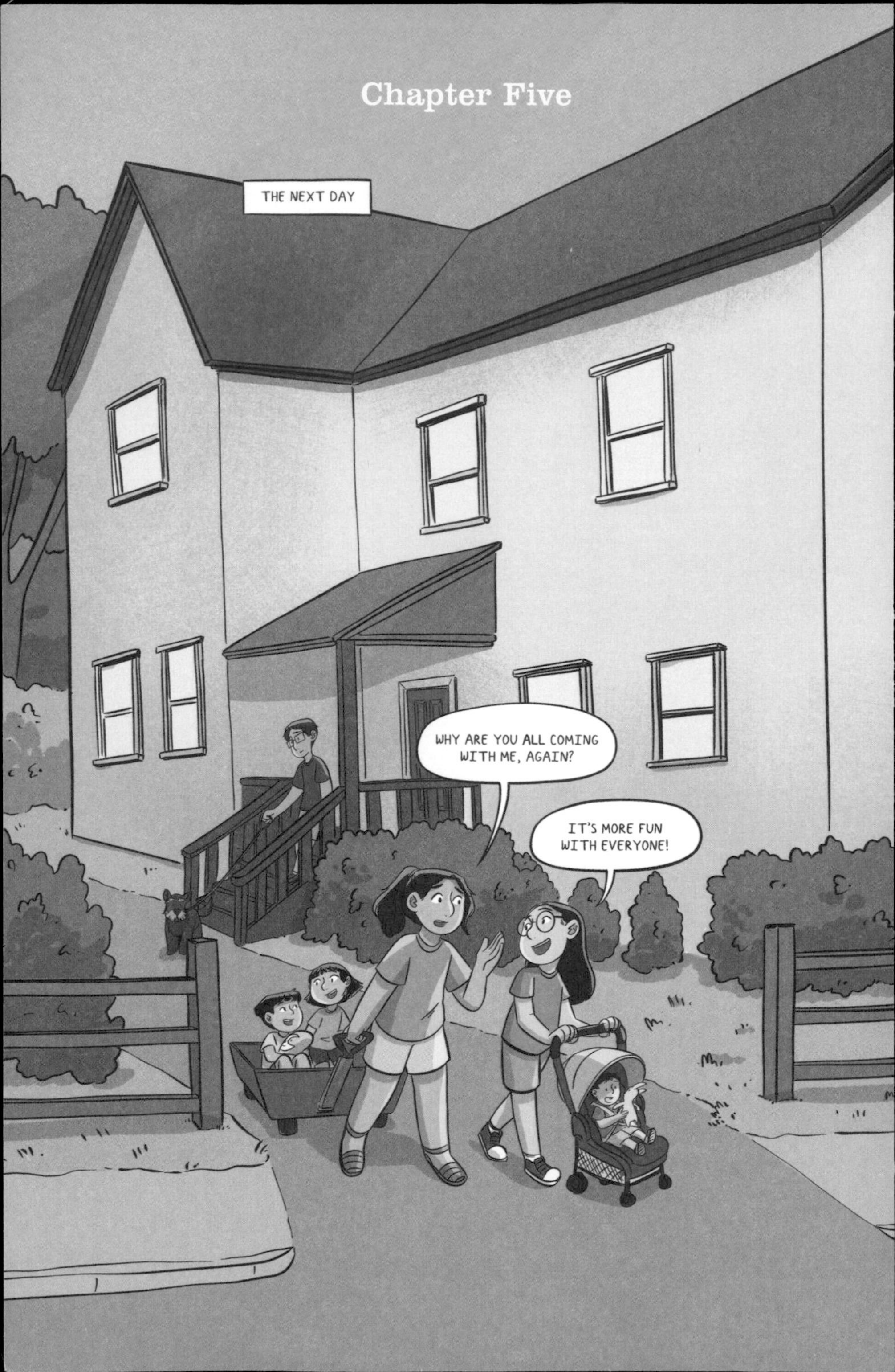
THE NEXT DAY
WHY ARE YOU ALL COMING WITH ME, AGAIN?
IT'S MORE FUN WITH EVERYONE!

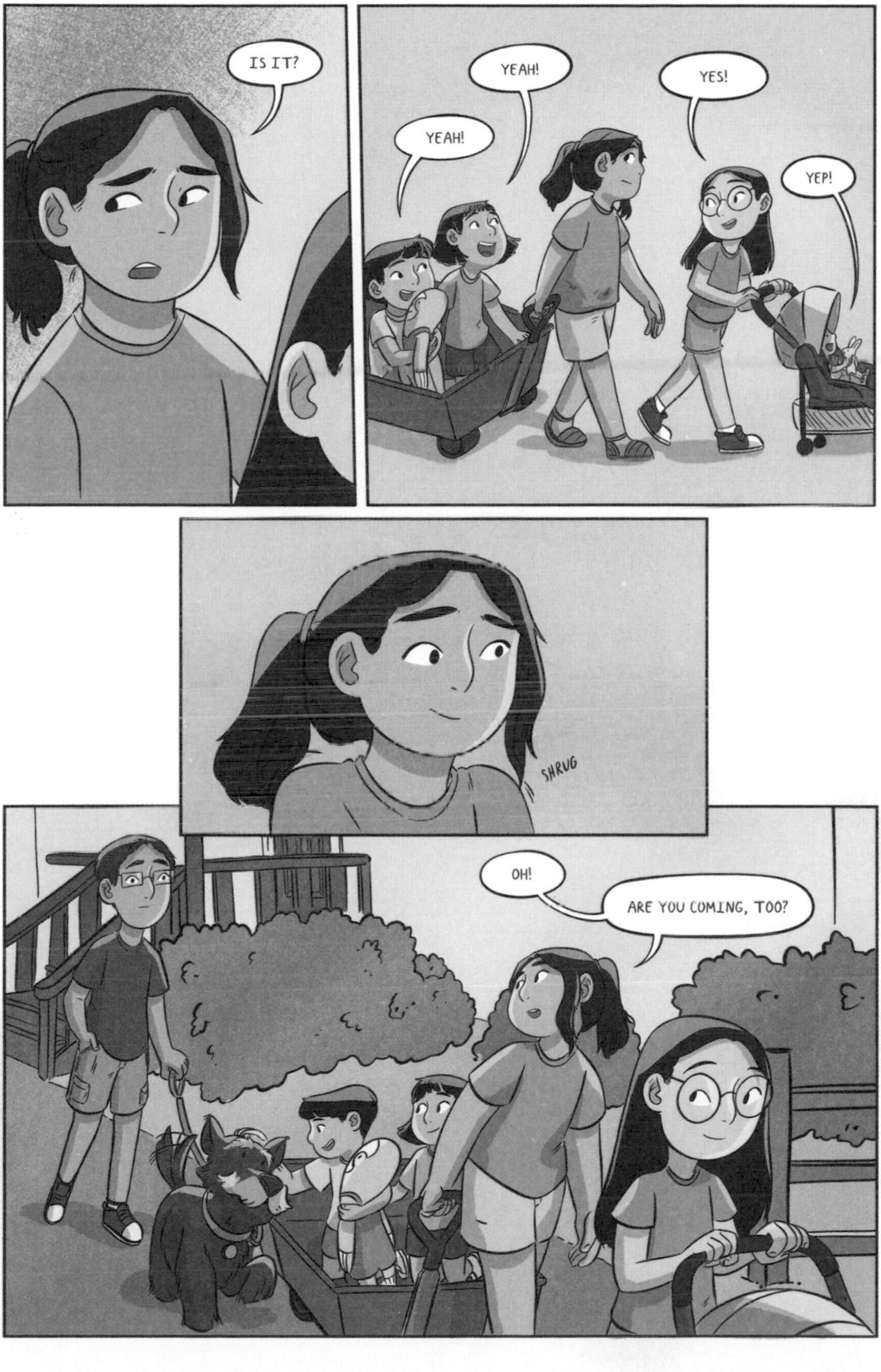
IS IT?
YEAH!
YEAH!
YES!
YEP!
SHRUG
OH!
ARE YOU COMING, TOO?

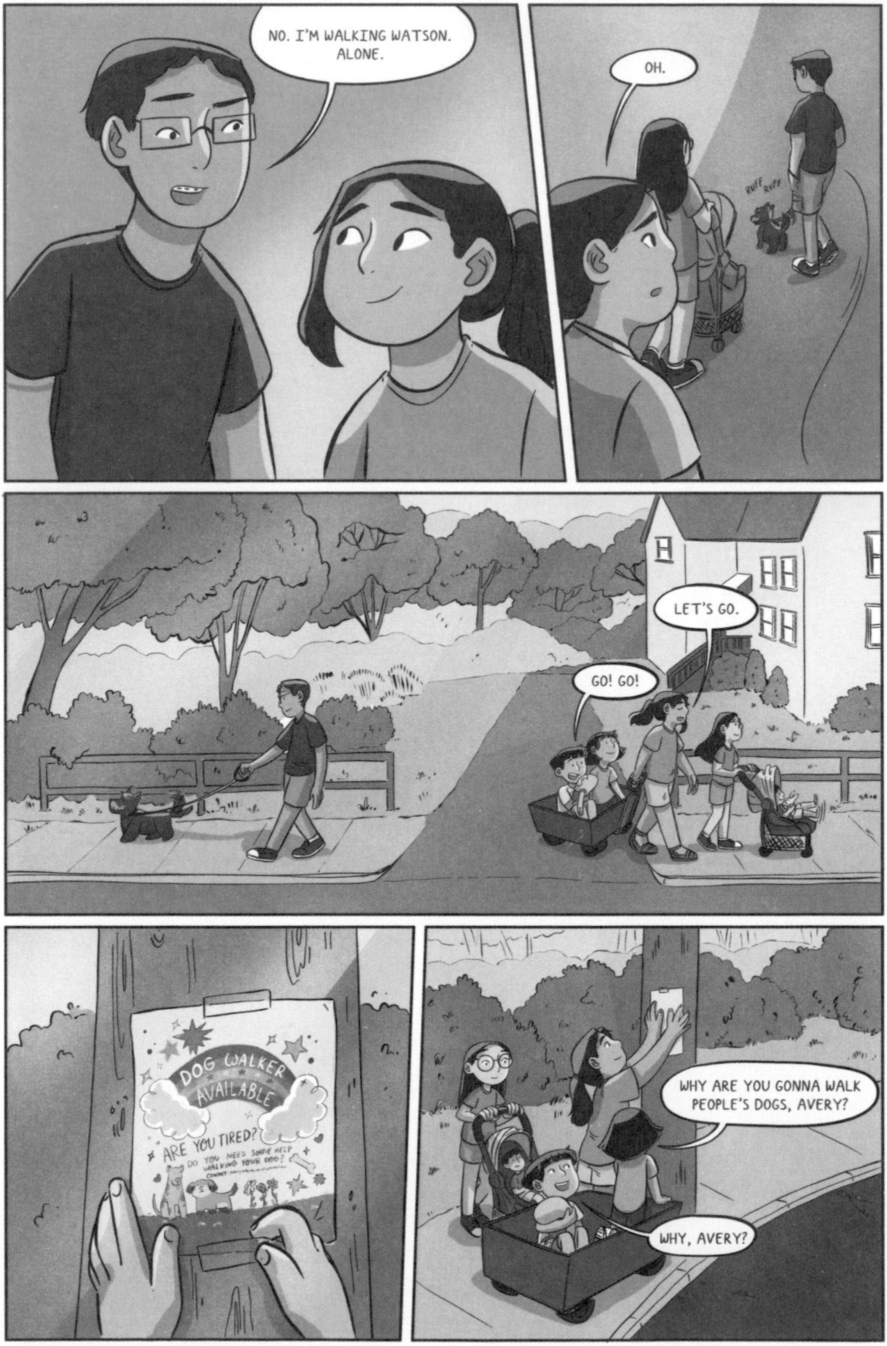
NO. I'M WALKING WATSON. ALONE.
OH.
RUFF RUFF
LET'S GO.
GO! GO!
DOG WALKER AVAILABLE
ARE YOU TIRED?
DO YOU NEED SOME HELP WALKING YOUR DOG?
WHY ARE YOU GONNA WALK PEOPLE'S DOGS, AVERY?
WHY, AVERY?

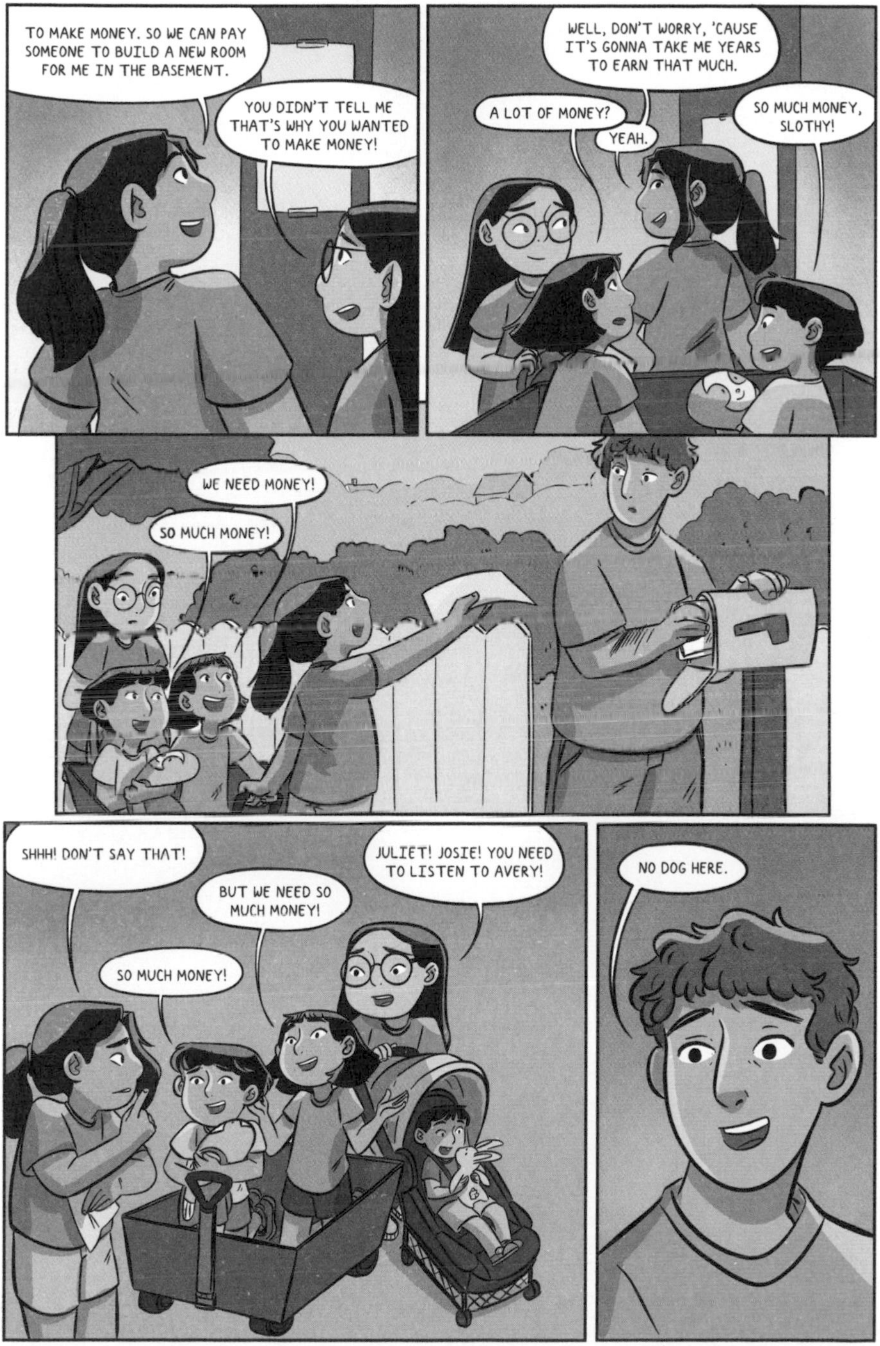
TO MAKE MONEY. SO WE CAN PAY SOMEONE TO BUILD A NEW ROOM FOR ME IN THE BASEMENT.
YOU DIDN'T TELL ME THAT'S WHY YOU WANTED TO MAKE MONEY!
WELL, DON'T WORRY, 'CAUSE IT'S GONNA TAKE ME YEARS TO EARN THAT MUCH.
A LOT OF MONEY?
YEAH.
SO MUCH MONEY, SLOTHY!
WE NEED MONEY!
SO MUCH MONEY!
SHHH! DON'T SAY THAT!
SO MUCH MONEY!
BUT WE NEED SO MUCH MONEY!
JULIET! JOSIE! YOU NEED TO LISTEN TO AVERY!
NO DOG HERE.

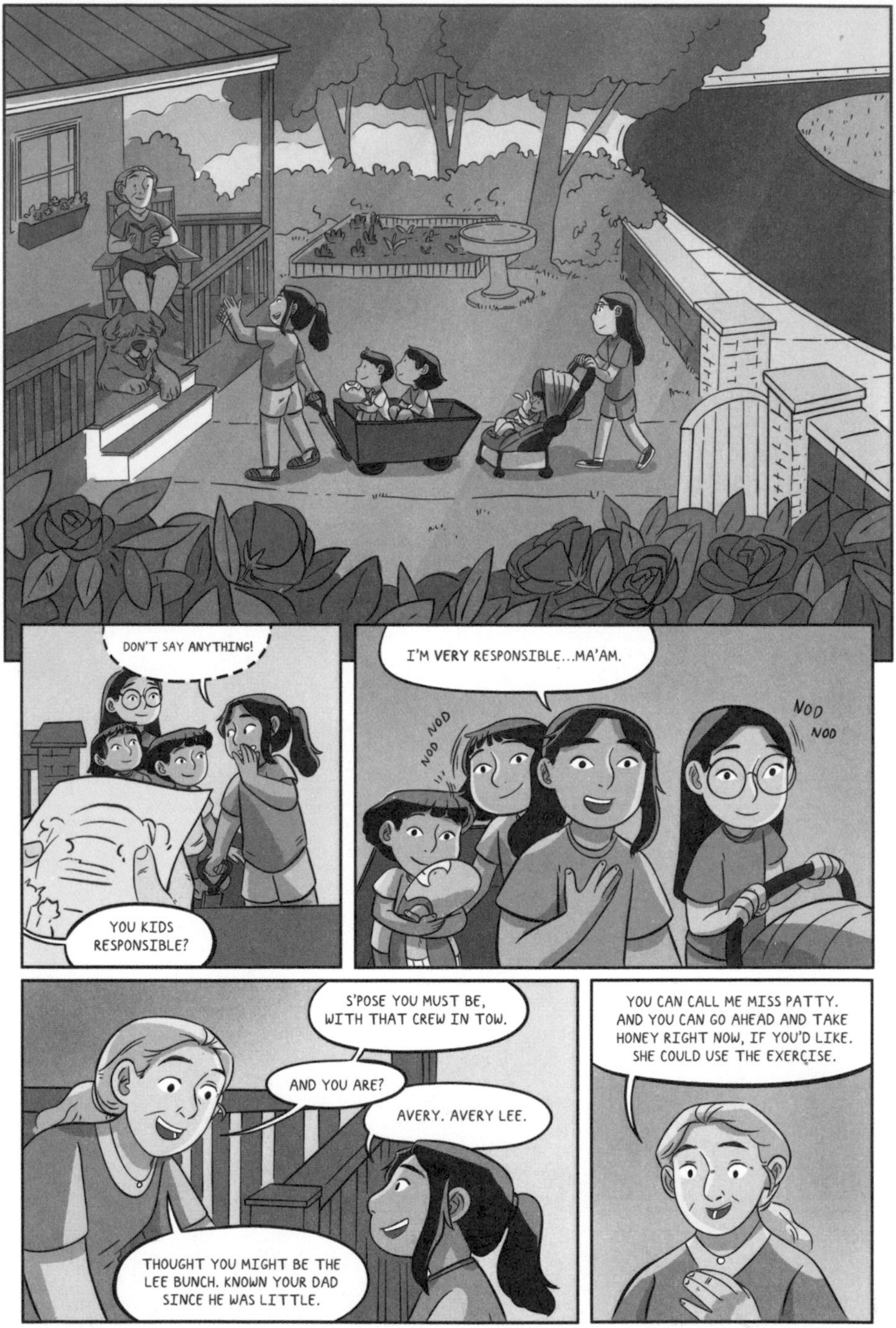

DON'T SAY ANYTHING!
YOU KIDS RESPONSIBLE?
I'M VERY RESPONSIBLE...MA'AM.
NOD NOD
NOD NOD
S'POSE YOU MUST BE, WITH THAT CREW IN TOW.
AND YOU ARE?
AVERY. AVERY LEE.
THOUGHT YOU MIGHT BE THE LEE BUNCH. KNOWN YOUR DAD SINCE HE WAS LITTLE.
YOU CAN CALL ME MISS PATTY. AND YOU CAN GO AHEAD AND TAKE HONEY RIGHT NOW, IF YOU'D LIKE. SHE COULD USE THE EXERCISE.

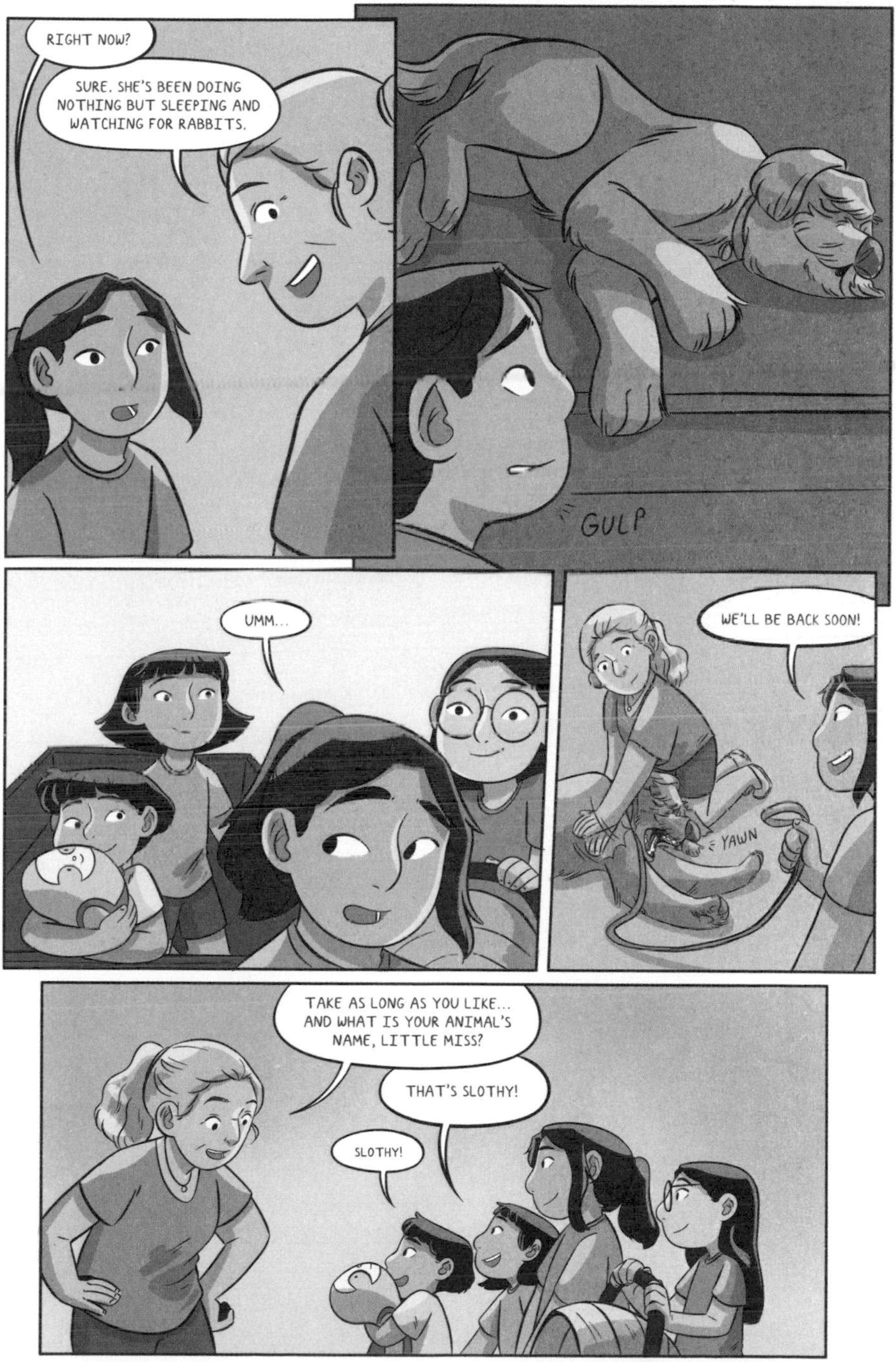
RIGHT NOW?
SURE. SHE'S BEEN DOING NOTHING BUT SLEEPING AND WATCHING FOR RABBITS.
GULP
UMM...
WE'LL BE BACK SOON!
YAWN
TAKE AS LONG AS YOU LIKE... AND WHAT IS YOUR ANIMAL'S NAME, LITTLE MISS?
THAT'S SLOTHY!
SLOTHY!

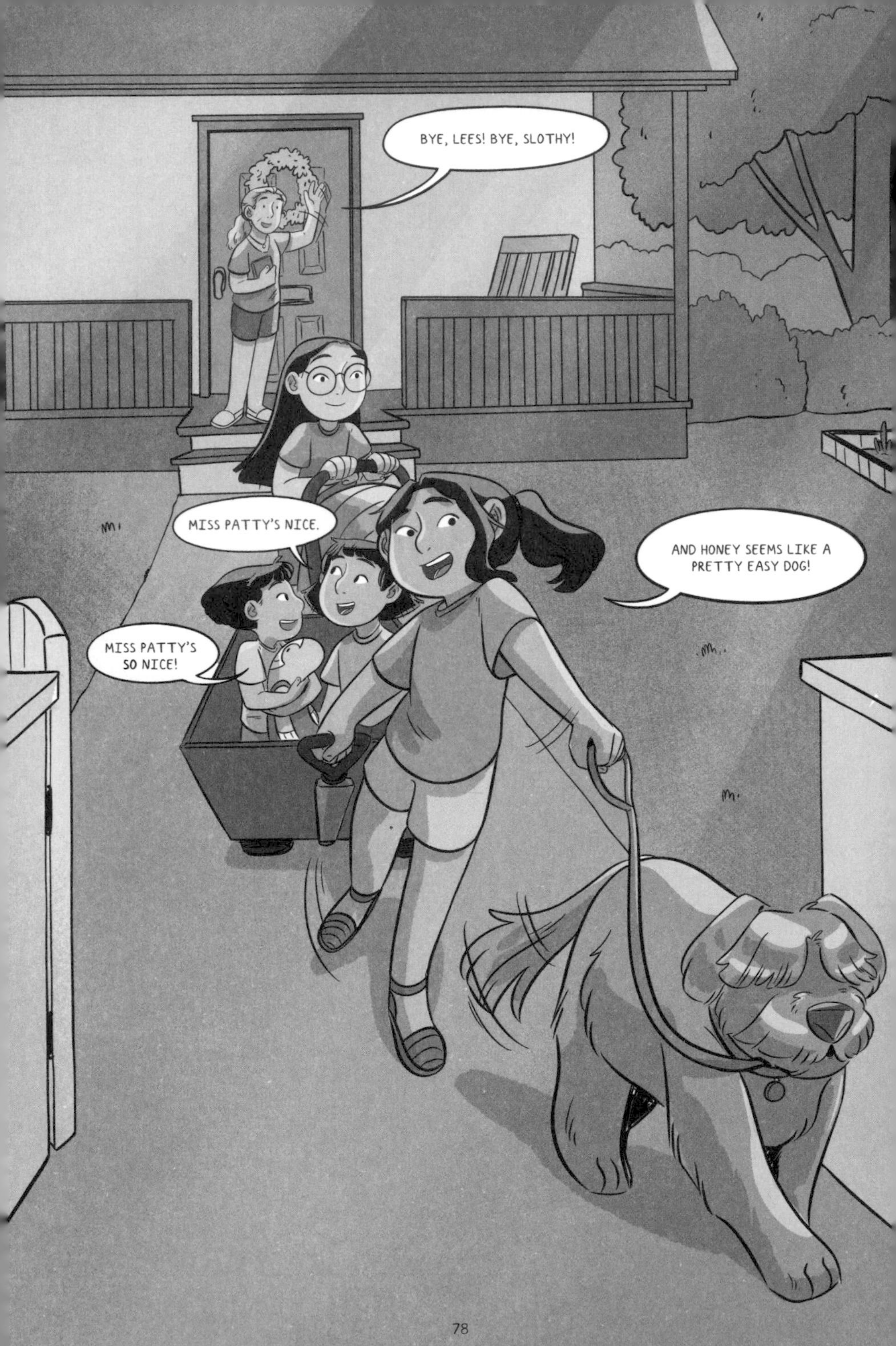
BYE, LEES! BYE, SLOTHY!
MISS PATTY'S NICE.
MISS PATTY'S SO NICE!
AND HONEY SEEMS LIKE A PRETTY EASY DOG!

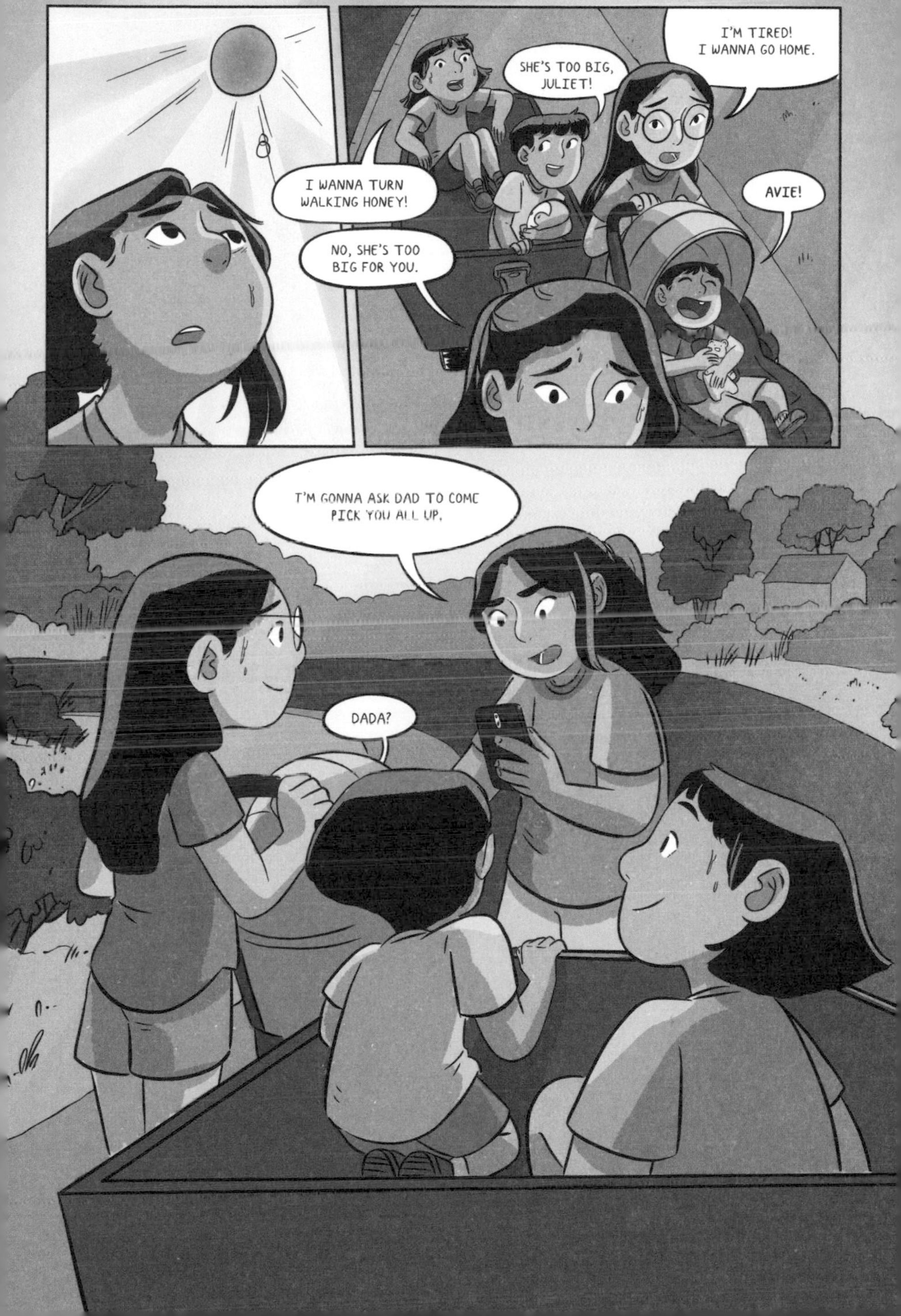
I'M TIRED!
I WANNA GO HOME.
SHE'S TOO BIG, JULIET!
I WANNA TURN WALKING HONEY!
AVIE!
NO, SHE'S TOO BIG FOR YOU.
I'M GONNA ASK DAD TO COME PICK YOU ALL UP.
DADA?

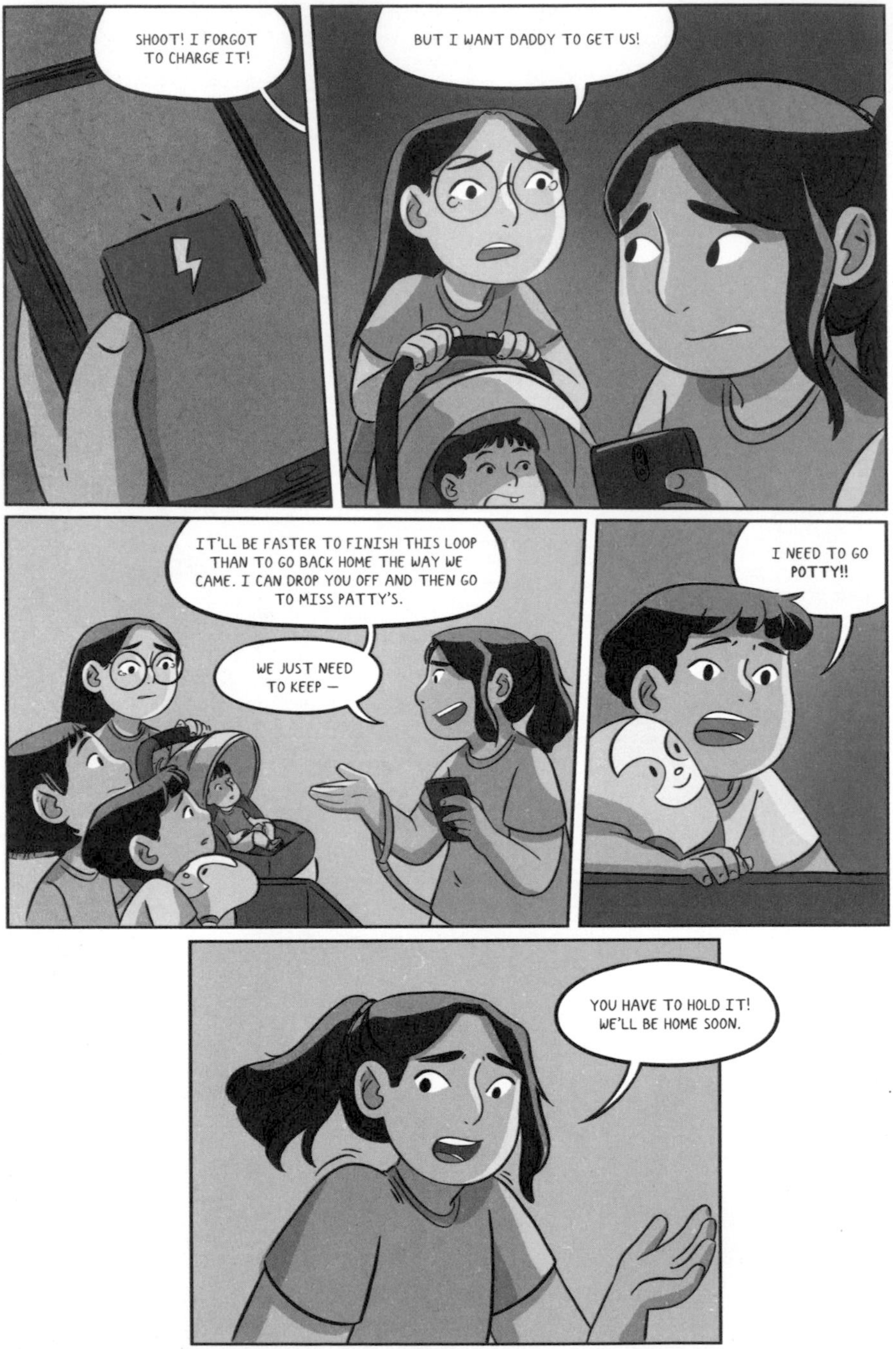
SHOOT! I FORGOT TO CHARGE IT!
BUT I WANT DADDY TO GET US!
IT'LL BE FASTER TO FINISH THIS LOOP THAN TO GO BACK HOME THE WAY WE CAME. I CAN DROP YOU OFF AND THEN GO TO MISS PATTY'S.
WE JUST NEED TO KEEP —
I NEED TO GO **POTTY!!**
YOU HAVE TO HOLD IT! WE'LL BE HOME SOON.

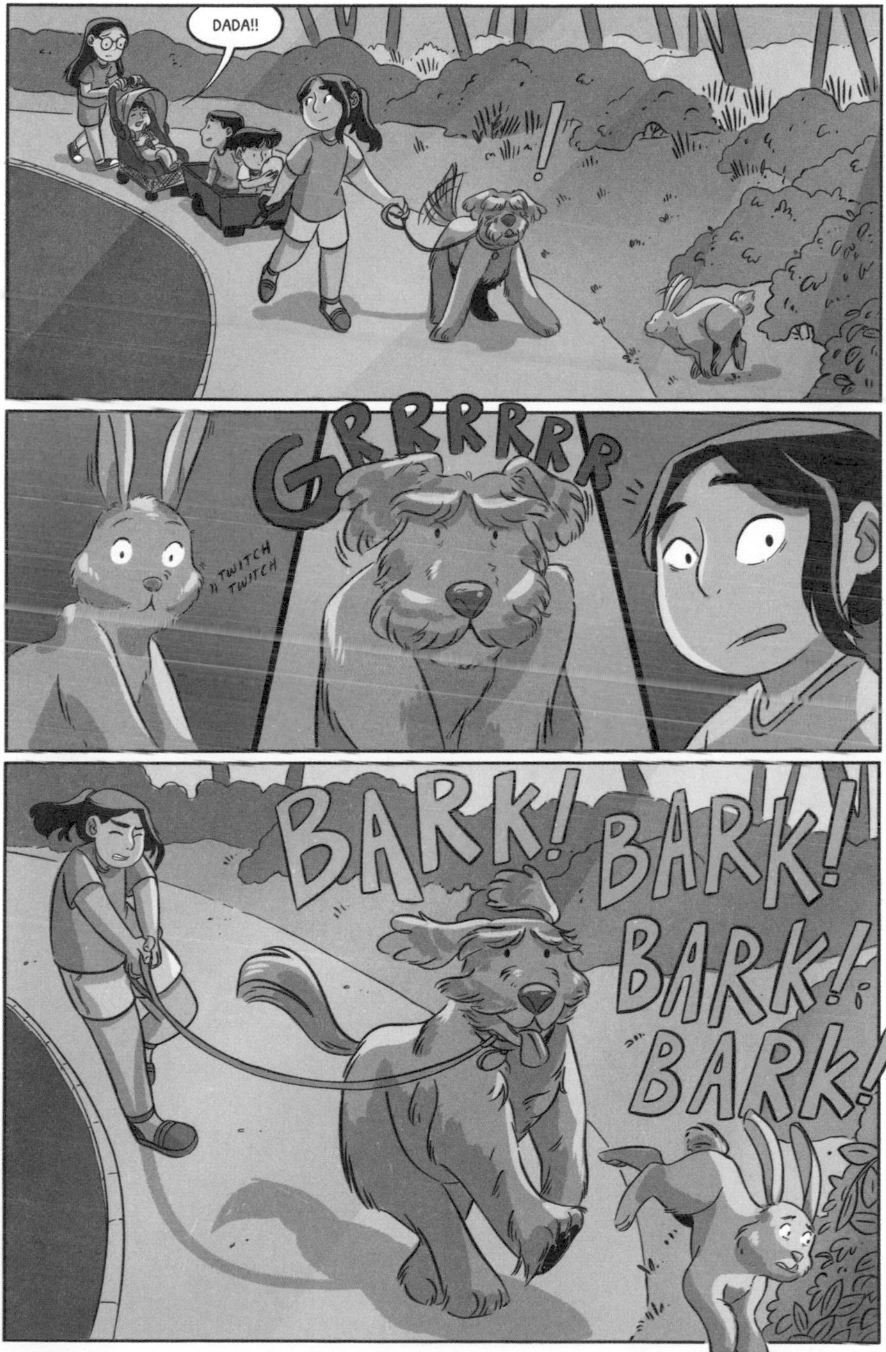
DADA!!
!
GRRRRRR
TWITCH TWITCH
BARK! BARK!
BARK!
BARK!

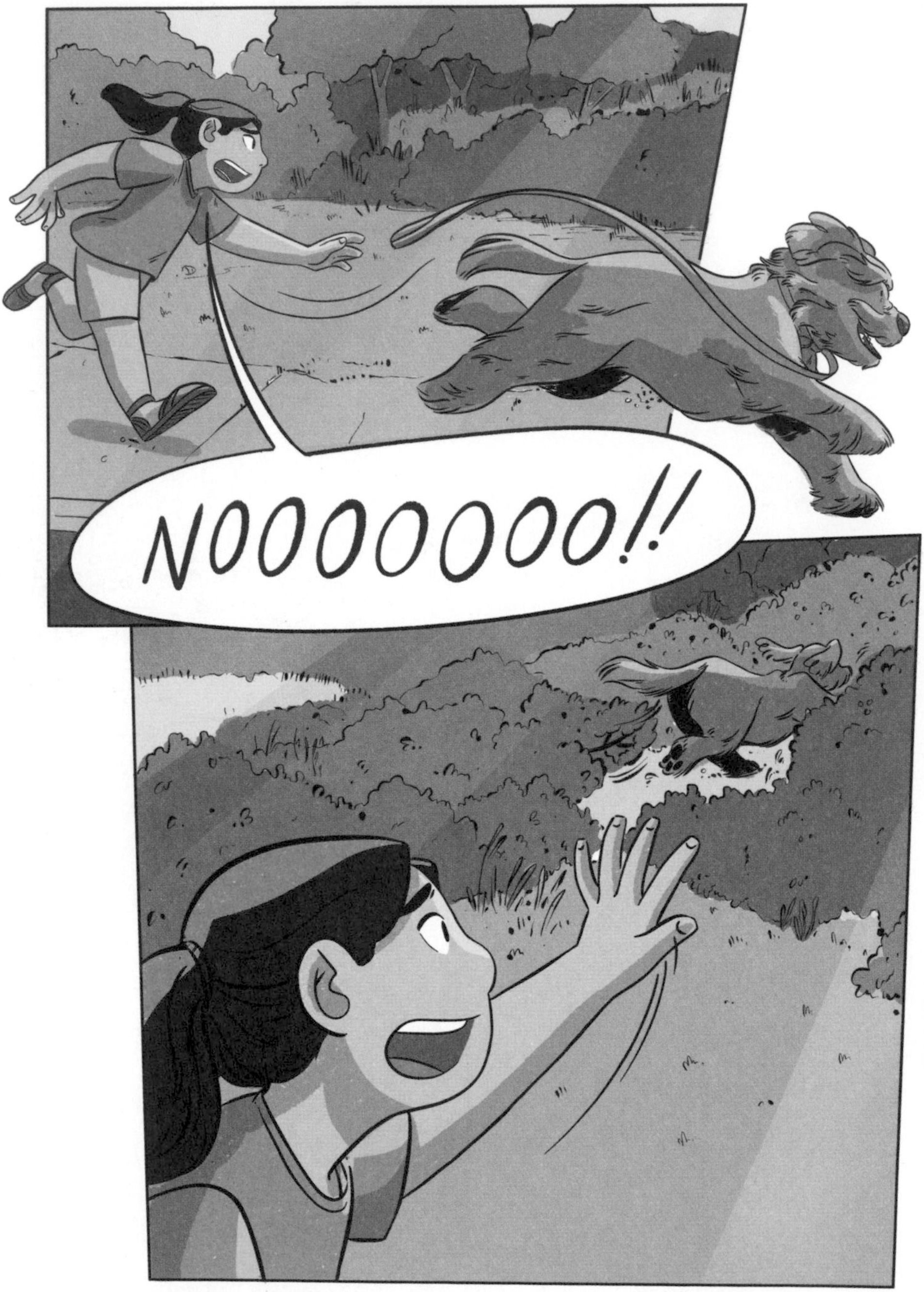
NOOOOOOO!!

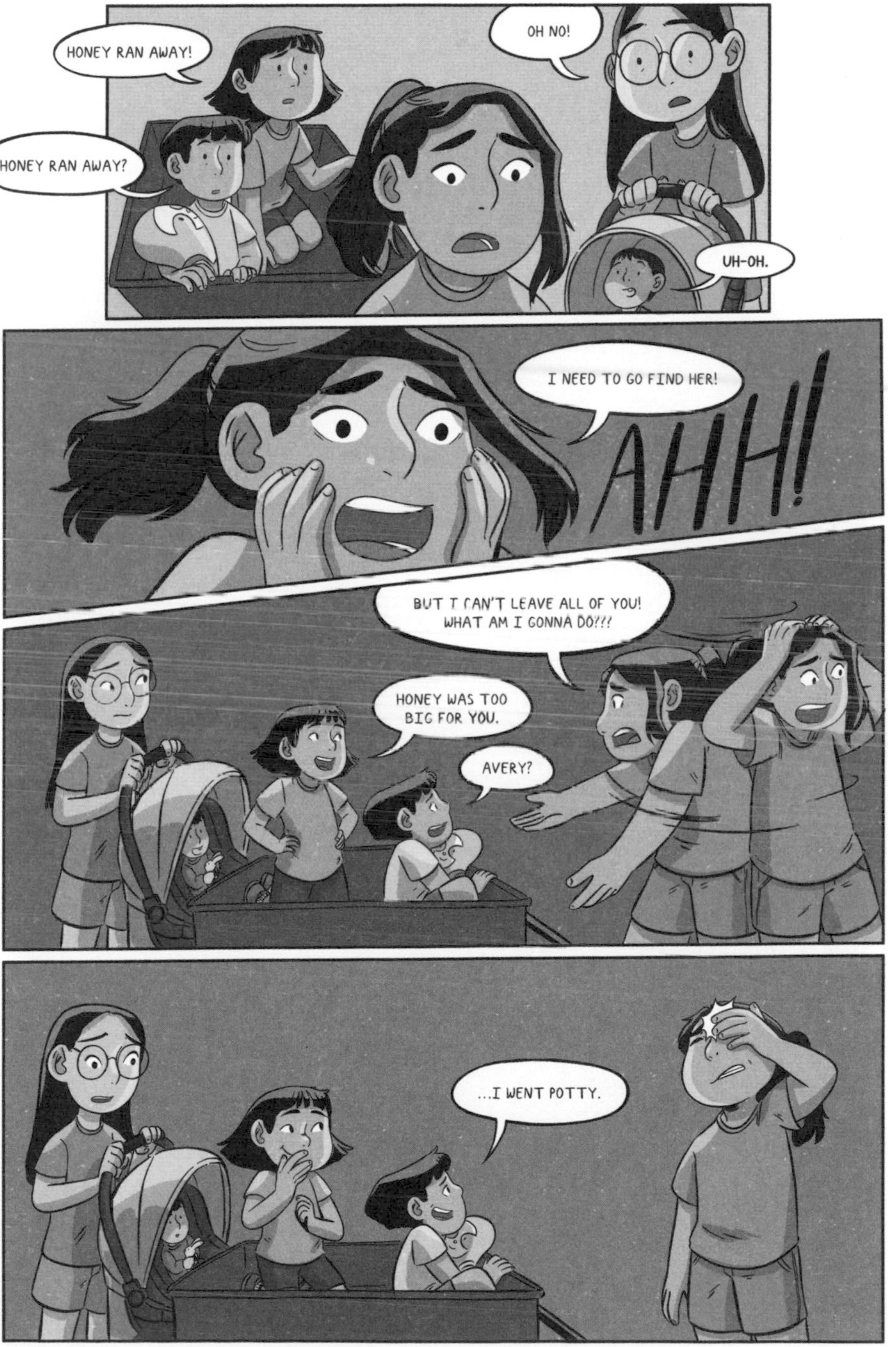
HONEY RAN AWAY!
HONEY RAN AWAY?
OH NO!
UH-OH.
I NEED TO GO FIND HER!
AHH!
BUT I CAN'T LEAVE ALL OF YOU! WHAT AM I GONNA DO???
HONEY WAS TOO BIG FOR YOU.
AVERY?
...I WENT POTTY.

Chapter Six

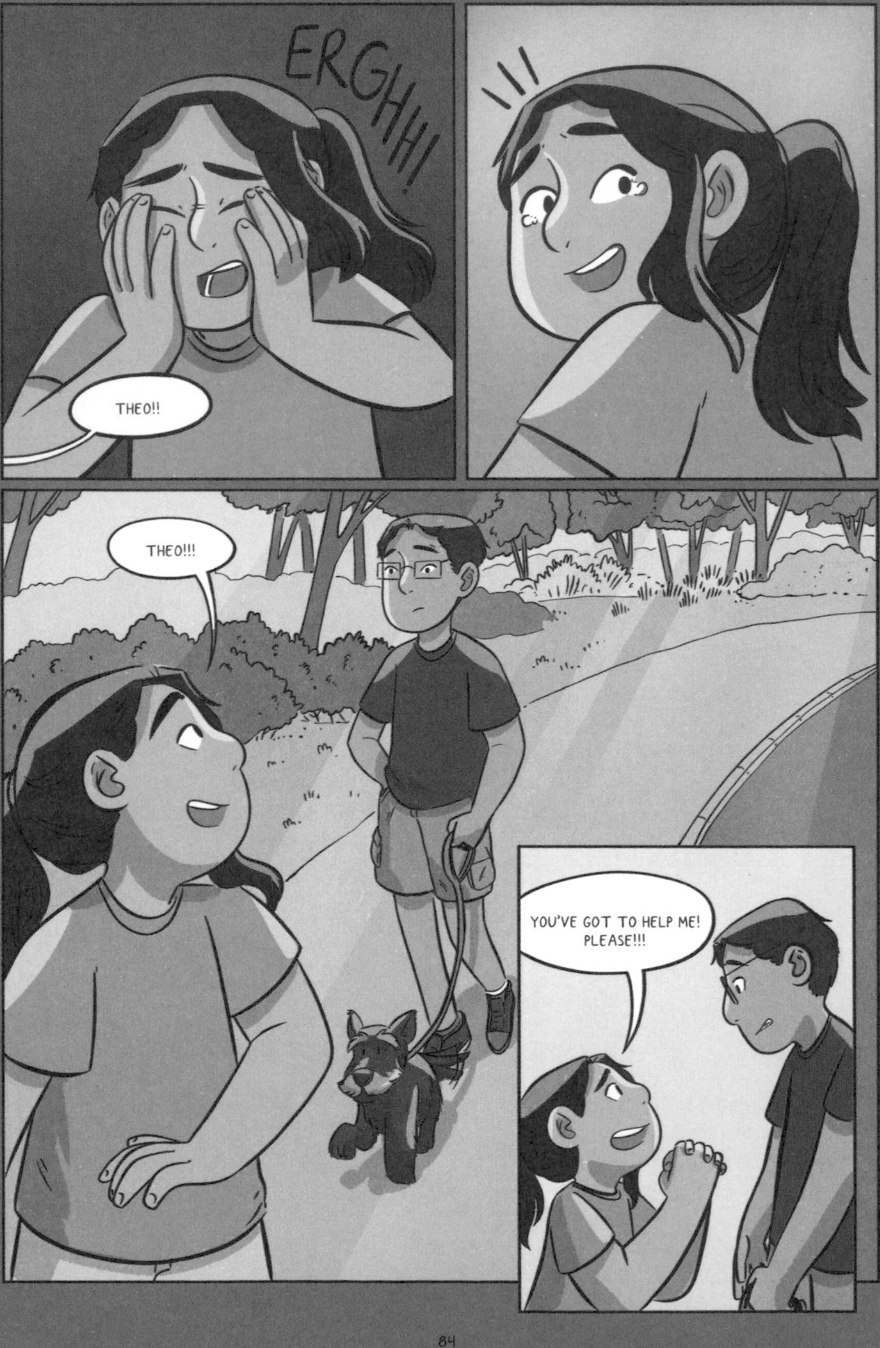
ERGHHH!
THEO!!
THEO!!!
YOU'VE GOT TO HELP ME! PLEASE!!!

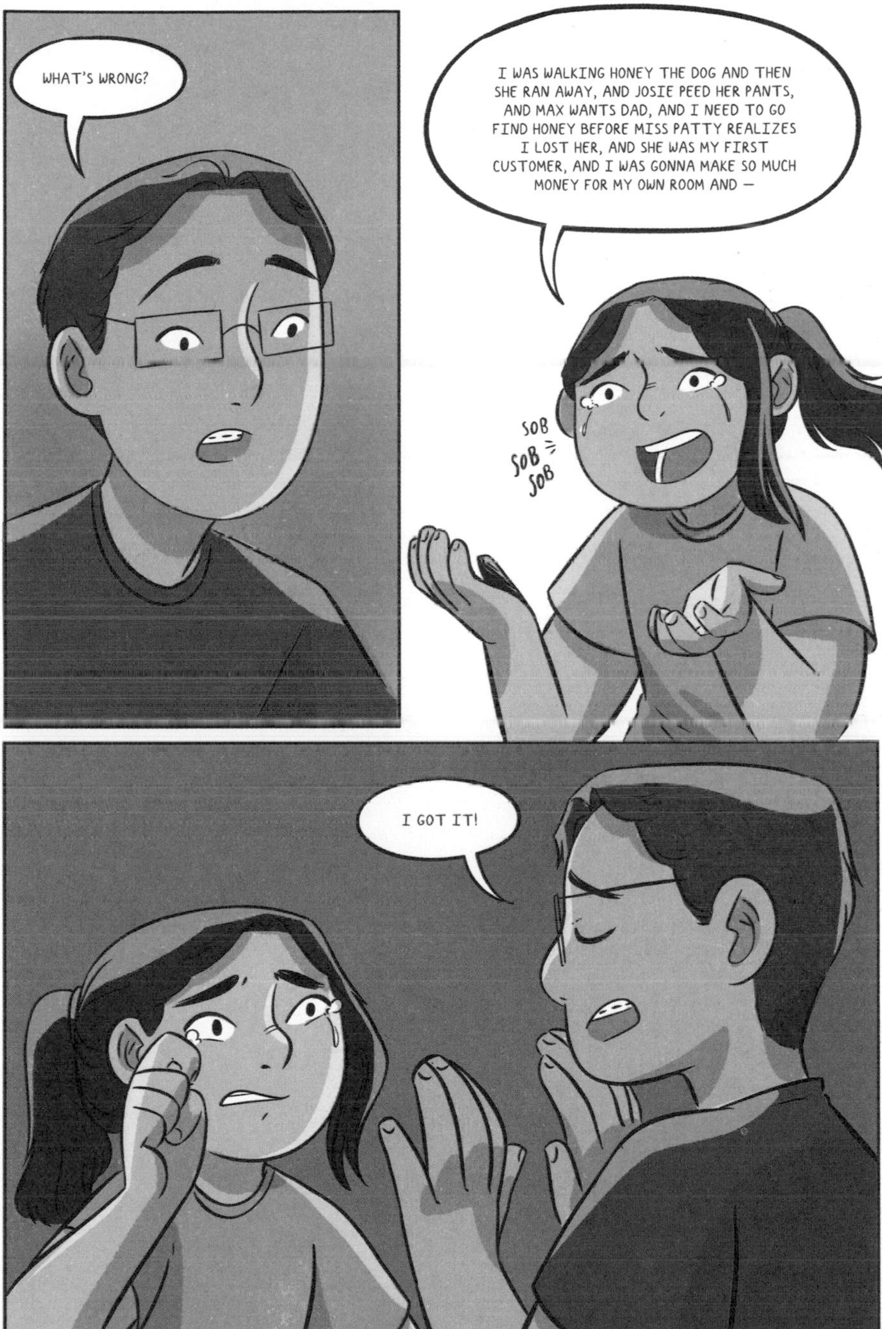
WHAT'S WRONG?
I WAS WALKING HONEY THE DOG AND THEN SHE RAN AWAY, AND JOSIE PEED HER PANTS, AND MAX WANTS DAD, AND I NEED TO GO FIND HONEY BEFORE MISS PATTY REALIZES I LOST HER, AND SHE WAS MY FIRST CUSTOMER, AND I WAS GONNA MAKE SO MUCH MONEY FOR MY OWN ROOM AND —
SOB SOB SOB
I GOT IT!

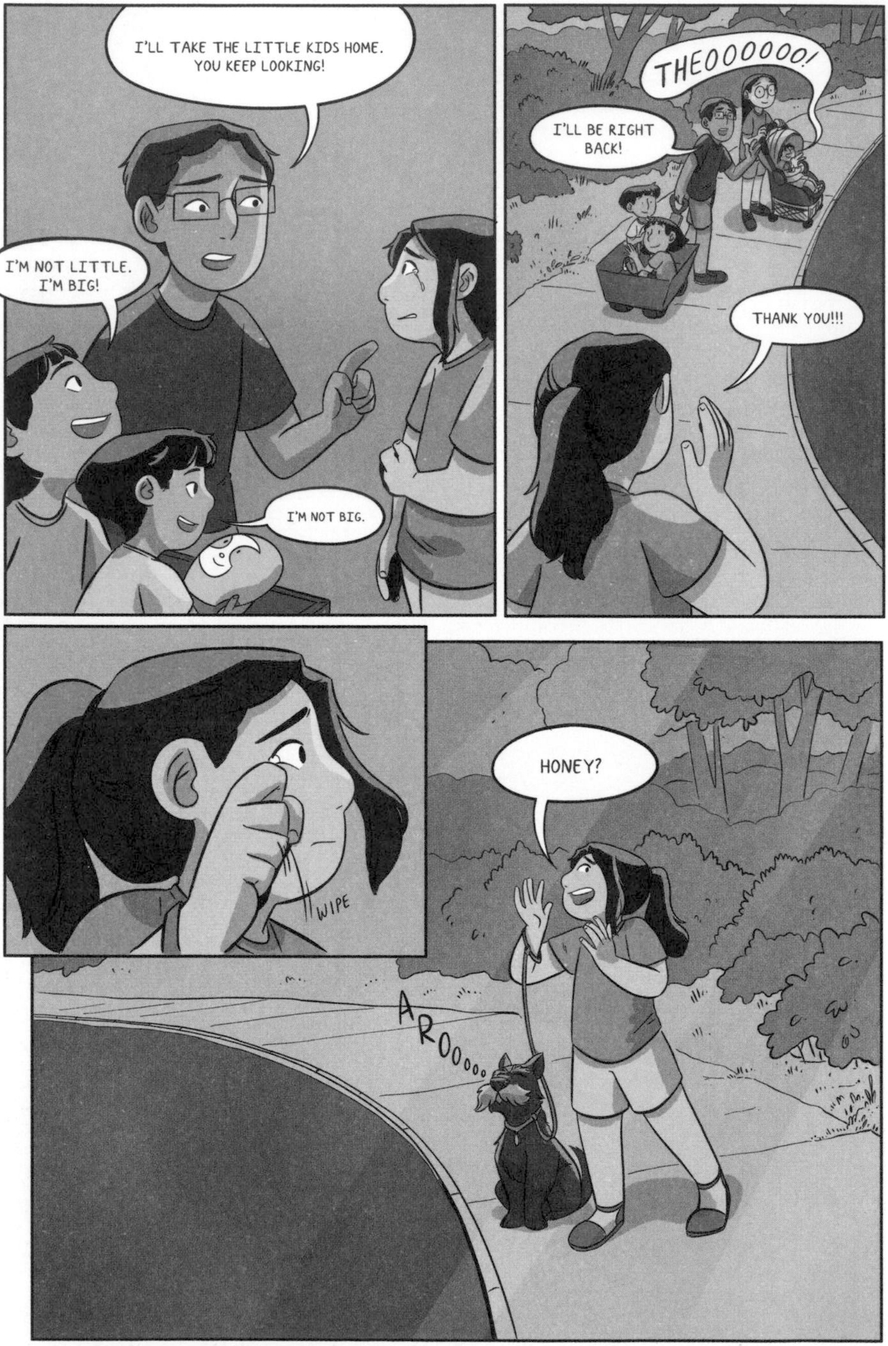
I'LL TAKE THE LITTLE KIDS HOME. YOU KEEP LOOKING!
I'M NOT LITTLE. I'M BIG!
I'M NOT BIG.
THEOOOOOO!
I'LL BE RIGHT BACK!
THANK YOU!!!
WIPE
HONEY?
AROOooo

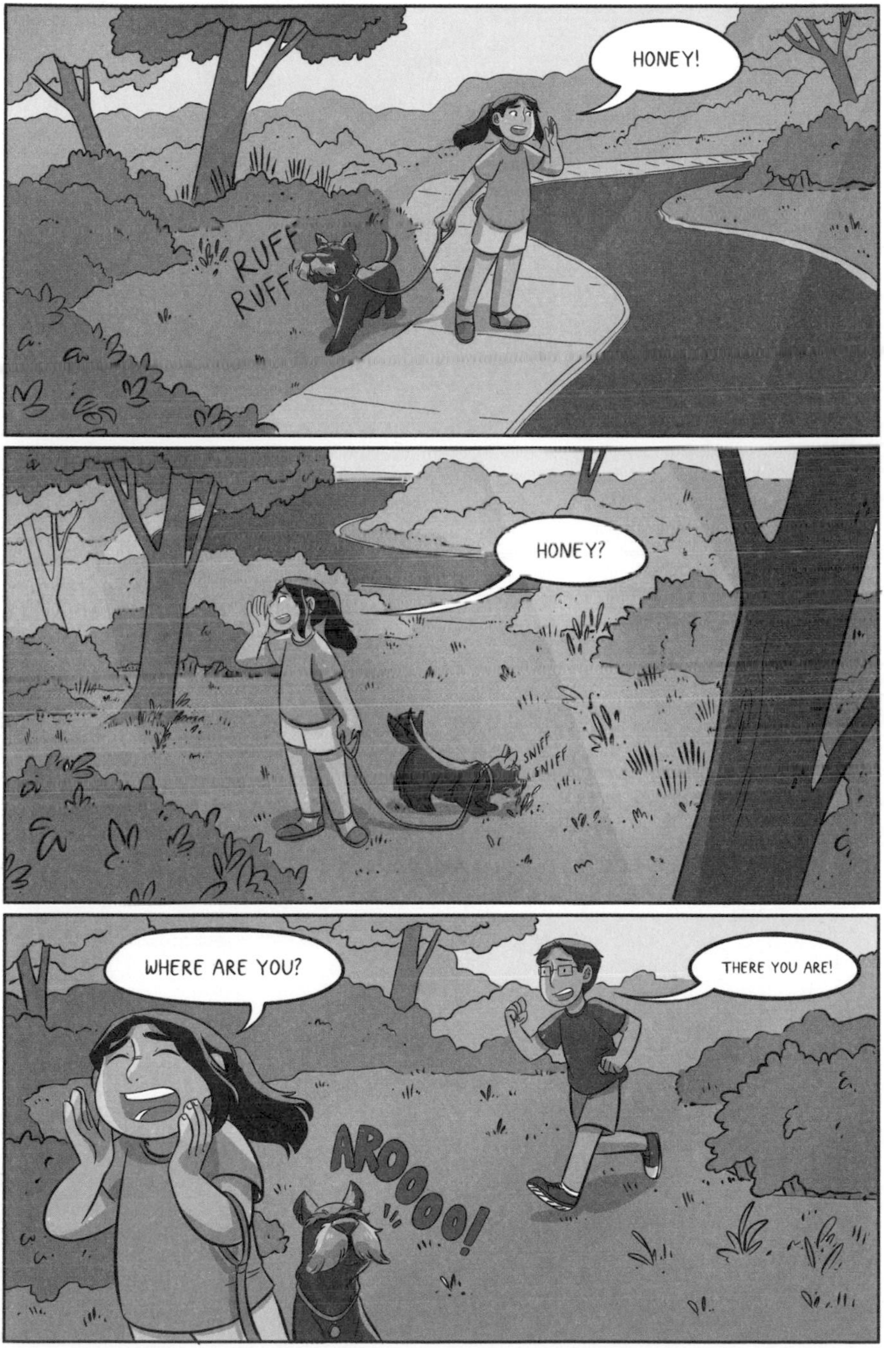
HONEY!
RUFF RUFF
HONEY?
SNIFF SNIFF
WHERE ARE YOU?
THERE YOU ARE!
AROOOO!

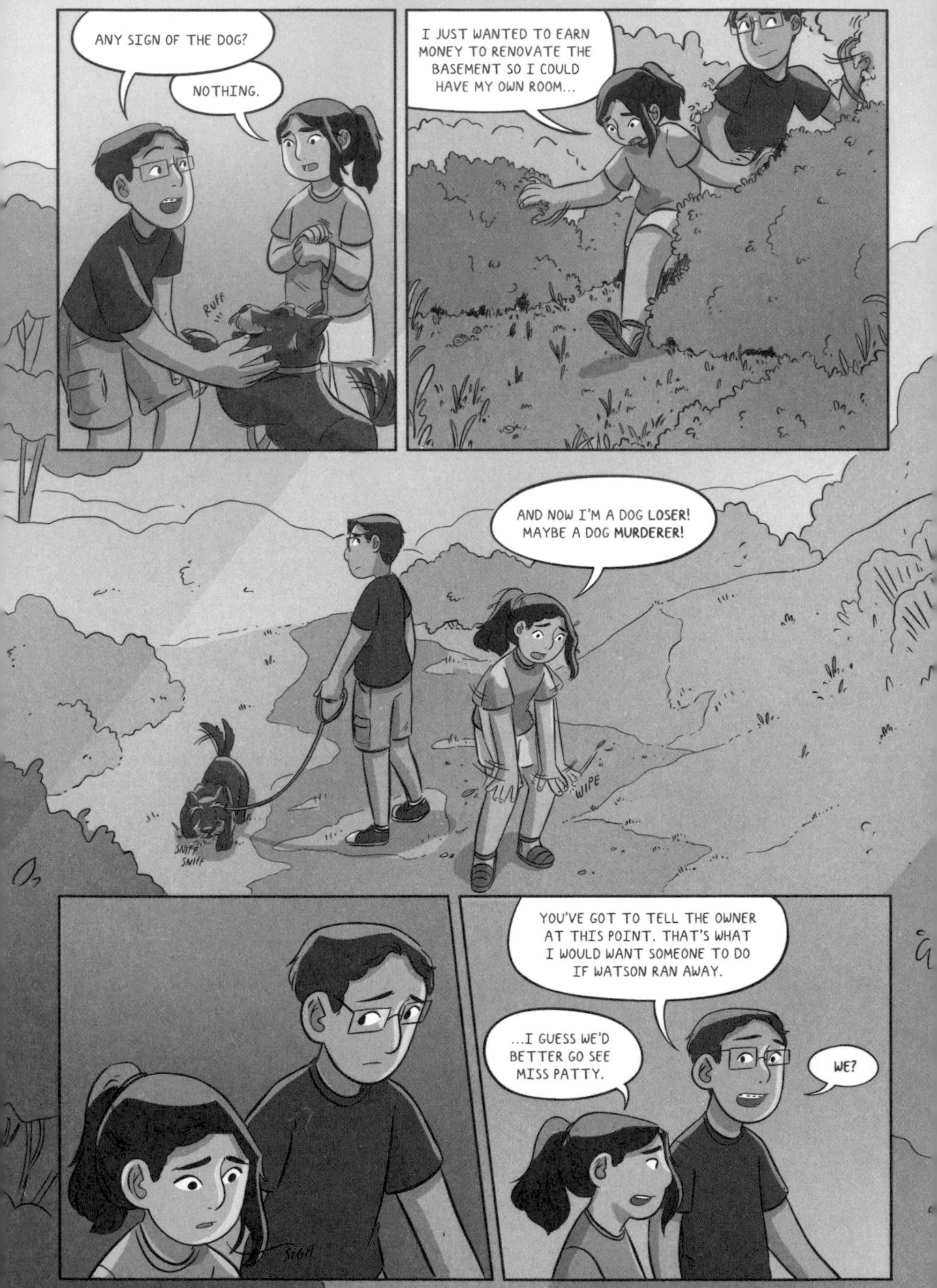
ANY SIGN OF THE DOG?
NOTHING.
RUFF
I JUST WANTED TO EARN MONEY TO RENOVATE THE BASEMENT SO I COULD HAVE MY OWN ROOM...
AND NOW I'M A DOG **LOSER**! MAYBE A DOG **MURDERER**!
SNIFF SNIFF
WIPE
SIGH
YOU'VE GOT TO TELL THE OWNER AT THIS POINT. THAT'S WHAT I WOULD WANT SOMEONE TO DO IF WATSON RAN AWAY.
...I GUESS WE'D BETTER GO SEE MISS PATTY.
WE?

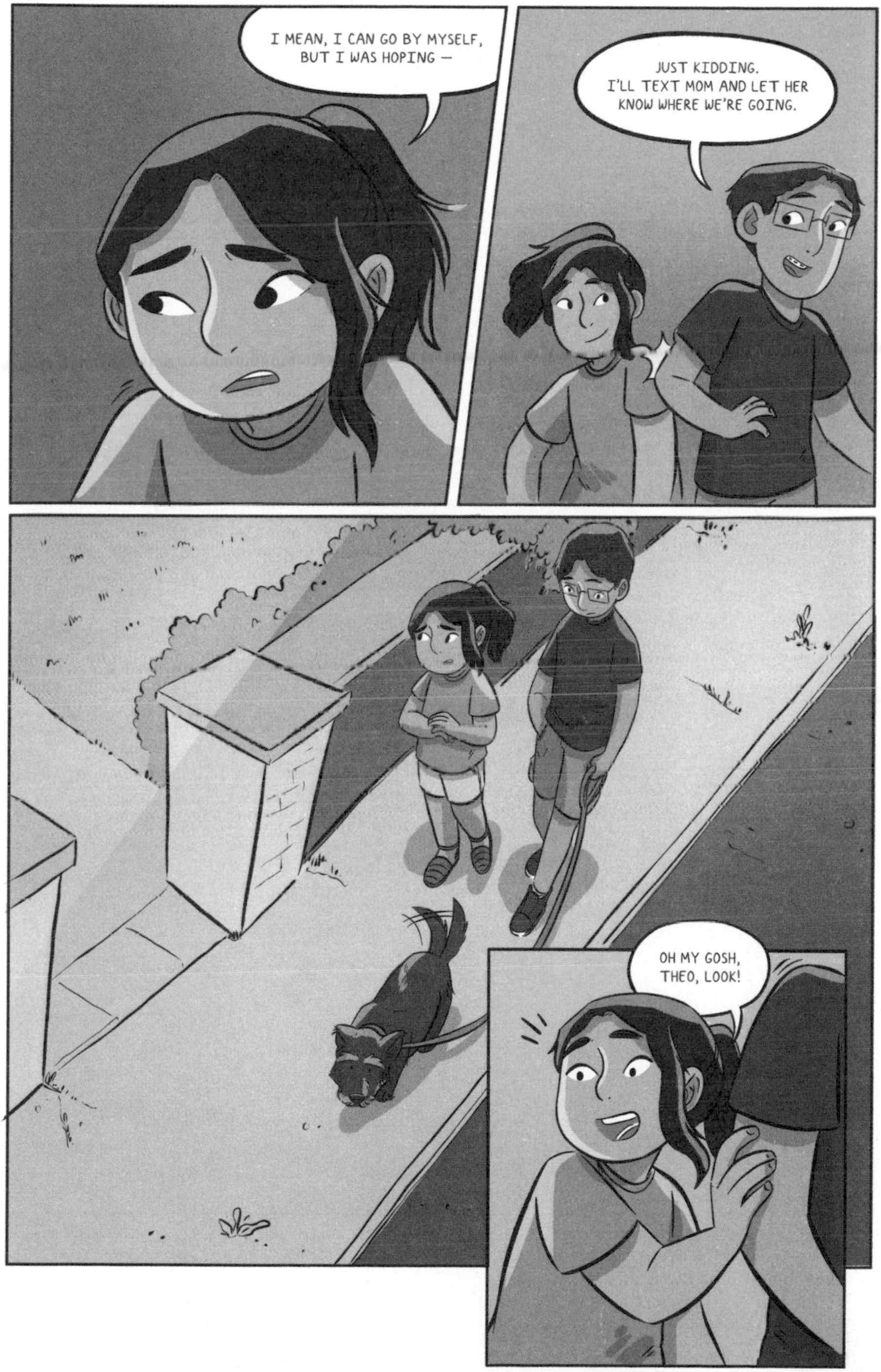
I MEAN, I CAN GO BY MYSELF, BUT I WAS HOPING —
JUST KIDDING. I'LL TEXT MOM AND LET HER KNOW WHERE WE'RE GOING.
OH MY GOSH, THEO, LOOK!

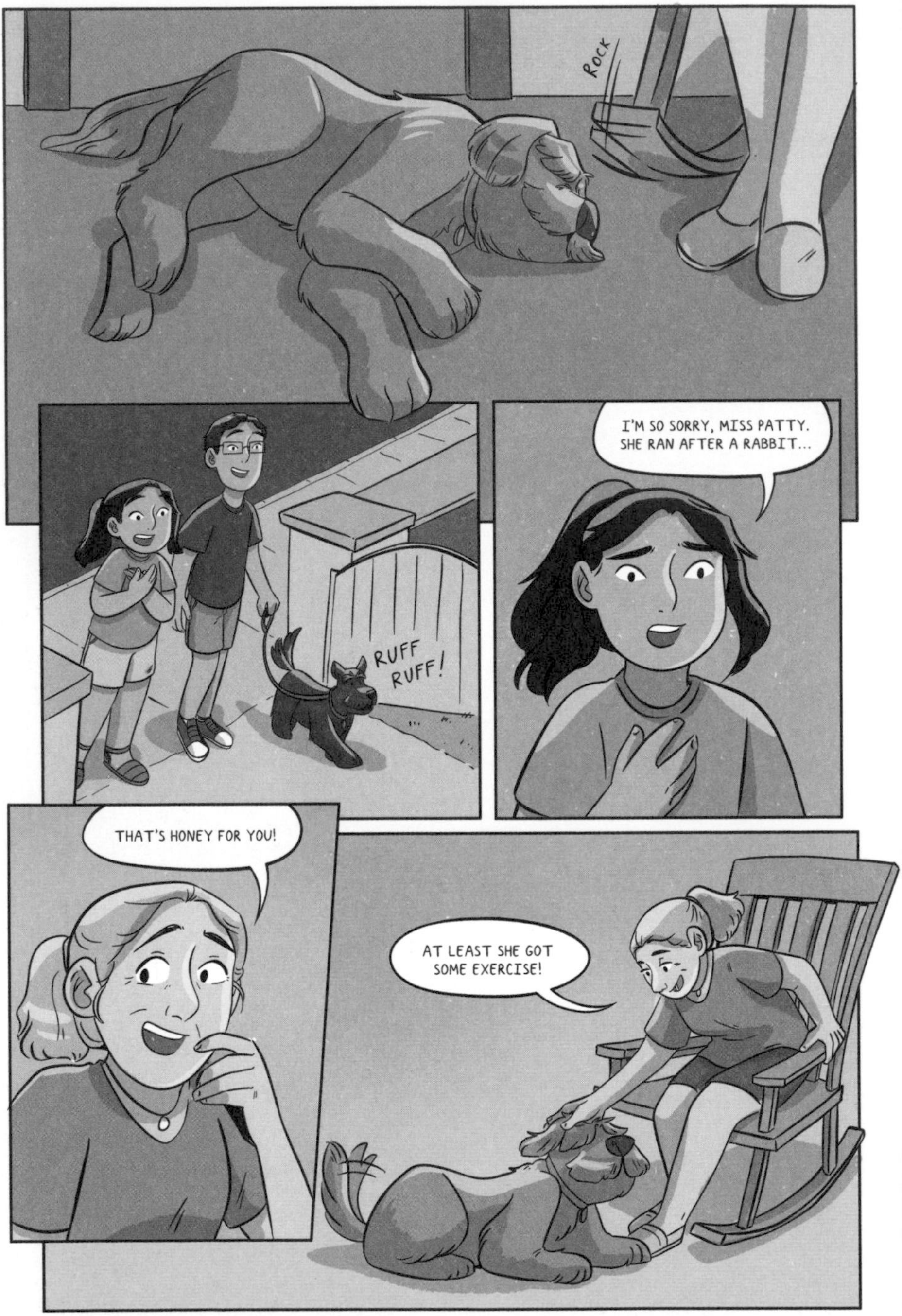
ROCK
RUFF RUFF!
I'M SO SORRY, MISS PATTY. SHE RAN AFTER A RABBIT...
THAT'S HONEY FOR YOU!
AT LEAST SHE GOT SOME EXERCISE!

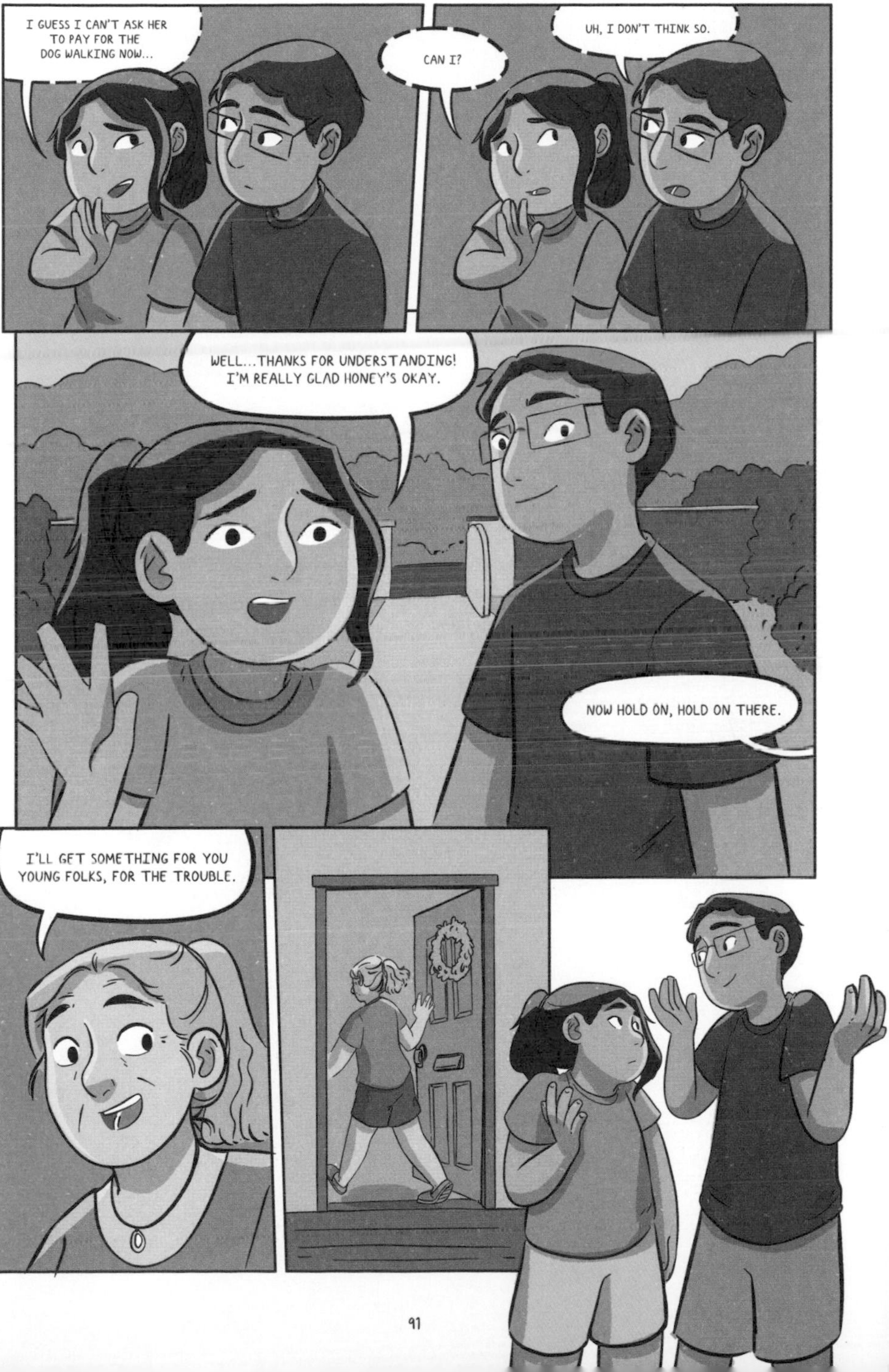

I GUESS I CAN'T ASK HER TO PAY FOR THE DOG WALKING NOW...
CAN I?
UH, I DON'T THINK SO.
WELL...THANKS FOR UNDERSTANDING! I'M REALLY GLAD HONEY'S OKAY.
NOW HOLD ON, HOLD ON THERE.
I'LL GET SOMETHING FOR YOU YOUNG FOLKS, FOR THE TROUBLE.

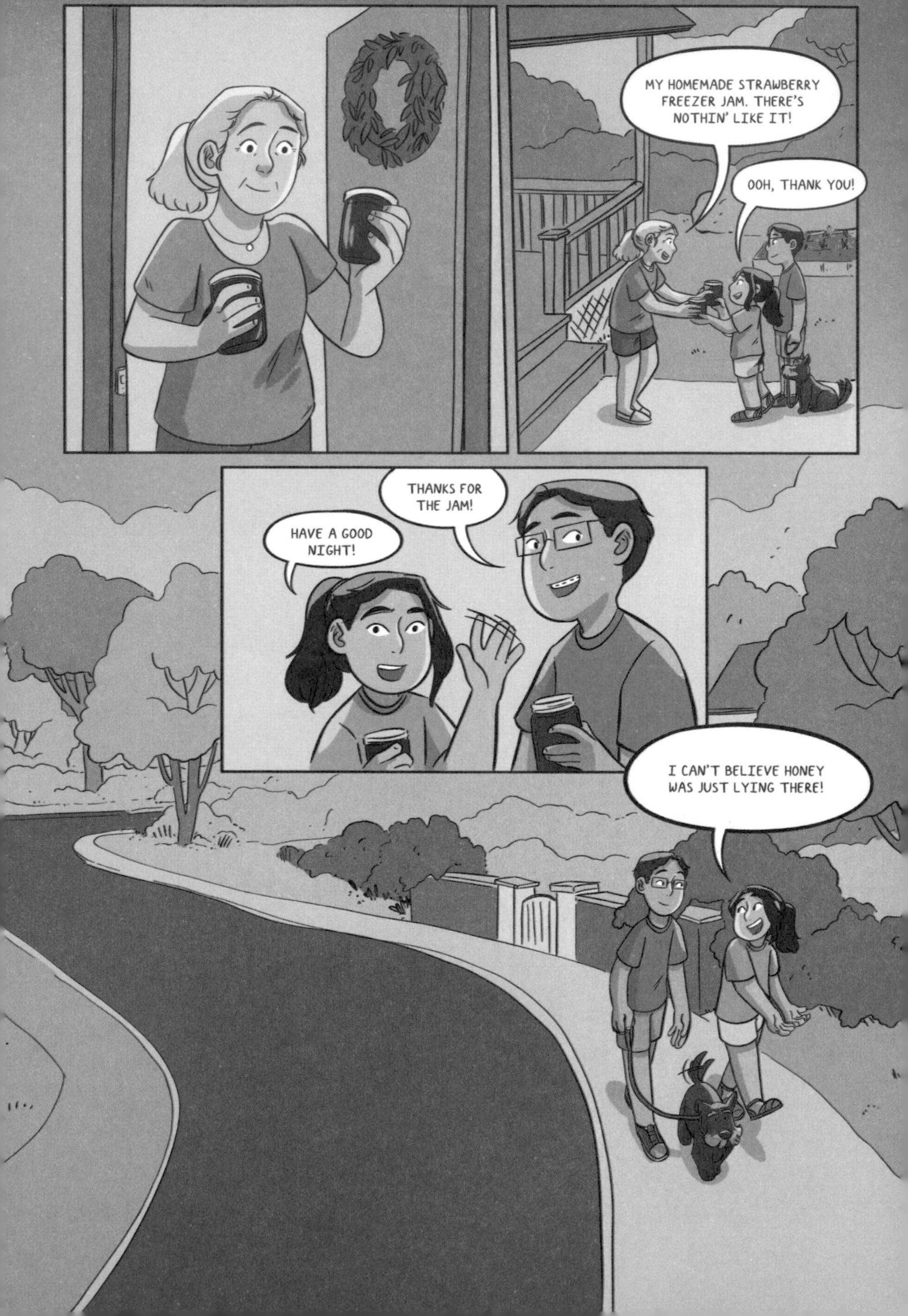
MY HOMEMADE STRAWBERRY FREEZER JAM. THERE'S NOTHIN' LIKE IT!
OOH, THANK YOU!
THANKS FOR THE JAM!
HAVE A GOOD NIGHT!
I CAN'T BELIEVE HONEY WAS JUST LYING THERE!

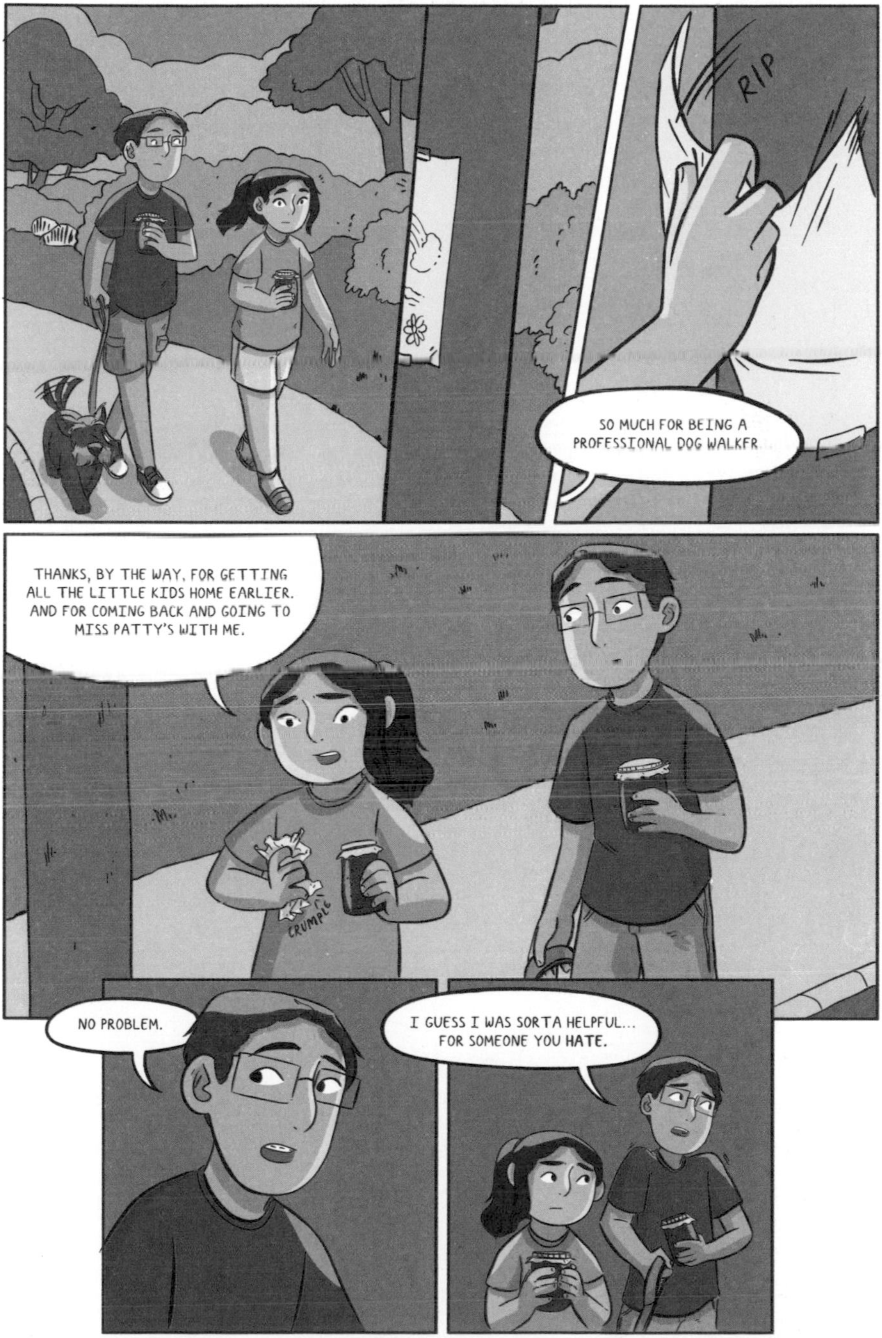
RIP
SO MUCH FOR BEING A PROFESSIONAL DOG WALKER.
THANKS, BY THE WAY, FOR GETTING ALL THE LITTLE KIDS HOME EARLIER. AND FOR COMING BACK AND GOING TO MISS PATTY'S WITH ME.
CRUMPLE
NO PROBLEM.
I GUESS I WAS SORTA HELPFUL... FOR SOMEONE YOU HATE.

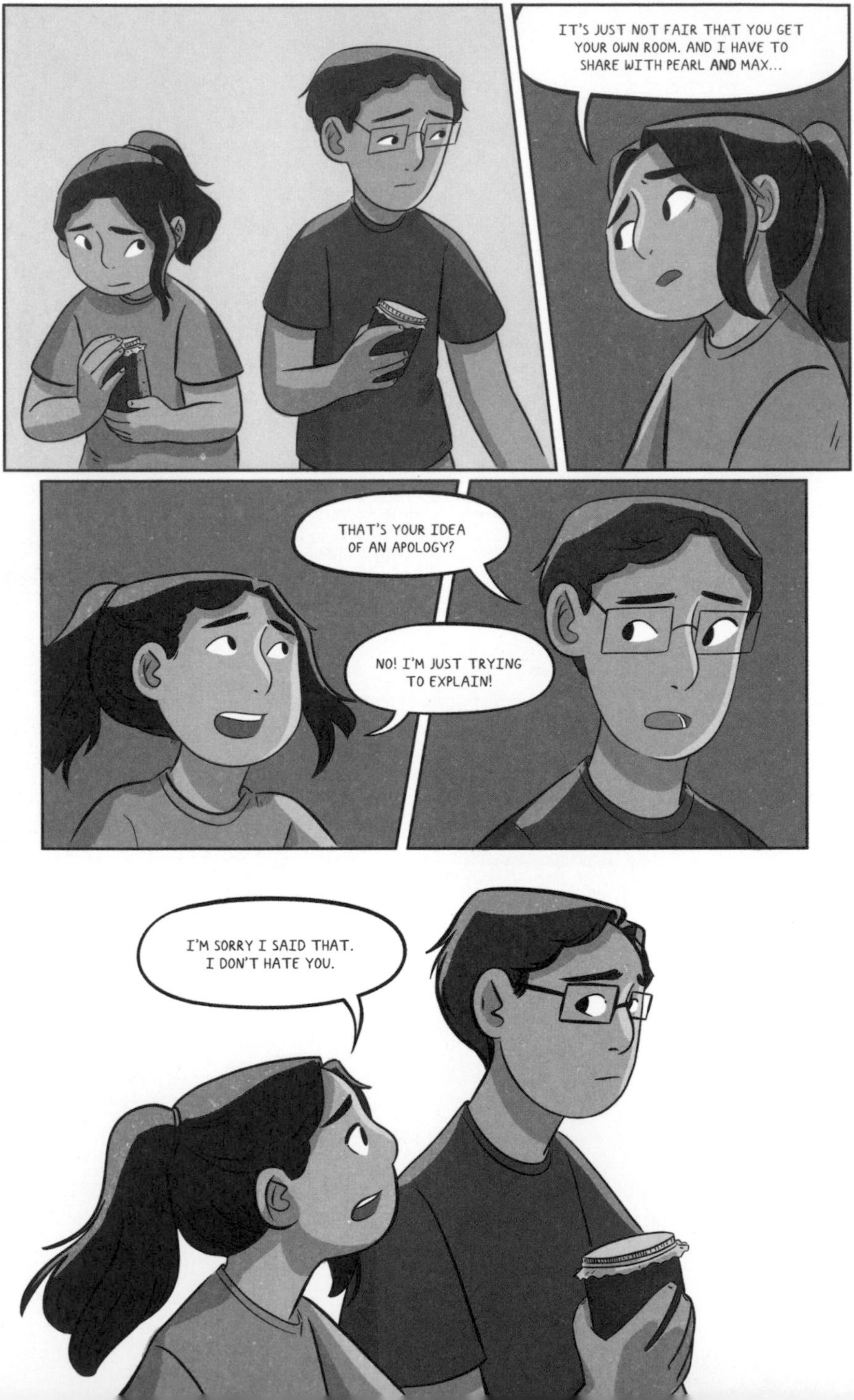
IT'S JUST NOT FAIR THAT YOU GET YOUR OWN ROOM. AND I HAVE TO SHARE WITH PEARL AND MAX...
THAT'S YOUR IDEA OF AN APOLOGY?
NO! I'M JUST TRYING TO EXPLAIN!
I'M SORRY I SAID THAT. I DON'T HATE YOU.

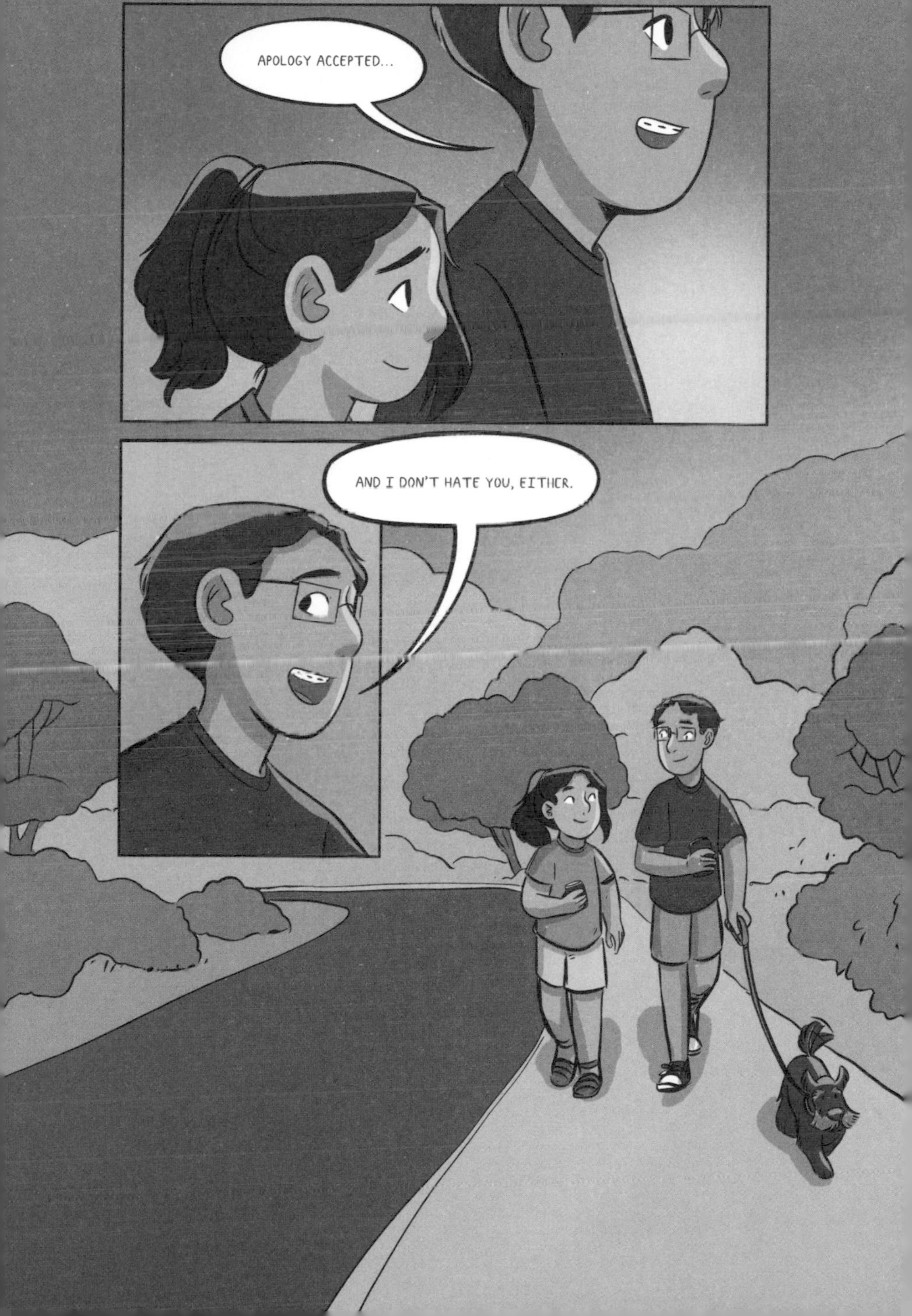
APOLOGY ACCEPTED...
AND I DON'T HATE YOU, EITHER.

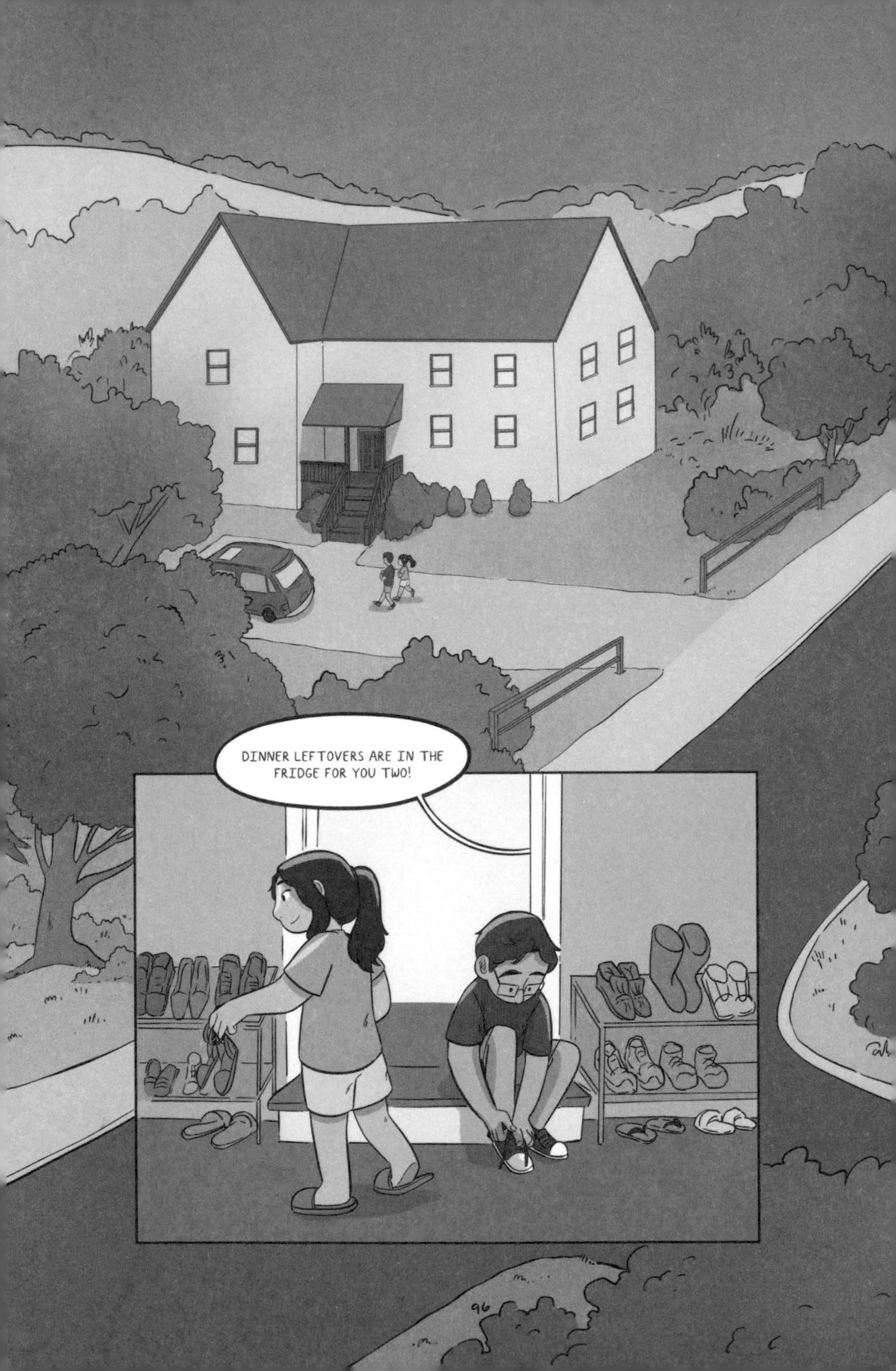
DINNER LEFTOVERS ARE IN THE FRIDGE FOR YOU TWO!

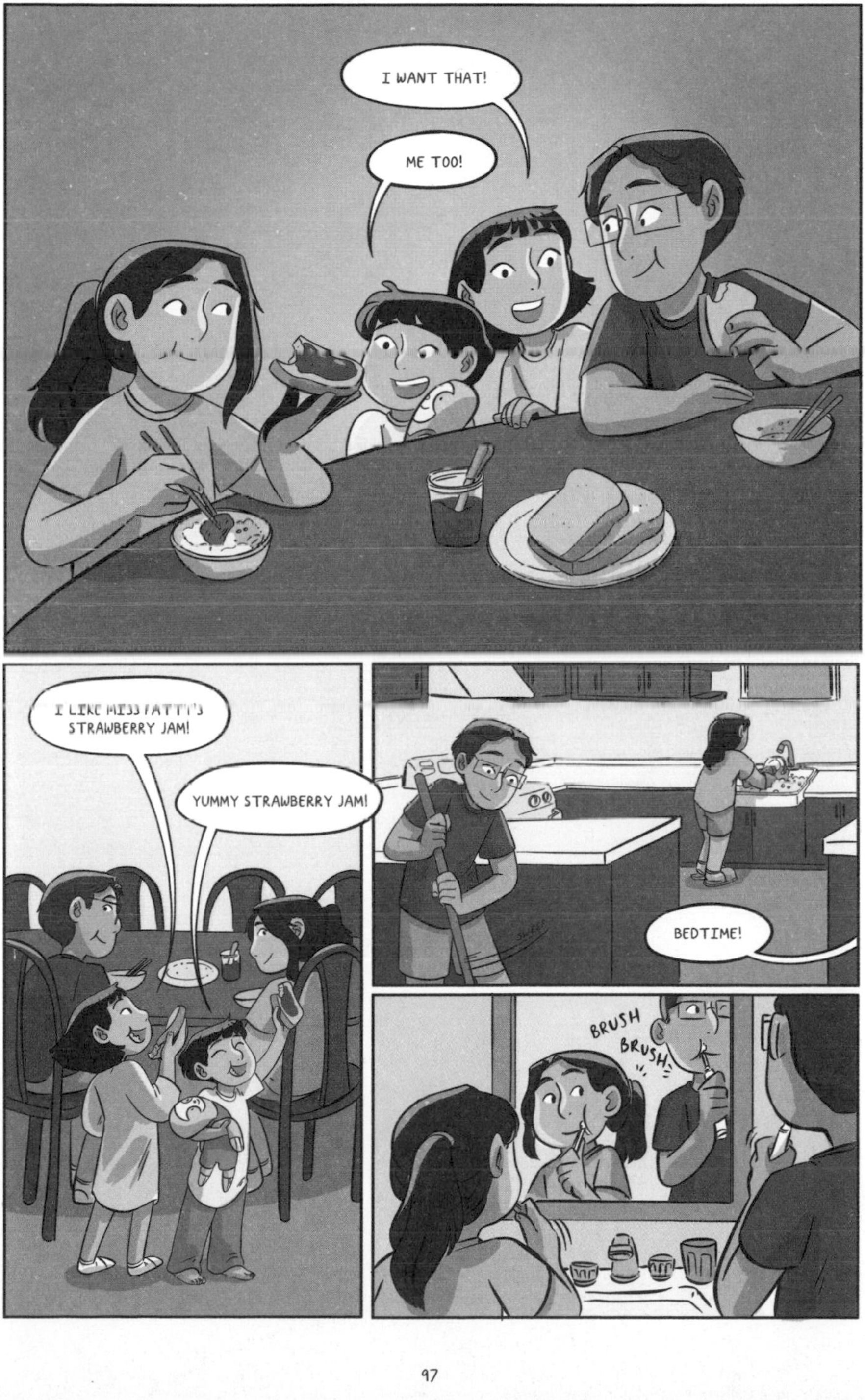
I WANT THAT!
ME TOO!
I LIKE MISS PATTI'S STRAWBERRY JAM!
YUMMY STRAWBERRY JAM!
BEDTIME!
BRUSH BRUSH

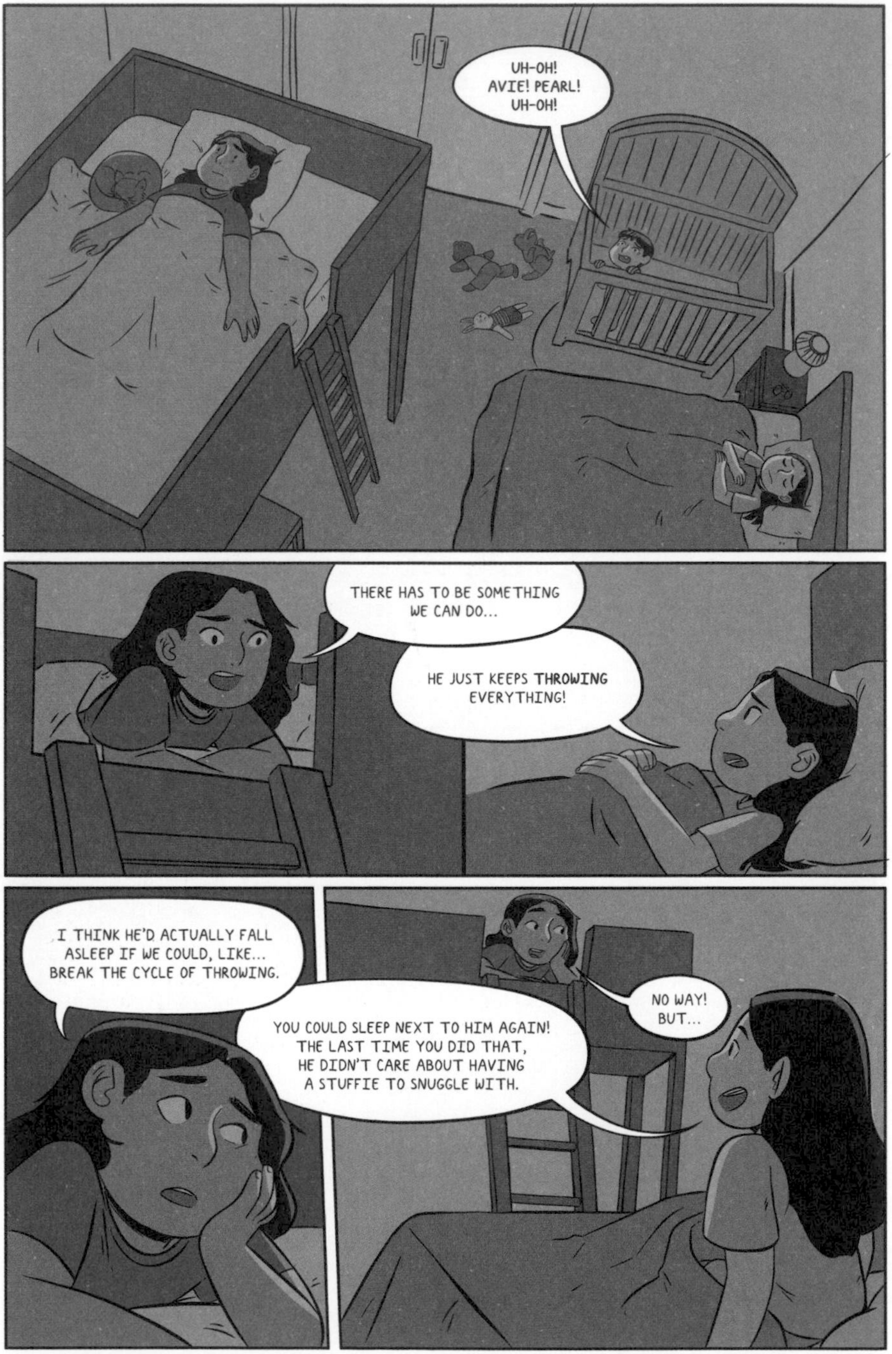
UH-OH! AVIE! PEARL! UH-OH!
THERE HAS TO BE SOMETHING WE CAN DO...
HE JUST KEEPS THROWING EVERYTHING!
I THINK HE'D ACTUALLY FALL ASLEEP IF WE COULD, LIKE... BREAK THE CYCLE OF THROWING.
YOU COULD SLEEP NEXT TO HIM AGAIN! THE LAST TIME YOU DID THAT, HE DIDN'T CARE ABOUT HAVING A STUFFIE TO SNUGGLE WITH.
NO WAY! BUT...

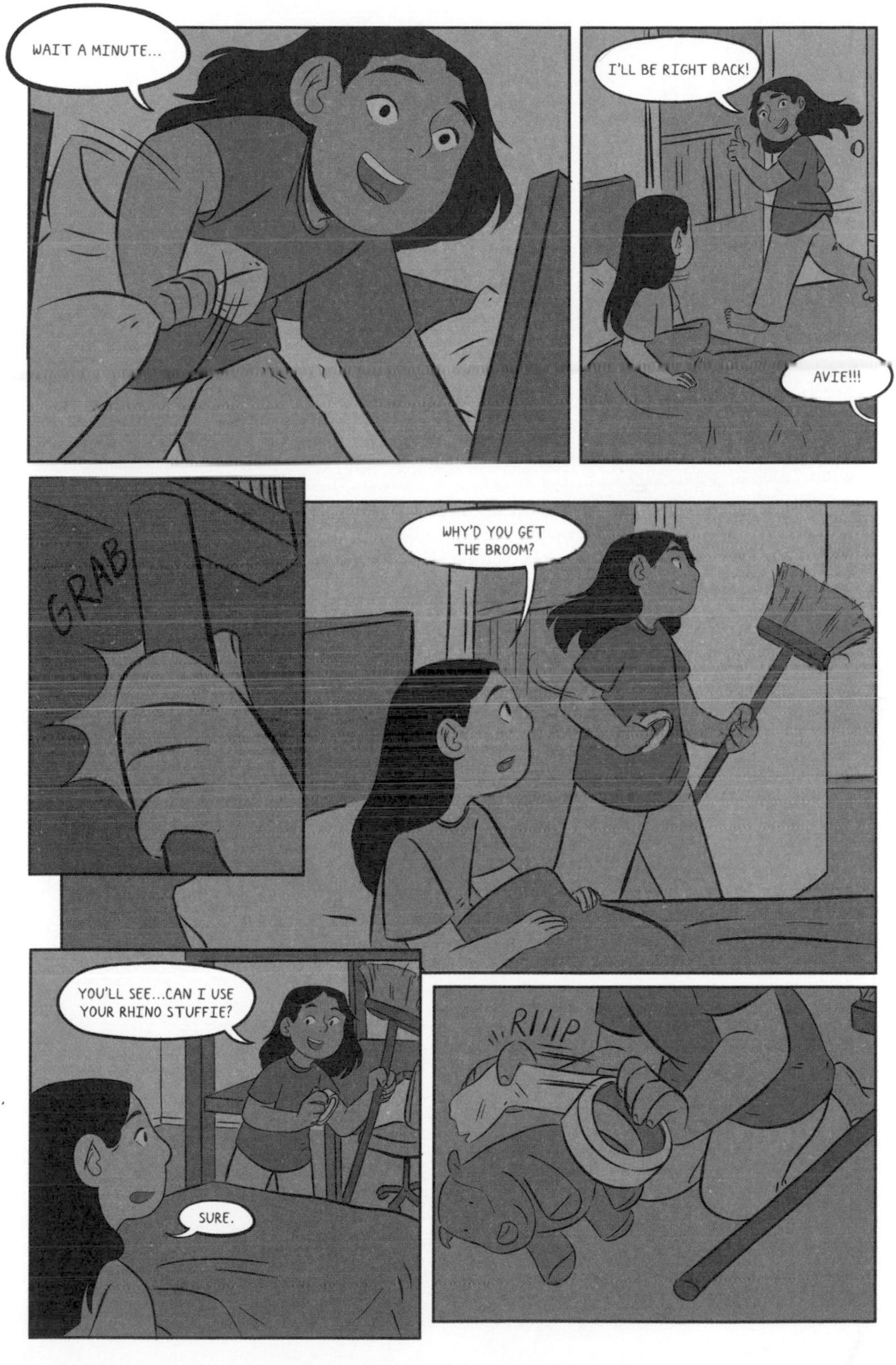
WAIT A MINUTE...
I'LL BE RIGHT BACK!
AVIE!!!
GRAB
WHY'D YOU GET THE BROOM?
YOU'LL SEE...CAN I USE YOUR RHINO STUFFIE?
SURE.
RIIIP

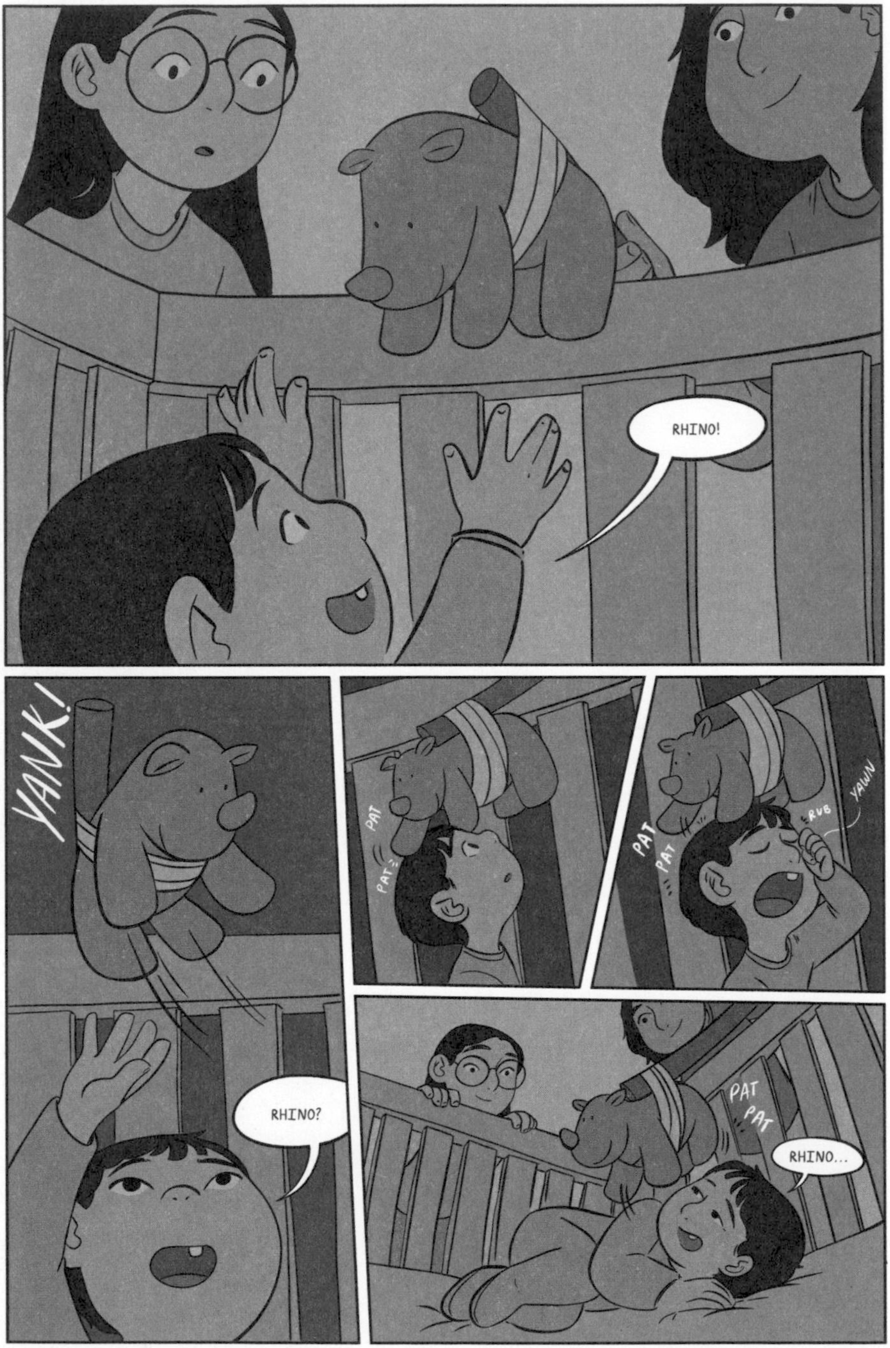
RHINO!
YANK!
PAT
PAT
PAT
PAT
RUB
YAWN
RHINO?
PAT
PAT
RHINO...

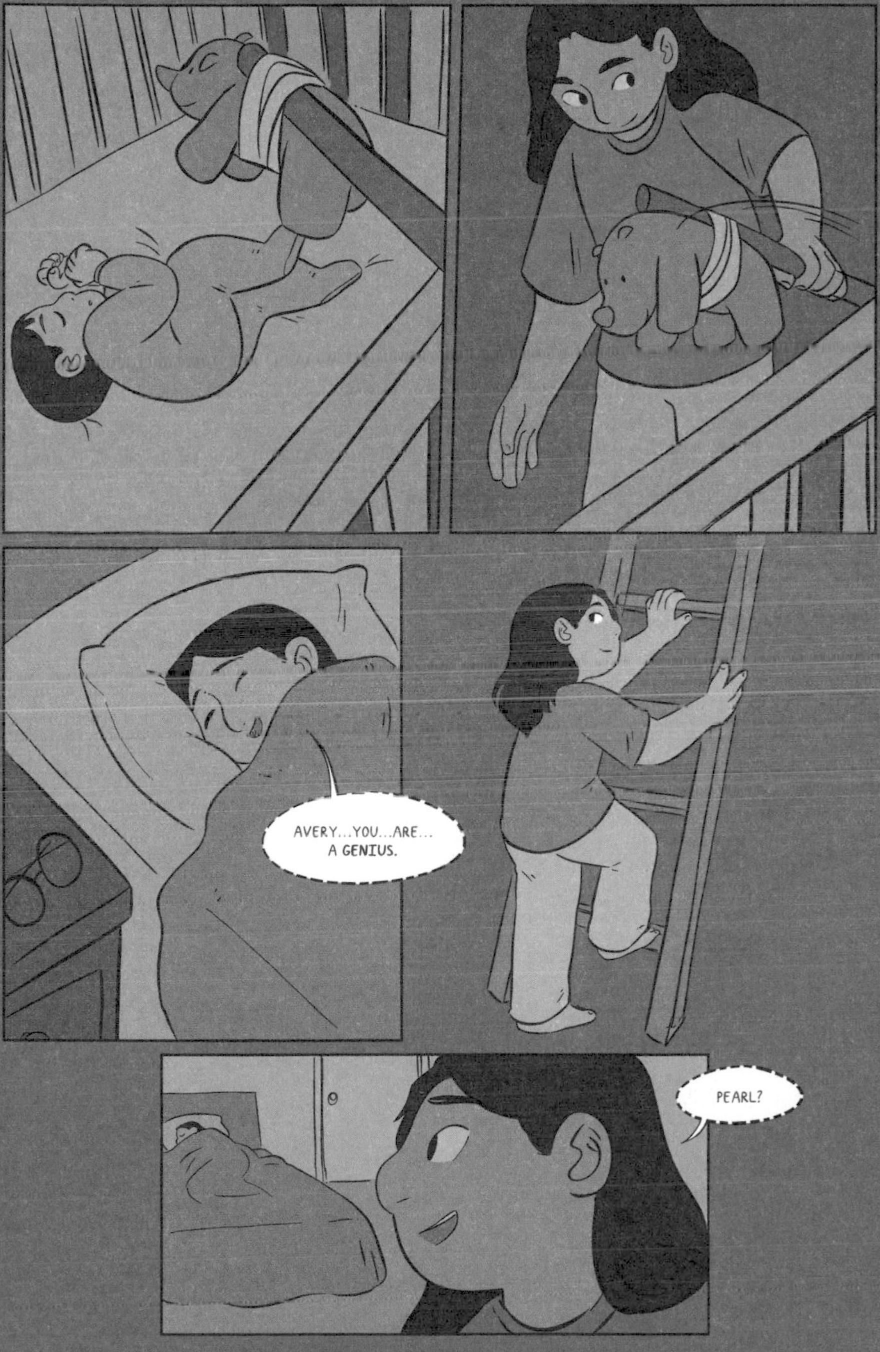
AVERY...YOU...ARE... A GENIUS.
PEARL?

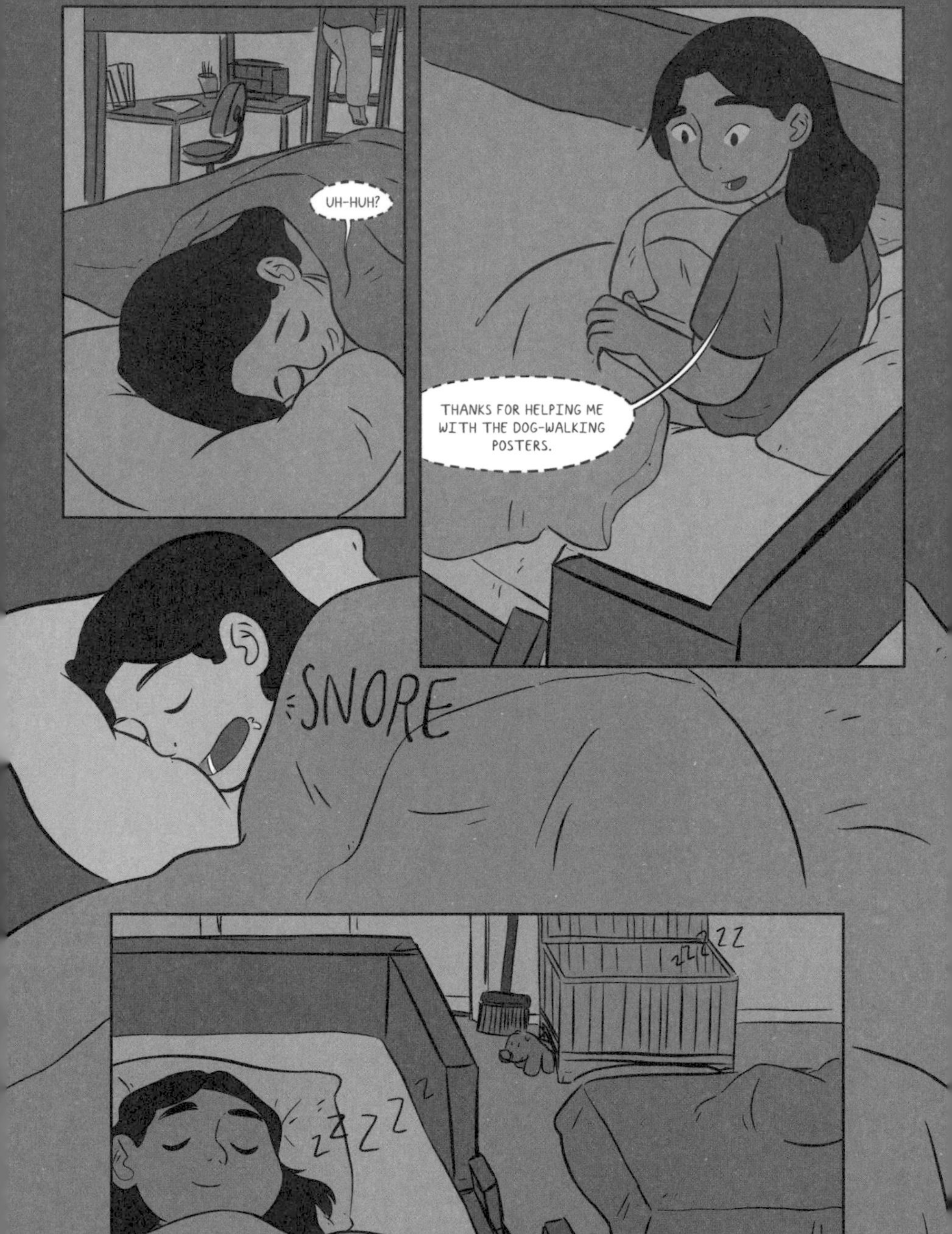

THANKS FOR HELPING ME WITH THE DOG-WALKING POSTERS.
UH-HUH?
SNORE
ZZZZ
ZZZZ

Chapter Seven

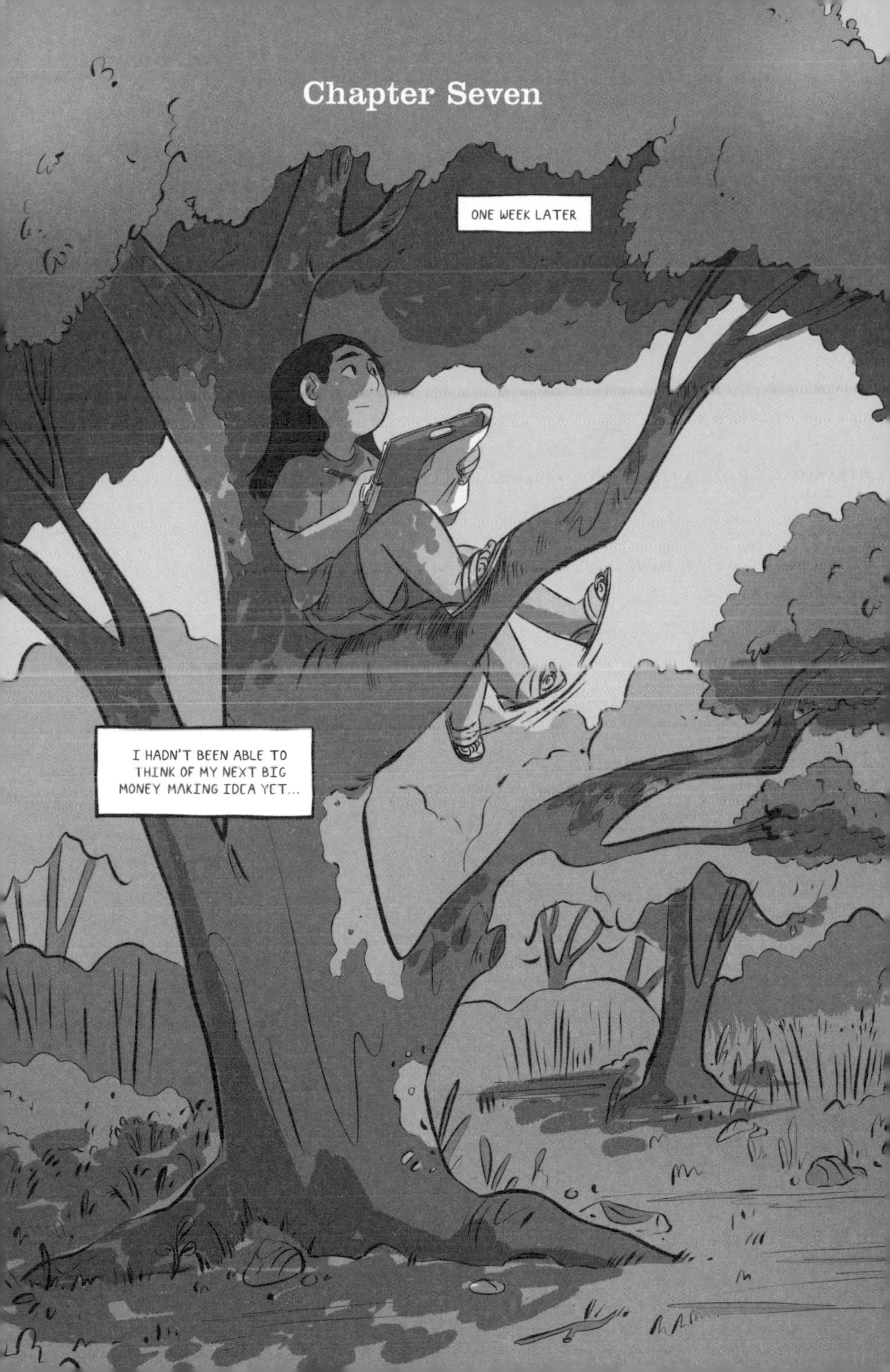
ONE WEEK LATER
I HADN'T BEEN ABLE TO THINK OF MY NEXT BIG MONEY MAKING IDEA YET...

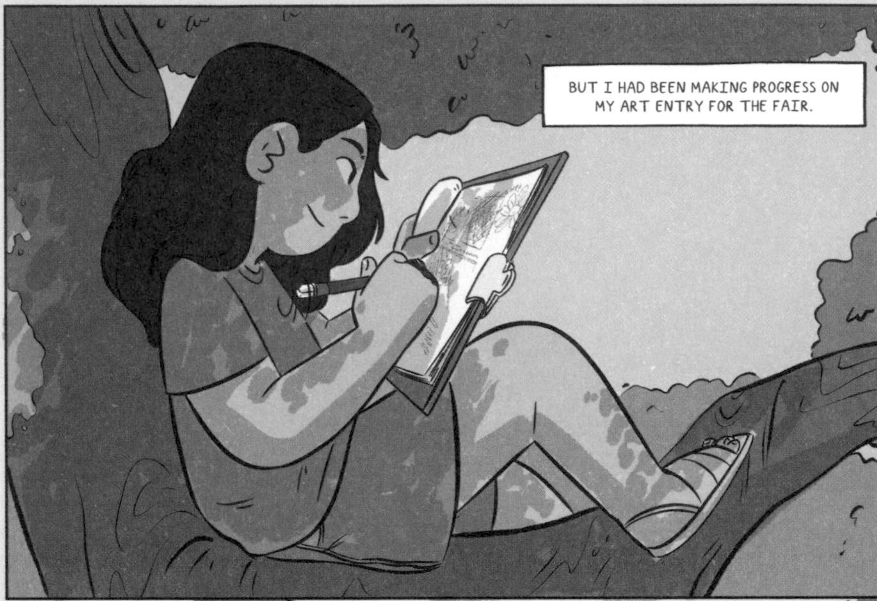
BUT I HAD BEEN MAKING PROGRESS ON MY ART ENTRY FOR THE FAIR.

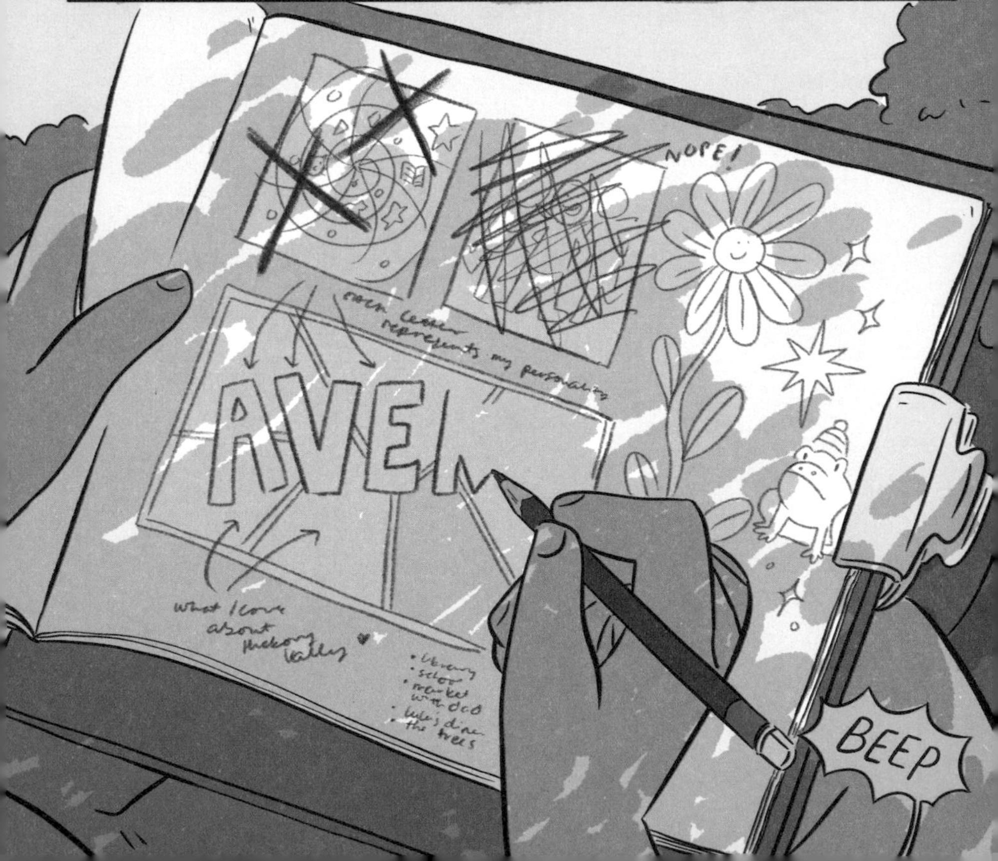
NOPE!
every letter represents my personality
AVE
what I love about
BEEP

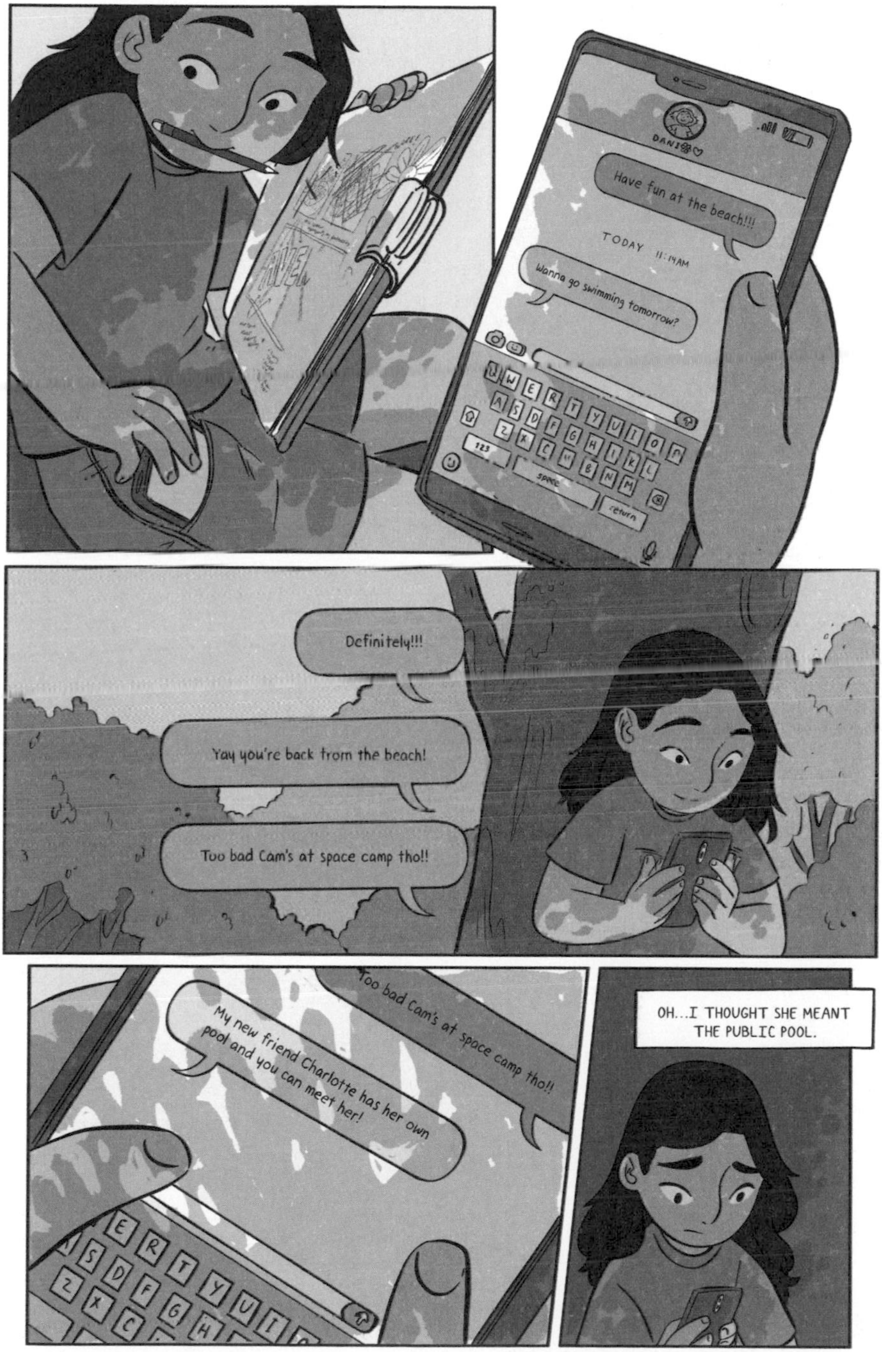

Have fun at the beach!!!
TODAY 11:14AM
Wanna go swimming tomorrow?
Definitely!!!
Yay you're back from the beach!
Too bad Cam's at space camp tho!!
Too bad Cam's at space camp tho!!
My new friend Charlotte has her own pool and you can meet her!
OH...I THOUGHT SHE MEANT THE PUBLIC POOL.

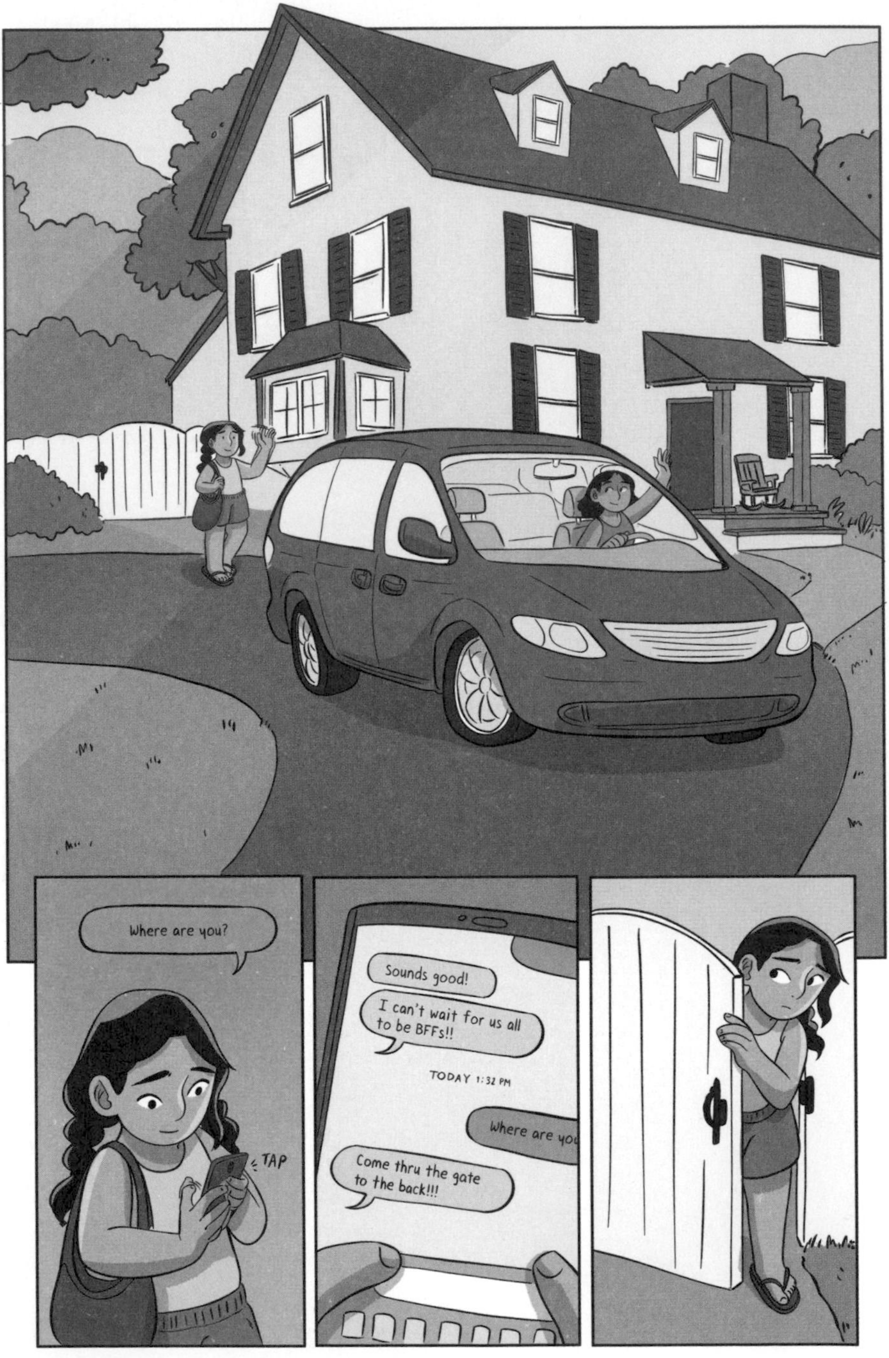
Where are you?
TAP
Sounds good!
I can't wait for us all to be BFFs!!
TODAY 1:32 PM
Where are you
Come thru the gate to the back!!!

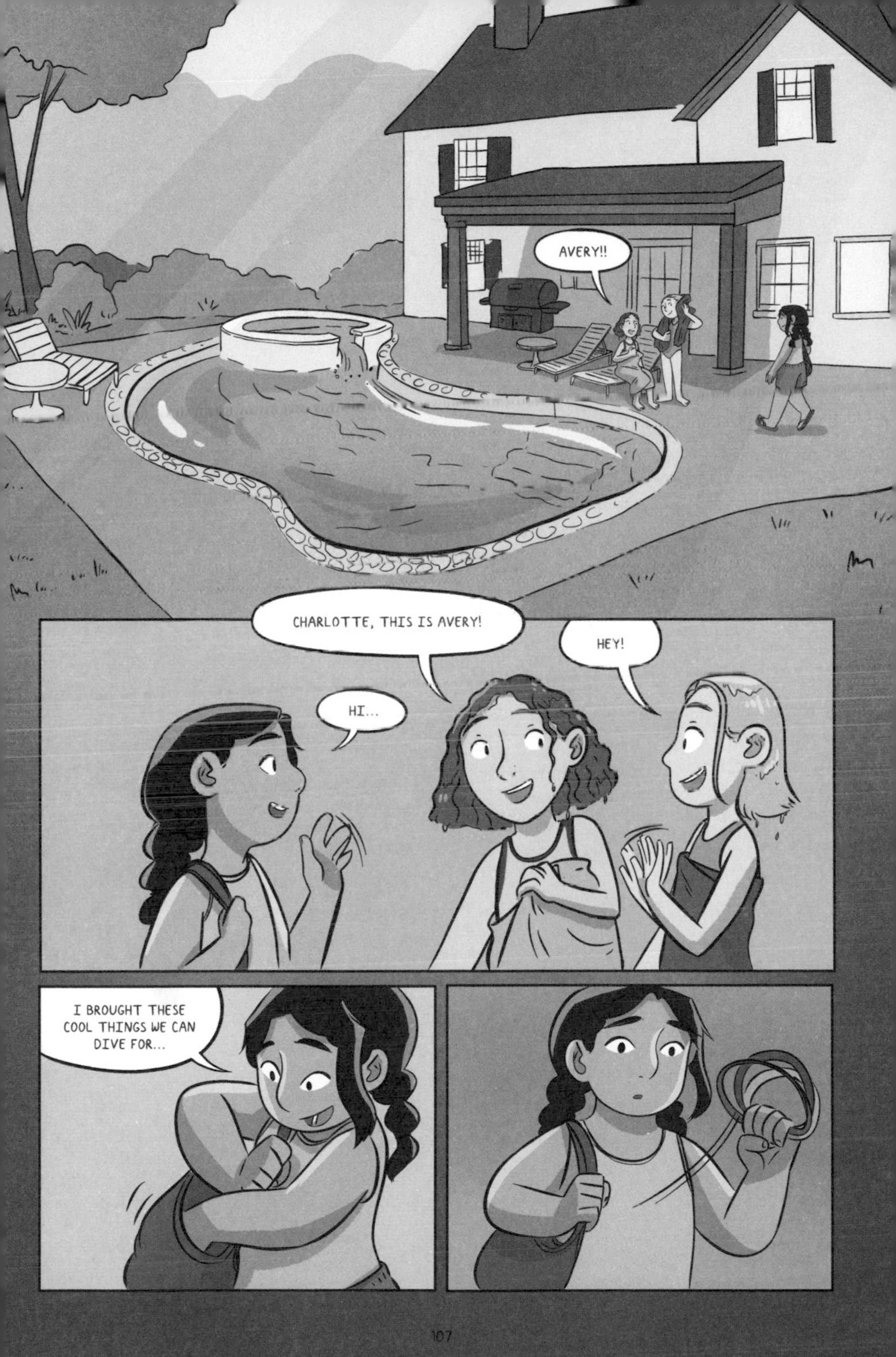
AVERY!!
CHARLOTTE, THIS IS AVERY!
HEY!
HI...
I BROUGHT THESE COOL THINGS WE CAN DIVE FOR...

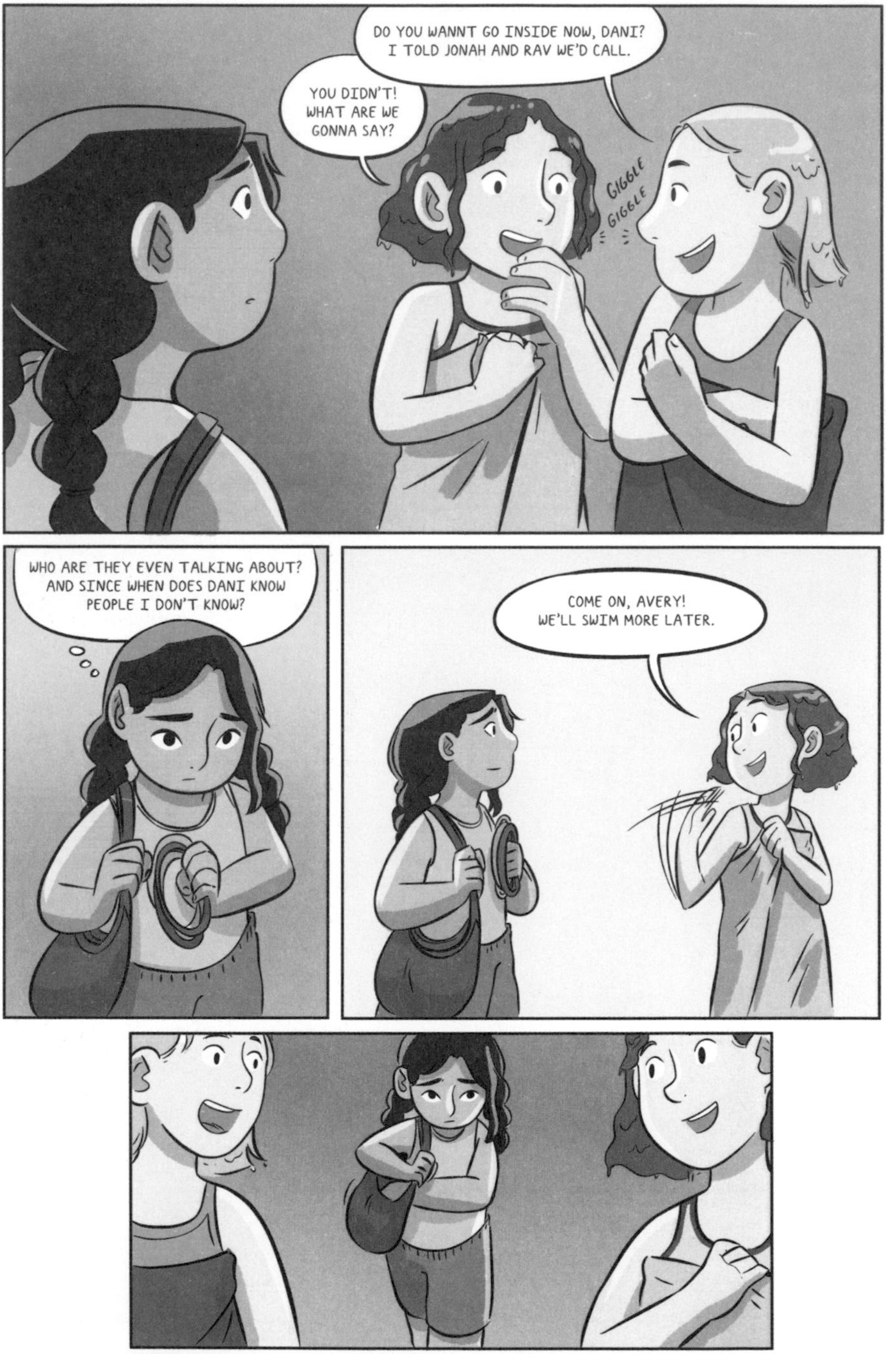
DO YOU WANN'T GO INSIDE NOW, DANI? I TOLD JONAH AND RAV WE'D CALL.
YOU DIDN'T! WHAT ARE WE GONNA SAY?
GIGGLE GIGGLE
WHO ARE THEY EVEN TALKING ABOUT? AND SINCE WHEN DOES DANI KNOW PEOPLE I DON'T KNOW?
COME ON, AVERY! WE'LL SWIM MORE LATER.

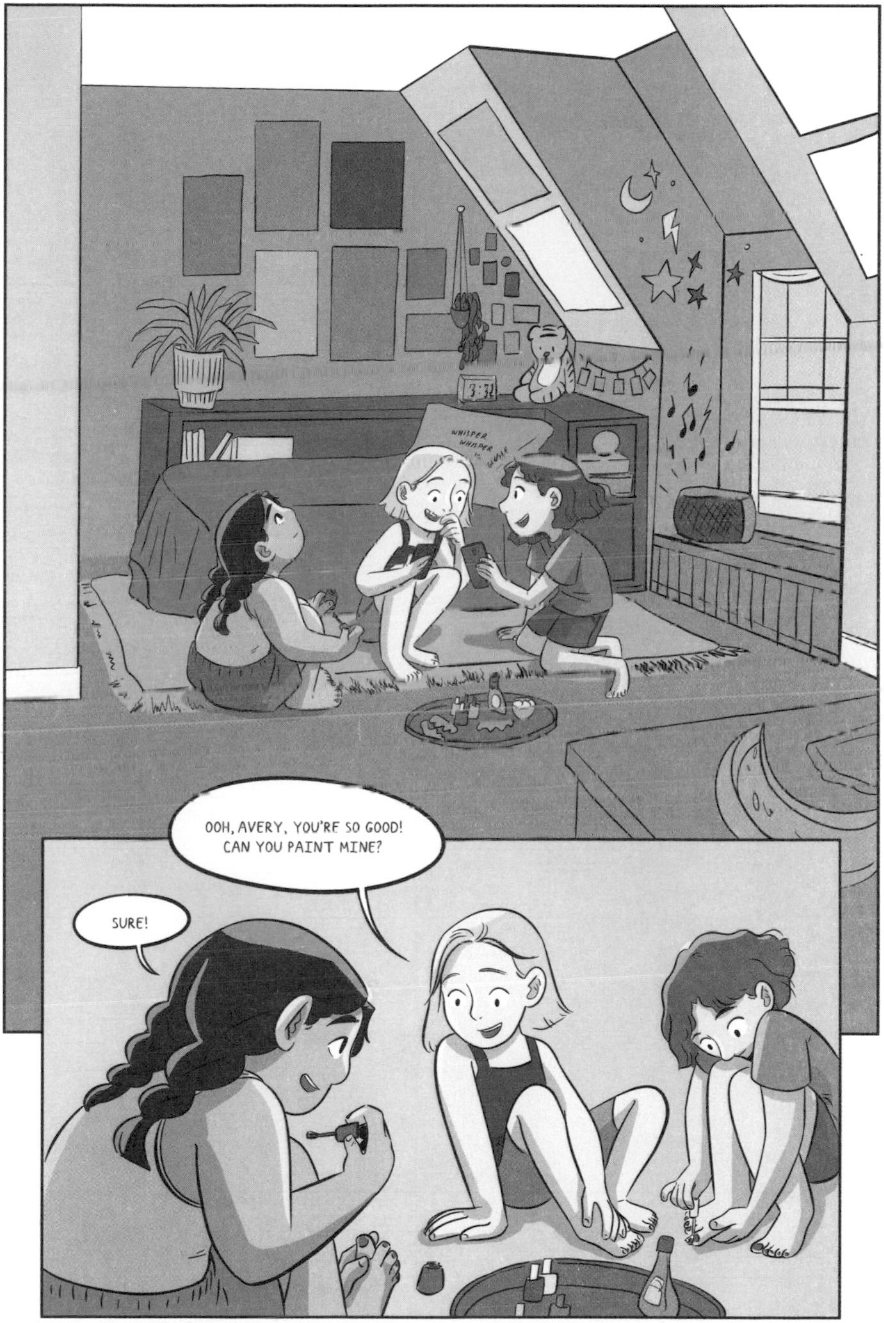
3:32
WHISPER
WHISPER
OOH, AVERY, YOU'RE SO GOOD! CAN YOU PAINT MINE?
SURE!

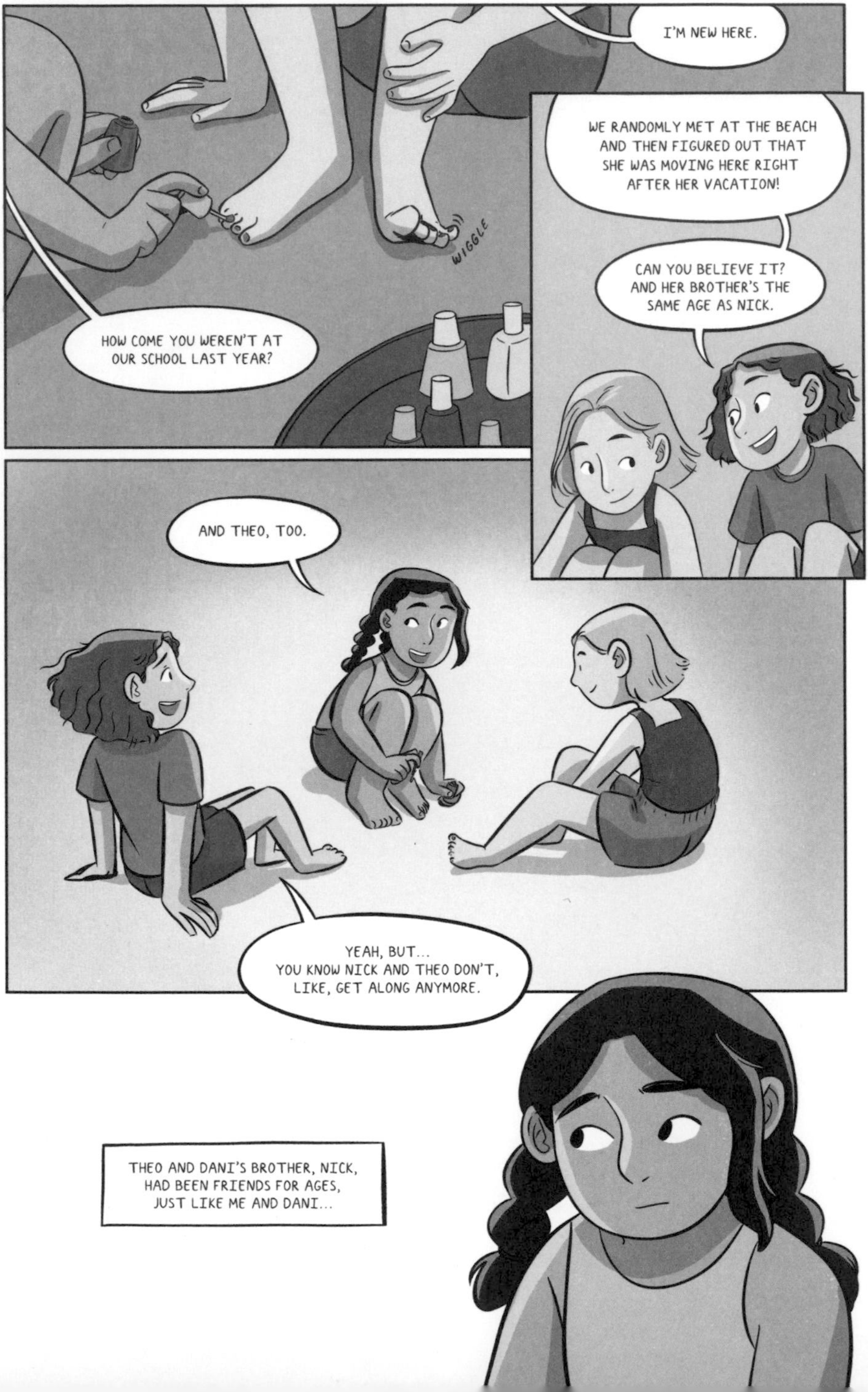
HOW COME YOU WEREN'T AT OUR SCHOOL LAST YEAR?
I'M NEW HERE.
WIGGLE
WE RANDOMLY MET AT THE BEACH AND THEN FIGURED OUT THAT SHE WAS MOVING HERE RIGHT AFTER HER VACATION!
CAN YOU BELIEVE IT? AND HER BROTHER'S THE SAME AGE AS NICK.
AND THEO, TOO.
YEAH, BUT... YOU KNOW NICK AND THEO DON'T, LIKE, GET ALONG ANYMORE.
THEO AND DANI'S BROTHER, NICK, HAD BEEN FRIENDS FOR AGES, JUST LIKE ME AND DANI...

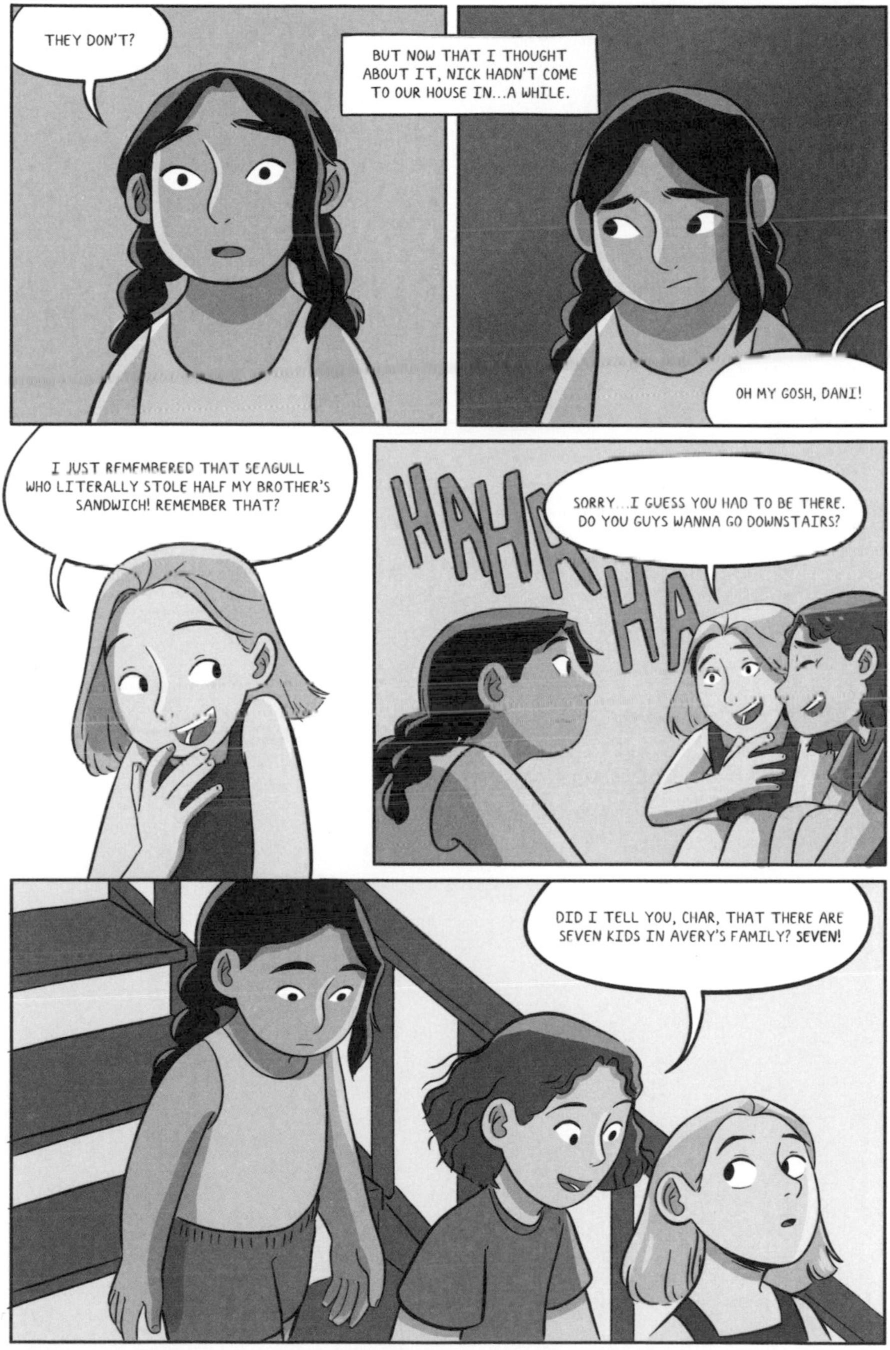
THEY DON'T?
BUT NOW THAT I THOUGHT ABOUT IT, NICK HADN'T COME TO OUR HOUSE IN...A WHILE.
OH MY GOSH, DANI!
I JUST REMEMBERED THAT SEAGULL WHO LITERALLY STOLE HALF MY BROTHER'S SANDWICH! REMEMBER THAT?
HAHAHA
SORRY...I GUESS YOU HAD TO BE THERE. DO YOU GUYS WANNA GO DOWNSTAIRS?
DID I TELL YOU, CHAR, THAT THERE ARE SEVEN KIDS IN AVERY'S FAMILY? SEVEN!

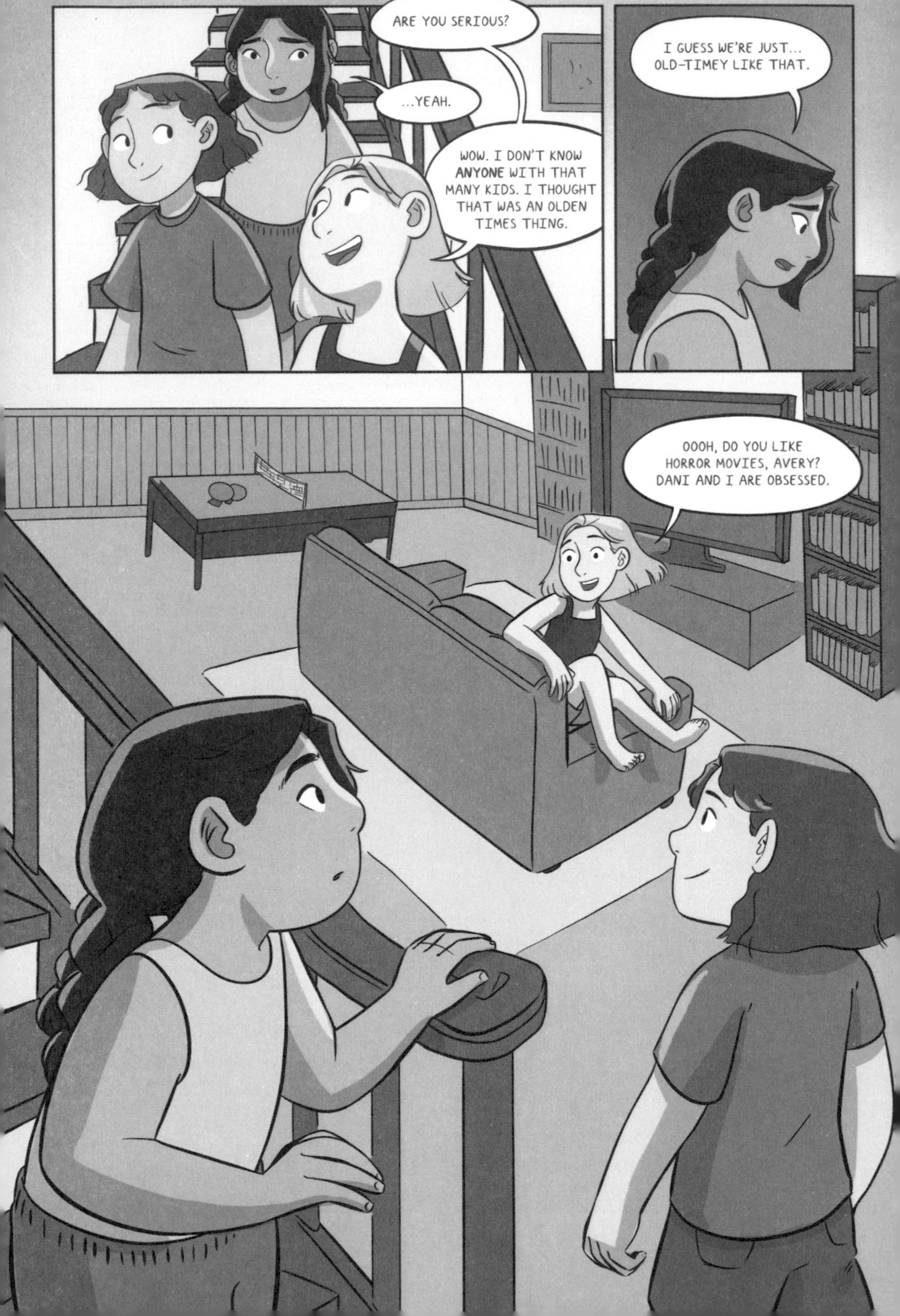
ARE YOU SERIOUS?
...YEAH.
WOW. I DON'T KNOW **ANYONE** WITH THAT MANY KIDS. I THOUGHT THAT WAS AN OLDEN TIMES THING.
I GUESS WE'RE JUST... OLD-TIMEY LIKE THAT.
OOOH, DO YOU LIKE HORROR MOVIES, AVERY? DANI AND I ARE OBSESSED.

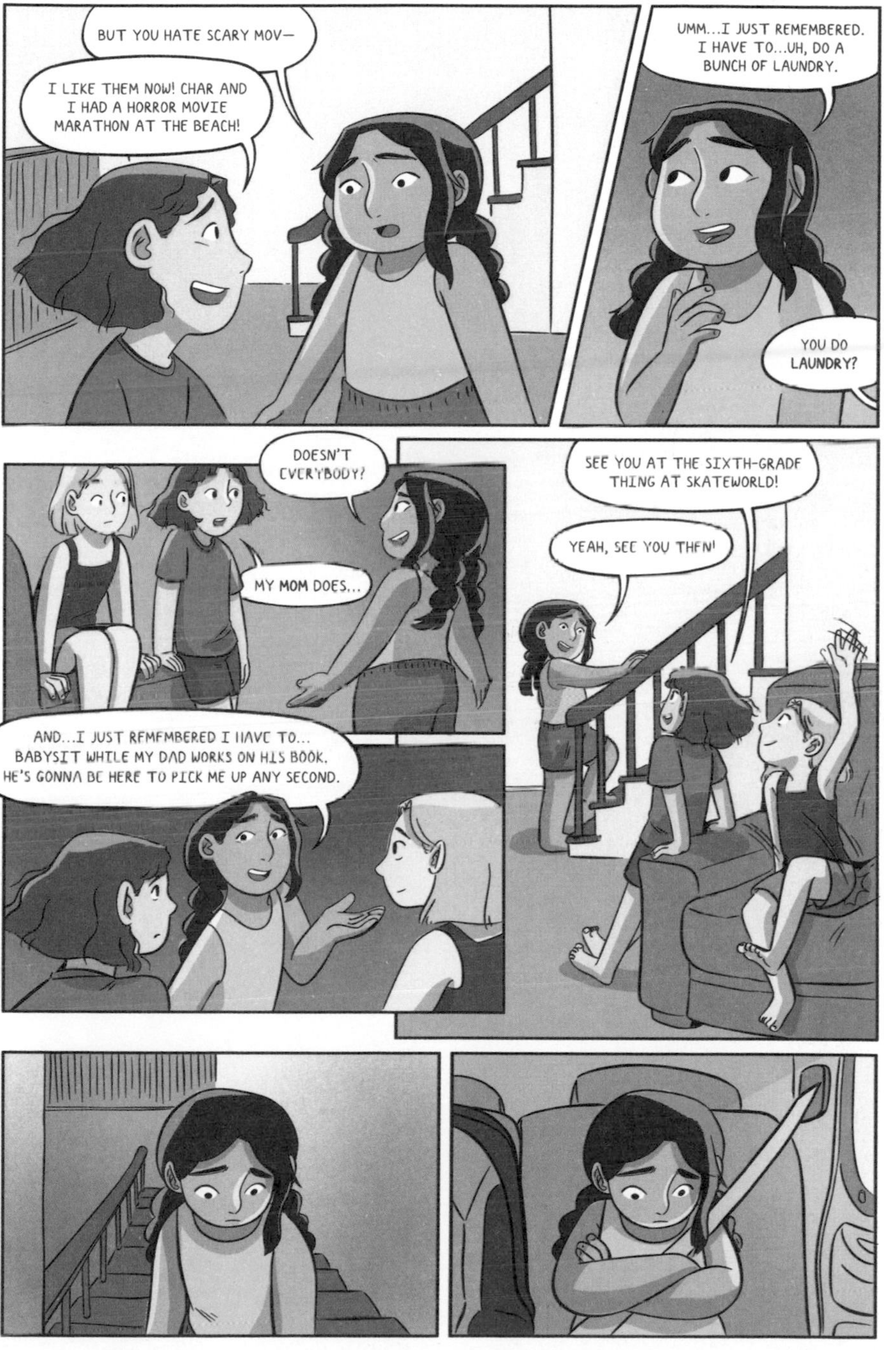
BUT YOU HATE SCARY MOV—
I LIKE THEM NOW! CHAR AND I HAD A HORROR MOVIE MARATHON AT THE BEACH!
UMM...I JUST REMEMBERED. I HAVE TO...UH, DO A BUNCH OF LAUNDRY.
YOU DO LAUNDRY?
DOESN'T EVERYBODY?
MY MOM DOES...
AND...I JUST REMEMBERED I HAVE TO... BABYSIT WHILE MY DAD WORKS ON HIS BOOK. HE'S GONNA BE HERE TO PICK ME UP ANY SECOND.
SEE YOU AT THE SIXTH-GRADE THING AT SKATEWORLD!
YEAH, SEE YOU THEN!

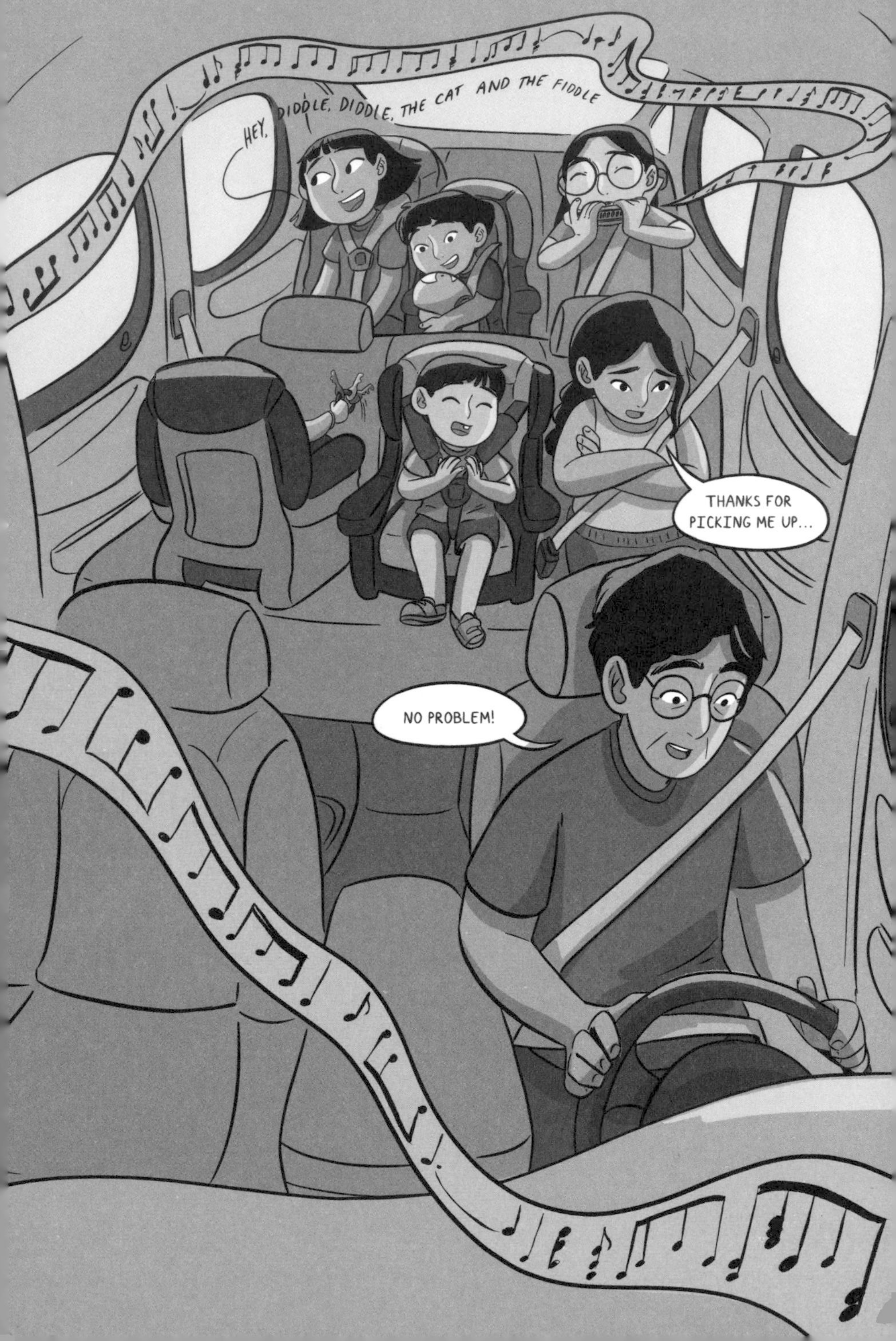
HEY, DIDDLE, DIDDLE, THE CAT AND THE FIDDLE
THANKS FOR PICKING ME UP...
NO PROBLEM!

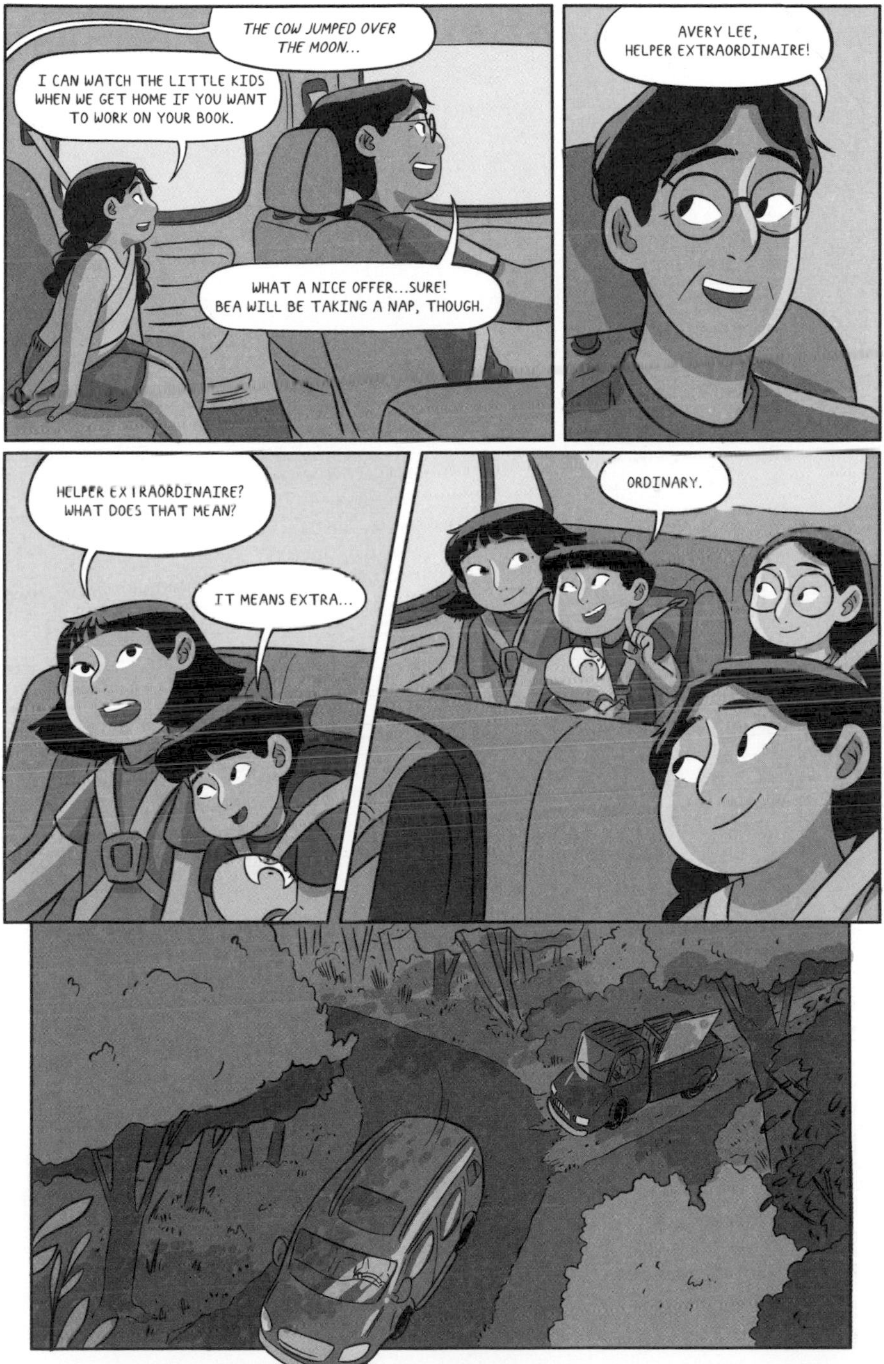
THE COW JUMPED OVER THE MOON...
I CAN WATCH THE LITTLE KIDS WHEN WE GET HOME IF YOU WANT TO WORK ON YOUR BOOK.
WHAT A NICE OFFER...SURE! BEA WILL BE TAKING A NAP, THOUGH.
AVERY LEE, HELPER EXTRAORDINAIRE!
HELPER EXTRAORDINAIRE? WHAT DOES THAT MEAN?
IT MEANS EXTRA...
ORDINARY.

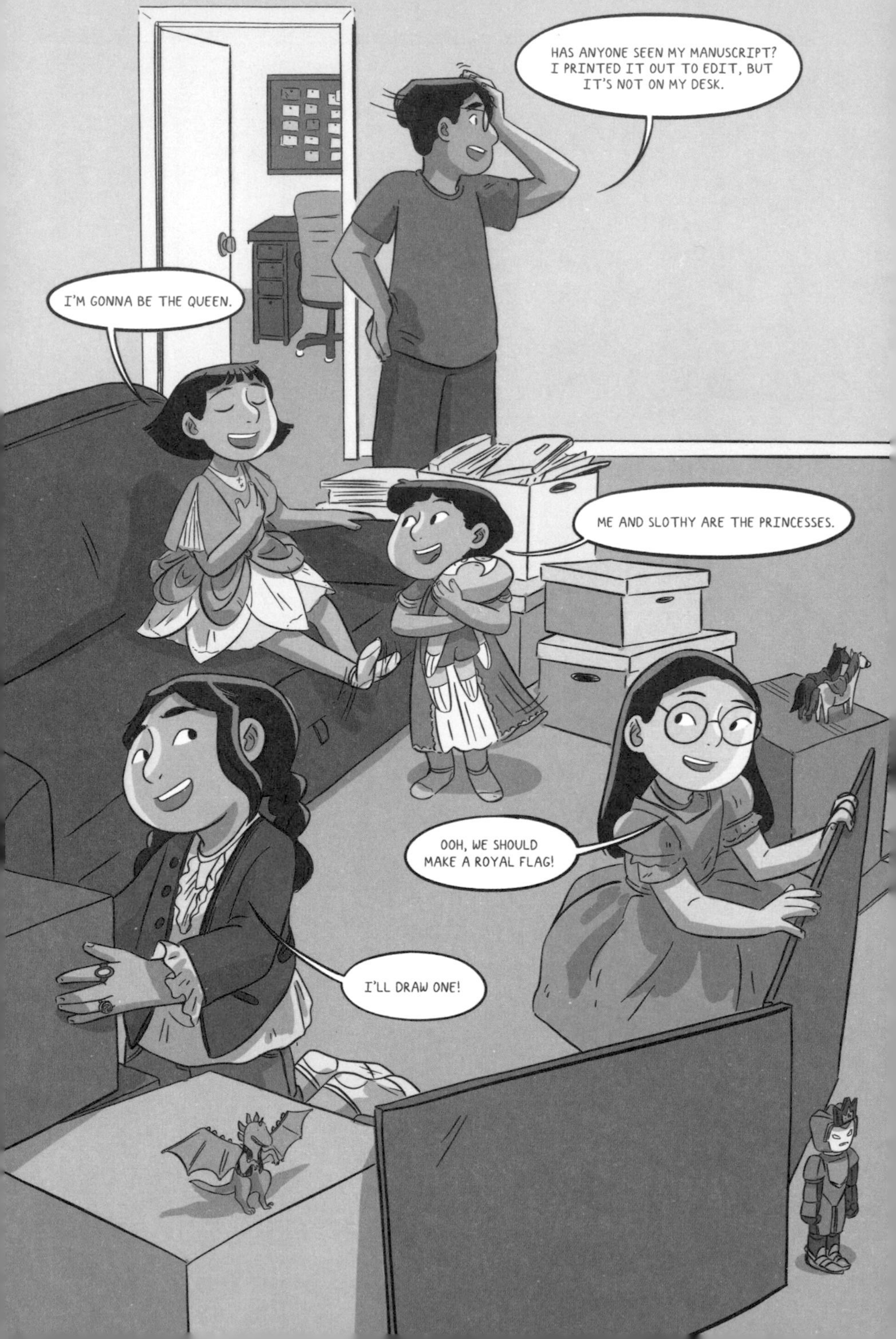
HAS ANYONE SEEN MY MANUSCRIPT? I PRINTED IT OUT TO EDIT, BUT IT'S NOT ON MY DESK.
I'M GONNA BE THE QUEEN.
ME AND SLOTHY ARE THE PRINCESSES.
OOH, WE SHOULD MAKE A ROYAL FLAG!
I'LL DRAW ONE!

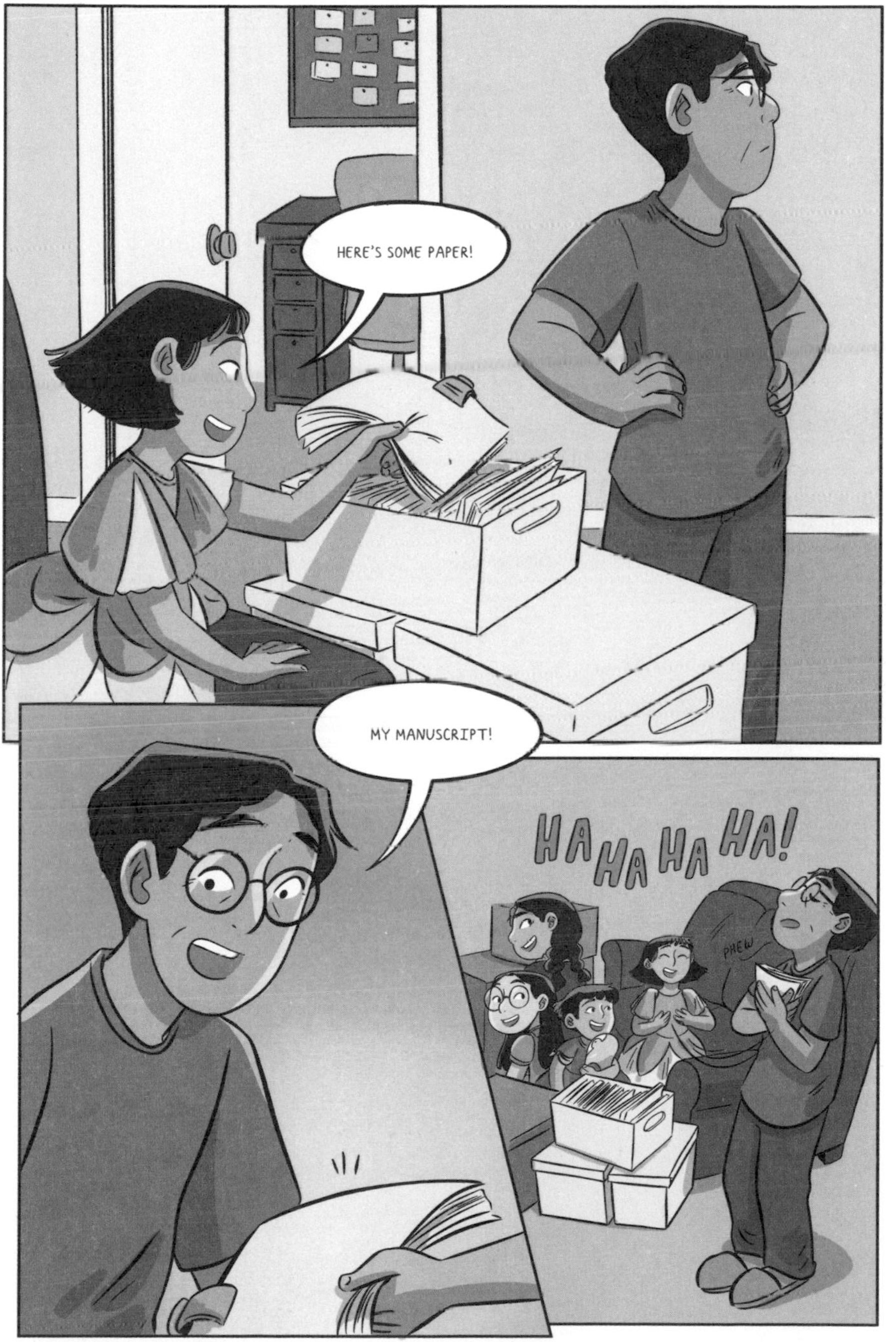
HERE'S SOME PAPER!
MY MANUSCRIPT!
HA HA HA HA HA!
PHEW

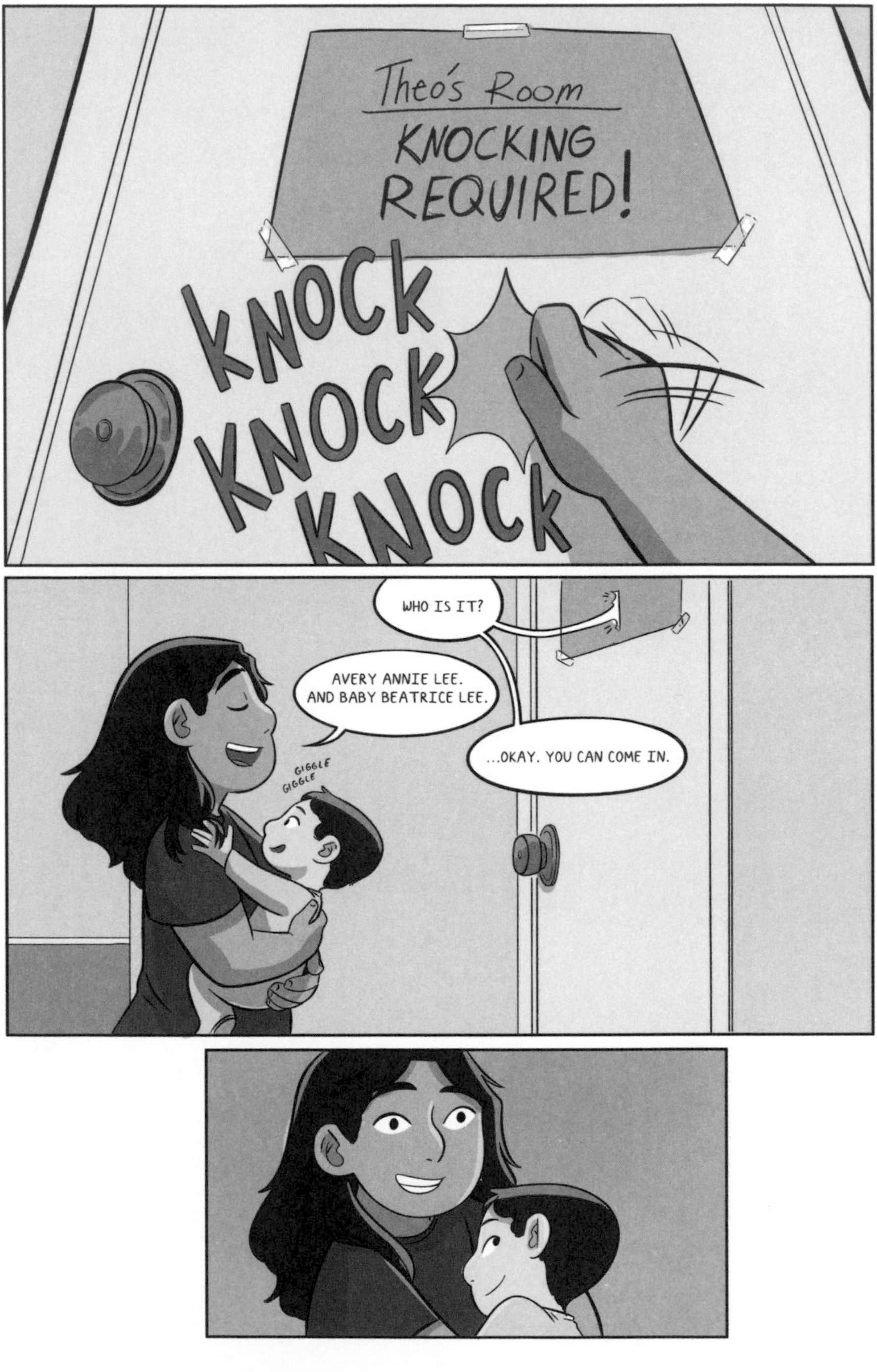
Theo's Room
KNOCKING REQUIRED!
KNOCK KNOCK KNOCK
WHO IS IT?
AVERY ANNIE LEE. AND BABY BEATRICE LEE.
GIGGLE GIGGLE
...OKAY. YOU CAN COME IN.

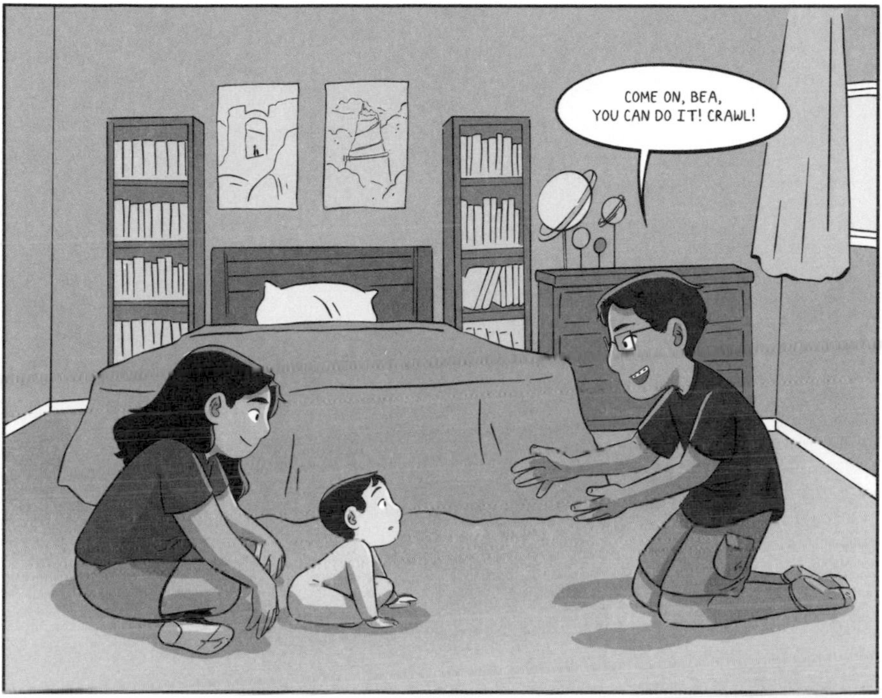
COME ON, BEA, YOU CAN DO IT! CRAWL!

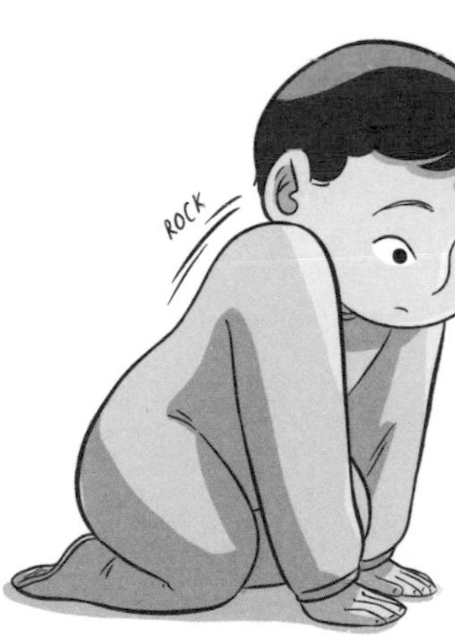
ROCK

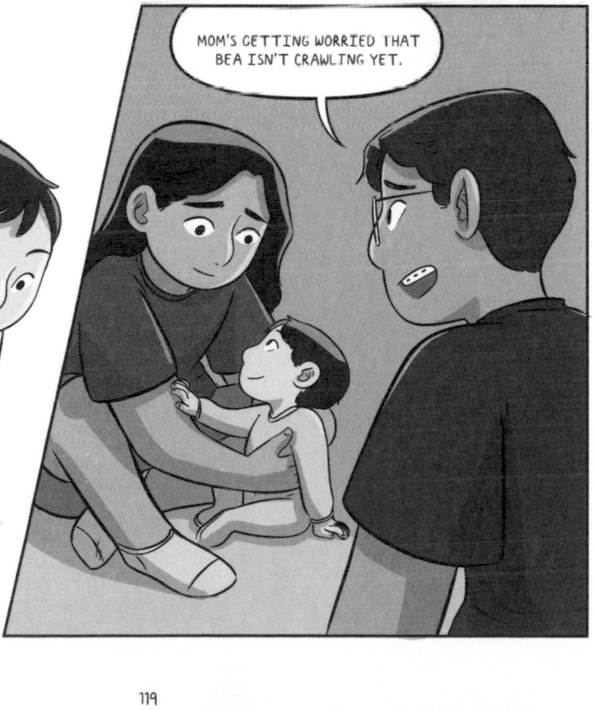
MOM'S GETTING WORRIED THAT BEA ISN'T CRAWLING YET.

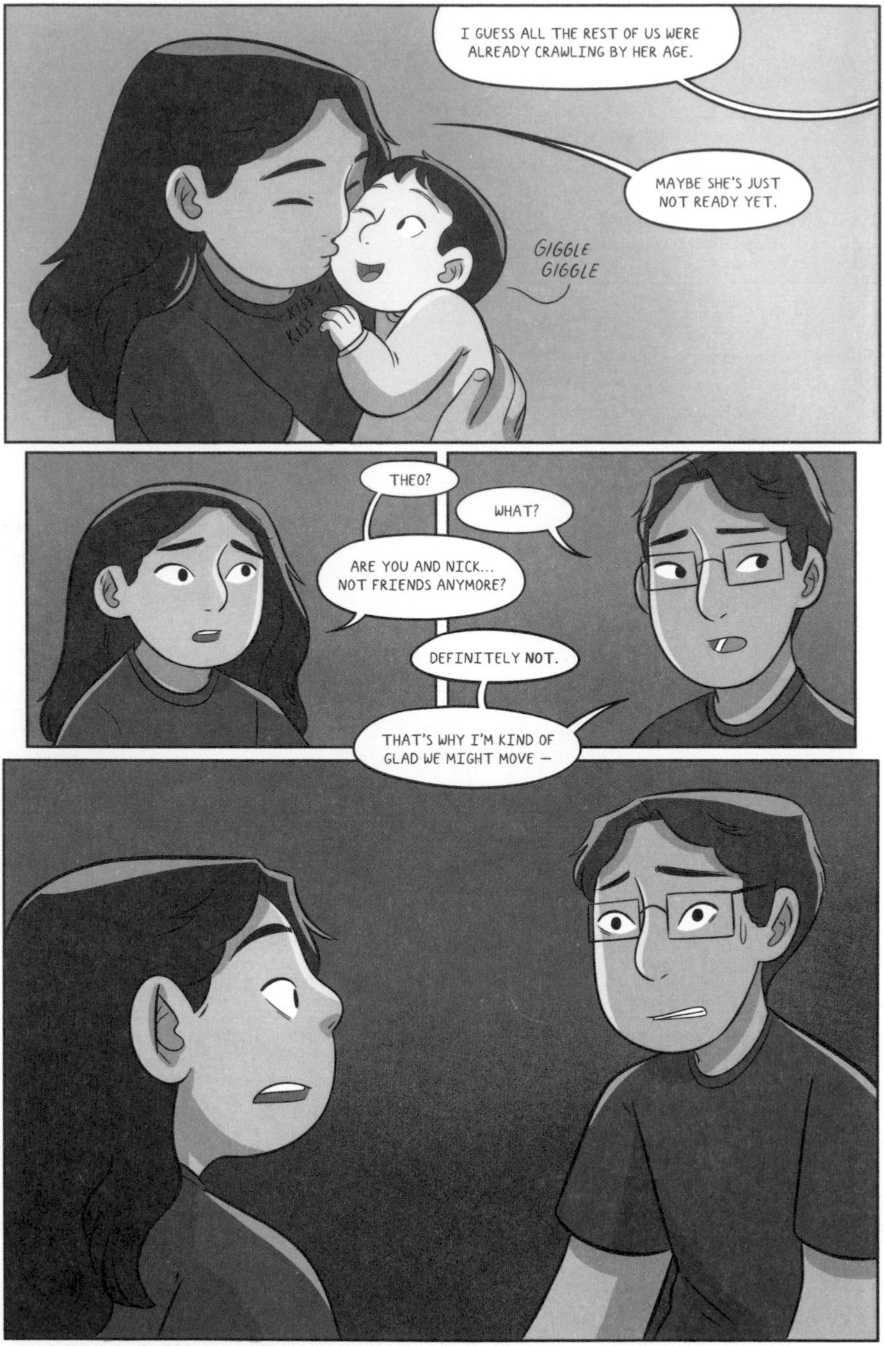
I GUESS ALL THE REST OF US WERE ALREADY CRAWLING BY HER AGE.
MAYBE SHE'S JUST NOT READY YET.
KISS KISS
GIGGLE GIGGLE
THEO?
WHAT?
ARE YOU AND NICK... NOT FRIENDS ANYMORE?
DEFINITELY NOT.
THAT'S WHY I'M KIND OF GLAD WE MIGHT MOVE —

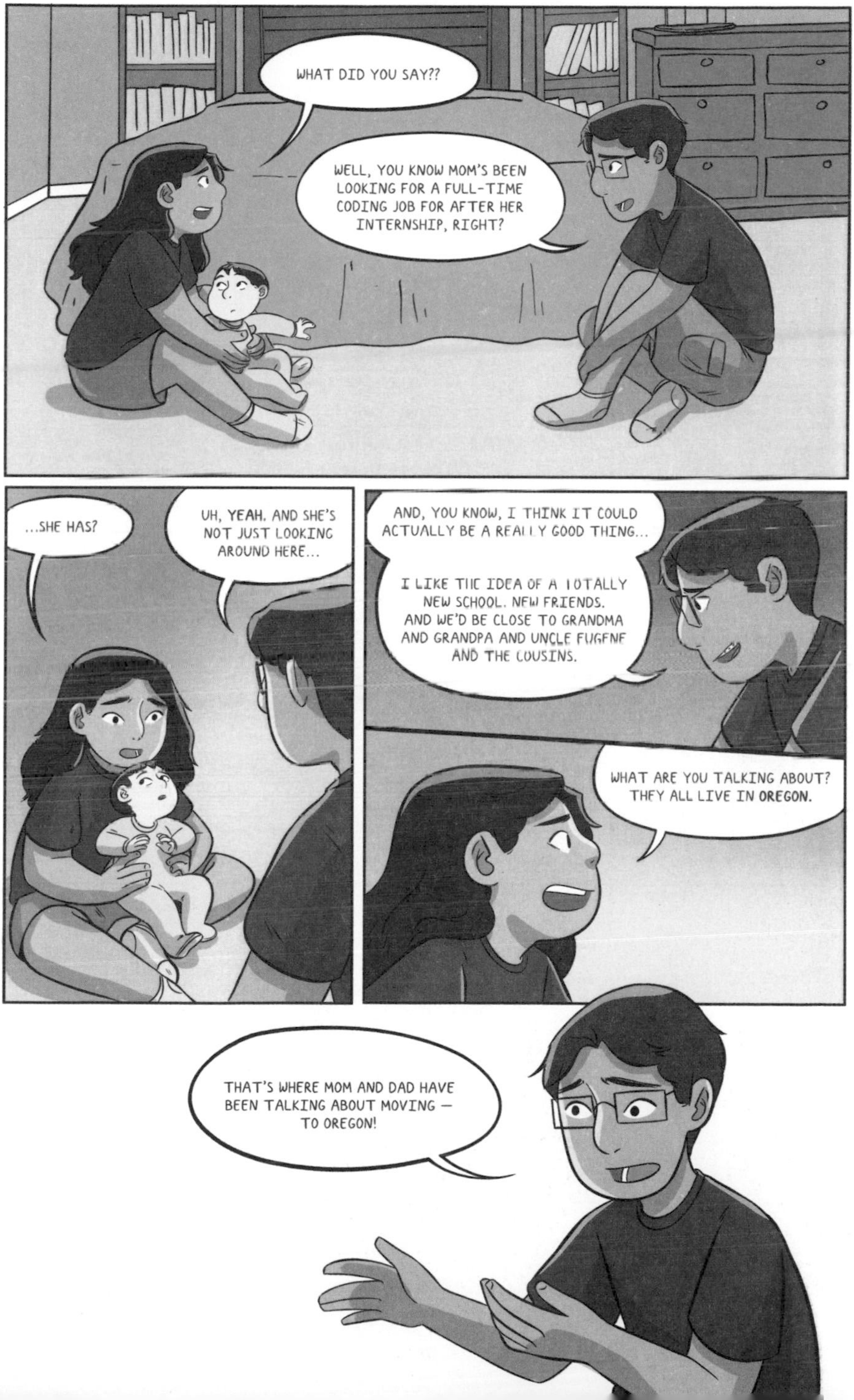
WHAT DID YOU SAY??
WELL, YOU KNOW MOM'S BEEN LOOKING FOR A FULL-TIME CODING JOB FOR AFTER HER INTERNSHIP, RIGHT?
...SHE HAS?
UH, YEAH. AND SHE'S NOT JUST LOOKING AROUND HERE...
AND, YOU KNOW, I THINK IT COULD ACTUALLY BE A REALLY GOOD THING...
I LIKE THE IDEA OF A TOTALLY NEW SCHOOL. NEW FRIENDS. AND WE'D BE CLOSE TO GRANDMA AND GRANDPA AND UNCLE EUGENE AND THE COUSINS.
WHAT ARE YOU TALKING ABOUT? THEY ALL LIVE IN OREGON.
THAT'S WHERE MOM AND DAD HAVE BEEN TALKING ABOUT MOVING — TO OREGON!

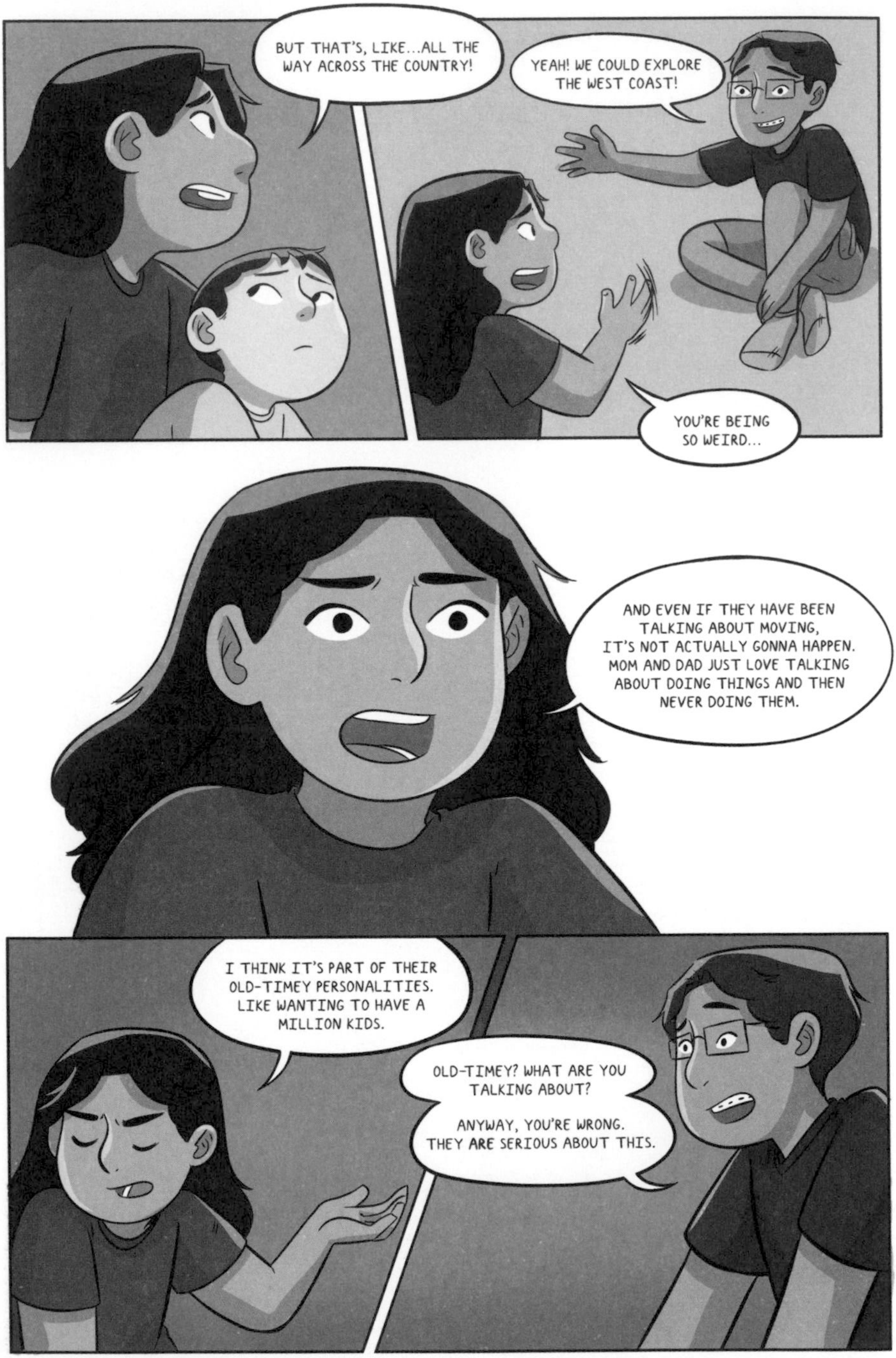
BUT THAT'S, LIKE...ALL THE WAY ACROSS THE COUNTRY!
YEAH! WE COULD EXPLORE THE WEST COAST!
YOU'RE BEING SO WEIRD...
AND EVEN IF THEY HAVE BEEN TALKING ABOUT MOVING, IT'S NOT ACTUALLY GONNA HAPPEN. MOM AND DAD JUST LOVE TALKING ABOUT DOING THINGS AND THEN NEVER DOING THEM.
I THINK IT'S PART OF THEIR OLD-TIMEY PERSONALITIES. LIKE WANTING TO HAVE A MILLION KIDS.
OLD-TIMEY? WHAT ARE YOU TALKING ABOUT?
ANYWAY, YOU'RE WRONG. THEY ARE SERIOUS ABOUT THIS.

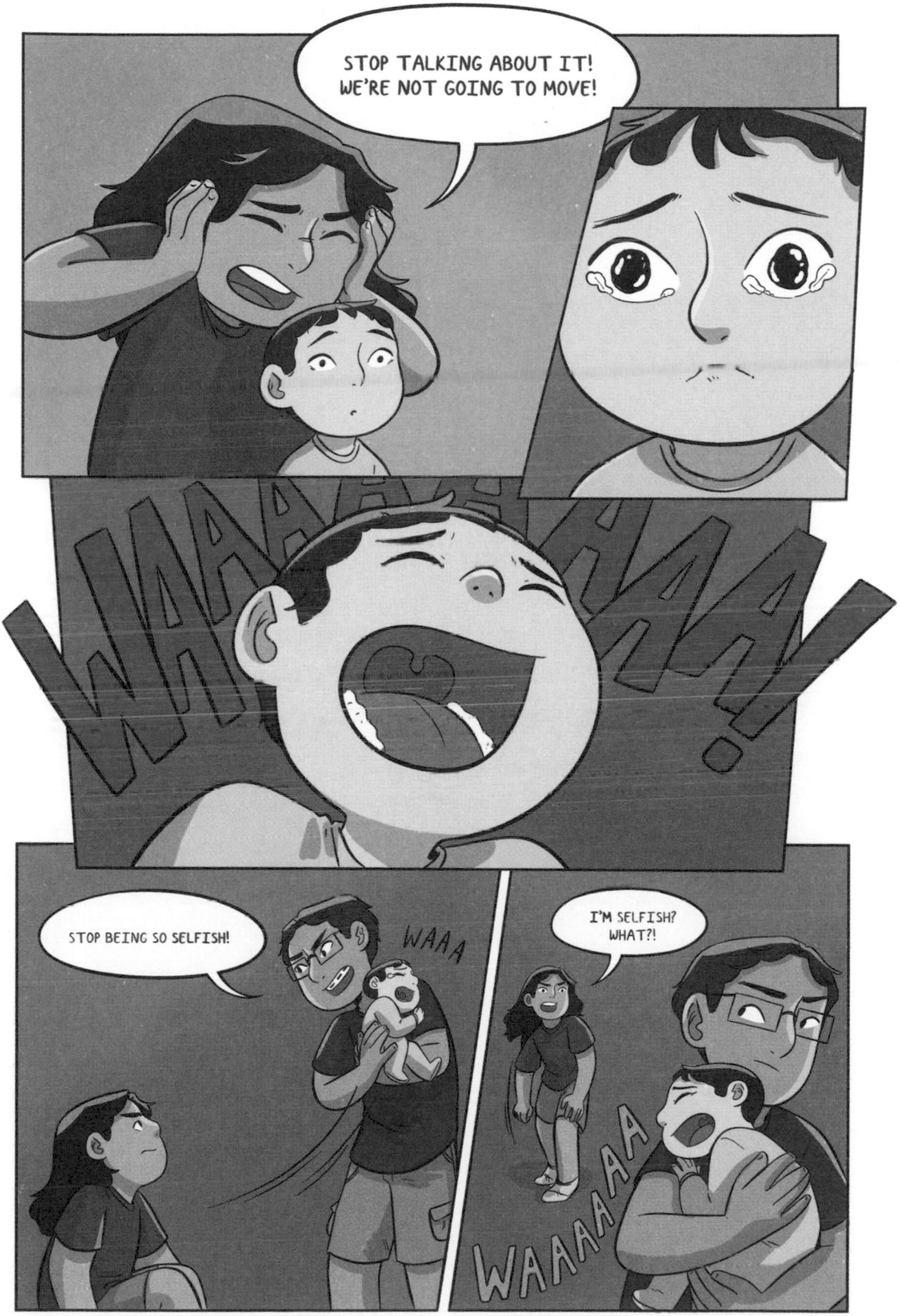

STOP TALKING ABOUT IT! WE'RE NOT GOING TO MOVE!
WAAAAAAAA!
STOP BEING SO SELFISH!
WAAA
I'M SELFISH? WHAT?!
WAAAAAA

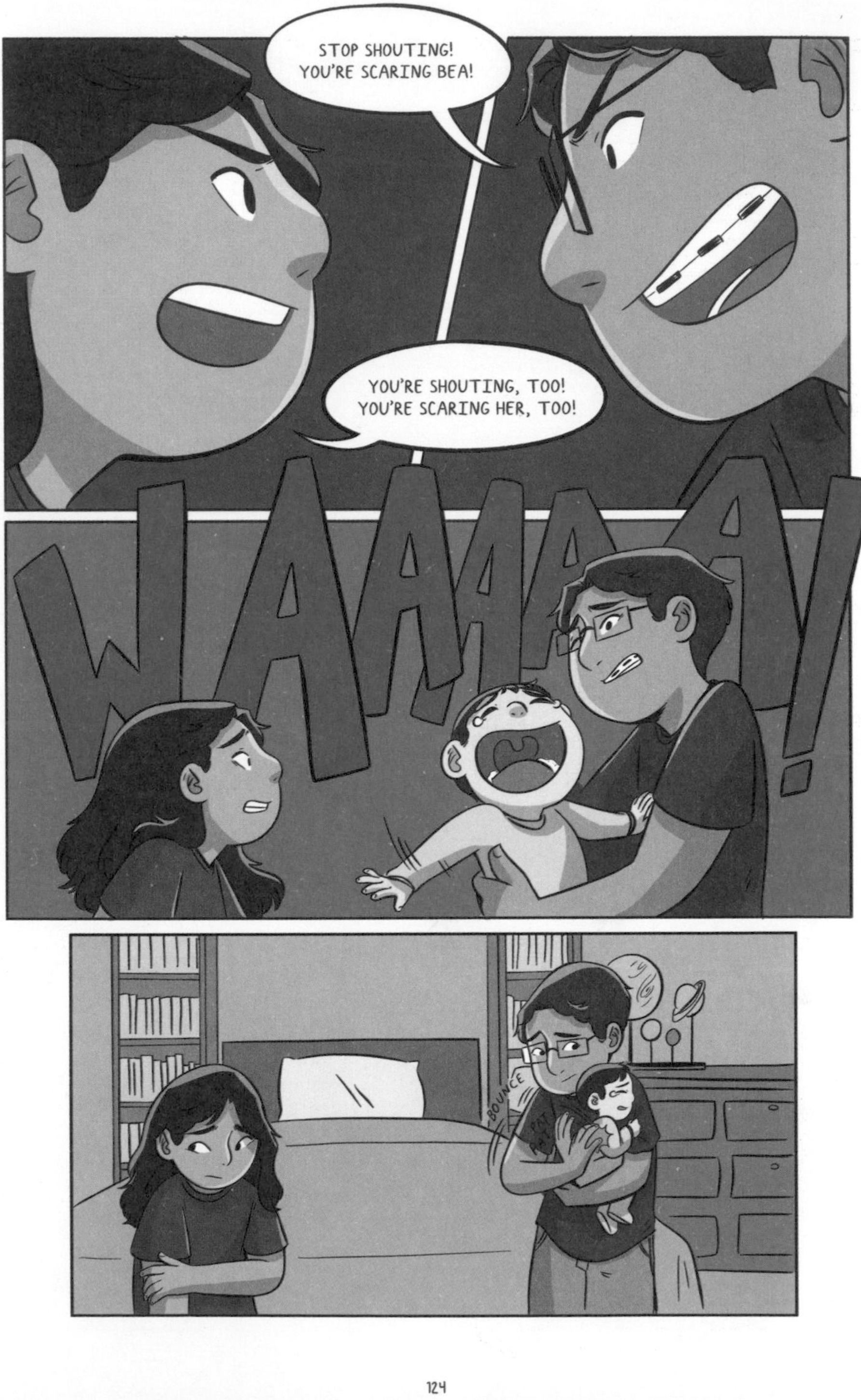
STOP SHOUTING! YOU'RE SCARING BEA!
YOU'RE SHOUTING, TOO! YOU'RE SCARING HER, TOO!
WAAAAAY!
BOUNCE
PAT

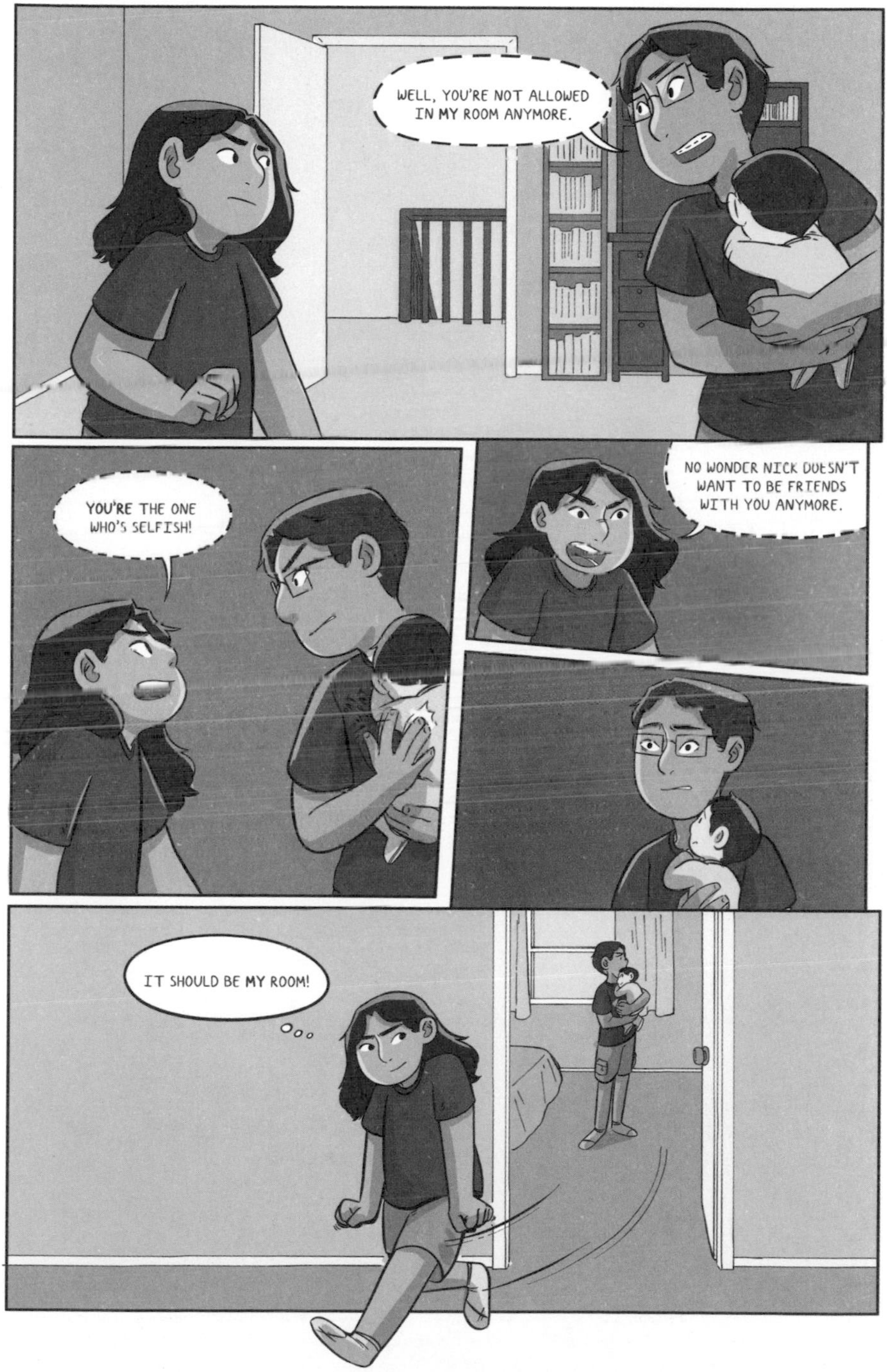

WELL, YOU'RE NOT ALLOWED IN MY ROOM ANYMORE.
YOU'RE THE ONE WHO'S SELFISH!
NO WONDER NICK DOESN'T WANT TO BE FRIENDS WITH YOU ANYMORE.
IT SHOULD BE MY ROOM!

Chapter Eight

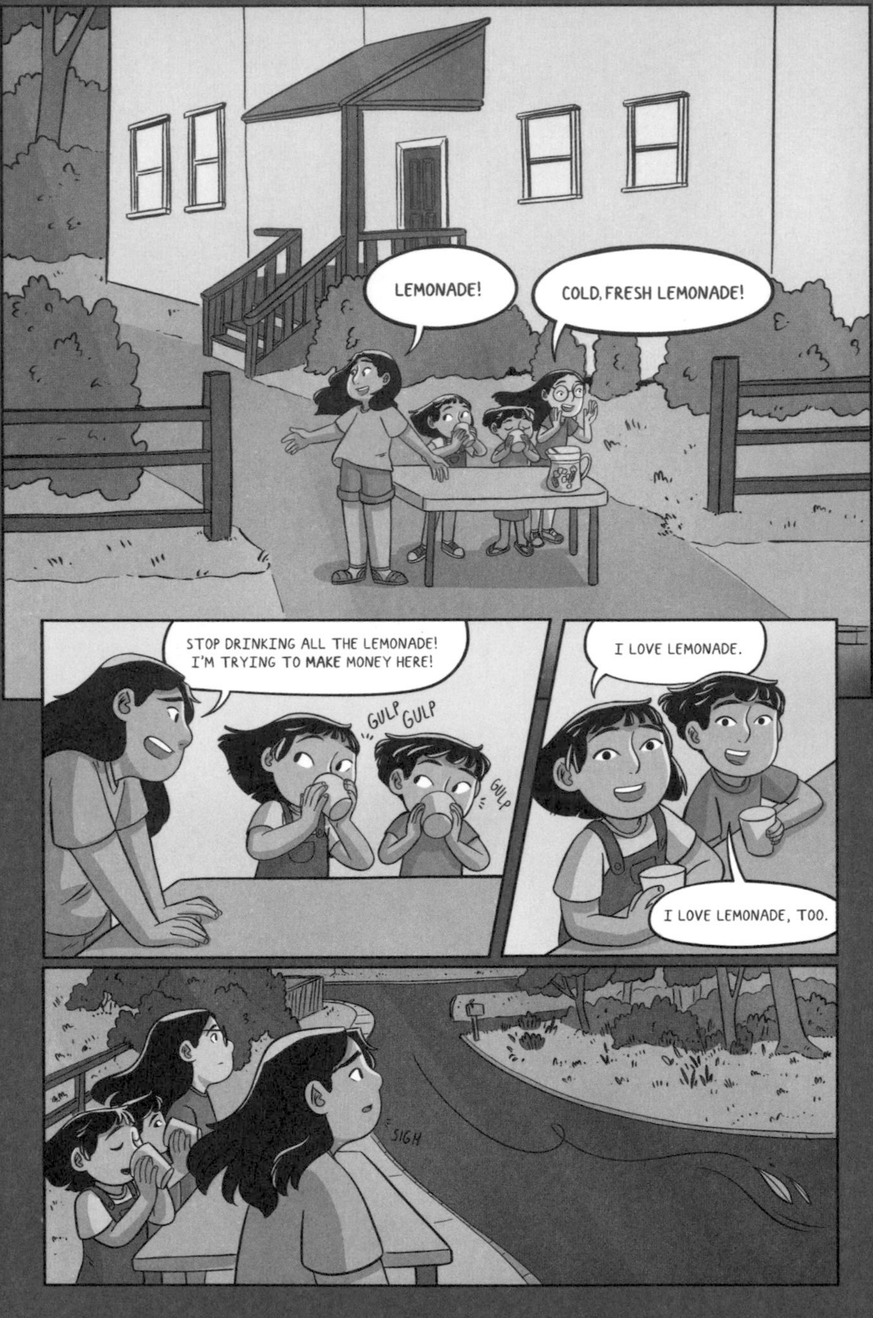
LEMONADE!
COLD, FRESH LEMONADE!
STOP DRINKING ALL THE LEMONADE! I'M TRYING TO MAKE MONEY HERE!
GULP GULP
GULP
I LOVE LEMONADE.
I LOVE LEMONADE, TOO.
SIGH

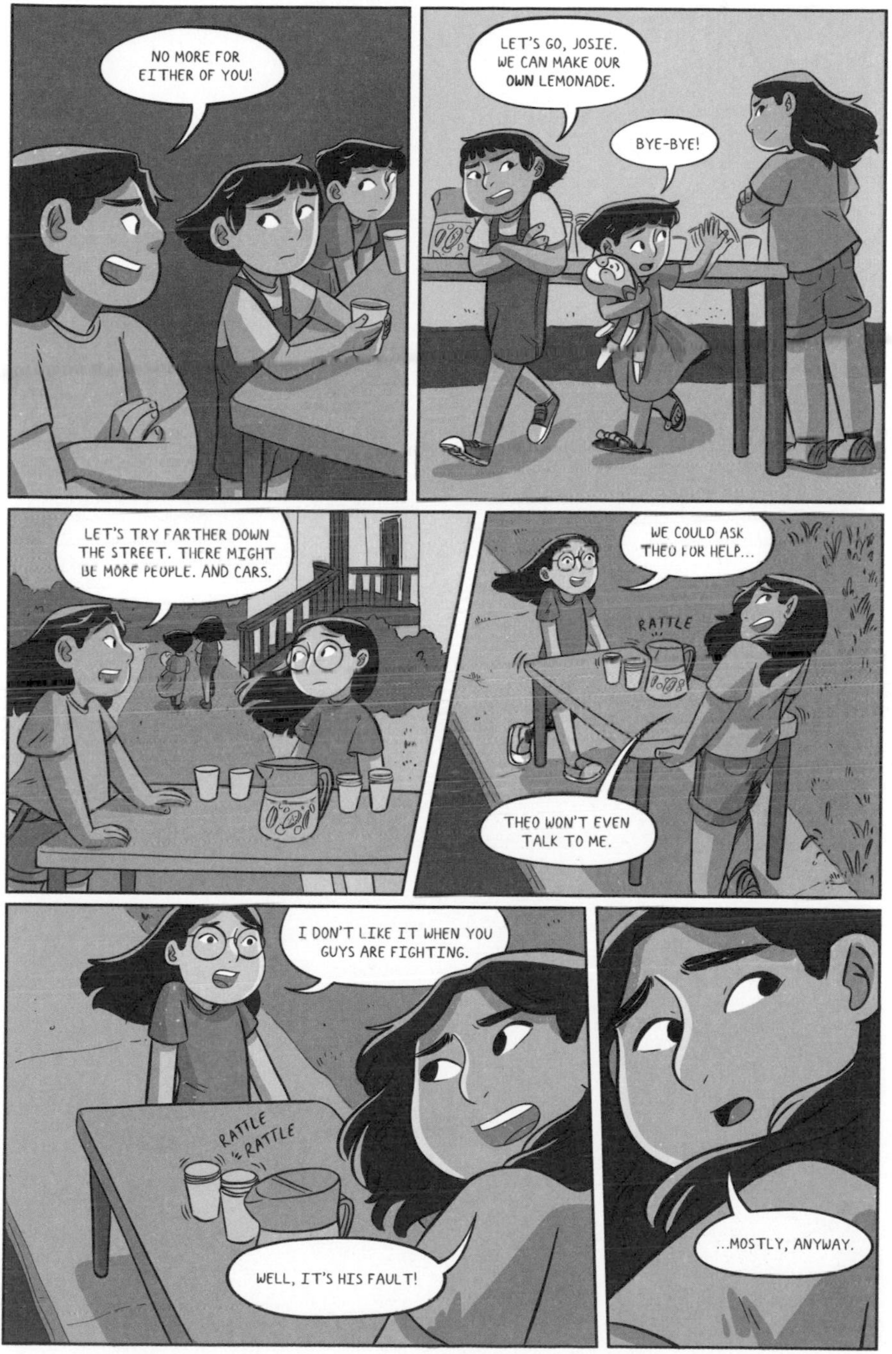
NO MORE FOR EITHER OF YOU!
LET'S GO, JOSIE. WE CAN MAKE OUR OWN LEMONADE.
BYE-BYE!
LET'S TRY FARTHER DOWN THE STREET. THERE MIGHT BE MORE PEOPLE. AND CARS.
WE COULD ASK THEO FOR HELP...
RATTLE
THEO WON'T EVEN TALK TO ME.
I DON'T LIKE IT WHEN YOU GUYS ARE FIGHTING.
RATTLE RATTLE
WELL, IT'S HIS FAULT!
...MOSTLY, ANYWAY.

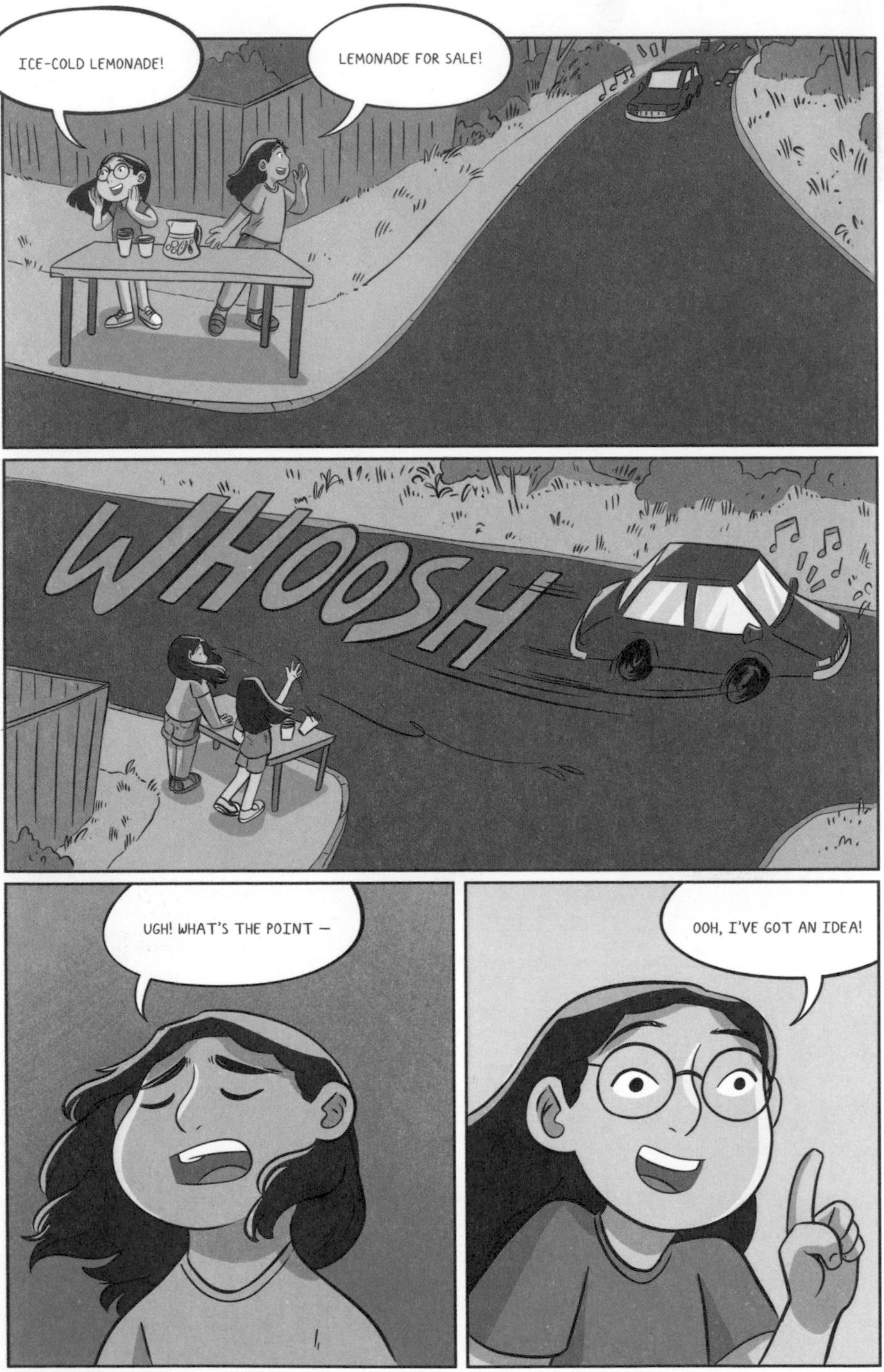
ICE-COLD LEMONADE!
LEMONADE FOR SALE!
WHOOSH
UGH! WHAT'S THE POINT —
OOH, I'VE GOT AN IDEA!

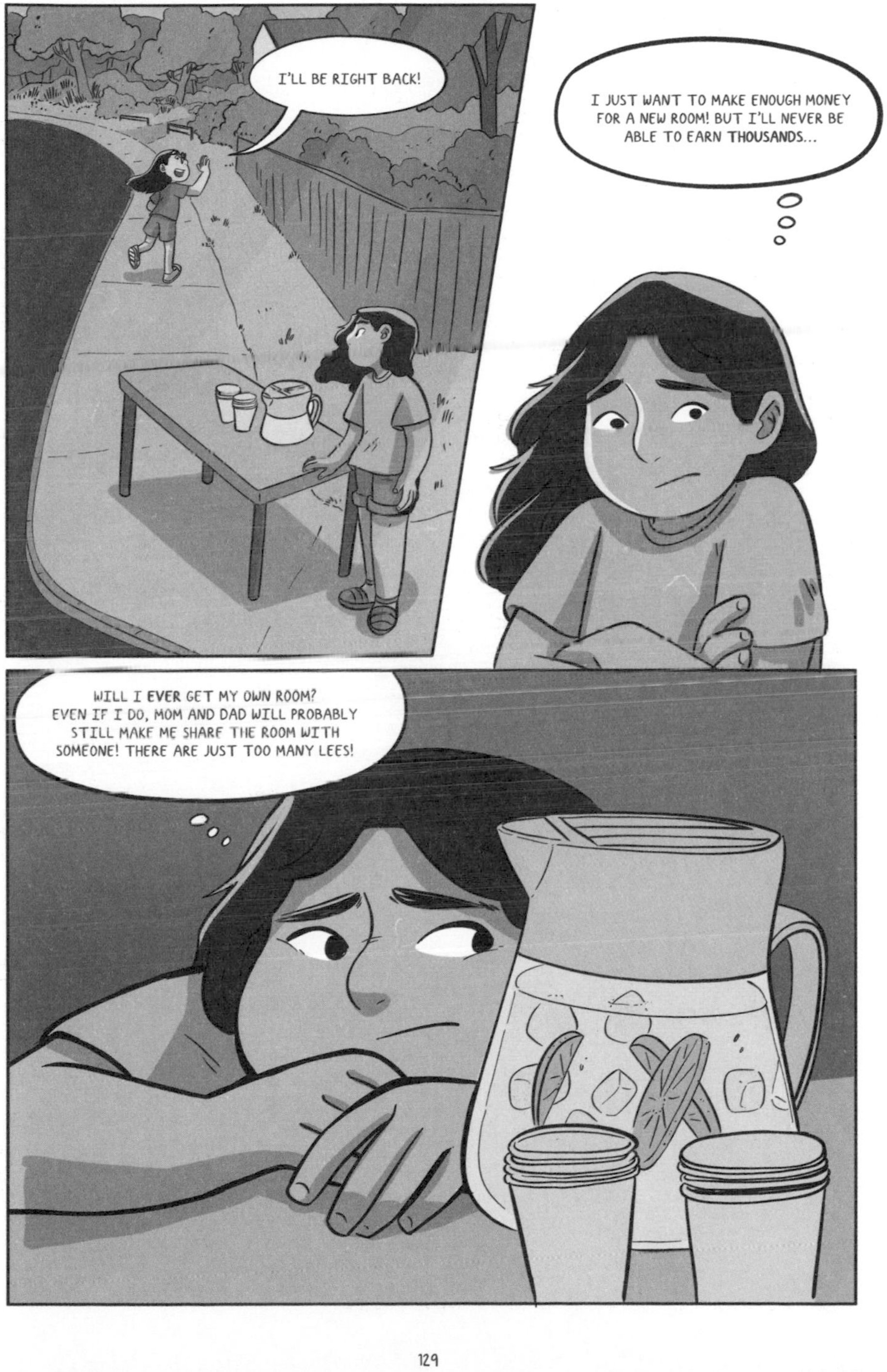
I'LL BE RIGHT BACK!
I JUST WANT TO MAKE ENOUGH MONEY FOR A NEW ROOM! BUT I'LL NEVER BE ABLE TO EARN THOUSANDS...
WILL I EVER GET MY OWN ROOM? EVEN IF I DO, MOM AND DAD WILL PROBABLY STILL MAKE ME SHARE THE ROOM WITH SOMEONE! THERE ARE JUST TOO MANY LEES!

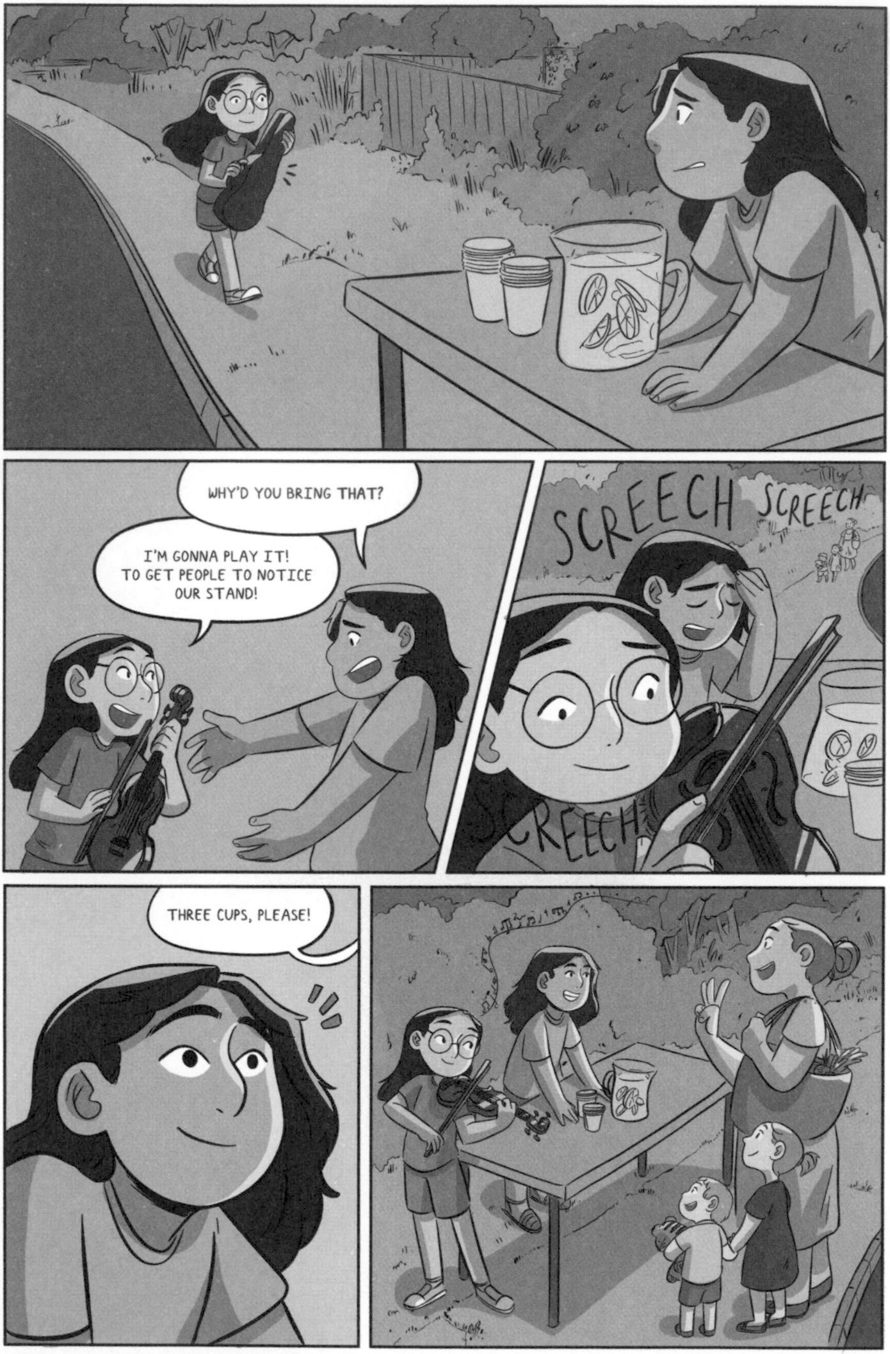
WHY'D YOU BRING THAT?
I'M GONNA PLAY IT! TO GET PEOPLE TO NOTICE OUR STAND!
SCREECH
SCREECH
SCREECH
THREE CUPS, PLEASE!

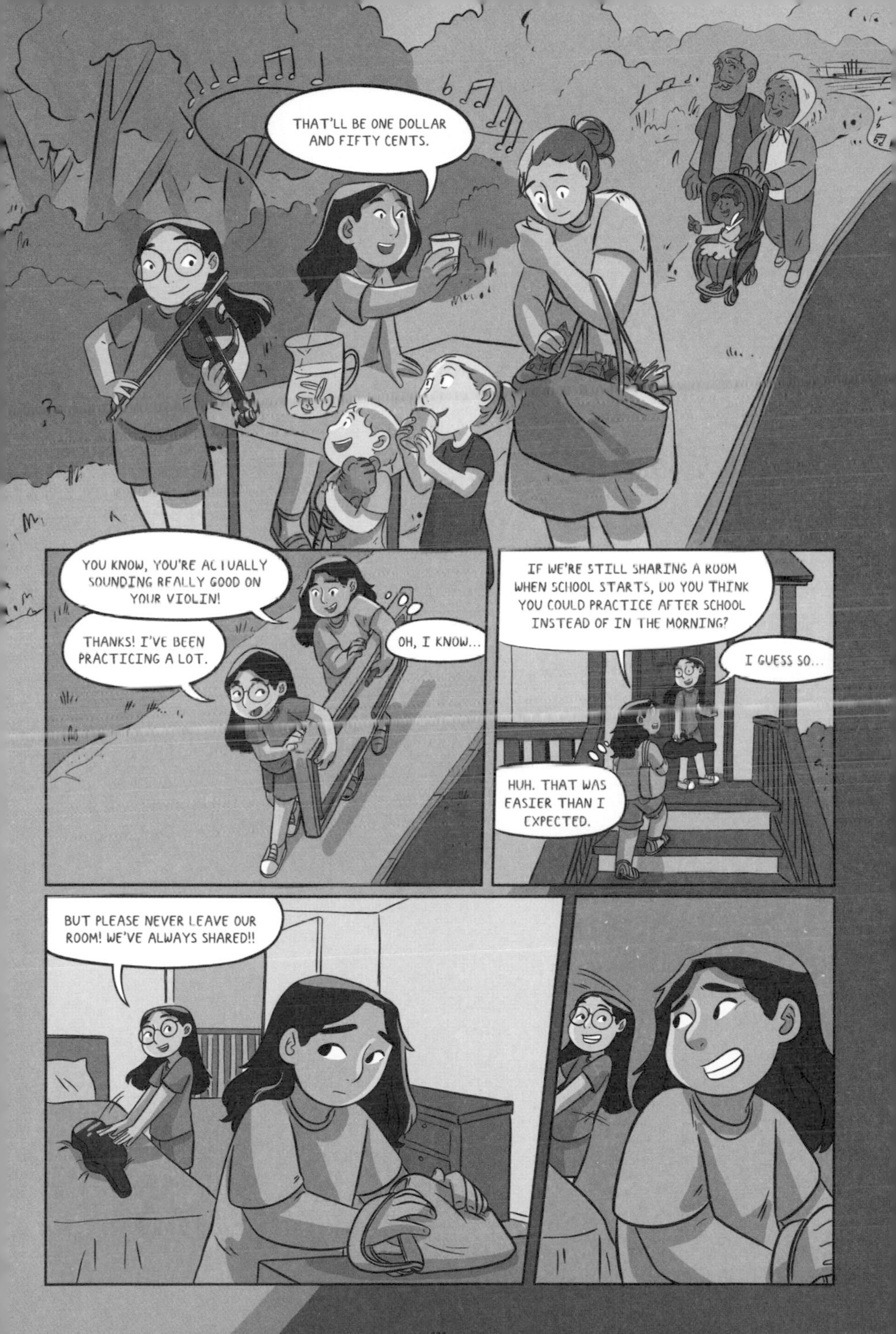
THAT'LL BE ONE DOLLAR AND FIFTY CENTS.
YOU KNOW, YOU'RE ACTUALLY SOUNDING REALLY GOOD ON YOUR VIOLIN!
THANKS! I'VE BEEN PRACTICING A LOT.
OH, I KNOW...
IF WE'RE STILL SHARING A ROOM WHEN SCHOOL STARTS, DO YOU THINK YOU COULD PRACTICE AFTER SCHOOL INSTEAD OF IN THE MORNING?
I GUESS SO...
HUH. THAT WAS EASIER THAN I EXPECTED.
BUT PLEASE NEVER LEAVE OUR ROOM! WE'VE ALWAYS SHARED!!

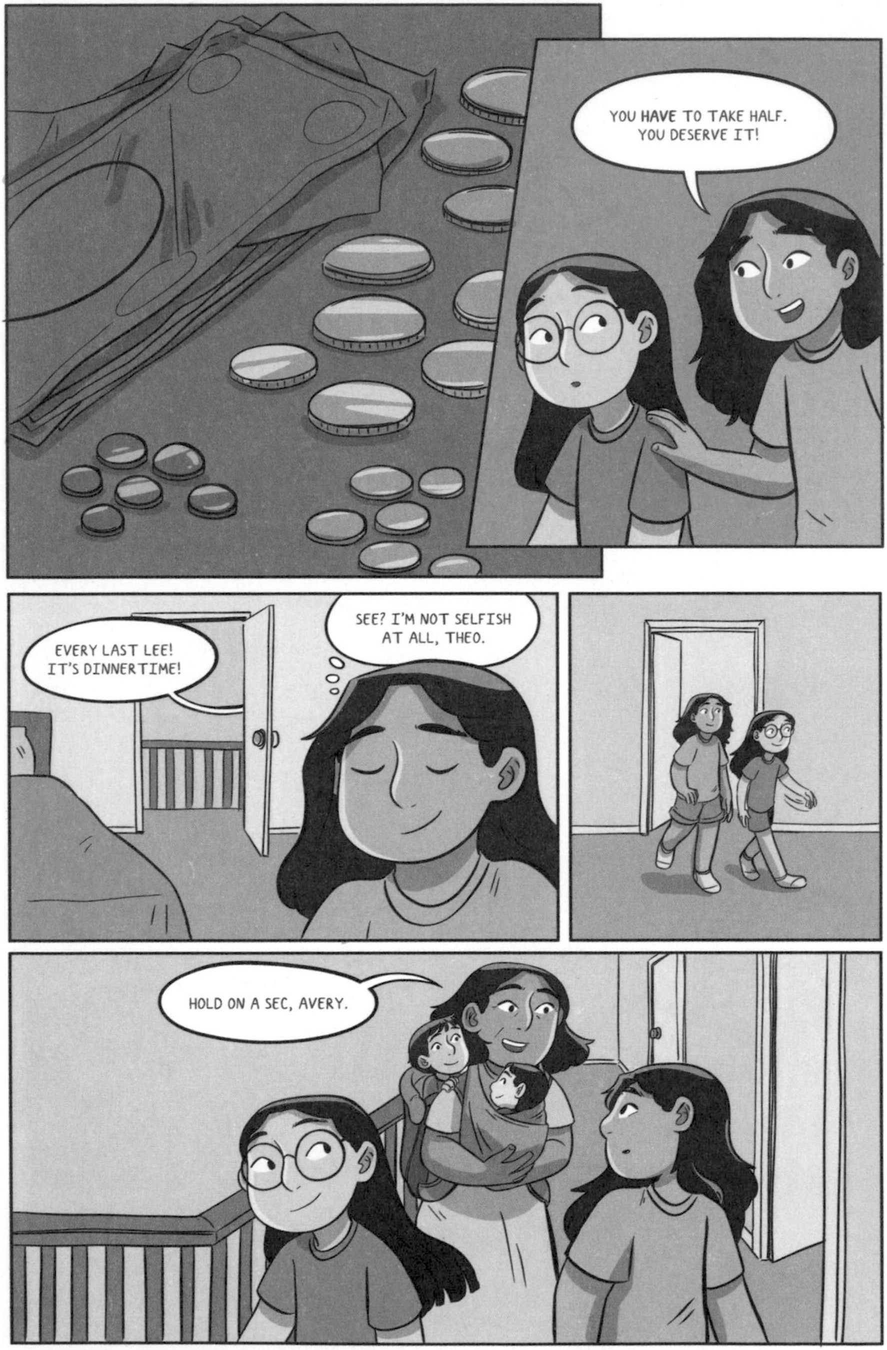
YOU HAVE TO TAKE HALF. YOU DESERVE IT!
EVERY LAST LEE! IT'S DINNERTIME!
SEE? I'M NOT SELFISH AT ALL, THEO.
HOLD ON A SEC, AVERY.

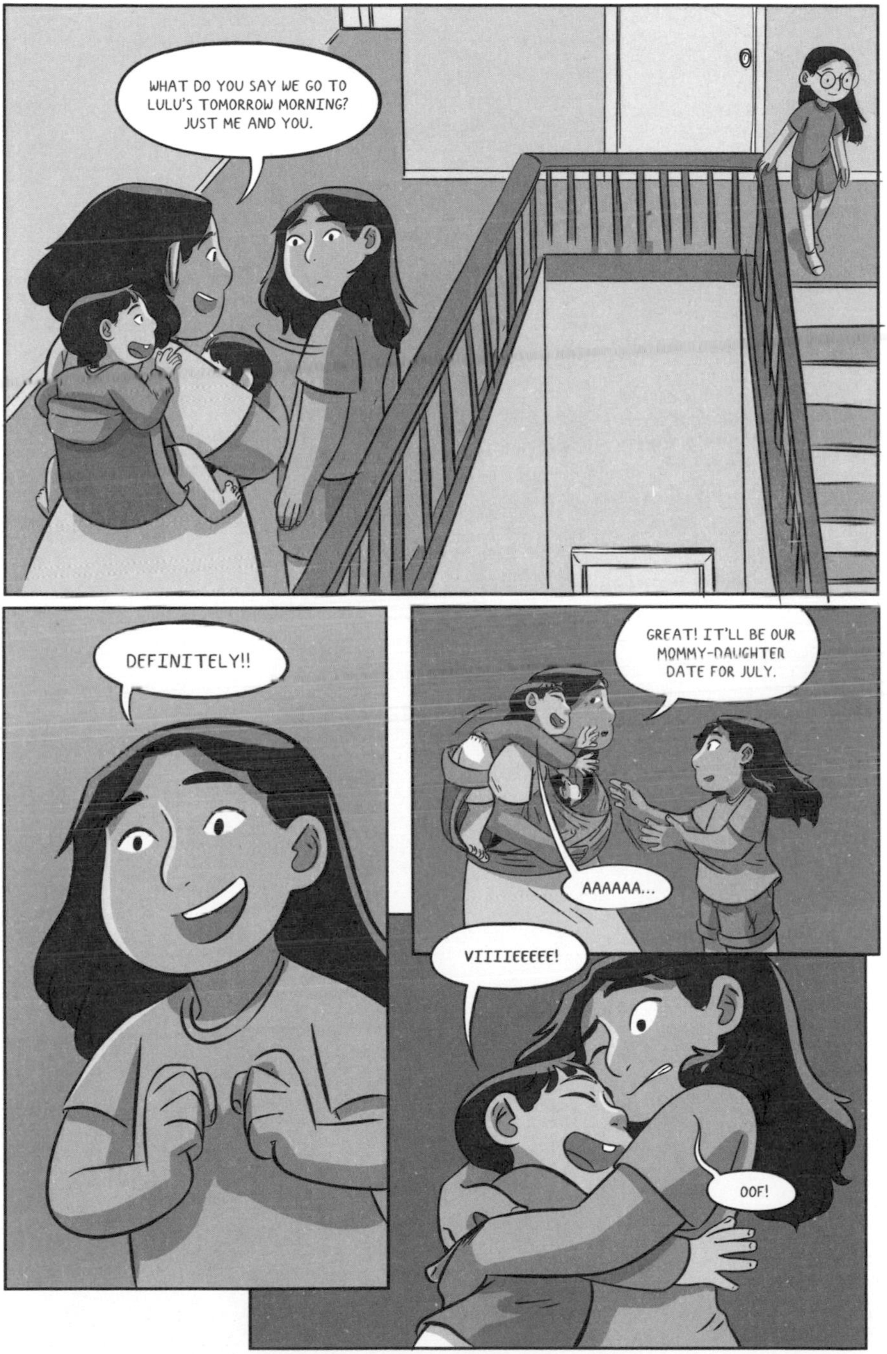
WHAT DO YOU SAY WE GO TO LULU'S TOMORROW MORNING? JUST ME AND YOU.
DEFINITELY!!
GREAT! IT'LL BE OUR MOMMY-DAUGHTER DATE FOR JULY.
AAAAAA...
VIIIIEEEEE!
OOF!

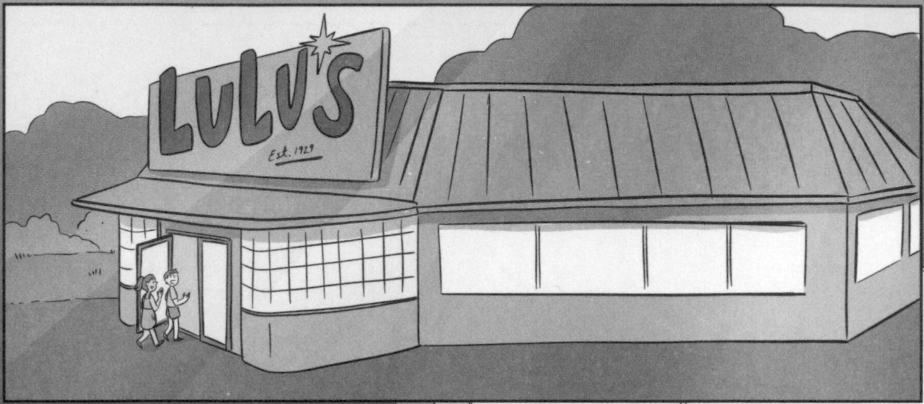
LULU'S
Est. 1929

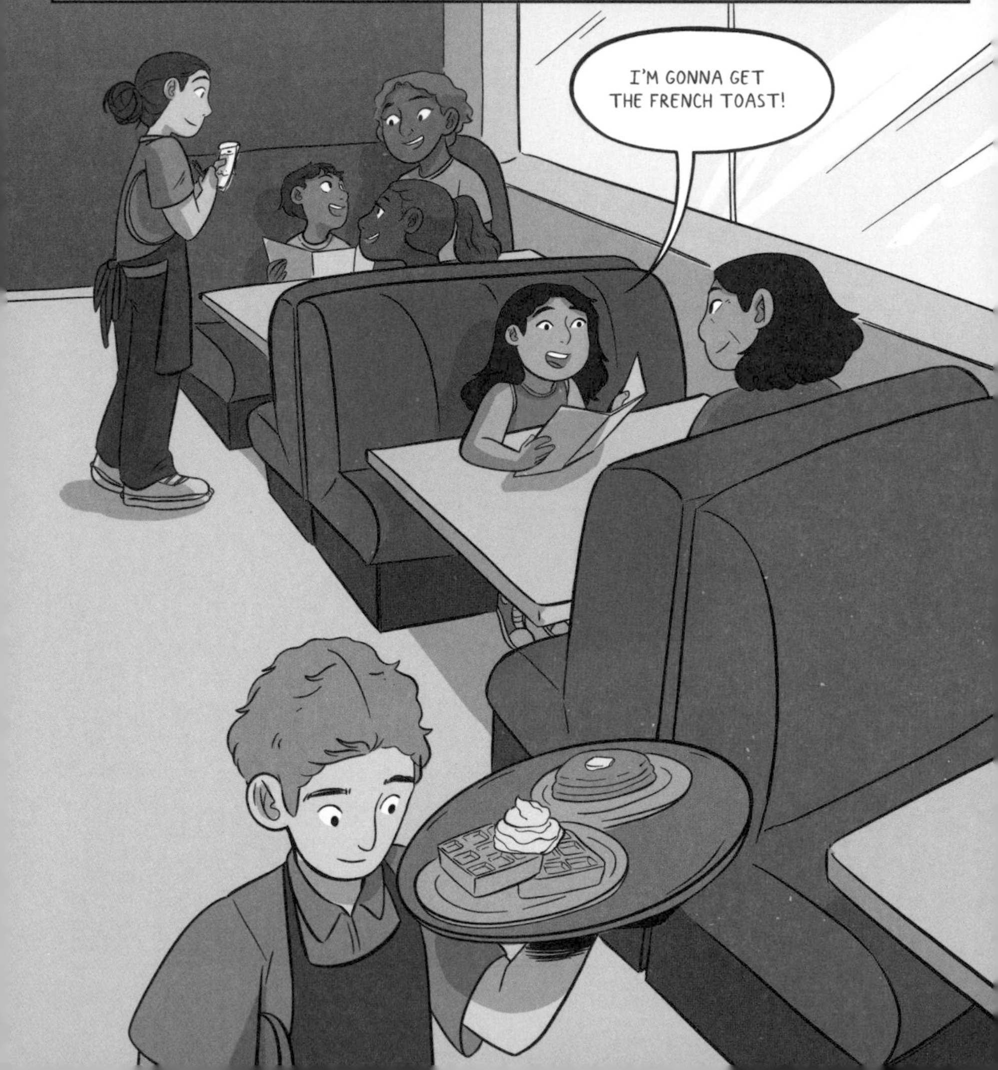
I'M GONNA GET THE FRENCH TOAST!

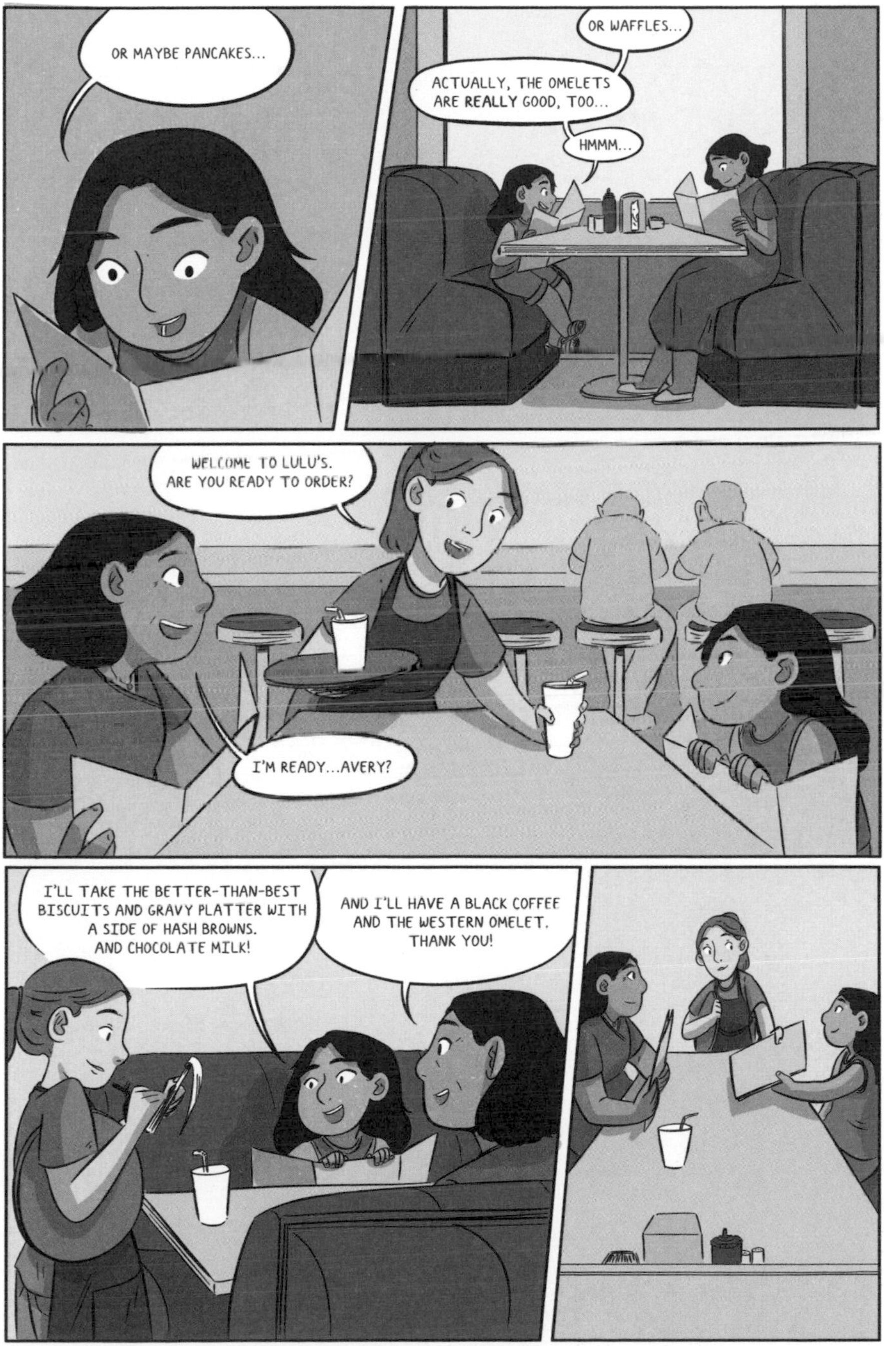
OR MAYBE PANCAKES...
OR WAFFLES...
ACTUALLY, THE OMELETS ARE REALLY GOOD, TOO...
HMMM...
WELCOME TO LULU'S. ARE YOU READY TO ORDER?
I'M READY...AVERY?
I'LL TAKE THE BETTER-THAN-BEST BISCUITS AND GRAVY PLATTER WITH A SIDE OF HASH BROWNS. AND CHOCOLATE MILK!
AND I'LL HAVE A BLACK COFFEE AND THE WESTERN OMELET. THANK YOU!

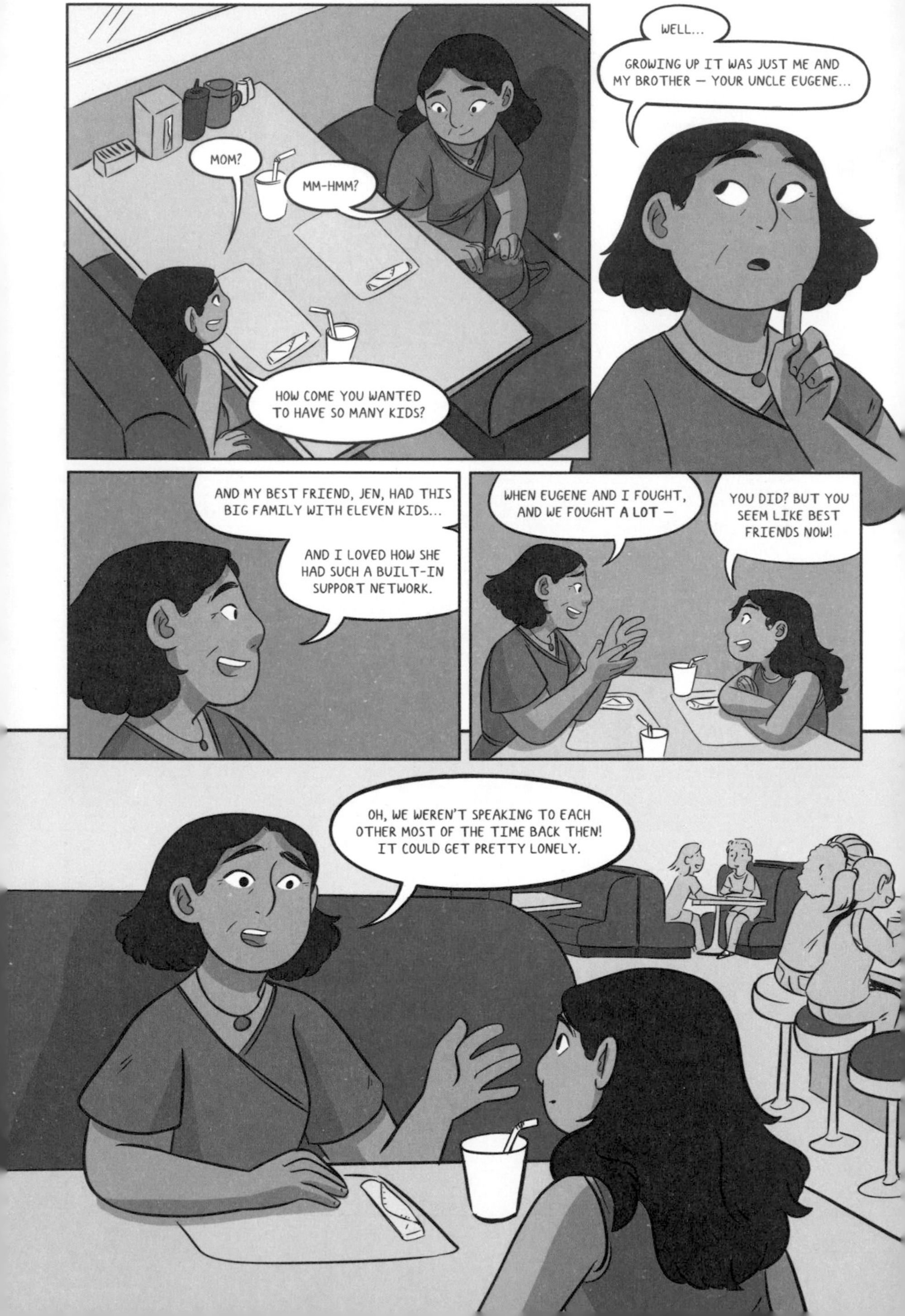
MOM?
MM-HMM?
HOW COME YOU WANTED TO HAVE SO MANY KIDS?
WELL...
GROWING UP IT WAS JUST ME AND MY BROTHER — YOUR UNCLE EUGENE...
AND MY BEST FRIEND, JEN, HAD THIS BIG FAMILY WITH ELEVEN KIDS...
AND I LOVED HOW SHE HAD SUCH A BUILT-IN SUPPORT NETWORK.
WHEN EUGENE AND I FOUGHT, AND WE FOUGHT A LOT —
YOU DID? BUT YOU SEEM LIKE BEST FRIENDS NOW!
OH, WE WEREN'T SPEAKING TO EACH OTHER MOST OF THE TIME BACK THEN! IT COULD GET PRETTY LONELY.

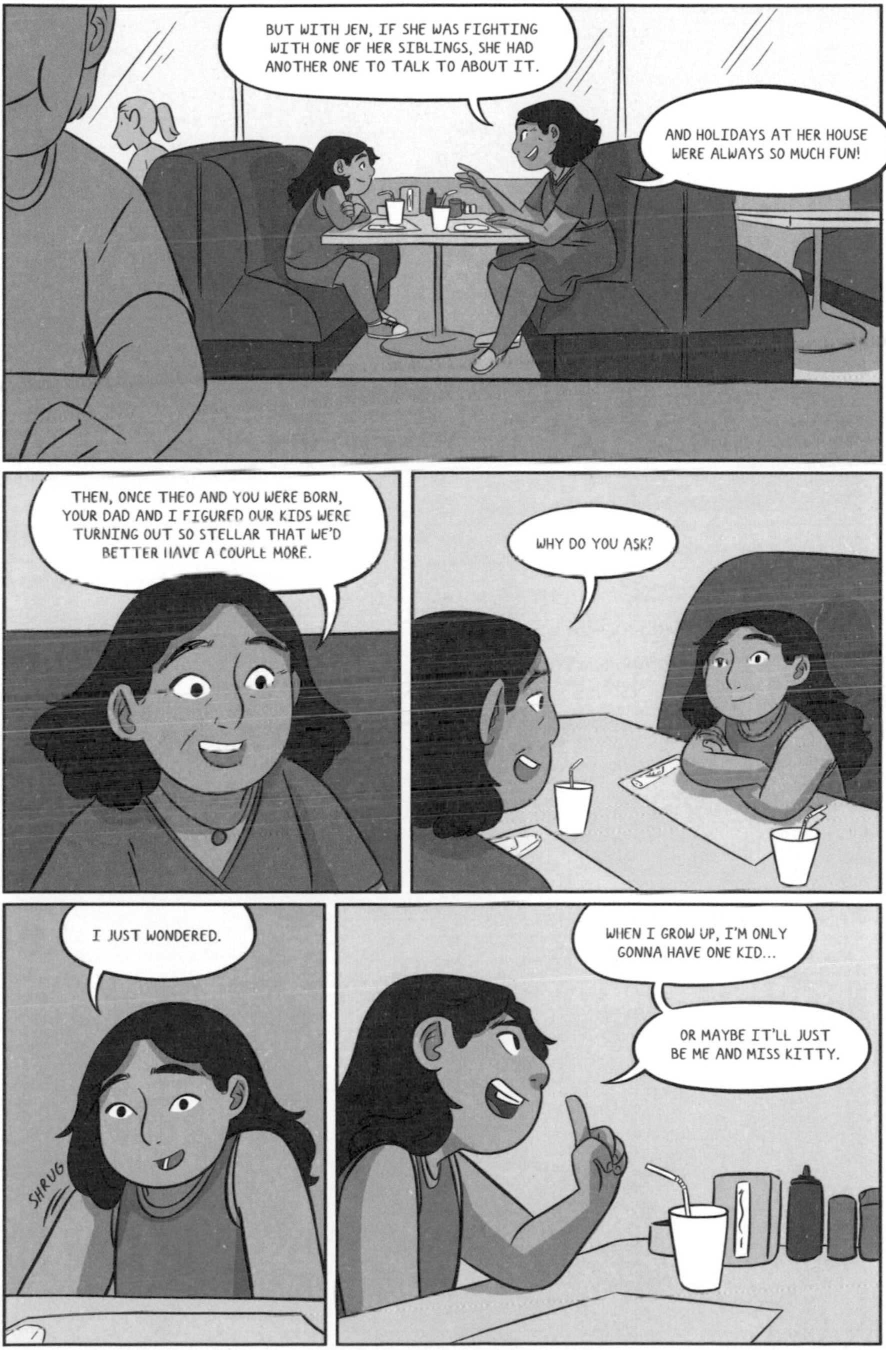
BUT WITH JEN, IF SHE WAS FIGHTING WITH ONE OF HER SIBLINGS, SHE HAD ANOTHER ONE TO TALK TO ABOUT IT.
AND HOLIDAYS AT HER HOUSE WERE ALWAYS SO MUCH FUN!
THEN, ONCE THEO AND YOU WERE BORN, YOUR DAD AND I FIGURED OUR KIDS WERE TURNING OUT SO STELLAR THAT WE'D BETTER HAVE A COUPLE MORE.
WHY DO YOU ASK?
I JUST WONDERED.
SHRUG
WHEN I GROW UP, I'M ONLY GONNA HAVE ONE KID...
OR MAYBE IT'LL JUST BE ME AND MISS KITTY.

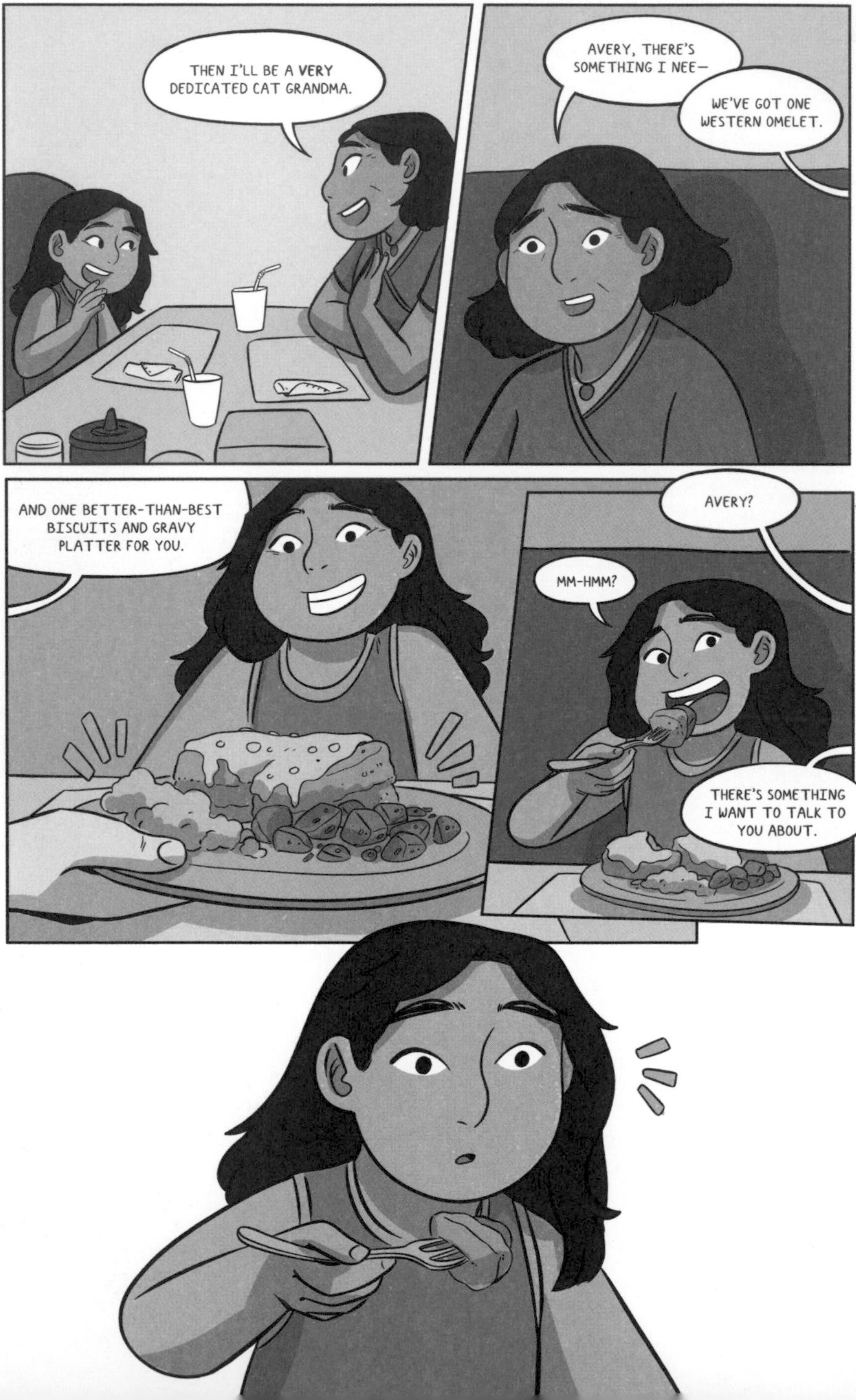
THEN I'LL BE A **VERY** DEDICATED CAT GRANDMA.
AVERY, THERE'S SOMETHING I NEE—
WE'VE GOT ONE WESTERN OMELET.
AND ONE BETTER-THAN-BEST BISCUITS AND GRAVY PLATTER FOR YOU.
AVERY?
MM-HMM?
THERE'S SOMETHING I WANT TO TALK TO YOU ABOUT.

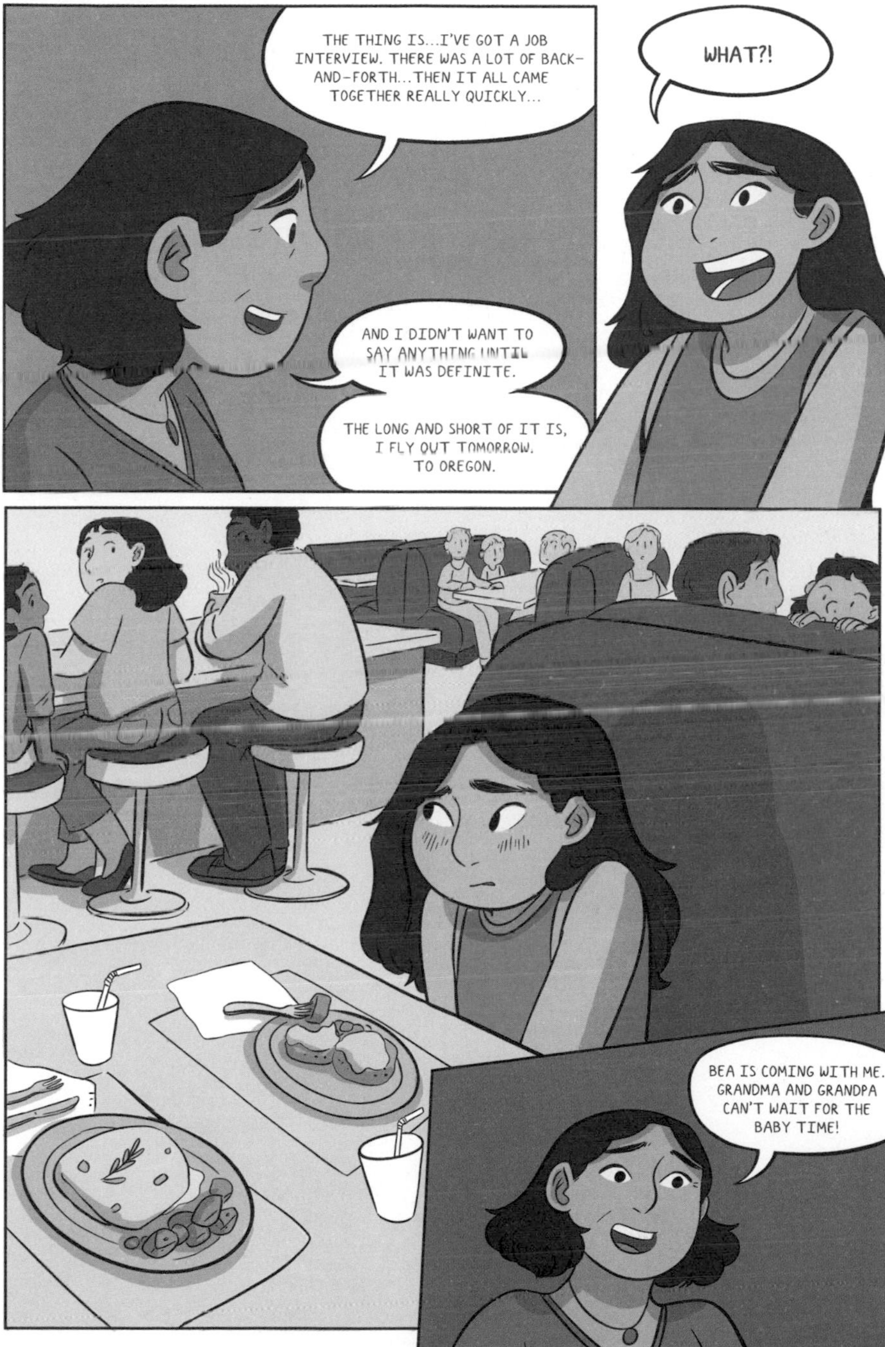
THE THING IS...I'VE GOT A JOB INTERVIEW. THERE WAS A LOT OF BACK-AND-FORTH...THEN IT ALL CAME TOGETHER REALLY QUICKLY...
WHAT?!
AND I DIDN'T WANT TO SAY ANYTHING UNTIL IT WAS DEFINITE.
THE LONG AND SHORT OF IT IS, I FLY OUT TOMORROW. TO OREGON.
BEA IS COMING WITH ME. GRANDMA AND GRANDPA CAN'T WAIT FOR THE BABY TIME!

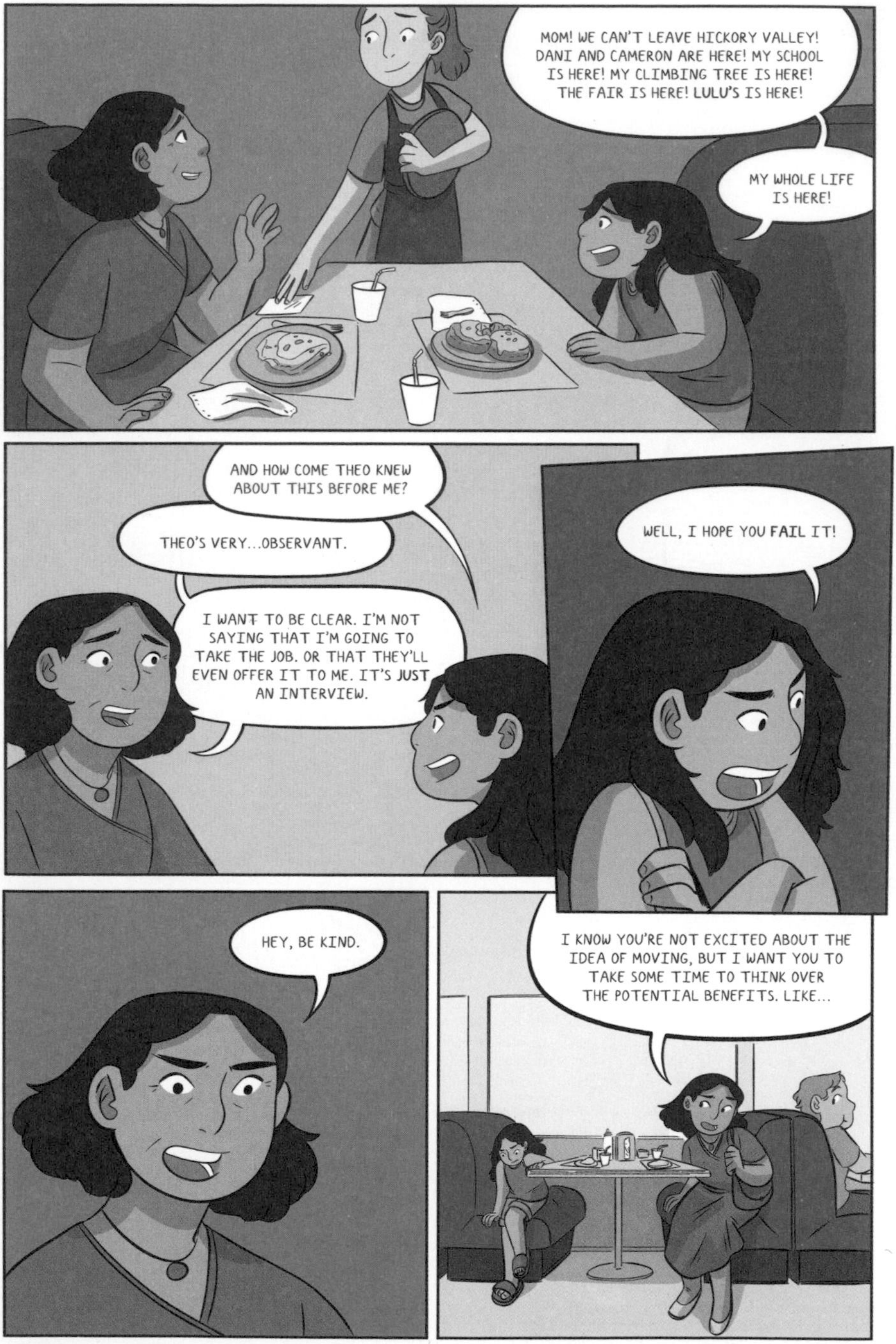
MOM! WE CAN'T LEAVE HICKORY VALLEY! DANI AND CAMERON ARE HERE! MY SCHOOL IS HERE! MY CLIMBING TREE IS HERE! THE FAIR IS HERE! LULU'S IS HERE!
MY WHOLE LIFE IS HERE!
AND HOW COME THEO KNEW ABOUT THIS BEFORE ME?
THEO'S VERY...OBSERVANT.
I WANT TO BE CLEAR. I'M NOT SAYING THAT I'M GOING TO TAKE THE JOB. OR THAT THEY'LL EVEN OFFER IT TO ME. IT'S JUST AN INTERVIEW.
WELL, I HOPE YOU FAIL IT!
HEY, BE KIND.
I KNOW YOU'RE NOT EXCITED ABOUT THE IDEA OF MOVING, BUT I WANT YOU TO TAKE SOME TIME TO THINK OVER THE POTENTIAL BENEFITS. LIKE...

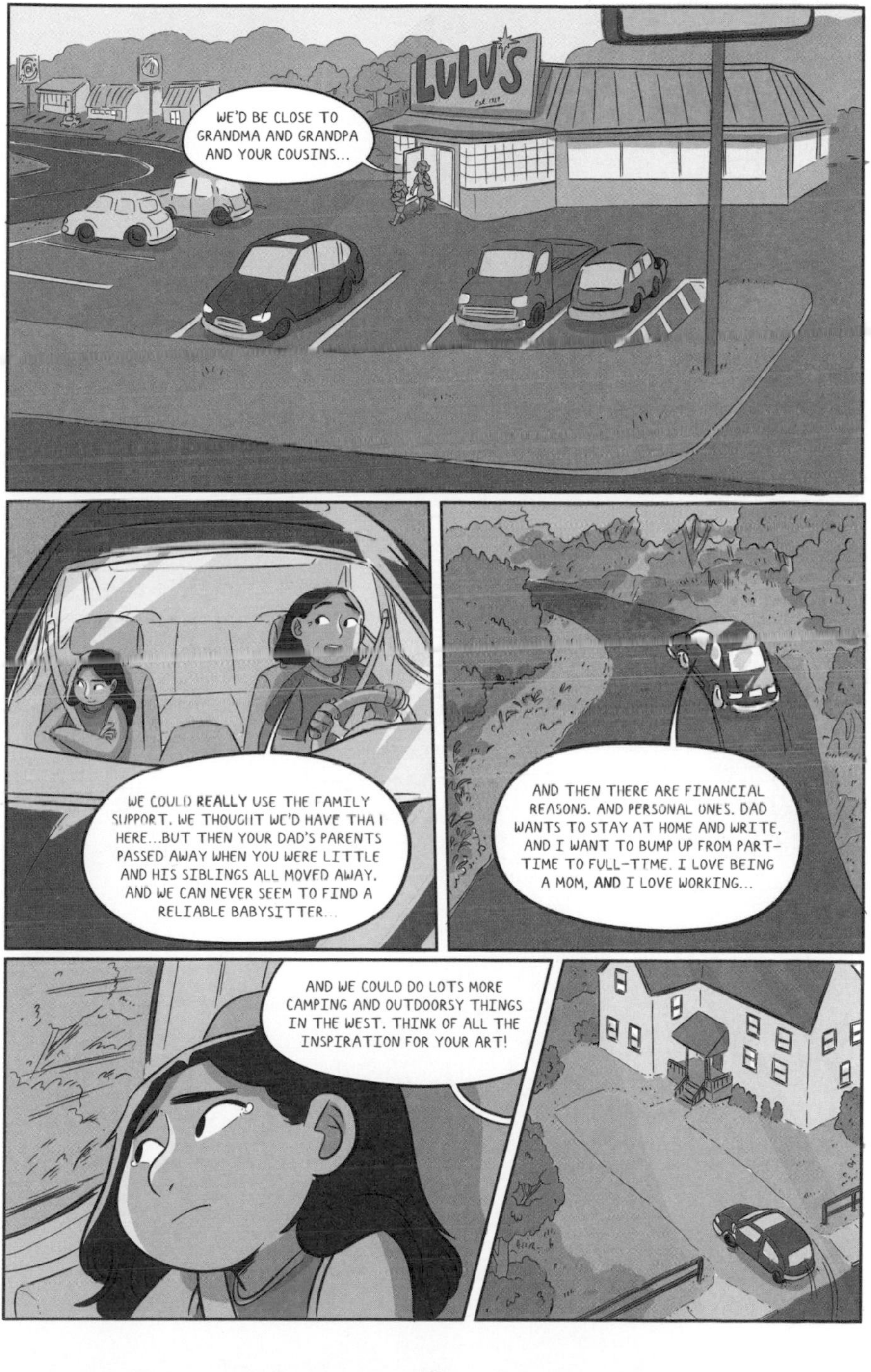
LULU'S
WE'D BE CLOSE TO GRANDMA AND GRANDPA AND YOUR COUSINS...
WE COULD **REALLY** USE THE FAMILY SUPPORT. WE THOUGHT WE'D HAVE THAT HERE...BUT THEN YOUR DAD'S PARENTS PASSED AWAY WHEN YOU WERE LITTLE AND HIS SIBLINGS ALL MOVED AWAY. AND WE CAN NEVER SEEM TO FIND A RELIABLE BABYSITTER...
AND THEN THERE ARE FINANCIAL REASONS. AND PERSONAL ONES. DAD WANTS TO STAY AT HOME AND WRITE, AND I WANT TO BUMP UP FROM PART-TIME TO FULL-TIME. I LOVE BEING A MOM, **AND** I LOVE WORKING...
AND WE COULD DO LOTS MORE CAMPING AND OUTDOORSY THINGS IN THE WEST. THINK OF ALL THE INSPIRATION FOR YOUR ART!

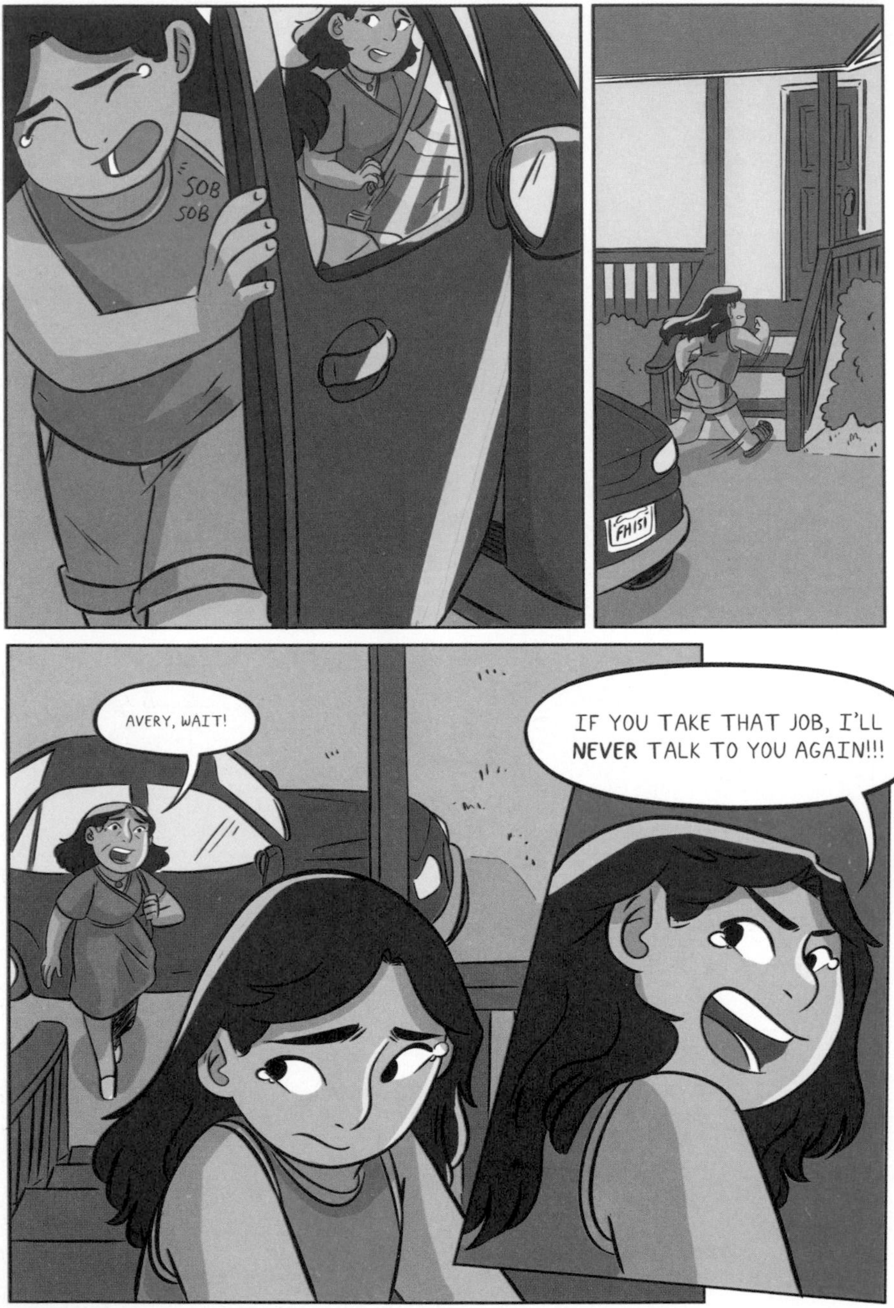
SOB
SOB
FHISI
AVERY, WAIT!
IF YOU TAKE THAT JOB, I'LL **NEVER** TALK TO YOU AGAIN!!!

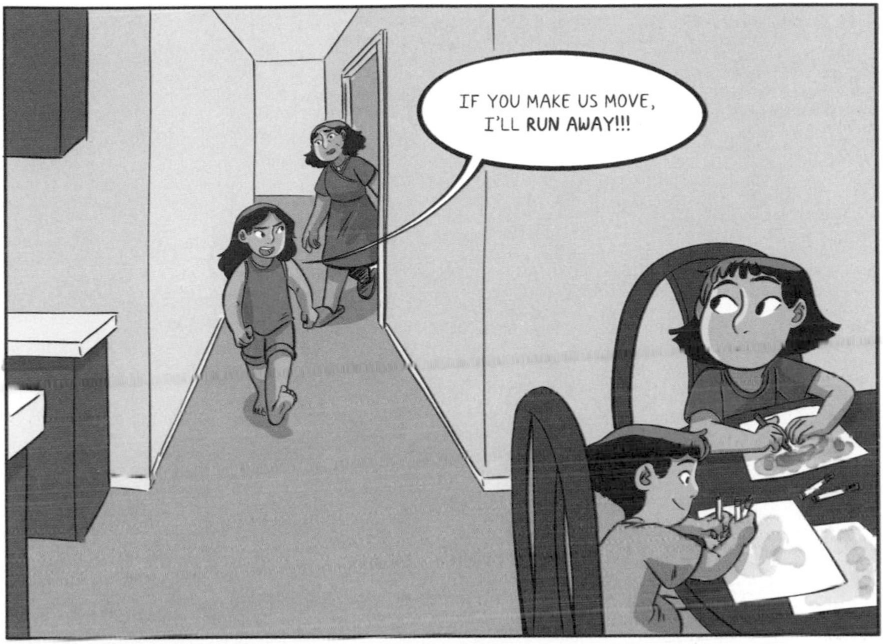
IF YOU MAKE US MOVE, I'LL RUN AWAY!!!

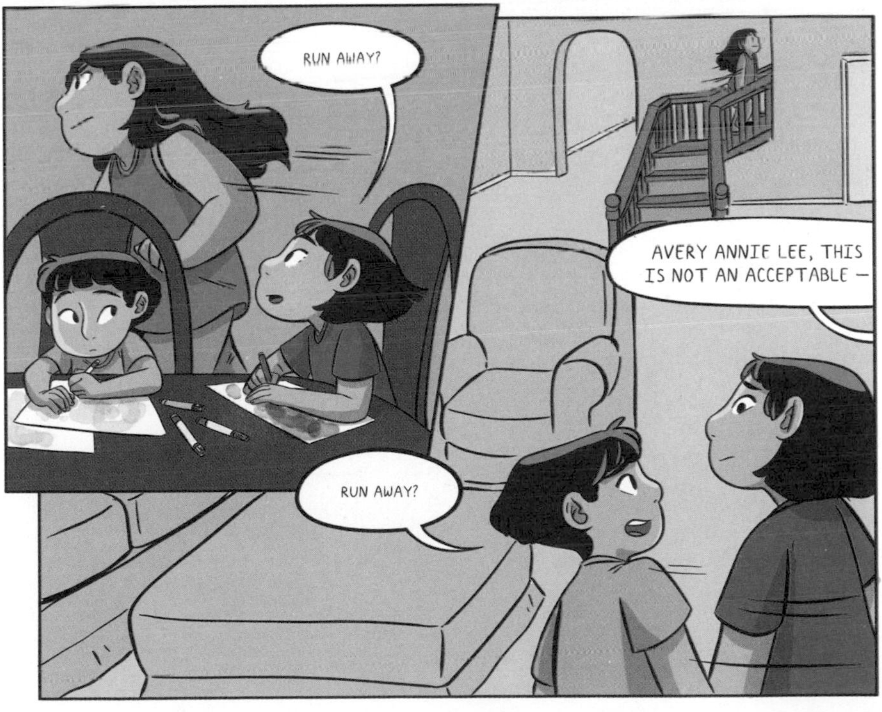
RUN AWAY?
AVERY ANNIE LEE, THIS IS NOT AN ACCEPTABLE —
RUN AWAY?

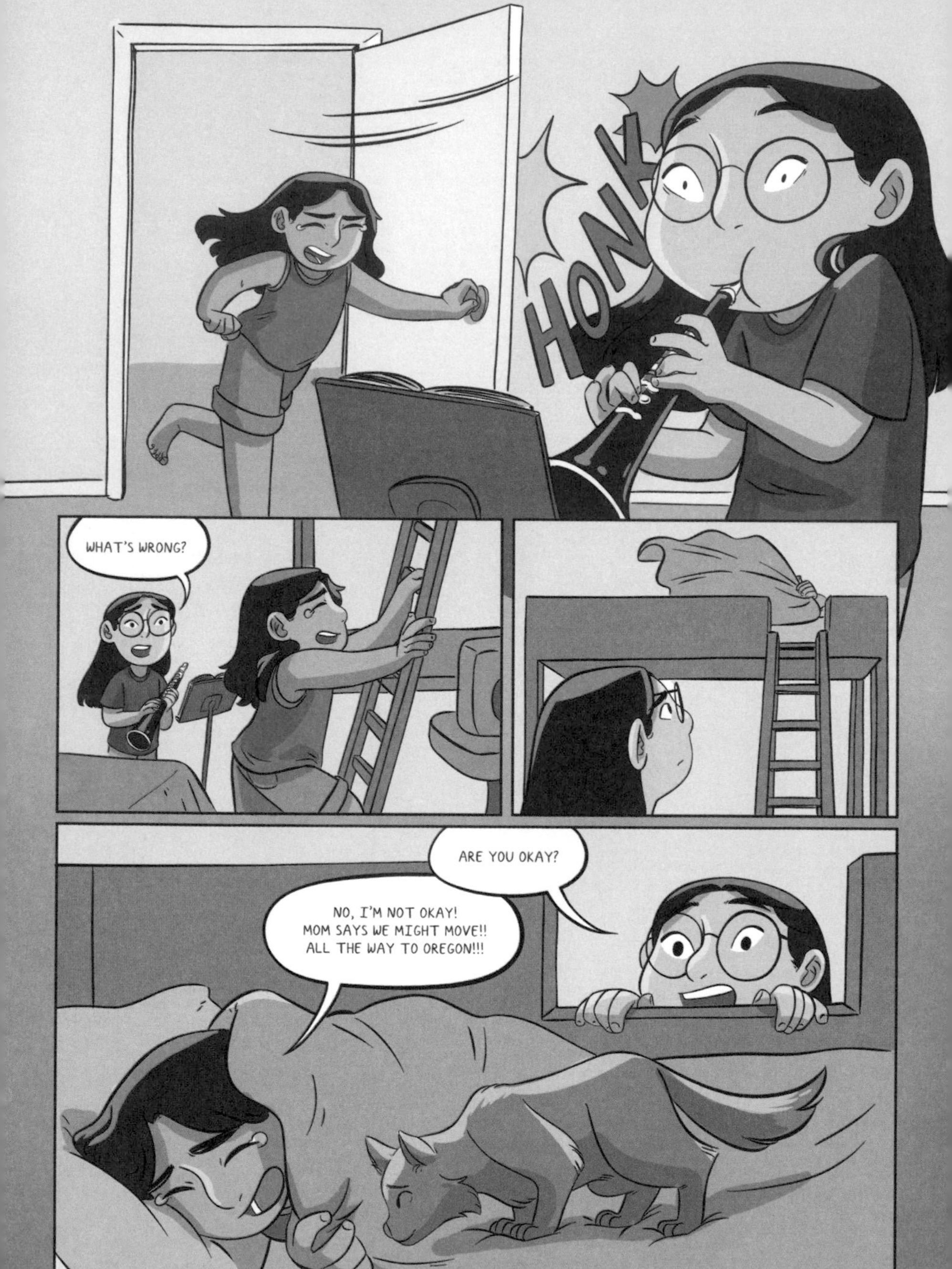
HONK
WHAT'S WRONG?
ARE YOU OKAY?
NO, I'M NOT OKAY!
MOM SAYS WE MIGHT MOVE!!
ALL THE WAY TO OREGON!!!

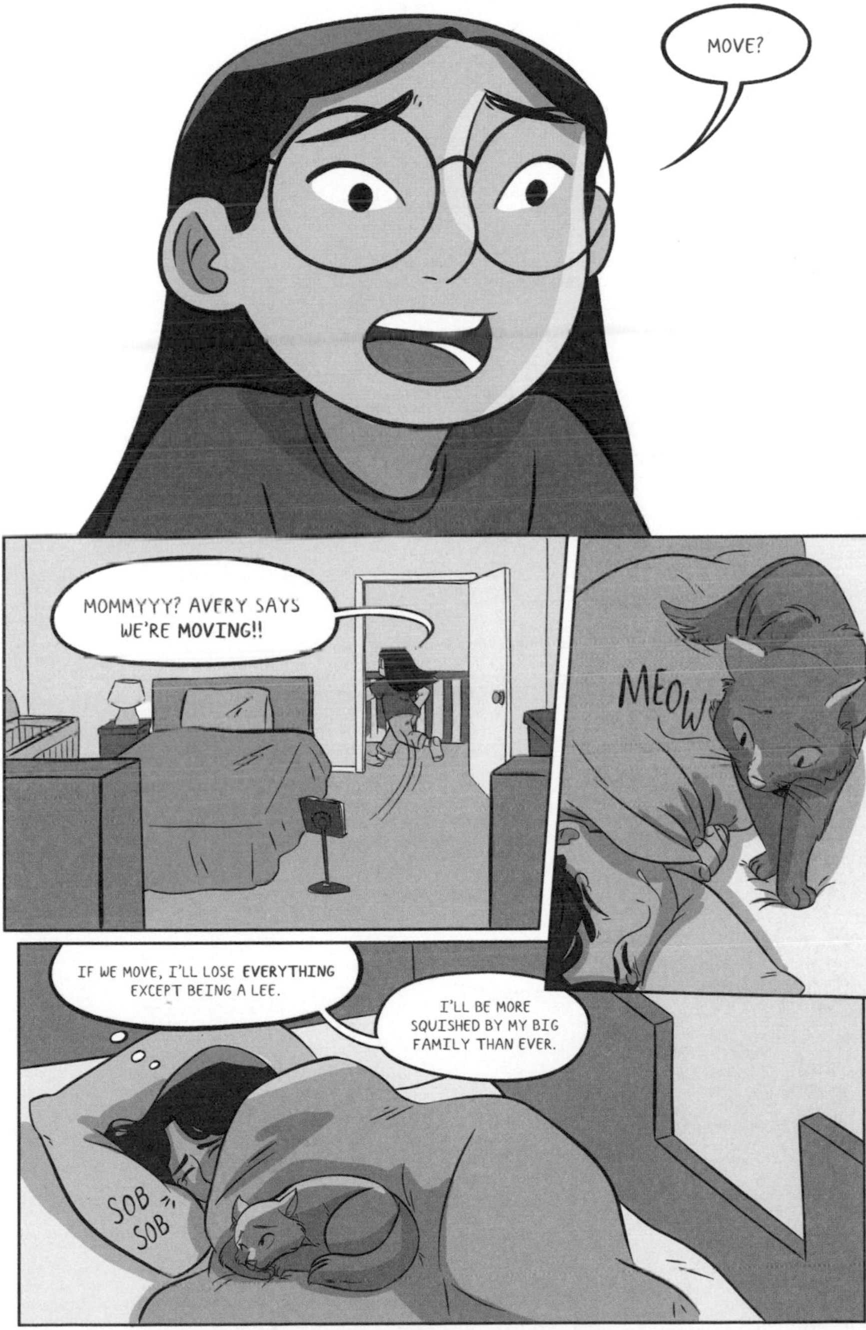
MOVE?
MOMMYYY? AVERY SAYS WE'RE **MOVING!!**
MEOW
IF WE MOVE, I'LL LOSE **EVERYTHING** EXCEPT BEING A LEE.
I'LL BE MORE SQUISHED BY MY BIG FAMILY THAN EVER.
SOB SOB

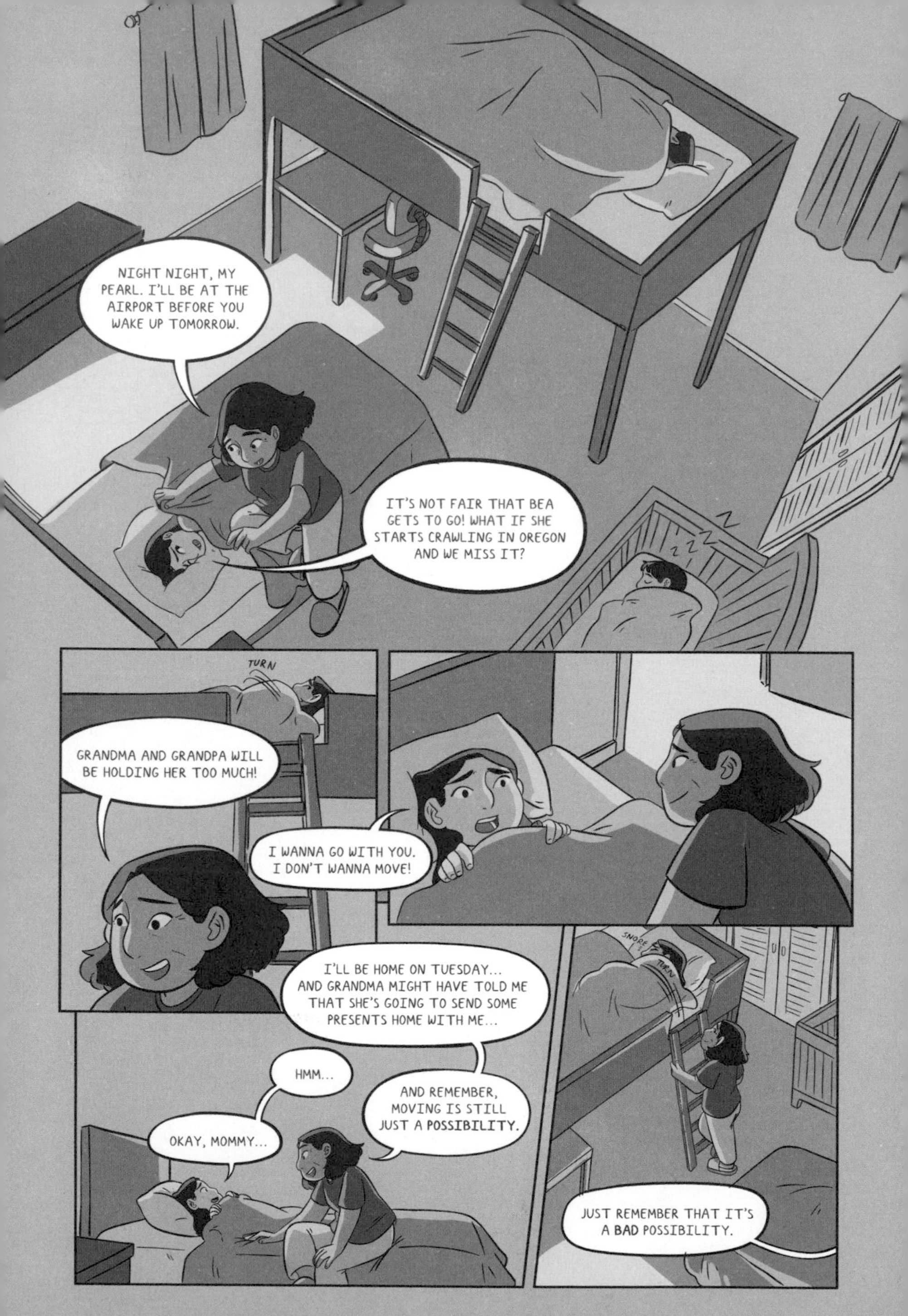
NIGHT NIGHT, MY PEARL. I'LL BE AT THE AIRPORT BEFORE YOU WAKE UP TOMORROW.
IT'S NOT FAIR THAT BEA GETS TO GO! WHAT IF SHE STARTS CRAWLING IN OREGON AND WE MISS IT?
Z Z Z
TURN
GRANDMA AND GRANDPA WILL BE HOLDING HER TOO MUCH!
I WANNA GO WITH YOU. I DON'T WANNA MOVE!
I'LL BE HOME ON TUESDAY... AND GRANDMA MIGHT HAVE TOLD ME THAT SHE'S GOING TO SEND SOME PRESENTS HOME WITH ME...
HMM...
AND REMEMBER, MOVING IS STILL JUST A **POSSIBILITY**.
OKAY, MOMMY...
SNORE
TURN
JUST REMEMBER THAT IT'S A **BAD** POSSIBILITY.

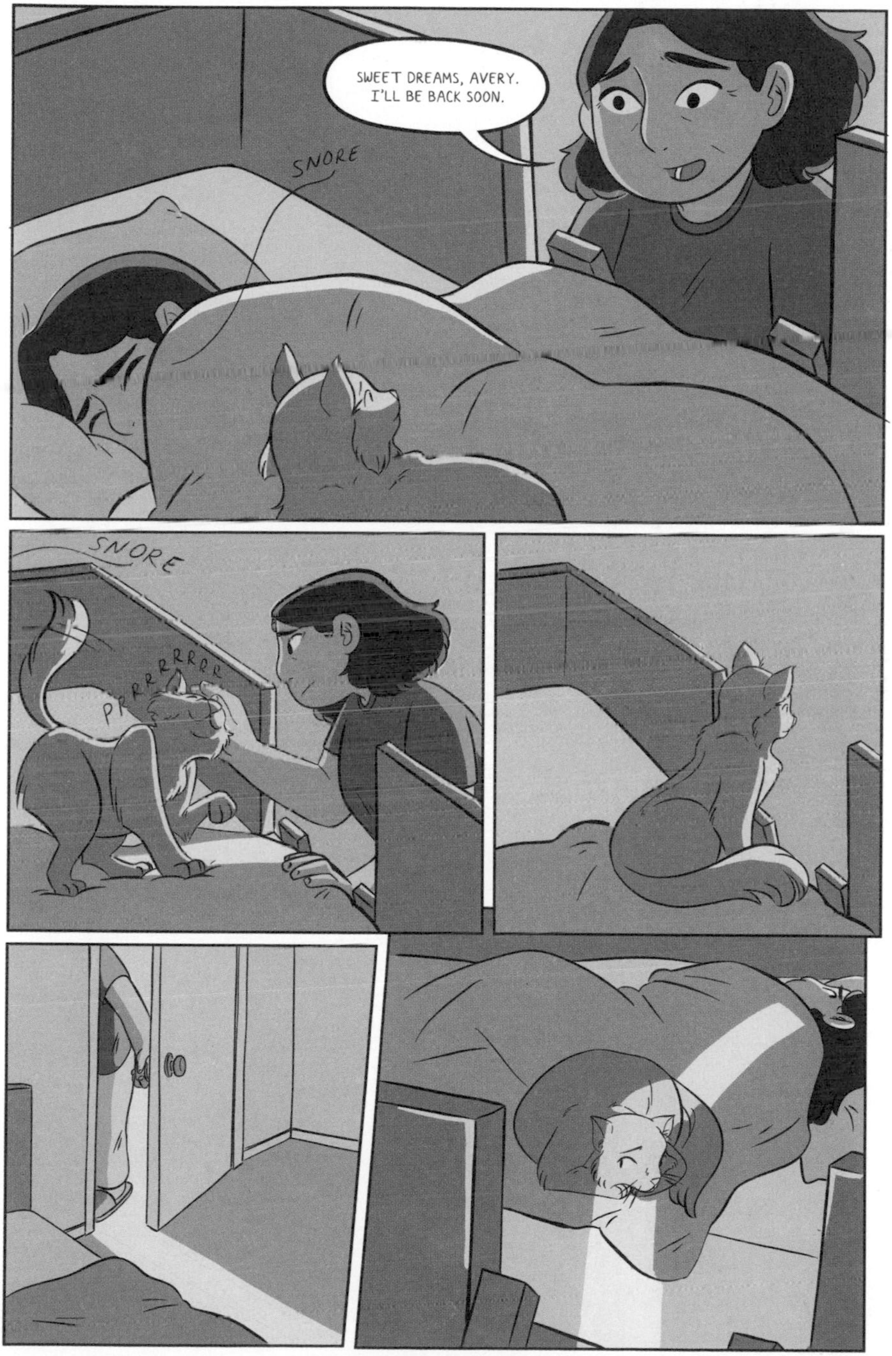
SWEET DREAMS, AVERY. I'LL BE BACK SOON.
SNORE
SNORE
PRRRRRRRRR

Chapter Nine

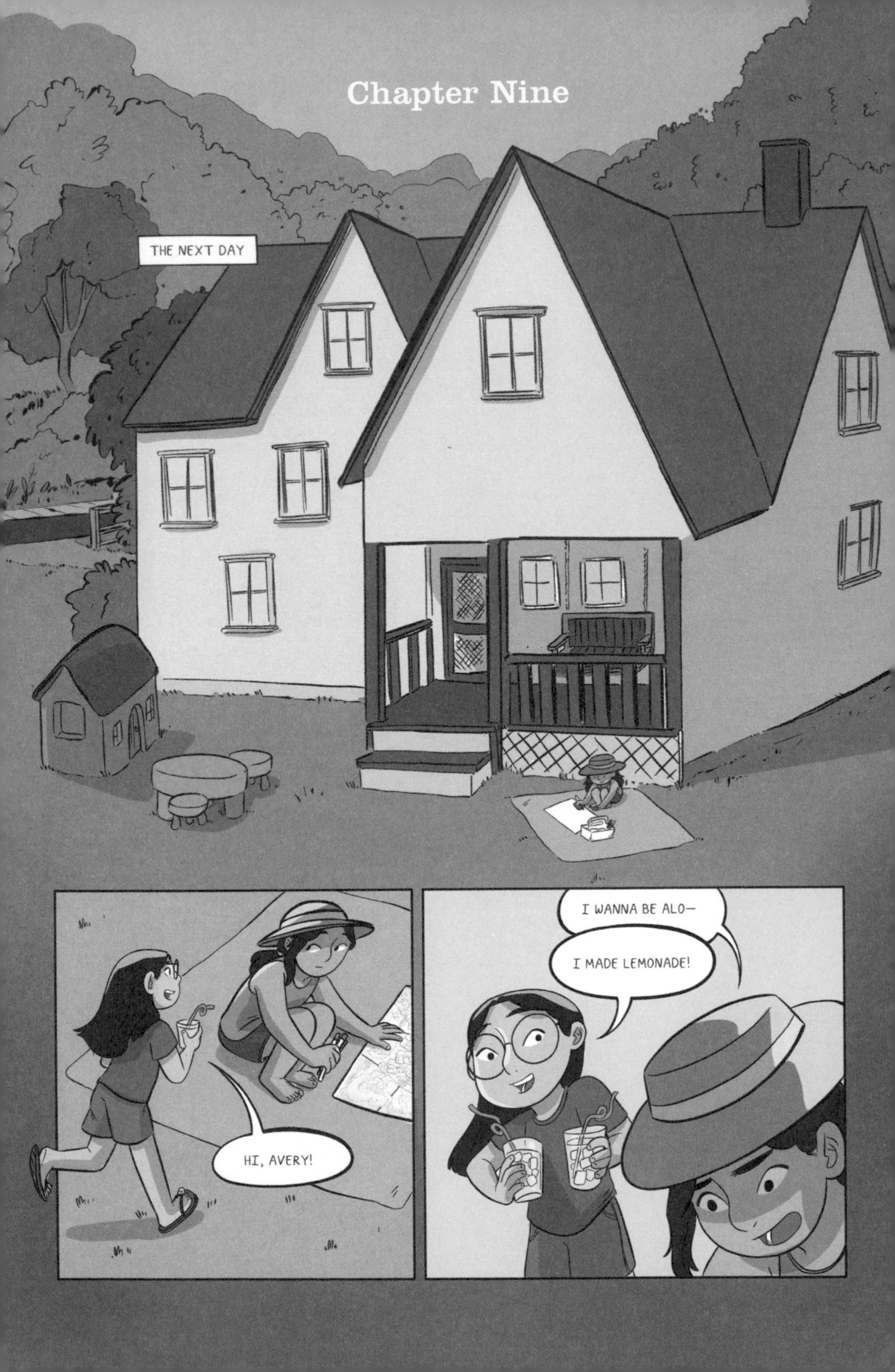
THE NEXT DAY
HI, AVERY!
I WANNA BE ALO—
I MADE LEMONADE!

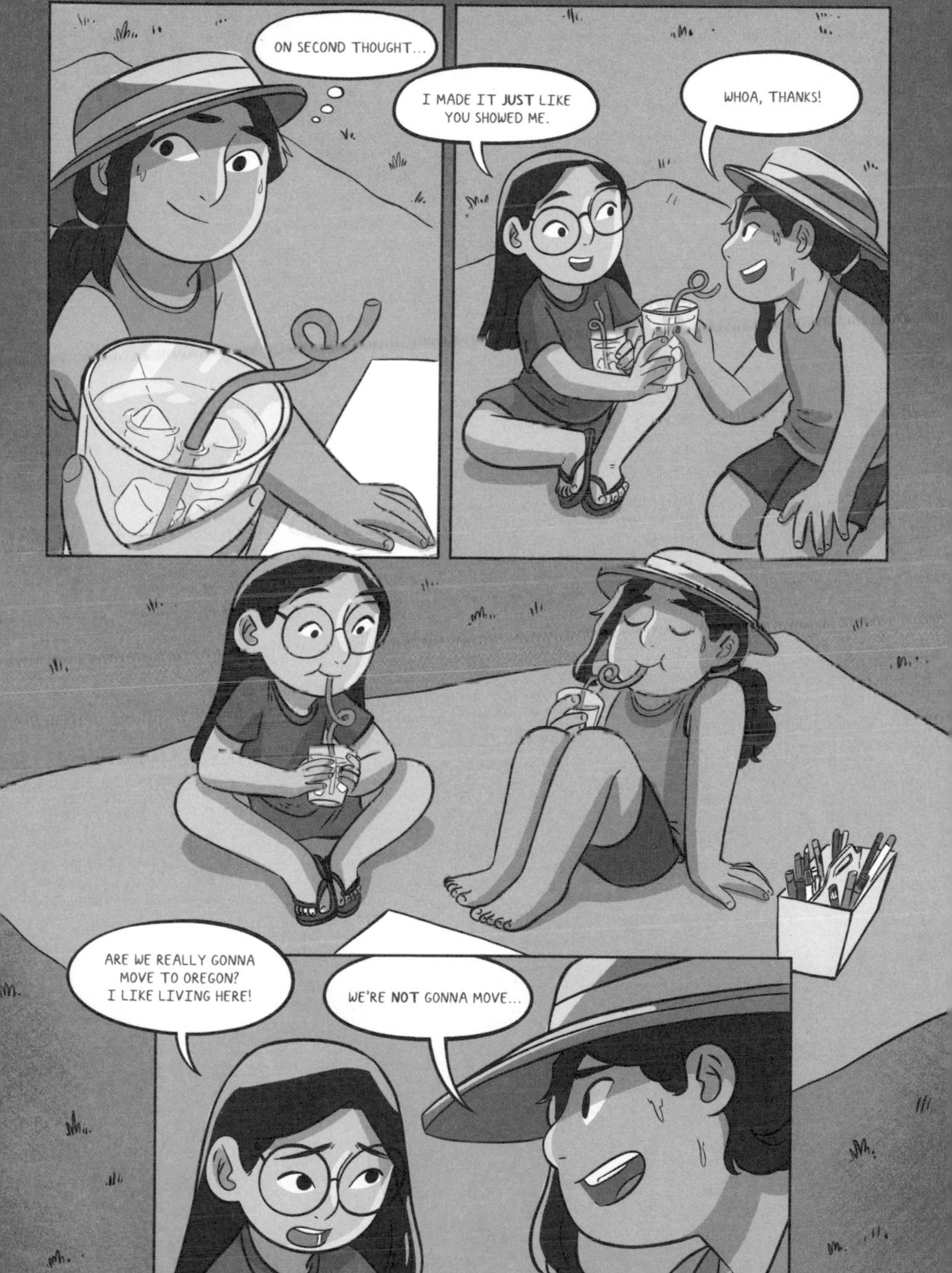
ON SECOND THOUGHT...
I MADE IT JUST LIKE YOU SHOWED ME.
WHOA, THANKS!
ARE WE REALLY GONNA MOVE TO OREGON? I LIKE LIVING HERE!
WE'RE NOT GONNA MOVE...

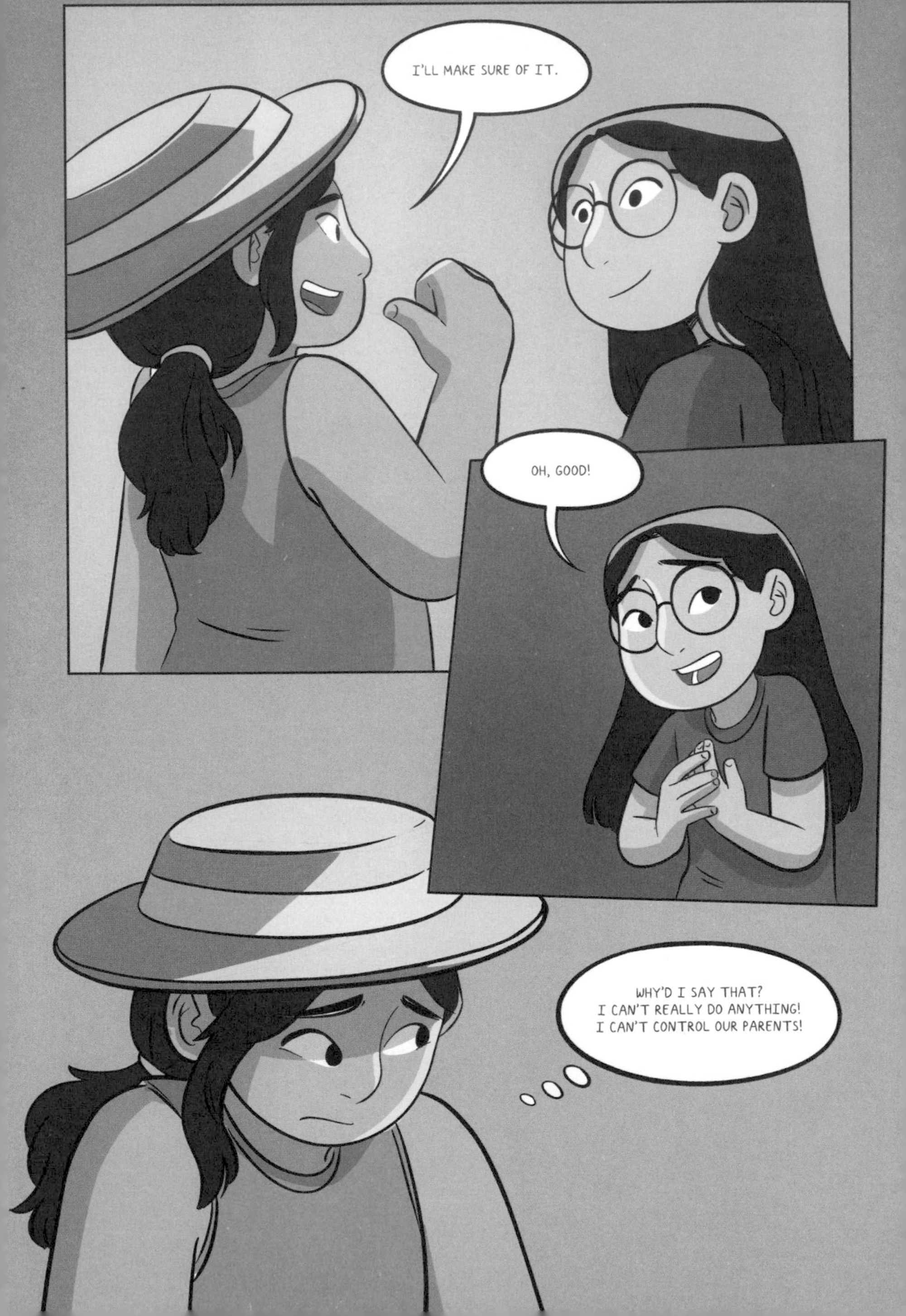
I'LL MAKE SURE OF IT.
OH, GOOD!
WHY'D I SAY THAT?
I CAN'T REALLY DO ANYTHING!
I CAN'T CONTROL OUR PARENTS!

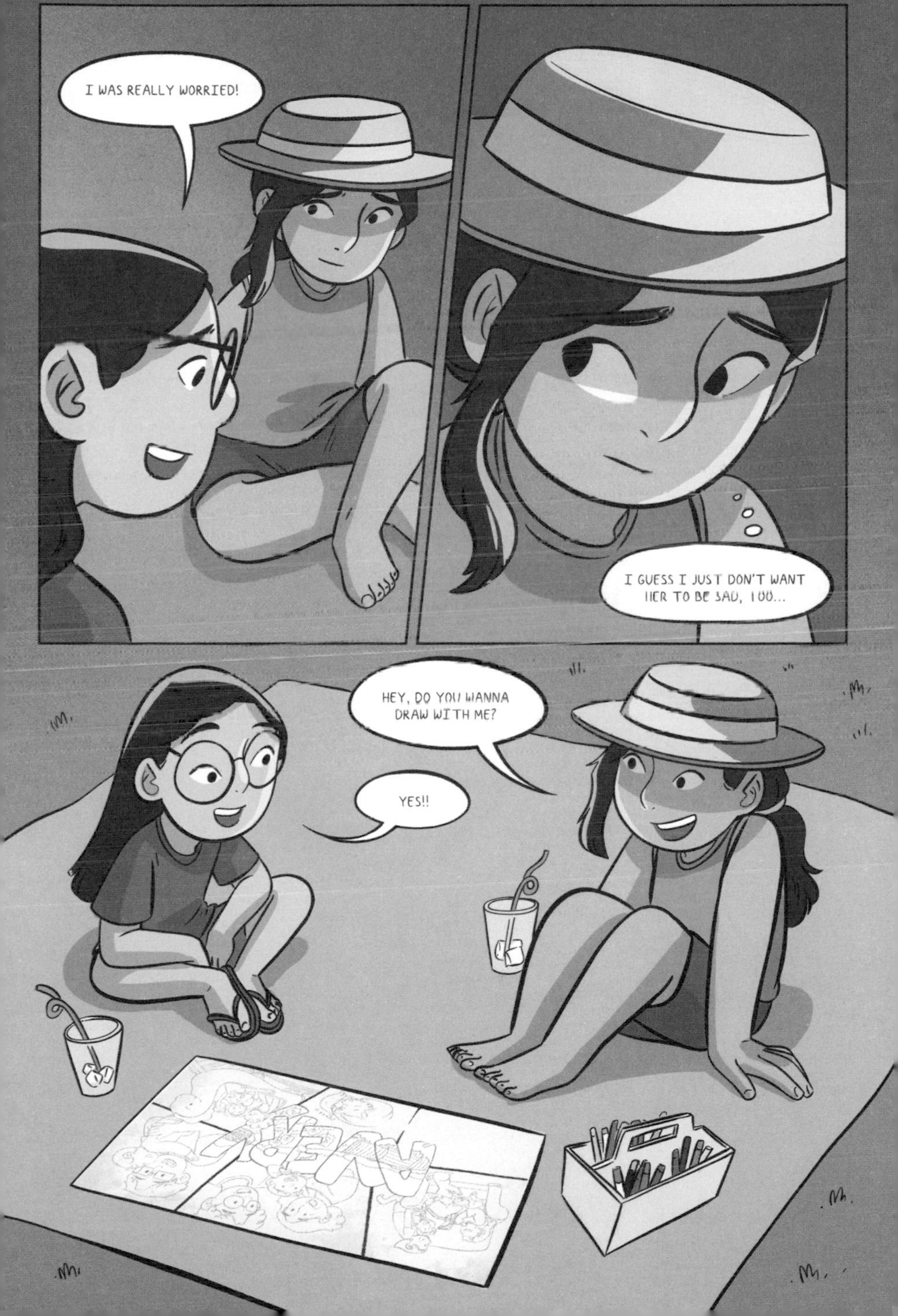
I WAS REALLY WORRIED!
I GUESS I JUST DON'T WANT HER TO BE SAD, TOO...
HEY, DO YOU WANNA DRAW WITH ME?
YES!!

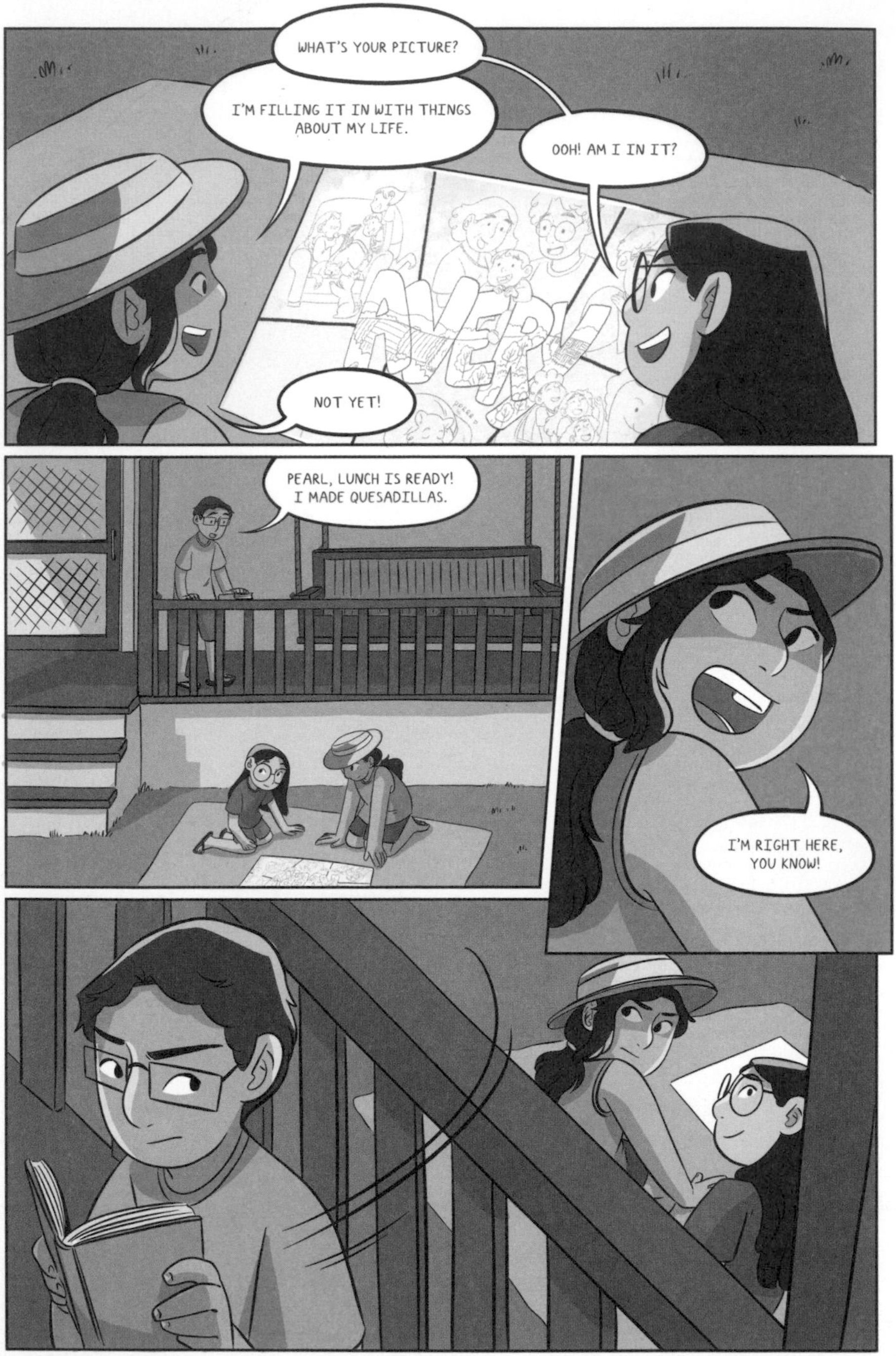
WHAT'S YOUR PICTURE?
I'M FILLING IT IN WITH THINGS ABOUT MY LIFE.
OOH! AM I IN IT?
NOT YET!
AVERY
PEARL, LUNCH IS READY! I MADE QUESADILLAS.
I'M RIGHT HERE, YOU KNOW!

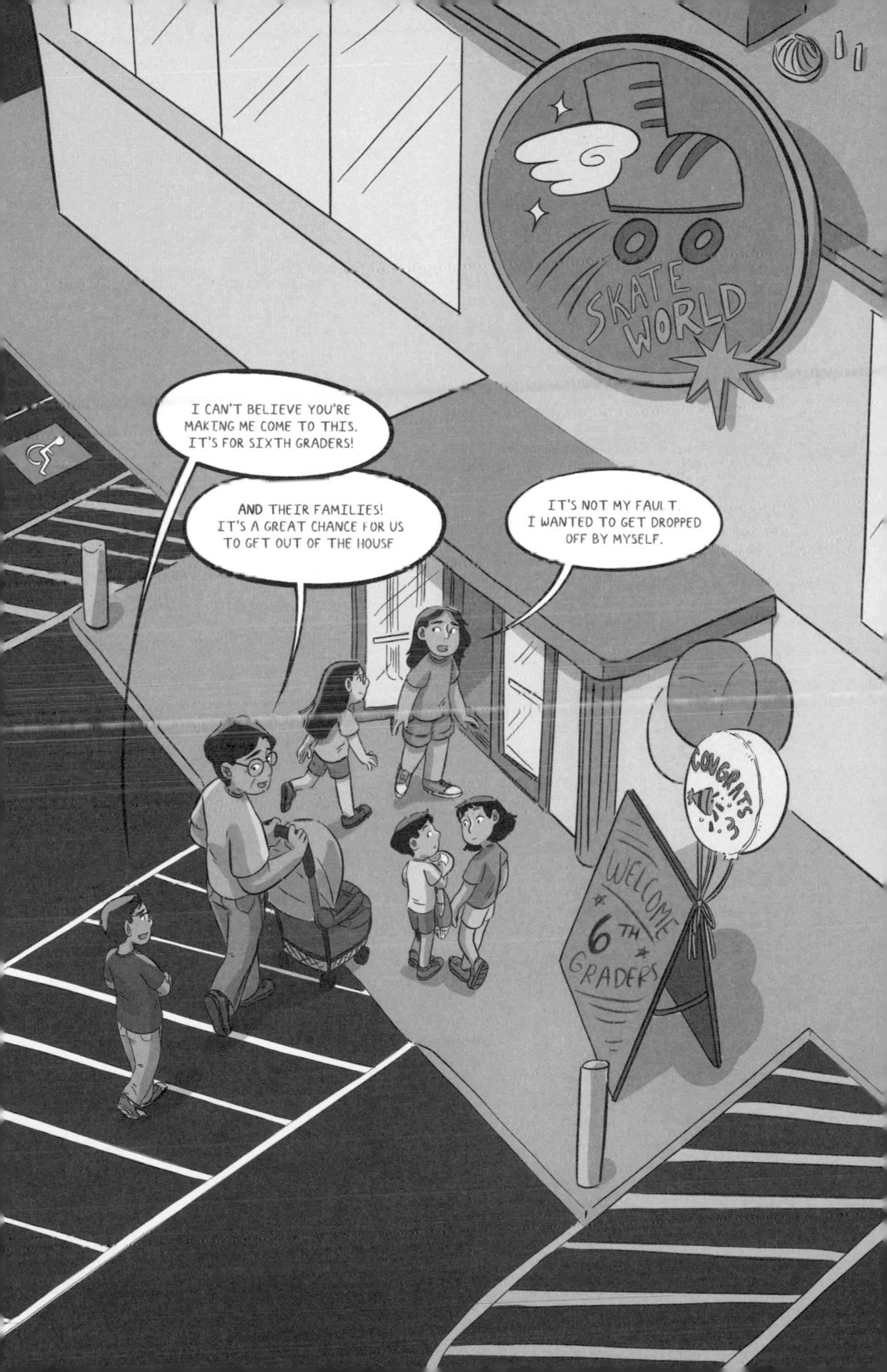
SKATE WORLD
I CAN'T BELIEVE YOU'RE MAKING ME COME TO THIS. IT'S FOR SIXTH GRADERS!
AND THEIR FAMILIES! IT'S A GREAT CHANCE FOR US TO GET OUT OF THE HOUSE.
IT'S NOT MY FAULT. I WANTED TO GET DROPPED OFF BY MYSELF.
CONGRATS
WELCOME 6TH GRADERS

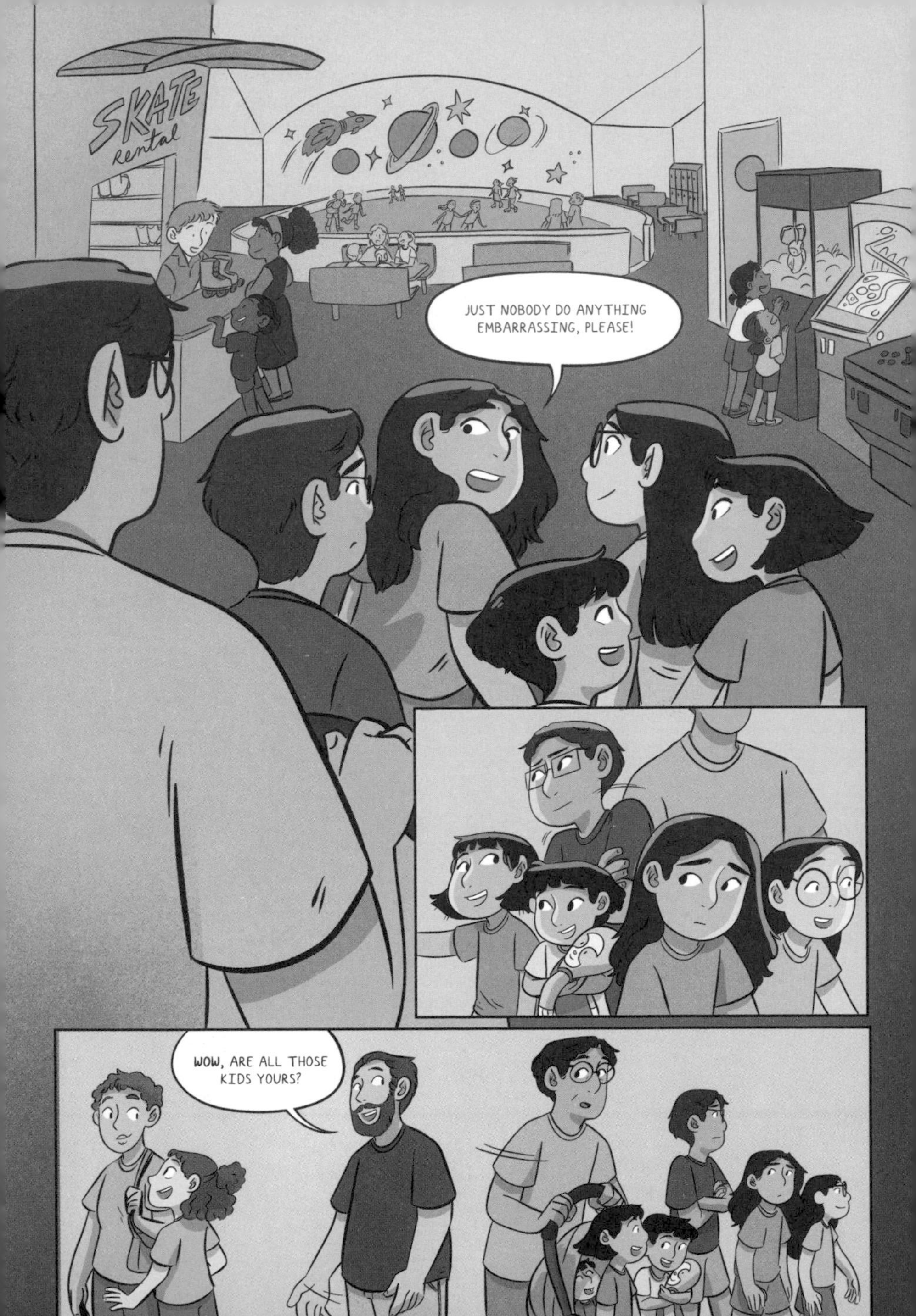
SKATE rental
JUST NOBODY DO ANYTHING EMBARRASSING, PLEASE!
WOW, ARE ALL THOSE KIDS YOURS?

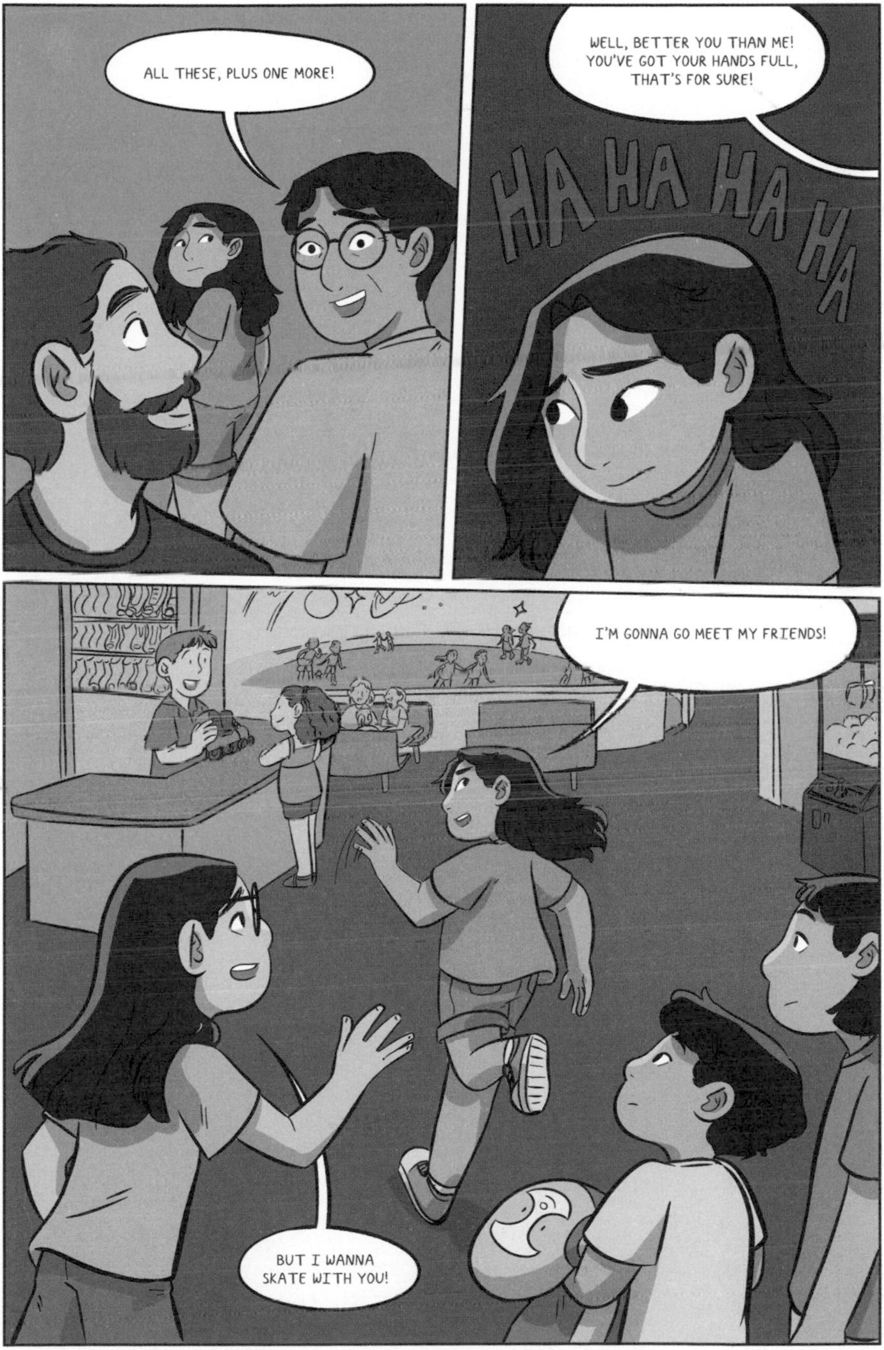
ALL THESE, PLUS ONE MORE!
WELL, BETTER YOU THAN ME! YOU'VE GOT YOUR HANDS FULL, THAT'S FOR SURE!
HA HA HA HA HA HA
I'M GONNA GO MEET MY FRIENDS!
BUT I WANNA SKATE WITH YOU!

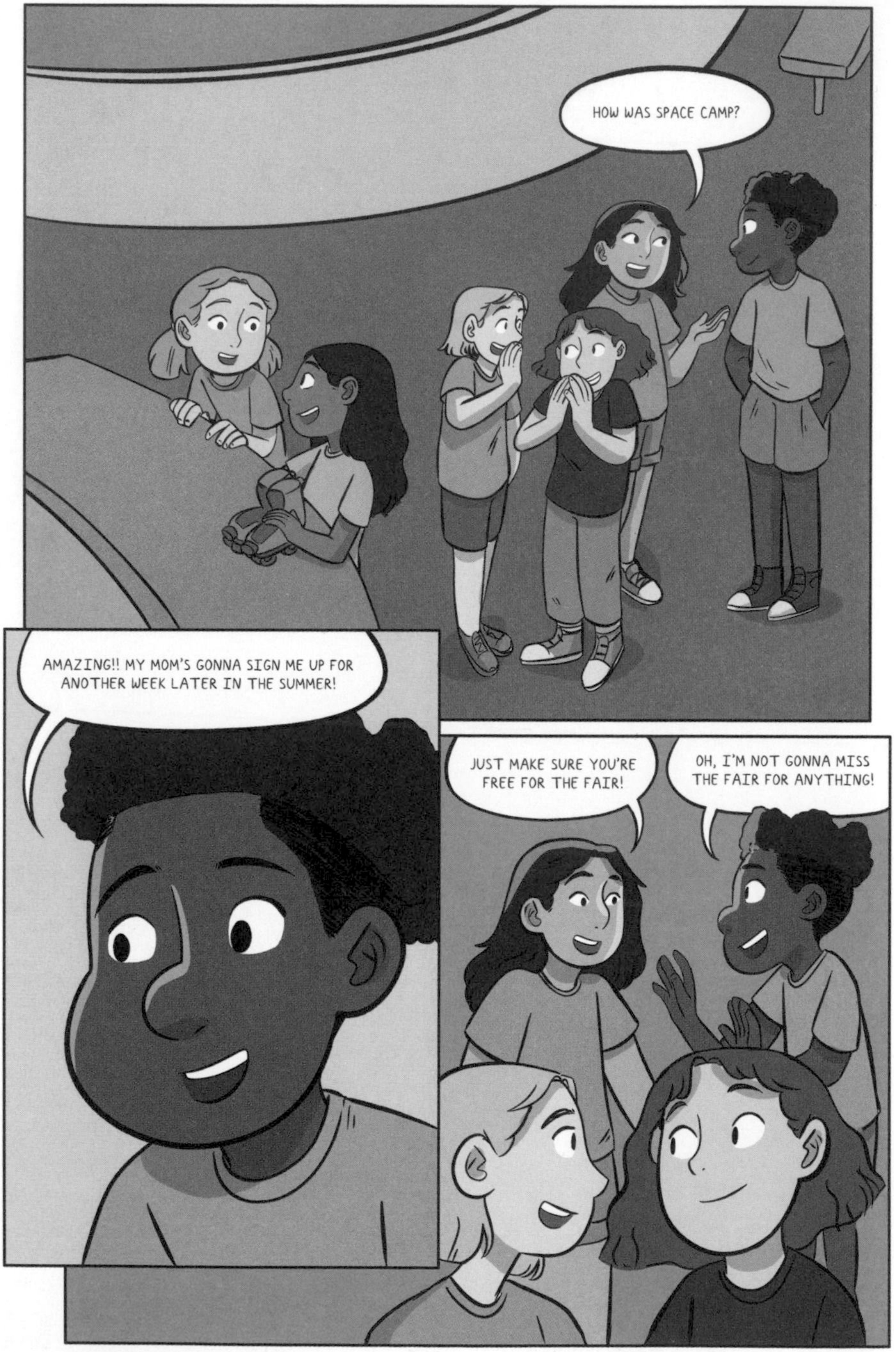
HOW WAS SPACE CAMP?
AMAZING!! MY MOM'S GONNA SIGN ME UP FOR ANOTHER WEEK LATER IN THE SUMMER!
JUST MAKE SURE YOU'RE FREE FOR THE FAIR!
OH, I'M NOT GONNA MISS THE FAIR FOR ANYTHING!

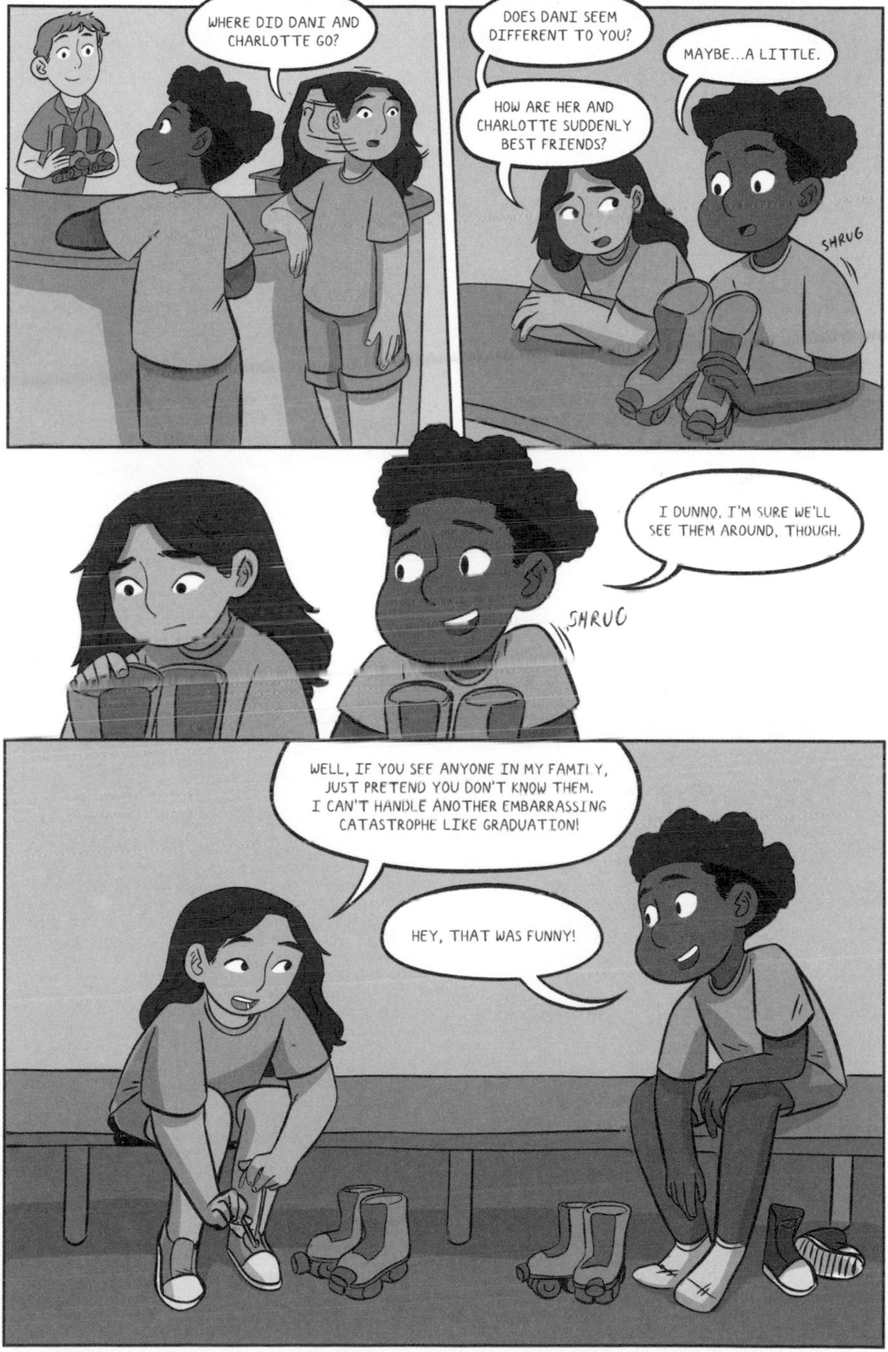

WHERE DID DANI AND CHARLOTTE GO?
DOES DANI SEEM DIFFERENT TO YOU?
HOW ARE HER AND CHARLOTTE SUDDENLY BEST FRIENDS?
MAYBE...A LITTLE.
SHRUG
I DUNNO. I'M SURE WE'LL SEE THEM AROUND, THOUGH.
SHRUG
WELL, IF YOU SEE ANYONE IN MY FAMILY, JUST PRETEND YOU DON'T KNOW THEM. I CAN'T HANDLE ANOTHER EMBARRASSING CATASTROPHE LIKE GRADUATION!
HEY, THAT WAS FUNNY!

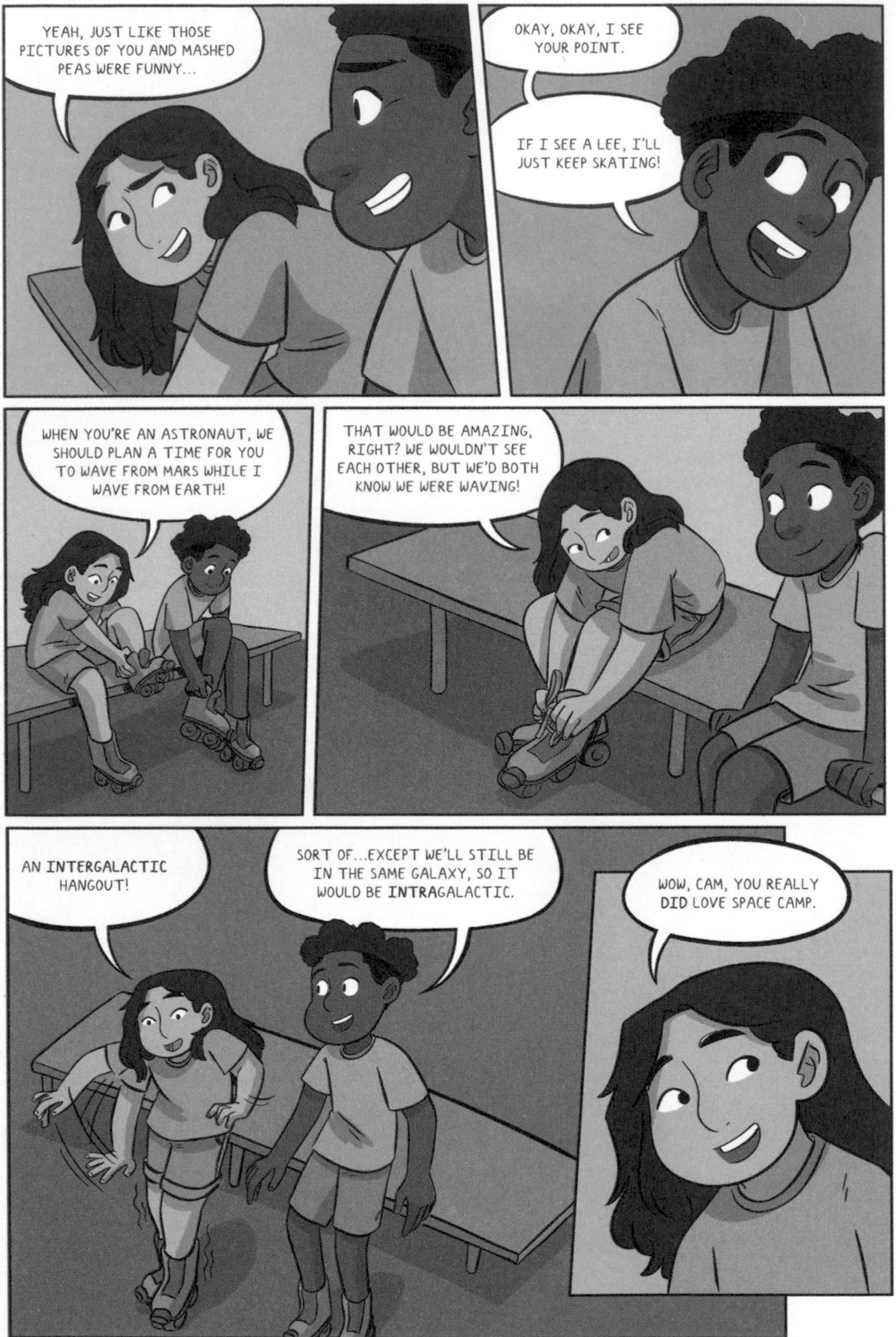
YEAH, JUST LIKE THOSE PICTURES OF YOU AND MASHED PEAS WERE FUNNY...
OKAY, OKAY, I SEE YOUR POINT.
IF I SEE A LEE, I'LL JUST KEEP SKATING!
WHEN YOU'RE AN ASTRONAUT, WE SHOULD PLAN A TIME FOR YOU TO WAVE FROM MARS WHILE I WAVE FROM EARTH!
THAT WOULD BE AMAZING, RIGHT? WE WOULDN'T SEE EACH OTHER, BUT WE'D BOTH KNOW WE WERE WAVING!
AN INTERGALACTIC HANGOUT!
SORT OF...EXCEPT WE'LL STILL BE IN THE SAME GALAXY, SO IT WOULD BE INTRAGALACTIC.
WOW, CAM, YOU REALLY DID LOVE SPACE CAMP.

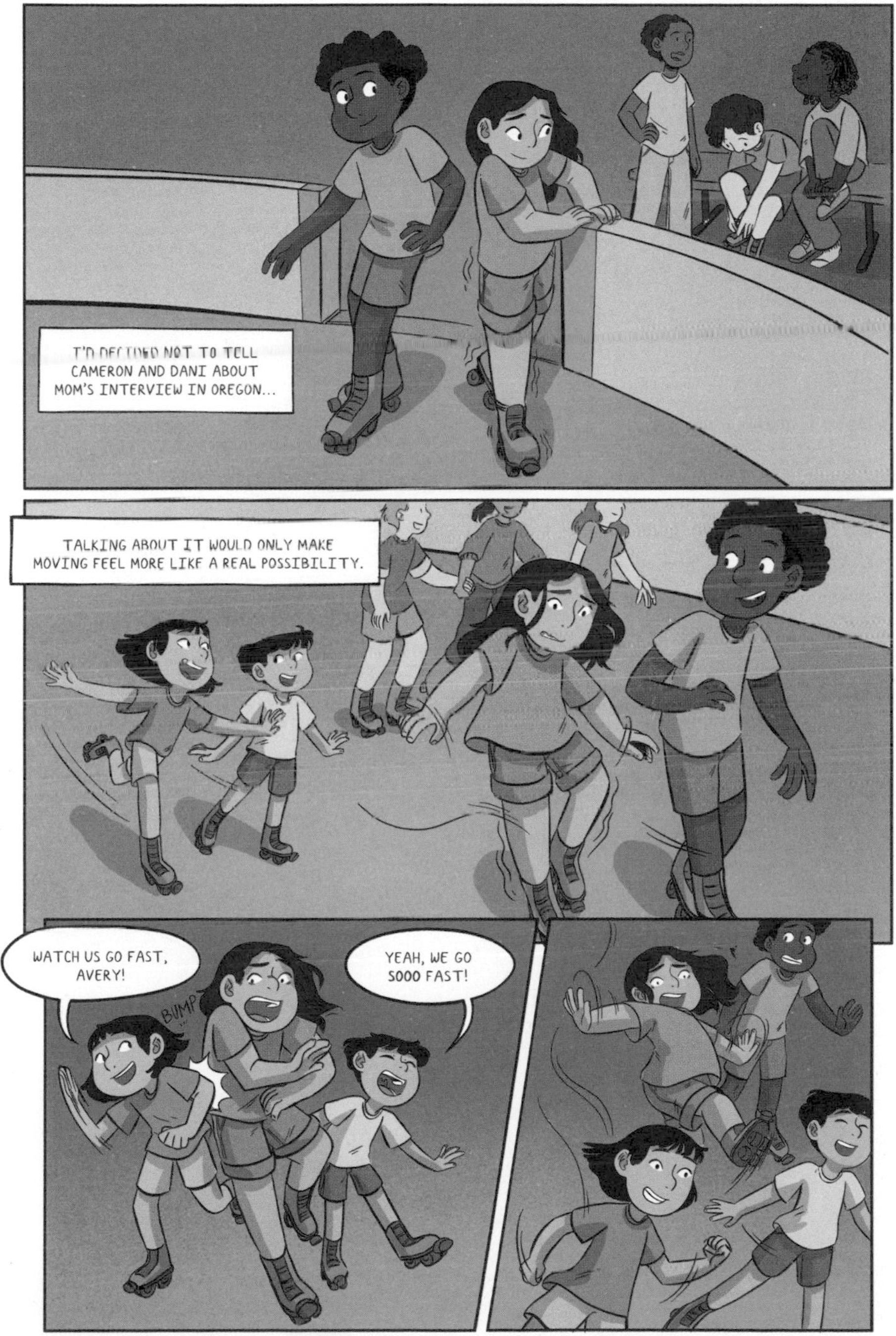
I'D DECIDED NOT TO TELL CAMERON AND DANI ABOUT MOM'S INTERVIEW IN OREGON...
TALKING ABOUT IT WOULD ONLY MAKE MOVING FEEL MORE LIKE A REAL POSSIBILITY.
WATCH US GO FAST, AVERY!
YEAH, WE GO SOOO FAST!
BUMP

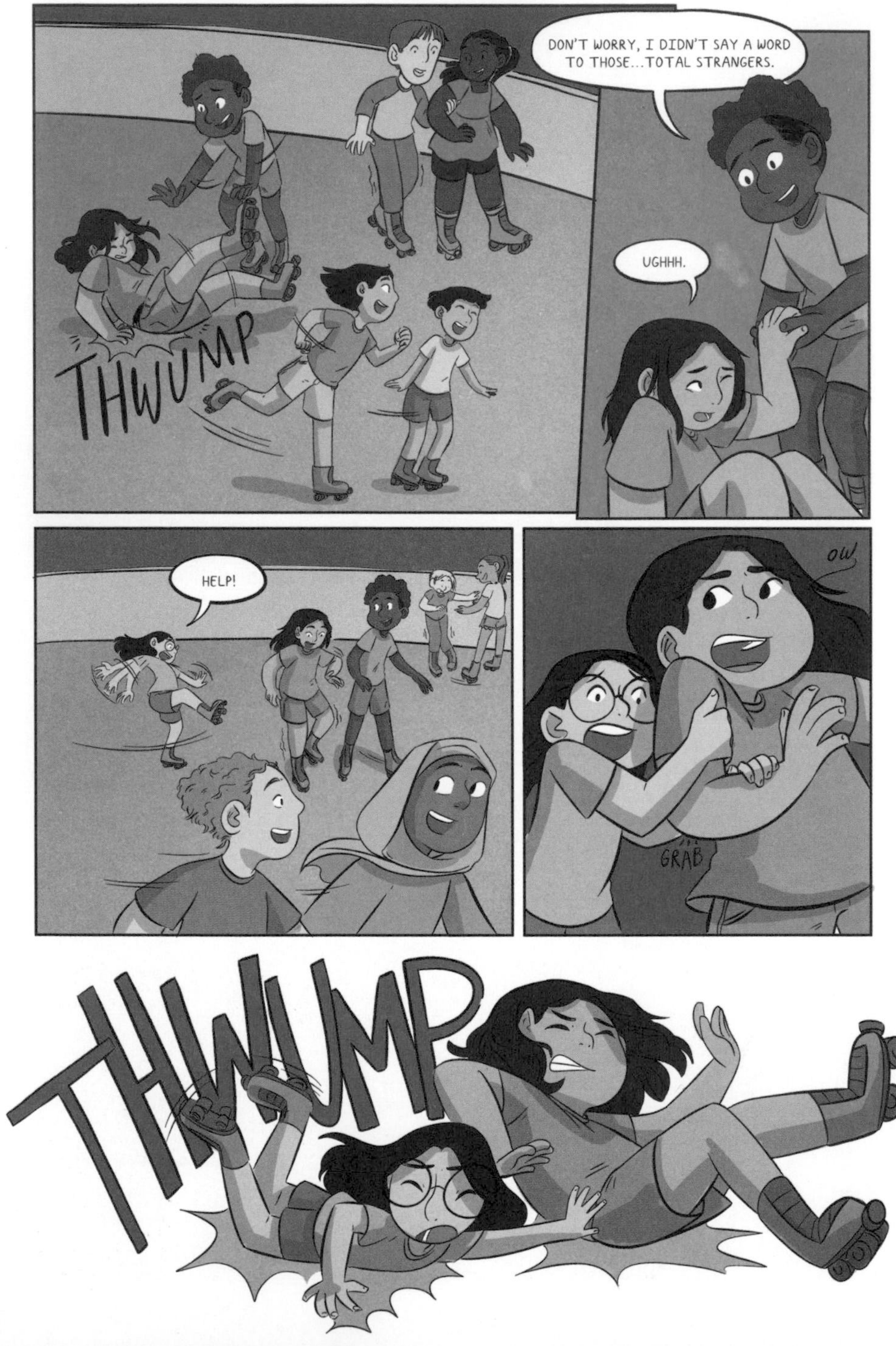
THWUMP
DON'T WORRY, I DIDN'T SAY A WORD TO THOSE...TOTAL STRANGERS.
UGHHH.
HELP!
OW
GRAB
THWUMP

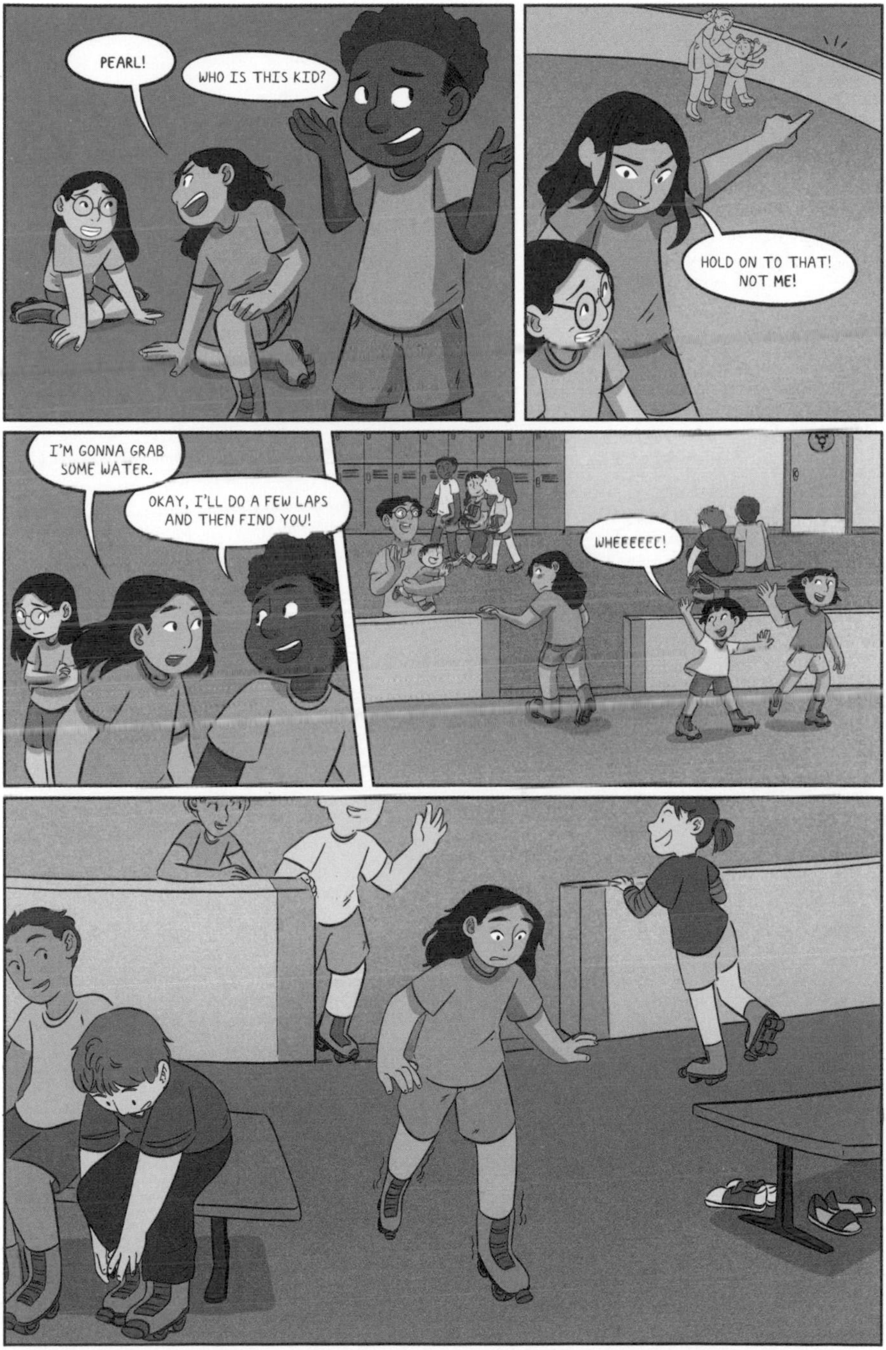
PEARL!
WHO IS THIS KID?
HOLD ON TO THAT! NOT ME!
I'M GONNA GRAB SOME WATER.
OKAY, I'LL DO A FEW LAPS AND THEN FIND YOU!
WHEEEEEE!

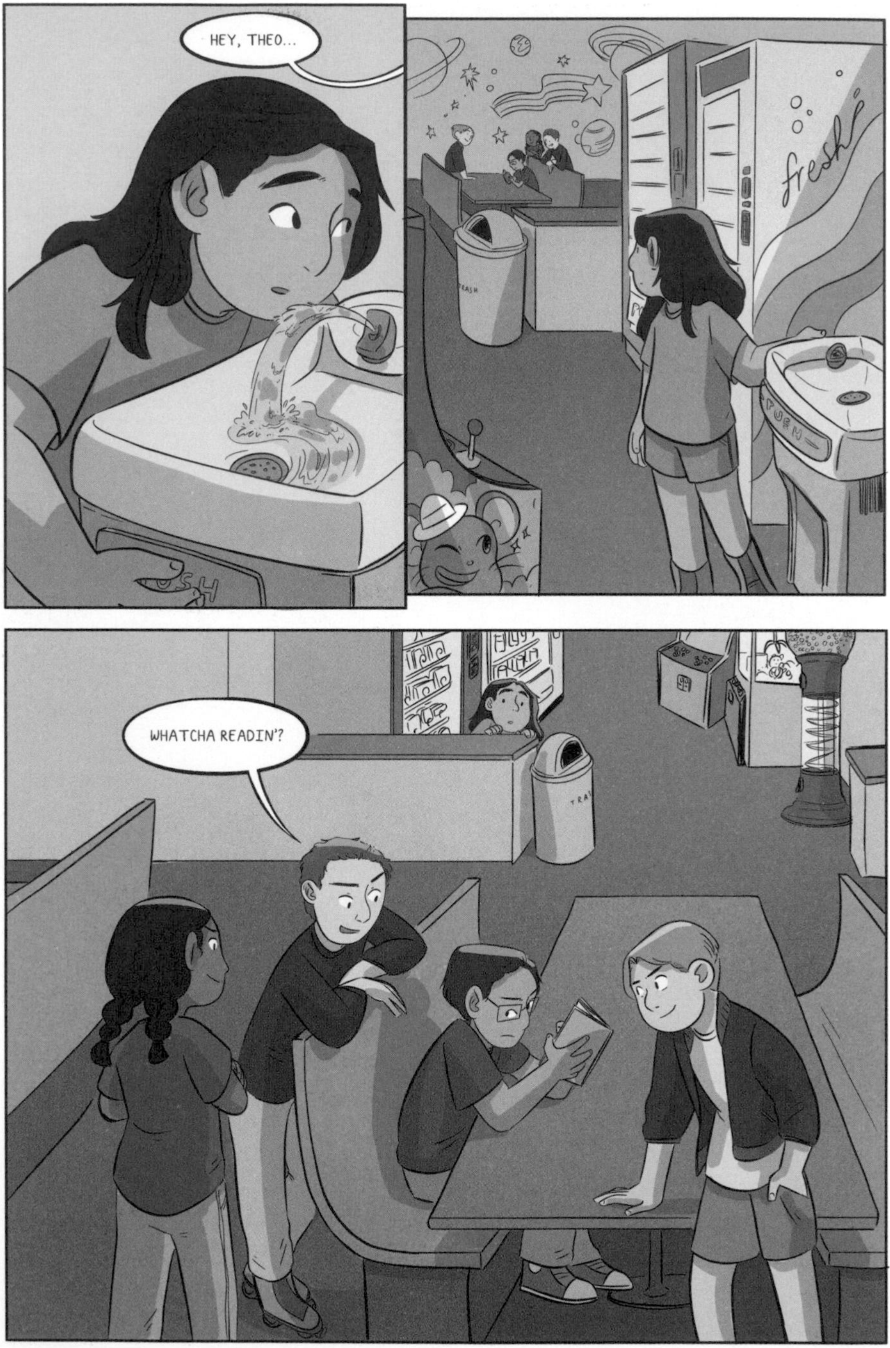
HEY, THEO...
fresh
WHATCHA READIN'?

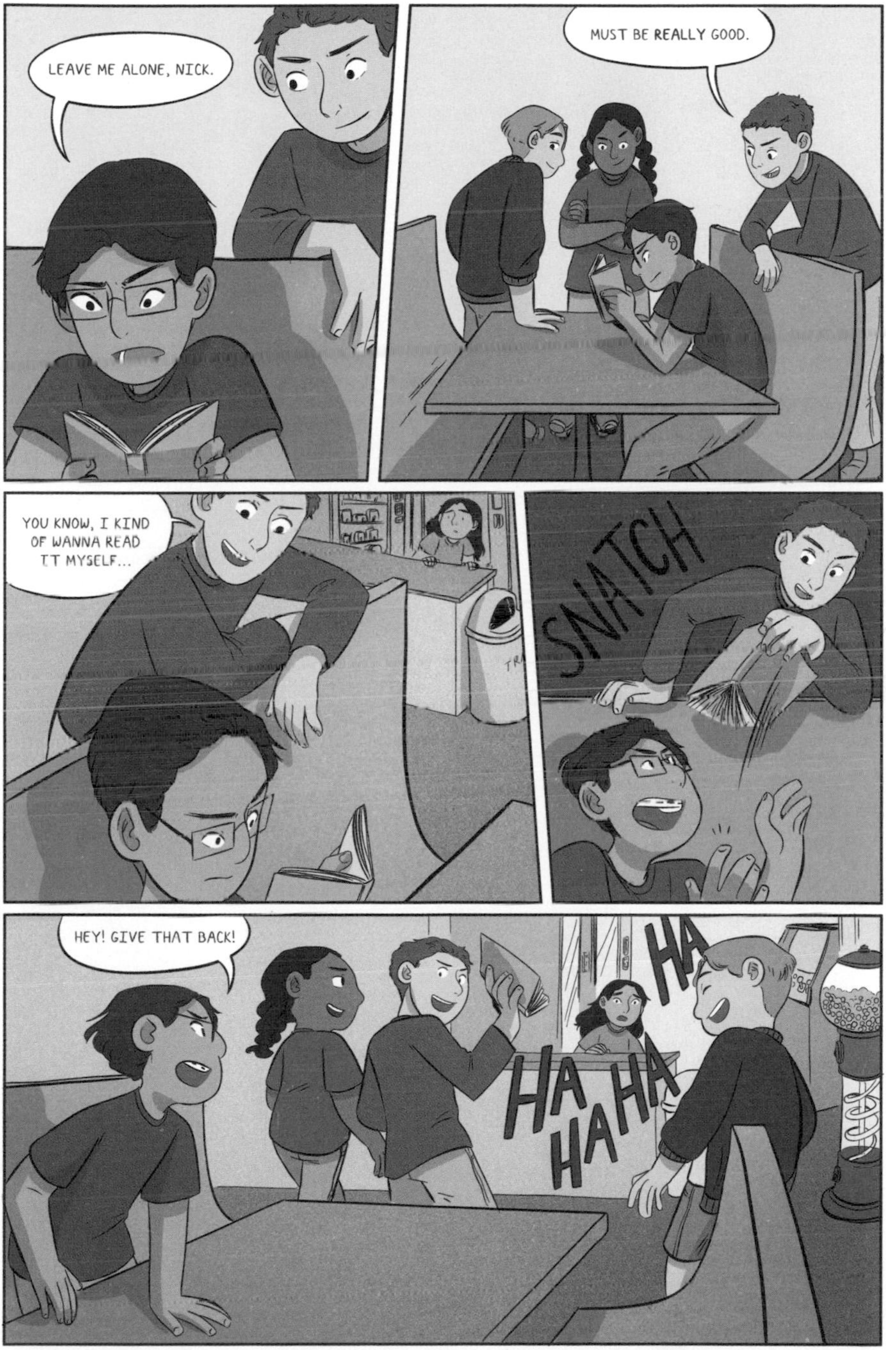
LEAVE ME ALONE, NICK.
MUST BE REALLY GOOD.
YOU KNOW, I KIND OF WANNA READ IT MYSELF...
SNATCH
HEY! GIVE THAT BACK!
HA HA HA HA HA

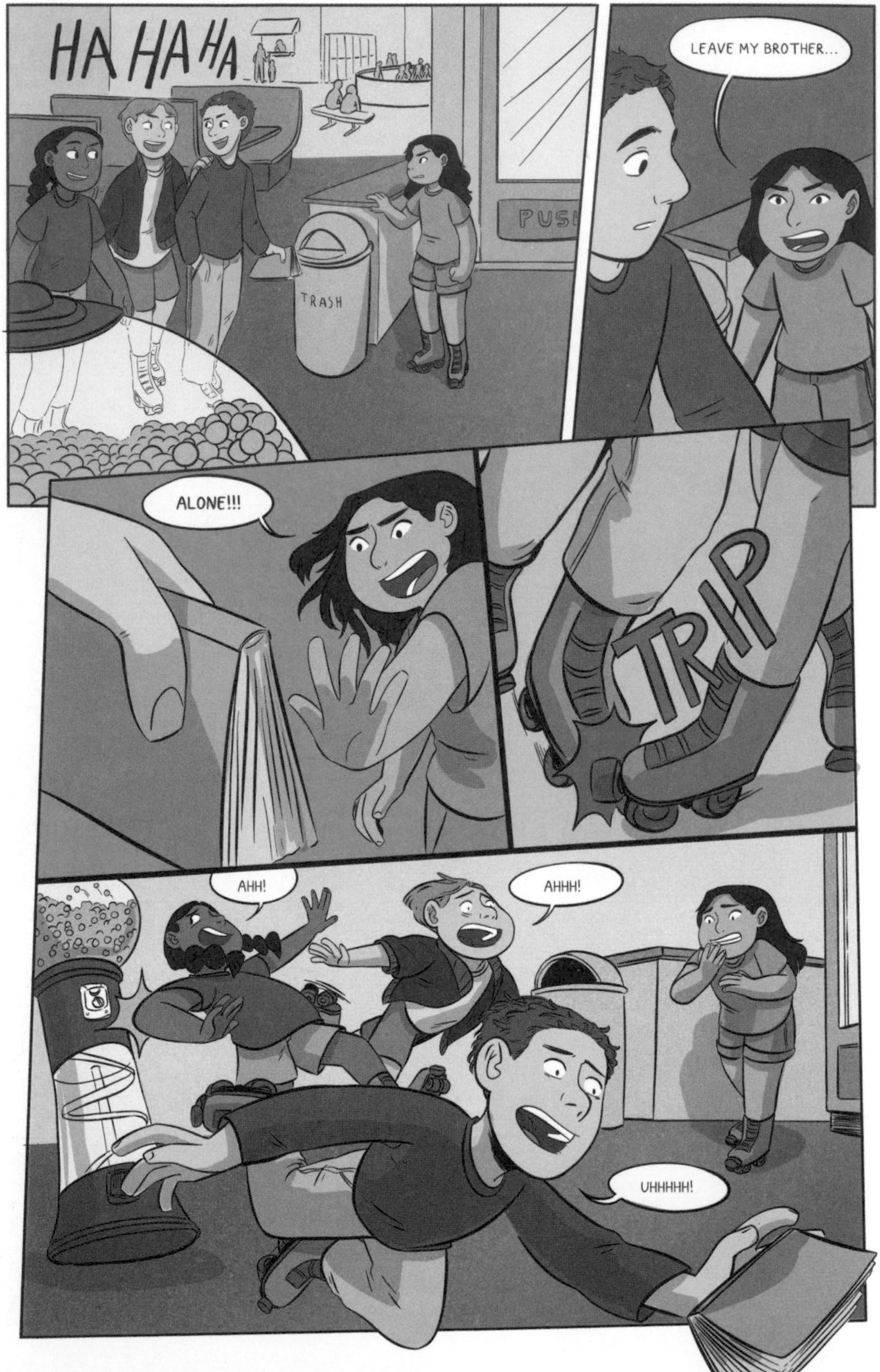
HA HA HA HA
TRASH
PUSH
LEAVE MY BROTHER...
ALONE!!!
TRIP
AHH!
AHHH!
UHHHHH!

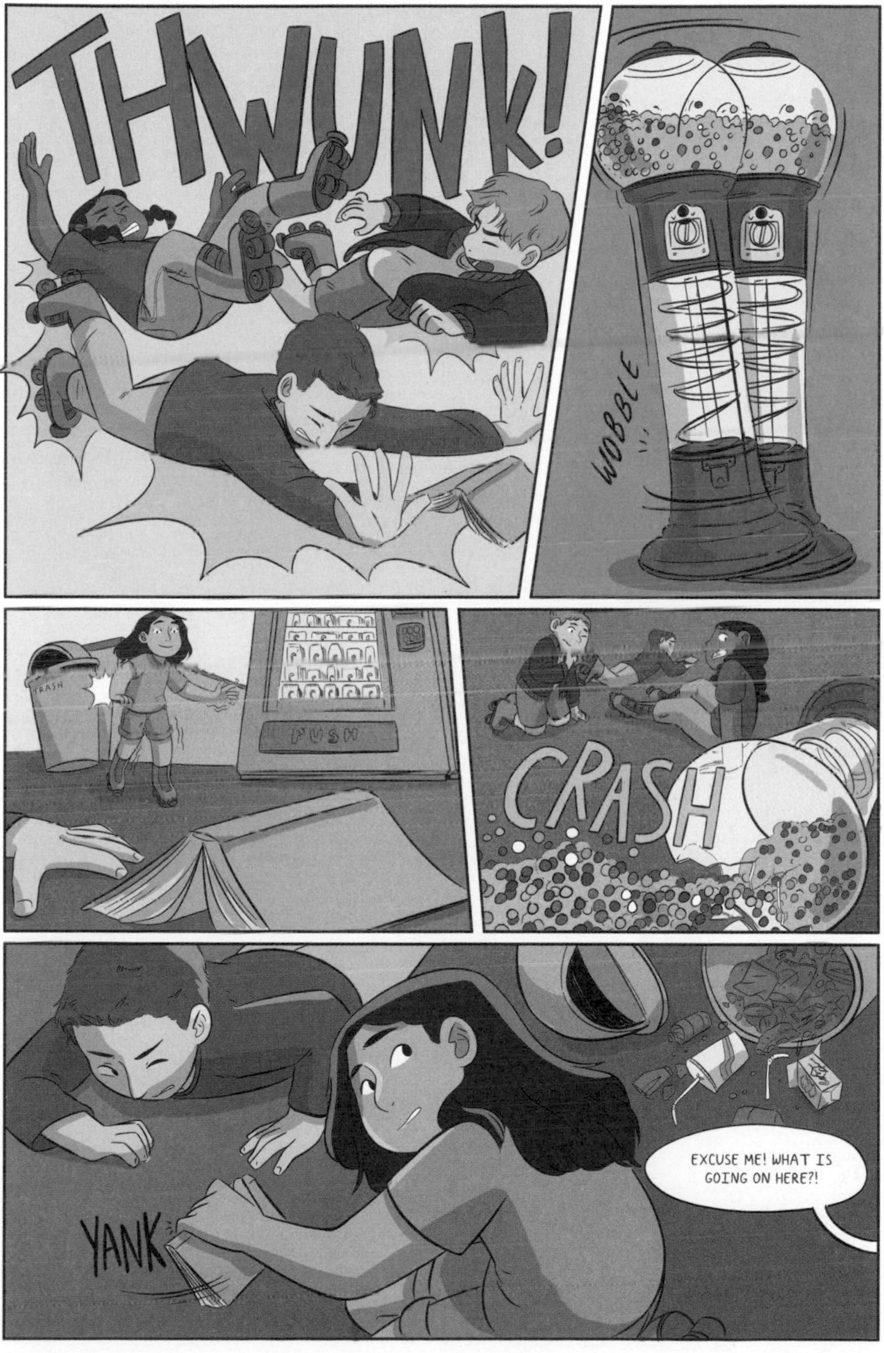
THWUNK!
WOBBLE
TRASH
PUSH
CRASH
YANK
EXCUSE ME! WHAT IS GOING ON HERE?!

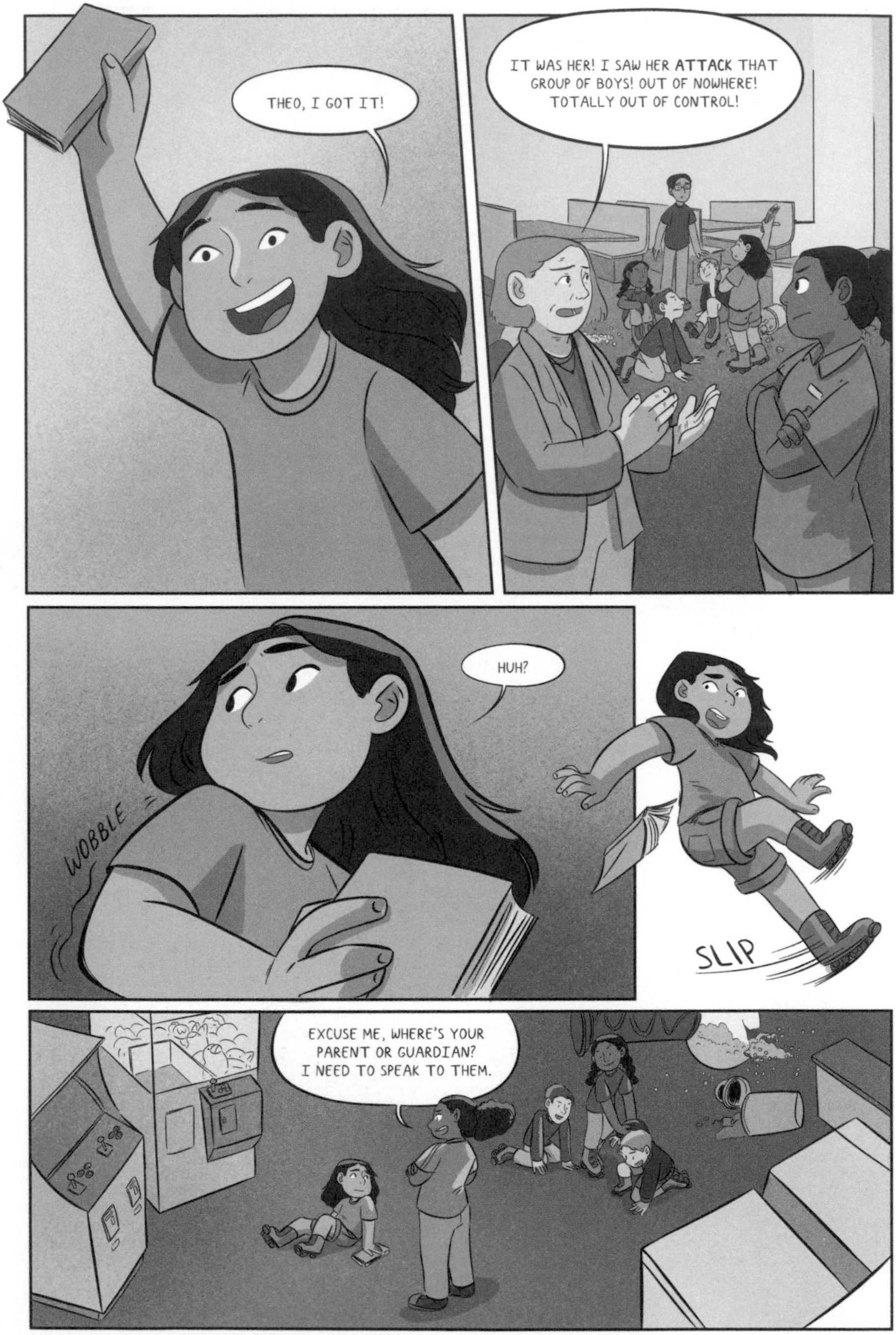
THEO, I GOT IT!
IT WAS HER! I SAW HER ATTACK THAT GROUP OF BOYS! OUT OF NOWHERE! TOTALLY OUT OF CONTROL!
HUH?
WOBBLE
SLIP
EXCUSE ME, WHERE'S YOUR PARENT OR GUARDIAN? I NEED TO SPEAK TO THEM.

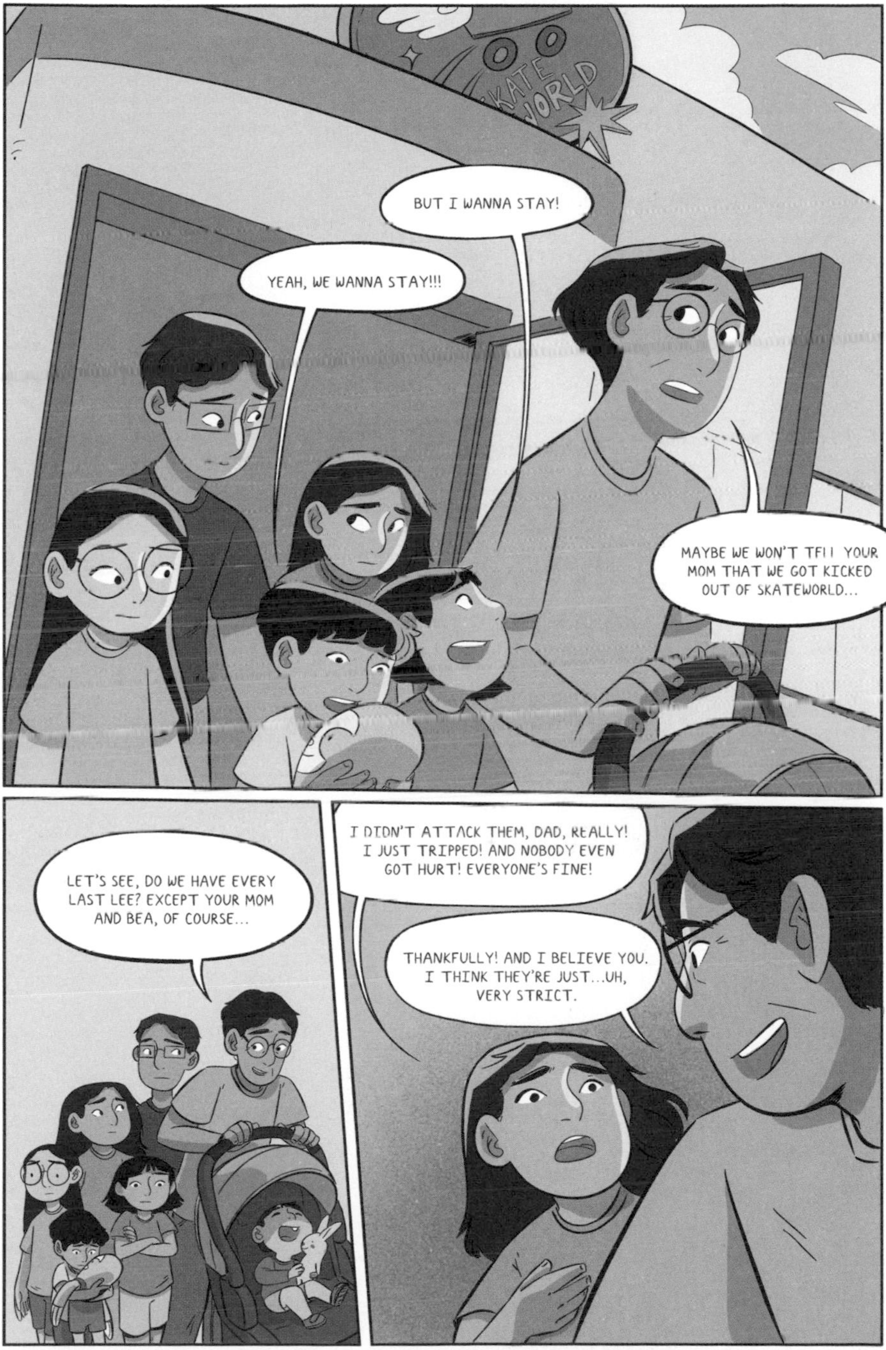

BUT I WANNA STAY!
YEAH, WE WANNA STAY!!!
MAYBE WE WON'T TELL YOUR MOM THAT WE GOT KICKED OUT OF SKATEWORLD...
LET'S SEE, DO WE HAVE EVERY LAST LEE? EXCEPT YOUR MOM AND BEA, OF COURSE...
I DIDN'T ATTACK THEM, DAD, REALLY! I JUST TRIPPED! AND NOBODY EVEN GOT HURT! EVERYONE'S FINE!
THANKFULLY! AND I BELIEVE YOU. I THINK THEY'RE JUST...UH, VERY STRICT.

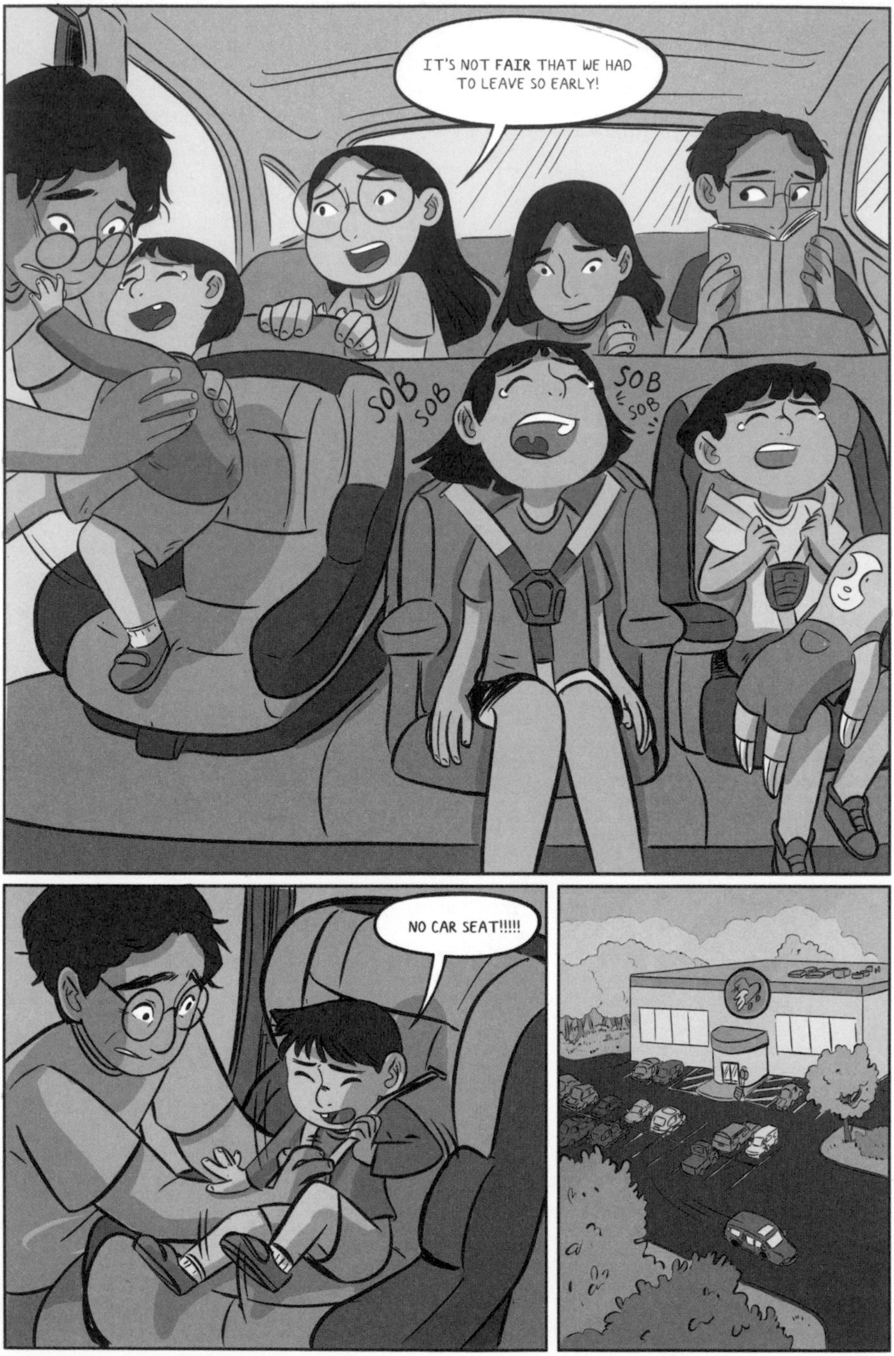
IT'S NOT **FAIR** THAT WE HAD TO LEAVE SO EARLY!
SOB SOB
SOB SOB
NO CAR SEAT!!!!!

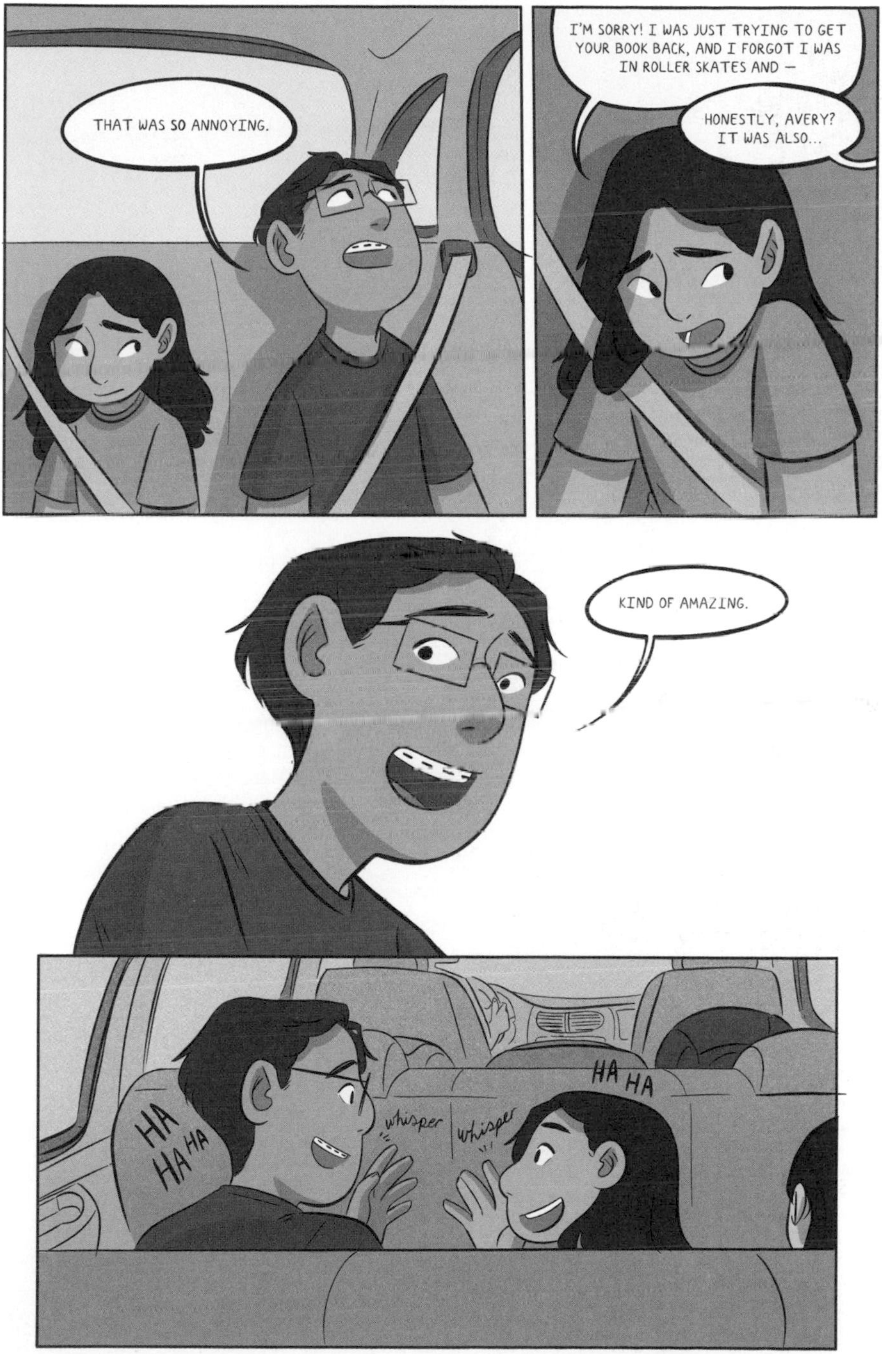
THAT WAS SO ANNOYING.
I'M SORRY! I WAS JUST TRYING TO GET YOUR BOOK BACK, AND I FORGOT I WAS IN ROLLER SKATES AND —
HONESTLY, AVERY? IT WAS ALSO...
KIND OF AMAZING.
HA HA
whisper
whisper
HA HA
HA HA HA

Chapter Ten

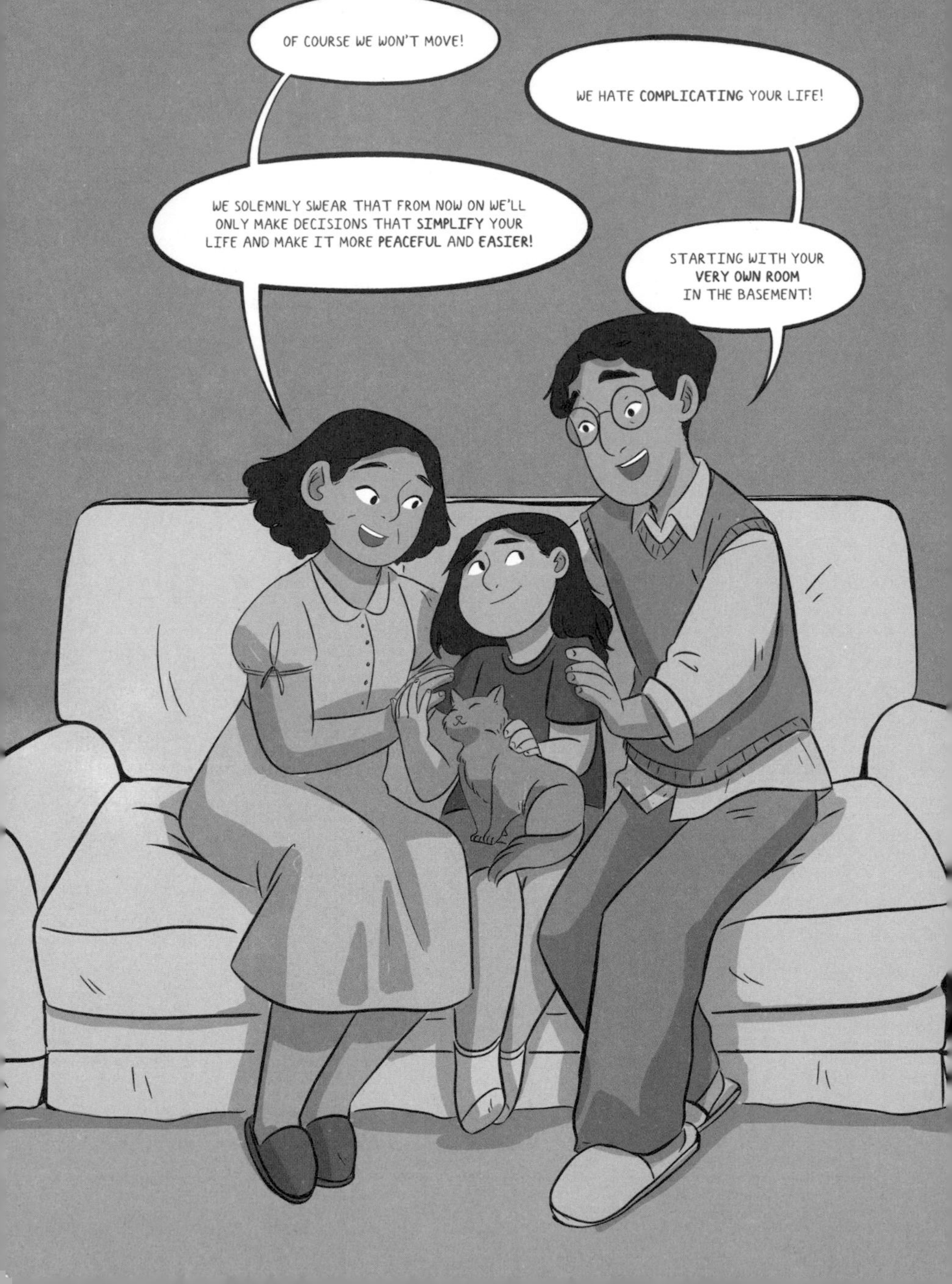
OF COURSE WE WON'T MOVE!
WE SOLEMNLY SWEAR THAT FROM NOW ON WE'LL ONLY MAKE DECISIONS THAT **SIMPLIFY** YOUR LIFE AND MAKE IT MORE **PEACEFUL** AND **EASIER!**
WE HATE **COMPLICATING** YOUR LIFE!
STARTING WITH YOUR **VERY OWN ROOM** IN THE BASEMENT!

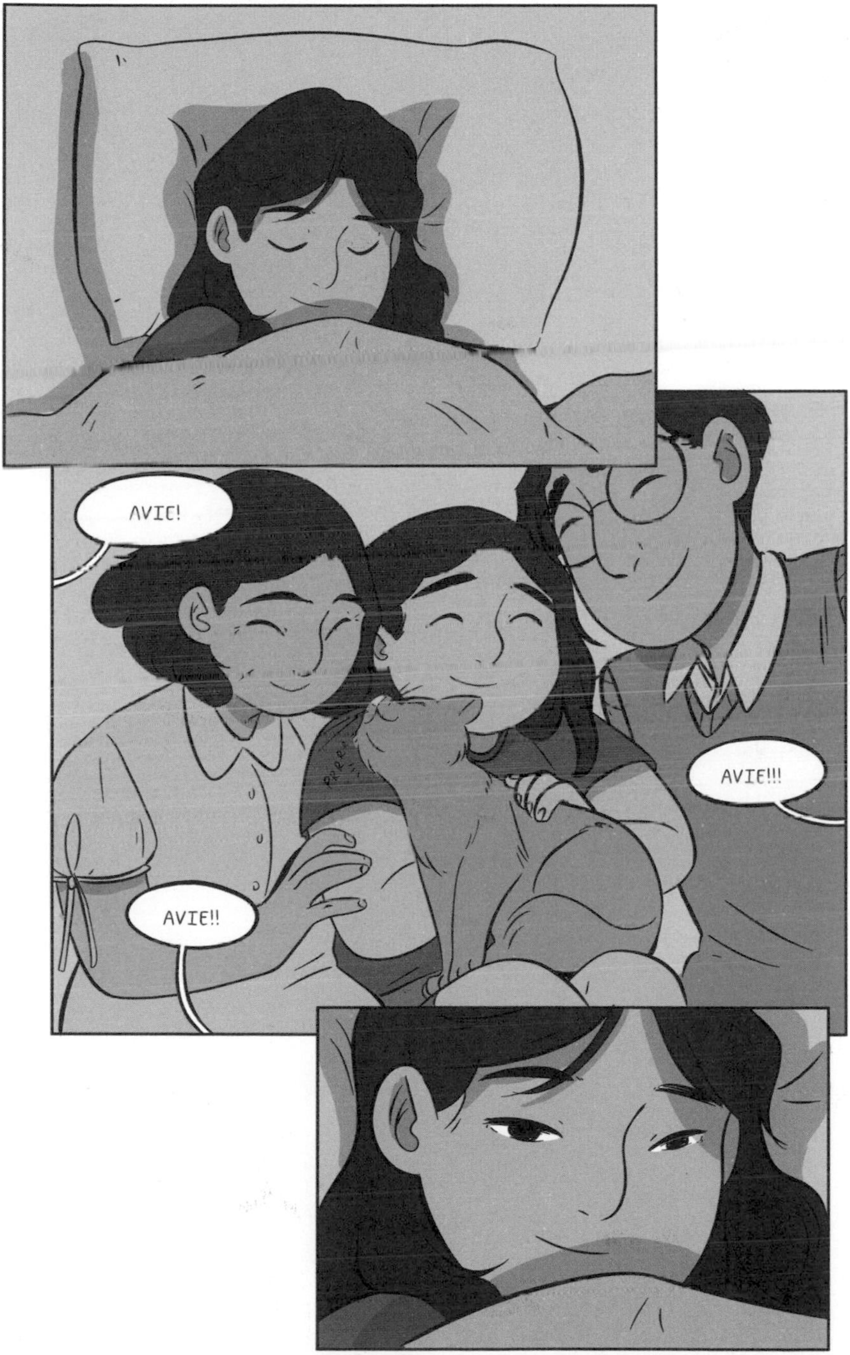
AVIE!
PRRR
AVIE!!!
AVIE!!

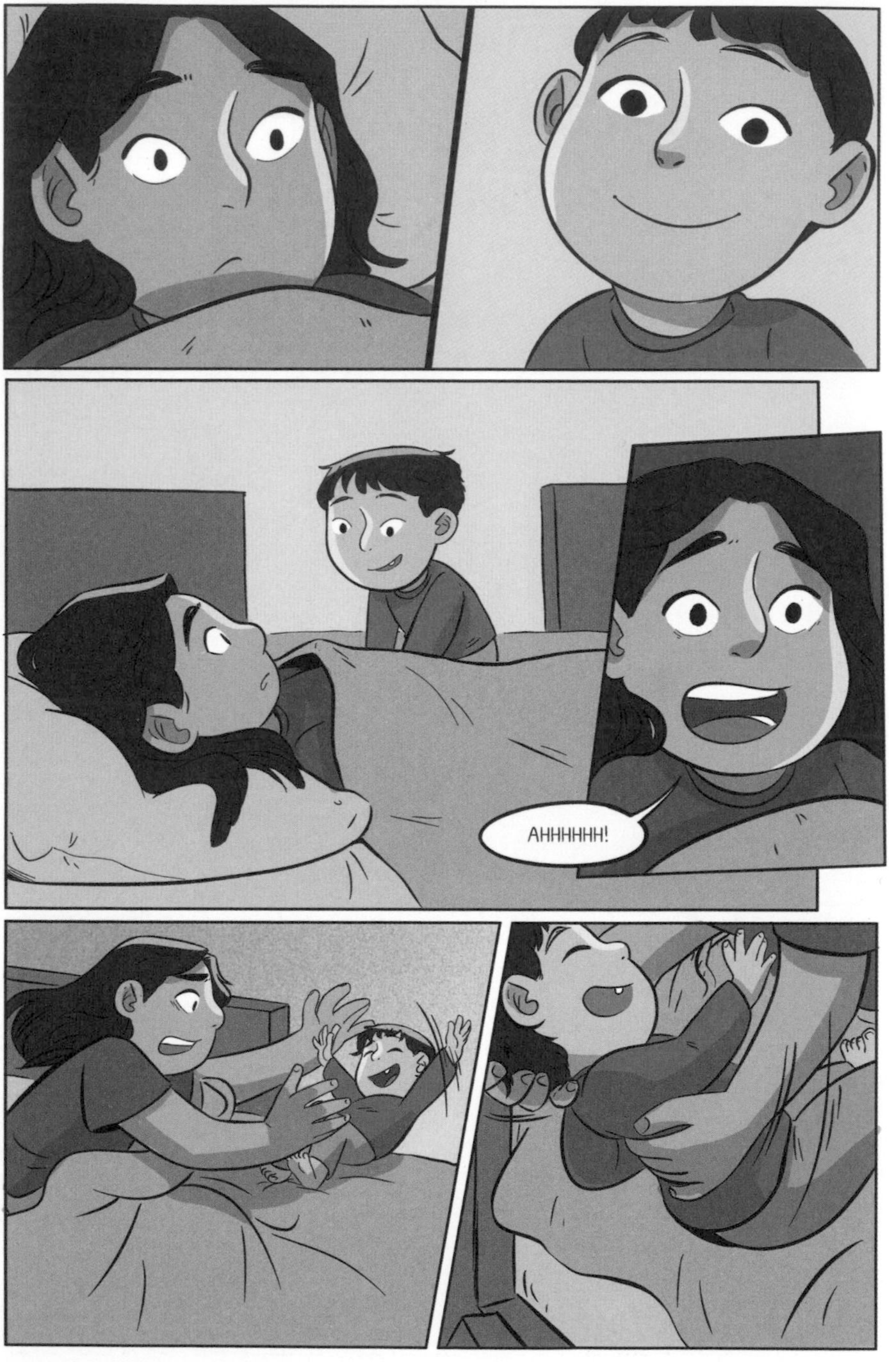
AHHHHHH!

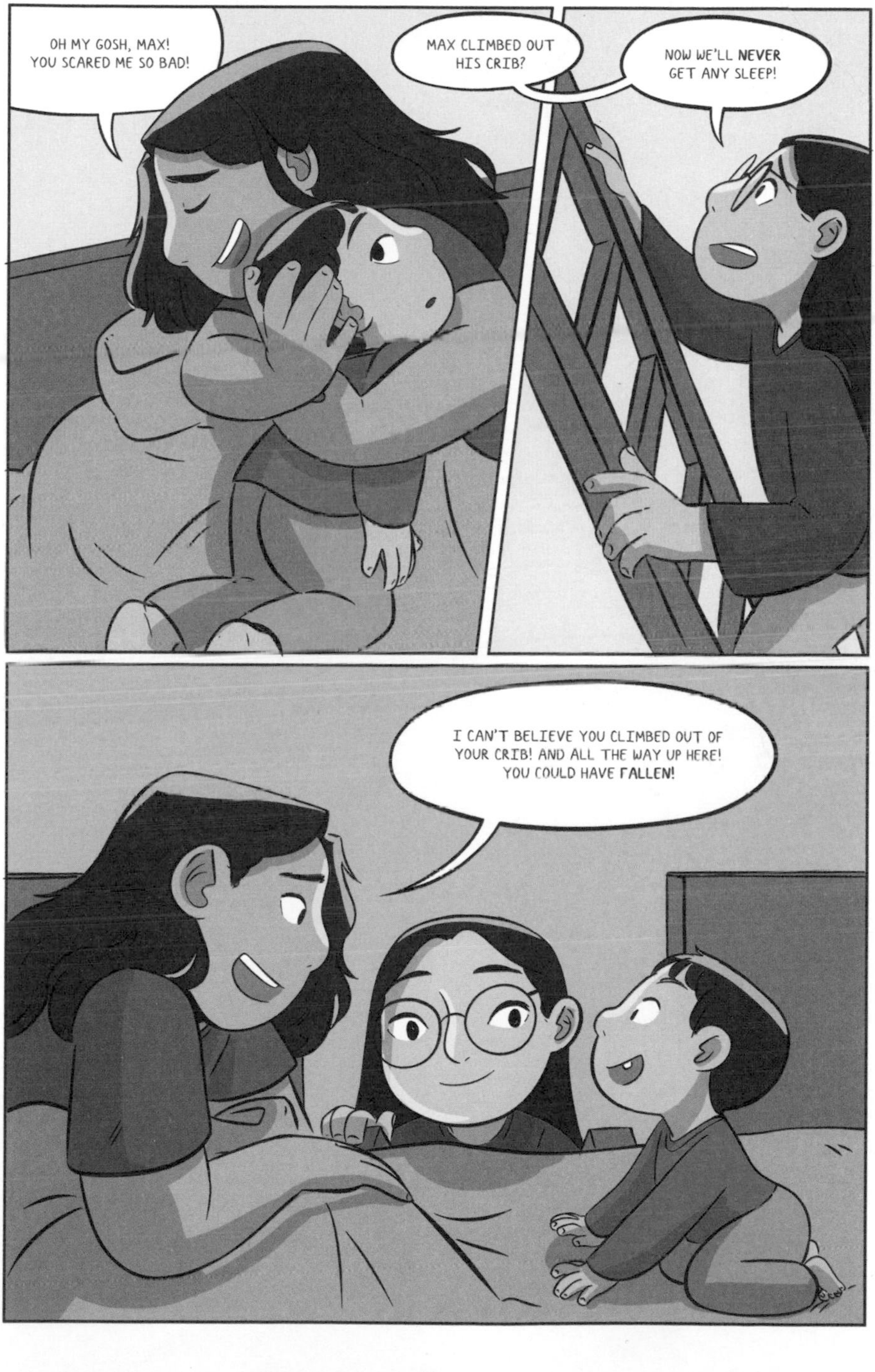
OH MY GOSH, MAX! YOU SCARED ME SO BAD!
MAX CLIMBED OUT HIS CRIB?
NOW WE'LL **NEVER** GET ANY SLEEP!
I CAN'T BELIEVE YOU CLIMBED OUT OF YOUR CRIB! AND ALL THE WAY UP HERE! YOU COULD HAVE **FALLEN!**

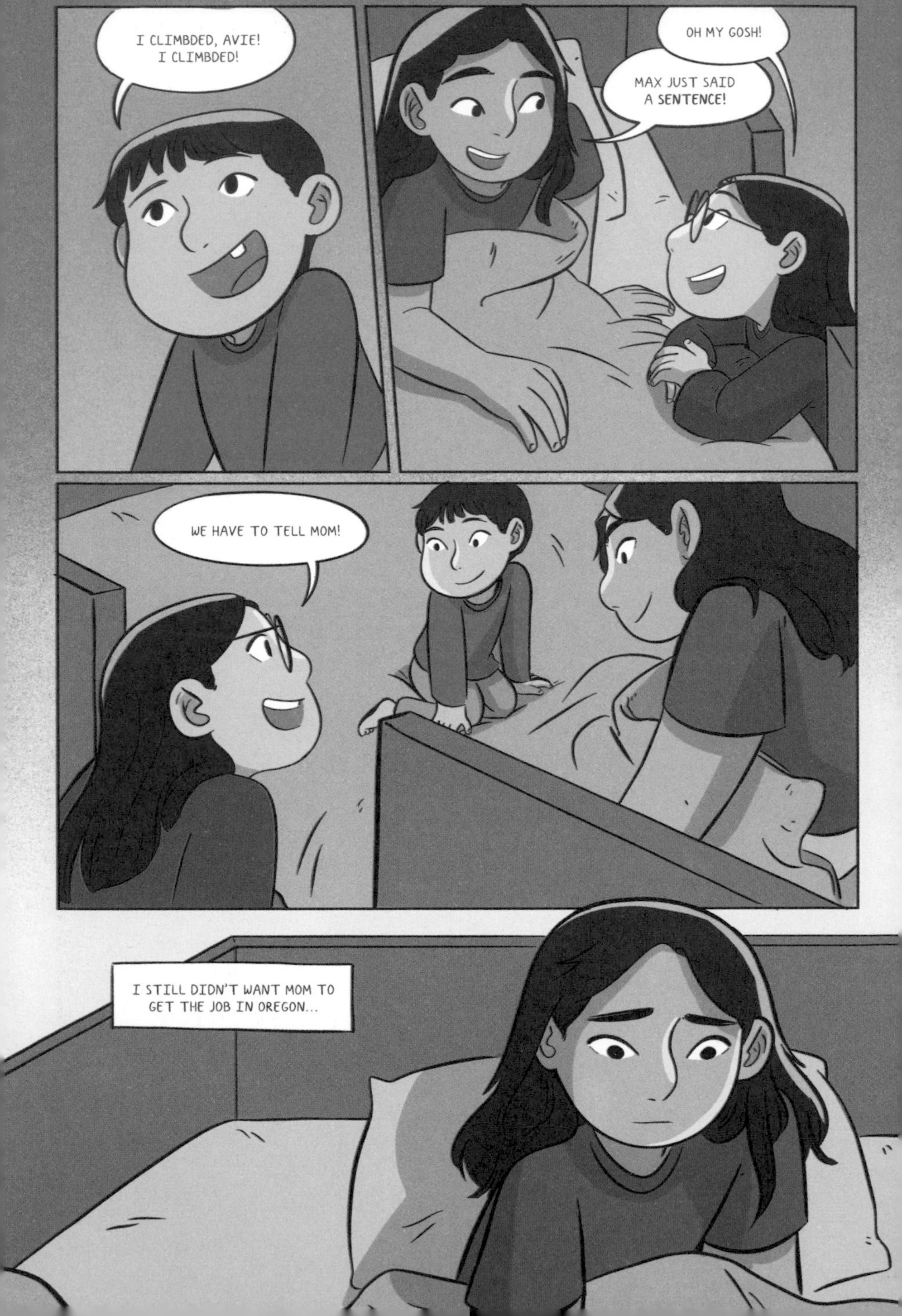
I CLIMBDED, AVIE! I CLIMBDED!
OH MY GOSH!
MAX JUST SAID A SENTENCE!
WE HAVE TO TELL MOM!
I STILL DIDN'T WANT MOM TO GET THE JOB IN OREGON...

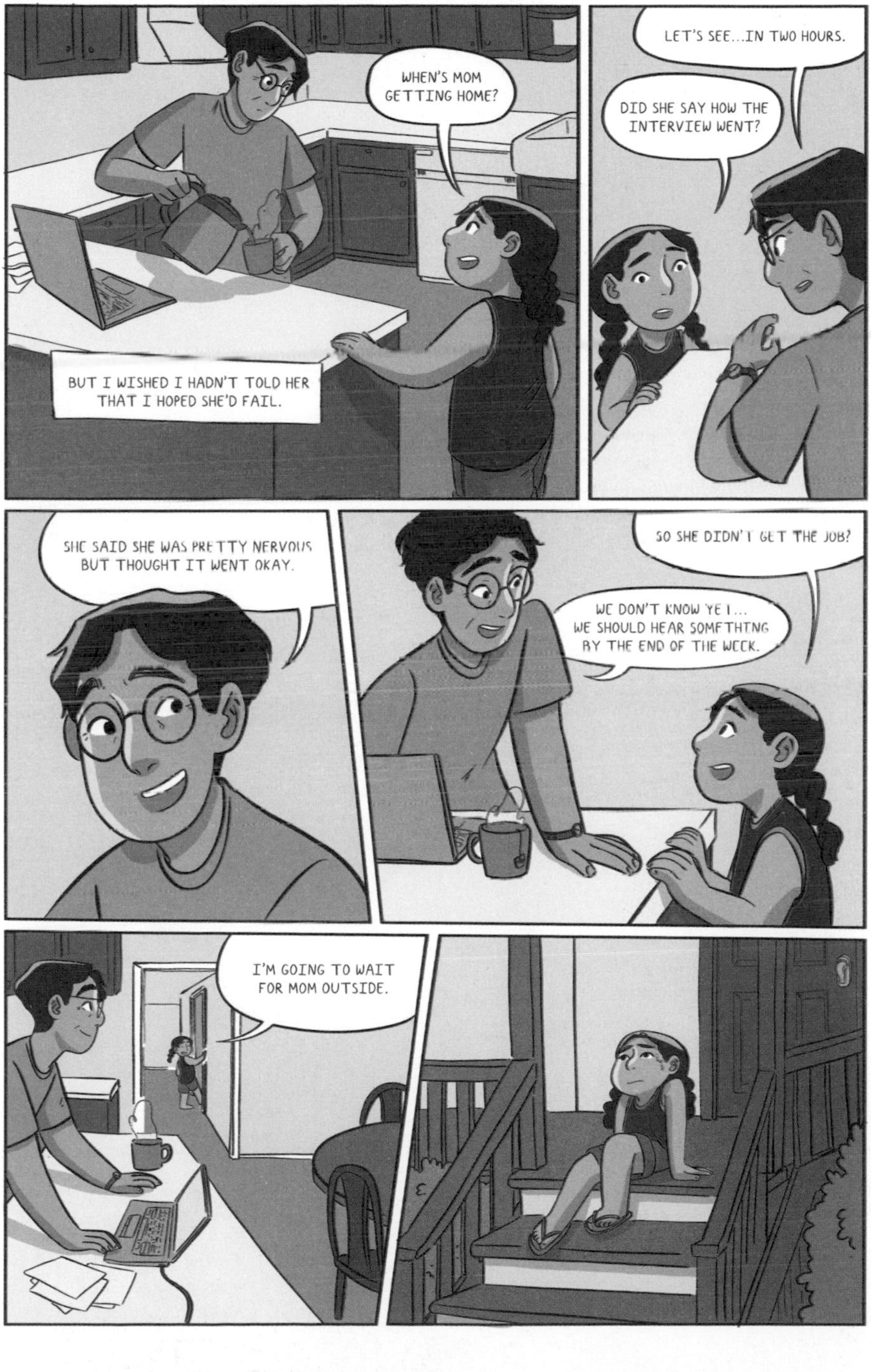
BUT I WISHED I HADN'T TOLD HER THAT I HOPED SHE'D FAIL.
WHEN'S MOM GETTING HOME?
LET'S SEE...IN TWO HOURS.
DID SHE SAY HOW THE INTERVIEW WENT?
SHE SAID SHE WAS PRETTY NERVOUS BUT THOUGHT IT WENT OKAY.
SO SHE DIDN'T GET THE JOB?
WE DON'T KNOW YET... WE SHOULD HEAR SOMETHING BY THE END OF THE WEEK.
I'M GOING TO WAIT FOR MOM OUTSIDE.

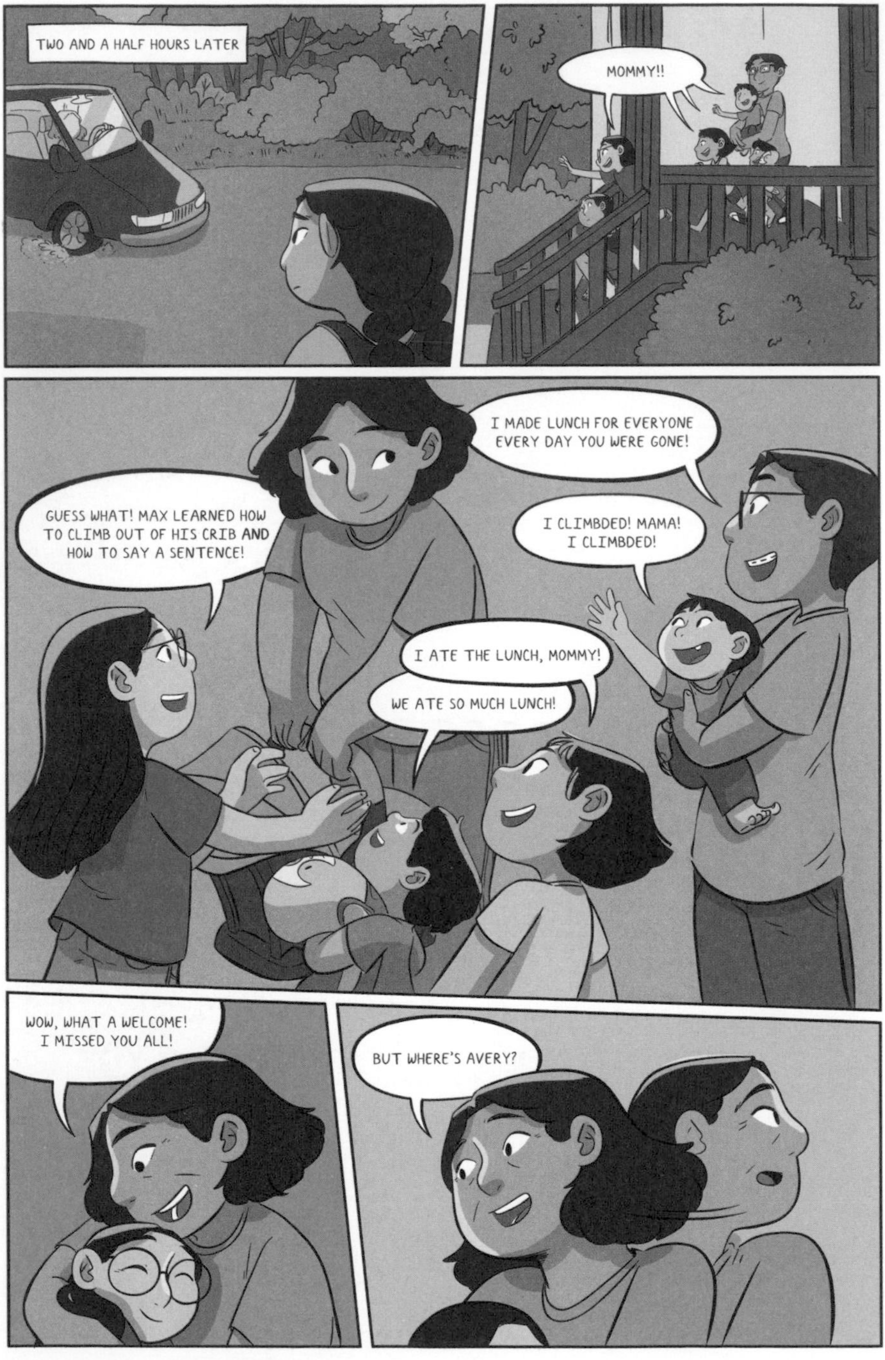

TWO AND A HALF HOURS LATER
MOMMY!!
I MADE LUNCH FOR EVERYONE EVERY DAY YOU WERE GONE!
GUESS WHAT! MAX LEARNED HOW TO CLIMB OUT OF HIS CRIB AND HOW TO SAY A SENTENCE!
I CLIMBDED! MAMA! I CLIMBDED!
I ATE THE LUNCH, MOMMY!
WE ATE SO MUCH LUNCH!
WOW, WHAT A WELCOME! I MISSED YOU ALL!
BUT WHERE'S AVERY?

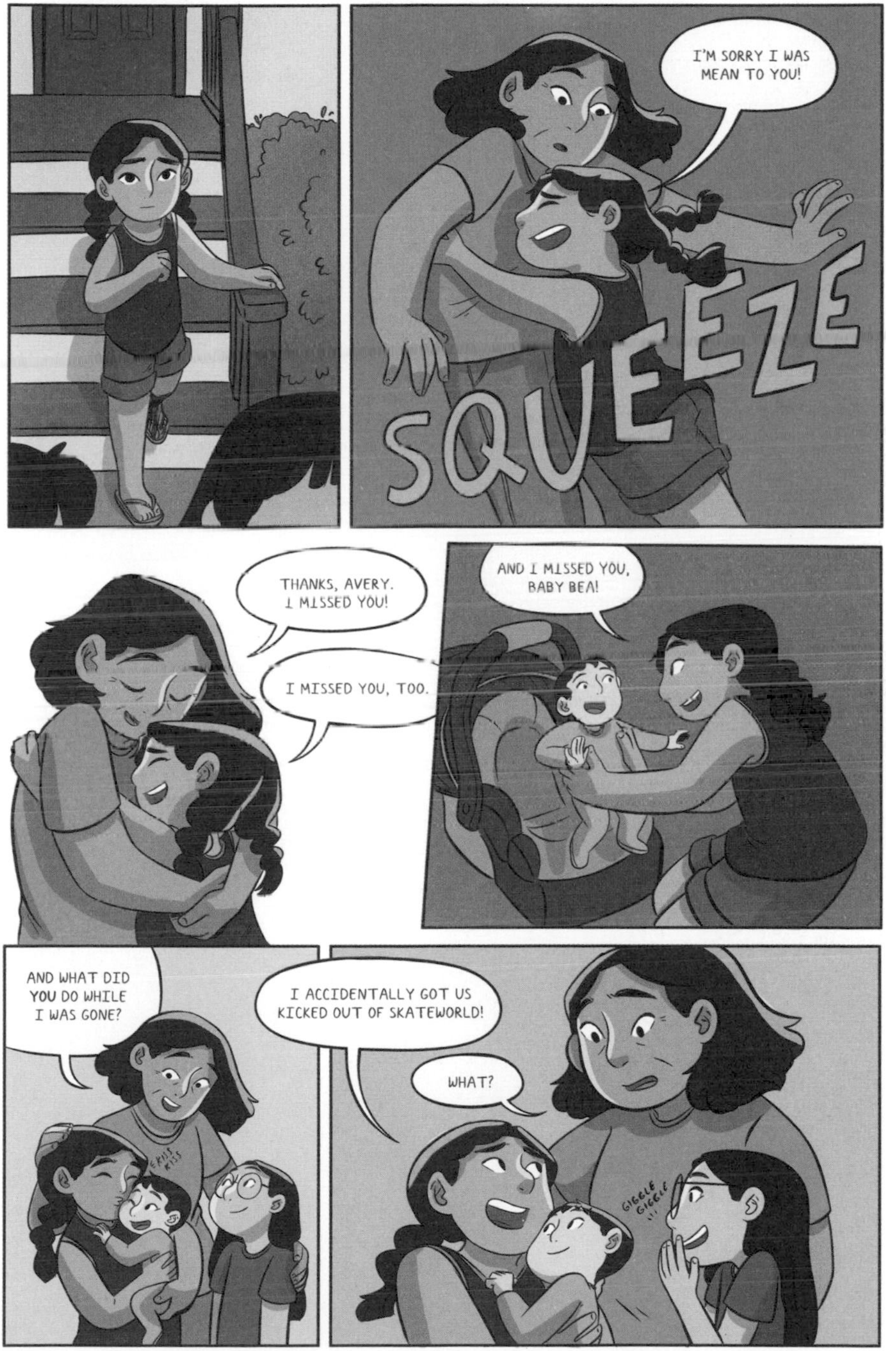
I'M SORRY I WAS MEAN TO YOU!
SQUEEZE
THANKS, AVERY. I MISSED YOU!
I MISSED YOU, TOO.
AND I MISSED YOU, BABY BEA!
AND WHAT DID YOU DO WHILE I WAS GONE?
I ACCIDENTALLY GOT US KICKED OUT OF SKATEWORLD!
WHAT?
GIGGLE GIGGLE

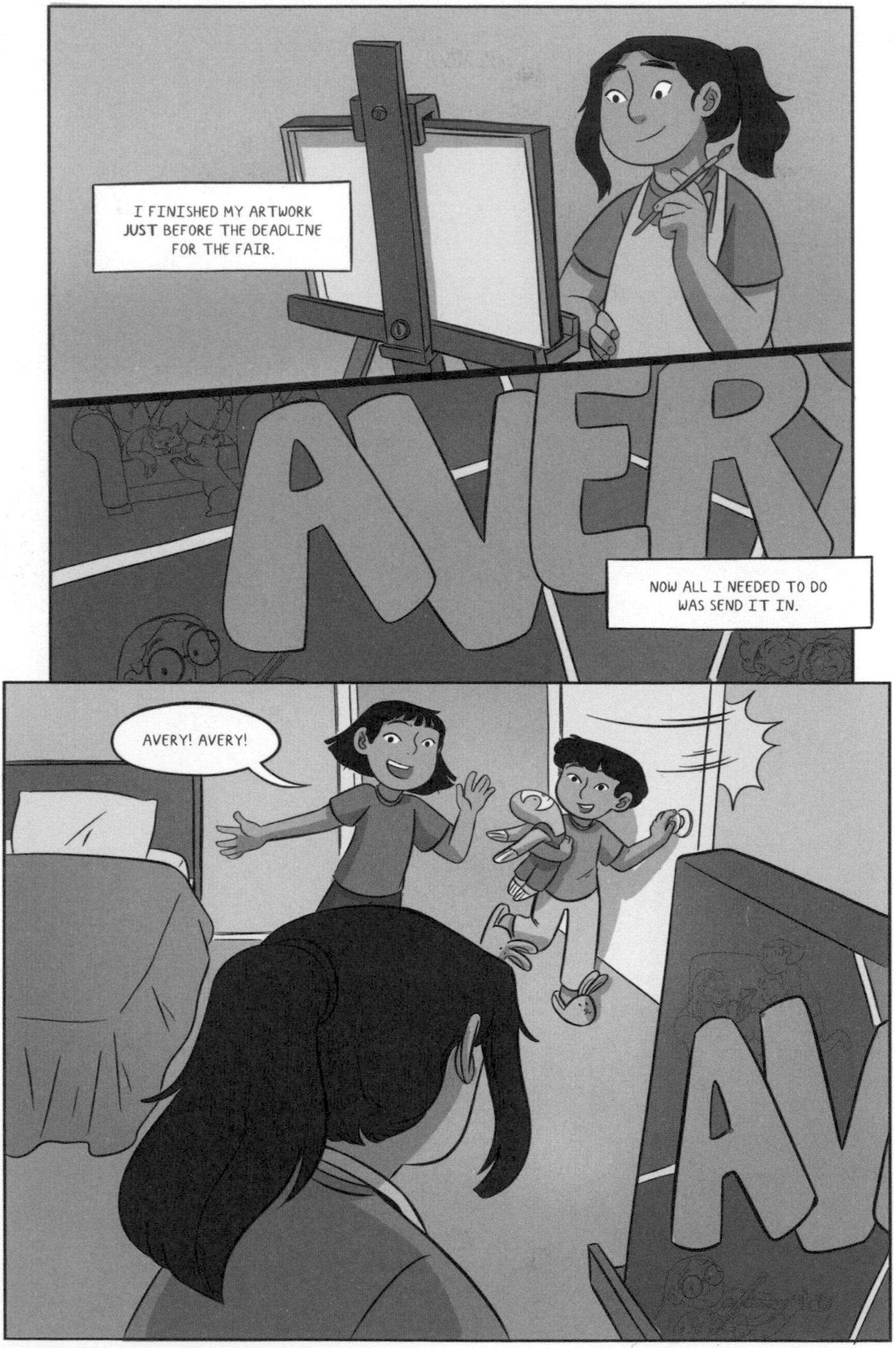
I FINISHED MY ARTWORK JUST BEFORE THE DEADLINE FOR THE FAIR.
AVERY
NOW ALL I NEEDED TO DO WAS SEND IT IN.
AVERY! AVERY!
AV

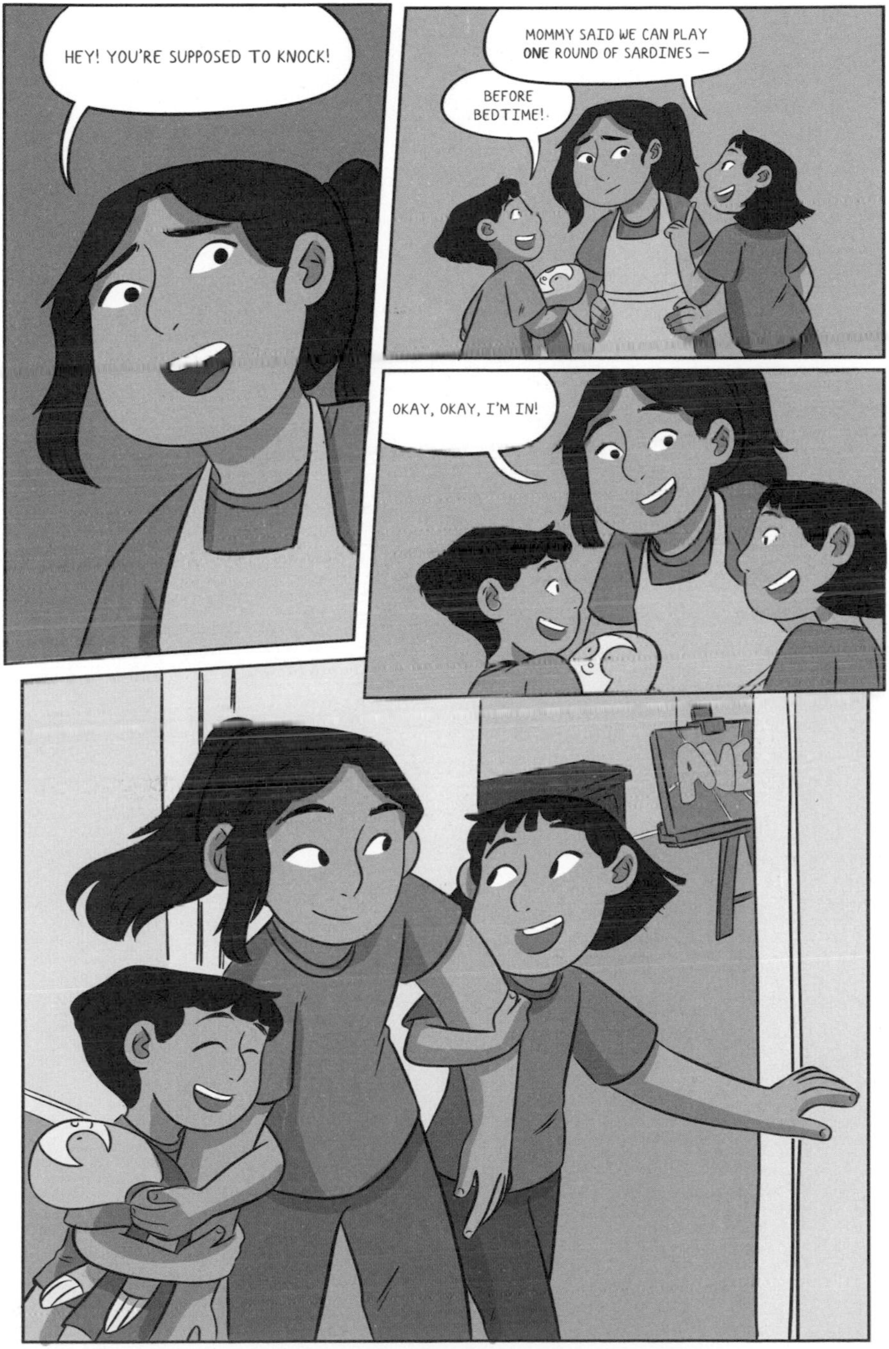
HEY! YOU'RE SUPPOSED TO KNOCK!
MOMMY SAID WE CAN PLAY ONE ROUND OF SARDINES —
BEFORE BEDTIME!
OKAY, OKAY, I'M IN!

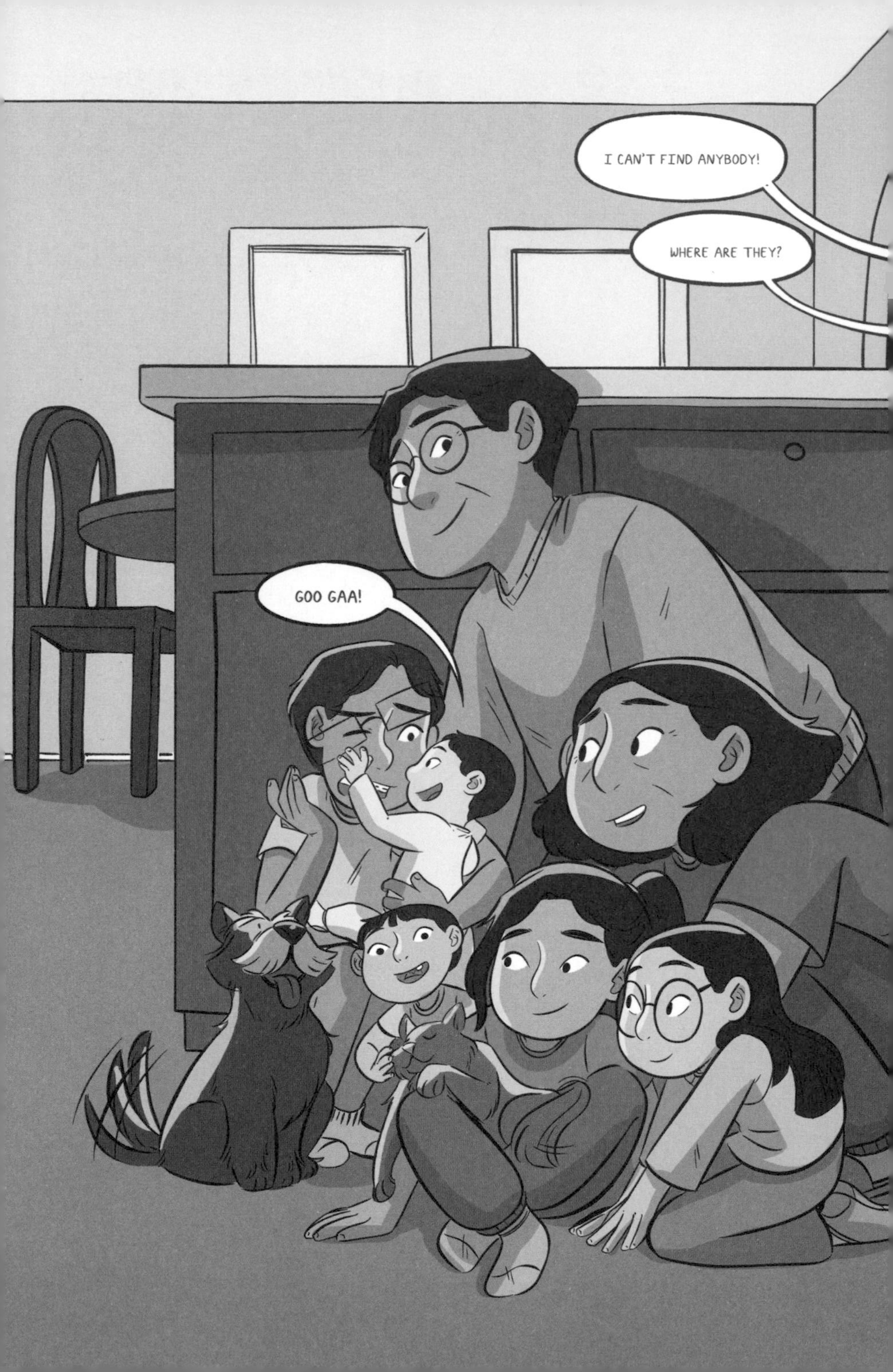
I CAN'T FIND ANYBODY!
WHERE ARE THEY?
GOO GAA!

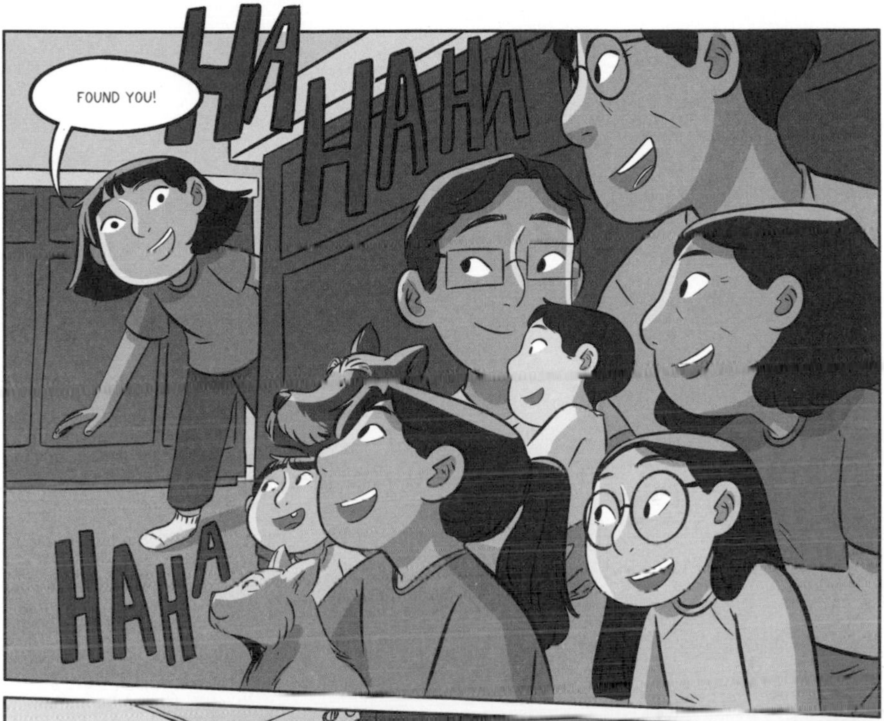
HA
HAHA
FOUND YOU!
HAHA
HA

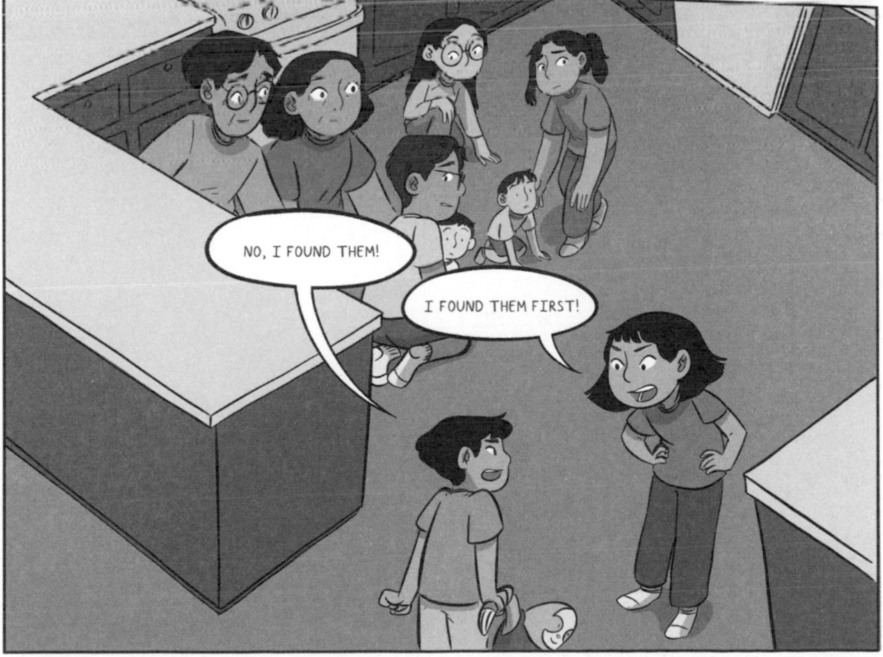
NO, I FOUND THEM!
I FOUND THEM FIRST!

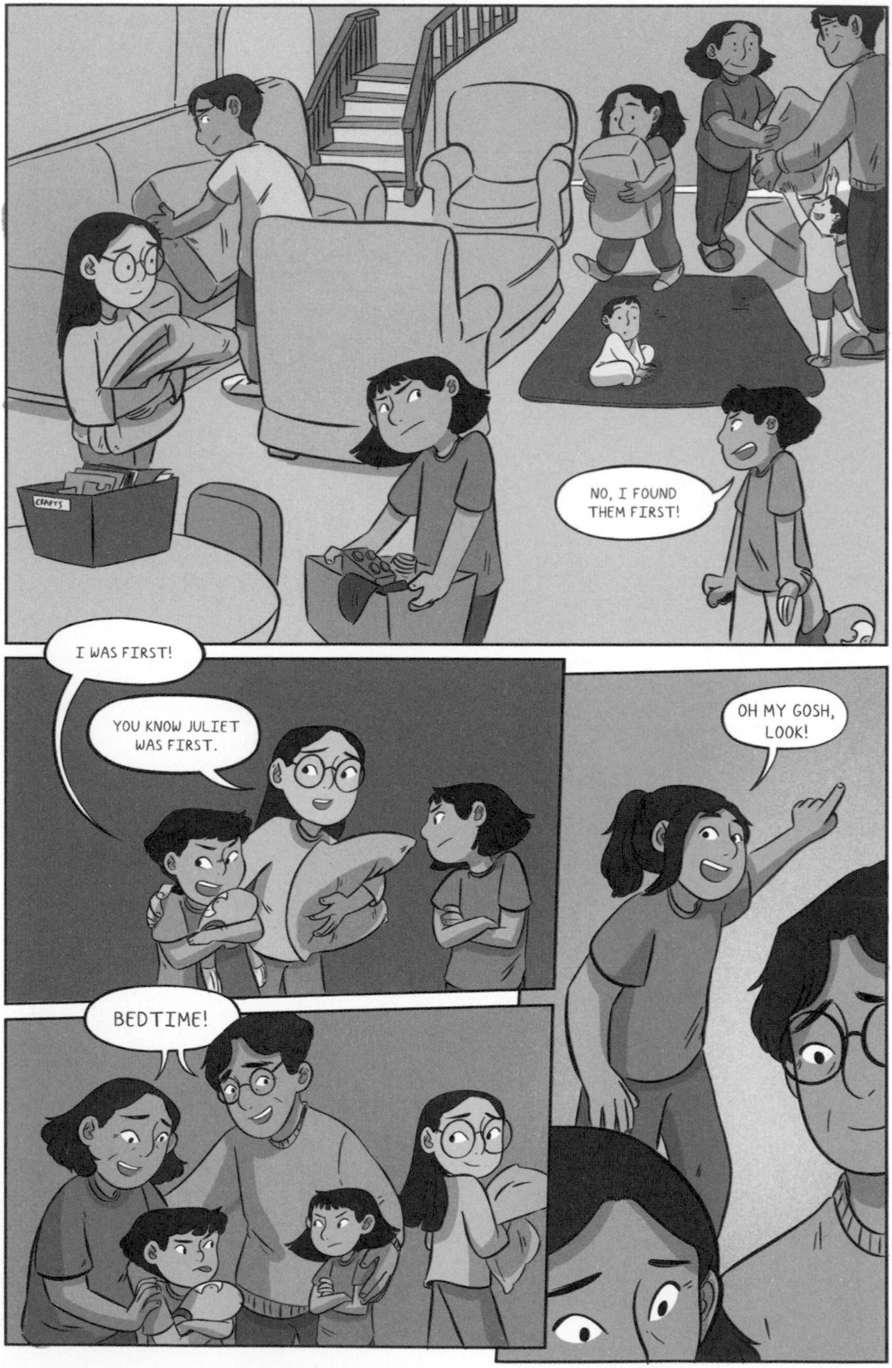
NO, I FOUND THEM FIRST!
I WAS FIRST!
YOU KNOW JULIET WAS FIRST.
BEDTIME!
OH MY GOSH, LOOK!

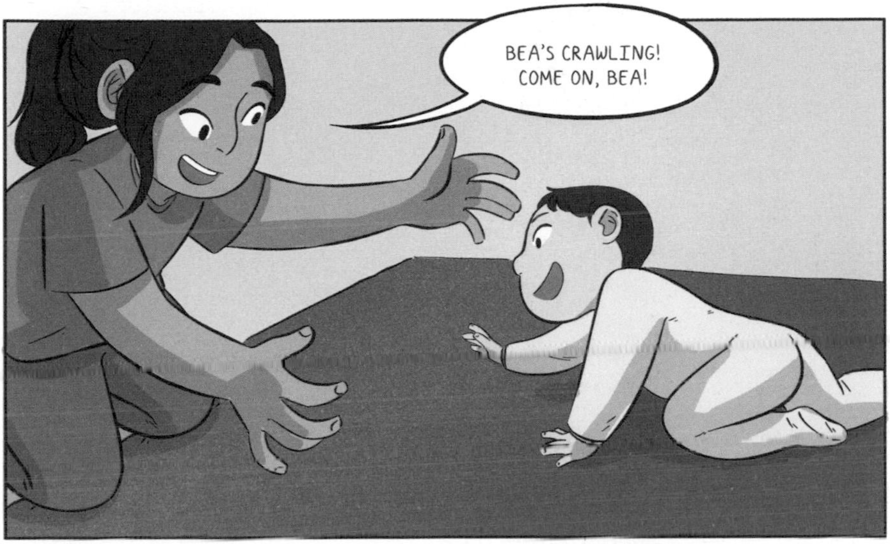
BEA'S CRAWLING!
COME ON, BEA!

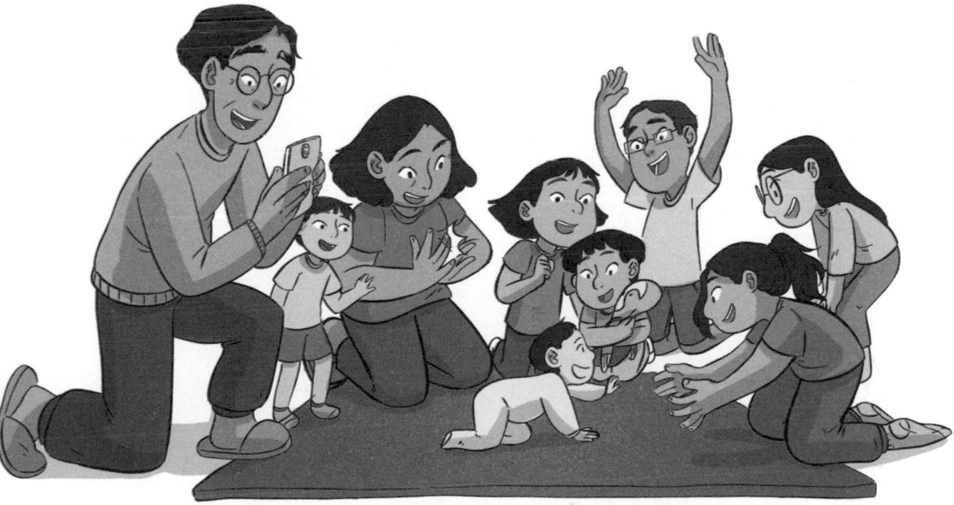

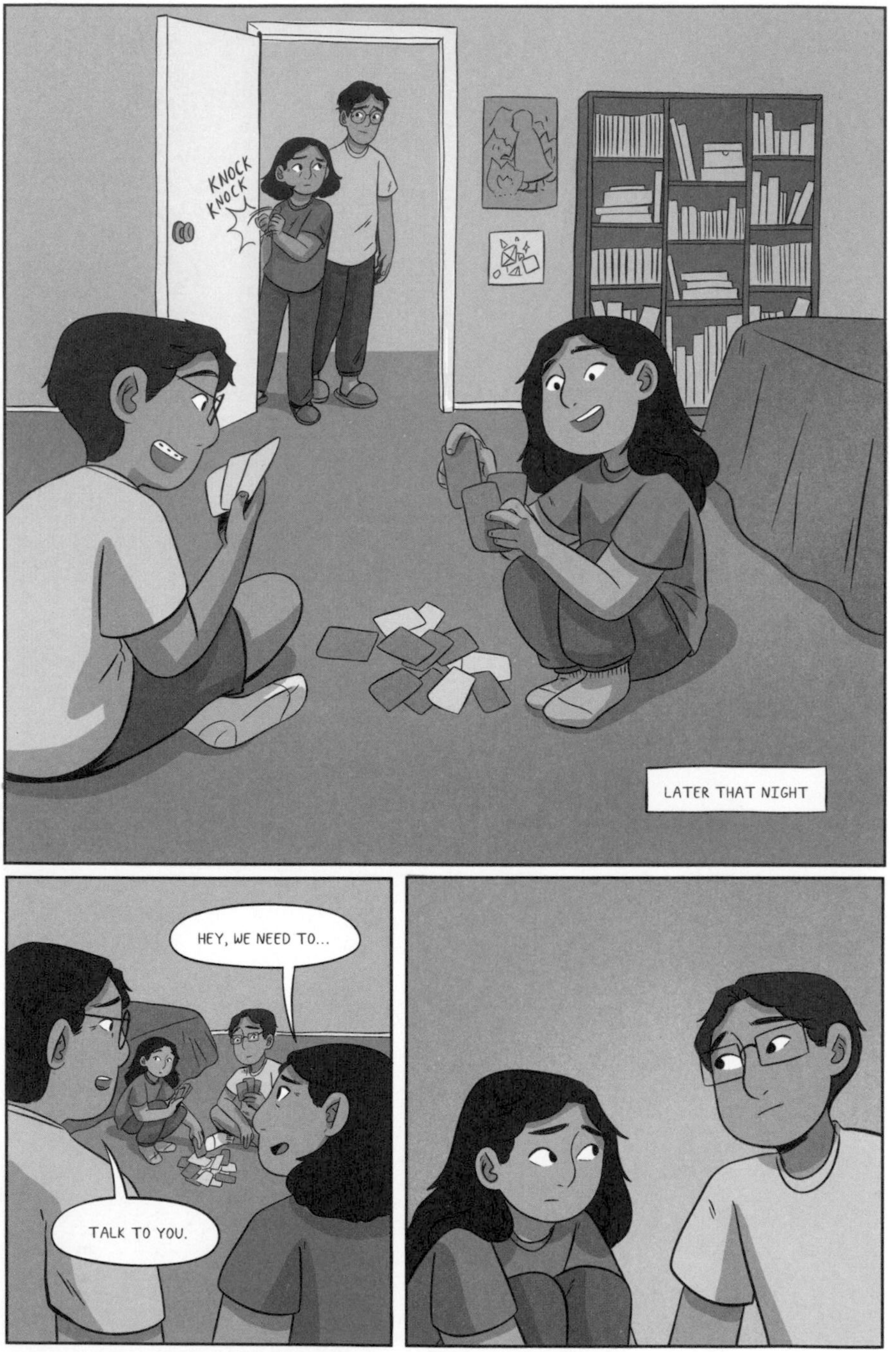
KNOCK
KNOCK
LATER THAT NIGHT
HEY, WE NEED TO...
TALK TO YOU.

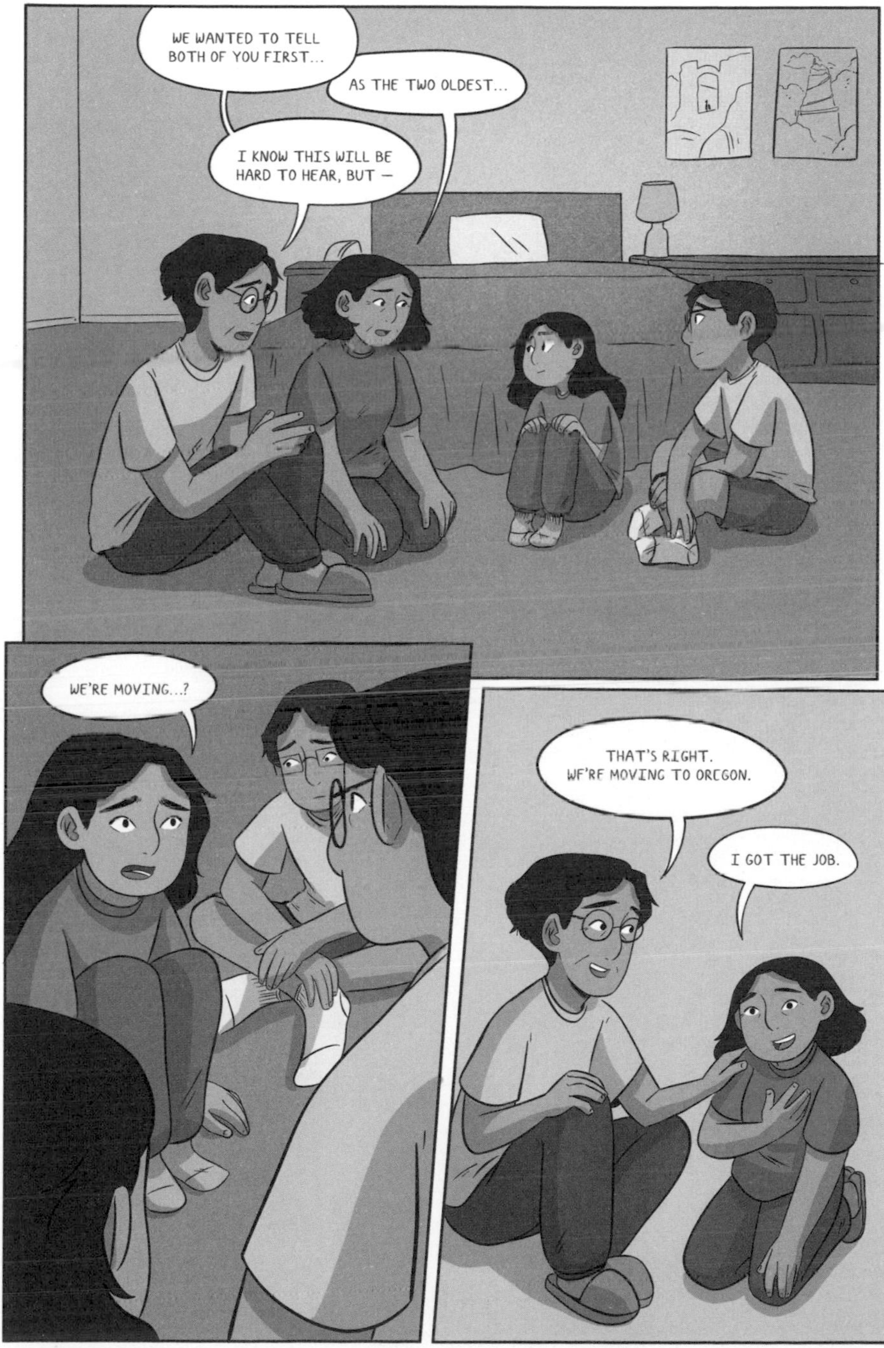
WE WANTED TO TELL BOTH OF YOU FIRST...
AS THE TWO OLDEST...
I KNOW THIS WILL BE HARD TO HEAR, BUT —
WE'RE MOVING...?
THAT'S RIGHT. WE'RE MOVING TO OREGON.
I GOT THE JOB.

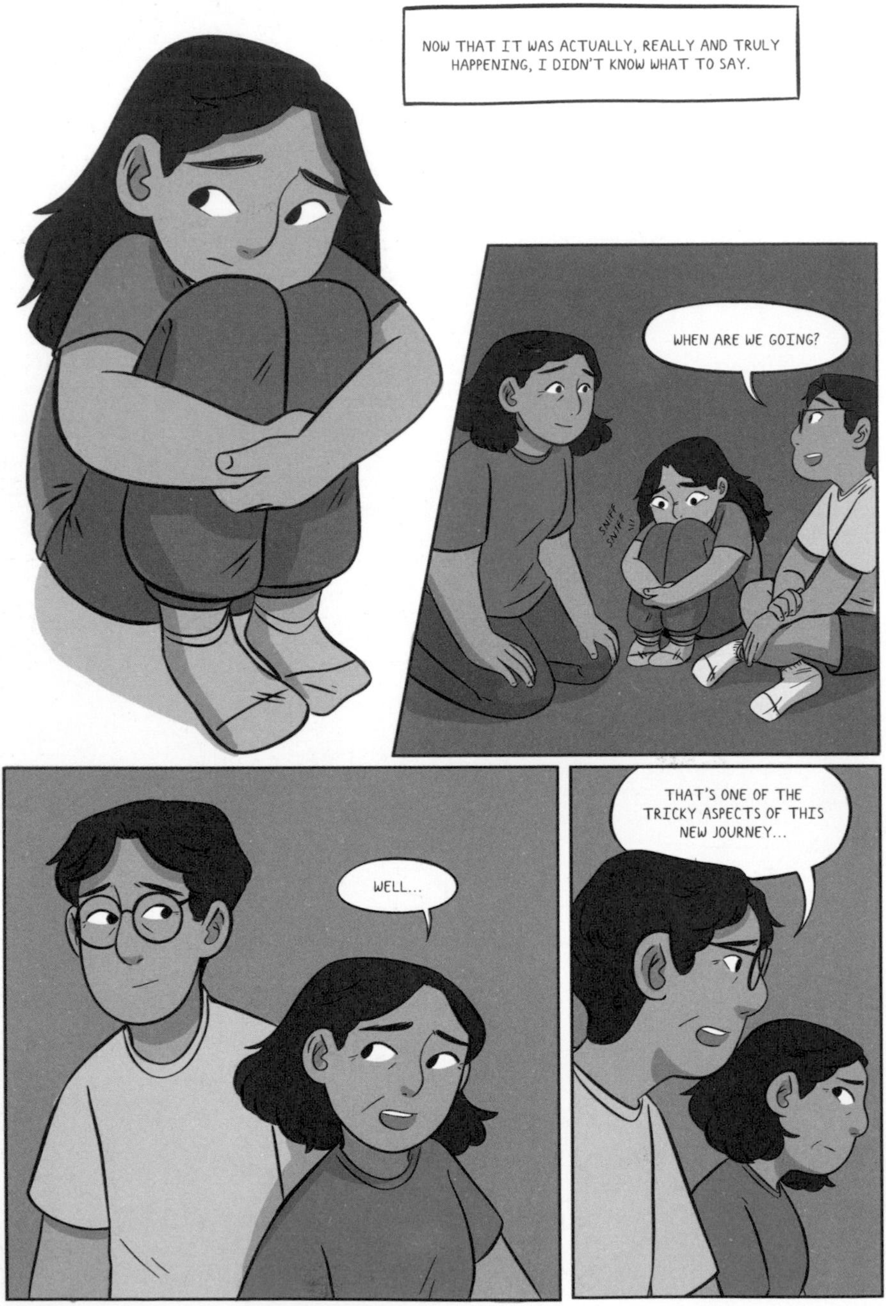
NOW THAT IT WAS ACTUALLY, REALLY AND TRULY HAPPENING, I DIDN'T KNOW WHAT TO SAY.
WHEN ARE WE GOING?
SNIFF SNIFF
WELL...
THAT'S ONE OF THE TRICKY ASPECTS OF THIS NEW JOURNEY...

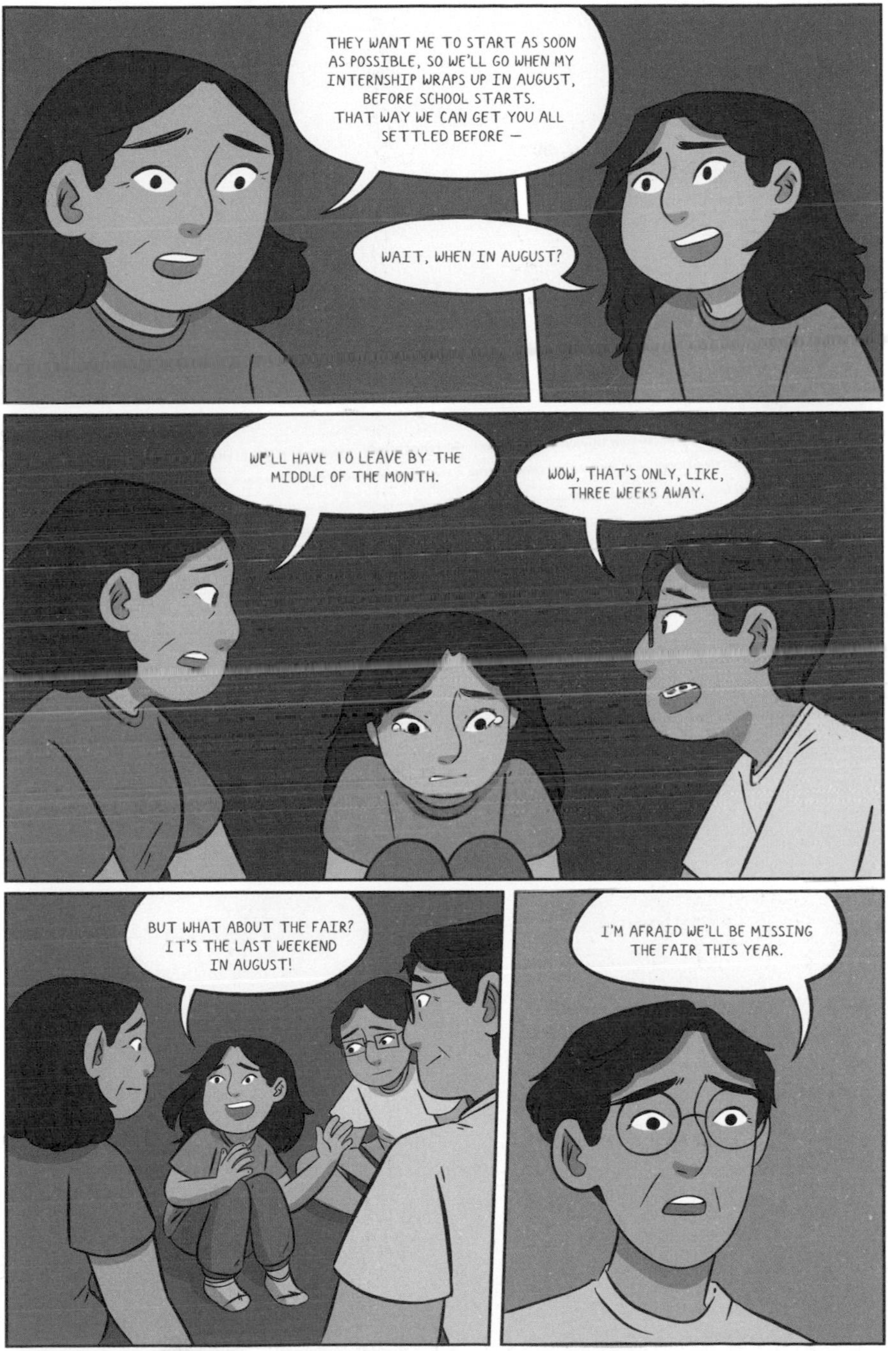
THEY WANT ME TO START AS SOON AS POSSIBLE, SO WE'LL GO WHEN MY INTERNSHIP WRAPS UP IN AUGUST, BEFORE SCHOOL STARTS. THAT WAY WE CAN GET YOU ALL SETTLED BEFORE —
WAIT, WHEN IN AUGUST?
WE'LL HAVE TO LEAVE BY THE MIDDLE OF THE MONTH.
WOW, THAT'S ONLY, LIKE, THREE WEEKS AWAY.
BUT WHAT ABOUT THE FAIR? IT'S THE LAST WEEKEND IN AUGUST!
I'M AFRAID WE'LL BE MISSING THE FAIR THIS YEAR.

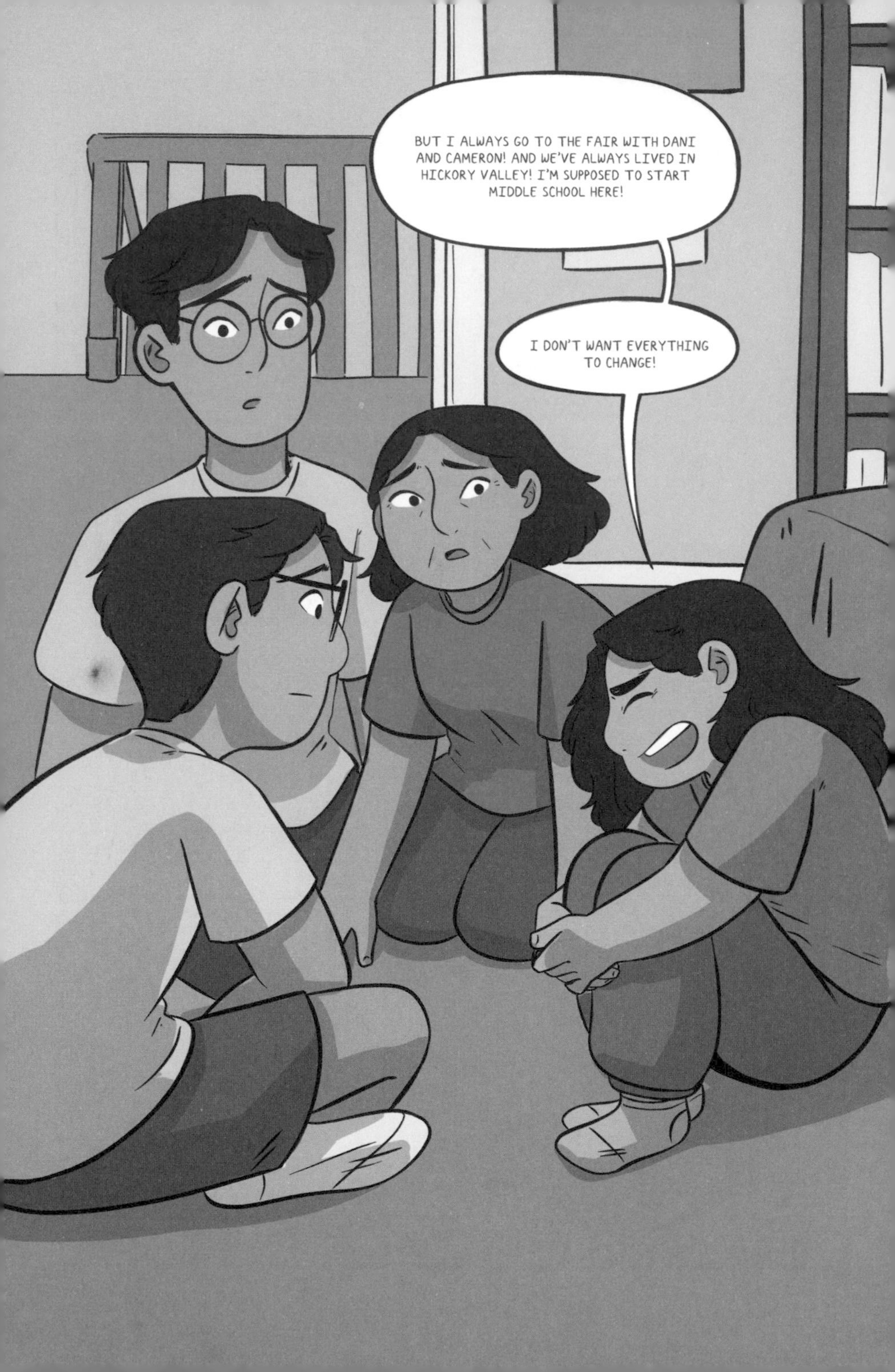
BUT I ALWAYS GO TO THE FAIR WITH DANI AND CAMERON! AND WE'VE ALWAYS LIVED IN HICKORY VALLEY! I'M SUPPOSED TO START MIDDLE SCHOOL HERE!
I DON'T WANT EVERYTHING TO CHANGE!

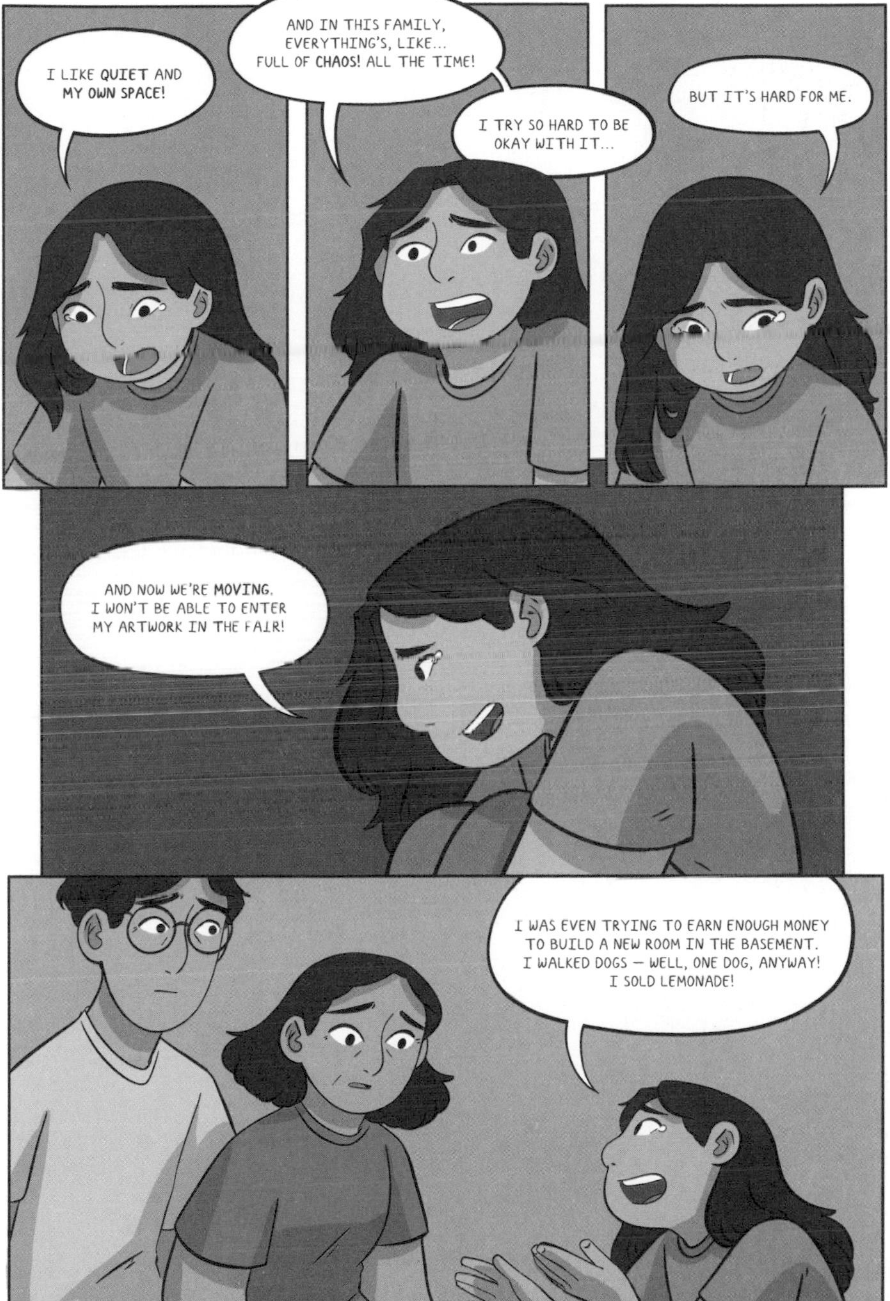
I LIKE QUIET AND MY OWN SPACE!
AND IN THIS FAMILY, EVERYTHING'S, LIKE... FULL OF CHAOS! ALL THE TIME!
I TRY SO HARD TO BE OKAY WITH IT...
BUT IT'S HARD FOR ME.
AND NOW WE'RE MOVING. I WON'T BE ABLE TO ENTER MY ARTWORK IN THE FAIR!
I WAS EVEN TRYING TO EARN ENOUGH MONEY TO BUILD A NEW ROOM IN THE BASEMENT. I WALKED DOGS — WELL, ONE DOG, ANYWAY! I SOLD LEMONADE!

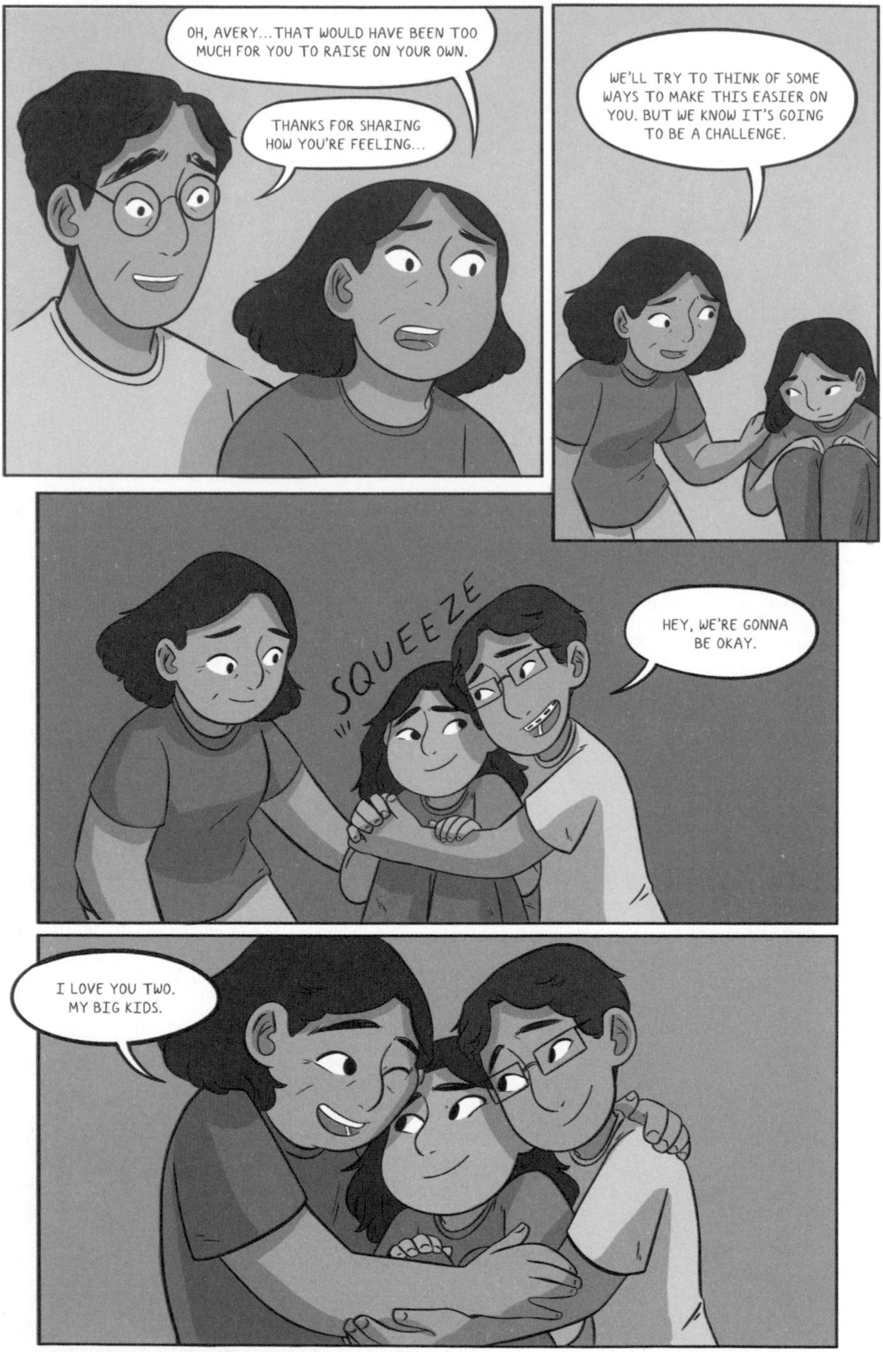
OH, AVERY...THAT WOULD HAVE BEEN TOO MUCH FOR YOU TO RAISE ON YOUR OWN.
THANKS FOR SHARING HOW YOU'RE FEELING...
WE'LL TRY TO THINK OF SOME WAYS TO MAKE THIS EASIER ON YOU. BUT WE KNOW IT'S GOING TO BE A CHALLENGE.
SQUEEZE
HEY, WE'RE GONNA BE OKAY.
I LOVE YOU TWO. MY BIG KIDS.

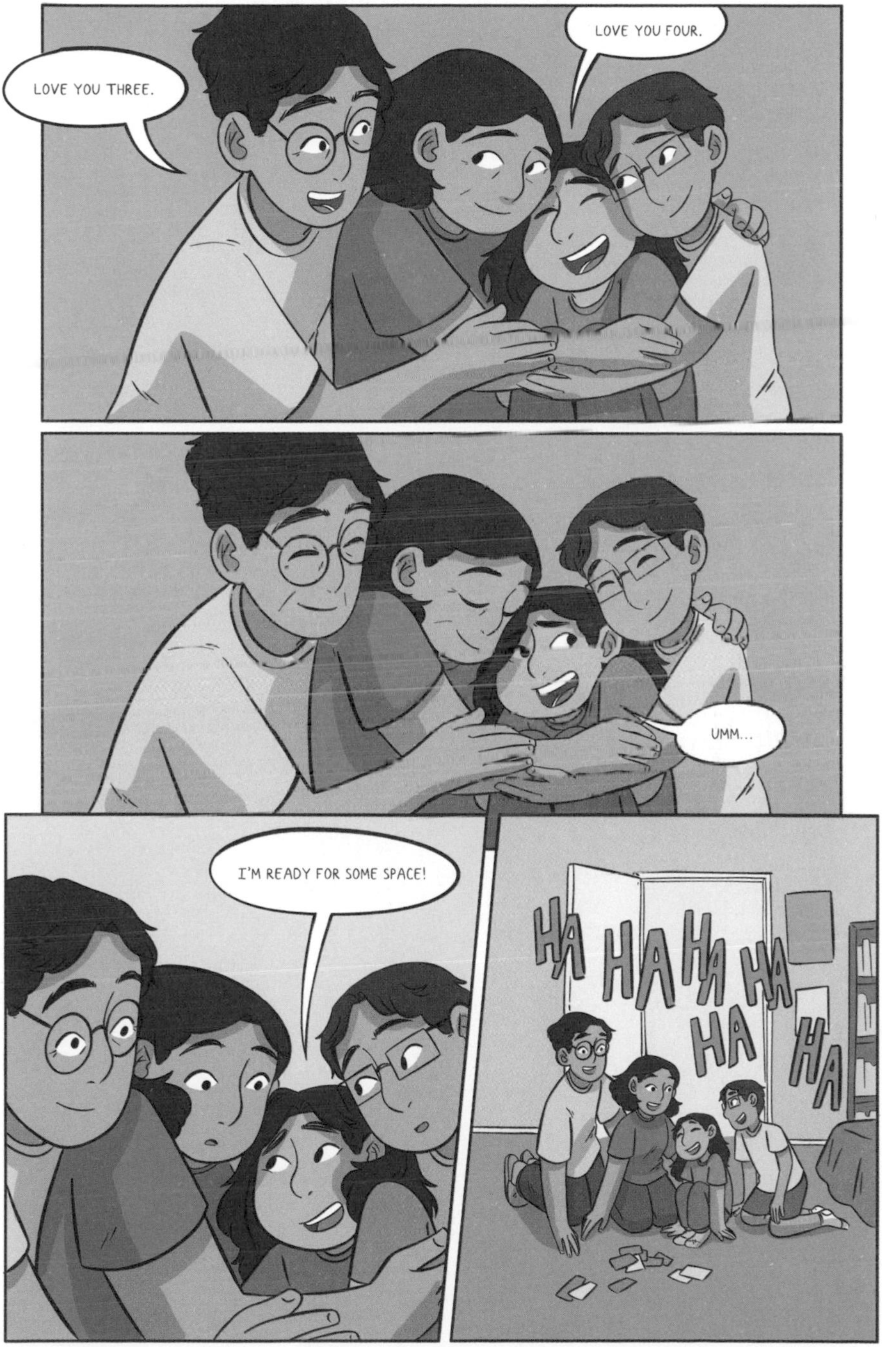
LOVE YOU THREE.
LOVE YOU FOUR.
UMM...
I'M READY FOR SOME SPACE!
HA HA HA HA HA HA HA

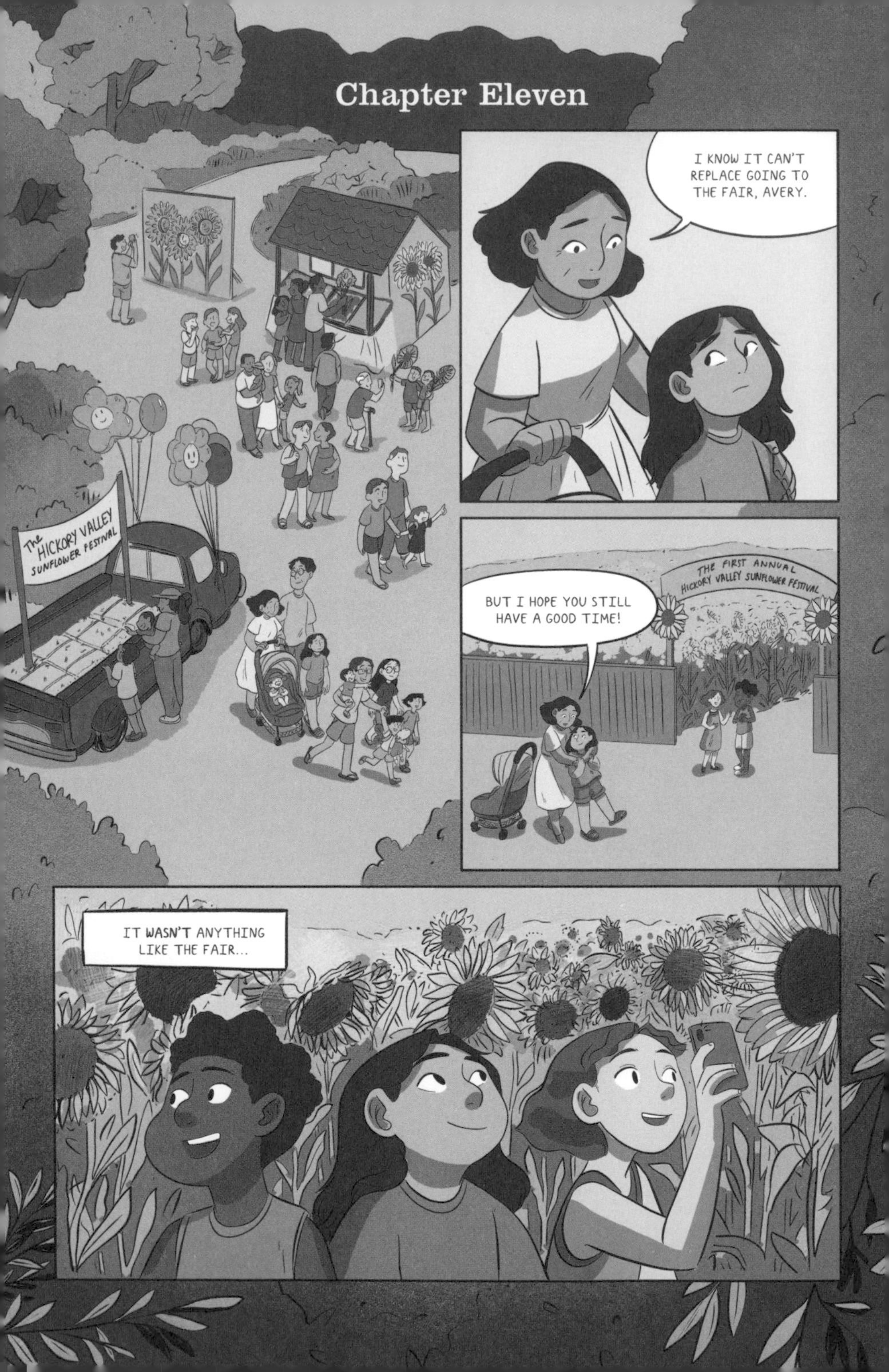
Chapter Eleven
The HICKORY VALLEY SUNFLOWER FESTIVAL
I KNOW IT CAN'T REPLACE GOING TO THE FAIR, AVERY.
THE FIRST ANNUAL HICKORY VALLEY SUNFLOWER FESTIVAL
BUT I HOPE YOU STILL HAVE A GOOD TIME!
IT WASN'T ANYTHING LIKE THE FAIR...

BUT IT WAS STILL FUN.

WE SHOULD COME HERE EVERY YEAR!

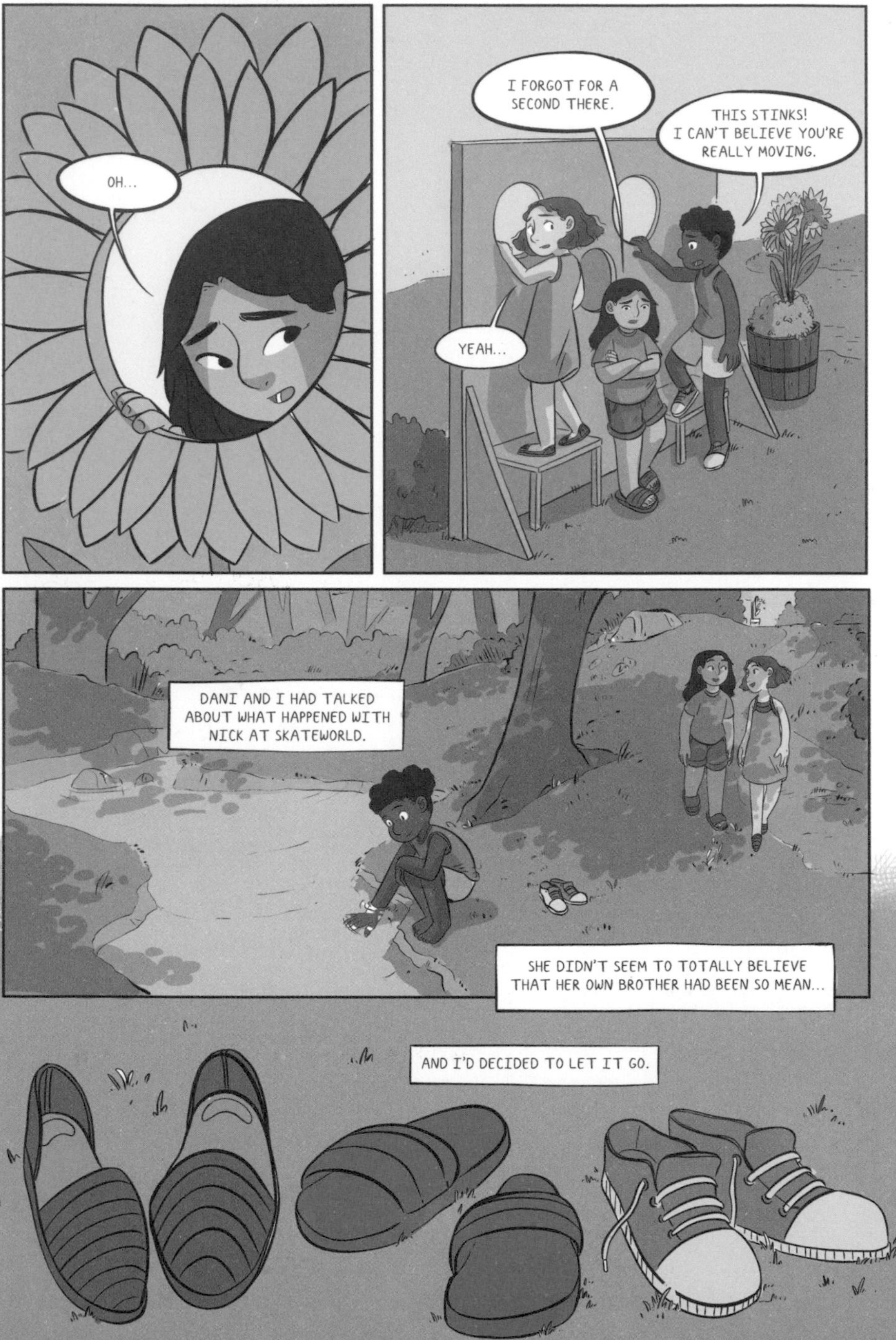
OH...
I FORGOT FOR A SECOND THERE.
THIS STINKS! I CAN'T BELIEVE YOU'RE REALLY MOVING.
YEAH...
DANI AND I HAD TALKED ABOUT WHAT HAPPENED WITH NICK AT SKATEWORLD.
SHE DIDN'T SEEM TO TOTALLY BELIEVE THAT HER OWN BROTHER HAD BEEN SO MEAN...
AND I'D DECIDED TO LET IT GO.

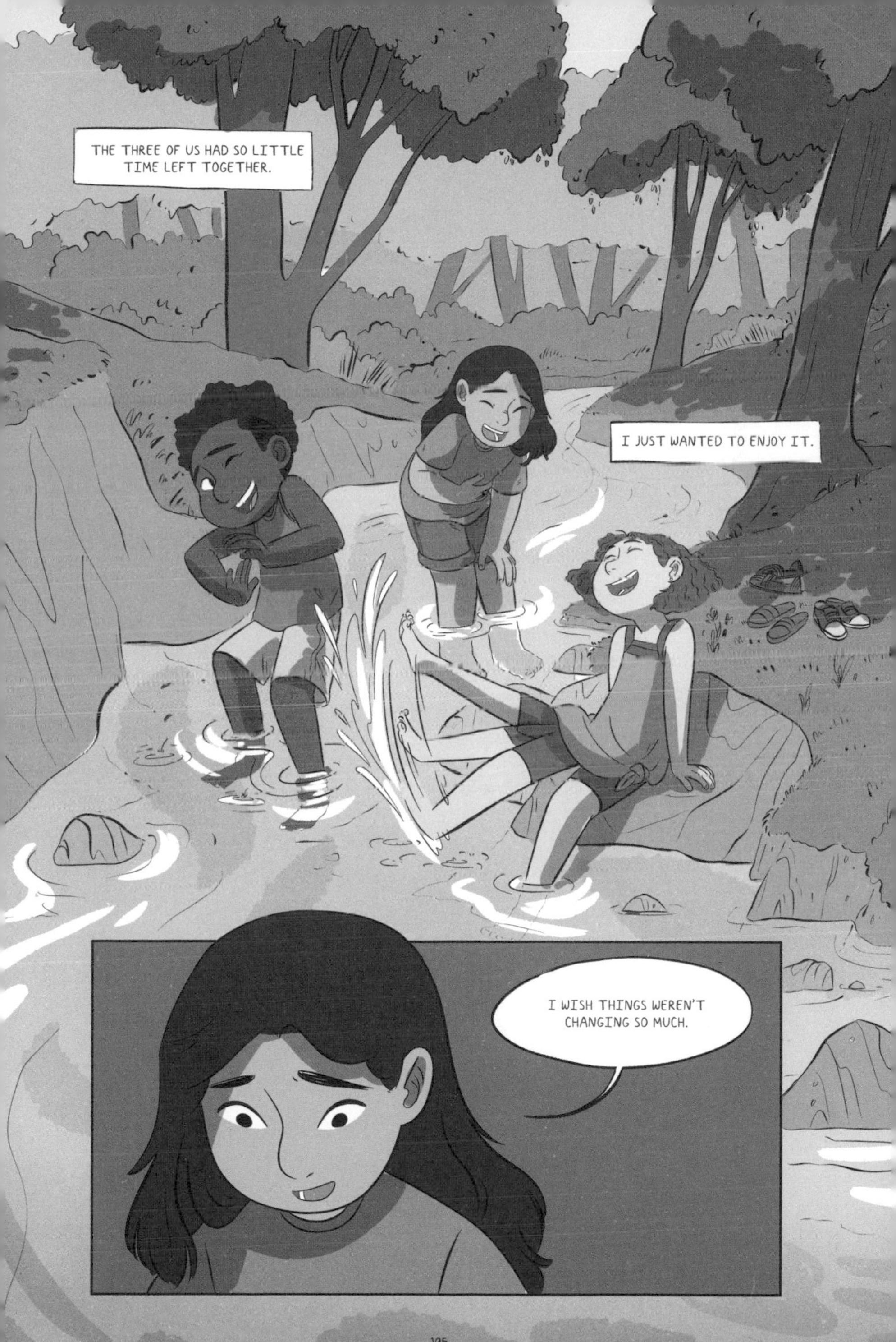
THE THREE OF US HAD SO LITTLE TIME LEFT TOGETHER.
I JUST WANTED TO ENJOY IT.
I WISH THINGS WEREN'T CHANGING SO MUCH.

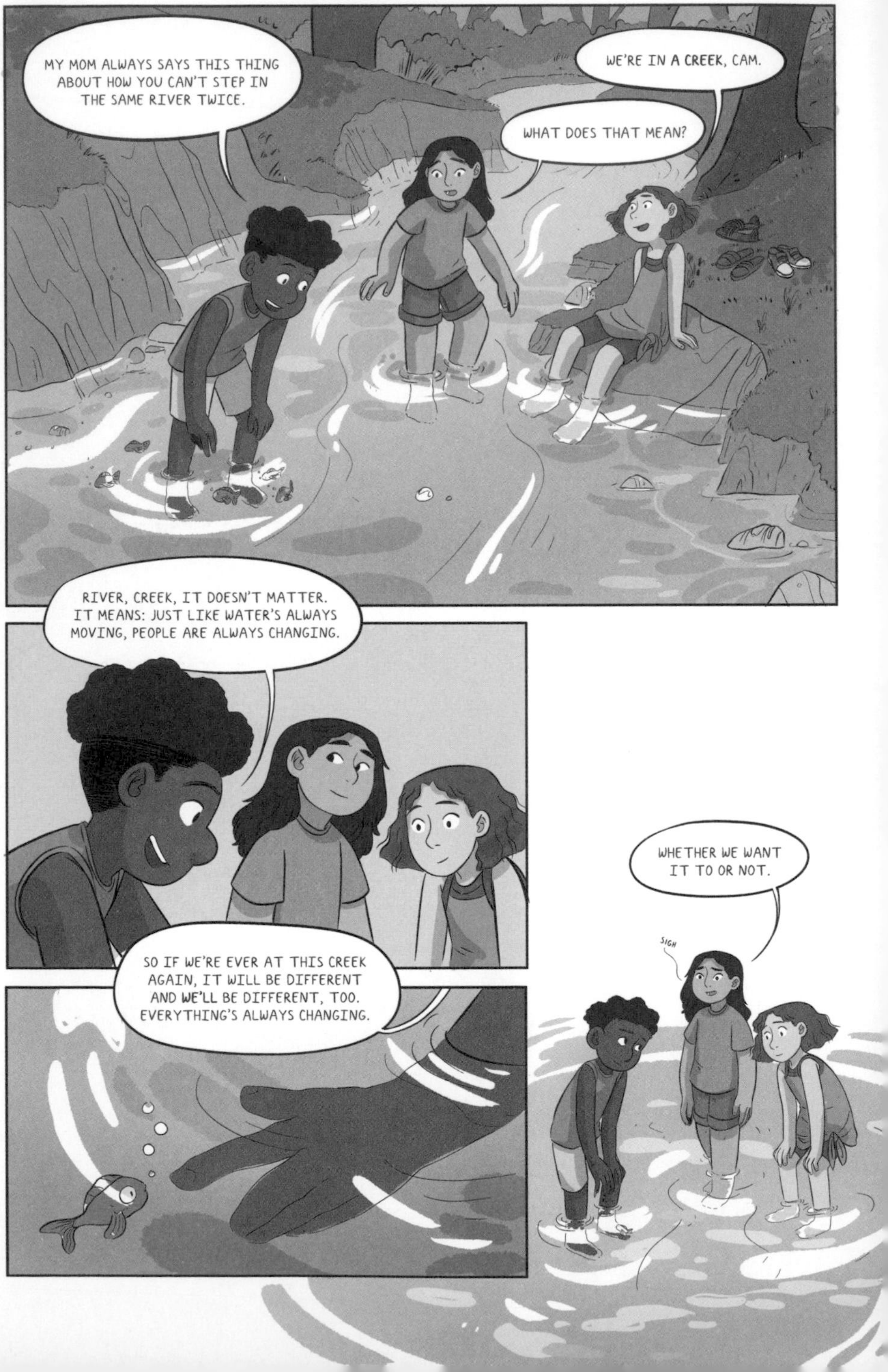
MY MOM ALWAYS SAYS THIS THING ABOUT HOW YOU CAN'T STEP IN THE SAME RIVER TWICE.
WE'RE IN A CREEK, CAM.
WHAT DOES THAT MEAN?
RIVER, CREEK, IT DOESN'T MATTER. IT MEANS: JUST LIKE WATER'S ALWAYS MOVING, PEOPLE ARE ALWAYS CHANGING.
SO IF WE'RE EVER AT THIS CREEK AGAIN, IT WILL BE DIFFERENT AND WE'LL BE DIFFERENT, TOO. EVERYTHING'S ALWAYS CHANGING.
SIGH
WHETHER WE WANT IT TO OR NOT.

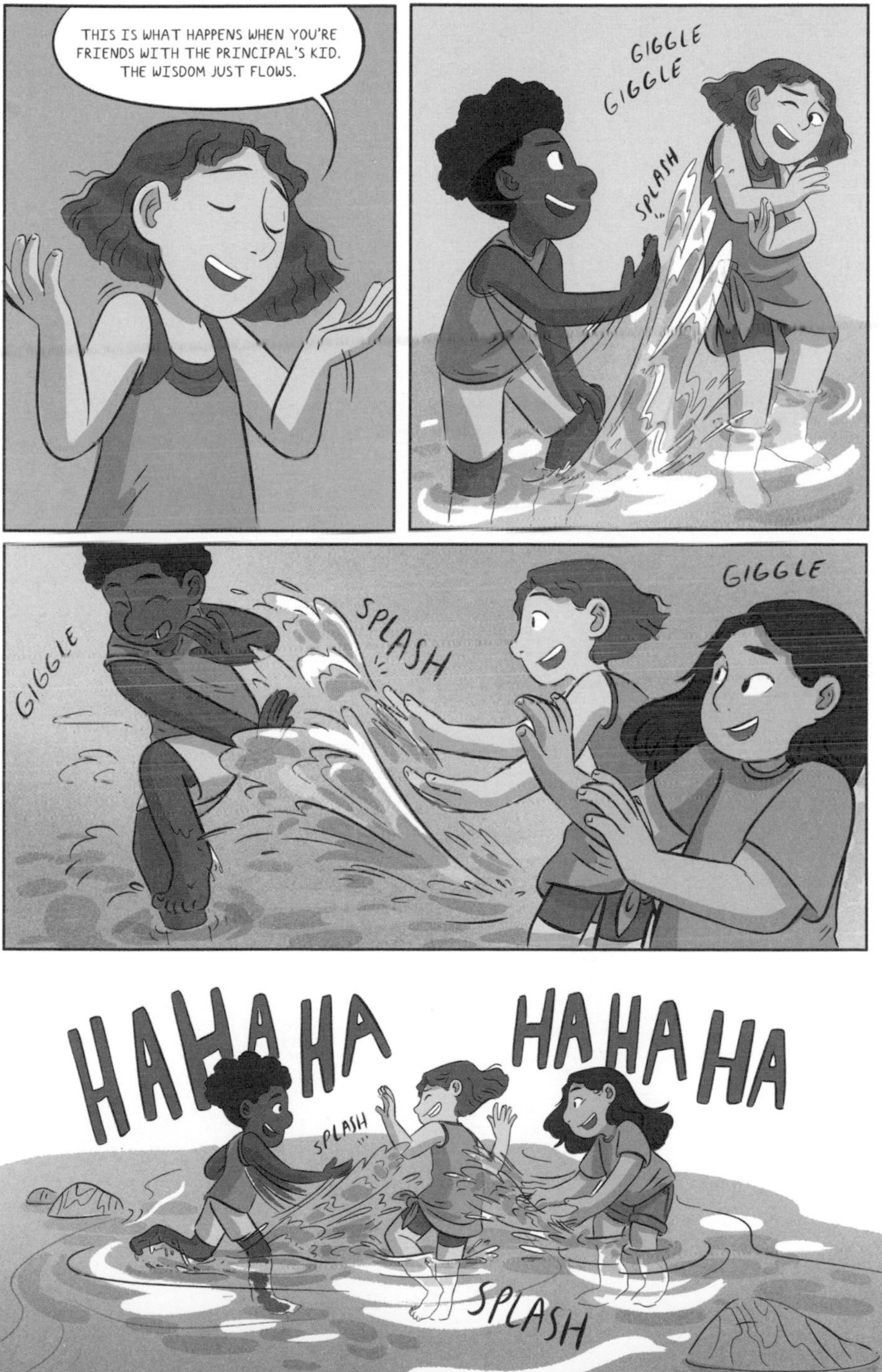
THIS IS WHAT HAPPENS WHEN YOU'RE FRIENDS WITH THE PRINCIPAL'S KID. THE WISDOM JUST FLOWS.
GIGGLE GIGGLE
SPLASH
GIGGLE
SPLASH
GIGGLE
HAHAHA
HAHAHAHA
SPLASH
SPLASH

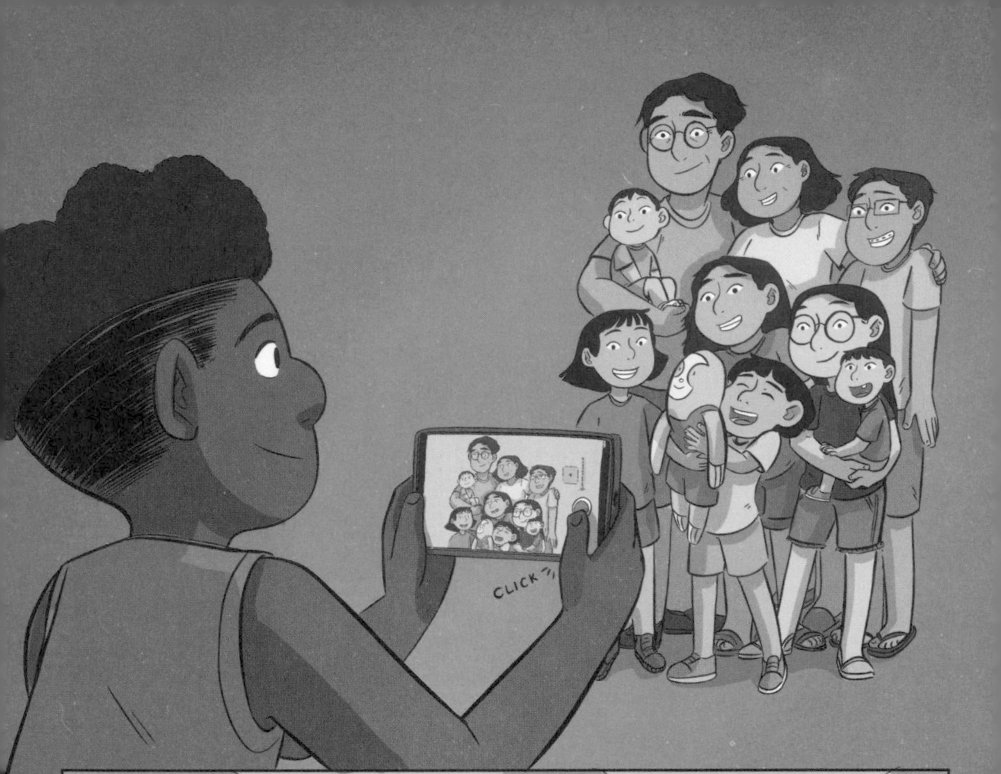

CLICK

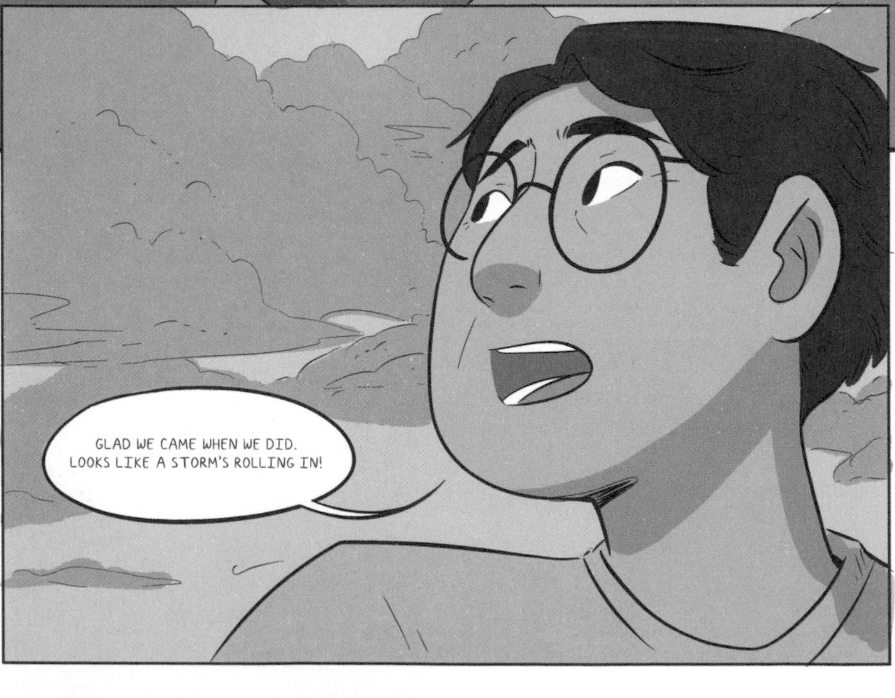

GLAD WE CAME WHEN WE DID.
LOOKS LIKE A STORM'S ROLLING IN!

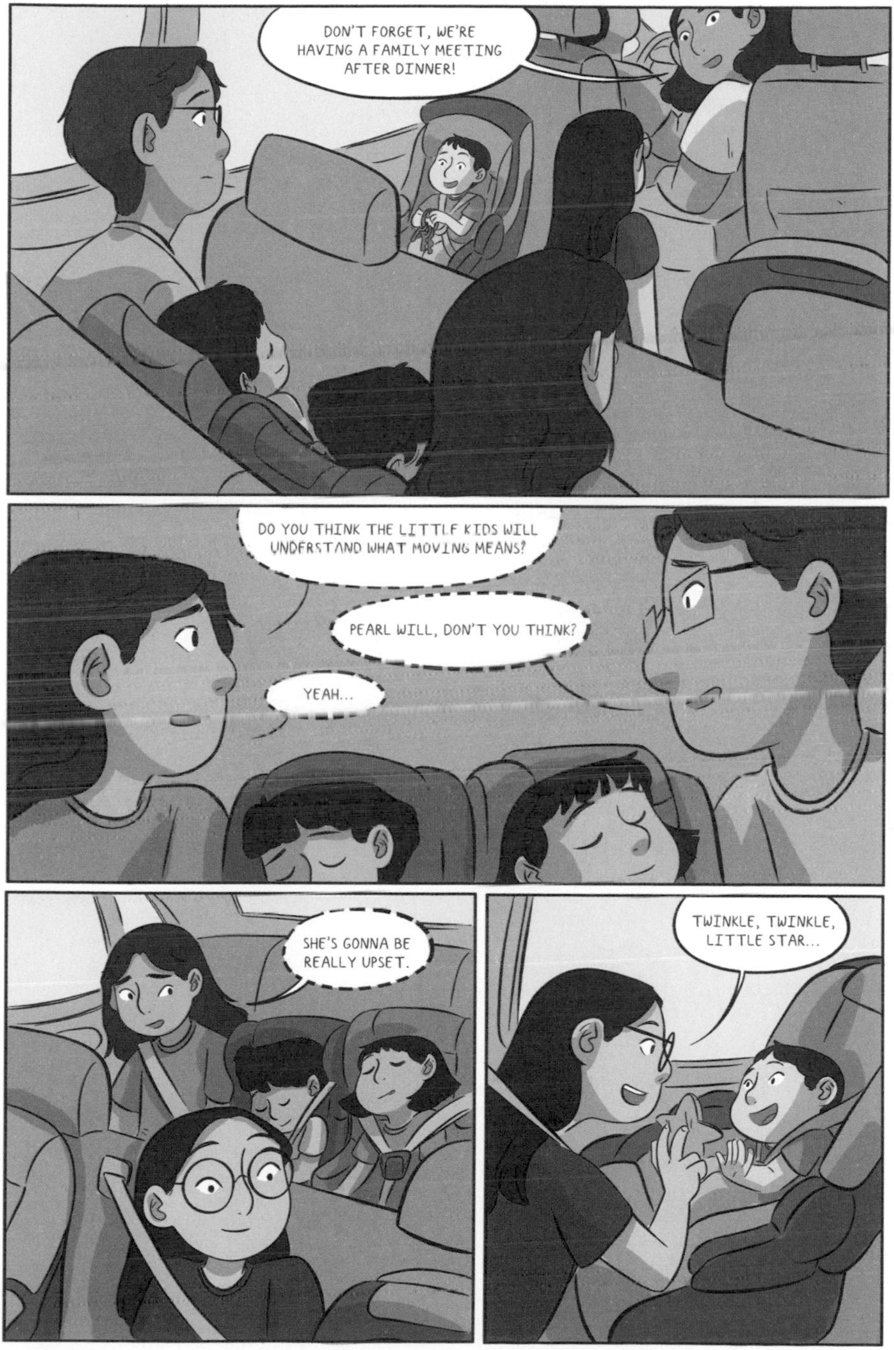
DON'T FORGET, WE'RE HAVING A FAMILY MEETING AFTER DINNER!
DO YOU THINK THE LITTLE KIDS WILL UNDERSTAND WHAT MOVING MEANS?
PEARL WILL, DON'T YOU THINK?
YEAH...
SHE'S GONNA BE REALLY UPSET.
TWINKLE, TWINKLE, LITTLE STAR...

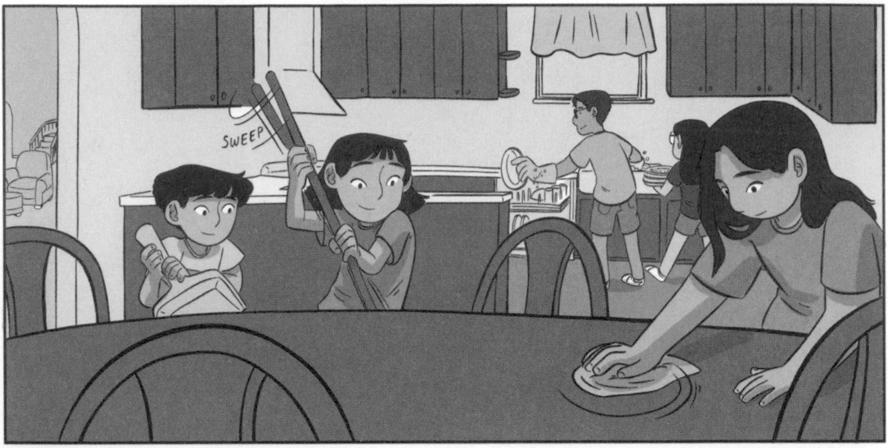
SWEEP

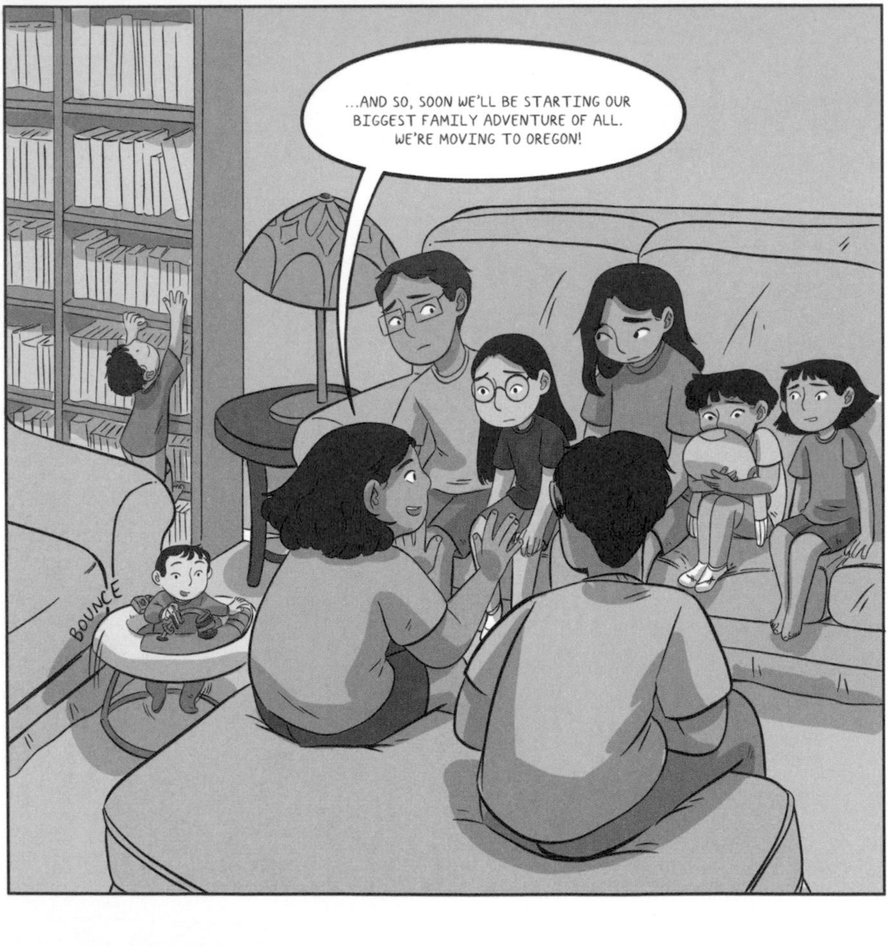
...AND SO, SOON WE'LL BE STARTING OUR
BIGGEST FAMILY ADVENTURE OF ALL.
WE'RE MOVING TO OREGON!
BOUNCE

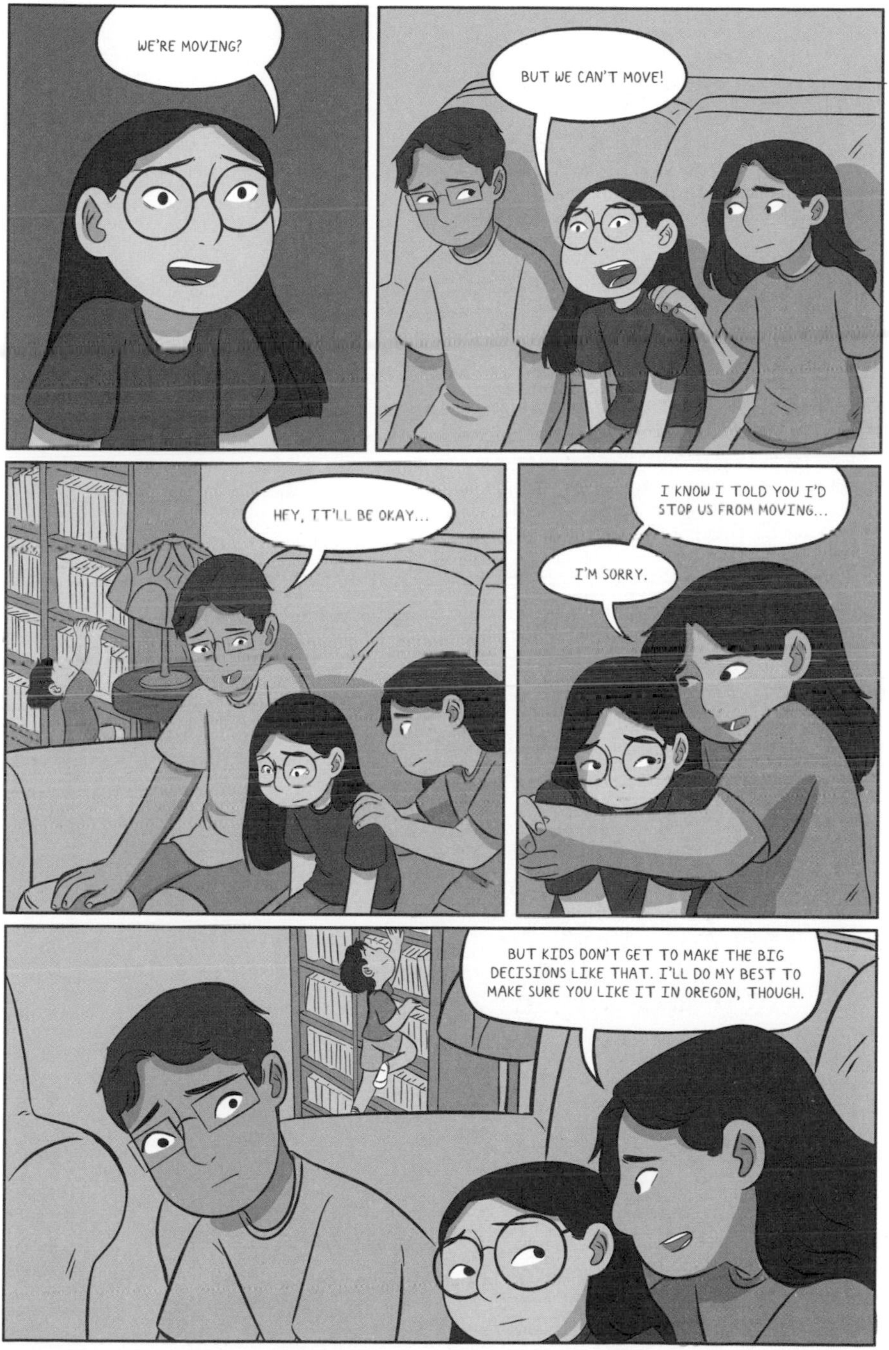
WE'RE MOVING?
BUT WE CAN'T MOVE!
HEY, IT'LL BE OKAY...
I KNOW I TOLD YOU I'D STOP US FROM MOVING...
I'M SORRY.
BUT KIDS DON'T GET TO MAKE THE BIG DECISIONS LIKE THAT. I'LL DO MY BEST TO MAKE SURE YOU LIKE IT IN OREGON, THOUGH.

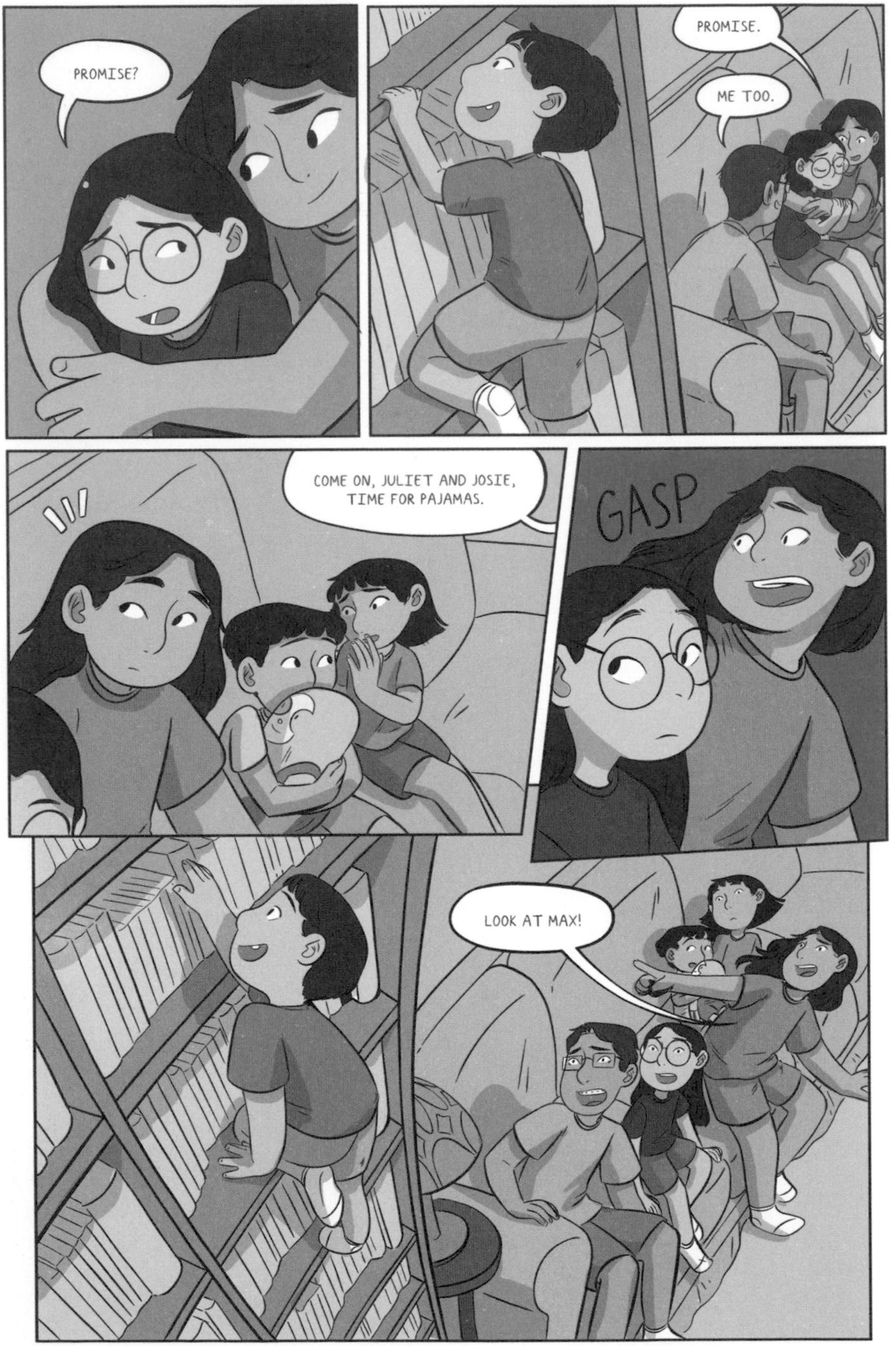
PROMISE?
PROMISE.
ME TOO.
COME ON, JULIET AND JOSIE, TIME FOR PAJAMAS.
GASP
LOOK AT MAX!

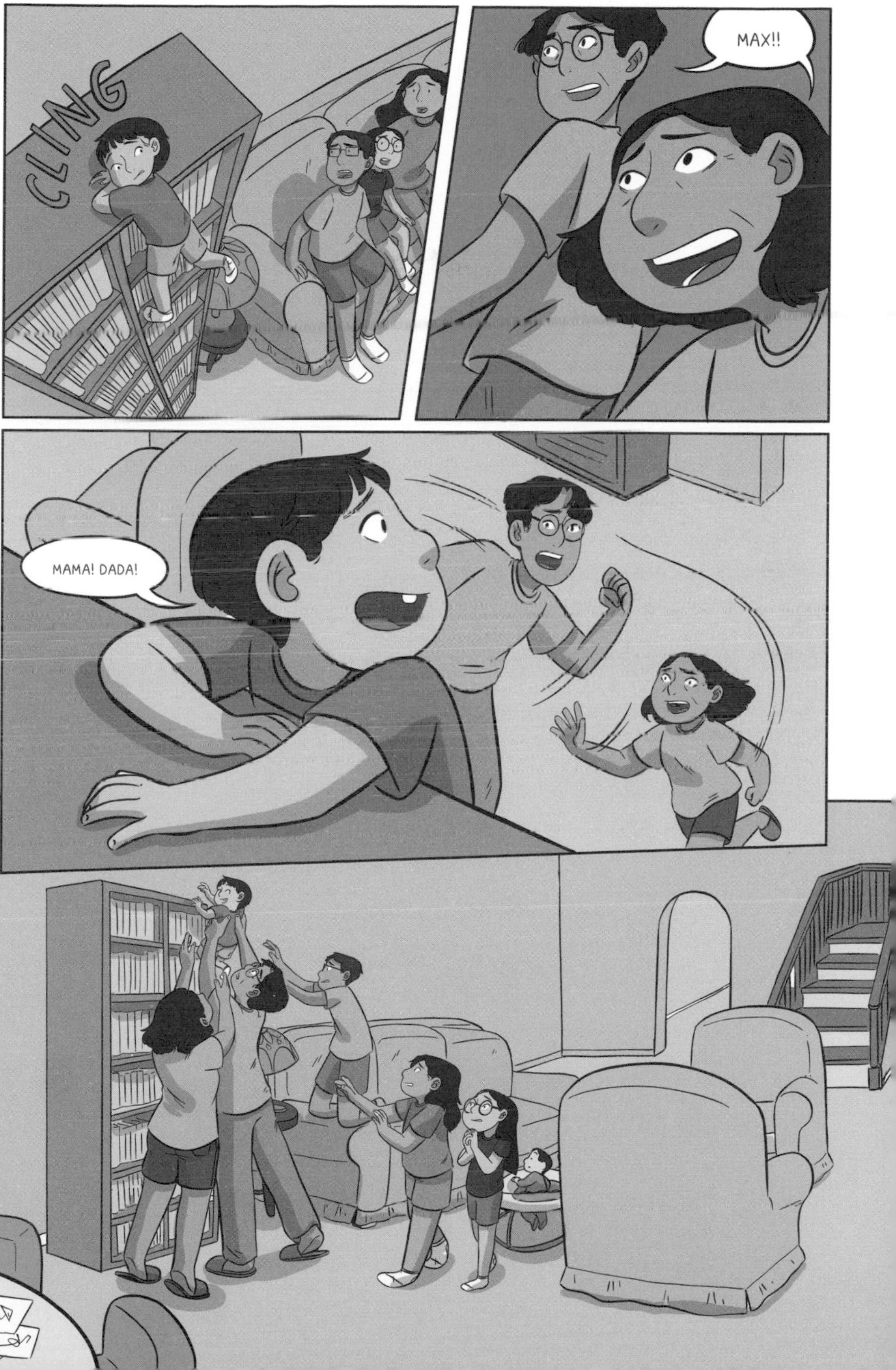
CLING
MAX!!
MAMA! DADA!

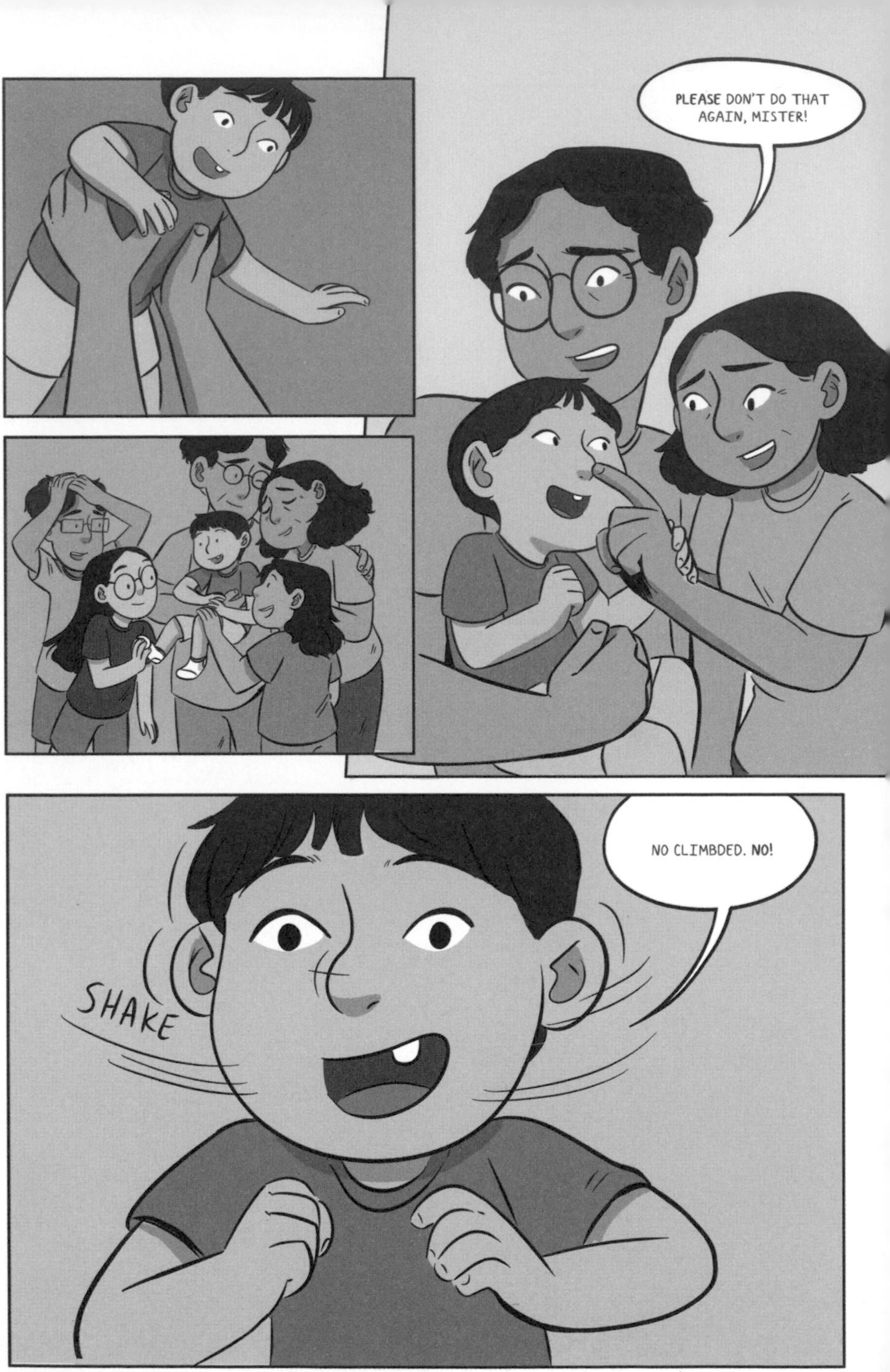
PLEASE DON'T DO THAT AGAIN, MISTER!
NO CLIMBDED. NO!
SHAKE

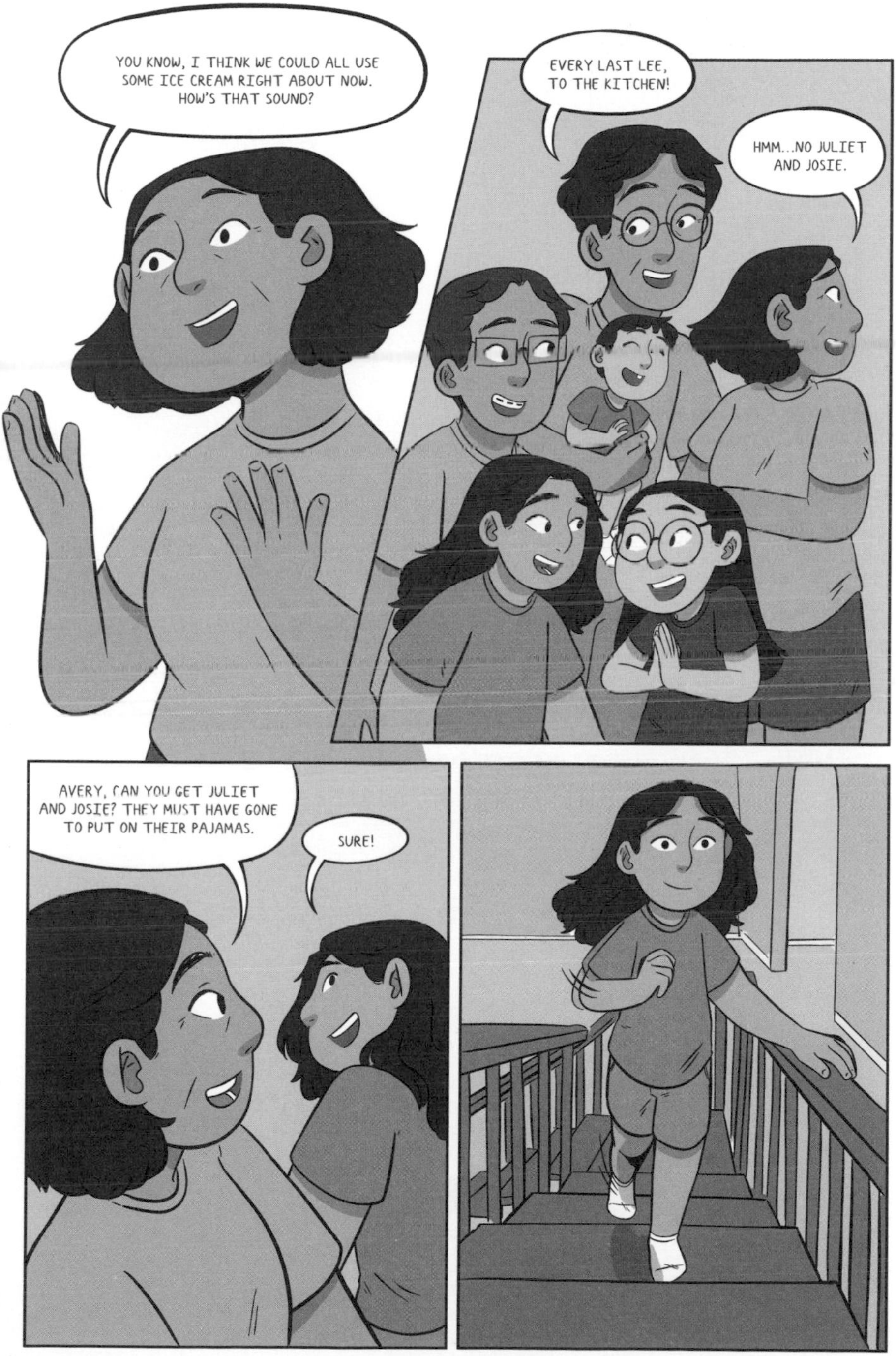
YOU KNOW, I THINK WE COULD ALL USE SOME ICE CREAM RIGHT ABOUT NOW. HOW'S THAT SOUND?
EVERY LAST LEE, TO THE KITCHEN!
HMM...NO JULIET AND JOSIE.
AVERY, CAN YOU GET JULIET AND JOSIE? THEY MUST HAVE GONE TO PUT ON THEIR PAJAMAS.
SURE!

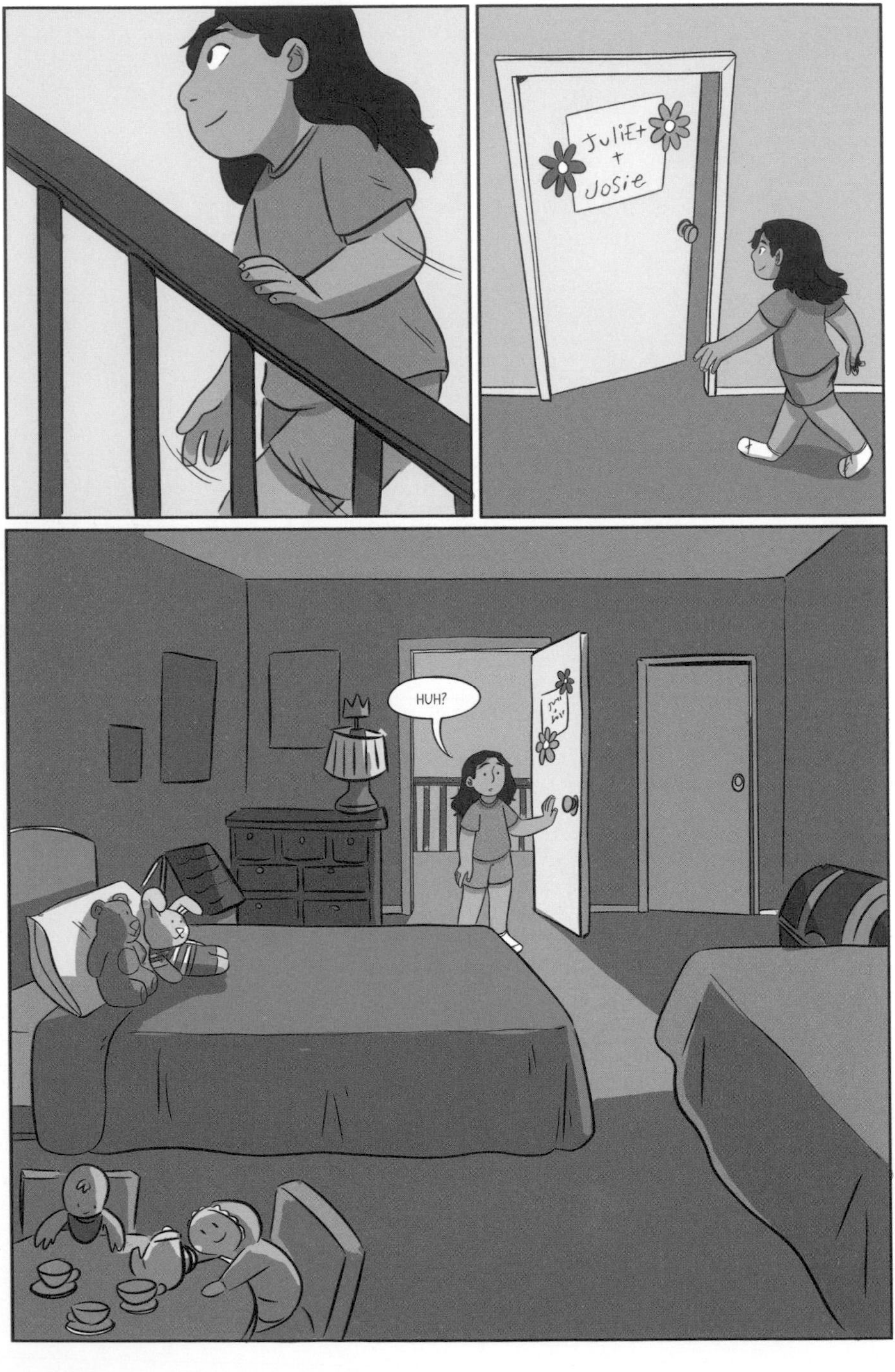
Julie
+
Josie
HUH?

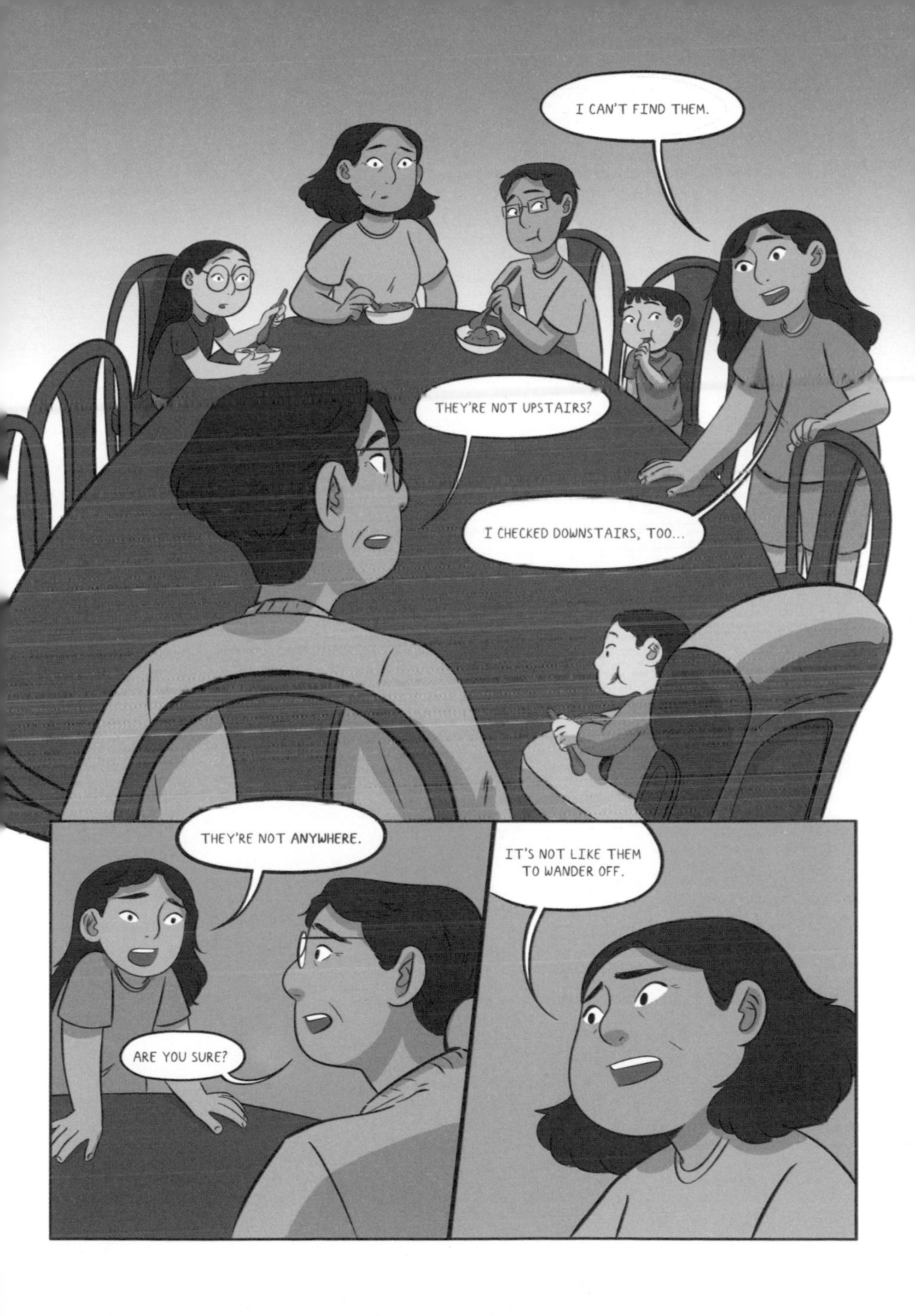
I CAN'T FIND THEM.
THEY'RE NOT UPSTAIRS?
I CHECKED DOWNSTAIRS, TOO...
THEY'RE NOT ANYWHERE.
ARE YOU SURE?
IT'S NOT LIKE THEM TO WANDER OFF.

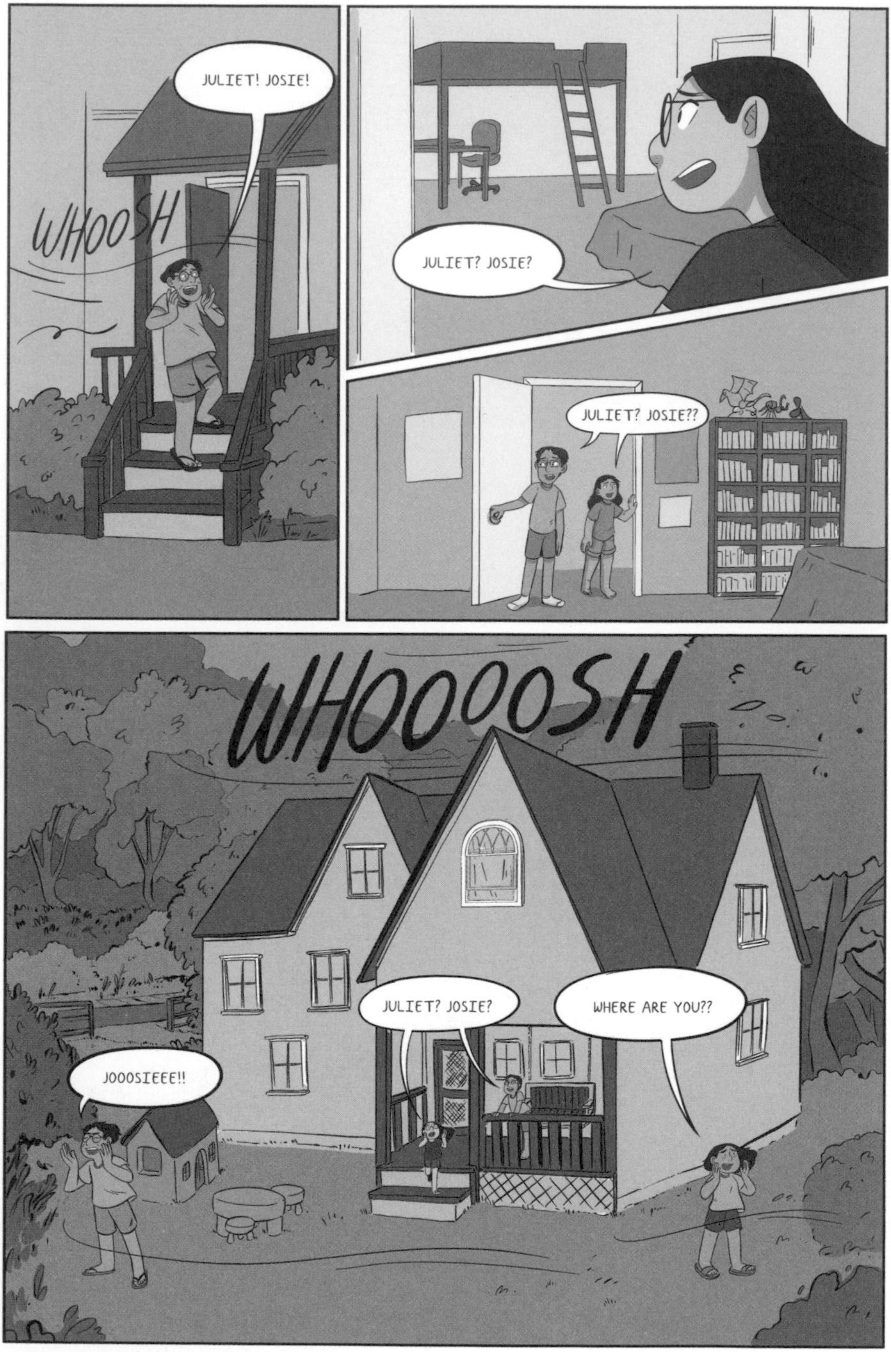
WHOOSH
JULIET! JOSIE!
JULIET? JOSIE?
JULIET? JOSIE??
WHOOOOSH
JULIET? JOSIE?
WHERE ARE YOU??
JOOOSIEEE!!

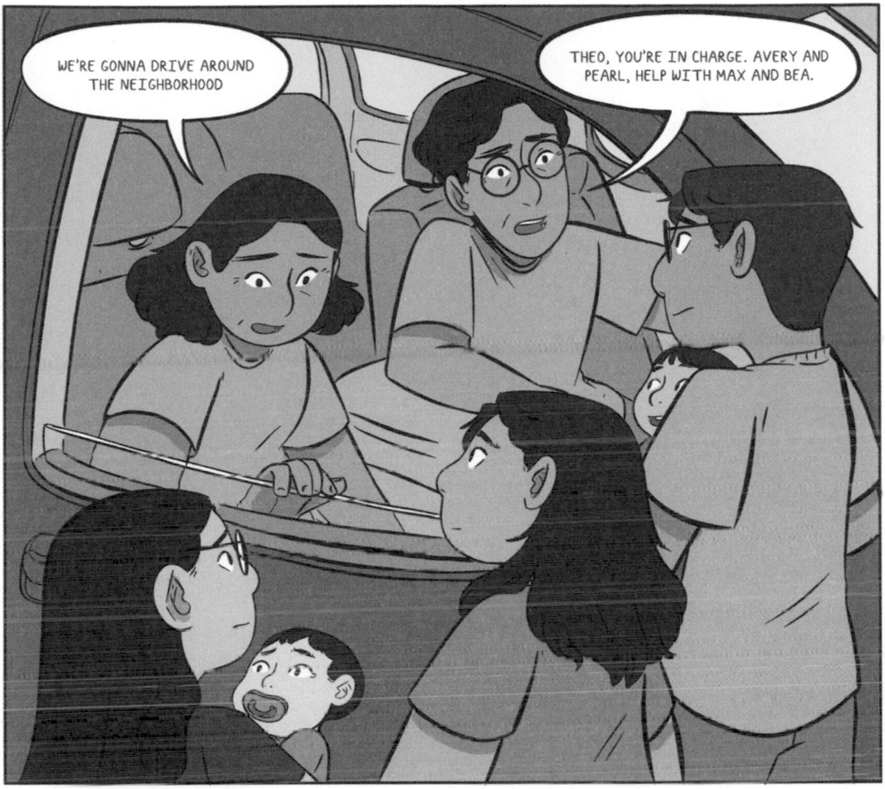
WE'RE GONNA DRIVE AROUND THE NEIGHBORHOOD
THEO, YOU'RE IN CHARGE. AVERY AND PEARL, HELP WITH MAX AND BEA.

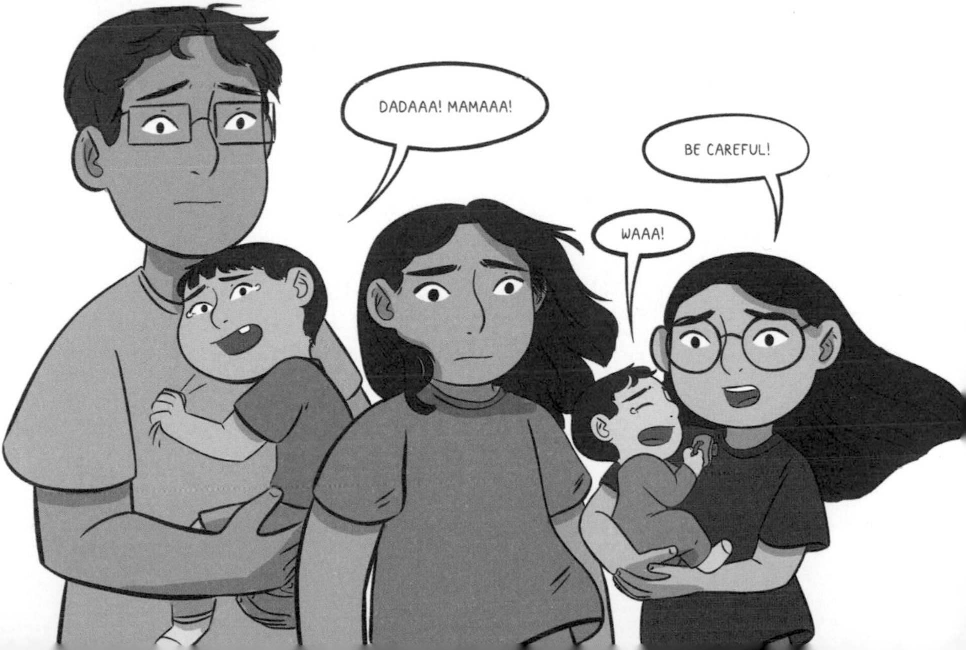
DADAAA! MAMAAA!
BE CAREFUL!
WAAA!

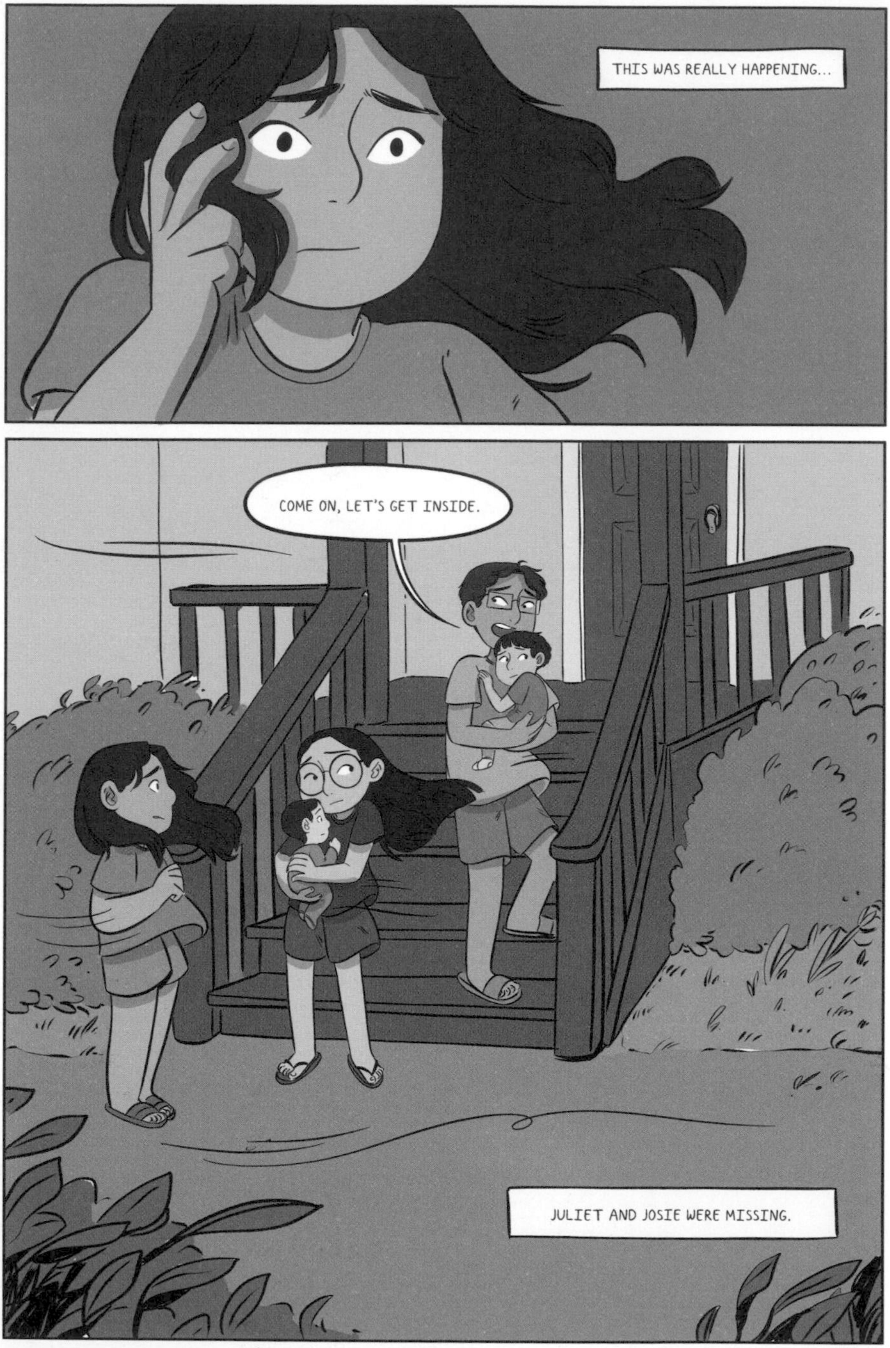
THIS WAS REALLY HAPPENING...
COME ON, LET'S GET INSIDE.
JULIET AND JOSIE WERE MISSING.

Chapter Twelve

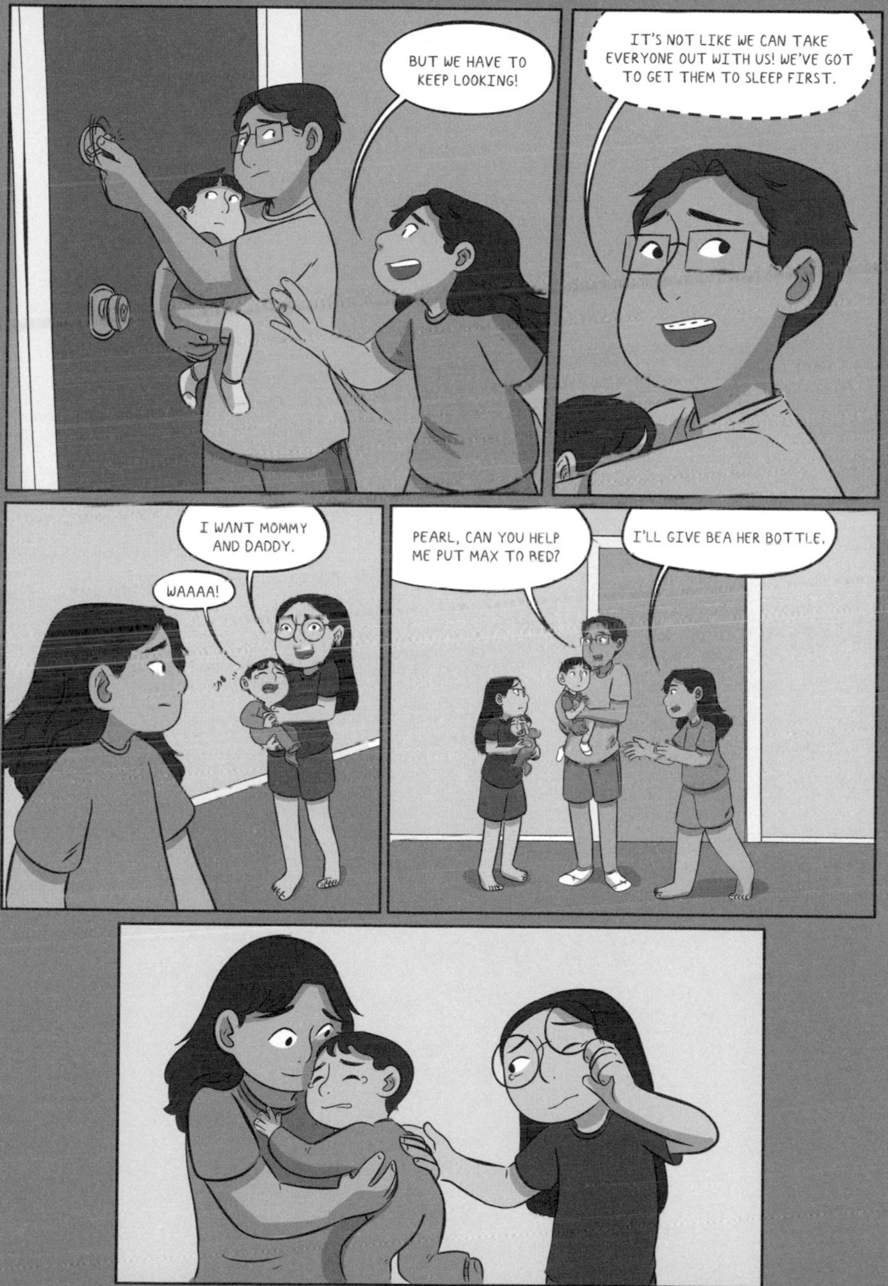

BUT WE HAVE TO KEEP LOOKING!
IT'S NOT LIKE WE CAN TAKE EVERYONE OUT WITH US! WE'VE GOT TO GET THEM TO SLEEP FIRST.
I WANT MOMMY AND DADDY.
WAAAA!
PEARL, CAN YOU HELP ME PUT MAX TO BED?
I'LL GIVE BEA HER BOTTLE.

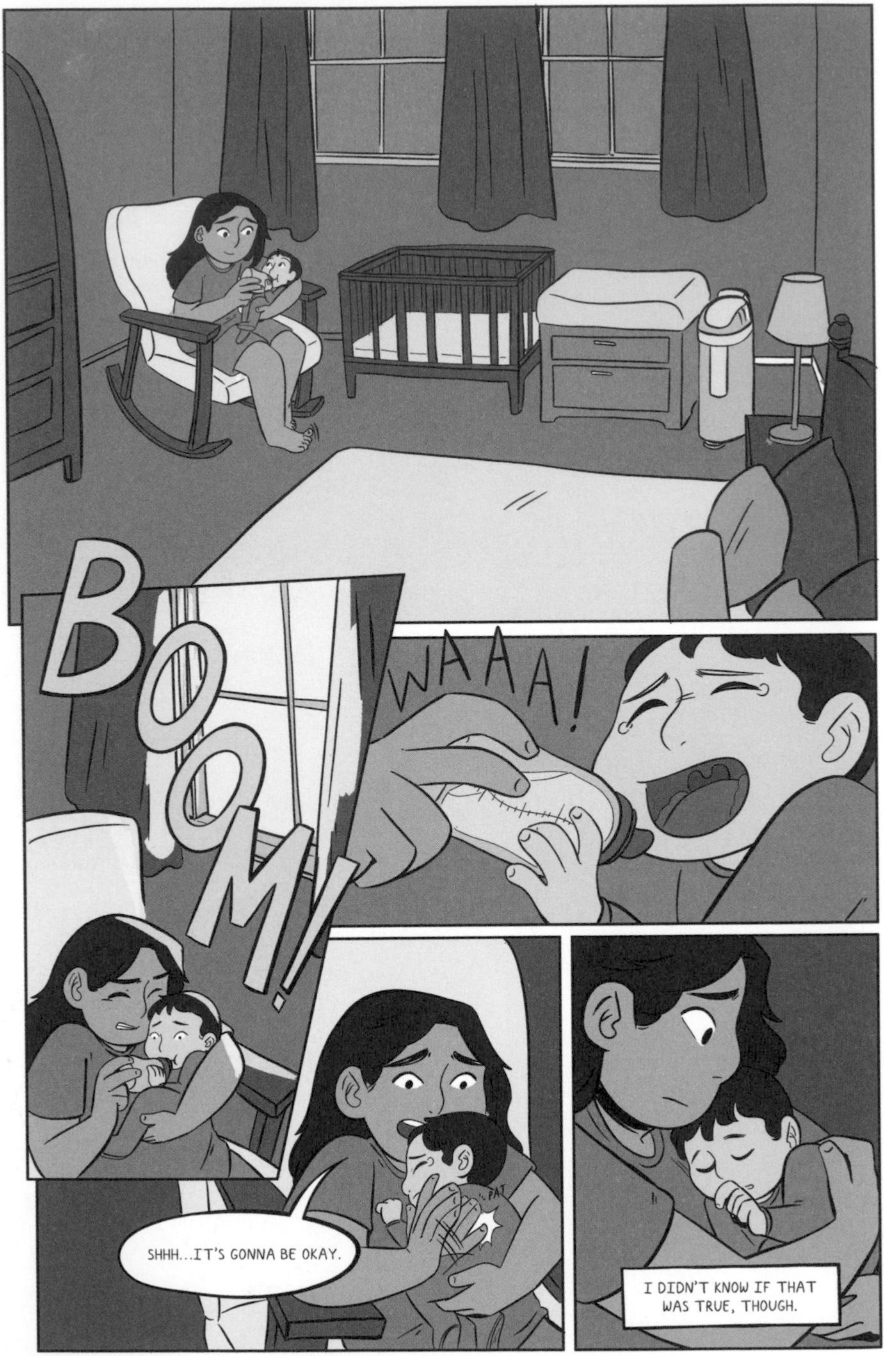
BOOM!
WAAAA!
PAT
SHHH...IT'S GONNA BE OKAY.
I DIDN'T KNOW IF THAT WAS TRUE, THOUGH.

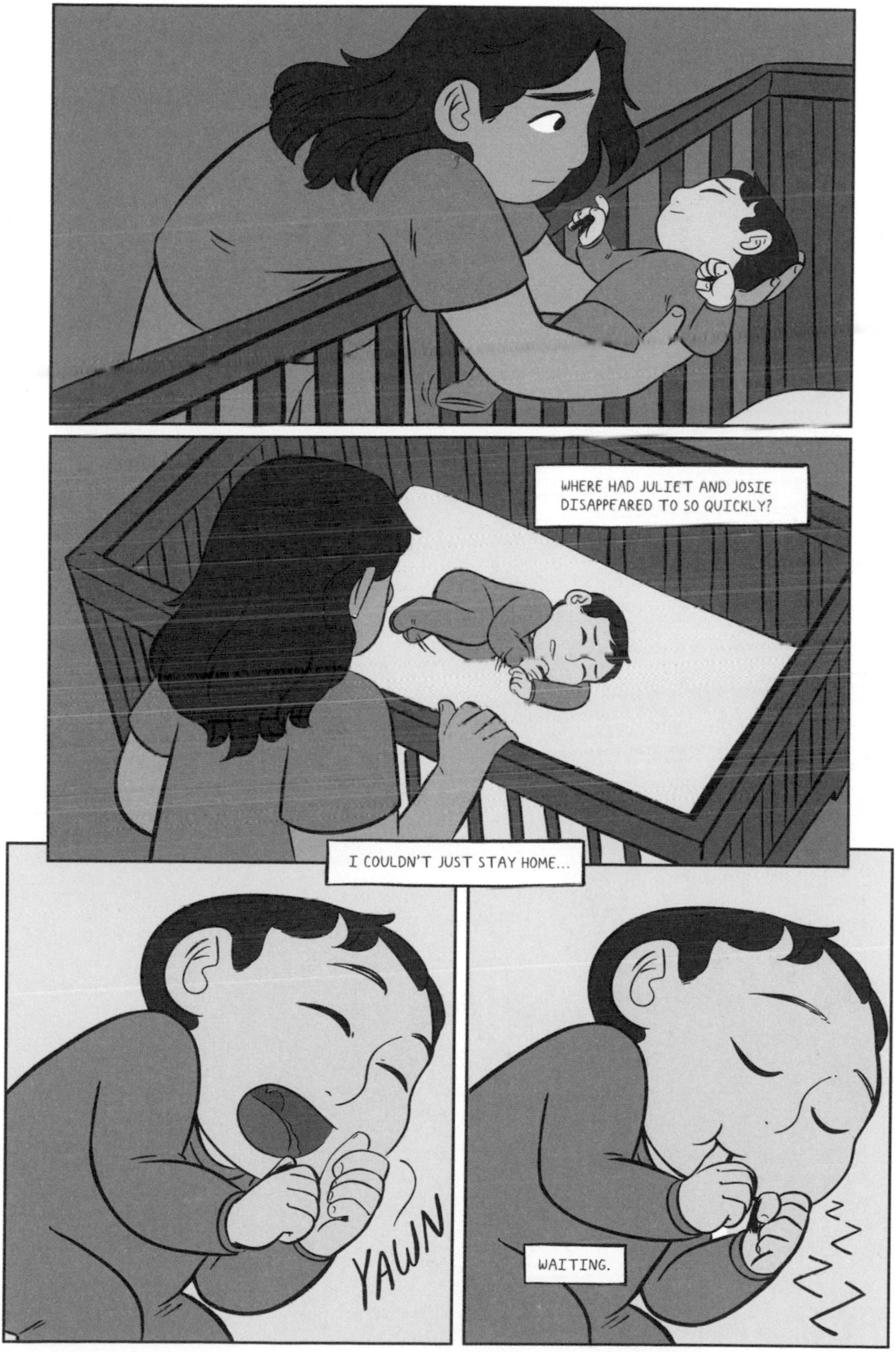
WHERE HAD JULIET AND JOSIE DISAPPEARED TO SO QUICKLY?
I COULDN'T JUST STAY HOME...
YAWN
WAITING.
ZZZ

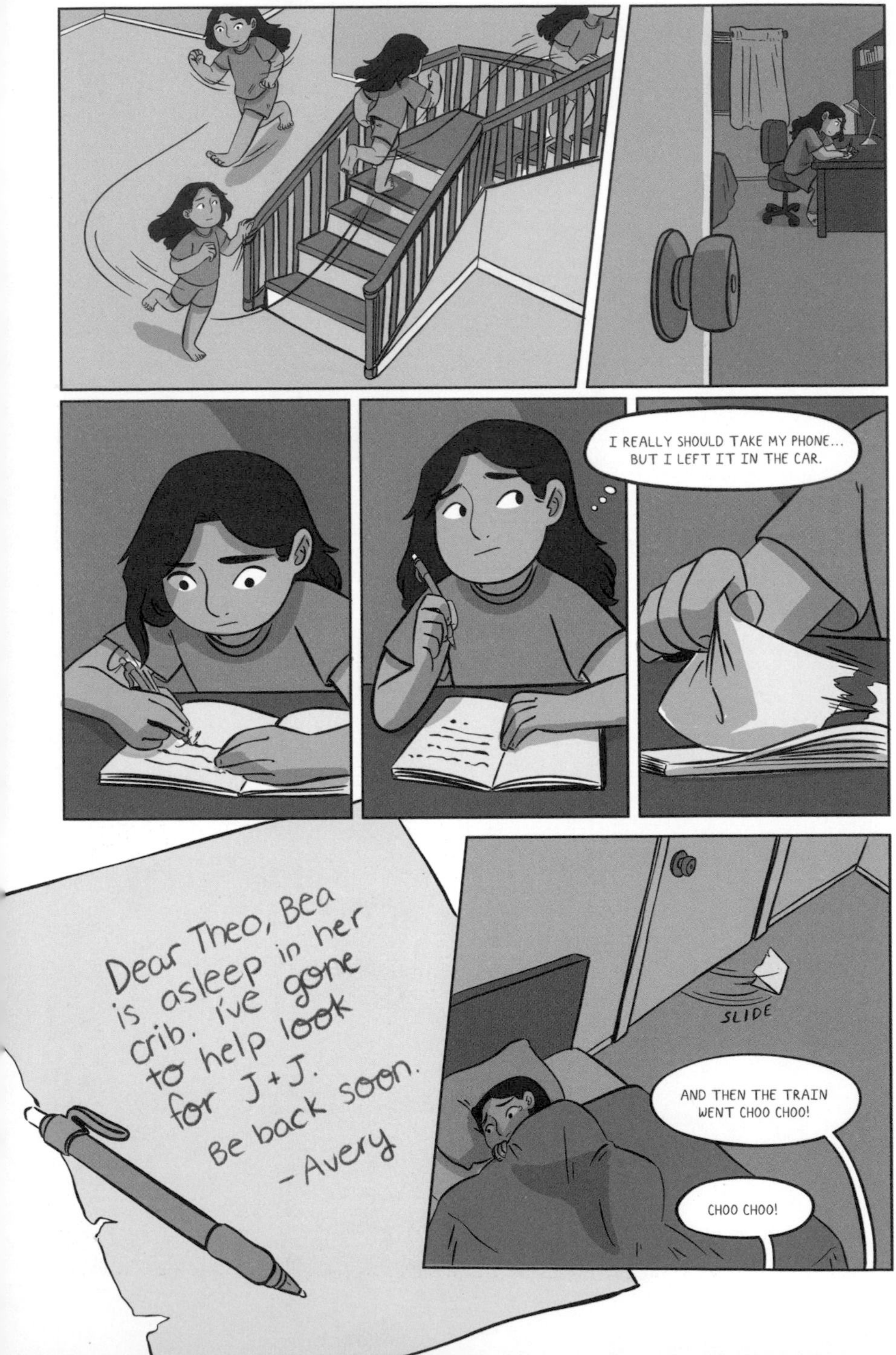
I REALLY SHOULD TAKE MY PHONE... BUT I LEFT IT IN THE CAR.
Dear Theo, Bea is asleep in her crib. I've gone to help look for J+J. Be back soon. -Avery
SLIDE
AND THEN THE TRAIN WENT CHOO CHOO!
CHOO CHOO!

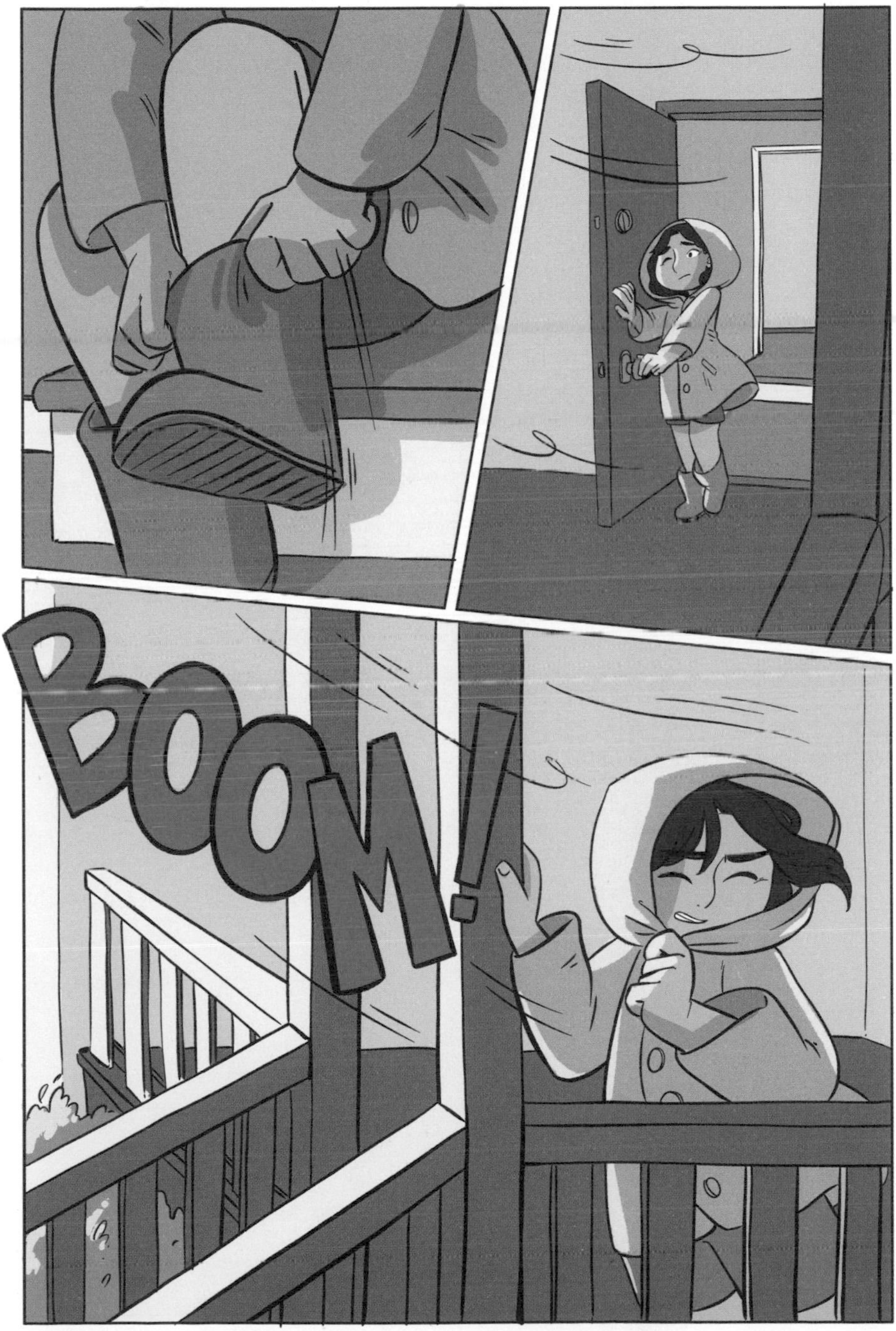
BOOM!

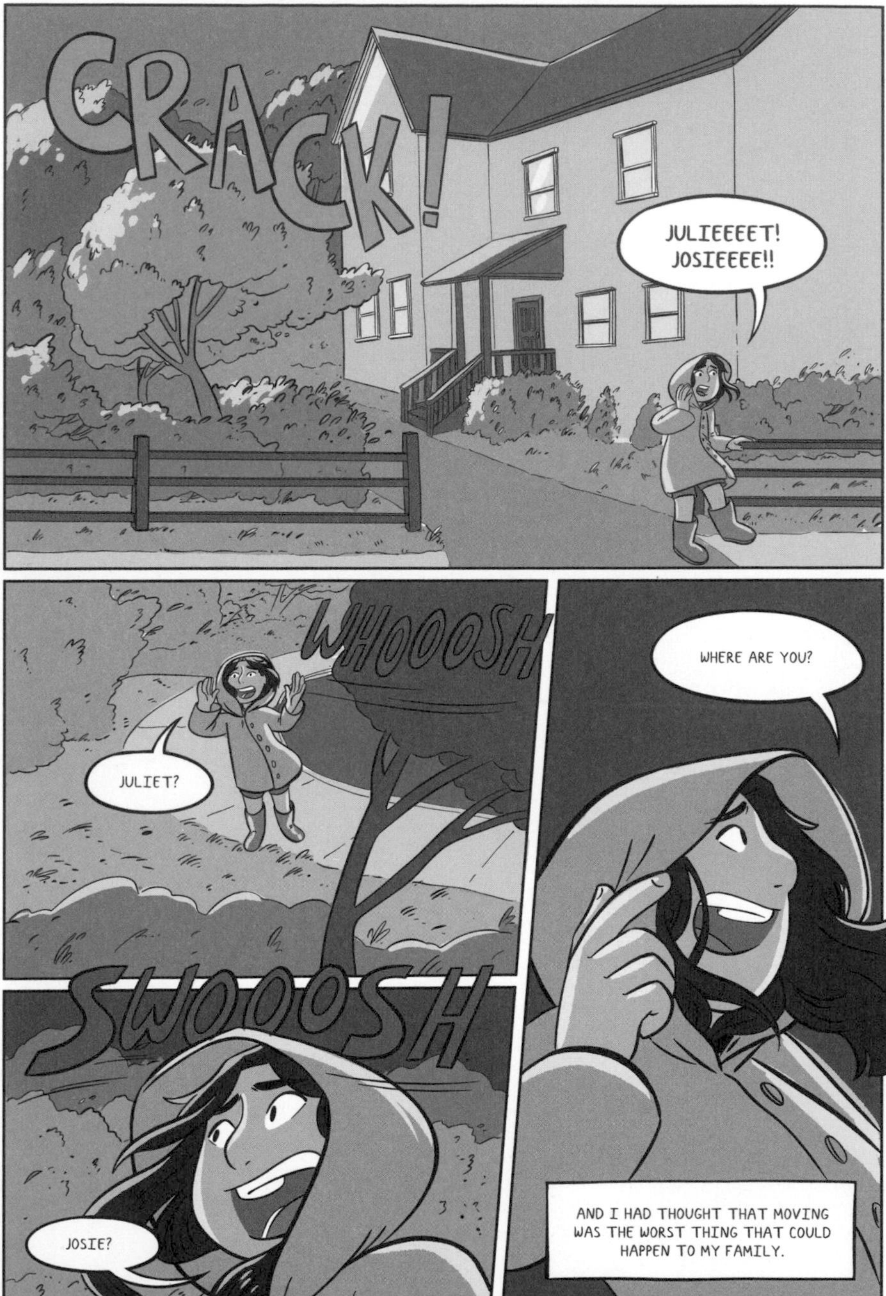
CRACK!
JULIEEEET! JOSIEEEE!!
WHOOOSH
JULIET?
WHERE ARE YOU?
SWOOOSH
JOSIE?
AND I HAD THOUGHT THAT MOVING WAS THE WORST THING THAT COULD HAPPEN TO MY FAMILY.

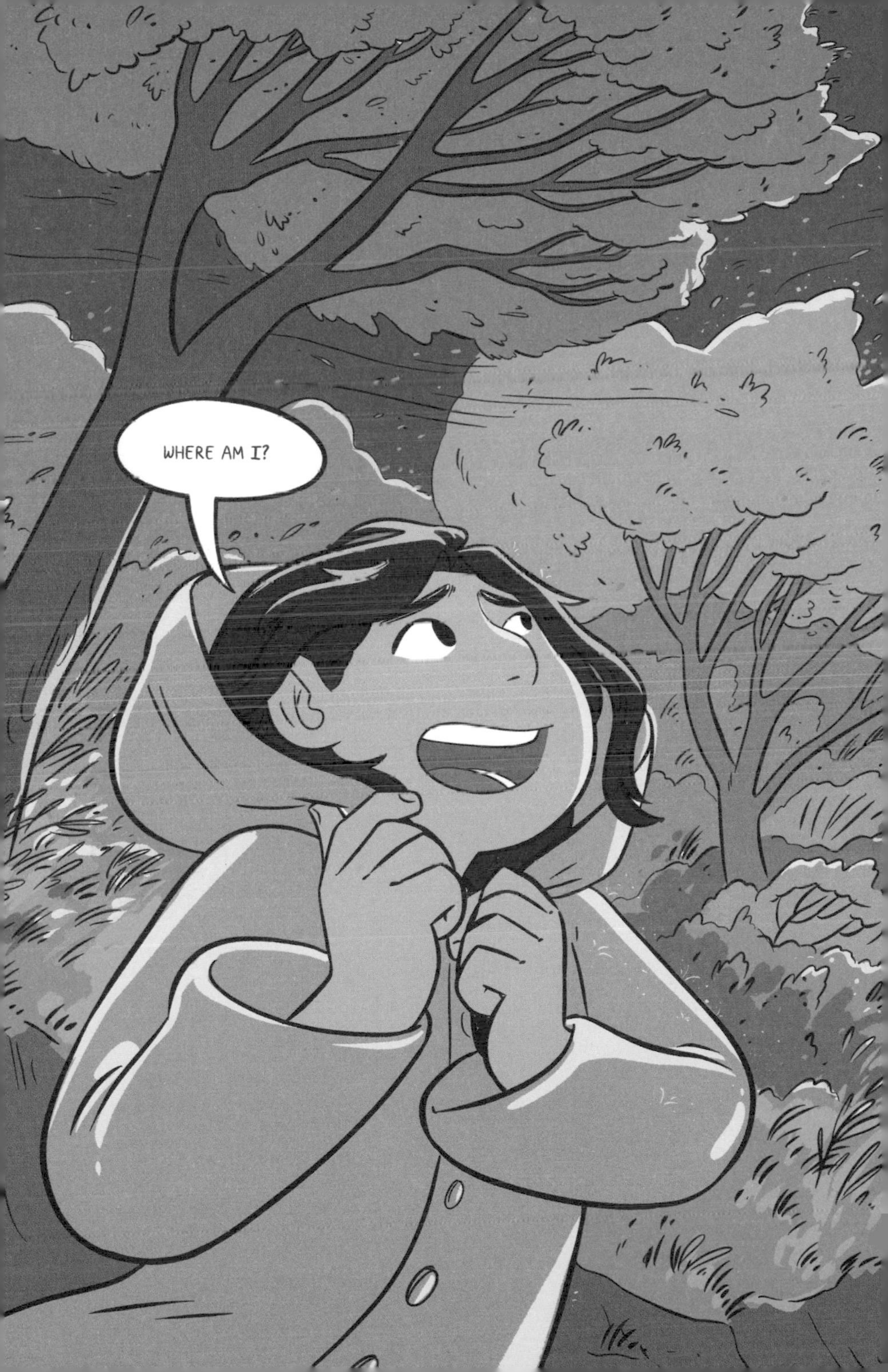
WHERE AM I?

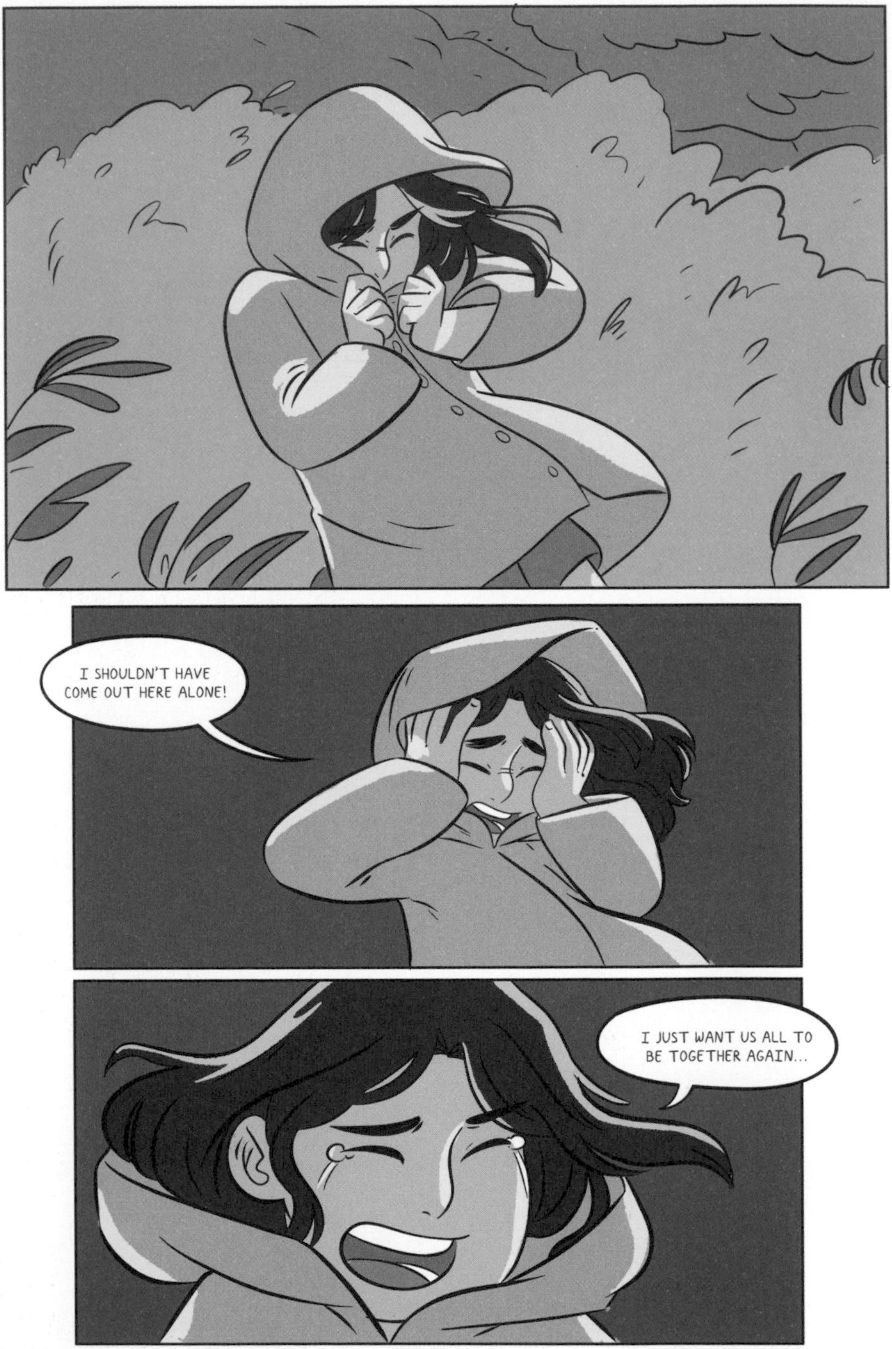
I SHOULDN'T HAVE COME OUT HERE ALONE!
I JUST WANT US ALL TO BE TOGETHER AGAIN...

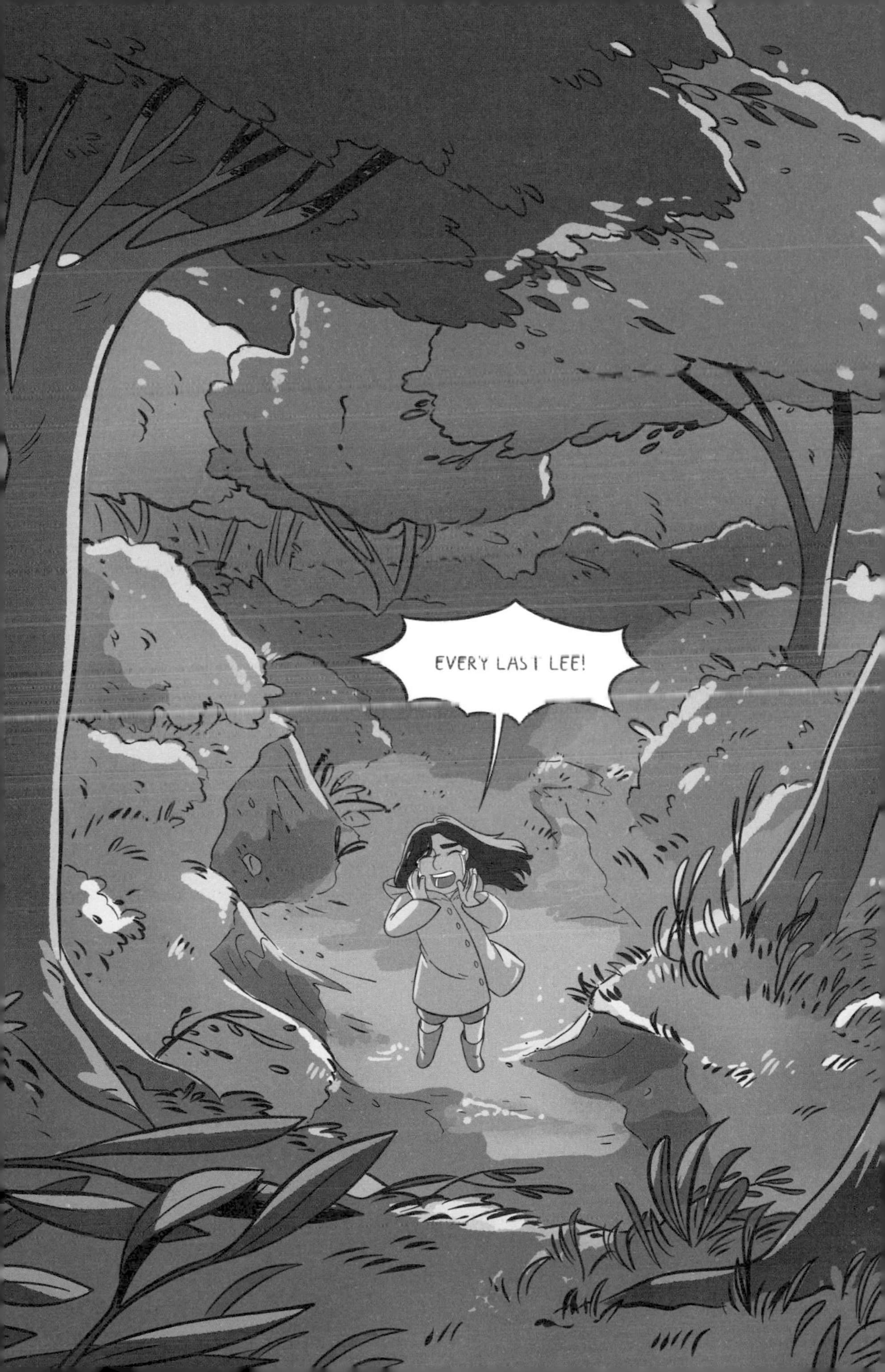
EVERY LAST LEE!

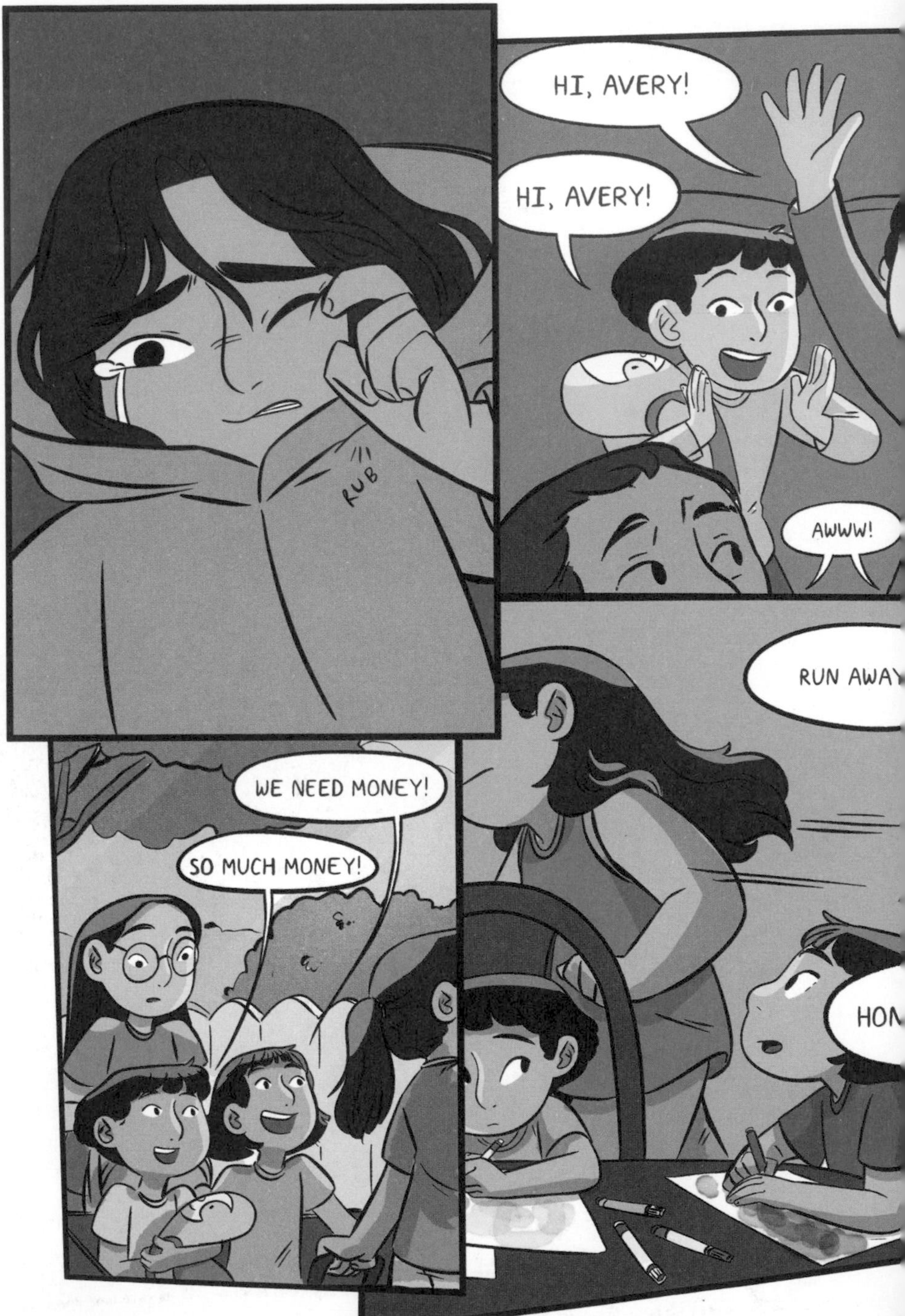
RUB
HI, AVERY!
HI, AVERY!
AWWW!
RUN AWAY
HOM
WE NEED MONEY!
SO MUCH MONEY!

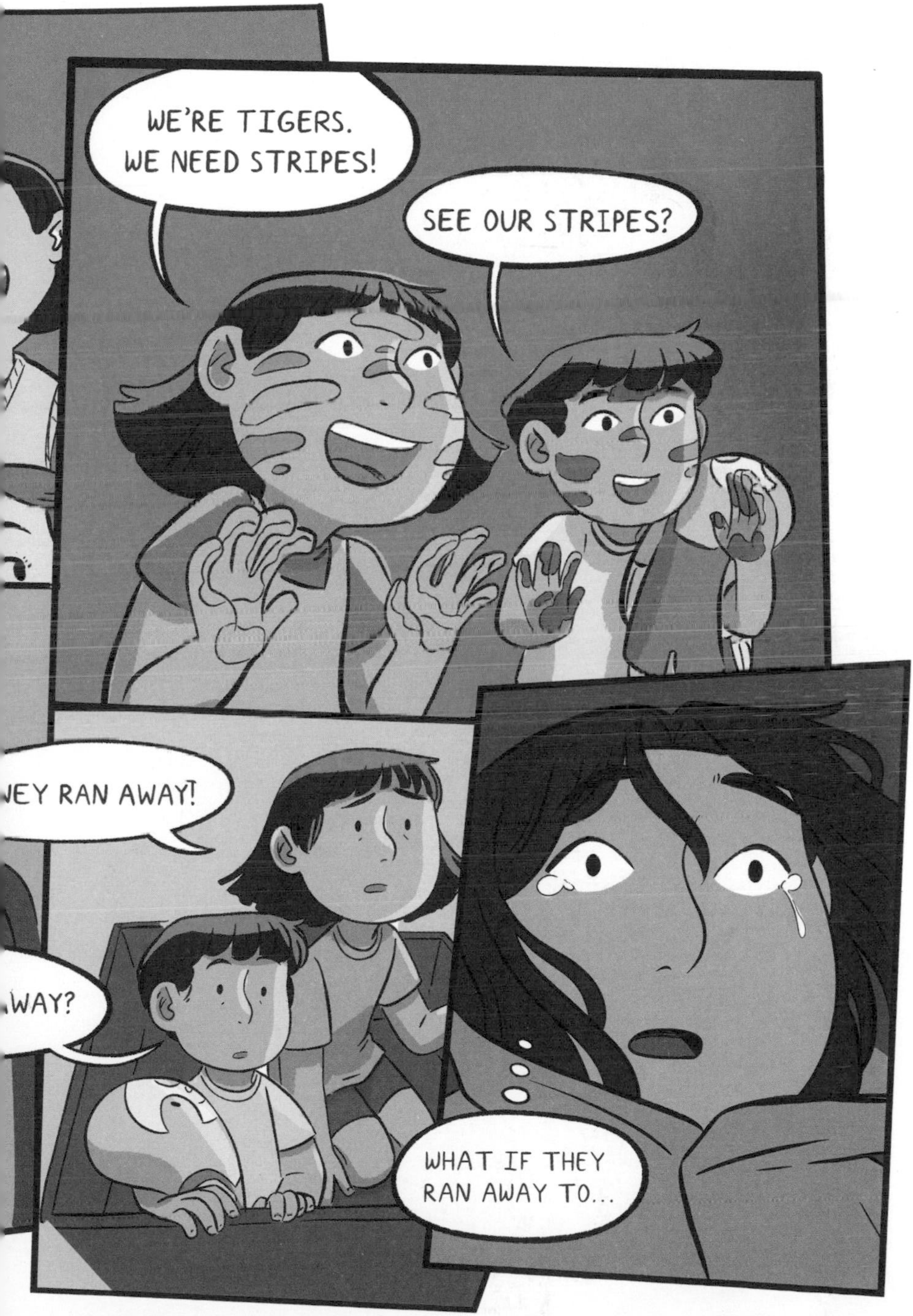
WE'RE TIGERS.
WE NEED STRIPES!
SEE OUR STRIPES?
EY RAN AWAY!
WAY?
WHAT IF THEY
RAN AWAY TO...

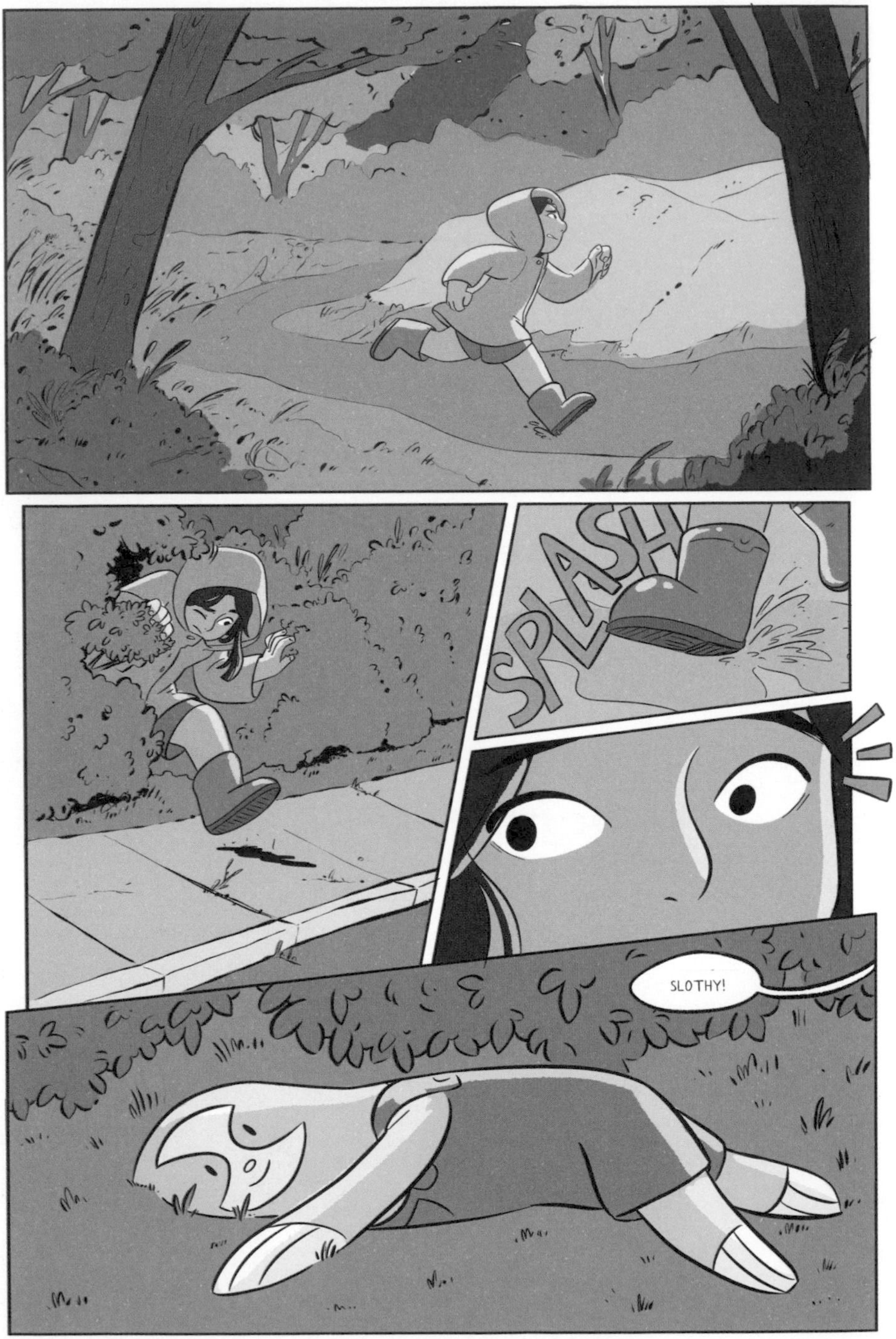
SPLASH
SLOTHY!

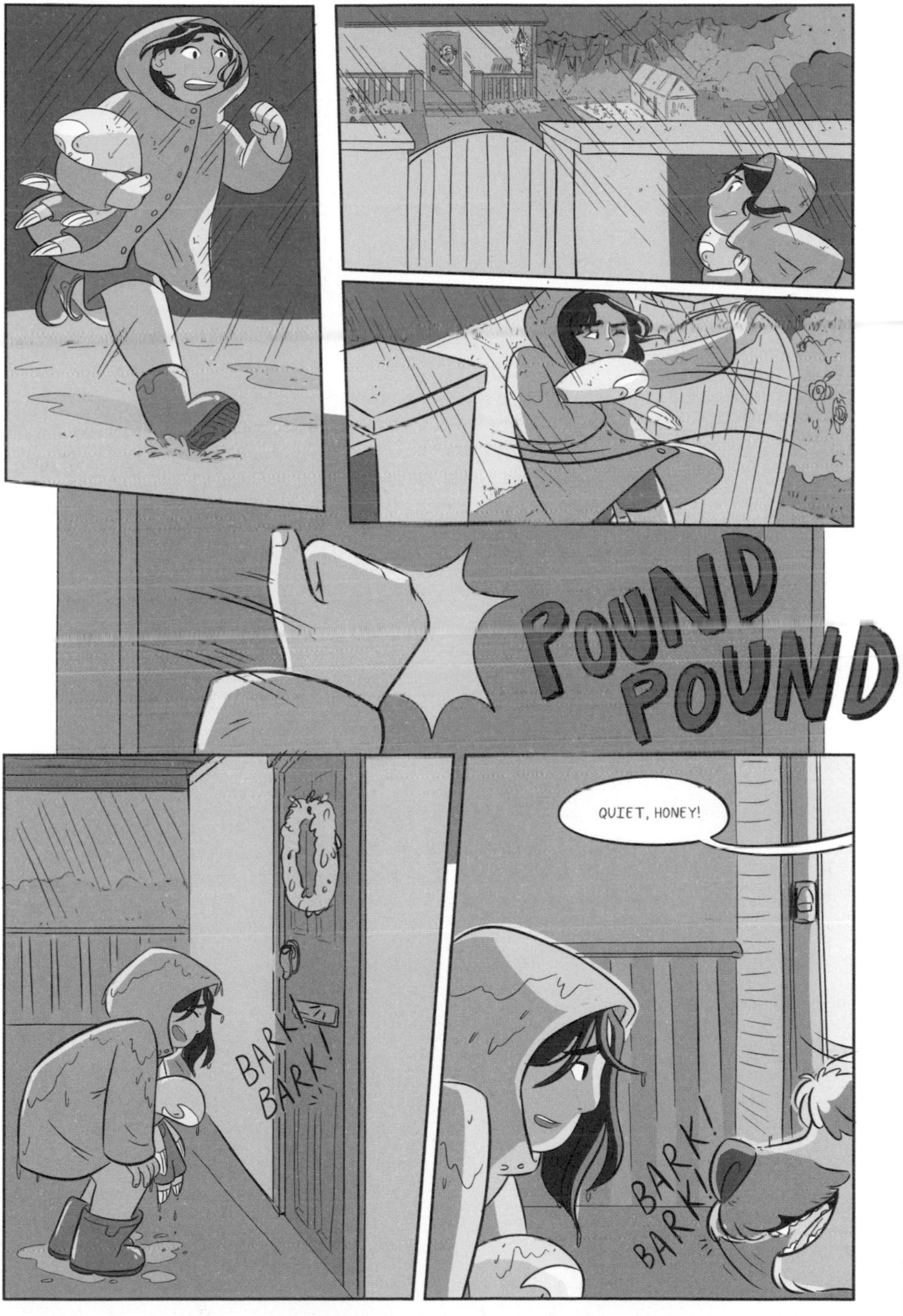
POUND
POUND
BARK!
BARK!
QUIET, HONEY!
BARK!
BARK!

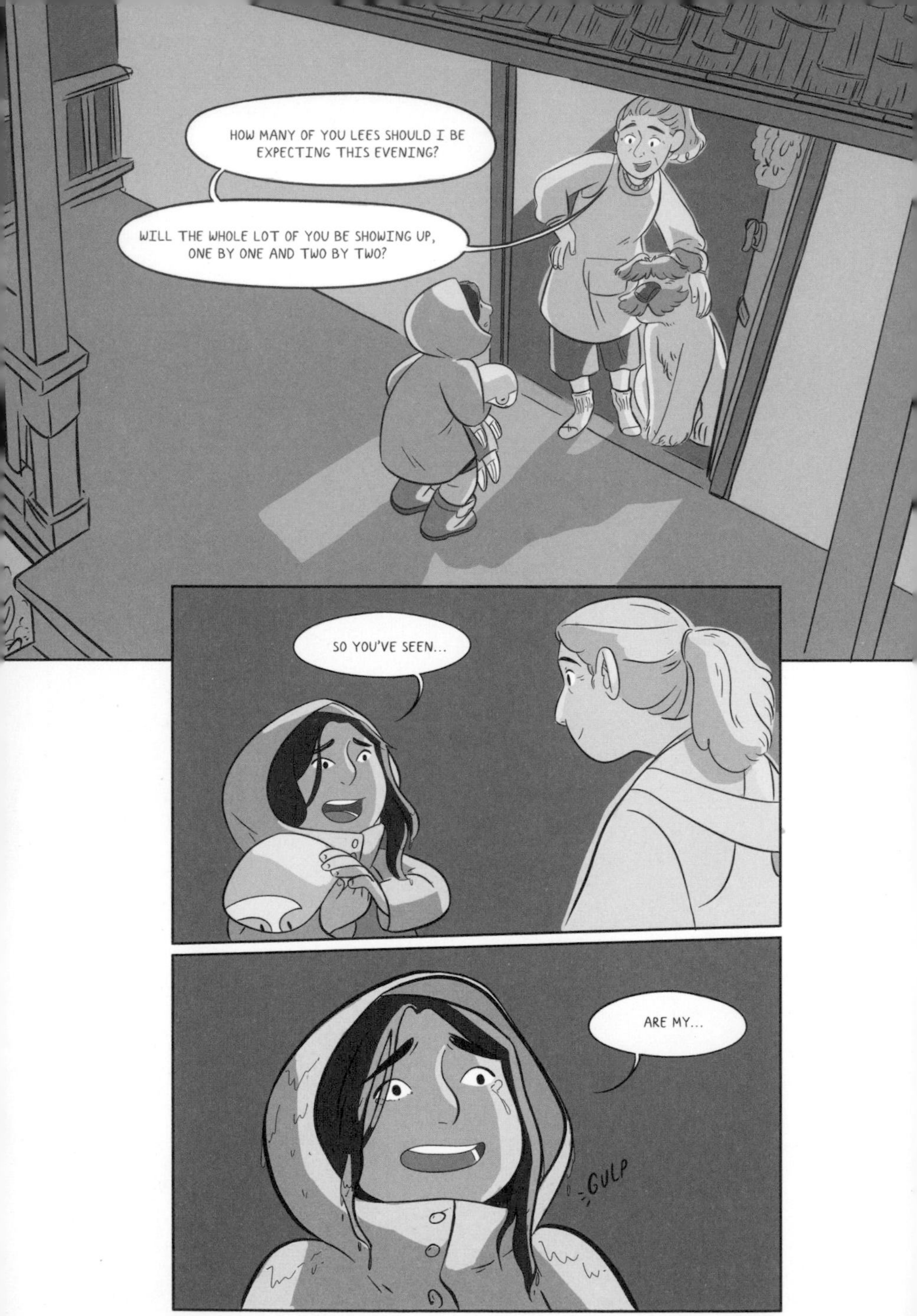
HOW MANY OF YOU LEES SHOULD I BE EXPECTING THIS EVENING?
WILL THE WHOLE LOT OF YOU BE SHOWING UP, ONE BY ONE AND TWO BY TWO?
SO YOU'VE SEEN...
ARE MY...
GULP

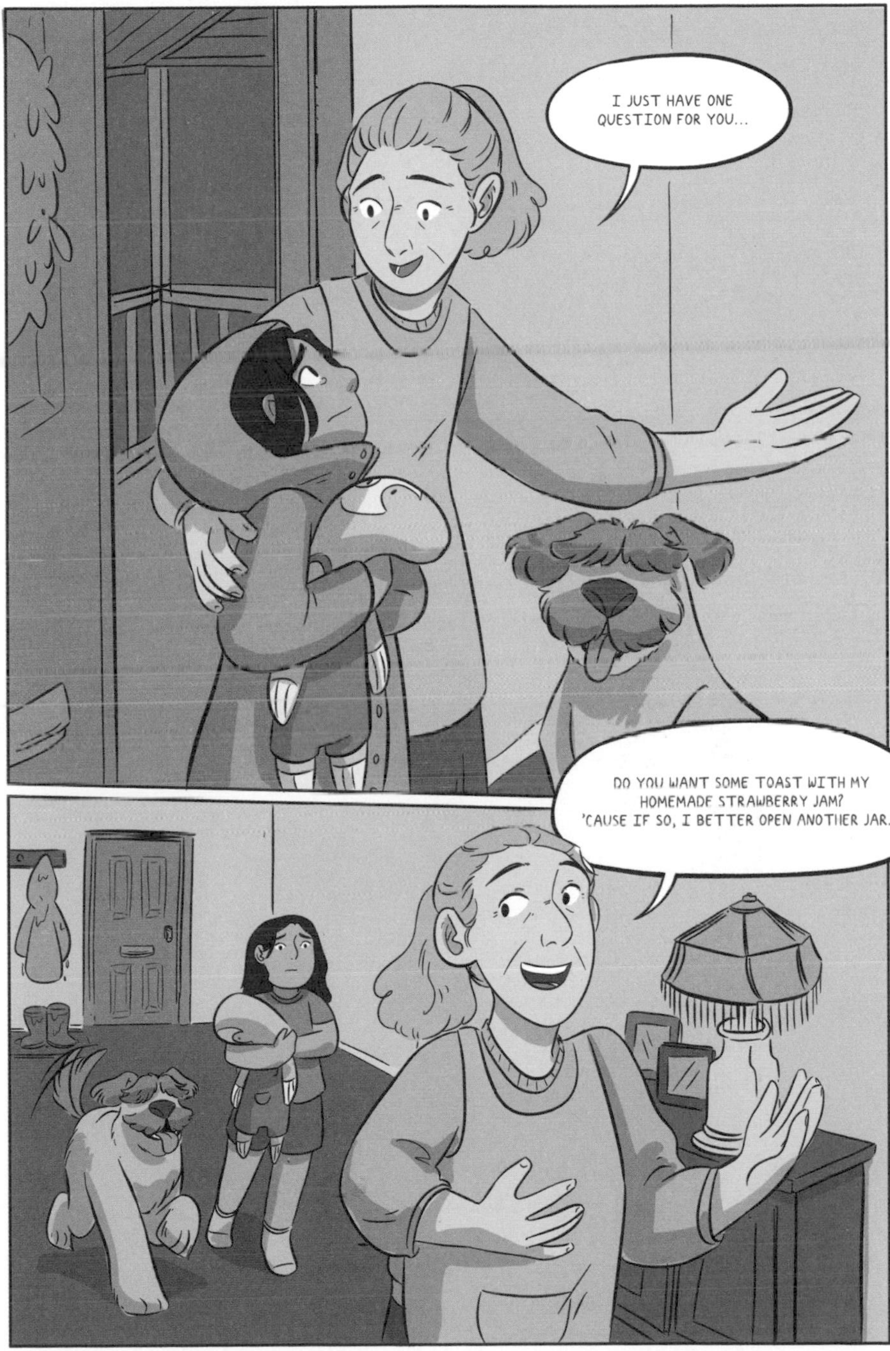
I JUST HAVE ONE QUESTION FOR YOU...
DO YOU WANT SOME TOAST WITH MY HOMEMADE STRAWBERRY JAM? 'CAUSE IF SO, I BETTER OPEN ANOTHER JAR...

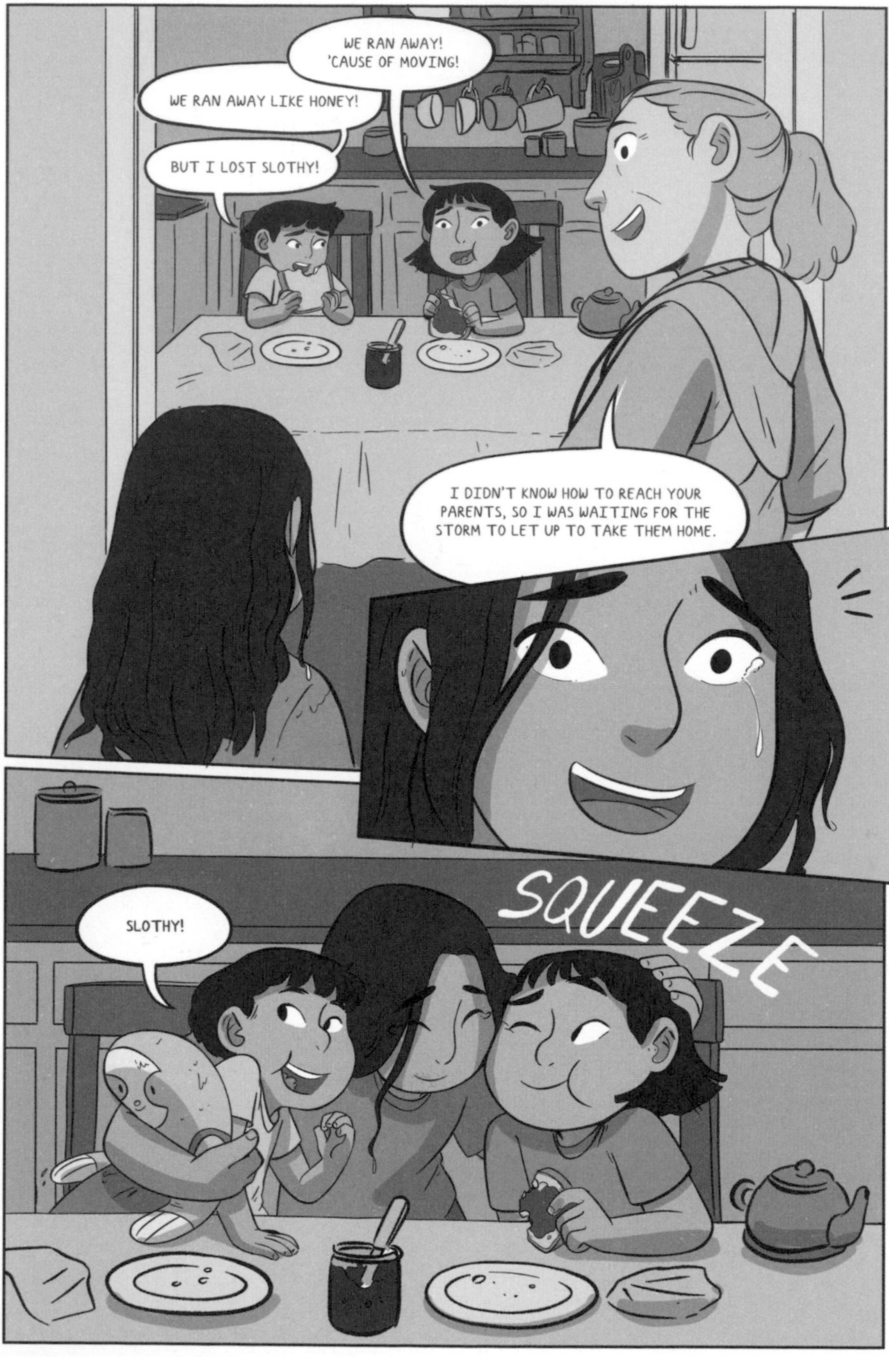
WE RAN AWAY LIKE HONEY!
BUT I LOST SLOTHY!
WE RAN AWAY! 'CAUSE OF MOVING!
I DIDN'T KNOW HOW TO REACH YOUR PARENTS, SO I WAS WAITING FOR THE STORM TO LET UP TO TAKE THEM HOME.
SLOTHY!
SQUEEZE

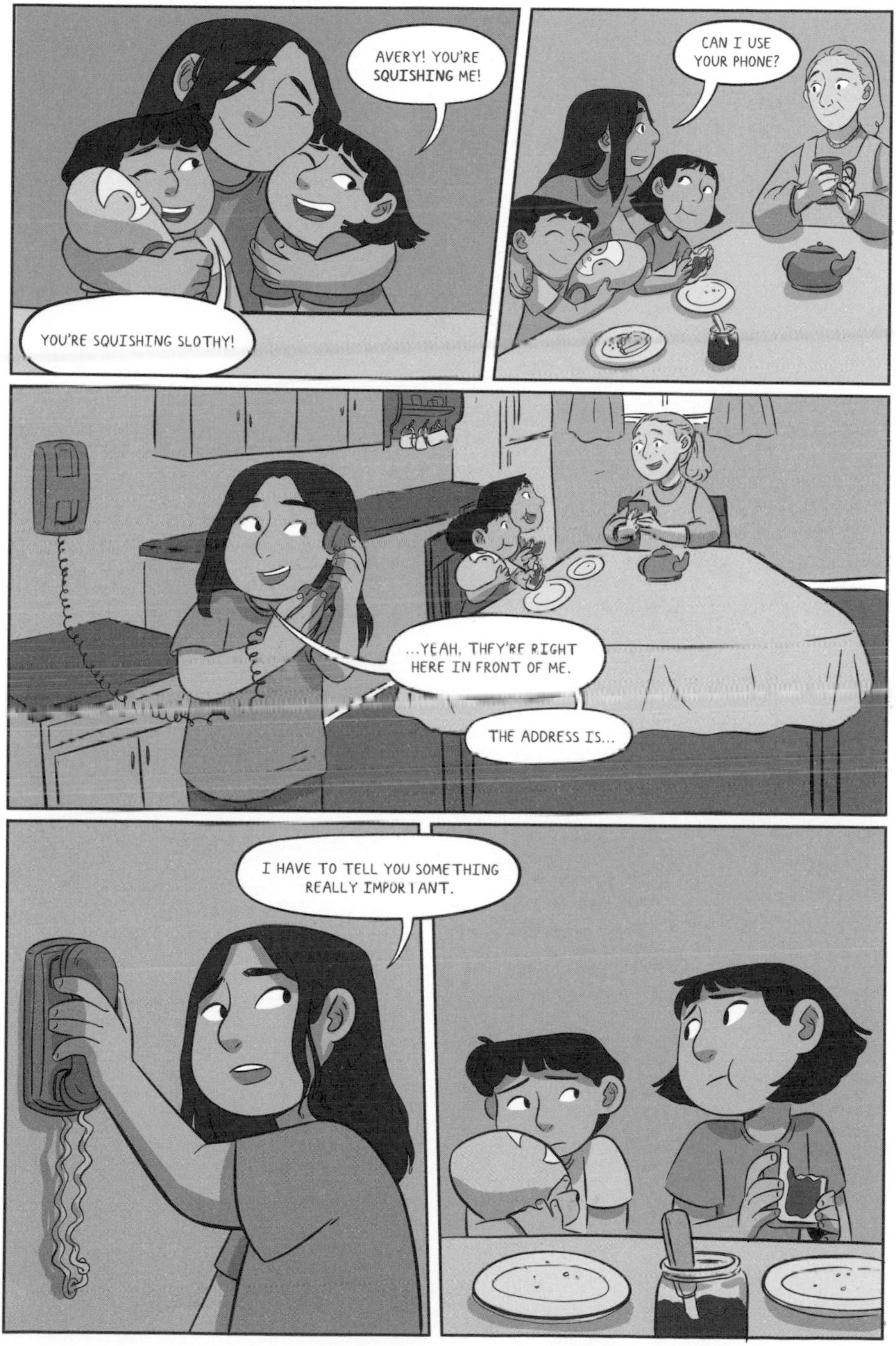
AVERY! YOU'RE SQUISHING ME!
YOU'RE SQUISHING SLOTHY!
CAN I USE YOUR PHONE?
...YEAH, THEY'RE RIGHT HERE IN FRONT OF ME.
THE ADDRESS IS...
I HAVE TO TELL YOU SOMETHING REALLY IMPORTANT.

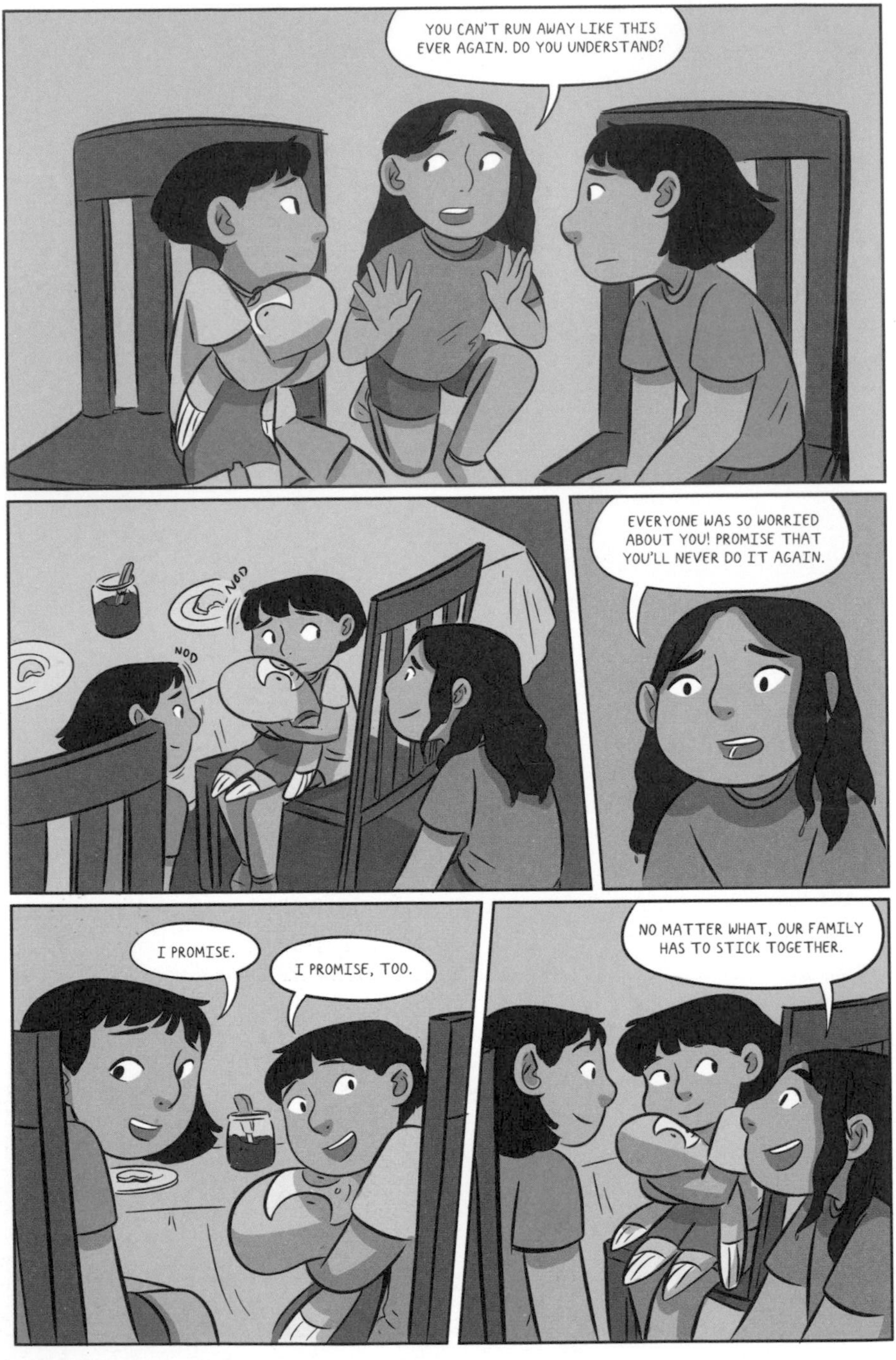
YOU CAN'T RUN AWAY LIKE THIS EVER AGAIN. DO YOU UNDERSTAND?
NOD
NOD
EVERYONE WAS SO WORRIED ABOUT YOU! PROMISE THAT YOU'LL NEVER DO IT AGAIN.
I PROMISE.
I PROMISE, TOO.
NO MATTER WHAT, OUR FAMILY HAS TO STICK TOGETHER.

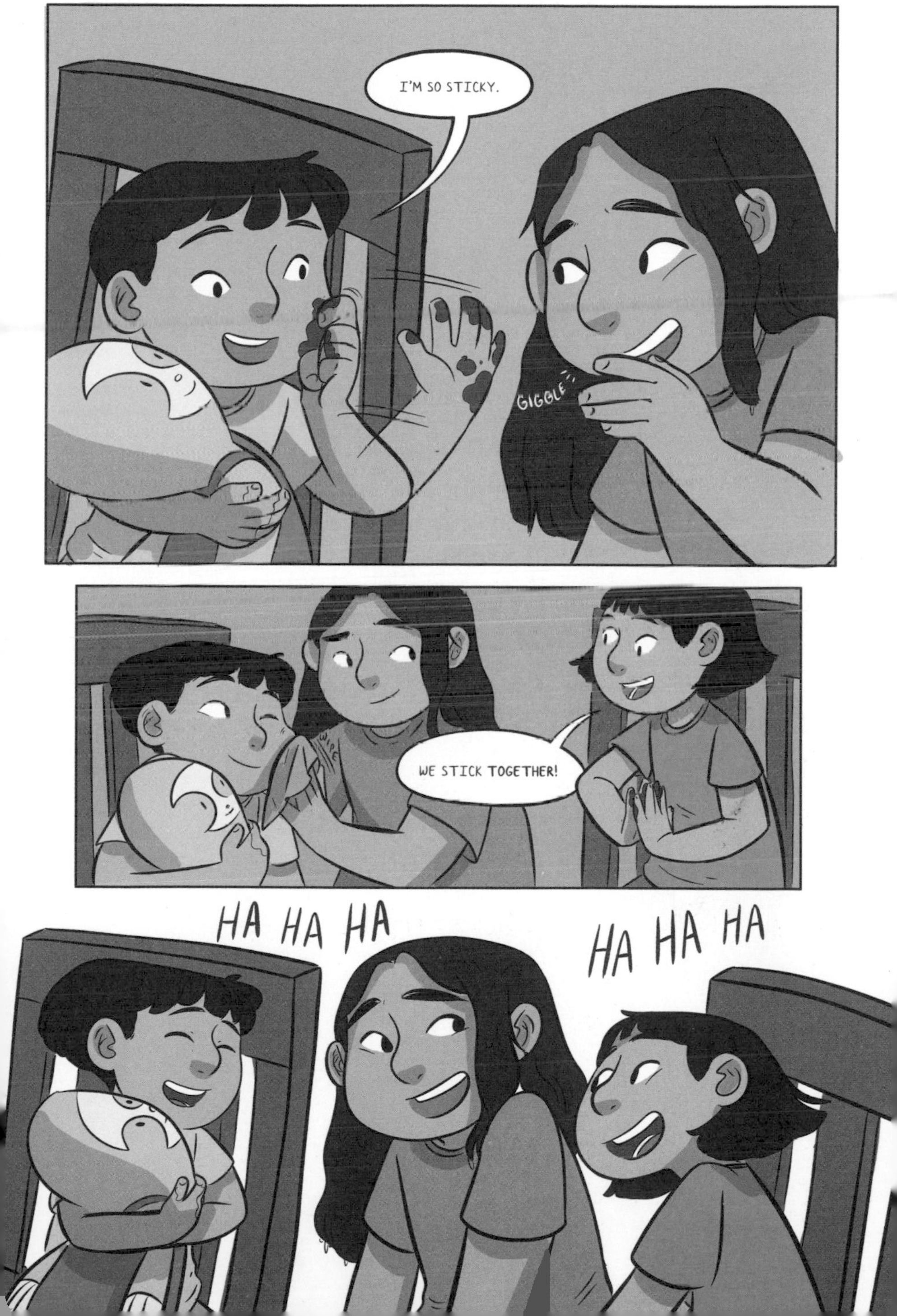
I'M SO STICKY.
GIGGLE
WIPE
WE STICK TOGETHER!
HA HA HA
HA HA HA

Chapter Thirteen

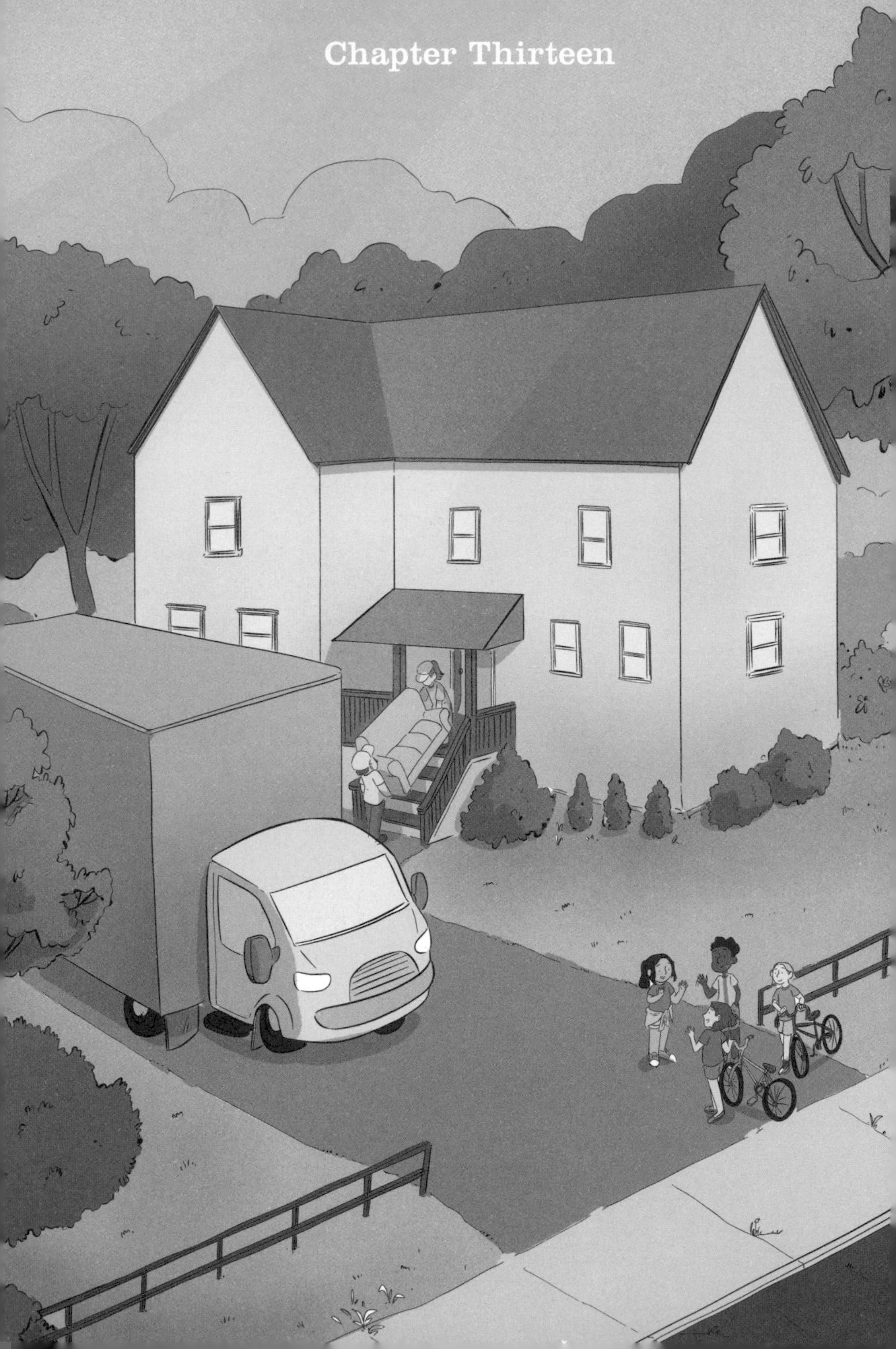

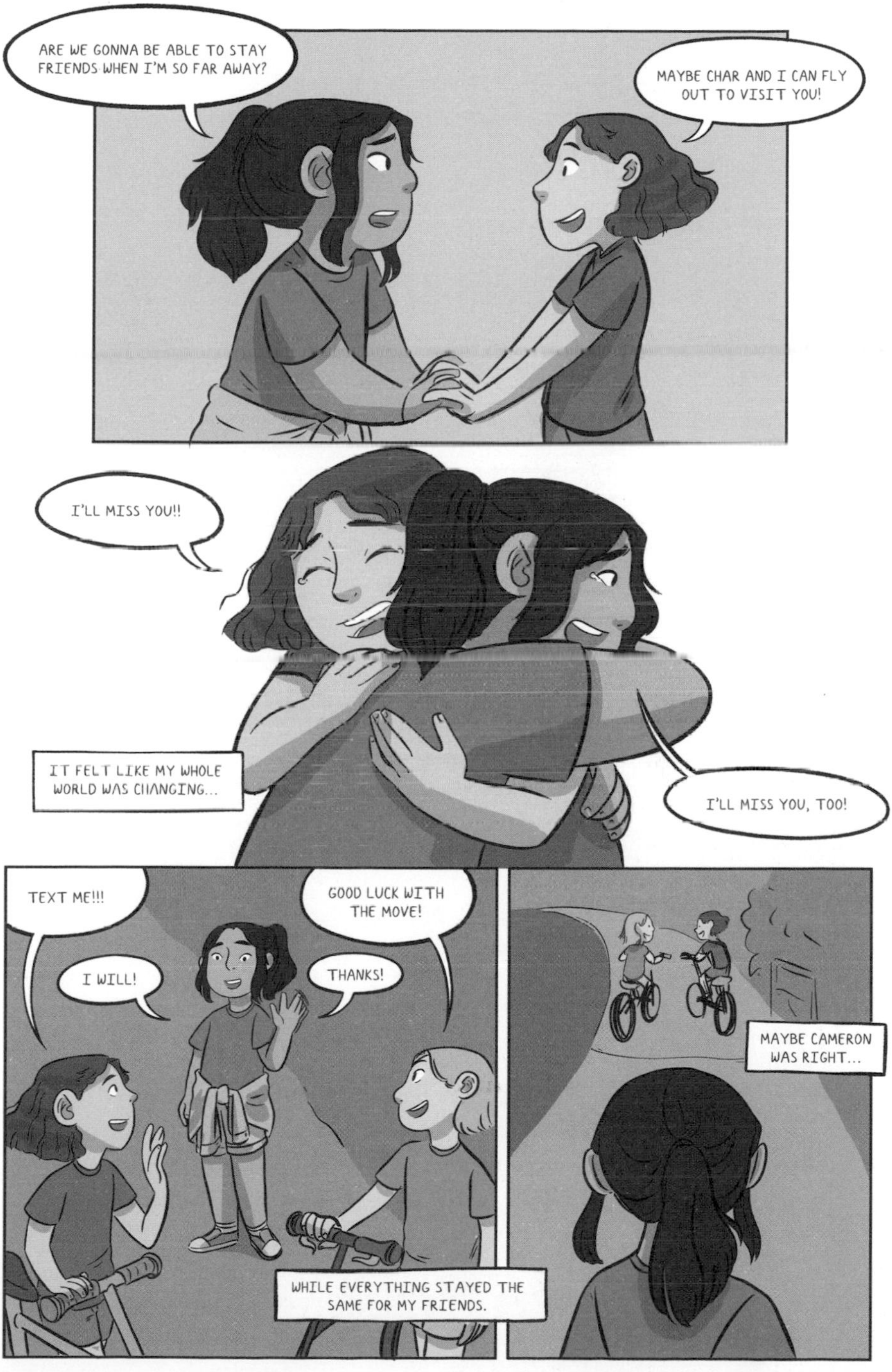
ARE WE GONNA BE ABLE TO STAY FRIENDS WHEN I'M SO FAR AWAY?
MAYBE CHAR AND I CAN FLY OUT TO VISIT YOU!
I'LL MISS YOU!!
IT FELT LIKE MY WHOLE WORLD WAS CHANGING...
I'LL MISS YOU, TOO!
TEXT ME!!!
I WILL!
GOOD LUCK WITH THE MOVE!
THANKS!
WHILE EVERYTHING STAYED THE SAME FOR MY FRIENDS.
MAYBE CAMERON WAS RIGHT...

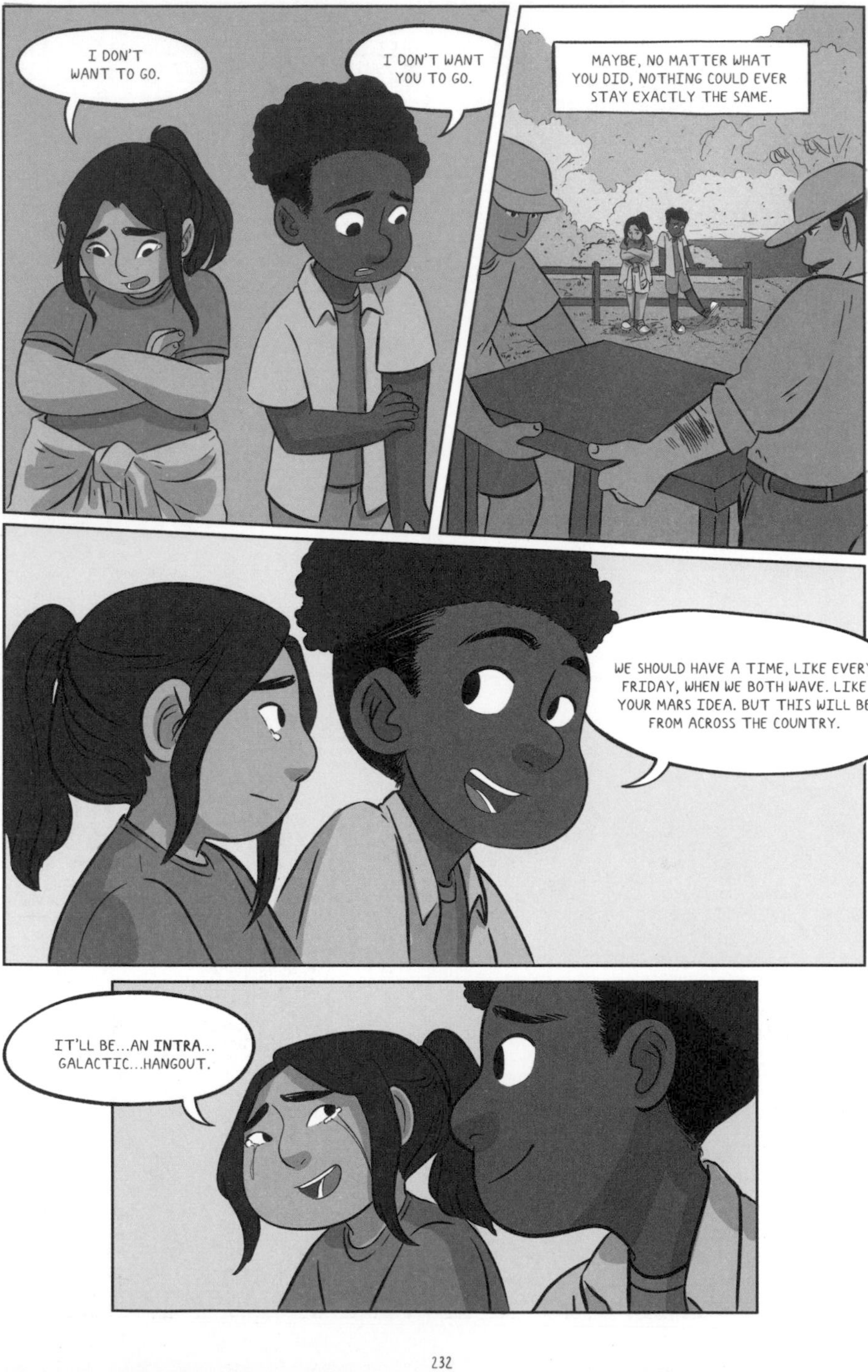
I DON'T WANT TO GO.
I DON'T WANT YOU TO GO.
MAYBE, NO MATTER WHAT YOU DID, NOTHING COULD EVER STAY EXACTLY THE SAME.
WE SHOULD HAVE A TIME, LIKE EVERY FRIDAY, WHEN WE BOTH WAVE. LIKE YOUR MARS IDEA. BUT THIS WILL BE FROM ACROSS THE COUNTRY.
IT'LL BE...AN INTRA... GALACTIC...HANGOUT.

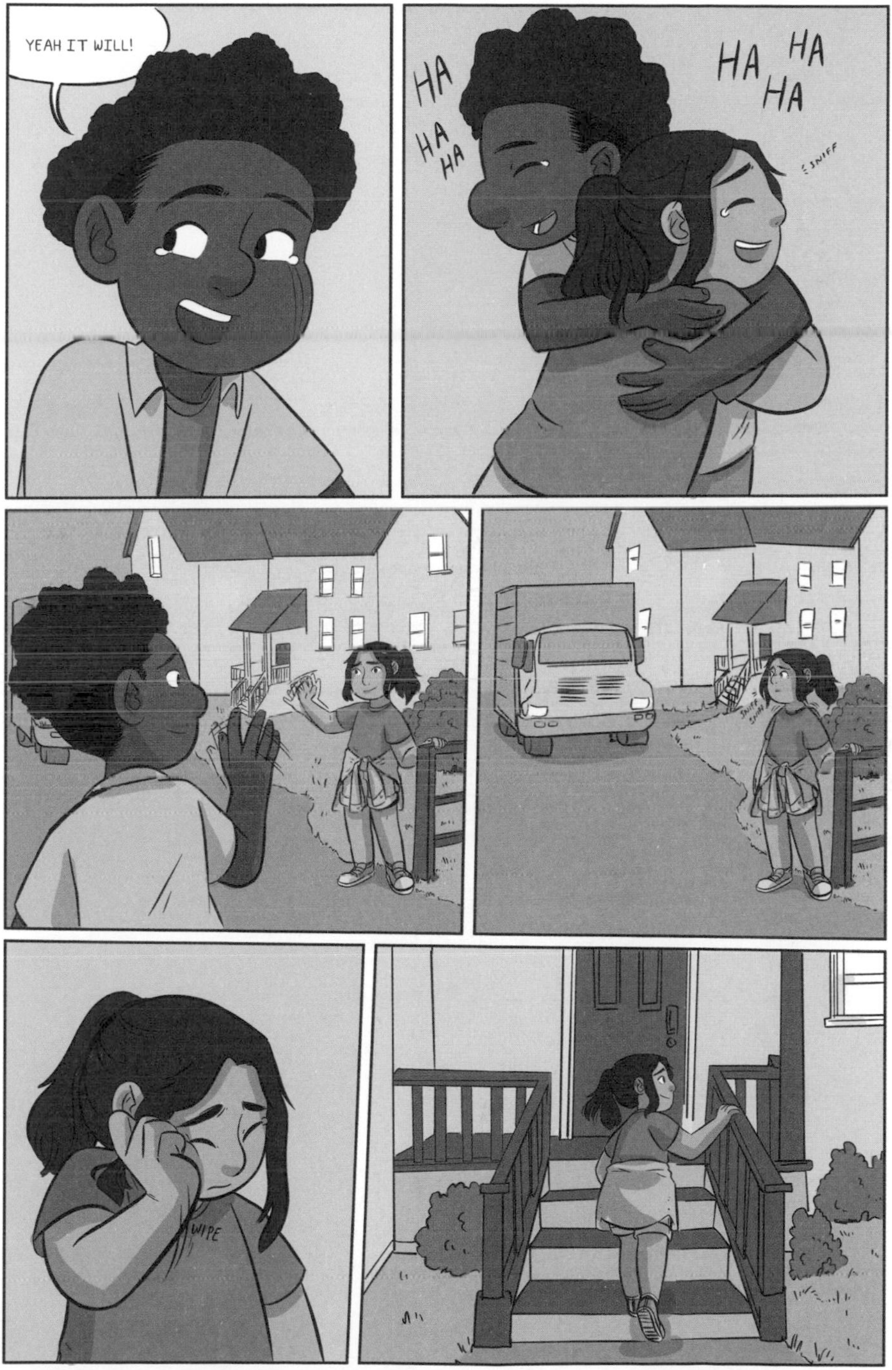
YEAH IT WILL!
HA HA HA
HA HA HA
SNIFF
SNIFF SNIFF
WIPE

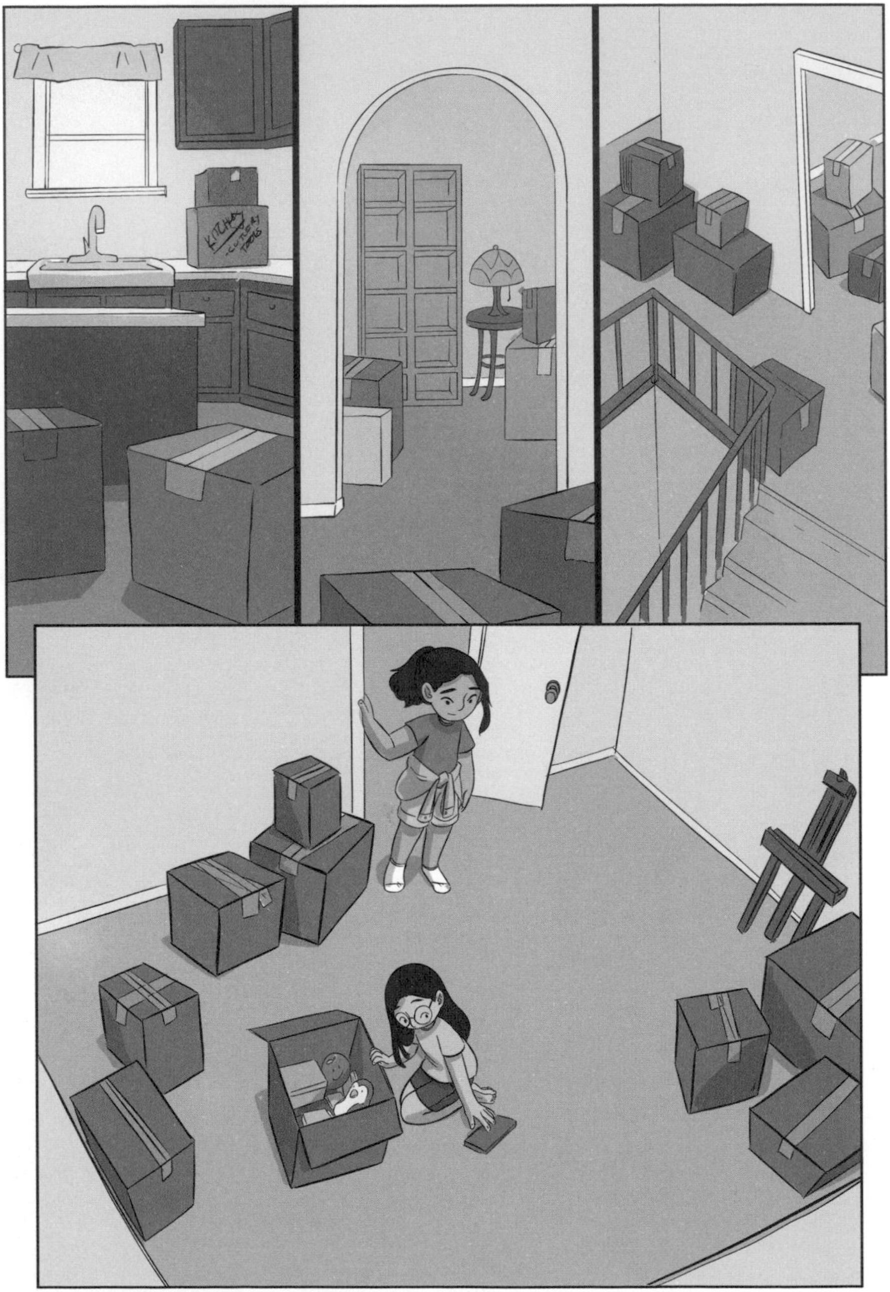
-CUTLERY TOOLS

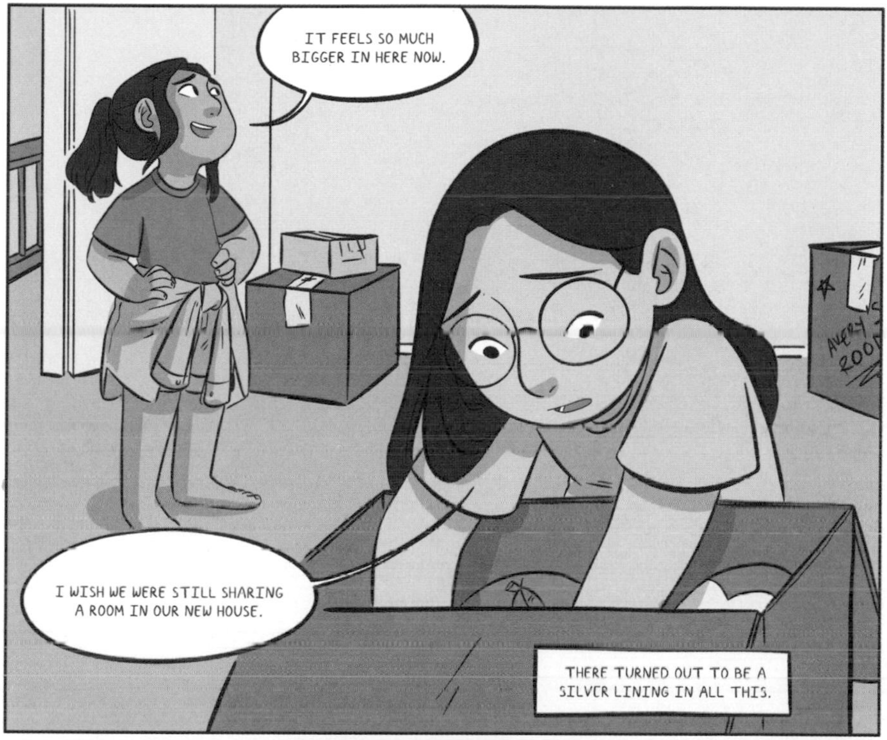
IT FEELS SO MUCH BIGGER IN HERE NOW.
I WISH WE WERE STILL SHARING A ROOM IN OUR NEW HOUSE.
THERE TURNED OUT TO BE A SILVER LINING IN ALL THIS.

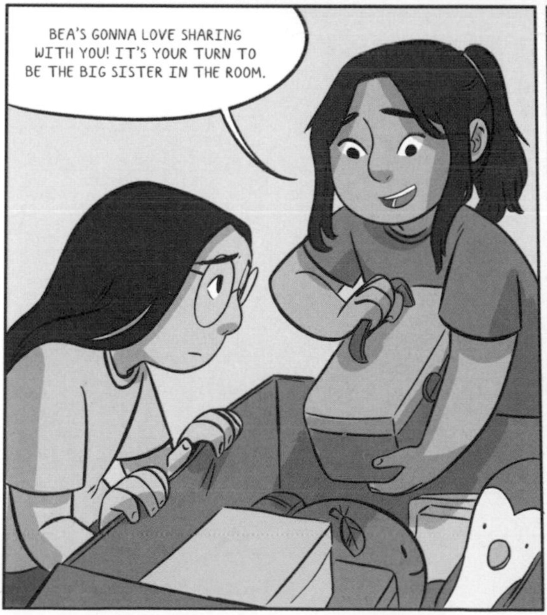
BEA'S GONNA LOVE SHARING WITH YOU! IT'S YOUR TURN TO BE THE BIG SISTER IN THE ROOM.

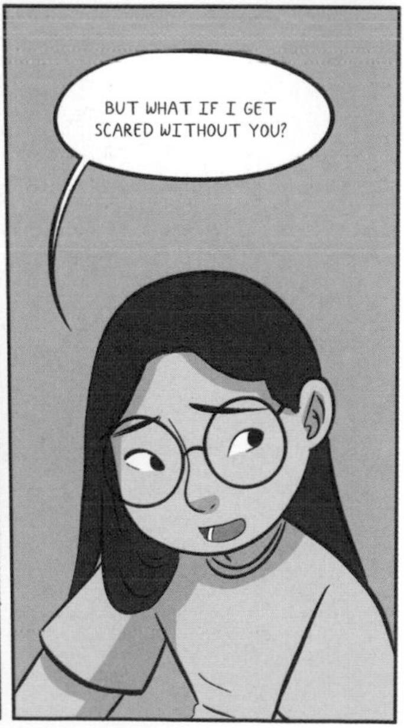
BUT WHAT IF I GET SCARED WITHOUT YOU?

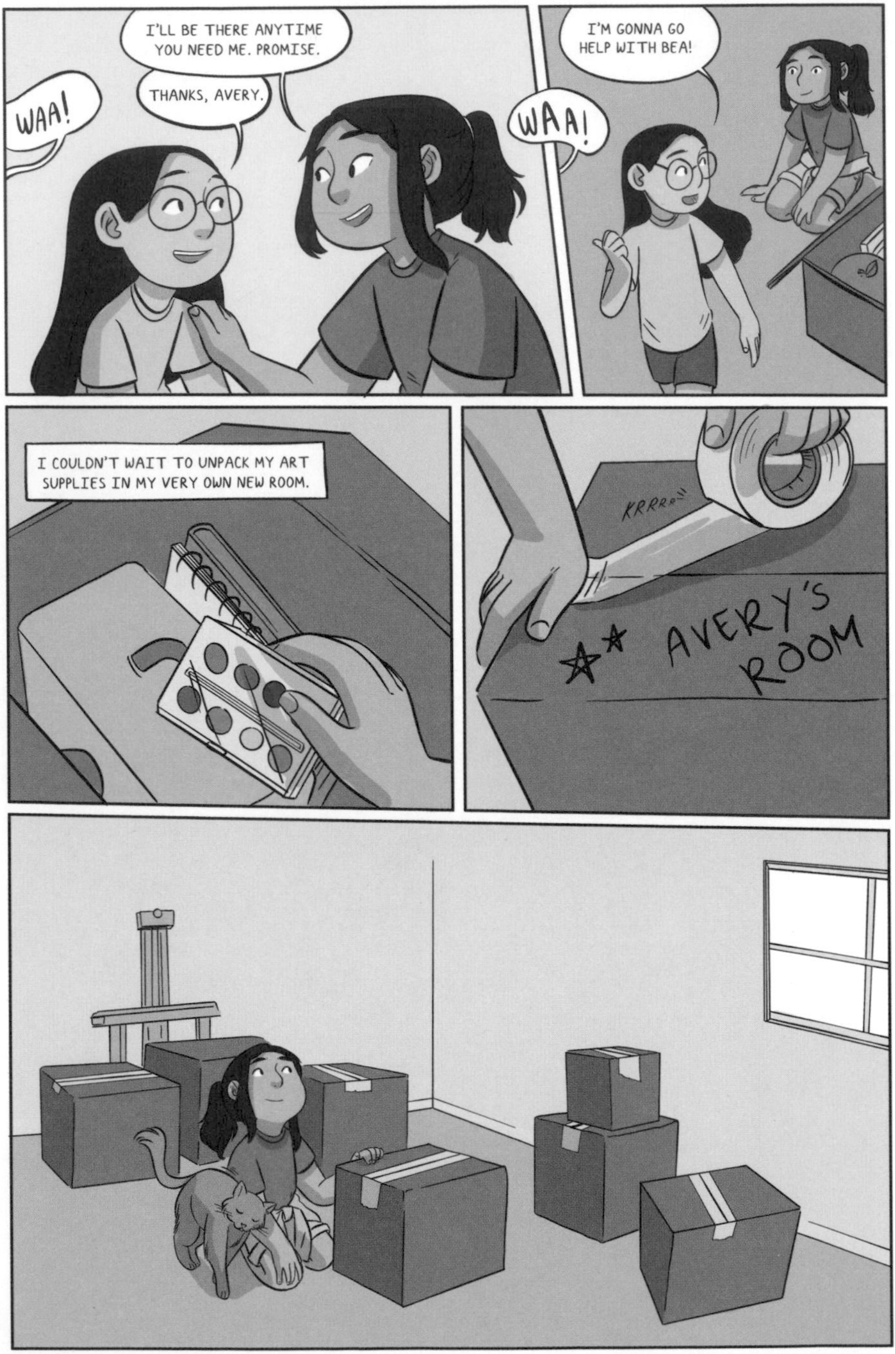
I'LL BE THERE ANYTIME YOU NEED ME. PROMISE.
THANKS, AVERY.
WAA!
I'M GONNA GO HELP WITH BEA!
WAA!
I COULDN'T WAIT TO UNPACK MY ART SUPPLIES IN MY VERY OWN NEW ROOM.
KRRRR
AVERY'S ROOM

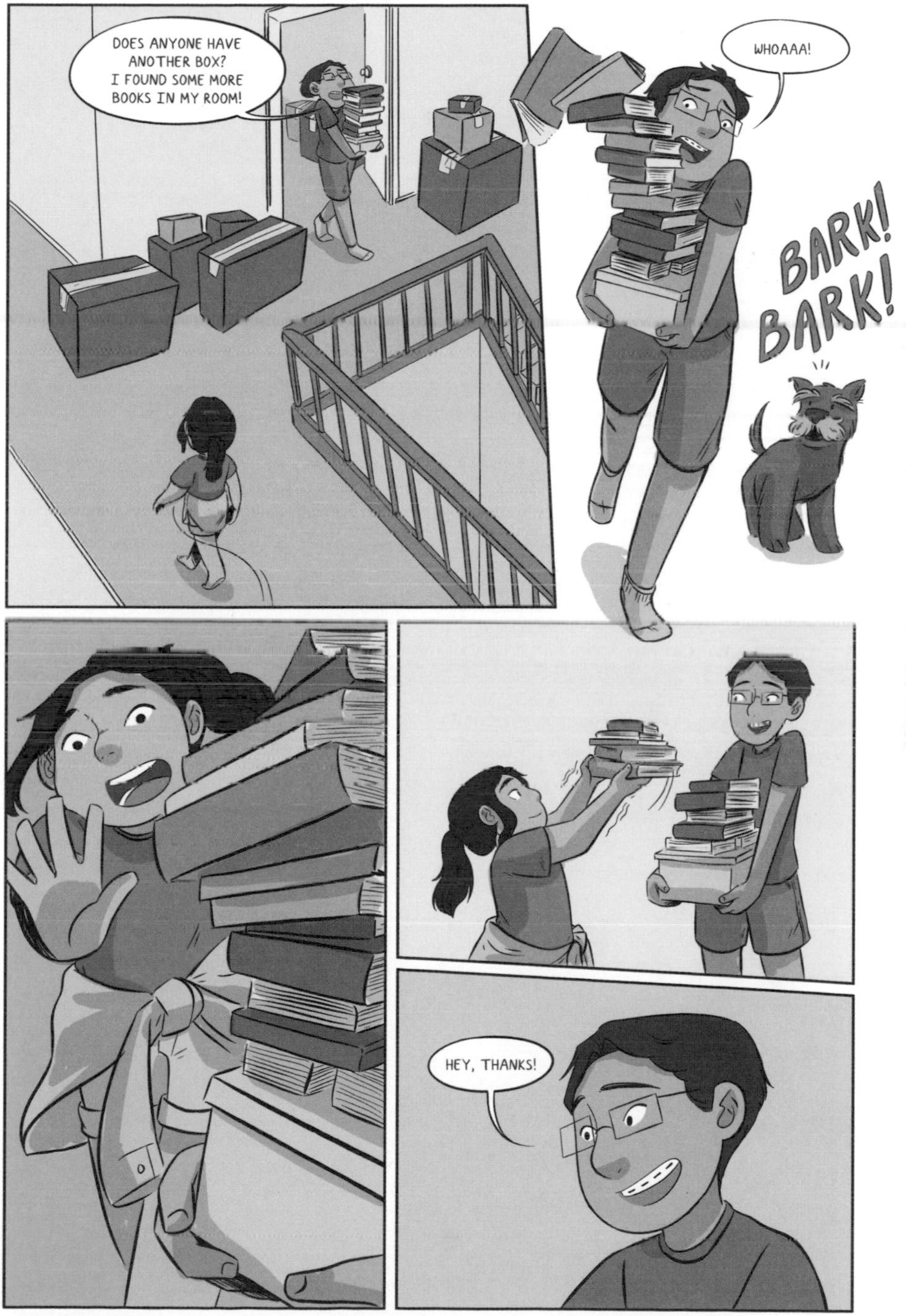
DOES ANYONE HAVE ANOTHER BOX? I FOUND SOME MORE BOOKS IN MY ROOM!
WHOAAA!
BARK! BARK!
HEY, THANKS!

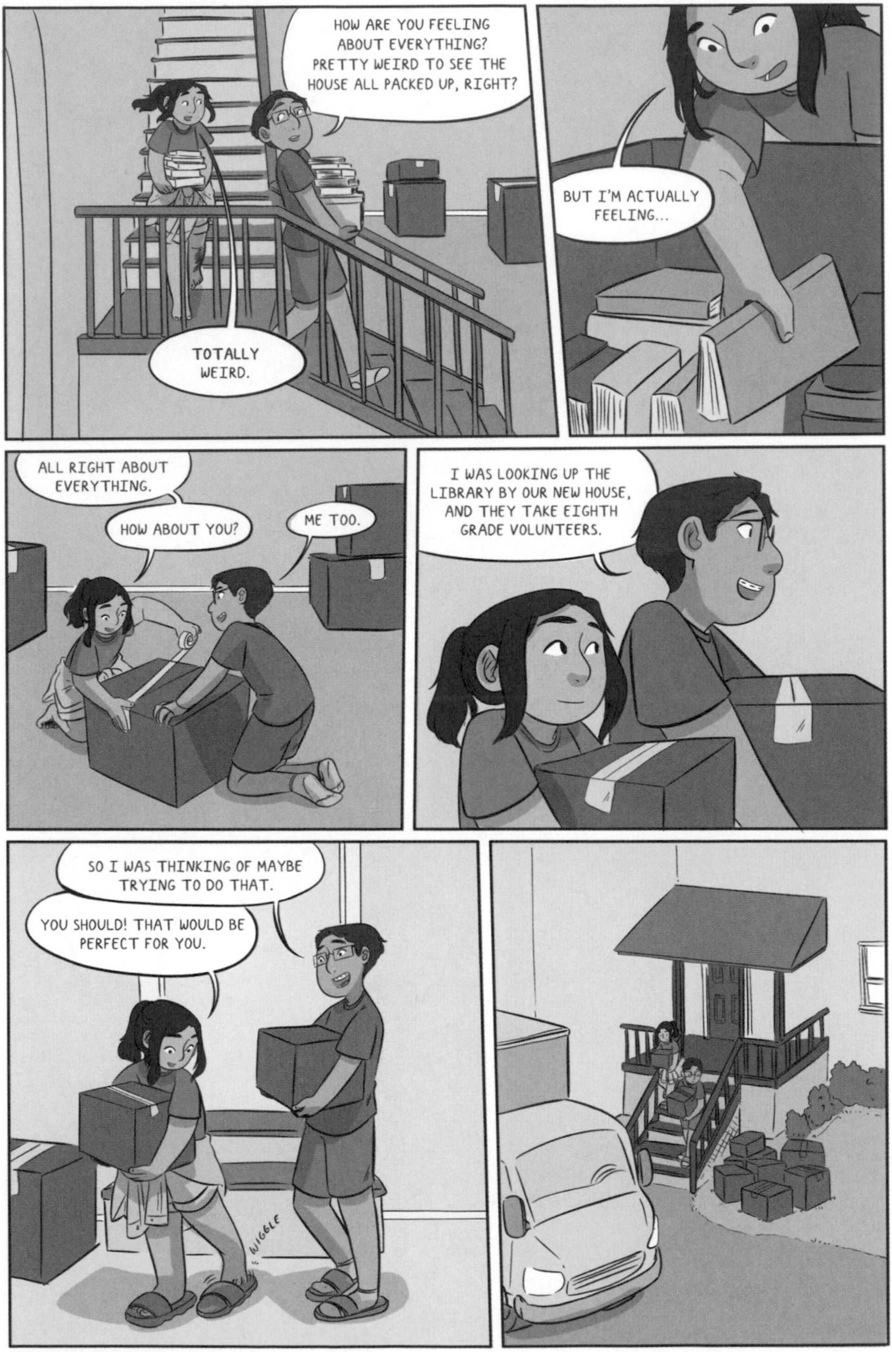

HOW ARE YOU FEELING ABOUT EVERYTHING? PRETTY WEIRD TO SEE THE HOUSE ALL PACKED UP, RIGHT?
TOTALLY WEIRD.
BUT I'M ACTUALLY FEELING...
ALL RIGHT ABOUT EVERYTHING.
HOW ABOUT YOU?
ME TOO.
I WAS LOOKING UP THE LIBRARY BY OUR NEW HOUSE, AND THEY TAKE EIGHTH GRADE VOLUNTEERS.
SO I WAS THINKING OF MAYBE TRYING TO DO THAT.
YOU SHOULD! THAT WOULD BE PERFECT FOR YOU.
WIGGLE

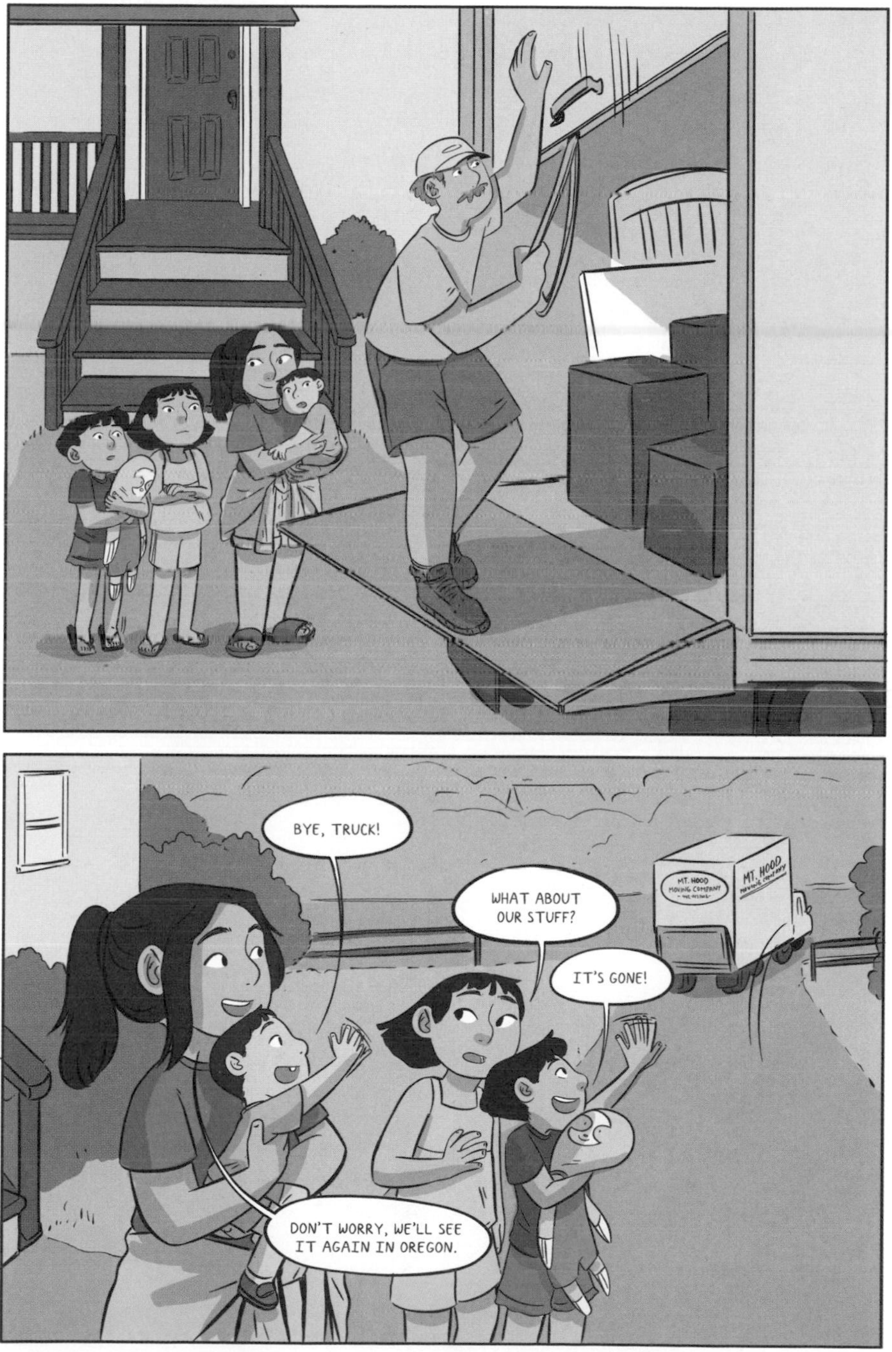
BYE, TRUCK!
WHAT ABOUT OUR STUFF?
IT'S GONE!
DON'T WORRY, WE'LL SEE IT AGAIN IN OREGON.

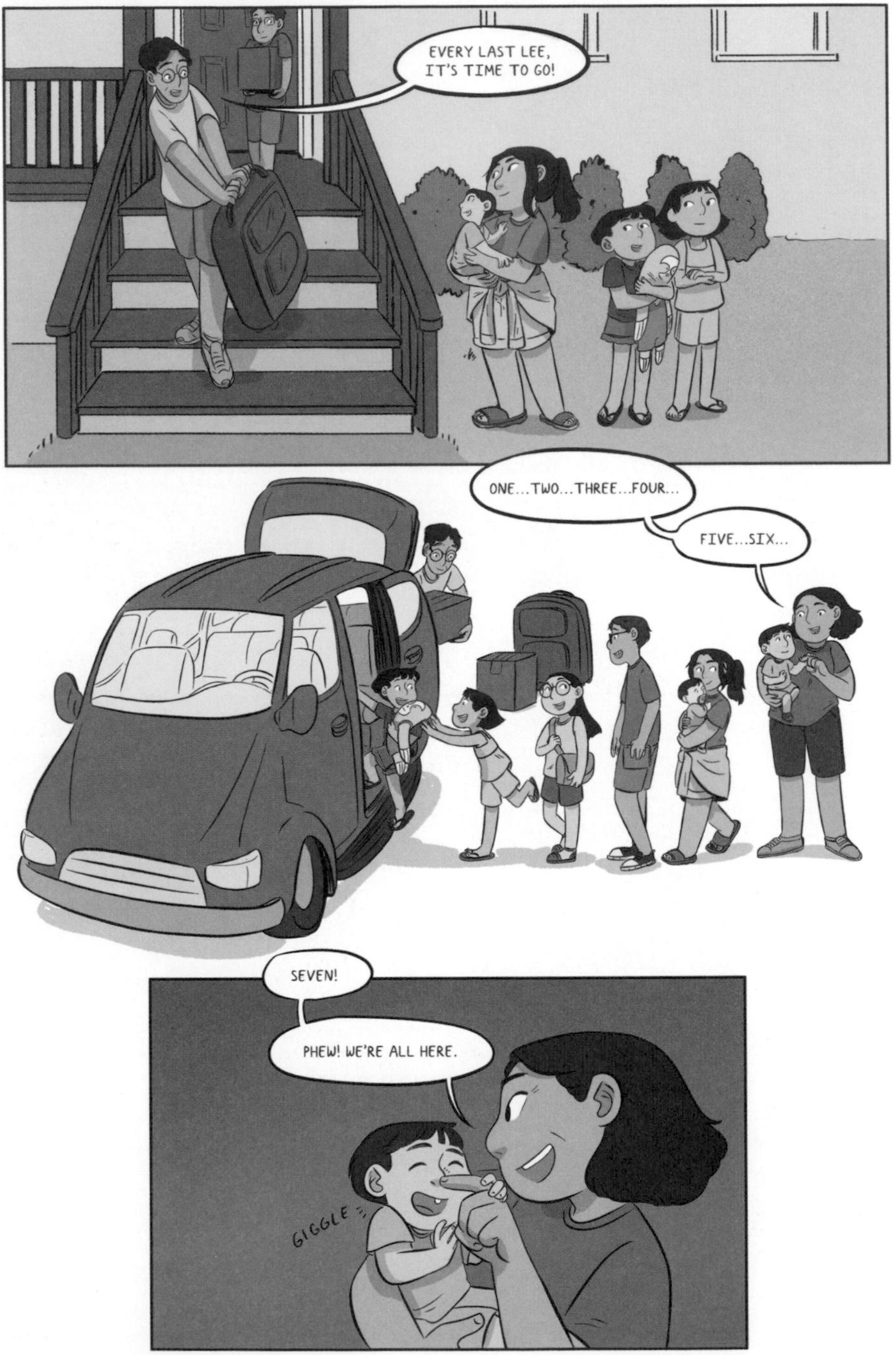
EVERY LAST LEE, IT'S TIME TO GO!
ONE...TWO...THREE...FOUR...
FIVE...SIX...
SEVEN!
PHEW! WE'RE ALL HERE.
GIGGLE

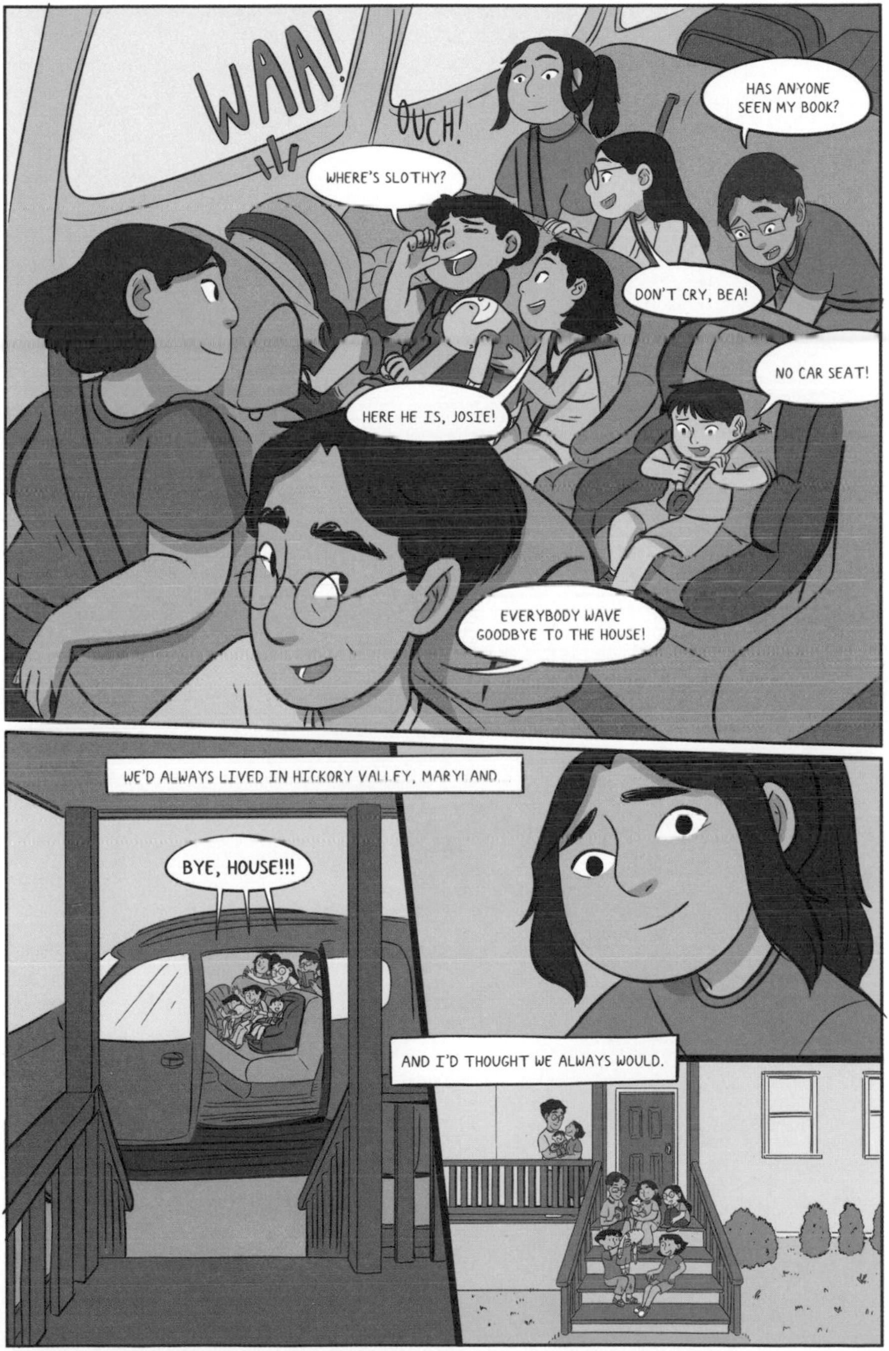
WAA!
OUCH!
HAS ANYONE SEEN MY BOOK?
WHERE'S SLOTHY?
DON'T CRY, BEA!
NO CAR SEAT!
HERE HE IS, JOSIE!
EVERYBODY WAVE GOODBYE TO THE HOUSE!
WE'D ALWAYS LIVED IN HICKORY VALLEY, MARYLAND...
BYE, HOUSE!!!
AND I'D THOUGHT WE ALWAYS WOULD.

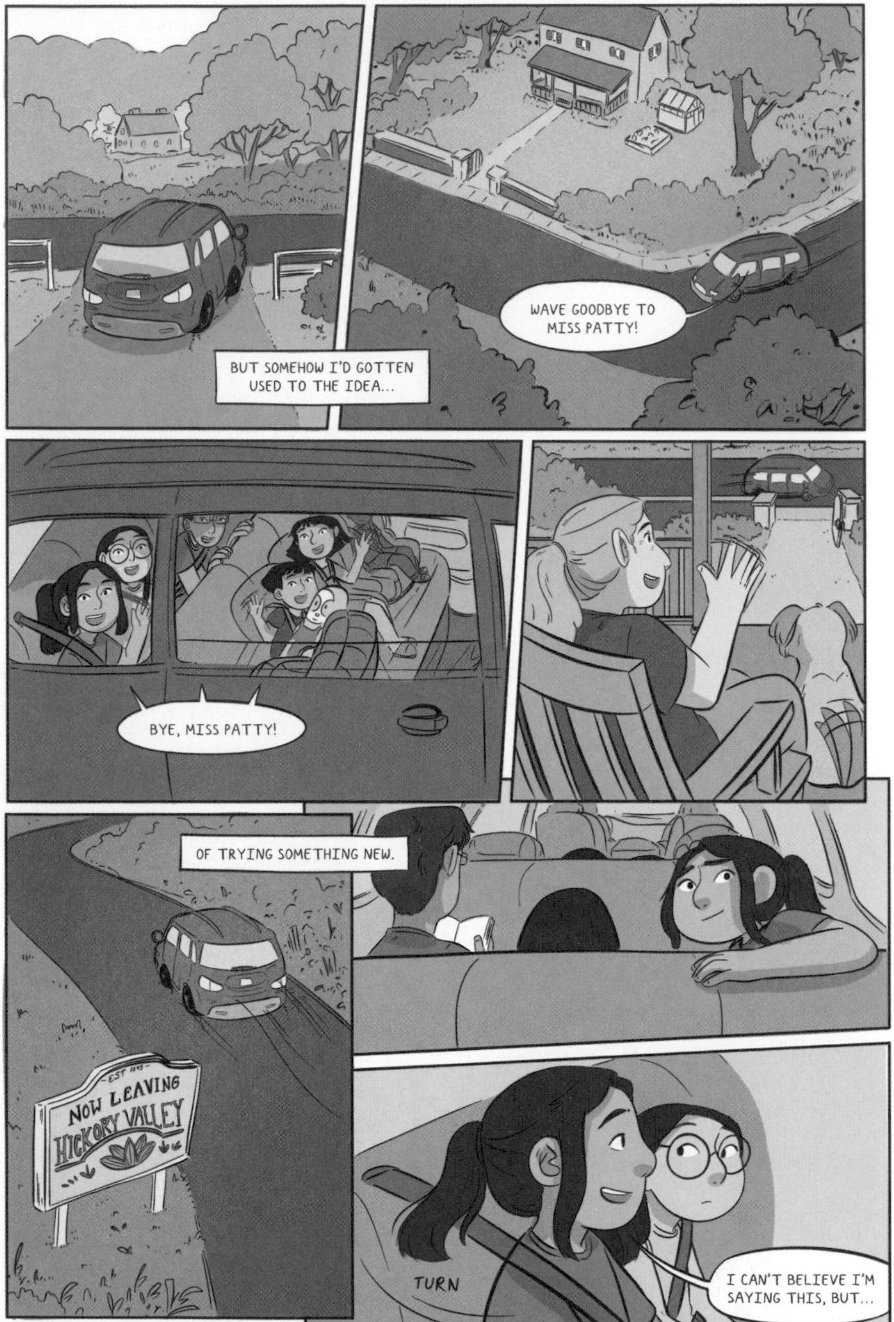
BUT SOMEHOW I'D GOTTEN USED TO THE IDEA...
WAVE GOODBYE TO MISS PATTY!
BYE, MISS PATTY!
OF TRYING SOMETHING NEW.
EST
NOW LEAVING
HICKORY VALLEY
TURN
I CAN'T BELIEVE I'M SAYING THIS, BUT...

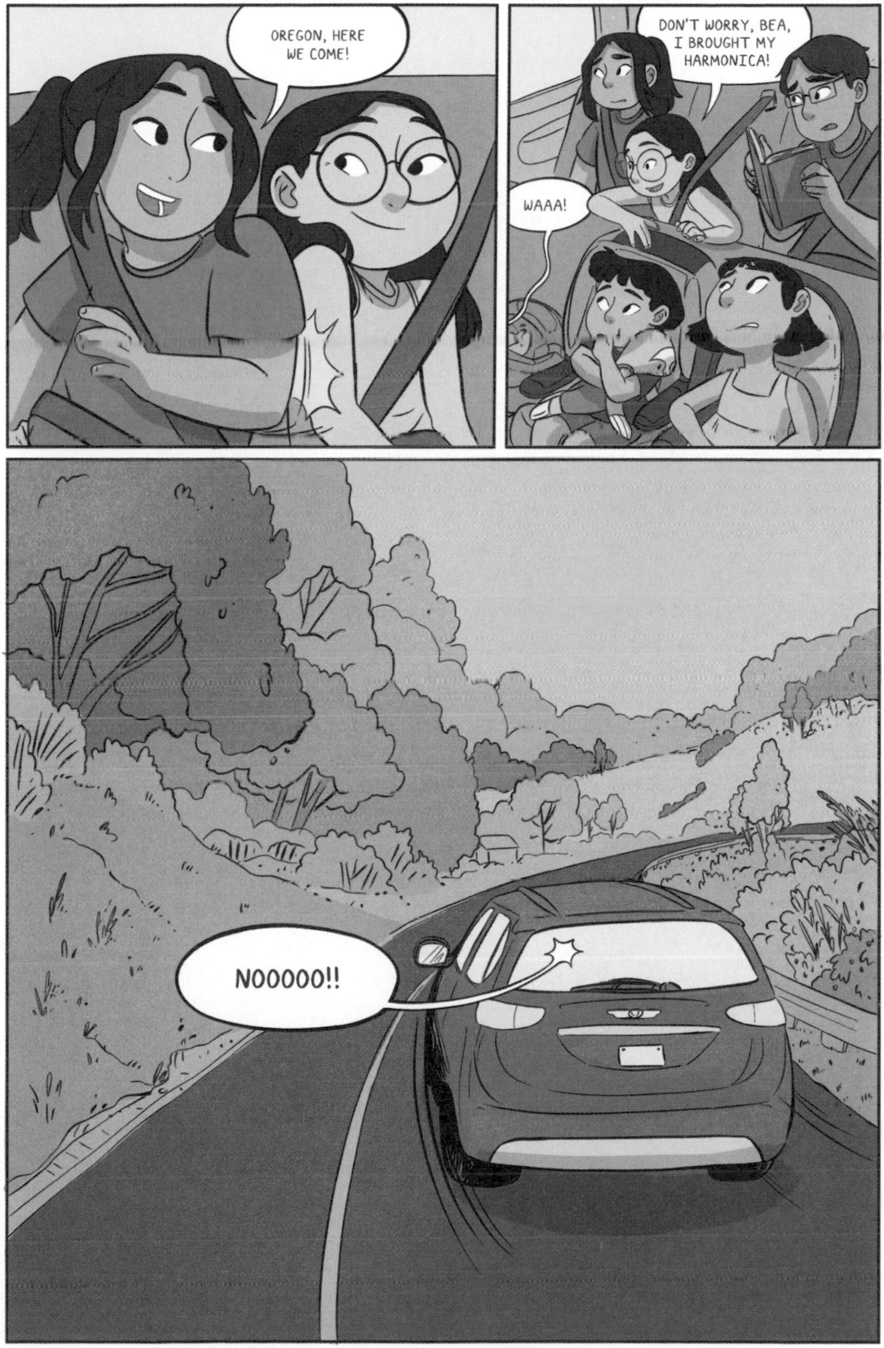
OREGON, HERE WE COME!
DON'T WORRY, BEA, I BROUGHT MY HARMONICA!
WAAA!
NOOOOO!!

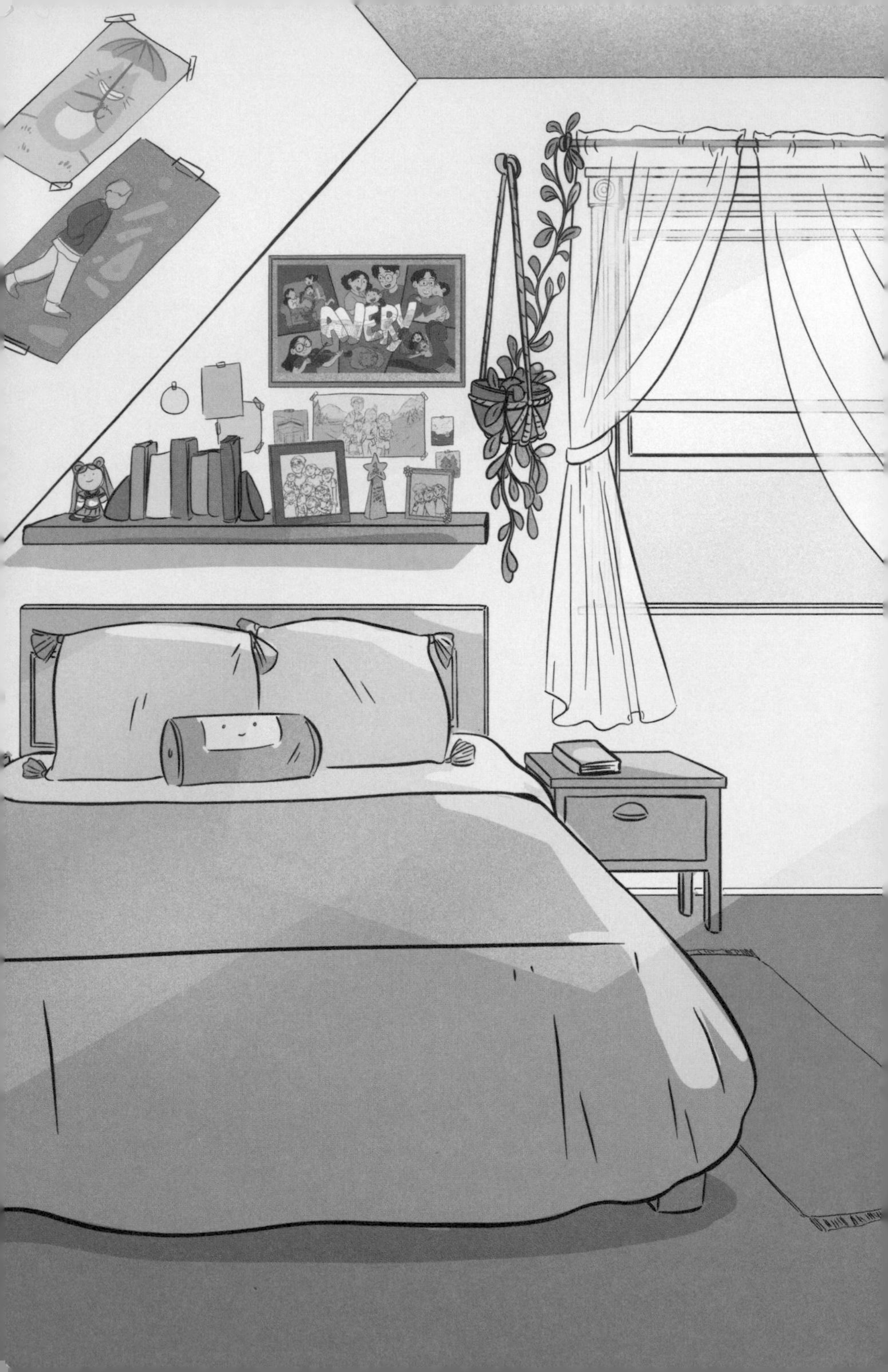
AVERY

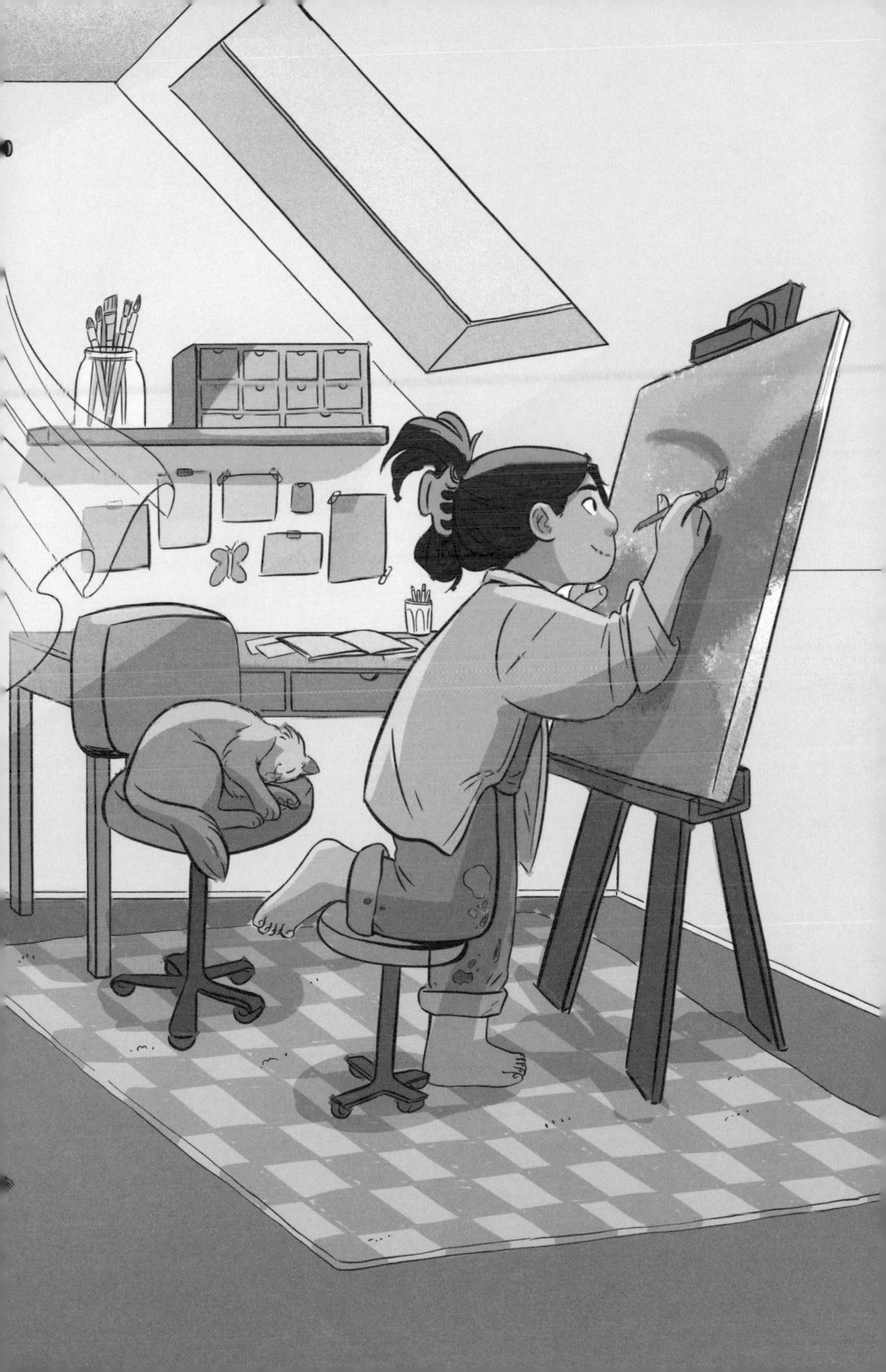

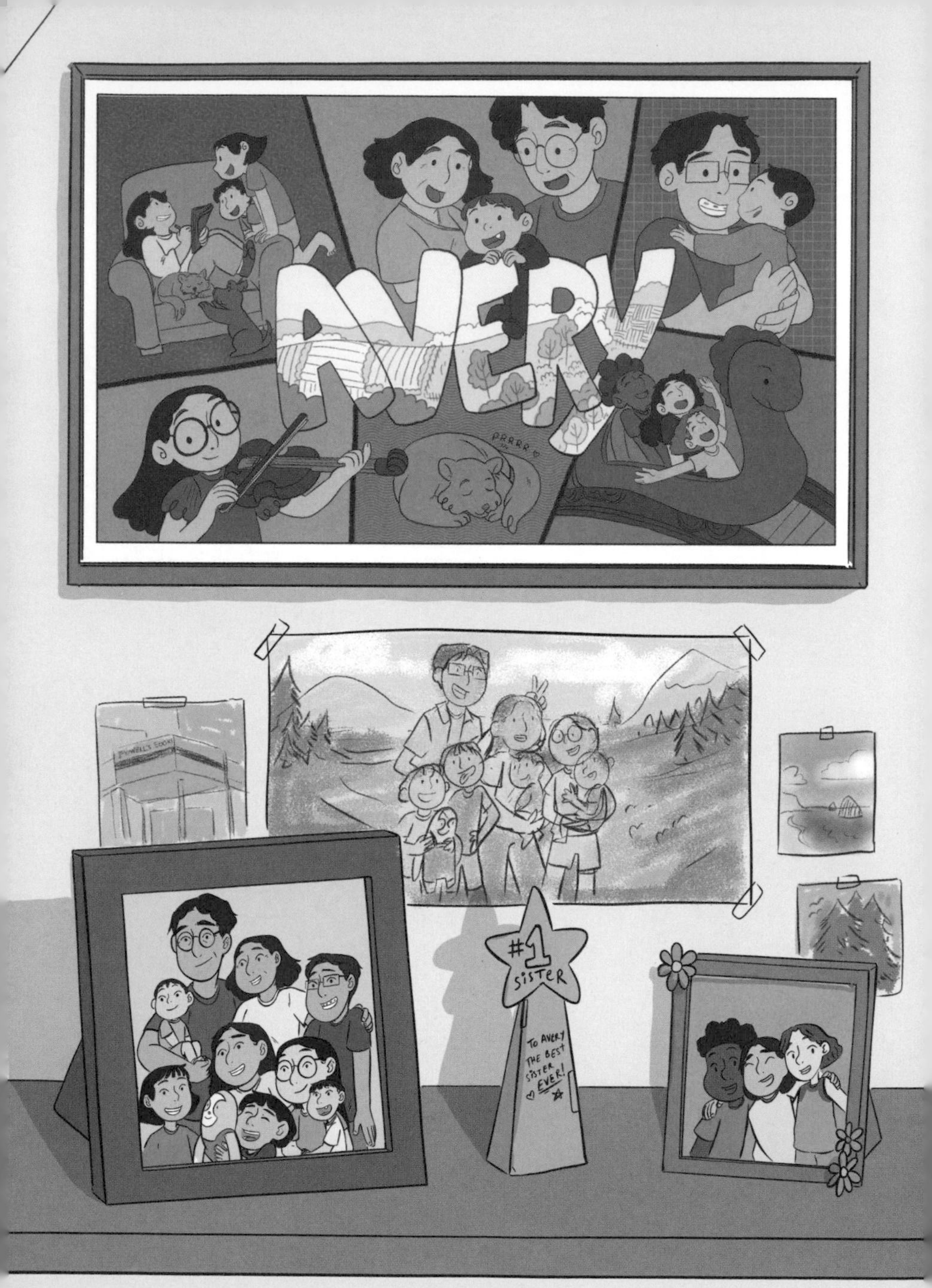
AVERY
PRRRR
POWELL'S BOOKS
#1
SISTER
TO AVERY
THE BEST
SISTER
EVER!

Also by Megan Wagner Lloyd and Michelle Mee Nutter

allergic

Megan Wagner Lloyd
and Michelle Mee Nutter

At home, Maggie is the odd one out. Her parents are busy getting ready for a new baby, and her younger brothers are twins and always in their own world. Maggie thinks that a puppy to call her own is the answer, but when she goes to select one from a shelter, she breaks out in hives and rashes. She's allergic to anything with fur! Can Maggie outsmart her allergies and find the perfect pet?

Working on this book has been amazing but also extremely challenging. There were a lot of times during this process when I doubted myself and struggled with the concept of being enough. I couldn't have gotten through it without the help of others. They cared for me, reminded me that my voice mattered, and made sure I rested a very injured arm. Creating the Korean American family in this book meant so much to me, particularly with the collective pain our AAPI community has felt. Thank you to everyone who has stood by our voices and continued to hold space for us. I'm here because of the continued love and support of those around me, especially:

Greg, you're an amazing partner. You're always in my corner and I love you so much. Thank you for keeping me fed amid deadlines — I don't think I would have eaten otherwise.

Megan, thank you for trusting me with your words. You're an amazing writer and friend. I love working with you.

Kelly, I'm so lucky to have you as my agent. Thank you for always guiding me toward work that excites me.

Cassandra, our editor, thank you for everything. You're the absolute best! I was able to create this book healthily because of your support.

Veda, my inking assistant, and Maddi, my flatter, I literally couldn't have completed this book without the two of you.

To my family, I love you all so much and I wouldn't be the person I am without you.

Last but not least, a huge thank-you to our whole Graphix team, indie booksellers, librarians, and teachers. To every single person who worked endlessly to get our books into the hands of kids. Your work is so deeply valued, and *Squished* wouldn't be here if it weren't for you.

Michelle

Acknowledgments

Endless gratitude and love to Seth, Izzy, Lucy, and Nelle — my favorite people to be squished at home with while I worked on this book in 2020.

A lifetime of thanks to my parents, siblings, kids, and niblings, for all the inspiring kid-silliness and joy.

Thank you to Izzy Lloyd for early drafting feedback, Doug Marshall for big family brainstorming, and Stacey Donoghue for outlining help.

Much appreciation to Cassandra Pelham Fulton and Emily Nguyen, for all the insightful guidance and feedback. With special thanks to Cassandra, for helping me stay true to the humor and heart with every step.

Thank you to the whole Graphix team for the myriad and much appreciated contributions.

Thank you to Ammi-Joan Paquette, for continuing support and encouragement.

And great big heaps of gratitude to incredible co-creator Michelle Mee Nutter, for bringing her talent and heart to *Squished* — and making it amazing.

Megan